R. E. LEE

Books by
Douglas Southall Freeman

GEORGE WASHINGTON

LEE'S LIEUTENANTS

THE SOUTH TO POSTERITY

R. E. LEE

Charles Scribner's Sons

R. E. LEE

A BIOGRAPHY

By

Douglas Southall Freeman

Volume II

A CHARLES SCRIBNER'S SONS BOOK
MACMILLAN PUBLISHING COMPANY
NEW YORK

Macmillan Publishing Company
866 Third Avenue, New York, NY 10022

Library of Congress Catalog Card Number 77-83150
ISBN 0-684-15483-8

Macmillan books are available at special discounts for bulk purchases for
sales promotions, premiums, fund-raising, or educational use.

For details, contact:
Special Sales Director
Macmillan Publishing Company
866 Third Avenue
New York, NY 10022

First Scribner / Macmillan Hudson River Edition 1988

10   9   8

Printed in the United States of America

CONTENTS

CONTENTS

ILLUSTRATIONS

ILLUSTRATIONS

MAPS

viii

ILLUSTRATIONS

ILLUSTRATIONS

ILLUSTRATIONS

R. E. LEE

CHAPTER I

LEE IS GIVEN AN IMPOSSIBLE ASSIGNMENT

DURING the terrible months Lee had been in western Virginia, mountains had broken the winds of contention and distance had kept from him the worst alarms. In South Carolina and in Georgia, engrossed in the details of a difficult defense, he had heard little of the confidential news that came only to the President and to the War Department. Now that he was back at the storm-centre of the Southern struggle, consulted by Davis and having free access to the files, he soon learned the dark inwardness of a situation that had changed much for the worse since he had left the Confederate capital in November.

Disaster was in the air. The defeats at Fort Henry and Fort Donelson had led the Confederates under Albert Sidney Johnston to evacuate most of Kentucky and part of western Tennessee. The newspapers that Lee read on his arrival in Richmond contained the gloomy intelligence that Fort Columbus, the advanced Confederate position on the Mississippi, thirty miles south of the confluence of the Ohio, had been abandoned by his old West Point friend, Leonidas Polk. There was danger that all the Southern posts on the river, from Columbus as far down as Memphis or beyond, would fall to the victorious and overwhelming Federal forces. Nowhere, since a small Federal column had been destroyed at Ball's Bluff on the Potomac, October 22, 1861, had there been a substantial Confederate success on land to relieve the gathering gloom. Southern commissioners in Europe had not been received at a single court. "Foreign intervention," which optimists had assured the country would certainly come by February 1, when the stores of cotton and tobacco would be exhausted overseas, seemed much more remote than it had been immediately after the victory at Manassas.[1]

[1] Charles Marshall: *An Aide de Camp of Lee*, edited by General Sir Frederick Maurice (cited hereafter as *Marshall*), 19.

The worst was not known, even to Congress. The Confederacy's supply of powder was nearly exhausted. The arsenals were almost bare of weapons. Expected shipments of arms from across the Atlantic were being delayed by a blockade that was already demonstrating the silent, decisive influence of sea-power, which the Confederates were powerless to combat. The army might soon be without the means to fight. Hope of relieving the blockade was raised for a day when the frigate *Merrimac,* cut down to the water's edge and covered with railroad iron, awkwardly steamed forth from Norfolk on March 8 as the Confederate ram *Virginia* and destroyed the *Congress* and the *Cumberland,* but she was challenged the next day by an ironclad as curious as herself, the *Monitor.*

The faith of the public had fallen with the misfortunes of their cause. Gone was the old boastfulness that had humiliated Lee. Silent were the platform-patriots who had predicted the complete defeat of the United States within ninety days after the first gun had been fired. The prophets had been confounded, the weak were despairing, the courageous were anxious. The South at length had realized, also, that the immensely larger man-power and resources of the North were being utilized in the creation of vast armies, perfectly equipped. In the passion of 1861. hotheads had relied on "Southern valor" and had refused to concede that 23,000,000 people had any advantage over an opposing 9,000,000; but now that Northern ports were receiving hundreds of tons of equipment from Europe, and Northern factories were being made ready to supply every want of any force that might be called into the field, the people of the South measured the odds against them accurately enough. Confederates no longer scoffed when indiscreet Northern newspapers and occasional Southern sympathizers who made their way through the lines told disquieting stories of the might and magnitude of the host that Lee's industrious friend of the Mexican campaign, General George B. McClellan, had brought together since he had taken command in Washington.

Not only were the Confederates depressed and outnumbered but they were preparing to abandon the lines that General Joseph E. Johnston had held, close to Washington, and almost on the frontier of Virginia, since the victory of Manassas eight months before. The news that Johnston was almost on the eve of a general retreat was the most alarming of all the secrets that Lee heard in the electric atmosphere of the President's office.

Five times during the winter, attacks on Johnston's inferior force had been predicted,[2] and with the coming of spring a great Federal advance was certain. Lee himself, similarly placed at a later time, held to a policy of open manœuvre, keeping the enemy as far from Richmond as possible and never abandoning the line of the Rappahannock if he could safely defend it. He probably would have declared for similar strategy had the choice been left to him now.[3] Johnston's withdrawal, however, had been agreed upon at a conference between himself and Davis on February 20. It was not Lee's nature to dispute what had already been determined by superior authority and was, moreover, virtually in process of execution. His observant eye must have discovered that the prospective movement was increasing the unhappy friction between Davis and Johnston that had antedated even the battle of Manassas. The President had accepted the view that the army could not successfully resist a heavy offensive by superior forces that could use their sea-power to land troops in rear of Johnston's right flank on the Potomac, just north of Fredericksburg, which Johnston believed they were preparing to do.[4] The advantages of standing on the line of the Rappahannock River, in closer touch with the other forces in Virginia, had not been overlooked by the President. Yet no sooner had the withdrawal been sanctioned than the nervous Davis and the irascible Johnston disagreed as to the time it should begin and the necessity of leaving stores behind. Davis admonished but Johnston kept his own counsel, determined to withdraw when and whither his judgment dictated.[5]

A week and more Lee spent in study of the general situation, without definite assignment to duty. On March 13 there were important developments. Davis then received his first official information that Johnston had evacuated the Manassas line on

---

[2] O. R., 5, 957 ff., 985, 997, 1006–7, 1019.

[3] Colonel John S. Mosby in his *Memoirs*, 375, affirmed that General Lee told him early in 1865 that Johnston should not have fallen back in 1862 but should have advanced on Washington.

[4] *Johnston's Narrative*, 101–2.

[5] O. R., 5, 1079, 1083, 1088; 1 *Davis*, 462 ff.; *Johnston's Narrative*, 96 ff.

March 8–9, had retreated twenty-five miles southward along the Orange and Alexandria Railroad, and had halted his army on either side of the north fork of the Rappahannock River.[6] The same day, unknown to the Confederates, a Union council of war at McClellan's headquarters decided on the line of advance for the vast Army of the Potomac that was now equipped to the last tent-peg.[7] And on that identical, ill-omened 13th, Lee received an impossible assignment to duty.

Behind it lay conflict between the President and Congress. The dissatisfaction of that body had been directed first to a campaign against Judah P. Benjamin, Secretary of War, who had been assailed for failure to send munitions to General Henry A. Wise at Roanoke Island, N. C.[8] Benjamin had the most valid of excuses—that there were no munitions to send—but both he and the President deemed it better to accept unmerited censure in silence than to expose to the enemy the weakness of the South.[9] The attack on Benjamin was so bitter that it manifestly would soon force the President to supplant him, but that was not the only grievance of Congress. Mr. Davis's disposition to direct military operations in person had provoked much criticism. Antagonism to him had been growing for some weeks,[10] though cool heads had sought a compromise. Reasoning that the first need was a new Secretary of War, and that the President had confidence in Lee, Congress had passed an act providing that, if a general of the army were appointed Secretary of War, he would not lose his rank.[11] This was a direct invitation to Mr. Davis to appoint Lee. When the President duly had signed the measure on February 27,[12] it was immediately assumed that Lee would be named,[13] but the President concluded that a soldier would not make a good secretary and made no appointment. Instead, he asked in effect that Congress provide him with two secretaries, one civil and one military, and that legislation creating the post of com-

---

[6] *Johnston's Narrative*, 103–4; *O. R.*, 5, 527, 1096, 1097, 1101–2.
[7] *O. R.*, 11, part 3, pp. 58–59.   [8] See *supra*, Vol. I, p. 625.
[9] *Marshall*, 16.   [10] 1 *R. W. C. D.*, 107.
[11] IV *O. R.*, 1, 954.   [12] *Ibid.*
[13] *Charleston Mercury*, Feb. 28, 1862; *O. R.*, 5, 1083. As if to prepare the way for the bill, *The Richmond Dispatch* of Feb. 18 had published a laudatory editorial on Lee, in which this language was employed: ". . . we venture to say that the time will yet come when his superior abilities will be vindicated, both to his own renown and the glory of his country."

4

manding general be enacted, so that the appointee could act, in a sense, as military or technical head of the War Department.[14] Congress acquiesced, but in drafting a new bill the President's enemies seem to have had equal hand with his friends. When the measure was finally laid before him, a few days after Lee's return, it provided for a commanding general, directed the President to nominate such an officer to the Senate, and authorized the officer so named to take personal command of any army in the field at any time.[15] Again it was expected that Davis would name Lee,[16] but the President saw in the move an invasion of his constitutional rights as commander-in-chief of the army and navy. Personal affronts he might swallow, with more of grace than usually was credited to him, but strict construction of the organic law was a matter of political conscience, for which he would do battle even if the enemy's divisions were at the doors of the capitol. On March 10 the bill came to him. Within three days his political experience had suggested a means of maintaining his rights as commander-in-chief and of accomplishing the desired object. He vetoed the measure and simultaneously assigned General Lee "to duty at the seat of government," charged "under the direction of the President"—that phrase asserted his authority—"with the conduct of military operations in the armies of the Confederacy." [17] Congress perforce sustained his veto and promptly re-enacted that part of the original bill providing a staff for the general so designated to duty.[18] Davis thereby won a tactical victory and followed it up by reorganizing his Cabinet on March 17, naming Benjamin as Secretary of State and placing the war office under George W. Randolph, a grandson of Thomas Jefferson and a very popular Virginian.[19] Lee's ability as an administrator gives interest to speculation as to what might have happened if he had been named Secretary of War, but his new position was manifestly difficult and anomalous. *The Charleston*

[14] This explanation is given in 2 *Southern Review,* 239–40. The article is unsigned but almost certainly was written by Doctor A. T. Bledsoe, who had been chief of the bureau of war and therefore spoke from personal knowledge.

[15] Text in IV *O. R.,* 1, 997–98. *Journal C. S. Congress,* 2, 35, 37, 47; 44 *S. H. S. P.,* 80.

[16] *Charleston Mercury,* March 8, 1862; Howell Cobb to John B. Lamar, in U. B. Phillips's *Correspondence of Toombs,* etc., 591.

[17] *O. R.,* 5, 1099; *National Intelligencer,* April 14, 1862.

[18] IV *O. R.,* 997–98, 1021; 1 *R. W. C. D.,* 117.

[19] IV *O. R.,* 1, 1005; *De Leon,* 164.

Mercury said that he was being reduced "from a commanding general to an orderly sergeant." [20] Lee himself said: "It will give me great pleasure to do anything I can to relieve [the President] and serve the country, but I cannot see either advantage or pleasure in my duties. But I will not complain, but do the best I can." [21] Few of his friends congratulated him: they knew too well the embarrassments Lee had to anticipate.[22]

Once appointed, Lee was not given an hour in which to organize his staff or to add to such understanding of the situation as he had been able to get from a brief study of the tangled records of the adjutant general's office during the interval between his arrival in Richmond and his assumption of command on March 14.[23] Every mail told of some added menace to Southern arms. The telegraph clicked off an endless report of new calamities. People, press, and politicians, in a spirit as dark as that of the dripping, mournful weather,[24] demanded action far beyond the feeble resources of a bewildered war office.

The duties of the post were to prove vexing and varied and were never to be finished. He could not know when the President would call him to a long, futile conference,[25] or what new problem from an unfamiliar field a hard-beset commander would present by telegraph with a plea for instant answer. One hour he might be puzzling over a complicated and obscure situation in Tennessee; the next he might be expected to advise which heavy guns should be moved from a Florida post and where they should be sent. Some dispositions were to be left completely to him by the President. Other matters Mr. Davis was to handle in person or was to take from him, half-completed. Within less than three months he was to be called upon to pass, in some form, on operations in every Southern state, and was besides to discharge some of the duties of the commissary general and quartermaster general. Broadly speaking, Davis entrusted to him the minor, vexatious matters of detail and the counselling of

[20] Quoted in *The National Intelligencer*, April 14, 1862. *Cf. Charleston Mercury*, March 24, 1862.

[21] Lee to Mrs. Lee, March 14, 1862; *R. E. Lee, Jr.*, 66–67.

[22] The only felicitations that appear in the records are those of General J. B. Magruder (*O. R.*, 9, 65–67) and General Humphrey Marshall (*O. R.*, 10, part 2, p. 34).

[23] For his study of the records, see *O. R.*, 5, 1098; *O. R.*, 10, part 2, pp. 320, 330–31.

[24] *McCabe*, 85.　　　　　　　　　　[25] *Marshall*, 7.

commanders in charge of the smaller armies. On the larger strategic issues the President usually consulted him and was often guided by his advice, but in no single instance was Lee given a free hand to initiate and direct to full completion any plan of magnitude.[26] He had to work by suggestion rather than by command, and sometimes, when he picked up a task that had been assigned him and then transferred to some one else, he was required to correct errors by swift action. Some public men were quick to see the good he accomplished, but in the hearts of others jealousies were aroused.[27] Sensitive spirits were encountered. Public confidence in his qualities as a commander was not what it had been in 1861. In his whole career there was not a period of more thankless service, but there were few, if any, during which he contributed more to sustain the Confederate cause.

[26] Cf. Richmond Whig, March 9, 1864: "The President never for a moment relinquished his rights as Commander-in-chief, and never entertained the first thought of doing so. This earth holds not the human being more jealous of his constitutional rights than Mr. Davis, and among those rights that to which he clings with death-like tenacity is well known to be the supreme and exclusive control of military operations. Nothing ever did or ever will induce him to relinquish one tittle of this right. If, during the short period in which General Lee occupied the complimentary position of Commanding General, any portion of the Confederacy was neglected, the fault was not Gen. Lee's. He had not the power, and, as we suspect, did not desire the power, to take the direction of military affairs out of the hands of the President. He was simply an adviser in military affairs, just as Mr. Mallory is in naval and Mr. Northrop in commissary affairs. He had no control, nor, of course, responsibility. That rests elsewhere."
[27] Cf. letters to T. R. R. Cobb, March 16, 20, 1862; 28 S. H. S. P., 291.

CHAPTER II

The Concentration on the Peninsula

It had been Lee's singular ill-fortune to assume each of his previous Confederate commands in an atmosphere of disaster. He had reached western Virginia when weary troops were still panting from an exhausting retreat. His arrival in South Carolina had been on the very day when the forts at the entrance of Port Royal Sound were being evacuated. And now almost the first dispatch that reached his desk announced that a strong Federal expedition had descended from Roanoke Island on the important North Carolina town of New Berne, had swept past the feeble Confederate lines that protected it, and had routed the defending force of 4000 men.[1] This might mean much or little, but the main railroad between Richmond and the South Atlantic states passed Goldsboro, less than sixty miles inland from New Berne. The possibilities were so serious and the available Confederate forces were so small that the President authorized Lee to detach a few regiments from Huger's force at Norfolk and two brigades of infantry, with two companies of artillery, from the right wing of Johnston's army, and to dispatch them to North Carolina. General S. G. French was immediately sent forward to assume general command.[2] For a day it seemed as if Lee would be compelled to accompany the troops, but Mr. Davis directed instead that they should be under General T. H. Holmes, a native North Carolinian, from whose immediate command part of them had been taken.[3]

This detachment was a serious matter, because it weakened by more than 10 per cent the strength of the principal Confederate army in Virginia and carried still further a deplorable if unescapable policy of scattering the troops that defended the frontier

[1] *O. R.*, 9, 197 ff., 443–45. [2] S. G. French: *Two Wars*, 143.
[3] *O. R.*, 9, 445, 449, 450; *O. R.*, 11, part 3, p. 391; *O. R.*, 12, part 3, p. 832; *O. R.*, 51, part 2, pp. 512, 514.

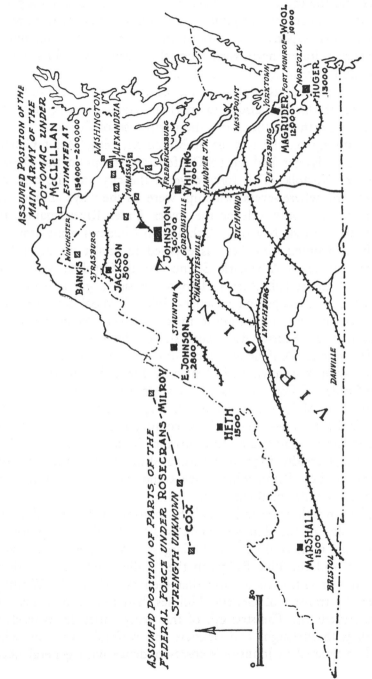

Distribution of the Confederate forces in Virginia, as of the morning of March 24, 1862, and the assumed positions of the opposing United States forces.

state and the capital city. There were at that time seven separate Southern forces in Virginia under six commanders, none of whom was responsible to any of the others. If one imagines a semicircle drawn northward from the Virginia-Carolina boundary, and extending from Norfolk to Bristol, the seven Confederate commands were spaced at irregular intervals roughly on the arc of this semicircle, to meet anticipated attack from the east, the northeast, the north, the northwest, or the west.

Beginning on the east, as of March 24, 1862, Major General Benjamin Huger had 13,000 Confederate troops in the Department of Norfolk. This force covered the city and the captured navy yard, where several warships were on the ways. Huger also guarded the south side of the lower James River against any attempt to mask Norfolk. Although no Federal army immediately confronted him, he was exposed to attack up the inland waterways from Albemarle Sound, North Carolina, which the Federals controlled. Across Hampton Roads a garrison of some 10,000 Union troops under General John E. Wool occupied Fort Monroe and was in position to make a descent on Huger at any time that the Federal fleet could silence the *Virginia*.

The second Confederate force, styled the Army of the Peninsula, lay at Yorktown and Gloucester Point, its outposts within three miles of Fort Monroe. Twelve thousand strong and commanded by Major General John B. Magruder, these troops had a two-fold function—to defend the country between the York and James Rivers against a Federal advance by land from Fort Monroe, and, secondly, to prevent Federal ships from passing up York River to West Point, where they could land troops within less than forty miles of Richmond.

The army that General Joseph E. Johnston had just withdrawn to the line of the Rappahannock was the third in geographical order and numerically much the largest in Virginia. Its left wing was west of the Blue Ridge, in the "Valley District." Its right, which was entrusted to Brigadier General W. H. C. Whiting, after the transfer of General Holmes, had been drawn back to Fredericksburg. The strength of this army varied from week to week with furloughs and sickness and probably was somewhat underestimated in Johnston's correspondence with general headquarters. The highest figure for the central divisions, the "main army," was 30,000, with an additional 7000 under Whiting.[4] This was the mobile, combatant force, weak in transport but well organized and fairly well equipped, though consisting largely of one-year recruits whose terms of enlistment were soon to expire. It had been located to prevent a turning movement from the Rappahannock, to dispute a Federal advance, to cover Richmond, and to protect the Virginia Central Railroad, which formed the only line of rail communication between Richmond and the Shenandoah Valley. The strength of the great Federal "Army of the Potomac," which was supposed to be confronting Johnston, was estimated by optimists at 150,000 and by pessimists at 200,000.[5]

The force in the Shenandoah Valley, consisting of 5000 men under Stonewall Jackson, was a part of Johnston's army and subject to his orders. It was geographically isolated, however, and had virtually to operate separately because it faced the enemy on two fronts. It unsuccessfully attacked a part of the opposing Federal army at Kernstown, near Winchester, on March 23, and on the 24th it halted at Woodstock. The enemy had not followed it from Winchester. Major General N. P. Banks, who was in general command in the valley, was attached to the Army of the Potomac in much the same manner as Jackson was to Johnston's army. Banks's strength was not known but was supposed to be much superior to Jackson's. West of the Appalachian range, beyond the Shenandoah Valley, the Federal command of Brigadier General W. S. Rosecrans lay potentially on Jackson's flank and rear. This force, which was soon to be transferred to Major General John C. Frémont, was scattered through western Virginia in unknown strength. Jackson's orders were to hold Banks in the valley, but, in manœuvring to do so, he had always to keep in mind the possibility that Rosecrans would cross the mountains at one or another of several passes and would sever his communications with Staunton and the upper valley.

The three remaining Confederate columns were small observation forces. West of Staunton, Brigadier General Edward John-

---

[4] Johnston's total force, including Jackson, on March 1, prior to the detachment of Holmes, had been 47,617 effectives; *O. R.*, 5, 1086. The Federals estimated the number, including Jackson, at 90,000, but General Sumner thought this figure was too high; *O. R.*, 11, part 3, p. 21.

[5] Actually, on March 1, 1862, it numbered 185,420 effectives; *O. R.*, 5, 732.

son with 2800 men guarded the Parkersburg road to Cheat Mountain of unhappy memory. In front of Lewisburg, leading into the valley of the Kanawha, Brigadier General Harry Heth had 1500.[6] At Lebanon, Russell County, Brigadier General Humphrey Marshall with 1500 covered the Virginia-Tennessee Railroad from attacks by raiders.[7] Heth and Johnson, like Jackson, were based on the Virginia Central Railroad. An offensive that brought the enemy to that road would cut them off from rail communication with Richmond.

All seven of these commands were under men who had received technical training as soldiers and had seen field service in the Mexican War. Except for Jackson and Marshall, all of them had continued in the United States army until 1861. The majority of the brigade commanders also were soldiers by profession.

Such was the distribution, not to say dispersion, of the Confederate forces shortly after Lee took nominal charge of the conduct of operations. "Our enemies are pressing us everywhere," he recorded at the time, "and our army is in the fermentation of organization. I pray that the great God may aid us, and am endeavoring by every means in my power to bring out the troops and hasten them to their destination."

And the enemy—what would he do? All agreed that he would assume the offensive speedily, for his numbers were vastly superior and his equipment was complete. At Johnston's headquarters the belief was that Richmond would be the immediate objective by one of four routes, but there was no agreement as to which of the four would be adopted.[8] The spies could discover little. Secret correspondence with Washington had been almost cut off. The cavalry could not penetrate far, though it was industriously led by Lee's former cadet and acting adjutant at Harpers Ferry, Brigadier General J. E. B. Stuart. To be in position to move quickly, Johnston withdrew a few miles southward on the 18th and put the Rapidan as well as the Rappahannock in front of him, but he was entirely in the dark as to the enemy's movements.[9] Lee was no better informed. He suspected that an attempt might be made on the Peninsula but he did not believe

[6] Cf. O. R., 5, 1077, 1098.   [7] O. R., 10, part 1, p. 34.
[8] Johnston's Narrative, 101, 108; O. R., 51, part 2, p. 504.
[9] Johnston's Narrative, 108.

a real offensive could be launched until the roads were firmer.[10]
If he knew how to profit by it, McClellan might have the priceless
advantage of surprise.

On March 24, 1862, Lee went, as usual, to his new office in the
War Department building, formerly the Mechanics Institute, on
Ninth Street, opposite the western end of Bank Street. Very soon
there came a sensational telegram from General Huger at Norfolk: More than twenty steamers, Huger reported, had come
down Chesapeake Bay the previous evening and had begun to
disembark troops at Old Point.[11] A little later, General Magruder
notified the Secretary of War that he believed the force confronting him had risen to 35,000.[12] Magruder did not suggest
that the troops had come from McClellan's army, nor could Lee
be sure, but by the next morning the information in hand[13]
rendered it probable that the new arrivals belonged to the Army of
the Potomac. If this were true, Lee had to consider three possibilities:

1. McClellan might have detached the troops to co-operate with
Burnside in North Carolina.

2. The new troops might have no connection with Burnside's
movements and might be designed to join with the 10,000 already
at Fort Monroe in an attack on Norfolk or up the Peninsula, while
McClellan advanced on Richmond from the north.

3. The reinforcements at Old Point might be the advanced
guard of McClellan's whole army which was preparing to march
up the Peninsula.

In dealing with these three possible movements, it was not
enough to draw a line and defend it. Norfolk could readily be
cut off, as Lee had pointed out during the mobilization of Virginia. The Peninsula afforded at least three good defensive
fronts, drawn from river to river, that could be held by an alert
force against odds, provided the James and the York were not
opened by the enemy. But if the attacking Federals used their
sea-power wisely and passed the batteries on either of these
streams, they could land in rear of the Confederates. This condition had led Lee in April, 1861, to put the obstruction and
defense of the rivers first in his programme and it was an im-

[10] O. R., 11, part 3, p. 385.   [11] O. R., 11, part 3, p. 394.
[12] O. R., 11, part 3, pp. 392–93.   [13] Cf. O. R., 11, part 3, p. 394.

portant factor in his strategy now. The appended sketch will show the Confederate defenses on the rivers and the exposed position of the army on the Peninsula:

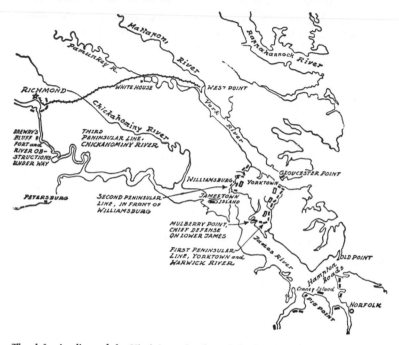

The defensive lines of the Virginia peninsula and the location of the earthworks on adjacent waters, March 27, 1862.

The time element was of even greater importance. The army must not be thrown into an active campaign, if this could be prevented, until the reorganization then in progress had been completed. Time was likewise needed to raise, to train, and to move forward other troops.

Weighing all the circumstances in conferences with the President and the Secretary of War, Lee developed a plan that is a most interesting example of provisional reconcentration to meet an undeveloped offensive. Perhaps the most remarkable thing about this plan is that it was devised and put in process of execution within thirty-six hours after Lee received news of the landing at Old Point. He had no doubt been canvassing the possibilities

14

for days, but the actual decisions, which could not be made until he had some inkling of the enemy's plan, were reached with great promptness. The course he chose was this:

1. Holmes's force in North Carolina was to be strengthened, so as to occupy Burnside, if possible, and to prevent his advance into North Carolina or his co-operation in any operations against Norfolk.

2. Both Huger and Magruder were notified to prepare their forces so that Huger could help Magruder if the attack were on the Peninsula, and Magruder could assist Huger if Norfolk proved to be the Federal objective.[14]

3. The ironclad *Virginia* could cover the mouth of the James River and prevent Federal interference with troop-movements by Magruder or Huger of Confederate forces across that stream, but she was then in drydock at Norfolk. Pending her return to service, Lee undertook the improvement of the water-batteries on the James, accumulated transportation on the river, and selected a point above the probable reach of Federal gunboats, where the infantry could cross.[15]

4. The scanty available reserves—a couple of regiments of infantry and some squadrons of cavalry then around Richmond—were at once ordered to Magruder.[16]

5. To give time for the reorganization and for the collection of new troops, Magruder was urged to stand on the first defensive line on the lower Peninsula, the line farthest from Richmond, and was instructed not to evacuate it voluntarily unless the Federals were able to turn it by carrying their gunboats up the York or the James.[17]

6. In case the lines on the lower Peninsula should be turned from the James or the York, Magruder was directed to prepare for a withdrawal to the third defensive line, that of the Chickahominy. In doing this, Magruder was to destroy the river landings. He was, moreover, to use his artillery on the river banks, as far as practicable, beyond the points covered by the water-batteries, in order to prevent the passage of the enemy high up the James or up the Pamunkey, the southern of the two streams that formed

14 *O. R.,* 11, part 3, pp. 396–97.   15 *O. R.,* 11, part 3, pp. 393, 397, 398, 400.
16 *O. R.,* 11, part 3, p. 396.   17 *O. R.,* 11, part 3, p. 399.

15

the York.[18] Lee's experience with this type of defense on the South Atlantic seaboard gave him a faith in it that was not possessed by those who had not seen how readily the Federal gunboats were deterred by such measures as these.

7. The enemy must be kept as far down the Peninsula as possible, at least until his full plan was disclosed. It might not be possible to do this with the force Magruder had, or with the reserves that could be sent him. Lee accordingly decided, with the President's approval, on this major movement: he would withdraw the greater part of Johnston's army from the Rapidan, would move it quickly to the lower Peninsula, would attack the Federals there, and then, if need be, would return Johnston's troops to their old position. Lee believed the situation in northern Virginia would make this possible, without excessive risk of losing Richmond, because he reasoned that so large a part of McClellan's army had already been transferred to the Peninsula that McClellan would not quickly advance on Richmond from the north with the forces left him. Johnston was asked what force he could dispatch to Richmond for this purpose and was instructed to be prepared for orders directing an immediate movement of his army.[19]

This was a bold plan to be formulated by an officer who had been at his post only a fortnight. It displayed the facility that Lee always exhibited in strategy, even from the beginning of his career in responsible command, and it embodied all that he had learned in South Carolina and in making dispositions for First Manassas. Execution, however, was not so easy as conception. Obstacles and objections were encountered in such numbers that the plan had to be revised almost as soon as it was formulated. Magruder held a council of war which decided, in something of a panic, that unless 10,000 reinforcements could be at once dispatched to that front, Yorktown should be evacuated. Lee reassured Magruder, cautioned him against over-large councils of war, and urged him to stand where he was as long as possible.[20] Magruder acquiesced, and that tangle was straightened out. It was otherwise with Johnston. He was a sworn devotee of con-

18 *O. R.*, 11, part 3, p. 398.   19 *O. R.*, 11, part 3, pp. 337, 409.
20 *O. R.*, 11, part 3, pp. 395, 398, 399; *Taylor's Four Years*, 38.

centration and he argued that all or none of his army should be transferred to the Peninsula. Soon he reported that Jackson was threatened by superior forces and that the enemy showed activity on his own front. Several days' exchange of correspondence with Johnston convinced Lee that his old friend would not willingly fall in with his plan. Then, for the first time, Lee displayed a quality of mind that was to become one of his greatest assets as a commander. It was this: he would make the best, for the time, of what he could not correct, but he would hold to what he believed the sound strategy and would look to time and circumstance for an opportunity of executing his plan. If Johnston would not consent to the dispatch of enough troops at one time to strengthen Magruder, Lee would take what Johnston would give him immediately, would extemporize, and then would get more as soon as he could. He exhibited, in short, a patient persistence in attaining his object. Patient persistence, indeed, was to become the measure of the man in many a difficult hour.

It is interesting to see how Lee applied this policy. In place of a speedy general movement, he effected a series of small transfers to the Peninsula. Johnston was willing, at the outset, to detach only two brigades. One of these was sent to the Peninsula; the other went to North Carolina.[21] As Magruder needed much more than this reinforcement, Lee ordered one of Huger's brigades to be ready to cross the James and sent two Alabama regiments to Yorktown. He even dispatched 1000 unarmed men to Magruder, in the hope that Magruder could give them, if necessary, the guns of soldiers then in hospitals.[22] This was the best he could do for them. Not even old flint-lock muskets could be supplied from Richmond. The arsenals were stripped of all arms that would fire, and preparations were being made to manufacture and issue pikes.[23] To this desperate plight had the battling Confederacy been brought!

During the march of these troops to Magruder's support, the Federals made no demonstration against his lines. This aroused Lee's suspicions and led him to apprehend that the real objective

21 O. R., 11, part 3, pp. 397, 401, 408–9; Johnston's Narrative, 109.
22 O. R., 11, part 3, pp. 409, 411.
23 For the shortage of arms and ammunition, see O. R., 5, 922–23; O. R., 10, part 2, p. 374; O. R., 12, part 3, pp. 842, 844–45; O. R., 51, part 2, p. 158.

of the enemy might be Norfolk, rather than the Peninsula. He accordingly began to strengthen Huger's little army and called for two of Johnston's brigades, to be employed on the Peninsula, at Norfolk or in North Carolina as the situation might demand.[24]

Either at Lee's suggestion or on his own initiative, Magruder all the while did his utmost to discourage the enemy both from attacking his line and from detaching troops for operations against Norfolk. Physically magnificent, though burdened by a curious lisp, Magruder had a certain innocent element of bluff in his makeup and could readily deceive a hesitating opponent. Working busily on the construction of the defenses and on the damming of Warwick River, which covered his front, he kept his troops in motion. One day, as if massing for some desperate business, he sent a column into a wood through which there ran a road in plain view of the Federal outposts. Hour after hour the Federals could see his gray troops emerge from a thicket, cross the road, and vanish again in the pines. The Federals must have counted thousands of files and must have wondered for what evil purpose so many brigades were being massed, but Magruder in reality was simply marching a few men in a circle, like an army of supernumeraries on a stage.[25] It was said of Magruder—"Prince John," they called him in the old army—that when war did not trouble, he delighted to dress a scene and to appear, a dazzling figure, in amateur theatricals, but rarely did he play a part so much to his country's good as in those anxious days at Yorktown, when Lee did not know how large a part of McClellan's army remained on the old battleground in northern Virginia or how many divisions were preparing to take ship for Hampton Roads.

Thus, for a time, all was well on the Peninsula. Whatever the enemy's plan there, he was slow in developing it. In northern Virginia, and in the Shenandoah Valley, the situation was obscured by doubt. Jackson reported the enemy advancing against him and called for reinforcements. Johnston, alarmed, detained one of the two brigades already ordered to Richmond and prepared to send half a division to Jackson if necessary.[26]

It seemed as likely on April 4 that the main offensive would be

[24] O. R., 11, part 3, pp. 413, 414, 419; O. R., 9, 455.
[25] R. Taylor, 93; Taylor's General Lee, 51–53; Sorrel, 66.
[26] O. R., 11, part 3, p. 419.

in northern Virginia as on the Peninsula. That same day, however, Lee received news through General Stuart that a flotilla of transports was under way down the Potomac for some unknown destination.[27] Simultaneously, word came from Magruder that heavy columns of Federals were moving out from Old Point in his direction as if to give battle. Lee concluded immediately that the two reports were related and that McClellan was moving more of his men to the Peninsula; but as Lee still was uncertain how large a part of the Army of the Potomac remained in Johnston's front, he decided for the time being not to attempt to send the remainder of Johnston's forces to Magruder's support. He continued, however, to order detachments until, by April 4, he had called a total of three divisions from the line of the Rapidan-Rappahannock.[28] It was done so quietly and so gradually that few protests were made.

These transfers, coupled with minor reinforcements to Magruder from other quarters, gave that officer the prospect of having a total force of 31,500 by April 11,[29] while Johnston was left with four divisions, roughly 28,000 men, including Jackson's 5000 in the Shenandoah Valley and Stuart's 1200 cavalry. This daring, piecemeal reconcentration was a matter of the greatest delicacy, the success of which depended on maintaining the morale both of Johnston and of Magruder, while interpreting accurately the very scant available information of the enemy's movements. If Lee underestimated the strength or the initiative of the Federals either in northern Virginia or on the Peninsula, Johnston or Magruder might be overwhelmed before help could be sent. A simultaneous attack on both, in such numbers as the Federals were known to have in the state, would inevitably be disastrous. And if disaster came in Virginia, it meant ruin everywhere.

For while Lee was in conference with Davis, hour after hour, calculating the risks on the Rapidan, in the Shenandoah Valley, and in Hampton Roads, the rival armies of Grant and of Albert Sidney Johnston were grappling on April 6–7 at Shiloh, near the

[27] O. R., 11, part 3, pp. 415–16; cf. ibid., 419.
[28] O. R., 11, part 3, p. 420; Johnston's Narrative, 109; W. H. Morgan: Personal Reminiscences (cited hereafter as Morgan), 97. The divisions sent to Magruder, including the units already dispatched, were those of Jubal A. Early, D. H. Hill, and D. R. Jones.
[29] O. R., 11, part 3, p. 436.

Tennessee-Mississippi boundary. The Confederate press claimed a victory on a hard-fought field, but the losses were heavy and Johnston was killed. Island No. 10, a Confederate stronghold on the Mississippi, was captured on April 8, with 7000 men. The bold bid of the South for the control of the upper Mississippi had been rejected by the fates. There was imminent danger that the Confederacy would be split in twain and that the Federals would then proceed to break up the riven halves. How could the South be saved if Virginia were lost?

The troops sent southward from the Rapidan moved steadily to the Peninsula, where the enemy was placing batteries and bringing up heavy artillery for a siege but showed as yet no disposition to assault. No general advance of the enemy in northern Virginia was reported. The threat against Jackson had not materialized. Several days passed without a new crisis, but by April 9 Magruder was satisfied that the greater part of the Army of the Potomac was in his front. A minister who had escaped from Alexandria, Reverend K. J. Stuart, confirmed this indirectly by giving a very accurate account of the departure of Federal troops, and of McClellan himself, from that city.

Risks would be taken, of course, in acting on this information, but an inferior force had to take them. On April 9, doubtless with Lee's full approval, the President made the final move in the reconcentration, ordered Johnston to report in Richmond, and directed that his two strongest divisions, Longstreet's and G. W. Smith's, be set in motion for the capital. Ewell's division of some 7000 or 8000 men was left on the Rappahannock to observe the enemy and to co-operate with Jackson, whose division of 5000 was slowly increasing in numbers. One brigade of Smith's command was left temporarily at Fredericksburg.[30] By this time, it was understood from Northern newspapers that the Federals remaining in northern Virginia were under Major General Irvin McDowell. Thereafter they were usually styled "McDowell's army," but of their strength and position very little was known.[31]

[30] *Johnston's Narrative*, 110; *O. R.*, 11, part 3, pp. 428–29.

[31] Actually, when the plan for an attack upon the Peninsula had been made, President Lincoln had stipulated that a sufficient force should be left in northern Virginia to make the capital secure. When McClellan failed to make what Mr. Lincoln regarded as adequate provision for this purpose, McDowell's division, which was to have joined McClellan, was detached on April 4 and McDowell was given command of this and other units east of the Blue Ridge (*O. R.*, 11, part 3, pp. 58–59, 65–66).

When Johnston arrived in Richmond, his command was enlarged to include Norfolk and the Peninsula,[32] and he was directed to visit that part of the front to see his problem at first hand. On April 13 he left. The next morning Lee received a summons to come to the President's office. When he entered, he learned that Johnston had returned unexpectedly and had made a disheartening report. The President was so much concerned that he had called a council of war, to which he had summoned Lee, Johnston, Secretary Randolph, and Major General Longstreet and Gustavus Smith, the two last-named at Johnston's instance. Discussion of the greatest moment followed. Johnston pronounced the situation at Yorktown an impossible one. The line, he said, was entirely too long for the force defending it. Magruder's men were beginning to show the effects of strain.[33] Inundations that had been prepared along the Warwick River might hold off McClellan on the land side but they would likewise render an offensive by the Confederates impossible. The superior Union artillery would soon batter down the Southern batteries covering York River, and when that happened McClellan's gunboats and transports could pass up the stream and turn the Confederate position. The most that could be done on the lower Peninsula would be to delay McClellan temporarily. It would be better, Johnston went on, to discard the plans under which they were operating, to abandon Norfolk and the Peninsula, to concentrate in front of Richmond all the troops in Virginia, the Carolinas, and Georgia, and to strike McClellan at a distance from his base. As a less desirable alternative, he proposed that Magruder stand siege in Richmond while the other Confederate forces carry the war into the enemy's country.[34]

The Secretary of War promptly opposed this change of plan because it would necessarily involve the evacuation of Norfolk, where the *Virginia* was based and where other ships were under construction. To lose Norfolk was to give up all hope of creating a navy to cope with the Federal sea-power.[35]

Lee was then asked to express his opinion. An early with-

---

[32] *O. R.*, 11, part 3, p. 438.   [33] *O. R.*, 11, part 3, p. 442.

[34] *Johnston's Narrative*, 112 ff.; 2 *Davis*, 87; G. W. Smith: *Confederate War Papers* (cited hereafter as *Smith*), 41; James Longstreet: *From Manassas to Appomattox* (cited hereafter as *Longstreet*), 66.

[35] II *N. O. R.*, 1, 716.

drawal, to his mind, would bring the armies dangerously close to the nerve-centre of the Confederacy and would complicate the reorganization then in progress. It would likewise make heavy fighting inevitable before the full armed strength of the South was in the field. From the lower South Atlantic coast a brigade or two might be spared, but no large reinforcement could be expected immediately. Fort Pulaski, the outpost of Savannah, had fallen just three days before. Losses in Tennessee had forced the War Department to send to that state six new regiments raised in Georgia and four from South Carolina.[36] Stripping the South Atlantic coast of men, as Johnston proposed, might involve the fall of Savannah and of Charleston. On the other hand, Lee had faith in the line on the lower Peninsula, where with his approval, if not on his initiative, the inundations of which Johnston complained had been effected.[37] He believed that invaluable time could be gained by delaying McClellan there as long as possible.[38]

Lee and Randolph argued against Johnston and Smith, with Longstreet saying little and Davis reserving judgment. The debate was continued with warmth until supper time, and after an hour's intermission, was kept up till 1 o'clock the next morning. Then Davis declared himself in favor of defending the lower Peninsula. It was undoubtedly a sound decision. Had Johnston's plan been adopted, Ewell would have been called to Richmond, Jackson could not have won the battle of Winchester the next month, the Federal troops remaining in front of Washington would have been available to co-operate with McClellan, and Johnston, in all likelihood, would have been defeated in front of Richmond or would have been compelled to uncover that city. The Confederacy could hardly have survived long.

In a more limited sense, Davis's decision in overruling Johnston had a direct effect on the operations of the next six weeks. Johnston made no protest at the time and seemingly acquiesced in the orders of the commander-in-chief, but he was of the same opinion still. Long afterward he recorded: "The belief that events on the

---

[36] *O. R.,* 10, part 2, pp. 370, 422.   [37] *O. R.,* 9, 68.

[38] Davis and Johnston, respectively, *loc. cit.,* mention only Lee's statement that the Peninsula was defensible and his warning that Charleston and Savannah might be lost by the concentration Johnston proposed. The other reasons here cited for Lee's opposition to the plan of Johnston are readily inferred from his dispatches of March 26 and April 9 to Magruder, *O. R.,* 11, part 3, pp. 398–99, 433–34.

Peninsula would compel the government to adopt my method of opposing the Federal army, reconciled me somewhat to the necessity of obeying the President's order." [39] He prepared, in other words, to go to the Yorktown front in the conviction that he would soon fall back on Richmond and would leave the President no alternative to that of bringing all possible forces from the South Atlantic seaboard for a battle near the capital.

Three days later, on April 17, Johnston assumed his new command.[40] Lee's part in the reconcentration was done. Operations on the Peninsula and the conduct of affairs at Norfolk were thereafter, until May 31, entirely under Johnston's direction. The only share Lee had in events that followed on those sectors was general supervision of the preparation of defenses near Richmond, particularly on James River, and the tender of such basic counsel on strategy as Mr. Davis sought.

The military achievement of Lee in effecting the reconcentration speaks for itself. Despite his anomalous position, his had been the guiding hand in shaping a policy that had held the Yorktown line with trifling losses until Magruder's 11,000 were in a fair way of being raised to 53,000[41] without any advance by the enemy south of the Rapidan River. Here, as on the South Atlantic coast, he had benefited by the extreme caution of his opponent. How much of that caution was due to the temperament of McClellan, and how much was dictated by sound dispositions that might have been mismanaged by a Confederate commander less capable than Lee, is a question that cannot be answered.

As if to dramatize the reconcentration, part of Longstreet's division and some of the cavalry marched through Richmond on the day that Johnston took command on the Peninsula. The infantry had made their long march afoot, often along muddy roads. They styled themselves for the time "Longstreet's Walking Division," and one of them grumblingly wrote: "I suppose that if it was intended to re-enforce Savannah, Mobile or New Orleans with our division, we would be compelled to foot it all the way." [42]

[39] *Johnston's Narrative*, 116.
[40] He so stated in his *Narrative*, 117, but his first order is dated April 18; *O. R.*, 11, part 3, p. 448.
[41] *Johnston's Narrative*, 117.
[42] Edwin —— to Miss Laura Jones, May 2–10, 1862, *MS.*, placed at the writer's disposal by Mason White, Esq., of Richmond.

At the sight of their soldiery, people who had been close to panic took heart again. The infantry moved down Main Street; the cavalry clattered along Franklin. It was the first anniversary of the secession of Virginia, a perfect spring day. The gardens were all abloom; the whole city was at the curb. Along with the best refreshments from their pantries, the women brought out to the sidewalk their jonquils and their hyacinths until the smell of grease and powder and unwashed men was subdued by the odors of flowers. Laughing boys took the blossoms from outstretched hands as they tramped eastward, and stuck them in their caps and gun-barrels, or strung them about their necks until the gray columns took on lively colors. The bands kept playing "Dixie," "My Maryland," and the "Bonnie Blue Flag," and the people cheered and waved and grew in confidence at the sight of so many men, until those dark words "Donelson" and "Shiloh" and "Island No. 10" lost their terror for the day.[43]

[43] *Miss Brock,* 119–20; *De Leon,* 192; *Mrs. McGuire,* 107.

CHAPTER III

LEE AND THE CONSCRIPTION ACT

IF Lee looked out at Longstreet's men as they marched down Main Street that 17th of April on their way to the Peninsula, he could not have been thinking of the flowers or of the cheers. His mind must have been on the size and number of the regiments. He must have asked himself what would be the probable effect of the law the President had signed the previous day. Would it fill the ranks that were soon to be decimated in the slaughter that every one now foresaw?

Ever since the early winter, he had been looking forward with the deepest concern to March and April, when the men who had clamored to join the colors in the first fervor of secession would come to the end of their twelve months' enlistment. Many, of course, would continue in service, but a sufficient number would leave the army to reduce its strength most dangerously. "At the beginning of the campaign," he had written in December, "when our enemies will take the field fresh and vigorous, after a year's preparation and winter's repose, we shall be in all the anxiety, excitement and organization of new armies. In what different condition will be the opposing armies on the plains of Manassas at the resumption of operations." [1] He had seen no way of meeting this condition except by conscripting the man-power of the South, and as early as December 26, 1861, it will be recalled, he had written Governor Letcher advocating a general draft in Virginia of all soldiers who did not re-enlist.[2] President Davis had advocated a like policy for the entire Confederacy, but he had encountered the opposition of extreme states-rights' politicians, and both in and out of Congress he had faced the inertia born of the belief that European countries would intervene to stop the war before another campaign opened. Not until December 11,

[1] O. R., 6, 350.   [2] 1 S. H. S. P., 462; see *supra*, vol. I, p. 622.

1861, had legislative action been taken, and then the law had been fashioned to please rather than to strengthen the army. The poor measure adopted was known as the "bounty and furlough act,"[3] and it demonstrated, as Ropes aptly remarked, that "the difference between an army and a congeries of volunteer regiments was not appreciated."[4] Every soldier who re-enlisted for three years or for the duration of the war was promised a bounty of $50 and a sixty-day furlough. He could choose his arm of the service, and if he did not like his company, he could join a new one. There was nothing in the law to keep an ambitious soldier from canvassing discontented men in established regiments to enter new units, where the solicitor hoped to win a commission. On the re-enlistment of the army, the men could elect their own officers, rewarding those who curried favor by laxity and demoting those who had enforced discipline. Once the elections were held, all commissioned vacancies in every regiment were thereafter to be filled by promotion, with the proviso that when new second lieutenants were to be named, they should be elected from the company in which the vacancy existed. A non-commissioned officer, therefore, who discharged his duties vigorously and aroused the antagonism of the indolent and the shirker, could be sure that when a new lieutenant was to be chosen, he had little chance of receiving a bar on his collar as a reward for performing his duty but was much more likely to be passed over for some popular private. A worse law could hardly have been imposed on the South by the enemy. Its interpretation was confusing,[5] its effect was demoralizing, and it involved nothing less than a reconstruction of the entire land forces of the Confederacy in the face of the enemy.[6] Upton did not err when he said later that the bounty and furlough law should have been styled "an act to disorganize and dissolve the provisional army."[7]

This mischievous measure had been enacted before Lee had returned to Virginia from the South Atlantic coast and its evil consequences were only too apparent when he assumed nominal

[3] O. R., 5, 1016.

[4] J. C. Ropes: The Story of the Civil War (cited hereafter as Ropes), 1, 219.

[5] O. R., 5, 1037, 1045, 1057, 1058–59, 1061, 1063. Johnston had favored inducements and furloughs for men who would re-enlist (O. R., 5, 974), but he protested often and warmly against the law as passed.

[6] Marshall, 13–14.   [7] Upton: The Military Policy of the United States, 460.

control of military operations. There had been nothing he could do about the existing law. He had been compelled to wait until necessity should convince Congress that if the South was to survive the casualties of even that single year, a sterner policy was demanded.

With the Virginia troops, the case had not been quite so discouraging. Moved by Lee's appeal from South Carolina, Governor Letcher had induced the general assembly of the commonwealth to provide in February for a general enrolment of all citizens between eighteen and forty-five years of age.[8] From the list so provided, 40,000 militia had been called to the colors on March 10, in response to a requisition from the War Department,[9] and the Confederate commanders had been authorized to use these men in any temporary emergency.[10] Replacements of militiamen were to be drafted to take the place of twelve-months' troops who declined to re-enlist for the war.[11] But these latter troops were not allowed to leave the service. Upon the expiration of their terms, they passed immediately into the militia, and, as all the militia had been embodied, Lee announced on April 11, in his capacity as commander of the military and naval forces of Virginia, that volunteers who fell into the militia on their failure to re-enlist could be drafted at once, "as far as practicable into the same companies to which they had lately belonged."[12] In this direct fashion, Virginia adopted compulsory service. Her regiments were in no danger of being wrecked by the reorganization.

Between the time the bounty and furlough law was enacted and the date of the conscription of the Virginians whose terms were expiring, Congress passed a series of weak and hurried measures, designed to increase recruiting with the bait of further promises to the men who re-enlisted.[13] These acts failed to effect any general re-enlistment. Within little more than a month after Longstreet's division marched through Richmond, the terms of not less than 148 Confederate regiments would expire. "There was," as the Secretary of War subsequently reported, "good reason to believe that a large majority of the men had not re-enlisted, and of those who had re-enlisted, a very large majority had entered

[8] IV O. R., 1, 1114–15.   [9] O. R., 51, part 2, p. 495.
[10] O. R., 5, 1097; cf. O. R., 12, part 3, p. 836.
[11] IV O. R., 1, 1011.   [12] O. R., 51, part 2, p. 534.
[13] Journals of the Confederate Congress, 1, 690, 692, 695, 711, 847, 848.

[new] corps which could never be assembled, or, if assembled, could not be prepared for the field in time to meet the invasion actually commenced." [14]

Seeing no way of preventing the disorganization of the army except by conscription, Lee made himself an opportunity, even during the crisis that followed the landing at Old Point on March 23, to review the subject fully with the new lawyer-member of his staff, Major Charles Marshall of Baltimore. Lee maintained, said Marshall, "that every other consideration should be subordinated to the great end of public safety, and that since the whole duty of the nation would be war until independence should be secured, the whole nation should for the time be converted into an army, the producers to feed and the soldiers to fight"—a principle that in 1917 America wisely adopted. [15]

Marshall was directed by Lee to draw up the heads of a bill providing for the conscription of all white males between eighteen and forty-five years of age. The finished paper Lee took to the President, who approved its principles and had it put into shape by Mr. Benjamin. Introduced in Congress, the bill was amended and mangled. Provision was made for the election of officers in re-enlisted commands, and most of the other useless paraphernalia of the bounty and furlough act were loaded on it. The upper age-limit was reduced from forty-five to thirty-five years, and a bill allowing liberal exemption was soon adopted. [16] The press had applause for the object of the bill and sharp words on its weaknesses. [17] In the army, those who had intended not to re-enlist on the expiration of their terms grumbled and charged bad faith on the part of the government, [18] but those who were determined to carry on the war to ruin or independence rejoiced that those who had stayed at home were at last to smell gun-

---

[14] IV *O. R.*, 2, 43.   [15] *Marshall*, 32.

[16] For the text, see IV *O. R.*, 1, 1095 *ff.* An unfavorable critique of the law will be found in *Marshall*, 33 *ff.* De Leon, *op. cit.*, 174 *ff.*, praised its good points. A. B. Moore, in his *Conscription and Conflict in the Confederacy*, 16 *ff.*, 115 *ff.*, discussed the reception and effects of the measure. To Doctor Moore's book the author is indebted for several of the references already cited.

[17] *Richmond Examiner*, April 14, 15; *Richmond Enquirer*, April 17, 18; *Richmond Dispatch*, April 14, 1862.

[18] Excellent examples will be found in J. W. Reid's letters home, published in his *History of the Fourth South Carolina Volunteers*, 68, 76. The act, he said, "will do away with all the patriotism we have. Whenever men are forced to fight, they take no personal interest in it."

powder. In the well-disciplined commands, men who went home at the expiration of their twelve months and returned as conscripts soon settled down to army routine.[19] The election of new officers resulted in the defeat of many good soldiers and in the choice of "good fellows" in their places, but, on the whole, the elections wrought less evil than could reasonably have been expected.[20] For his part Lee realized the danger involved in reorganizing the army to the accompaniment of Federal bullets, but he read in the law a promise that recruits would ere long fill the regiments which passed down Main Street that April day, and for that promise he must have been grateful. It probably never occurred to him that chief credit for the conscript act was his own.

[19] Dickert's *History of Kershaw's Brigade*, 104–5.
[20] *Ibid.*, 106–7; letters of T. R. R. Cobb, 28 *S. H. S. P.*, 292.

CHAPTER IV

The Genesis of Jackson's Valley Campaign

THE enactment of the conscript law and the assumption by Johnston of command on the Peninsula did not lessen Lee's labors. They simply turned them into other channels. More time was allowed him during which to study a military situation elsewhere that called for the best judgment the administration could exercise. Affairs on all the fronts were tangled and on some were desperate. Lee was called upon by the President to advise regarding the movements of the army in northern Mississippi, the command of which had passed to Beauregard on the death of Albert Sidney Johnston.[1] In East Tennessee, a small force under General Kirby Smith was in the deepest need of equipment and reinforcement, and the task of helping it was assigned to Lee.[2] The few scattered regiments in western and southwestern Virginia were threatened by superior Federal forces; unable to send more men, Lee could only urge a slow withdrawal to strong natural positions and the best preparation of the ground for defense.[3] To Lee, also, was given the difficult rôle of diplomatist in dealing with Governor Brown of Georgia;[4] on his shoulders fell part of the burden of apportioning such arms as reached the Confederacy from abroad;[5] on occasion he helped in the work of the commissary and quartermaster-general.[6] From West Florida and Alabama,[7] from the trans-Mississippi,[8] then and thereafter,

---

[1] Lee had been consulted by the President prior to Johnston's demise and had drafted an important dispatch at the instance of Mr. Davis. W. P. Johnston: *Life of Albert Sidney Johnston*, 521. For Lee's later instructions to Beauregard, see *O. R.*, 10, part 1, p. 775, part 2, p. 546.

[2] *Cf. O. R.*, 10, part 2, pp. 321, 366, 368–69, 393, 397–98, 425–26, 479.

[3] *O. R.*, 5, 1098, 1101; *O. R.*, 10, part 2, pp. 322–23, 349, 364–65, 428; *O. R.*, 12, part 3, pp. 827, 829–31, 833–34, 836, 853, 855, 856.

[4] *O. R.*, 53, 244–45; 3 *Confederate Records of Georgia*, 169, 186, 210, 221–22, 225–26.

[5] See *supra*, Vol. I, p. 611.

[6] *Marshall*, 44; *O. R.*, 51, part 2, p. 515; *O. R.*, 14, 491.

[7] *O. R.*, 6, 874, 880, 881–82, 884.

[8] *O. R.*, 6, 652–53; *O. R.*, 8, 791; *O. R.*, 9, 713, 716; *O. R.*, 13, 824.

came calls for reinforcements and appeals for instruction. An unpleasant controversy involving Ripley and Pemberton at Charleston had to be relieved, as far as practicable, a little later.[9] In dealing with all these distant operations, Lee laid down the sound principle, expressed in a letter to the commanding officer in Florida, that where he did not know the "particular necessities" of a local situation he could only make general suggestions and would not send "definite instructions." [10]

His chief attention, after April 17, Lee gave to operations in northern Virginia and in the Shenandoah Valley. When Johnston had left the Rapidan, he had directed Jackson and Ewell to communicate with him through the adjutant general's office.[11] The President evidently reasoned that Johnston would be engrossed in operations on the Peninsula and that the campaign north and northwest of Richmond could be managed more promptly and satisfactorily from the capital than from Johnston's headquarters. No formal orders were issued and the nominal command of Johnston over Ewell and Jackson was not reduced, but dispatches from them were referred to Lee, evidently with instructions to supervise the movements of these two officers as long as Johnston was at a distance from Richmond. It was a most embarrassing arrangement. Johnston was excessively sensitive on all that touched his authority. Lee had to defer to the chief executive, as always, while avoiding offense to Johnston. He had to fashion operations of the utmost gravity, but with no assurance whatsoever that he would be allowed to complete the strategical combinations he might undertake. His work, in short, had to be one of tactful substitution, now for Davis, now for Johnston.

It was pressing work, too, because important changes had occurred since Johnston had marched from the Rapidan, leaving on that line and at Fredericksburg only a thin detachment of observation. The strength of the Federals under McDowell in northern Virginia was still unknown but was assumed to be great. On April 21 this army, or a large part of it, was believed to be debarking at Aquia Creek, north of Fredericksburg. Its

[9] O. R., 14, 502, 503–4, 515–16, 523, 524, 527–28.
[10] O. R., 14, 477. For correspondence regarding Florida, see O. R., 6, 660, 868, 878; O. R., 14, 483, 484–85; O. R., 53, 226, 234, 245, 247.
[11] Johnston's Narrative, 128–29.

31

advanced guard, estimated at 5000, had reached the Rappahannock opposite that city. In its front was only Field's brigade, about 2500 men, which had withdrawn fourteen miles south of Fredericksburg to get behind streams that were then very high.

Forty-seven miles west of Fredericksburg, at Gordonsville, lay the greater part of Ewell's division, now 8500 strong.[12] This force was the mobile reserve designed to be moved eastward to Fredericksburg or Richmond or across the Blue Ridge to support Jackson, as required. At Swift Run Gap, twenty-five miles northeast of Staunton, Jackson had 6000 men, in the face of General N. P. Banks, whose strength in the Shenandoah Valley was not known but was thought to be much in excess of Jackson's.[13] Detachments from Banks and from McDowell were vaguely reported at various points between Winchester and Manassas Junction.

Among them Field, Ewell, and Jackson had 17,000 men from east to west over a front of eighty-three miles. The only other troops then available in Virginia, outside Johnston's enlarged command east of Richmond, were the three insignificant forces covering the roads from western Virginia—Edward Johnson's 2800, Heth's 1500, and Marshall's 1500. Marshall was at too great a distance to help Jackson. Heth probably was too remote. Edward Johnson's little command on the Parkersburg road had been compelled to withdraw close to Staunton in the face of Milroy's advanced guard of Frémont's army, which was believed to outnumber it very greatly.[14] Johnson was more apt to need help than to be able to render it.

On April 21 the Federals had the greatest opportunity the war in Virginia was to offer them until the late winter of 1864-65. Correspondingly, the Confederate position was one of acutest danger. The odds against the troops north, west, and northwest of Richmond were even greater than the Confederates supposed —65,000 to 24,000.[15] If Banks and Frémont occupied Jackson and

---

[12] Including artillery.   [13] Actually it was around 21,000, somewhat scattered.

[14] In reality, Frémont had 4087 in the Cheat Mountain district on April 30, according to his return, 8494 in the District of the Kanawha, and on his lines of communication, 4640; total, 17,221 (*O. R., 12*, part 3, p. 121).

[15] These figures of Federal strength include Blenker's division, which was moved about so much as to be almost useless. McDowell, whose strength in April is hard to determine, is here credited with 30,000. His May returns, which include some units previously with Banks, show 47,484 (*O. R., 12*, part 3, p. 309).

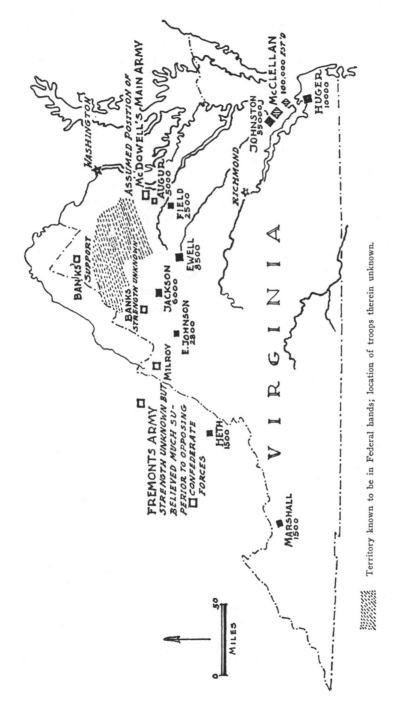

Distribution of Confederate forces and assumed position of the Union armies in Virginia, April 21, 1862.

Territory known to be in Federal hands; location of troops therein unknown.

VIRGINIA

WASHINGTON

ASSUMED POSITION OF McDOWELL'S MAIN ARMY

McCLELLAN 100,000 EST'D

HUGER 10000

JOHNSTON 55000

RICHMOND

AUGUR 5000

FIELD 2500

EWELL 8500

BANKS (SUPPORT)

BANKS STRENGTH UNKNOWN

JACKSON 6000

E. JOHNSON 2800

MILROY

FREMONTS ARMY STRENGTH UNKNOWN BUT BELIEVED MUCH SUPERIOR TO OPPOSING CONFEDERATE FORCES

HETH 1500

MARSHALL 1500

MILES
0   50

Ewell, then a sudden thrust across the Rappahannock by the force under McDowell would of course overwhelm Field's little command. Richmond would be only sixty miles to the southward, less than five easy marches, and McDowell would be on Johnston's line of communications before that officer could return to Richmond. Indeed, a quick attack by McClellan might mean the destruction of Johnston ere he could reach the defenses of the capital. Even if the Federal armies were not then capable of launching four offensives simultaneously, it seemed almost certain that McClellan and McDowell could unite in front of Richmond. They could invest the city from the north, the east, and the south and either reduce it with their superior artillery or force the immediate retreat of Johnston to North Carolina. Thus the least result of vigorous, joint action by the Federals would be that they would soon occupy the whole of Virginia, and the reasonably attainable outcome would be the decisive defeat of the one formidable army then under the Southern flag. The downfall of the Confederacy by midsummer was a distinct possibility.

Johnston and Lee were both alive to this danger, but they took fundamentally different views of the best method to meet it. Johnston changed his proposals from time to time, as was natural, but, generally speaking, he continued to urge that concentration be met with concentration—that as McClellan and McDowell were almost certain to form a junction, they should be allowed to advance to a great distance from their bases and should then be attacked by all the Confederate forces from the Rapidan to the Savannah. Lee's strategy, on the other hand, reduced to the simplest formula, was not to meet concentration with concentration but to occupy the Federals on the Peninsula and to undertake an offensive-defensive in northern Virginia that would prevent a Federal concentration. Lee's was the bolder policy, but in a long view it was the more prudent course. It was better to keep the Federals away from Richmond than to attempt to fight a battle there, much less to stand a siege. Knowing the strength of the North, Lee never willingly accepted investment in a fixed position. His study of Napoleon warned him of the danger of such a course. He sought always to keep the enemy at a distance from his base, and when a siege was threatened, his impulse was to avoid it by a counter-stroke. If a siege was inevitable or the enemy was concentrated in a single army, then, of course, Lee was as insistent as Johnston could have been on the fullest possible concentration.

Because great stakes hung on the throw, and because troop-movements in northern Virginia from April 17 to May 25 represent the first development of some of the most distinctive methods Lee was subsequently to employ, the student of war will find interest in every line of the correspondence that now opened between Lee and the commanding officers on the Rappahannock and in the valley.

Lee's fundamental problem was to prevent the reinforcement of McClellan from any quarter. Immediately, as he saw it, the point of danger was Fredericksburg, where McDowell might establish a base for an advance to McClellan's flank.[16] The Rappahannock city was so feebly defended that Field's little brigade could not retard, much less halt, a Federal offensive. Before anything else was done, therefore, the Fredericksburg line had to be strengthened against demonstrations that might show the weakness of the defending force. Lee felt out Johnston to see if that officer could release any of the troops recently sent to the Peninsula, but was assured that this was impossible.[17] Reinforcements had to come from elsewhere. Lee could not strip the Carolina and Georgia coast, as Johnston had suggested, but, as he had no other source from which to get men, he adopted the expedient of calling for small forces from several quarters, on the theory that he would not take enough men from any army to destroy its powers of resistance. In case it were attacked, the force from which he drew reinforcements would still be strong enough to hold out until he could replace the men he had ordered elsewhere. Like a hard-pressed debtor, he had to borrow where he could to meet his most pressing obligations, trusting that, if his new creditors became troublesome, the future would bring the means with which to repay them. Already, on April 19, Lee had ordered to Richmond one regiment from North Carolina, one from South Carolina, and one from Georgia.[18] Now,

---

[16] O. R., 12, part 3, p. 859.
[17] O. R., 11, part 3, pp. 456, 458. Lee's first dispatch is missing from the records.
[18] O. R., 9, 461.

as Burnside was quiet on the North Carolina coast, Lee decided
to take the chance that he would remain so, or could be delayed
if he attempted to advance. He accordingly ordered to Virginia
Anderson's brigade of 4000 from Holmes's North Carolina
army.[19] From South Carolina Gregg's fine brigade of 3500 was
called, and a regiment was scraped together around Richmond
to complete it.[20] In this way the force at Fredericksburg, which
was to pass to the direct command of General Jos. R. Anderson,
would be raised to 13,000 men by April 28, or about that time.[21]
Pending the arrival of Anderson with these reinforcements,
Field's orders were "to preserve a firm front to the enemy, to
keep yourself accurately advised of his strength and movements,
and to communicate anything of importance that may occur at
once to this office." [22]

Thirteen thousand troops on the Rappahannock manifestly could
put up a more formidable resistance than 2500 could, but they
could not prevent an advance by such an army as McDowell was
rightly assumed to command. Something more must be done.
Either enough additional force had to be gathered on the Rappahannock to resist McDowell successfully, and to prevent his union
with McClellan in front of Richmond, or else McDowell had to be
held north of the Rappahannock and deterred from advancing.
Only the 8800 of Jackson and Edward Johnson in the Shenandoah
Valley and Ewell's 8000 at Gordonsville could be counted on for
either purpose, and they, of course, were threatened by Banks and
Frémont.

Lee promptly decided how he would utilize these troops in the
crisis. On April 21, before any of Field's reinforcements had
reached him, Lee wrote one of the most historic of all his military
dispatches. It was addressed to Jackson. In it, Lee outlined the
situation in front of Fredericksburg and suggested three possibilities. First, if Jackson felt that he could drive Banks down the
valley by calling up Ewell's division, he was advised to do so.
This, said Lee, "will prove a great relief to the pressure on

[19] O. R., 9, 459, 462. For Lee's further correspondence regarding the situation in
North Carolina, see ibid., 9, 448, 450, 452 ff., 455, 457, 458, 462.
[20] O. R., 14, 480, 481.
[21] Cf. O. R., 11, part 3, p. 458. [22] O. R., 12, part 3, p. 859.

Fredericksburg." If, secondly, Banks was too strong to be attacked, and Jackson thought that Ewell should be in supporting distance, it would be well to place Ewell between Richmond and Fredericksburg, that was to say, in front of the line of the Virginia Central Railroad, near Hanover Junction, whence he could be moved with equal speed by rail to support Jackson, Field, or even Johnston, in case the battle went against the Confederates on the Peninsula. If, in the third place, Jackson believed that he could hold Banks without assistance, then Lee recommended that Ewell be made ready to reinforce Field.[23] In a word, instead of waiting for Frémont and Banks to crush Jackson and Ewell, while McDowell disposed of Field and moved to unite with McClellan, Lee proposed to anticipate all of them, to take the initiative, and so to occupy McDowell that he could not advance from the line of the Rappahannock. "I have hoped," he wrote Jackson four days later, "in the present divided condition of the enemy's forces that a successful blow may be dealt them by a rapid combination of our troops before they can be strengthened themselves either in position or by re-enforcements." [24]

While submitting three plans to Jackson, over whom, it must be remembered, he had no formal command, Lee manifestly favored an attack by Jackson and Ewell on Banks. In the course of his correspondence with the two Confederate commanders during the fortnight following the letter of April 21, Lee wrote few dispatches in which he did not dwell on this possibility. When it seemed that Jackson could not attempt to assail Banks directly, Lee suggested that Jackson and Ewell advance east of the main Federal force in the Shenandoah Valley and destroy Banks's communications, either around Warrenton or at White Plains and Salem. He was altogether for an immediate offensive-defensive. "The blow, wherever struck, must, to be successful, be sudden and heavy"—such was his admonition.[25]

Jackson, at this time, did not feel strong enough to attack

23 *O. R.*, 12, part 3, pp. 859–60. *Cf.* Lee to Ewell, *ibid.*, 869. This is improperly addressed to Ewell in "Somerset County." A photostat in the Library of Congress reads "near Sommerset, Va."

24 *O. R.*, 12, part 3, p. 865.

25 *O. R.*, 12, part 3, p. 866. For his further references to an attack on Banks, see *ibid.*, 875, 878.

Banks, even with Ewell's support, unless Lee could send him 5000 men. Lee could not do this,[26] though he cherished a momentary hope of being able to dispatch Heth to his support.[27] As an alternative to an immediate offensive against Banks, Jackson proposed that he unite with Edward Johnson, who was being pressed back on Staunton. He could then attack Milroy, leading Frémont's advanced force, Jackson reasoned, and if he succeeded in defeating Milroy, he could take Edward Johnson and Ewell, strike Banks, and then come east of the Blue Ridge to Fredericksburg or to any other threatened point. Doubtful whether it was practicable at that moment to attack Banks, Lee, on May 1, approved Jackson's plan for joint operations with Edward Johnson west of Staunton, but he kept reverting to the desirability of an offensive against Banks. Lee was willing that the offensive should be undertaken at Fredericksburg, if nothing else could be done, but he continued of opinion that the best way to hold the line of the Rappahannock was to strike in the valley.[28]

It has generally been assumed that, in urging this course, Lee was actuated by a conviction that he could play on President Lincoln's fears for the safety of Washington. Those who argue this do so in a knowledge of facts with which Lee could not possibly have been acquainted at this time. After the battle of Winchester, Lee discovered that President Lincoln would make almost any military sacrifice and forego any offensive plan in order to save Washington from the risk of capture, but in early May Lee's strategy was based on military considerations only. He believed that an advance down the valley would so threaten the communications of an army operating north of the Rappahannock as to keep it from advancing on Richmond. No evidence of any larger purpose than this, on Lee's part, can be adduced as of this date.

Lee's dispatch of May 1 to Jackson, authorizing him to use his discretion in attacking Frémont west of Staunton, marked the end of the first stage of the preliminaries to Jackson's renowned

---

26 *O. R.*, 12, part 3, p. 875. This letter was prepared with much care. The original draft in the *Taylor MSS.* is dated April 29 and shows interlineations that appear in a still-different form in the printed text. These differences are not very material, but they emphasize Lee's concern lest any reduction of force in front of Fredericksburg endanger Richmond or threaten the rear of the army on the Peninsula.

27 *O. R.*, 12, part 3, pp. 870, 873.   28 *O. R.*, 12, part 3, pp. 871, 872, 875, 878.

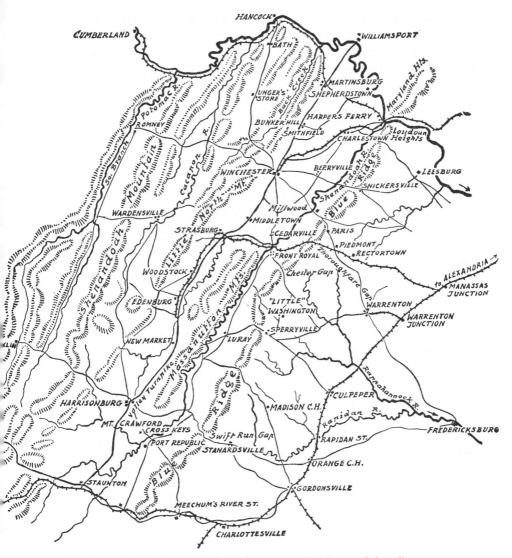

The Shenandoah Valley and the field of manœuvre directly east of the valley.

valley campaign. Jackson silently marched away on his mission to join Edward Johnson west of Staunton and, after his wont, entrusted neither to the mails nor to the telegraph any intimation of his purpose or his progress. Lee had to wait, and wait not less to see his judgment of Jackson vindicated than to see their joint

39

strategy work out. For Lee was gambling on Jackson as well as on the veteran McDowell, the adventurer Frémont, and the politician-soldier Banks. Jackson did not then have great reputation. His personal appearance was all against him. "Cavalry boots covered feet of immense size, a mangy cap with visor drawn low, a heavy dark beard, weary eyes" were his.[29] Stern in his discipline, uncommunicative in his dealings with his officers, darkly Calvinistic in his manner, this strange young soldier of thirty-eight was regarded by some of his comrades as eccentric to the point of madness. Ewell confided to his friends that Jackson was insane beyond all doubt.[30] His hard marching during the previous winter had created much ill-will against him. Ashby, who commanded his cavalry, obeyed his orders but would not permit him to organize, much less to discipline, his troopers.[31] The Romney campaign and the battle of Kernstown were accounted defeats that had effaced the distinction he had won at Manassas. Yet Lee from the outset saw in Jackson qualities that some overlooked or discredited. He had not forgotten Jackson's work at Harpers Ferry, when he had been able to communicate with him as soldier to soldier and not as deferential diplomat to sensitive individualist. To Jackson's discretion he had now entrusted operations that immediately affected the whole strategic plan for saving Richmond. The laurels of many a man of larger military reputation than Jackson had already been withered in the heat of that war. Would the new operations against Milroy justify Lee's judgment of the man or repeat the fiasco of Romney and the half-defeat of Kernstown?

[29] *R. Taylor,* 49.   [30] *R. Taylor,* 37.   [31] *O. R.,* 12, part 3, p. 880.

CHAPTER V

The Battle Brought Closer to Richmond

AFFAIRS were more desperate than ever when Lee made his gamble on Jackson and that strange man led his regiments mysteriously away into the mountains. Admiral Farragut on April 24 passed with his fleet the forts guarding the Mississippi, and the next day captured New Orleans, the largest, richest city of the Confederacy. Civilian Richmond trembled to think that what had happened in the Louisiana metropolis might be repeated on their streets.[1] The Federals under Burnside waked up. On the 26th they occupied Fort Macon, the evacuation of which Lee had previously urged.[2] Signs were multiplying that Grant was preparing to launch an offensive against Beauregard in northern Mississippi. The news from the Virginia Peninsula was bad. Almost every message from Johnston after April 24 contained some hint of an early retreat from Yorktown, which he expected the Federals to turn with their gunboats as soon as they had silenced the batteries.[3] In the face of strong arguments to the contrary by the Secretary of War,[4] Johnston on April 27 had notified the President that he was preparing to abandon his position and had renewed his argument for a general concentration in front of Richmond.[5] His dispatches had requested that bridges across the Chickahominy be constructed as rapidly as possible—an intimation that he purposed to retire close to the city.[6] In a letter to Lee on the 29th Johnston mentioned the evacuation of Richmond as a possibility that had to be considered.[7]

Then, on May 1, the very day when Lee sanctioned Jackson's move against Milroy, word came from Johnston that he intended to evacuate Yorktown on the night of May 2-3. Davis at once

---

[1] De Leon, 191. [2] O. R., 9, 458.
[3] O. R., 11, part 3, pp. 461, 464, 469, 470. Cf. ibid., 455–56, for Johnston's view of the situation on April 22: "Nobody but McClellan would have hesitated to attack."
[4] E.g., O. R., 11, part 3, p. 464. [5] Johnston's Narrative, 118–19, 127.
[6] O. R., 11, part 3, p. 469. [7] O. R., 11, part 3, p. 473.

urged Johnston to delay his retreat long enough to permit the removal of the invaluable naval supplies from Norfolk,[8] where Huger, by his own admission, was in a *cul de sac.*[9] The Secretary of War and the Secretary of the Navy prepared to go to Norfolk to see what could be saved there.[10] Lee did not lose faith, but even he was shaken and, as always, he looked to Heaven for deliverance. "We have received some heavy blows lately," he wrote on April 26, "from the effects of which, I trust, a merciful God will deliver us."[11] His was not a nature, however, to leave to God what man could perform. Still believing that the enemy could be delayed on the lower Peninsula,[12] he undertook to see if Johnston would not try to hold on a few days longer. Johnston had changed his mind about the general strategy and had reverted to the second of the two plans he had presented at the council of war at Richmond on April 14—the plan, that is, for a general offensive across the Potomac instead of a concentration and battle in front of Richmond.[13] Lee assured him the President was considering the feasibility of such a move—to be undertaken at a later date of course—and the next day, May 2, he wrote Johnston again, explaining that time was needed to complete the evacuation of Norfolk and, if possible, to bring the unfinished gunboats up James River. Lee went on: "All the time that can be gained will facilitate these operations. It is not known under what necessity you are acting or how far you can delay the movements of the enemy, who it is presumed will move up York River as soon as opened to him to annoy your flank. His advance on land can be retarded, and he might be delayed in effecting a landing on York River until your stores are withdrawn. The safety of all your ammunition is of the highest importance, and I feel every assurance that everything that can be accomplished by forethought, energy and skill on your part will be done. If it is possible for the *Virginia,* which upon the fall of Norfolk must be destroyed, to run into Yorktown at the last minute and destroy the enemy's gunboats and transports, it would greatly cripple his present and

---

[8] *O. R.,* 11, part 3, pp. 484–85.

[9] *O. R.,* 11, part 3, pp. 474–75.

[10] 2 *Davis,* 92–93.

[11] To Charlotte Lee, *Jones,* 390.

[12] J. S. Mosby, *Memoirs,* 375; J. S. Mosby's conversation with Walter Watson, *Watson's Notes on Southside Virginia,* 245.

[13] *O. R.,* 11, part 3, pp. 477, 485.

future movements, relieve your army from pursuit, and prevent its meeting the same army in Northern Virginia." [14]

It was in vain that Lee held out in his final sentence the possibility that the administration might ultimately approve Johnston's plan for a new offensive in the territory from which his army had withdrawn. Johnston had made up his mind that McClellan would soon silence his water-batteries. He had been advised, moreover, that the pilots did not believe the *Virginia* could run past the Federal fleet in Hampton Roads and reach the York or enter Poquoson River in rear of McClellan's army. [15]

On the 4th came news that Johnston, without further notice to the War Department, had removed his whole army from the Yorktown line and was retreating up the Peninsula. [16] Simultaneously Lee received the ominous tidings that Federal gunboats had passed up the York and had reached West Point, thirty-seven miles from Richmond. Lee at once telegraphed to Johnston, tactfully inquiring if light artillery might be sent to the Pamunkey to prevent the Federal ascent of that river from West Point. [17] No reply came from Johnston, nor any report on his movements. The authorities in Richmond were at least as much in the dark as the enemy was, concerning the plans of the general whose 55,000 troops were the chief reliance of the Confederacy.

The day of the evacuation of Yorktown was a Sunday, when all Richmond went to church to pray for the army. As anxious worshippers started home, word spread that the sick from the lower Peninsula were arriving and were making their way to the hospital at Camp Winder. Carriages at once were hurried to the street; wagons were hitched; Sunday dinners, uneaten, were sent to the hungry, muddy men. [18] They could tell little of what had happened except that when they had been sent from Yorktown, the army was preparing to leave the heavy guns in position [19] and to take the road toward Richmond.

---

[14] *O. R.*, 11, part 3, p. 488.

[15] *O. R.*, 11, part 3, p. 488; there are many references to the difficulties of running the *Virginia* past Fort Monroe and taking her into the York, as Lee had several times proposed. *Cf. O. R.*, 51, part 2, pp. 440–41, 539.

[16] For the order of evacuation, see *O. R.*, 11, part 3, p. 489. The evacuation, set for the night of May 2–3, was delayed until the night of May 3–4.

[17] *O. R.*, 11, part 3, 493. This same dispatch, wrongly dated March 5, also appears in *O. R.*, 5, 1090.

[18] *De Leon*, 193–94.   [19] Fifty-four were lost; *O. R.*, 11, part 3, 134.

Monday, the 5th, brought rumors of a bloody action at Williamsburg; Tuesday confirmed the story and added dark details of a stubborn rearguard battle, so closely contested that Johnston had been forced to leave his wounded in the rain and to hurry on without making a stand on the support-line that Lee had drawn in front of Williamsburg.[20] And still nothing official from Johnston! All that Lee could do, in the absence of any precise knowledge of Johnston's plans, was to prepare for a battle close to Richmond. Despite high water, he endeavored to speed the slowly progressing work on the James River defenses and channel obstructions, seven miles below the city.[21] From Norfolk, he sought to remove to Richmond the heavy guns that might supplement those already being placed to keep the enemy from ascending the river.[22] He urged, moreover, that the *Virginia* hold the mouth of the river as long as possible, to cover Johnston's flank on that stream.[23] Lee's chief hope of saving Richmond he still pinned to the projected operations in northern Virginia. Looking beyond Jackson's attack on Milroy to his cherished offensive against Banks,[24] he was scouring the seaboard for troops to reinforce Ewell, while Johnston's unhappy troops were marching up the Peninsula, with the enemy in leisurely pursuit.

At last, on May 7, came a dispatch from Johnston, the first that appears in the published records bearing date subsequent to the evacuation of Yorktown. It told of the presence of a fleet of ironclads and transports at West Point and of Johnston's apprehension for the safety of Richmond. There was no reference in the message to Johnston's plan of operations and no hint of any purpose to make an early stand. Lee had to draw his own inference from the fact that Johnston was then at Barhamsville, only thirty-five miles from Richmond, and mentioned that his army was moving in two columns, up roads that led straight to the capital. The only reassurance to be had from the paper was

---

[20] Federal casualties were 2239; Confederate, not accurately reported, were put at 1560.

[21] *O. R.*, 11, part 3, pp. 476, 485–86, 493; *O. R.*, 51, part 2, pp. 338–39, 507, 548–49.

[22] *O. R.*, 11, part 3, p. 497.

[23] *O. R.*, 11, part 3, p. 499. The *Raleigh* and *Jamestown* had already been sent up the river for this purpose, *ibid.*, 450.

[24] *Cf. infra*, p. 51.

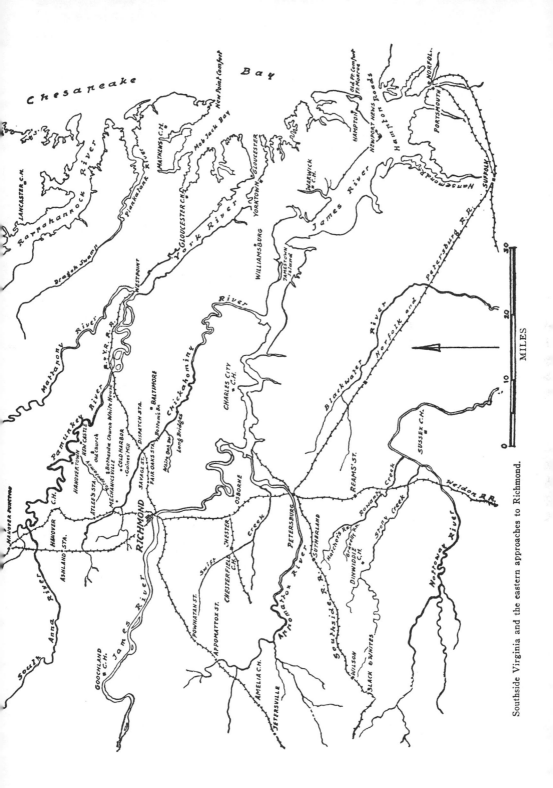

Southside Virginia and the eastern approaches to Richmond.

that Johnston held a position from which he could meet any offensive directed against his flank by way of York River.[25]

The next day brought even more disquieting evidence of the field-commander's state of mind. His known and deplored jealousy as to his prerogatives broke out, most inopportunely, in a long, sharply phrased letter of many complaints: Without his knowledge, he said, troops under his command on the south side of the James had been ordered about by Lee; he had not been informed concerning operations on the Fredericksburg front; nothing had been said to him as to the placing of obstructions in the Pamunkey: he had no control over work on the Richmond defenses. "My authority," he said, "does not extend beyond the troops immediately around me. I request therefore to be relieved of a merely nominal geographical command. The service will gain thereby the unity of command, which is essential in war." [26]

The feeling disclosed in this letter had been shown before by Johnston in smaller things, when the possible consequences of discord had not been so serious. After Bull Run he had wrathfully refused to accept a staff officer because he thought Lee had no right to send him,[27] and his grievance over rank had increased as he had meditated upon it.[28] Truth was, Johnston possessed very great ability as a strategist and was in many of his impulses generous and warm-hearted, but his temper was apt to get out of control when he felt his authority was ignored. Although he was able to win and to hold the affection of his subordinates, he was suspicious, reserved, and wholly lacking in the arts of conciliation when dealing with his superiors. In this crisis, burdened with responsibility, and conscious that he did not possess the good opinion of the President, he appeared at his

---

[25] *O. R.*, 51, part 2, pp. 552–53. On the day that Johnston wrote, May 7, General G. W. Smith repulsed an enemy force at Eltham Landing (*Johnston's Narrative*, 126; *G. W. Smith*, 47). General Hood, *op. cit.*, 153, said that Johnston told a volunteer aide, during the retreat up the Peninsula, that he expected to be compelled to evacuate Richmond. The evidence as to this assertion is second-hand, though it probably is a fact that Johnston did not believe he would be able to hold the city.

[26] *O. R.*, 11, part 3, pp. 499–500. [27] *D. H. Maury*, 144.

[28] See *supra*. Johnston's formal statement of his case appears in IV *O. R.*, 1, 605 *ff.* Davis's contention was that Johnston's commission as a brigadier general, U. S. A., had been as quartermaster general, a staff appointment, with specific prohibition on the command of troops, and that Johnston's rank as a line officer was below that of those to whom he claimed to be senior.

worst and was a most difficult man with whom to work. Lee, however, understood from old acquaintance that Johnston usually cooled as quickly as he boiled. Knowing and admiring the man, Lee had no intention of permitting Johnston's testiness to ruin a friendship of thirty-five years' standing or to endanger a cause to which he knew Johnston was sincerely devoted. With patient tact, therefore, in a long letter, he smoothed down Johnston's ruffled sensibilities, explained all the matters of which Johnston complained, and ignored his request to be relieved of responsibility for the troops on the south side of the James.[29] The incident, however, was a new warning of what might be expected in dealing with Johnston, and this, in turn, added to the difficulty of a situation that now seemed to be hurrying to a tragic climax.

For Johnston's army had continued its retreat and now was less than thirty miles from Richmond and only fifteen from the Chickahominy, the last natural barrier in McClellan's way.[30] Stragglers were streaming into Richmond, some of them men who had thrown away their arms on the field of Williamsburg;[31] on May 10 the Federals entered Norfolk—an irreparable loss;[32] the valiant *Virginia* was blown up on the 11th, being unable to pass up James River and having no harbor;[33] Huger was in retreat up the south side of the James toward Petersburg, destroying the railroad as he went;[34] Federal gunboats were in the river,[35] the defenses below the capital were still so weak that field artillery had to be hurried down to support the guns in fixed positions;[36] panic had again seized Richmond and was driving hundreds southward;[37] the archives were packed for removal and a conference was held on the disposition of reserve rations;[38] committees waited on the President to know if he intended to hold the city, and went away scarcely reassured by his calm announcement that he would.[39] News reached Richmond that Jackson had

---

[29] *O. R.*, 11, part 3, pp. 502–3.

[30] Johnston's headquarters on May 9 were at New Kent Courthouse; *O. R.*, 11, part 3, p. 502.

[31] *O. R.*, 11, part 3, 505, 506, 514.   [32] *O. R.*, 11, part 3, p. 162.

[33] *O. R.*, 11, part 3, 163–64.   [34] *O. R.*, 11, part 3, p. 507.

[35] *O. R.*, 51, part 2, pp. 553–54. *O. R.*, 11, part 3, p. 505.

[36] *O. R.*, 11, part 3, p. 516; *O. R.*, 51, part 2, pp. 555–56.

[37] *Miss Brock*, 129; T. R. R. Cobb, in 28 *S. H. S. P.*, 292.

[38] *O. R.*, 11, part 3, 504, 512–13. McCabe stated, *op. cit.*, 94–96, that Congress adjourned precipitately about this time, but actually it had adjourned on April 21.

[39] *De Leon*, 197; *Mrs. McGuire*, 113.

won a victory over Milroy at the village of McDowell on May 8, and had driven the Federals westward from in front of Staunton, but this did not ease the mind of a public which did not understand that the battle was the auspicious preliminary to the fulfillment of larger plans. Jackson was declared "too rash" and a whisper that he was crazy when under excitement went the rounds.[40] The President was bitterly assailed. Lee was criticised for what he had not directed on the Peninsula and for what he could not now prevent.[41]

Had Lee been of a nature to heed criticism of this sort, he would not have had time to trouble himself with it. Every energy was bent on the preparation of the defenses at Drewry's Bluff. That was now a more important position than even the line of the Chickahominy, toward which Johnston's columns were slowly marching. When Johnston finally made a stand and fortified himself, he could at least hold off McClellan for a time. But the Federal ironclads were coming up the James; the lower defenses of the river had all been abandoned; nothing stood between the Union fleet and Richmond except the incomplete batteries perched there on the cliff at Drewry's. A brief bombardment might decide the fate of that fortification and of Richmond any day the Federals saw fit to attack.

All the resources of the breathless capital were requisitioned to finish the obstructions and batteries, if possible, before the enemy's ships hove in sight. The seasoned, confident gunners of the abandoned *Virginia* were sent to Drewry's to reinforce the garrison.[42] The crude machines that had been used to drive piles across the James were worked furiously. Ships that had been brought up from Norfolk were sunk below the bluff. A brigade from Huger's division was sent there by forced marches. Troops were posted on both sides the river to punish the incautious when the ships hove in sight. General William Mahone, as the most experienced construction engineer, was placed in charge of the defensive preparations.[43]

Twice the President and General Lee went down the river to examine in person the condition of the defenses.[44] To them, to

---

[40] *Mrs. McGuire*, 112.
[41] *Mrs. McGuire*, 113.
[43] *O. R.*, 11, part 3, pp. 515, 516, 518.
[42] *N. O. R.*, 7, 799.
[44] *Mrs. McGuire*, 113–14.

anxious Richmond, and to the panting engineers who battled
with mud and high water, the work at Drewry's seemed to progress with torturing slowness. The chances of success or disaster
appeared to be about even. While Lee was struggling to better
the odds, the President had to consider what should be done if
the enemy passed the batteries on the bluff. His courage was as
staunch as Lee's own, but after what had happened on the York,
he could not decline to ask himself how the army could escape
from the front of Richmond in case of disaster, and where it
would make its next stand.

The counsel of Lee was sought on this dark question. He was
summoned to a cabinet meeting and was asked what line south
of Richmond the army of Johnston could best take up if forced
to evacuate that city. The answer was not difficult from a military
point of view: The next good line was that of the Staunton
River, nearly one hundred miles to the southwest rather than to
the south. Usually, Lee would have answered the President's
question and would have said no more, but now his fighting-
blood was up. The army could occupy a good position on the
Staunton if Richmond fell, "but," he said—and tears rose in his
eyes—"Richmond must not be given up; it shall not be given
up!" His words were an amazement to men who had come to
look on his self-control as invulnerable. "I have seen him on
many occasions," Postmaster-General Reagan subsequently wrote,
"when the very fate of the Confederacy hung in the balance;
but I never saw him show equally deep emotion." [45]

Early on the morning of May 15, Lee rode down the valley of
the James for a further examination of the river defenses. He had
not gone far when across the flats there came the roar of the
heaviest guns that had ever echoed over that quiet country. The
Federals were attacking Drewry's Bluff! A few hours would tell
which flag would float at nightfall over the capitol. Quickly the
ordnance on the cliff took up the challenge. Farther down the
river, on either bank, there was the bark of small arms as the
Southern sharpshooters sought to hold the Federal sailors below

---

[45] J. H. Reagan: *Memoirs* (cited hereafter as *Reagan*), 139. The date of this meeting, as of many incidents during the exciting days of May, 1862, cannot be fixed with
certainty. Although there is no date into which all the related facts fit so well as approximately May 14, it is possible that the incident came later.

decks. For three hours and twenty minutes thunder followed thunder. Then the fire died away and the calm of the country-side settled once again.

It was not long before Lee and the anxious city behind him heard what had happened. The redoubtable *Monitor,* the iron-clad *Galena,* and three other ships had steamed up the river almost to the obstructions and had engaged the garrison of the unfinished fortification. The Southern gunners had met this attack with a deliberate, accurate fire. The Confederate ship *Patrick Henry,* above the obstructions, had added the weight of its metal. *Galena,* badly mauled, her thick iron plates rent and buckled, had finally quit the fight, and, with the other vessels, had dropped down the stream, out of sight. The repulse was as decisive as it was surprising.[46]

Would the enemy renew the battle on the river, would he attempt to take Drewry's from the land side, or would the next thrust be across the marshes of the sluggish Chickahominy? Lee was not certain,[47] but, so far as his limited authority went, he prepared to make the best resistance he could with the water-batteries and on either side of the James. Tactfully he urged Johnston to challenge McClellan's advance before the Federal army established contact with the fleet on James River.[48] Vigorously he pushed the construction of works on the north bank, in the expectation that, if Johnston were forced to withdraw closer to Richmond, he would rest his right flank on that stream, opposite Drewry's Bluff.[49] And all the while he kept looking to Jackson for the move by which, and perhaps by which alone, he believed that Richmond could be saved.

[46] *N. O. R.,* 7, 356 *ff.;* 2 *B. and L.,* 270. *McCabe, op. cit.,* 95, said that Lee and Davis witnessed the fight, and Taylor, *O. R.,* 11, part 3, 518, stated that Lee went down the river, but Lee's reference to the affair in his letter of May 16 to Jackson, *O. R.,* 12, part 3 p 893, does not read like the account of an eye-witness. It is probable that Lee was on the north side of the James, above Drewry's Bluff, and did not reach Chaffin's Bluff, if he went there at all, until the action was over. In 29 *S. H. S. P.,* 284, Major A. H. Drewry denied the published report that the crew of the *Virginia* beat off the attack.
[47] *Cf.* his letter of May 16 to General Huger, *O. R.,* 11, part 3, pp. 519–20.
[48] *O. R.,* 11, part 3, p. 523.   [49] *O. R.,* 11, part 3, p. 521.

CHAPTER VI

"Drive Him Back Toward the Potomac"

From the time Drewry's Bluff was first threatened, about May 12, until the end of that month, Lee's position was increasingly difficult. Two games of chess, so to speak, were in progress under his eyes. Johnston was playing one, Jackson the other. Over Johnston's game Lee had no control. Jackson's moves he had been directed to supervise, under Davis's verbal orders. Yet Johnston, also, could direct Jackson. Lee had to advise the commander in the valley without knowing when Johnston would look up from his own board and tell Jackson what to do. The closer Johnston came to Richmond, the more certain it was that he would resume his command of Jackson's operations. So far as Lee's own sensibilities were concerned, it made no difference when Johnston again took charge of affairs in the valley. Lee would have been glad at any time to be relieved of responsibility where he lacked commensurate authority. But the strategy of Jackson was complicated and might easily be upset by conflicting orders, whereas, if the most were made of his opportunities, the rapid execution of his plans might change the whole dark situation in Virginia.

When Jackson had marched off into the mountains, by roundabout roads, to move against Milroy, west of Staunton, he had left Ewell at Swift Run Gap, in the Blue Ridge. From that point Ewell could watch Banks or move eastward to support Anderson at Fredericksburg in case that officer was assailed. The inactivity of the Federals in the valley and at Fredericksburg puzzled Lee. He could not understand why so large a column as was reported to be just north of Fredericksburg remained quiet for so long a time. He began to doubt if this army of McDowell's was so large as it was supposed to be,[1] and he suspected that McDowell

[1] O. R., 12, part 3, p. 887.

50

might really be waiting for reinforcements from Banks in the valley. In that case, it was very desirable to keep Banks from sending troops to McDowell, for if McDowell were strengthened, he would certainly march on Richmond. Accordingly, Lee ordered Branch's brigade from North Carolina, where he saw no further evidence of any intention on Burnside's part to move inland toward the railroad that connected Richmond with the South.[2] Branch was dispatched to Gordonsville on May 5 to support Ewell, in the hope that this enlarged force would be strong enough to make a raid on Banks's communications and tie him down in the Shenandoah Valley.[3] Twice after Branch's arrival Lee urged Ewell to undertake this raid if he were not needed to support Jackson, or if it should develop that Banks was leaving the valley.[4] Ewell, however, had received a very important piece of news: Banks had ordered three days' rations cooked. Evidently he was preparing to move. Would it be on Staunton, or down the valley to Winchester, or across the mountains to Fredericksburg or Alexandria? Ewell did not know and, until he could be sure, he decided not to start the raid Lee had authorized. He notified Jackson of Banks's signs of activity, and received orders to remain in the valley as long as Banks did or at least until Jackson could return from his expedition against Frémont's army.[5]

Jackson, meantime, had been in something of a quandary. Having reached Staunton by a little-used route, he had joined Edward Johnson and, on May 8, had struck Milroy at the village of McDowell and had forced him back with losses. This was the battle the news of which had failed to lift the pervading gloom in Richmond, because Jackson had been accounted "too rash." The victory, in fact, had been by no means decisive but it had discouraged further Federal advances along the Parkersburg road and it probably had created in the minds of the Federals an exaggerated idea of the Confederate strength in the valley. Jackson's efforts to follow up the enemy had yielded no results and he had been debating a northward movement, along a road west

---

[2] *O. R.*, 9, 467–68.
[3] *O. R.*, 12, part 3, pp. 887, 880–81. The editors of the *Official Records* enter Lee's letter of May 5 under that date but suggest in a foot-note that the proper date may have been May 15. Subsequent correspondence shows May 5 to have been correct.
[4] *O. R.*, 12, part 3, pp. 883, 885, 887. [5] *O. R.*, 12, part 3, pp. 887–88.

of the Shenandoah Mountains, in an attempt to get in Banks's rear. On receipt of the news that Banks was cooking three days' rations he resolved his quandary by deciding to return to Ewell *via* the shortest route.

As far as Lee knew of the development of these plans, he approved them step by step, leaving all details to Jackson's discretion, but when his adjutant general wrote Jackson to congratulate that officer on the victory at McDowell, he once more reverted to the plan that Lee had put first. General Lee, wrote Taylor, "thinks that if you can form a junction with General Ewell with your combined forces you would be able to drive Banks from the valley." [6]

This letter was dated May 14 and it ended the brief period of unhampered direction of Jackson's movements that Lee had enjoyed since Johnston had gone to the Peninsula. In two somewhat sharp letters to Lee, Johnston reasserted his right to the direction of operations in northern Virginia and he now proceeded to exercise it.[7]

Johnston's military method was quite different from that of Lee. A general design Johnston could fashion very soundly, but he was careless of details, and, if his larger strategic plans did not work out, he was disposed to extemporize from day to day, retreating if necessary and waiting for some good opportunity to attack. Lee's impulse, one might almost say his military instinct, was to devise a broad general plan, or to develop one from circumstance, and to watch the details so closely that he did not have to change his basic strategy so often as Johnston did. Lee disliked to direct remote operations, because he insisted that he could understand a situation only when he examined the ground, but his method was better suited to such work than Johnston's was. Now that Johnston again assumed control, there was danger that his natural desire to reinforce his own army would lead him to minimize the value of Lee's simple plan to drive Banks from the Valley.

Johnston's first orders to Ewell and to Jackson were issued on May 13. They provided that if Jackson and Ewell were strong

[6] *O. R.*, 12, part 3, p. 889.   [7] *O. R.*, 11, part 3, pp. 503, 505, 506, 510–11.

enough, they should attack Banks. "Should the latter cross the Blue Ridge," Johnston wrote Ewell, "to join General McDowell at Fredericksburg, General Jackson and yourself should move eastward rapidly to join either the army near Fredericksburg, commanded by Brig. Gen. J. R. Anderson, or this one. I must be kept informed of your movements and progress, that your instructions may be modified as circumstances change." Branch was to remain with Jackson and Ewell.[8] Lee could have known nothing of these orders, else he would not have urged Jackson, the following day, to fall on Banks with Ewell's support.

Two plans of action were thus presented Jackson, both of them contingent. Johnston regarded a joint attack on Banks by Ewell and Jackson as desirable; Lee saw in it the supreme opportunity of the campaign. If Jackson and Ewell could not attack Banks in the valley, Johnston was quite content to have them join Anderson at Fredericksburg or come to Richmond. Lee felt that if the offensive could not be taken in the valley, Jackson and Ewell should strike at Banks as he moved eastward or else assail his line of communication. Only in case of inability to do this was he inclined to send Jackson and Ewell to Fredericksburg. Fundamentally, Lee was determined to keep McDowell from joining McClellan.[9] Johnston had less faith than Lee in the success of any attempt to stop McDowell's march to McClellan. He had previously cherished the hope that this might be done,[10] but he had virtually abandoned it.[11] The whole tone of his correspondence again indicated a belief, never fully expressed, that he must effect a general concentration around Richmond, because he could not prevent the junction of McDowell and McClellan.

Before either Johnston's conditional orders or Lee's reiterated suggestion of an attack on Banks reached him, Ewell got word that Banks had started to retire northward, down the valley, and that two of his brigades were at Front Royal. This might mean either that Banks was withdrawing for fear he would be outflanked by Jackson, or that he was preparing to leave the valley and join McDowell or McClellan. Under orders from Jackson,

---

[8] *O. R.*, 12, part 3, 888.
[9] *Cf.* Lee to Johnston, April 23, 1862, *O. R.*, 11, part 3, p. 459.
[10] *O. R.*, 11, part 3, pp. 455–56.   [11] *O. R.*, 11, part 3, p. 506.

Ewell on May 14 put his column in motion after Banks,[12] while Jackson hurried on to overtake Ewell.

Advised of these movements by Ewell, Lee did not feel that he should issue orders supplementing those that Johnston had given, but he could not altogether forgo advocacy of a plan of which he expected so much. On May 15 he informed Ewell of Jackson's approach and once again reminded him that "if upon the junction of yours and General Jackson's forces a blow could be struck at Banks, it would make a happy diversion in our favor in other directions."[13] Writing to Jackson the next day, May 16, he informed him of the general situation and tactfully sought to reconcile Johnston's orders of May 13 with his own suggestion of operations against Banks. He explained that Banks might be planning to join McDowell or to take shipping at Alexandria and reinforce McClellan. "Whatever may be Banks' intention," he said, "it is very desirable to prevent him from going either to Fredericksburg or the Peninsula, and also to destroy the Manassas Gap road. A successful blow struck at him would delay, if it does not prevent, his moving to either place, and might also lead him to recall the re-enforcements sent to Fremont from Winchester. . . ." He went on: "But you will not, in any demonstration you may make in that direction, lose sight of the fact that it may become necessary for you to come to the support of General Johnston, and hold yourself in readiness to do so if required."[14]

On the 17th, the day after Lee sent this letter, Jackson was at Mount Solon, Augusta County, twelve miles southwest of Harrisonburg, and was headed for the valley turnpike. Ewell was marching after Banks. That same day fresh reports reached Jackson: Banks had halted his northward movement and was fortifying at Strasburg, eighteen miles south of Winchester. Simultaneously, Ewell heard that Shields's command, which had been with Banks, had crossed the Blue Ridge bound for Warren-

[12] O. R., 12, part 3, pp. 889, 890.   [13] O. R., 12, part 3, p. 891.

[14] O. R., 12, part 3, pp. 892–93. The last-quoted sentence has often been cited as marking the genesis of the plan that Lee later developed to bring Jackson from the valley in order that he might participate in the campaign of the Seven Days. The fact is, as early as April 23, this particular movement had been accepted as part of a general concentration around Richmond in case of necessity (O. R., 11, part 3, pp. 456, 459). Lee's reference to the matter on May 16, in the writer's opinion, was simply, as set forth in the text, to reconcile his own suggestions with Johnston's orders.

ton.[15] This meant, of course, that Banks's strength was reduced. The opportunity of attacking him, as Lee had proposed, seemed to have come. But there was one very serious obstacle. It threatened to upset the whole strategic plan at the very moment when its execution was possible: Johnston's orders to Ewell were that if Banks crossed the Blue Ridge, Ewell must follow him. Ewell was always strict in his construction of orders and he felt that Shields's departure was such a move as Johnston had contemplated. He accordingly considered that he should halt his march down the valley and turn eastward, paralleling Shields. He so advised Jackson, who, in turn, communicated with Johnston telling him what Banks was supposed to be doing at Strasburg. "I have been moving down the valley for the purpose of attacking Banks," Jackson wrote, "but the withdrawal of General Ewell's command will prevent my purpose being executed. I will move on toward Harrisonburg, and if you desire me to cross the Blue Ridge please let me know by telegraph." [16]

The decision Johnston was called upon to make on receipt of this telegram was of the sort that brings out a commander's natural caution or daring, a quality of mind that usually tips the beam one way or the other when arguments seem to be balanced. Lee's whole inclination would have been to take the lesser risks for the sake of the great gain that would follow a defeat of Banks. Johnston's conservatism and his concern for his own army in front of Richmond led him to give contrary orders. "If Banks is fortifying near Strasburg," he told Ewell, "the attack would be too hazardous. In such an event we must leave him in his works. General Jackson can observe him and you can come eastward. If, however, Shields is on the Orange and Alexandria railroad near the Rapidan, it might be worth while for your joint forces to attack him, then for you to move on, while Jackson should keep Banks away from McDowell. We want troops here; none, therefore, must keep away unless employing a greatly superior force of the enemy. In your march communicate with Brigadier-General Anderson, near Fredericksburg; he may require your assistance. My general idea is to gather here all the troops who do not keep away from McClellan's greatly superior

[15] O. R., 12, part 3, pp. 894, 895.   [16] O. R., 12, part 3, pp. 894–95.

forces." [17] Branch's brigade, Ewell's support in the vicinity of Gordonsville, was directed to move to Johnston's left flank.[18]

These orders brought the valley campaign to its first crisis. The opportunity of destroying Banks was to be forgone. Jackson was to be left to face Banks in his front and Frémont on his flank or in his rear, as soon as Frémont's army recovered from the minor defeat of Milroy at McDowell. The best that could possibly be gained would be to put Shields *hors de combat*. Then Ewell and Anderson probably would be called to Johnston, the line of communications between Richmond and Jackson's army might be cut, and Johnston, plus Ewell and Anderson, might have to face McClellan's and McDowell's combined forces. If, on the other hand, Banks were defeated, McDowell's communications might be so threatened that he would not dare advance, and Anderson could join Johnston for an attack on McClellan alone. Johnston could hardly have given more dangerous orders.

Lee probably did not know that his cherished plan of an early attack on Banks was threatened with immediate wreck. There is no evidence that the answer of General Johnston to Jackson's telegram was communicated to him. Probably the first he heard of the crisis came in this telegram:

Camp near New Market, Va.,
May 20, 1862.

General R. E. Lee:

I am of opinion that an attempt should be made to defeat Banks, but under instructions just received from General Johnston I do not feel at liberty to make an attack. Please answer by telegraph at once.

T. J. JACKSON,
Major-General.[19]

Jackson, in other words, had courageously met the crisis. He saw his opportunity lost if Johnston's orders were obeyed. Every impulse, every report of his scouts, every reflection upon the situation, convinced him that Lee's strategy was preferable. The

17 *O. R.*, 12, part 3, pp. 896–97. The text reads "who do not keep away from McClellan's greatly superior forces." The context makes *McClellan*, rather than *McClellan's*, the correct word.
18 *O. R.*, 12, part 3, p. 897.   19 *O. R.*, 12, part 3, p. 898.

execution of orders was a part of Jackson's religion not less than of his military code, but in this instance, knowing the greatness of the stakes and the weight of the loss if he failed to attack Banks, he had countermanded the movement of Ewell to the east of the mountains and had appealed to headquarters. It was one of the most important acts of his career and it made possible the movements that were soon to win him a place among the great captains of war.

The copious records of the campaign curiously enough do not show precisely what Lee did when he received Jackson's appeal for a revocation of the orders of Johnston. Whether he spurred to Johnston's quarters and prevailed upon that officer to countermand his instructions, or whether he took the question directly to the President, it is impossible to say. The probabilities are that he did not lose the time that a reference of the subject to Johnston inevitably would have involved. The answer, which could only be of one sort, went forward quickly, and at dawn on May 21 Jackson set his column in motion down the valley to join Ewell in an attack on Banks, fortifications or no fortifications.[20] Then, for the second time within a month, the curtain of Jackson's military caution was dropped between Richmond and the valley, and days passed before Lee knew what was happening.

[20] G. F. R. Henderson: *Stonewall Jackson and the American Civil War* (cited hereafter as *Henderson*), I, 313.

CHAPTER VII

An Anxious Fortnight Ends in a Memorable Ride

JACKSON was a hundred miles from Richmond when he started in pursuit of Banks; Johnston was only half an hour's ride away. Following the repulse of the Federal gunboats at Drewry's Bluff on May 15, Johnston decided to bring the greater part of his army across the Chickahominy River both to give it safety and to cover the land defenses being constructed on the north side of the James opposite the cliff where the garrison of Drewry's Bluff had fought so valiantly against the *Galena* and her sister-ships. The Chickahominy's course is roughly parallel to that of the James for many miles and its upper stretch is only some five miles north of Richmond. At the point where the river is nearest to Richmond, it is crossed by the Virginia Central Railroad, the main line of communication with the Shenandoah Valley. A little farther westward lies the Richmond, Fredericksburg and Potomac Railroad. As it was necessary to guard these railways, Johnston put part of one division north of the Chickahominy. The right flank of his main force he gradually drew in until on May 22 it was across the Charles City Road, about five miles from the corporate limits of Richmond. Thence his line ran generally northward to the vicinity of the Chickahominy. His left was close to the Fairfield race-course, almost within the northeastern suburbs of the city,[1] but his outposts were north of the Chickahominy as far as Mechanicsville. McClellan, advancing cautiously, was known to have two corps of his army at Cold Harbor, about eight miles northeast of Richmond and was believed to be preparing to extend his right flank to form a ready junction with McDowell, whenever that officer moved southward from Fredericksburg. The rest of McClellan's army, on the 22d, was crossing the Chickahominy at Bottom's Bridge, fifteen miles

---

[1] *O. R.*, 11, part 3, p. 533.

east of Richmond, and was advancing up the Williamsburg road. If Johnston had to withdraw his left, he would expose the railroads but he would find good cover for his troops on the high hills overlooking the Chickahominy on the side nearest Rich-

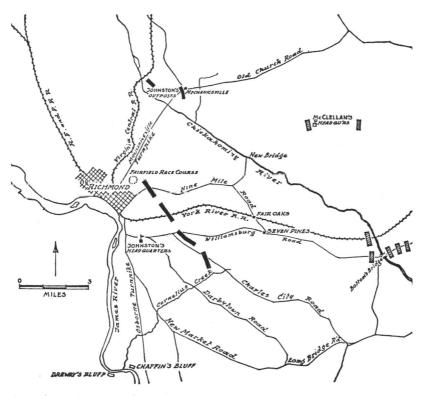

Approximate situation in front of Richmond, about May 22, 1862, showing defensive disposition of Johnston's army and the approach of McClellan.

mond. If he retired his right, however, it would have had to move across a flat country and could find no cover except scattered woods and an incomplete line of earthworks that had been thrown up, chiefly after Lee's return from Savannah.[2] It was a line so dangerously close to Richmond that the sound of a heavy action would almost certainly be heard in President Davis's office. Should the Confederate line break in a rout, two hours' pursuit would bring the Federals into the streets of Richmond.

[2] *Taylor's General Lee*, 46.

Close as Johnston was to Richmond, he had shown no intention of giving battle, and had not informed the President when he intended doing so. Soon after he crossed the Chickahominy, Davis and Lee rode out to his headquarters in order that the President might be apprized of the situation. The General was absent at the time, visiting his troops, but he returned and spent the evening with his guests. It was not a satisfactory conference. Johnston was reticent and seemed to have no definite plan, though the three talked together until too late for the President to return that night. The next morning, as Davis and Lee rode back toward Richmond, the President spoke of their discussion. Loath as Lee was to criticise a fellow-soldier, he was compelled to confess that he had been able to draw only one inference from Johnston's remarks: Johnston apparently planned to improve his position as best he could and would wait to attack the enemy at some favorable opportunity.[3]

Subsequently, Lee asked Johnston to come to Richmond to review the situation with the President, but Johnston did not answer.[4] Three days later, on May 21, Lee again wrote to ask a report in the name of Mr. Davis and renewed his suggestion that Johnston communicate in person with the chief executive.[5] Now, on the 22d, the President and Lee rode out to Mechanicsville, where they found a disheartening lack of organization.[6] "My conclusion," Davis wrote Johnston, after this ride, "was, that if, as reported to be probable, General Franklin, with a division, was in that vicinity he might easily have advanced over the turnpike toward if not to Richmond."[7] It was difficult for Davis and doubly difficult for Lee to assist in a defense concerning which the field-commander did not see fit to advise them.

At length, probably on May 24, General Johnston came into Richmond and doubtless had an interview with Mr. Davis,[8] but apparently he did not explain his plan. The same day the enemy occupied Mechanicsville,[9] only five miles from Richmond, and

[3] 2 *Davis*, 101–2. The date of this interview is not given by Davis. It must have been about May 14.

[4] *O. R.*, 11, part 3, p. 526.   [5] *O. R.*, 11, part 3, p. 530.

[6] *O. R.*, 11, part 3, p. 536. T. R. R. Cobb (28 *S. H. S. P.*, 292) gave the date as the 23d, but he must have been mistaken unless there were two such journeys on successive days.

[7] *O. R.*, 11, part 3, p. 536.

[8] *O. R.*, 11, part 3, p. 541.   [9] *O. R.*, 11, part 1, p. 651.

an admirable position from which to form a junction with Mc-
Dowell when the latter came down from the north. There was
nothing to stop him from doing so. For Johnston had ordered
Anderson back from the line of the Rappahannock. At that very
time, also, Johnston was preparing to abandon the Virginia Central Railroad west of Hanover Junction. Branch's brigade from
Gordonsville had already come down and was stationed at Hanover Courthouse in an exposed position.[10] Everything indicated
the loss of northern Virginia and the early junction of the two
Federal forces, immediately in front of Richmond, with a strength
not much below 150,000. To oppose them, Johnston would not
have more than 72,000 after Anderson's troops from the Rappahannock had formally united with him. Only one of three
things could save Richmond—a miracle, a successful attack by
Johnston on McClellan before McDowell could arrive, or the
failure of McDowell to advance.

Impatient at Johnston's failure to make any movement or to
confide his plan, despite their recent interview, Davis expressed
to Lee his deep dissatisfaction. The President's concern was so
manifest, and the possible effects of a continued misunderstanding
were so serious that Lee once more volunteered to act as a peace-
maker. "General Johnston," he said to Davis, "should of course
advise you of what he expects or proposes to do. Let me go and
see him, and defer this discussion until I return." Riding out to
Johnston's headquarters, Lee must have had a more satisfactory
interview with Johnston than on his previous visit in the company of the President, for he brought back news that Johnston
intended on the 29th to attack that part of the Federal army
north of the Chickahominy.[11]

At last the prospect of an offensive against McClellan! And
with it the news of an event that might add vastly to its success.
Rumor had been bringing reports of battles in the valley, behind
the screen of Jackson's secret manœuvres, but there had been
nothing definite and nothing official. Now, on the 26th, came a
messenger with dispatches from Jackson. The very first word

[10] *O. R.,* 11, part 3, pp. 535, 537, 540, 543, 544.
[11] 2 *Davis,* 120. Mr. Davis gave no date, but his mention of "Thursday" makes it
plain that he referred to the attack projected for May 29. As he probably had seen Johnston on the 24th and as he would not have sent him an envoy the very next day, it seems
likely that the 26th was the date of Lee's visit, but the chronology is doubtful.

of the letter to the adjutant general was an assurance of a victory, for the paper was dated at Winchester, which had been eighteen miles behind Banks's lines at last reports:

"General S. Cooper:

"During the last three days God has blessed our arms with brilliant success. On Friday [23d] the Federals at Front Royal were routed, and one section of artillery, in addition to many prisoners, captured. On Saturday Banks's main column, while retreating from Strasburg to Winchester, was pierced, the rear part retreating towards Strasburg. On Sunday the other part was routed at this place. At last accounts Brig. Gen. George H. Steuart was pursuing with cavalry and artillery and capturing the fugitives. A large amount of medical, ordnance, and other stores have fallen into our hands.

T. J. Jackson,

Major-General, Commanding." [12]

Faith in the eccentric Jackson had been vindicated. The often-urged, much-debated attack on Banks had been delivered. Private messages that followed Jackson's telegram described a rout indeed, with Banks's scattered troops driven back to the Potomac. Northern papers, smuggled across the lines, made no attempt to conceal the magnitude of the defeat.[13]

What would be the effect? On the answer might hang the outcome of the battle that Johnston was preparing in front of Richmond. "Whatever movement you make against Banks," Lee had written Jackson on May 16, "do it speedily, and if successful drive him back toward the Potomac, and create the impression, as far as practicable, that you design threatening that line." [14] Jackson had executed the first part of this plan and could be counted on to spread the fear of a farther advance. His returning messenger carried Lee's suggestion that Jackson demonstrate with vigor.[14] Would McDowell ignore that warning? Would Johnston's plan to strike on the 29th be thwarted by a southward advance of the

---

[12] *O. R.,* 12, part 1, p. 701. The dispatch bore date of May 26, 1862.

[13] 2 *Davis,* 107–9; *Baltimore American,* May 26, 1862, p. 1, col. 1; *Philadelphia Inquirer,* May 26, 1862, p. 1, col. 3; *New York Tribune,* May 26, 1861, p. 1.

[14] *O. R.,* 12, part 3, p. 893.   [15] 1 *Henderson,* 345.

Federals? If so, Jackson's movement might simply have eliminated Banks temporarily as a factor in the situation. But if the threat on the Potomac halted or delayed McDowell's advance, until Johnston could drive against McClellan, then a victory at Richmond might break up the whole stupendous combination against the capital. So much depended on Johnston's proposed offensive that every nerve of the Confederacy was strained to reinforce him. The War Department and General Lee labored feverishly to place Huger in supporting distance of Johnston, to expedite the movement of two regiments under General Ripley, who had been ordered from Charleston on May 23, and to hurry northward units of Holmes's force in North Carolina that Lee now determined to bring to Richmond at the risk of a possible advance by Burnside.[16]

Everywhere, on the morning of May 27, the question was the same— What news of McDowell? Had he started across the Rappahannock? He had four days' march ahead of him and that, of course, would prevent him from arriving in front of Richmond before Johnston attacked McClellan on the 29th. At the same time, the line of McDowell's advance would lie in rear of Johnston's assaulting columns. Consequently, if McDowell were close at hand by the day set for the battle, the risk to the numerically inferior Confederate force would be too great for it to assume the offensive. It was raining hard at Richmond, and that was encouraging. A heavy downfall north of the city would inevitably slow up McDowell's advance.

Before noon, the worst possible news reached Johnston's headquarters in a telegram from General Anderson, whose force was strung out on the road leading from Hanover Junction to Richmond: Anderson's videttes, covering his rear, reported that McDowell had started to march on Richmond! The main Federal column was already six miles south of Fredericksburg and the advanced guard was at Guiney's, less than forty miles from Richmond.[17] Had Lee been mistaken in his strategy? Had Jackson's demonstration been in vain?

Later in the day, this grim question seemed to be answered by

16 O. R., 14, 518, 519; O. R., 11, part 3, pp. 547, 552, 555, 559. Lee had already ordered Anderson's brigade to Virginia from Holmes. Cf. supra, p. 36.
17 G. W. Smith, 146–47.

what the Confederates regarded as an ominous happening. A strong Federal force struck Branch's brigade at Hanover Courthouse during the afternoon and forced it back.[18] The Southern strategists reasoned that McClellan was extending his right flank to meet McDowell. With Hanover Courthouse in Federal hands, the gap between McDowell's advanced guard and McClellan's right was reduced to less than twenty-five miles. Cavalry contact might readily be established the next day, May 28. The outlook seemed almost hopeless.

Thick clouds obscured the sky on the morning of the 28th. The rain continued to pour down. The traditional "long spell in May" had seen a succession of heavy storms, broken only by a day or two of sunshine. The worst of it was now brewing. The Chickahominy, whose sluggish waters ran through a wide, low valley, was higher than it had been in twenty years.[19] In Richmond, curiously enough, panic had died away. Not knowing the weakness of the reinforcements that had been brought up, the people believed the army ample for the defense of the city.[20] Quietly they went about the work of cleaning and preparing the hospitals for the army of wounded they expected after the battle that every one knew the Confederates would have to fight within a day or two.[21] Even an order for the removal of the government archives[22] created no new apprehension.

Lee spent the morning in final efforts to bring up the troops hurrying northward from the Carolinas. Johnston was satisfied that McDowell was approaching.[23] There seemed nothing to do except to prepare for the inevitable—and either to strike McClellan, as planned, in the desperate hope of defeating him decisively before McDowell could come up, or else to draw in the lines for a stubborn defense against overpowering odds. Huger, Holmes, and Ripley might bring up the total force to 80,000, perhaps to 85,000, but what could they do against an estimated 150,000 Federals with superior artillery?

Night brought no news to Richmond, though couriers were hurrying about on the lines and long conferences were being

[18] O. R., 11, part 1, pp. 33–34, 679; part 3, p. 196.
[19] O. R., 11, part 1, p. 31; part 3, p. 193.
[20] 1 R. W. C. D., 128.
[21] Mrs. McGuire, 118.
[22] O. R., 11, part 3, p. 557.
[23] O. R., 11, part 3, p. 555.

held. On the morning of the 29th, the day of the promised Confederate attack, nervous thousands listened and strained their ears but heard no sound of battle. Did contrary wind and a heavy atmosphere drown the roar of the guns, or had there been some hitch, some unexplained change of plans, when a day's delay in attacking McClellan might mean ruin?

Davis hurried through his office-work and took the road to Mechanicsville. Lee could not remain behind. To sit in the office, to listen and hear nothing, to wait and know nothing, to be an adviser when he yearned to be a participant, was a more terrific ordeal than even he could endure. It would be worse, by far, than his experience on the 21st of the previous July, when Johnston and Beauregard had been fighting at Manassas, and President Davis had hastened away on a special train, leaving him there in Richmond in suspense and regret. He must do something. Quickly he ordered his horse and went out, probably to Johnston's headquarters.

He found no battle in progress but he heard news that meant as much as victory, news that would have thrown an army on its knees in the middle ages with a cry of "Miracle, miracle!" Young Jeb Stuart had put a cavalry outpost close to McDowell on the previous day, and late in the night he had reported that McDowell, hurrying southward to join McClellan, had halted his columns in the road on the 28th and then had turned them around and had marched back to Fredericksburg! It seemed incredible, but Stuart vouched for it.[24]

There might be speculation as to the reasons for this astounding deliverance, but what was more reasonable than to suppose that the victory at Winchester, the rout of Banks, and Jackson's intelligent discharge of his orders to threaten the line of the Potomac had led the Washington government to order McDowell closer to Washington? Lee had believed that a successful attack on Banks would "relieve pressure" on Fredericksburg, and that

[24] *Johnston's Narrative*, 131-32. McDowell, in reality, had begun to reduce force on May 25, in order to guard the approaches to Washington from the valley, in accordance with orders from Washington (*O. R.*, 11, part 1, pp. 30, 32-33, 35; part 3, p. 190; *O. R.*, 12, part 3, pp. 229 ff.). The movement on the 27th was simply a scout to determine whether Anderson had retreated toward Richmond or had moved to support Jackson (*O. R.*, 12, part 3, p. 253). McClellan was assured that reinforcements would be sent him as soon as Jackson was defeated (*O. R.*, 11, part 3, p. 194).

had been the chief reason he had so often urged Jackson forward amid a thousand difficulties. And now the "relief" had come when it might be the salvation of the Confederacy. It was not Lee's nature to exult or to count personal performance, least of all in comparison with that of other men, but as he stood, an observer in the midst of actors, he could have reflected that Johnston might fight the battle, but that he had made the victory possible with the stout aid of Jackson.[25]

The great news that McDowell was marching away from Richmond, instead of toward it, had led G. W. Smith to argue on the night of the 28th–29th for a change of plan, on the ground that the Federal flank north of the Chickahominy rested on a very strong natural barrier, Beaver Dam Creek, which it was not desirable to attempt to storm if there was no immediate necessity of striking McClellan in the expectation that he was about to be reinforced by McDowell. The question had been argued at length, and a decision had been reached to call off the battle and to regroup the forces for an attack south of the river.[26] That was why Lee found no action under way.

Lee rode back to the city that afternoon[27] but he had been in the tense atmosphere of approaching conflict and he could no longer restrain himself. He must have an active part in the defense of Virginia, no matter what his rôle. Rather the command of a brigade, a regiment, even service as a voluntary aide on Johnston's staff, without authority, than inaction behind office walls. So, on the morning of May 30, though entirely uninformed as to when Johnston proposed to attack on the south side of the Chickahominy, he sent Colonel A. L. Long, his military secretary, out to Johnston's headquarters with a personal message. He had no desire, he bade Long tell the general, of interfering with his command but he would be glad to serve in the field in any capacity during the coming action.[28]

While waiting for an answer, restlessness overcame him. There

[25] The evidence as to Lee's movements on the 29th is far from satisfactory. The little that is known of them rests on a dispatch by the correspondent of *The Memphis Appeal*, bearing that date, and reproduced in *The National Intelligencer* of June 16, 1862, p. 2, col. 2. This dispatch raises some rather confusing questions, but as it is not contradicted, the writer has accepted it as evidence. Davis's failure to mention Lee's presence with him makes it likely that the two went out separately.

[26] G. W. Smith, 149 *ff*.

[27] *National Intelligencer*, June 16, 1862, p. 2, col. 2.   [28] *Long*, 158,

had been some confusion whether McClellan's flank extended to the Virginia Central Railroad north of Richmond. Unable to perform any better service, Lee determined to ride out Brook road and reconnoitre. Accompanied by a few members of his staff, he went to the crossing of the Telegraph road over the Chickahominy, talked with a few officers he met there, and satisfied himself that the Federals had moved their advance guard eastward, back from the railroad.[29] Then he trotted homeward— with what thoughts, one wonders. The war had been on for thirteen months, and during all that time he had not fought a battle for his country! Was he doomed to remain always a headquarters general? Had his long preparation brought him only to this?

Back in Richmond, in the anxious twilight, he dispatched a report to Johnston of what he had found. Presently Long came in, bringing a polite, indefinite answer to his message: Johnston would be happy to have him ride out to the field, and, meantime, would Lee send him all the reinforcements he could collect?[30] Johnston did not tell Long, nor did Long learn from any other source, when the battle for Richmond would open. Still uncertainty; still suspense! That evening there was thunder in the heavens and the heaviest storm that had been visited on the territory around Richmond during the whole of the drenching spring,[31] but no sound of conflict came from the east or the northeast. It was simply another dark, anxious night, with nothing to indicate that on the morrow a bloody milestone was to be set in the career of the anxious soldier who doubtless ended the day on his knees in his gloomy room at the Spotswood Hotel.

Saturday morning, May 31, dull and cloudy,[32] found Lee still restless. No commanding duties held him at his office. Huger's troops were across James River, in good position to be used by Johnston when and where they were needed. Holmes had been ordered to Richmond.[33] Ripley had arrived from South Carolina.[34] All the troops from in front of Fredericksburg had joined Johnston. Chances had been taken that the minor fronts might be penetrated. To Loring, who was calling for troops in western

29 O. R., 11, part 3, p. 560.
31 Longstreet, 88.
33 O. R., 11, part 3, p. 559.
30 Long, 158–59.
32 Miss Brock, 133.
34 Cf. O. R., 11, part 3, p. 563.

Virginia, word was sent that no reinforcements were available and that he must make the best defense in his power.[35] The concentration of every unit that could be brought to Richmond in time for the battle had either been effected or was so nearly completed that the rest was routine. A last-minute call was sent Pemberton in South Carolina for two regiments to replace some of the men soon to fall.[36] This final bit of business transacted, an irresistible desire to see what was happening on the front of the opposing armies led Lee to take horse and ride out with some of his lieutenants to Johnston's headquarters. These had been moved from the Harrison house on the Williamsburg road, near the junction of the Darbytown road, and had been established about three miles from the city on the Nine Mile road, a thoroughfare that led to the enemy's main position east of Richmond and south of the Chickahominy.

Learning that Johnston had gone forward, Lee went on to the point where the New Bridge road turned off to the left from the Nine Mile road. Magruder's headquarters were there, and his men were in line of battle across the road ahead. Here, in a house on the right, slightly off the highway, Lee found General Johnston. There was a tenseness in the air. Officers were coming and going. Johnston was preoccupied. A general movement evidently was afoot. That obvious fact Johnston must have announced to Lee. He may have added that he was disposing his troops anew for an attack on the Federals supposed to be around Seven Pines and Fair Oaks, two miles ahead, but he did not explain his plan in detail or tell Lee when the battle was to open.

Noon passed. Presently, from the southeast, came the intermittent mutter of heavy guns and, very faintly, after 3 o'clock, a sound that Lee's ear took to be the sound of musketry. But, no, Johnston explained; it could only be an artillery duel. He did not elaborate and Lee did not argue. Ere long, orders reached the troops waiting at the forks of the road, the word of command was passed, and Whiting's men hurried down the road that led toward the enemy. And still, as if in subdued accompaniment to the feet of the soldiers, Lee heard that strange, indefinite sound from the south.

[35] *O. R.,* 12, part 3, pp. 901, 903.   [36] *O. R.,* 14, 528.

Now a familiar mounted figure turned into the lane from the road. It was the President. A moment later—either by chance or with intent to avoid an embarrassing meeting[37]—Johnston rode away across the field, in the direction of Whiting's march. Lee went out to meet Mr. Davis. The President's first question was what the musketry-fire meant. Had he heard it? Lee asked. Assuredly, Davis answered—what was on? Lee explained that he had thought it was musketry, but had been assured by Johnston that only artillery was in action. Together the two walked to the rear of the house and listened. There was now no mistaking the sound, faint though it was. Either a heavy skirmish or a battle was in progress somewhere down the way where the Nine Mile road turned to Fair Oaks Station on the Richmond and York River Railroad, above the homely settlement of Seven Pines.

Davis, always a soldier at heart, could never resist the impulse to ride to the sound of firing, and with a few words he returned to his horse and started forward. Equally anxious, Lee rode with him. It was now late afternoon, with every promise of an early twilight in that wooded country. If a battle was being fought, night would soon end it, one way or another. They went down the road for nearly a mile, with a thick wood on their right and open ground on their left. Then, beyond a lane leading off toward the Chickahominy, they found a heavy tangle of timber on their left also. Close by was a field on which a crop of oats was growing. The troops they had followed up the road, Whiting's and Pettigrew's brigades, had left the road near this point and had deployed on the left, driving back the Federal pickets to an unseen line that was assumed to run almost perpendicular to the railroad.

Before they knew it, Lee and Davis were under a hot fire, in a scene of the greatest confusion.[38] To their left, hidden Federal batteries, almost in rear of the Confederate forces farther down the road, were pouring a regular and well-placed fire into charging ranks that floundered over fallen logs and through the bushes, vainly seeking the Federal infantry. On the right, beyond a belt of woods, another column was engaged. The clouds hung

[37] E. P. Alexander: *Military Memoirs of a Confederate* (cited hereafter as *Alexander*), 92; 2 *Davis*, 122.
[38] N. A. Davis: *The Campaign from Texas to Maryland* . . ., 39.

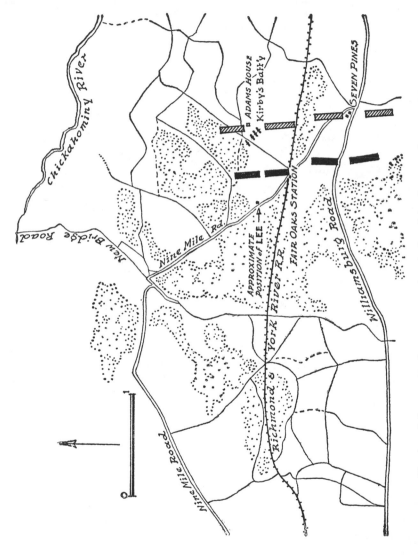

Situation of the opposing forces at Seven Pines (Fair Oaks), afternoon of May 31, 1862, as understood by Lee upon his arrival on the field of battle

low; the smoke was everywhere. Already the wounded were limping to the rear; the line on the left was making little or no progress. Johnston was somewhere down the road in the thickest of the fire; Smith, who commanded that wing of the army, had also gone ahead; the Secretary of War, other Cabinet officers, and a few members of Congress were galloping about. Nobody seemed to know anything except that the enemy was strong and resisting hotly, and that, away on the right, an even more desperate action was in progress. It was apparent that unless the Federal flank on the left of the Nine Mile road was turned and the batteries in that locality silenced, Whiting's troops would sustain a bloody repulse. Lee was merely an observer and could not act, even in such an emergency, but Davis made a hurried reconnaissance and sent off one messenger and then another to find General Magruder and to direct him to throw a Confederate brigade beyond the Federal right, up a path in the woods. Magruder, like the others, was in the battle. Search for him was vain. Davis was starting in person to look for him when a returning courier reported that he had located General Richard Griffith, one of Magruder's brigadiers, and had delivered the message to him.[39]

It was beginning to get dark. From the right, through the woods and over a little field, the left of Hood's Texas brigade of Smith's division was coming forward to support the troops beyond the Nine Mile road.[40] Griffith's men were being assembled for the advance on the left. But it was too late. Before the flanking column could start, Whiting's troops began to stream back from the thickets. They had not been able to reach the Federal line in the woods. Dusk made it almost impossible to distinguish blue coat from gray. Further effort would be a waste of life. Davis suspended Griffith's movement.

The Federal fire continued. The troops waited to see if it would be followed by a counter-attack. Presently up rode Postmaster-General Reagan, a Texan, who had come to the battlefield to cheer Hood's men in action. He had been farther to the southward and had found General Johnston in great danger, in a most exposed position. Davis, he instantly observed, was taking

[39] 2 *Davis*, 123.   [40] *G. W. Smith*, 180.

like chances needlessly. He protested warmly against the President's remaining where a bullet might strike him down at any minute. Davis refused to leave. And now a courier passed by from the left, with the news that General Wade Hampton had been shot. On his heels rode another mounted messenger who told them—they gasped as they heard it—that General Johnston had been wounded, some thought fatally.

Darkness, a joined battle, crowded confusion, a multitude of wounded and the army left without the one man who knew all the dispositions: Was the story of Shiloh to be repeated, when a mortal injury to another Johnston had lost the South a great victory, as all Southerners believed?

Before Lee and Davis had time to think of the possible effects of this loss, up the road came litter-bearers bringing General Johnston, conscious, but in so much pain from two serious wounds that he had not been able to stand the jostling of the ambulance in which he had first been placed. Gone on the instant was the coolness that Davis had felt. With warm, friendly words he expressed his deep regret and his hope that Johnston would soon be able to take the field again. Lee, of course, cherishing no malice for Johnston's petulance and secretiveness, saw only the friend of his youth, the companion of happier days, stricken and helpless, and his warm affection went out to him.

It was a desperate hour and it promised a desperate tomorrow. Fortunately, the enemy had suffered heavily and was quite content to leave the issue as it was. No counter-charge was pressed through the woods where the dead lay among the blood-soaked logs, under the shattered trees and in the underbrush that was reddened as if with the touch of autumn. The broken regiments reformed beyond and across the road and prepared to sleep on their arms, in exhaustion so complete that even the groans of the wounded and the ghostly creaking of the ambulances would not awaken them.

And now General Smith had come up. From him, for the first time, Davis and Lee learned as much as he knew of the battle they had witnessed but had not understood. Johnston, they were told, had expected by a sudden attack to overwhelm that part of McClellan's army on the south side of the Chickahominy at a time when he believed the rise in the waters of that river would prevent the dispatch of Federal reinforcements from the ample divisions north of that whimsical stream. D. H. Hill, with four brigades, was to have advanced down the Williamsburg road and was to have opened the battle, with Huger on the Charles City road to turn the left of the enemy. Smith had understood that Longstreet was to have moved down the Nine Mile road to form on Hill's left, but, he explained, in some manner unknown to him, Longstreet had gone over to the Williamsburg road and had attacked there. Smith's own command, General Johnston had told him, was to occupy the extreme Confederate left, to serve as a support for Longstreet, if needed, and to watch against a possible movement by the Unionists from across the Chickahominy. For reasons that Smith did not know, the opening of the action had been long delayed. Then heavy fighting had broken out on the right and Longstreet had called for help, Smith said; Federal troops had unexpectedly arrived from the north of the Chickahominy, and the greater part of Smith's troops, under Whiting, had been brought up and thrown into action. Whiting, Smith concluded, had been heavily engaged. Did Davis know anything of the battle on the right? Had he received any word from Longstreet later than a message sent to Johnston at 4 o'clock?[41]

Davis had no information, and, as Smith was the senior major-general on the field, the President asked him what his plans were. Smith, who was manifestly under heavy nervous strain, naturally could not answer on such short notice. He could make no decision, he said, until he could ascertain how the battle had gone on the front of D. H. Hill and Longstreet, from neither of whom he had heard. It might be necessary, he said, to withdraw closer to Richmond and form a new line. He might, on the other hand, be able to hold his ground. Davis suggested that if he remained where he was, the Federals might fall back during the

---

[41] All this, of course, is controverted, but whether Longstreet was out of place, and whether the main fault lay with him or Huger in his slow crossing of Gillies's Creek, are questions that have no place in a biography of Lee. Smith's views were given in *op. cit.*, 158 *ff.* and his statement of his explanation to the President appeared in *ibid.*, 181. A later *résumé* of Smith's version of the controversy will be found in 2 *B. and L.*, 220 *ff.* Longstreet's account is in *op. cit.*, 85 *ff. Johnston's Narrative*, 132 *ff.*, displayed much reticence regarding the engagement and mentioned very briefly the misunderstandings that arose.

night and thereby give the Confederates the moral effect of a victory. Smith could only reply that he would not retire unless compelled to do so. If the outcome of the action on the right had not been more serious than on his own part of the line, he saw no reason for retreating.[42]

There was no more to be said. After a few minutes, Davis bade farewell to Smith and turned his horse's head back up the Nine Mile road toward Richmond. Lee went with him. Along the deeply trampled highway, past the woods where the reserves were sleeping, and on by the endless line of ambulances,[43] bound the same way as themselves, the two rode in darkness. They must have talked, of course, of the frightfully mismanaged battle they had witnessed, and the forthright Davis must have commented on Smith's manifest confusion, on the lack of staff-work, and on the strange misunderstanding of Longstreet's route. Then, perhaps, the two riders lapsed into silence, each pondering his duty in the confused situation that existed. At length, Davis uttered the few and simple words that were to change the whole course of the war in Virginia. "General Lee," he said, in effect, "I shall assign you to the command of this army. Make your preparations as soon as you reach your quarters. I shall send you the order when we get to Richmond." [44]

[42] *G. W. Smith*, 181–82.

[43] Mrs. Burton Harrison, *op. cit.*, 82–83, presented a graphic description of the arrival of the wounded in Richmond.

[44] The narratives of Lee's movements on this historic day in his career are so uncertain and contradictory that the writer has had to weigh probabilities and reconcile differences. The principal sources are: 2 *Davis*, 122 *ff.*, 130; *G. W. Smith*, 159 *ff.*; *Marshall*, 57; *Long*, 159; *Taylor's Four Years*, 40; *Johnston's Narrative*, 138; *Alexander*, 75 *ff.*, particularly, 92 n.; *Reagan*, 140–42; *N. A. Davis*, 39. The best critical account of the battle is Alexander's. Smith's report is in *O. R.*, 11, part 1, pp. 989 *ff.* The chief point of difficulty in the narrative is the unavoidable assumption that, though Lee was with Johnston most of the day, Johnston told him little or nothing about the impending battle. The writer has taken almost at its face value Davis's statement (2 *Davis*, 122), apropos of the unexplained firing he and Lee had heard while they were at the New Bridge fork of the Nine Mile road: "It is scarcely necessary to add that neither of us had been advised of a design to attack the enemy that day." Johnston must surely have told Lee something, but his singular unwillingness to discuss his plans with his superiors, and Lee's reticence in questioning a field commander over whom he had no direct authority, account for a silence that would otherwise be unbelievable. A very good account of the battle, as seen by a man in the ranks, is given in a letter from Newton Walker to Reverend Robert Lamb, June 9, 1862, *MS.* kindly lent the writer by Miss Josephine Sizer of Richmond.

CHAPTER VIII

"Tête de l'Armée"

THE battle probably would be renewed with the dawn. That meant infinitely more to Lee than personal advancement or opportunity. He could not attempt to direct the fighting immediately, for that would be as dangerous to the army as it would be unfair to Smith. What, then, could he do to help Smith?

Over that question Lee wrestled after he returned to Richmond. Before 5 o'clock on the morning of the 1st, a courier was knocking at his door with a dispatch from Smith, telling of his dispositions and asking for more troops and additional engineers. In his own hand Lee answered at once—answered with a consideration for Smith's feelings that reflected not a pose but an honest wish for the success of a comrade-in-arms.

> Richmond, 1st June, 1862
> 5 A.M.
>
> General:
>
> Your letter of this morning just received. Ripley will be ordered and such forces from General Holmes as can be got up will be sent. Your movements are judicious and determination to strike the enemy right. Try and ascertain his position and how he can best be hit. I will send such engineers as I can raise. But with Stevens, Whiting, Alexander, etc., what can I give you like them. You are right in calling upon me for what you want. I wish I could do more. It will be a glorious thing if you can gain a complete victory. Our success on the whole yesterday was good, but not complete.
>
> Truly,
> R. E. Lee, *General*.

He addressed it to "Genl. G. W. Smith, Comdg. Army of N. Va." and sent it off.[1] Then he set himself to redeeming the promise of his letter. At this he was laboring when he received

[1] *G. W. Smith*, 205–6.

a brief, formal communication from the President. Davis explained that the wounding of Johnston "renders it necessary to interfere temporarily with the duties to which you were assigned in connection with the general service, but only so far as to make you available for command in the field of a particular army," [2] which was a diplomatic way of serving notice to all and sundry that there was no occasion to renew the agitation for the appointment of a commanding general. Other dispatches came; every hour brought new calls; time had to be found to draft an address for publication to the army when Lee took command; preparations had to be made to move the office. It was about 1 P.M., June 1, 1862, an historic hour in the military history of the United States, when Lee was able to start with his staff for the battlefield.

He was now aged fifty-five and had been in the service of the Confederacy more than thirteen months, without having participated in a single general engagement. Only once—and then but the day previously—had he been under close fire since, in September, 1847, the guns of Chapultepec had been silenced. He was as old as Haig was when he succeeded Sir John French, three years older than Ludendorff when that officer became quartermaster general, eight years younger than Joffre at the Marne, and thirteen years the junior of Hindenburg in 1914 and Foch in 1918. Wellington, at thirty-seven, had seven years in which to fix the fame he had won in Spain; to Marlborough, after he was fifty-two, a decade of campaigning as supreme commander remained; Napoleon, a general in Italy at twenty-seven, was destined to have nineteen years before Waterloo. From Lee, Appomattox was distant only thirty-four months.

In what spirit did Lee approach the sprawling, weary lines of the army he was henceforth to lead? He did not confide his thoughts to his staff officers as they trotted along, but his feelings probably were those he put on paper the next day in a letter to his daughter-in-law. "I wish," said he, "that [Johnston's] mantle had fallen upon an abler man, or that I were able to drive our enemies back to their homes. I have no ambition and no desire

---

2 *O. R.,* 11, part 3, pp. 568–69. Orders from the Adjutant-General, announcing that Lee would succeed Johnston, bear date of June 2 and appear in *ibid.,* 571.

but the attainment of this object, and therefore only wish for its accomplishment by him that can do it most speedily and thoroughly."[3] It was the profession of a simple soul, and such a soul was Lee's.

Riding out the Nine Mile road, Lee found President Davis and General Smith at the Hughes house, about a mile closer to Richmond than the headquarters occupied the previous day. The battle around Seven Pines had been renewed during the morning, as Lee had expected, but Smith had not been successful in winning a victory. Instead, the action at that hour seemed to be dying indecisively away. Davis had already notified Smith that Lee was to supersede him, so explanations were unnecessary, and an immediate conference could be held to acquaint Lee with the exact dispositions.[4] At its conclusion Lee and Smith went over to the headquarters of General Longstreet on the Williamsburg road. They found that Longstreet's troops had broken off the battle, but that their commander was anxious to renew it, confident of victory. The forces on the flanks, however, were not in hand for immediate co-operation, so Lee ordered the whole army back to the lines it had occupied before the battle of the previous day.

Thereupon Lee returned to the Nine Mile road, where he opened headquarters in a house belonging to Mrs. Mary C. Dabbs, widow of Josiah Dabbs, a property about a mile and a half from the outskirts of the city.[5] One of his first acts was to issue as an order the address he had prepared before leaving Richmond. It is worth quoting in full, for two reasons. It was the first of a series that was to range every chord of resolution, triumph, and exhortation before the solemn finale was sounded at Appomattox. In the second place, this order gave the army the name it was to make famous. Lee, and Lee alone, had already styled it "The Army of Northern Virginia" in various references to it, but never before had it been so addressed in its own orders.[6] It was by

---

[3] Lee to Charlotte Lee, June 2, 1862; *Jones,* 390.

[4] 2 *Davis,* 129; *G. W. Smith,* 211–13.

[5] The Dabbs farm, since renowned, was known as High Meadows. Its owner, Mrs. Dabbs, subsequently married Reverend J. B. Jeter, D.D. See W. E. Hatcher: *Life of Jeremiah B. Jeter,* 265, 271, 274. For the history of this property, the writer is indebted to his friend Thomas C. Fletcher.

[6] Johnston had continued to call it the "Army of the Potomac" long after Oct. 22, 1861, when the "Department of Northern Virginia" had been established (*O. R.,* 5, 913; *cf. ibid.,* 1061; *O. R.,* 51, part 2, p. 553). As late as March 17, Lee had addressed John-

happy chance and not through deliberate design that Lee christened the army the very day he assumed command.

Special Orders,
   No. 22
                              Headquarters,
                              Richmond, Va., June 1, 1862
   I. In pursuance of the orders of the President, General R. E. Lee
assumes command of the armies of Eastern Virginia and North
Carolina.

   The unfortunate casualty that has deprived the army in front
of Richmond of the valuable services of its able general is not
more deeply deplored by any member of his command than by
its present commander. He hopes his absence will be but temporary, and while he will endeavor to the best of his ability to
perform his duties, he feels he will be totally inadequate to the
task unless he shall receive the cordial support of every officer
and man.

   The presence of the enemy in front of the capital, the great
interests involved, and the existence of all that is dear to us appeal
in terms too strong to be unheard, and he feels assured that
every man has resolved to maintain the ancient fame of the Army
of Northern Virginia and the reputation of its general and to
conquer or die in the approaching contest.

   II. Commanders of divisions and brigades will take every precaution and use every means in their power to have their commands in readiness at all times for immediate action. They will
be careful to preserve their men as much as possible, that they

ston as "commanding Army of the Potomac" (O. R., 5, 1105), but on March 25, he had
written him as "commanding Army in Northern Virginia" (O. R., 11, part 3, p. 397)
and on March 28, in a letter to Johnston, he had first styled his command the "Army of
Northern Virginia." This represented nothing more than the application of the name
of the department to the army, but perhaps it had other implications to the soldier whose
home, now in the hands of the enemy, had been in northern Virginia. Prior to June 1,
the only reference to the "Army of Northern Virginia" in an official order seems to have
been made by Lee on April 12 when he announced in the President's name that the departments of Norfolk and of the Peninsula were to be embraced, for the time, within the
line of operations of "The Army of Northern Virginia" (O. R., 11, part 3, p. 438).
Neither Johnston nor Davis adopted the name. After the army moved to the Peninsula,
Davis spoke of the forces that remained on the Rappahannock and in the valley as the
"Army of the North" (O. R., 11, part 3, p. 485) and on June 2, the day after Lee had
christened it in his orders, Davis addressed the men facing McClellan as the "Army of
Richmond" (O. R., 51, part 2, p. 565). The more famous name that Lee bestowed upon
the army rested thereafter on usage, not on formal, authorized adoption.

may be fresh when called upon for active service. All surplus baggage, broken down wagons, horses, and mules, and everything that may embarrass the prompt and speedy movement of the army will be turned into depot. Only sufficient transportation will be retained for carrying the necessary cooking utensils and such tents or tent-flies as are indispensable to the comfort and protection of the troops.

By order of General Lee:

W. H. Taylor,
Assistant Adjutant-General.[7]

The troops politely cheered when this order was read to them,[8] but no enthusiasm attended the announcement of the selection of Lee as commander of the army. The newspapers had been requested to omit all reference to the wounding of Johnston and consequently most of them had no comment on the choice of his successor. The single violation in Richmond of this voluntary censorship was a mild expression of hope by the hostile *Richmond Examiner* that Lee would "prove himself a competent successor to General Johnston and complete his great undertaking." This tepid commendation was coupled with an encomium on Johnston: "Time may yet produce another, but no living man in America is yet ascertained to possess a military character so profound, or a decision of character so remarkable."[9] A few loyal admirers expressed the belief that the change of commanders would bring victory.[10] Up in the valley, the inimitable Ewell, Jackson's right-hand man, announced that he would not be "scared" to fight under Lee.[11]

Most of Johnston's lieutenants, taking their cue from him, had been very critical of the Richmond government, and they resented the selection of a "staff officer" to lead them. There were "misgivings" as to Lee's "power and skill for field service" and fears that he would not be aggressive.[12] Smith felt that he should be left to direct operations; the best that Longstreet could say

7 *O. R.*, 11, part 3, p. 569.   8 *Richmond Examiner*, June 4, 1862, p. 1, col. 1.
9 *Richmond Examiner*, June 4, 1862, p. 2, col. 2.
10 *E.g.*, 1 *R. W. C. D.*, 133.
11 F. M. Myers: *The Comanches* (cited hereafter as *F. M. Myers*), 61.
12 *Longstreet*, 112; *Alexander*, 110; E. M. Law in *Southern Bivouac*, new series, 2, no. 11 (April, 1887), 652.

for the change was that it afforded a happy relief from the halting policy of the unhappy Smith.[13] Aside from Davis, the only man of station who seemed to realize what Lee might accomplish in the field was Johnston himself. His petulance vanished with a few days' rest and ere long he saw clearly how the friction between him and the administration had endangered the defense of Richmond. When told by a friend that his wounding was a calamity to the South, Johnston manfully answered, "No, sir. The shot that struck me down is the very best that has been fired for the Southern cause yet. For I possess in no degree the confidence of our government, and now they have in my place one who does possess it, and who can accomplish what I never could have done—the concentration of our armies for the defence of the capital of the Confederacy."[14] Neither the army nor the swelling anti-Davis cabal in Richmond knew that this was the opinion of Johnston when his nerves were restored and his shoulders eased of responsibility. In some quarters, "disparagement, sarcasm and ridicule" were the lot of Lee.[15]

The new commander wasted no time in answering or in mollifying critics but bent himself to the task of saving Richmond. Circumstance gave him the necessary time. McClellan had been shaken by the impetuous attacks at Seven Pines, and though his casualties were less by 1103 than the Confederates had sustained, his cautious nature prompted him to delay further operations until reinforcements made good his casualties. Lee had no information of this, of course, nor was he aware that most of the eleven bridges that McClellan had been constructing across the Chickahominy had been washed away,[16] but he could judge the effects of the weather on the roads McClellan would be compelled to use. And that weather was of the worst. The day Lee took command the battle-ground was so heavy that President Davis's mount had been mired knee-deep.[17] There was rain on June 3, a heavy storm during the night of June 3-4, a downfall on the 4th,

13 *Longstreet*, 112.

14 *D. H. Maury*, 161. After Johnston recovered and was about to take command in the West, he was toasted at a farewell breakfast as the "only man who can save the Confederacy." Johnston replied, "The man you describe is now in the field in the person of General Robert E. Lee. I will drink to his health" (De Leon, *Belles and Beaux and Brains of the 'Sixties*, etc., 400–402).

15 *Richmond Whig*, July 15, 1862, p. 1, col. 1.

16 *O. R.*, 11, part 1, pp. 30–31, 44.   17 *Reagan*, 143.

no sunshine on the 5th, showers during the night of the 5th–6th, and a near-deluge on the morning of the 6th.[18] The Chickahominy bottom was covered with three or four feet of water; the whole face of the country was a bog; General Burnside, visiting there, took four and one-half hours to go nine miles on horseback.[19] "You have seen nothing like the roads on the Chick-[ahomin]y bottom," Lee told Davis on the 5th.[20]

Behind the temporary barrier of these mud-courses, Lee reasoned fast. His first concern, of course, was a position of immediate security for the army. Should it remain where it was, or should it fall back closer to Richmond? After a conference with Longstreet, Lee decided to hold the ground on which the troops then rested, as he believed this would keep McClellan's army astride the Chickahominy.[21]

This settled, Lee's next task, of course, was to prevent the capture of Richmond. On this he was determined. The sentiments he had expressed at the Cabinet meeting, about the time of the attack on Drewry's Bluff, were stronger now that he had the responsibility of command. He told one politician that if he had to evacuate Richmond, he would fall back to the mountains, "and," he added, "if my soldiers will stand by me I will fight those people for years to come."[22] It was manifest, however, that Richmond could not be held indefinitely against McClellan's larger army, possessed as the Federals were of ample artillery of superior range. The way to save the capital was to drive McClellan off, before his army was overwhelming or his guns close enough to shell the city. To attack McClellan, Richmond must be so protected by earthworks that it could be defended by a small force while the rest of the army attacked. Preparation of works would take time, and the outcome of an offensive was of course doubtful. Consequently, it was necessary to keep reinforcements from McClellan and, at the same time, to make it difficult for him to bring up heavy ordnance with which to open parallels.

[18] Waldrop in *Contributions to the History of the Richmond Howitzers Battalion* (cited hereafter as *Richmond Howitzers*), part 3, pp. 39–40; *O. R.*, 11, part 1, p. 45; part 3, p. 217.

[19] *O. R.*, 11, part 1, p. 46; *ibid.*, part 3, p. 224.

[20] D. S. Freeman, editor: *Lee's Dispatches* (cited hereafter as *Lee's Dispatches*), 8.

[21] J. A. Early, to W. H. Taylor, *MS.*, April 29, 1876, quoting Charles Marshall, *Taylor MSS.*

[22] To Lieutenant Governor R. L. Montague, *Jones*, 295.

This was Lee's initial analysis of his military problem, an analysis quickly completed and immediately applied. His first move was to provide for the construction of the earthworks. "I desire you," he wrote his chief engineer, Major W. H. Stevens, on June 3, "to make an examination of the country in the vicinity of the line which our army now occupies, with a view of ascertaining the best position in which we may fight a battle or resist the advance of the enemy. The commanding points on the line I desire to be prepared for occupation by our field guns and the whole line strengthened by such artificial defences as time may permit. My object is to make use of every means in our power to strengthen ourselves and to enable us to fight the enemy to the best advantage. It is not intended to construct a continuous line of defence or to erect extensive works. Having selected the line and put the works in progress of construction, I desire you to resume the examination and see what other positions can be taken nearer Richmond in case of necessity. . . . I have to request that you will push forward the work with the utmost diligence." [23] The next day he organized a pioneer corps of 300 men from each division and placed them under Stevens's command to work on the entrenchments.[24] He had little faith in military labor by slaves, though later he had to employ it.

So much for the first steps. With good speed and good fortune, Richmond would be safe enough, in two or three weeks, for him to make a thrust at his adversary. But how was he to keep the industrious McClellan from pounding his way by regular approaches within striking distance of Richmond? "McClellan," he told Mr. Davis, "will make this a battle of posts. He will take position from position under cover of his heavy guns and we cannot get at him without storming his works, which with our new troops is extremely hazardous." [25] The roads, Lee reasoned, were so heavy that McClellan could not haul siege guns over them. He must use the Richmond and York River Railway. If, therefore, some method could be devised to keep the Federals from employing the railroad for this purpose, a bombardment might be avoided until Lee was ready for an offensive. It was a new

[23] O. R., 11, part 3, pp. 571–72. Cf. Richmond Dispatch, July 9, 1862, p. 2, col 1.
[24] G. O. No. 62, A. N. Va., O. R., 11, part 3, p. 573.
[25] Lee to Davis, June 5, 1862: Lee's Dispatches, 8.

problem in war. Lee solved it by proposing to mount and armor a heavy gun upon a railroad truck, which could be run down the Richmond and York River line, outranging the Federal ordnance on the swampy ground.[26] This was the birth of railway ordnance. Simultaneously, he directed an immediate reorganization of the Confederate artillery to render it more mobile and more efficient.[27]

Cover was being prepared for an offensive. An untried weapon for halting the movement of the Federal heavy artillery was to be fashioned. How, next, was he to guard against the possibility that McDowell would move southward again, reinforce McClellan, and envelop Richmond with a force against which an offensive would be merely a waste of life?

Jackson's victory at Winchester had been an immense relief—"of great advantage" as Lee conservatively put it,[28] but the demonstration on the Potomac had been short-lived. Frémont from the west and Shields from the east had threatened the rear of the Army of the Valley and had forced Jackson to withdraw. Only his daring and his hard marching had enabled his 16,000 men to elude the Federals' 60,000 and more.[29] Once out of the Federal pincers, Jackson had immediately projected a new thrust at the enemy. He had sent to Lee a Confederate congressman, A. R. Boteler, with a statement of his situation. Placed where he was, Jackson had bidden Boteler to tell Lee, he believed he could strike successfully at Shields, but, he went on, if Lee could send him enough reinforcements to raise his army to 40,000 men, he could invade the North. In talking with Boteler, about June 3 or 4, Lee did not see how he could do more than replace Jackson's losses, which he was already preparing to make good,[30] and he perhaps told Boteler that before he could give Jackson 40,000 reinforcements, Jackson would have to unite with him and drive McClellan from in front of Richmond—a possibility which, on June 2, he had discussed with Davis.[31] With this message,

[26] *Lee's Dispatches,* 7–8; *O. R.,* 11, part 3, pp. 574, 575–76, 610, 615.
[27] Susan P. Lee: *Memoirs of William Nelson Pendleton* (cited hereafter as *Pendleton*), 187, 198; J. C. Wise: *Long Arm of Lee* (cited hereafter as *Wise*), 1, 198 ff.
[28] *O. R.,* 11, part 3, pp. 582–83.
[29] 1 *Henderson,* 346 ff.   [30] *O. R.,* 12, part 3, p. 906.
[31] So Davis, *op. cit.,* 2, 131, and R. L. Dabney: *Life and Campaigns of Lieut.-Gen. Thomas J. Jackson* (cited hereafter as *Dabney*), 431. Colonel Boteler, in his account, 40 *S. H. S. P.,* 161, did not state that Lee then insisted that Jackson join him in defeating

Boteler returned to the valley. Pondering the question, however, Lee saw the immense possibilities of an offensive in the North and he decided to make an effort to comply with Jackson's request. "After much reflection," he wrote the President on June 5, "I think if it was possible to reinforce Jackson strongly, it would change the character of the war. This can only be done by the troops in Georgia, S. C. and N. C. Jackson could in that event cross Maryland into Penn. It would call all the enemy from our Southern Coast and liberate those states. If these states will give up their troops I think it can be done." [32] In other words, if the South Atlantic states would take the risks, Jackson could assume the offensive and undertake an invasion of the North. That would lead to the immediate evacuation of the Georgia and Carolina coast and, at the same time, would prevent the reinforcement of McClellan on any large scale. The danger that would result from stripping these states of their defenders was not excessive, for there was reason to believe the Union forces had been reduced along the coast. Besides, the heat and the mosquitoes had settled over the swamps and were as effective a barrier to a Federal advance as would have been a bristling, bayoneted line, crowded with troops. The situation had changed much, in this respect, since Lee had left Savannah—had changed for the better, indeed, since he had opposed the withdrawal of forces from that front at the time of the council of war preceding Johnston's move to the Peninsula in April. Heretofore, Lee had held strictly to the defensive, in order that the South might gather strength. Now, looking beyond the relief of Richmond, Lee for the first time could consider a new phase of the war, an offensive-defensive at a distance from Richmond. The immediate success of such a change of policy depended not merely on good strategy but also on the mental attitude of the Georgia and Carolina people. The President, of course, could order the brigades northward, and they would come; but could a new government, dependent on the support of sovereign states, afford to risk a panic

McClellan before launching a large-scale offensive against the North. Boteler did, however, quote Lee to this effect in an interview on June 14 (*ibid.*, 173). It is possible that Henderson and Dabney confused the two conversations, but as Lee on June 3–4 had certainly considered bringing Jackson to Richmond, the conflict of testimony is not material.
[32] *Lee's Dispatches*, 5–6.

or to create the impression that Virginia was being defended at the expense of her sisters? The influences that were to thwart the efforts of the administration in later attempts to effect large-scale concentration were already operative and had to be taken into account. The Southern states were allies, not a united nation, and the conduct of military operations was subject to nearly all the difficulties, save that of language, that weaken most alliances. Would they have the larger vision now? Were the much-cherished states' rights, which were so potent a factor in leading the South to declare its independence, to prove an obstacle to the attainment of that independence?

CHAPTER IX

LEE AS THE "KING OF SPADES"

WHILE Davis undertook to negotiate for the transfer of troops from the South Atlantic states, in order that Jackson might invade Pennsylvania, Lee gave himself for a few days to expediting the construction of the defenses, and to improving the army's discipline and organization. It was not easy work. Many of the soldiers had never done manual labor. In many cases even privates had their body-servants to perform their menial duties about the camp.[1] Scorning the shelter of fortifications as unworthy of gentlemen in arms, the troops were not disposed to construct them. Much they grumbled at the orders of their engineer-general, the "King of Spades" as they dubbed him. One element of the press was equally antagonistic. "Gen. Jackson's two maxims," carped *The Richmond Examiner,* " 'to fight whenever it is possible,' and in fighting, to 'attack at once and furiously,' are worth all the ditches and spades that Gen. Lee can display on this side of the Chickahominy."[2] Lee was puzzled and provoked at this attitude. "Our people are opposed to work," he told President Davis, "our troops, officers, community and press. All ridicule and resist it. It is the very means by which McClellan has and is advancing. Why should we leave to him the whole advantage of labour. Combined with valour, fortitude and boldness, of which we have our fair proportion, it should lead us to success. What carried the Roman soldiers into all Countries, but this happy combination? The evidences of their labour last to this day. There is nothing so military as labour, and nothing so important to an army as to save the lives of its soldiers."[3] Thus convinced, he did not stand back because of antagonism or doubting minds. Almost daily he went out to the lines, encouraging the soldiers and complimenting them on their progress

[1] *Cf. Eggleston,* 29–37. [2] June 17, 1862, p. 2, col. 2.
[3] Letter of June 5, 1862; *Lee's Dispatches.* 8.

86

Soon they began to take pride in his praise and looked for his visits. The works began to rise satisfactorily, not a strong line compared with that which girdled Richmond in 1864 but ample for the immediate purpose.[4] Fortification was continued until the eve of the battle of Mechanicsville, but after the first two weeks of June, Lee felt no further concern regarding it. The Federals at the same time were digging furiously, felling timber in front of their defenses, building bridges, and constantly watching Confederate movements from their observation balloons.[5]

To stiffen the discipline and improve the organization of the army was a task even more difficult. The obstacles were manifold. Perhaps if he reflected in his active life on his reading of Everett's *Life of Washington* in the winter of 1861–62, Lee saw the parallel between his condition and that of Washington in 1776, as pictured by the biographer:

"The position of affairs was one of vast responsibility and peril. The country at large was highly excited, and expected that a bold stroke would be struck and decisive successes won. But the army was without organization and discipline; the troops unused to obey, the officers for the most part unaccustomed, some of them incompetent to command. A few of them only had had a limited experience in the Seven Years' War. Most of the men had rushed to the field on the first alarm of hostilities, without any enlistment; and when they were enlisted, it was only till the end of the year. There was no military chest; scarce anything that could be called a commissariat. The artillery consisted of a few old field-pieces of various sizes, served with a very few exceptions by persons wholly untrained in gunnery." [6]

In some of its aspects, discipline had been lax under Johnston; drunkenness had been frequent; many things were at loose ends.[7]

[4] *Long*, 164–67; *Marshall*, 79; *Longstreet*, 114; *Richmond Whig*, July 15, 1862, p. 1, col. 1. *The Richmond Dispatch*, July 9, 1862, p. 2, col. 1, greatly exaggerated the strength of these works.

[5] Dickert, in his *History of Kershaw's Brigade*, 122, told a diverting story of a South Carolina sentinel who called his officer one night and reported that the enemy was putting up a balloon. The officer insisted it was a star that the soldier had seen. "Star hell," the man answered. "I tell you, it's a balloon. Are the Yankees smart enough to catch the stars?"

[6] *Everett*, 112–13.   [7] *Cf.* 1 *R. W. C. D.*, 133; IV *O. R.*, 1126–27.

Some of the regiments reported a third of the troops sick.[8] Lee worked as fast as he could to improve the condition of the men. The commissary and the quartermaster's service were improved. Favoritism in granting details for service in the rear was ended.[9] Before he had been two weeks in the field, a friendly Richmond newspaper noted: "Since Gen. Lee has assumed command many things have been done for the benefit of the public service and the soldier individually which have been overlooked or neglected."[10] The Federals, of course, were not aware at this time of what Lee was doing toward the improvement of discipline, but later they were fully conscious of the effects. One Northern correspondent wrote after the Seven Days: "The shell . . . which wounded . . . General Johnston, although it confused the Rebels, was the saddest shot fired during the war. It changed the entire Rebel tactics. It took away incompetence, indecision and dissatisfaction and gave skilful generalship, excellent plans and good discipline. . . . Before the battle of Fair Oaks, Rebel troops were sickly, half fed and clothed, and had no hearts for their work. . . . [After Lee took command], the troops improved in appearance. Cadaverous looks became rare among prisoners. The discipline became better; they went into battles with shouts, and without being urged, and, when in, fought like tigers. . . . A more marked change for the better never was made in any body of men than that wrought in his army by the sensible actions of General Lee."[11]

The labors to which Federals paid tribute took many hours of the busy days of June. Lee was ceaselessly astir. Not only did he have to supervise a hundred undertakings on the line, but he had to direct, in some measure, those distant operations that had been under his care when he was assigned to field duty. The army of Kirby Smith in Tennessee continued for some weeks to be his special charge.[12]

In dealing with the officers, Lee proceeded as though there was no opposition to him. The day after he took command he sum-

---

[8] *History of the Fourth South Carolina Volunteers*, 94.

[9] *O. R.*, 11, part 3, pp. 581, 585–86; cf. *ibid.*, 599.

[10] *Richmond Dispatch*, June 13, 1862, p. 3, col. 1.

[11] Joel Cook: *The Siege of Richmond*, 246–47. This contemporary narrative by the correspondent of *The Philadelphia Press* is cited hereafter as *Joel Cook*.

[12] *O. R.*, 10, part 2, pp. 584, 590, 597; *O. R.*, 15, 756.

moned all the generals to a council of war at a place on the Nine Mile road styled "the Chimneys."[13] Smith had left the army with some obscure nervous ailment.[14] The other division commanders were somewhat scandalized at what they considered incaution on Lee's part in discussing a plan of operations in the presence of the brigadiers.[15] They might as well have spared their feelings. Lee simply asked for opinions on the state of affairs and listened as the brigade commanders reported. One by one they took the floor. When the turn of General W. H. C. Whiting came, his gloomy temperament displayed itself. As he was describing how McClellan's long-range guns would make it possible for him to hammer his way into Richmond, President Davis came into the room and quietly took a seat. Whiting kept on, mathematically demonstrating his thesis. "Stop, stop," said Lee, "if you go to ciphering we are whipped beforehand." Davis took heart from the warning.[16] Presently D. H. Hill made a humorous observation on an unmilitary remark by General Robert Toombs, and the conversation drifted into less serious channels.[17] Lee at length bade his lieutenants good-day without the slightest intimation of what he intended to do.

The generals rode away none the wiser for their conference, some of them assured of Lee's ability,[18] others convinced that he had simply called them together to see what manner of men they were.[19] He could hardly have been disappointed in them as a group. The policy of the administration, well sustained in previous months by Johnston's persistent appeal for trained men, had put at the disposal of Lee an unusual number of professional soldiers of high intelligence. Counting those who were yet to join him, Lee was to go into the Seven Days' Battle with forty-nine general officers, whose average age was slightly over forty years. Thirty-one of these were West Point graduates, and only a handful could be accounted as "political generals" in the accepted Northern use of that unhappy term. Thirteen were to be major generals and twelve lieutenant generals. Sixteen were to be

---

13 *Marshall*, 77.
14 *G. W. Smith*, 193; 2 *B. and L.*, 261; *O. R.*, 11, part 3, pp. 685–86.
15 *Longstreet*, 112–13.
16 17 *S. H. S. P.*, 369. For Whiting's despondency, see *O. R.*, 5, 1092.
17 *Longstreet*, 113.　　18 *Pendleton*, 187–88.　　19 *Longstreet*, loc. cit.

killed or were to die of wounds; thirteen were to share with Lee the last dreadful hours of Appomattox. Seventeen came from Virginia, eight from North Carolina, and seven from Georgia.

In addition to Longstreet, A. P. Hill, and a few others who were to be in daily association with their chief, the council and the camps then contained many interesting personalities, some of them soldiers who were not to sustain the reputation they then enjoyed, others of them fated to rise to high position by valor and by skill. Magruder has already been introduced. Benjamin Huger, commanding a division, has been observed at Norfolk, ere its evacuation. He was comparatively an old man by the standard of that youthful army, being fifty-six. Behind him were some of the finest Huguenot traditions of South Carolina, as well as connection with the great house of Pinckney.

Among Huger's brigadier generals were three unusual men. L. A. Armistead, son of a general in the War of 1812 and himself an Indian fighter of distinction, was destined to play a conspicuous part in Malvern Hill and to fall the next year in a dramatic hour at Gettysburg. William Mahone was a small, wiry man of thirty-six, who had already established his reputation as an imaginative consolidator of railroads, the Southern Harriman of his day. Ambrose R. Wright, of Georgia, was a lawyer and a "political general," but he was to justify by hard blows the confidence of his people who, when he had enlisted as a private, had forthwith elected him a colonel. He was never to be a brilliant soldier but he was to exhibit a noble fidelity.

In Magruder's conglomerate command, one division was under a stocky, bearded Georgian, Lafayette McLaws, a West Pointer and a veteran of the Mexican War, whose name was to be linked with Longstreet's until an unhappy disagreement. The most interesting of McLaws's brigadiers at this time was a magnificent South Carolinian, Joseph B. Kershaw, a lawyer, who had been chosen to lead Bonham's famous brigade.

The nervous, impetuous A. P. Hill had excellent brigadiers. One of them, Charles W. Field, of Kentucky, then forty-two, was to be transferred to Longstreet and, at the very end of the war, was to have the honor of leading on the field of surrender the largest division that survived the last ordeal. Maxcy Gregg of South Carolina, another of Hill's brigadiers, was to win an Homeric fame at Second Manassas and was to fall at Fredericksburg, cheering a wild counter-attack. Still another brigadier of this division was the small, vigorous, and soldierly William D. Pender of North Carolina, a classmate of Custis Lee's and of Jeb Stuart's. He was only twenty-eight and he had won his wreath and his three stars by his able leading of the Sixth North Carolina at Seven Pines. He was to receive his mortal wound at Gettysburg, before he had attained the full measure of his potential achievements.

The brigades of Longstreet's division were well-served. At the head of one was a Virginian of thirty-seven, a romantic person, who loved to wear his hair in ringlets. He was to give his name to the most famous charge of the war—George E. Pickett. Cadmus M. Wilcox, thirty-two, was a slow, meticulous, and scholarly soldier, an authority on rifle-fire. "Dick" Anderson, then forty-one, was the most brilliant but at that time the most erratic of the group, a soldier all his life and one of the witnesses of the initial tragedy at Fort Sumter.

In Whiting's division was a physically magnificent brigadier of thirty-one, John B. Hood, who had been a lieutenant of cavalry in Lee's old regiment—a man of great activity on the field, but more sociable than diligent off it. The prince of the South Carolina planters, Wade Hampton, a powerful man of forty-four, had just been promoted brigadier general and was limping from the wound received at Seven Pines.

Busy with their commands on the lines around Richmond were a host of others whose names were to have eminence— E. Porter Alexander, then acting chief of ordnance and soon to be the most brilliant of all Lee's artillerists; John B. Gordon, not yet thirty, and the diligent commander of the 6th Alabama, Samuel MacGowan, who was to be Maxcy Gregg's successor and was then the colonel of the 14th South Carolina; John R. Cooke, twenty-nine, a Harvard man, a civil engineer and commander of the 27th North Carolina, soon to win a glorious name at Sharpsburg; W. T. Wofford of the 18th Georgia, who was to develop into one of the most capable of all Lee's brigadiers— these were only a few. Young R. F. Hoke, Stephen D. Ramseur, and A. M. Scales were all of them at this time colonels of North Carolina regiments; the queer, cynical Jubal A. Early, West Pointer by training but prosecuting attorney by impulse and choice, was absent, wounded. So was another and younger officer of much capacity, R. E. Rodes. Nearly all the men who were later to be Lee's renowned cavalry commanders were colonels at the time, and the youthful John Pelham was a captain of the horse artillery attached to Stuart.

With surprising rapidity, considering their devotion to Johnston and their secret disdain of the staff, nearly all of these officers were won over to Lee's support by his manner, his energy, and his modest but unmistakable willingness to assume the responsibilities of leadership. He neither flattered them nor dealt with them austerely, but they could not fail to see that he knew his duty and was determined to discharge it, regardless of their opinion of him. He was careful in his appointments to fill vacancies, studiously just in his judgment of qualifications, and unwilling to recommend officers of whose ability he was doubtful.[20] One thing helped him greatly—the confidence imposed in him by those who knew him well. Major E. P. Alexander, for instance, chanced to be riding with Colonel Joseph Ives, who had been Lee's engineer in South Carolina and was now on President Davis's staff. They fell to talking of Lee. "Ives," said Alexander, "tell me this. We are here fortifying our lines, but apparently leaving the enemy all the time he needs to accumulate his superior forces, and then to move on us in the way he thinks best. Has General Lee the *audacity* that is going to be required for our inferior force to meet the enemy's superior force—to take the aggressive and to run risks and take chances?" Ives reined in his horse, stopped. and turned to his companion. "Alexander," he said, "if there is one man in either army, Confederate or Federal, head and shoulders above every other in *audacity,* it is General Lee! His name might be Audacity. He will take more desperate chances, and take them quicker than any other general in this country, North or South; and you will live to see it, too." [21] Such confidence begat confidence.

Before Lee had progressed far in preparing for the offen-

[20] *Lee's Dispatches,* 10–12.   [21] *Alexander,* 110–11.

sive against McClellan, it became apparent that no such reinforcements as Jackson would require for the invasion of Pennsylvania could be expected from the South Atlantic seaboard.
Brigadier-General A. R. Lawton had a large Georgia brigade
that he was anxious to bring to Virginia and he started northward.[22] But at Charleston, General Pemberton talked of the
danger of an attack on his line and was so involved in dis-
agreements with some of his officers that a movement was on
foot to have him removed to another command. Large detachments from that quarter might break the morale of the Palmetto
state. A proposal to send green North Carolina troops to Charleston to take the place of more seasoned regiments that might be
ordered to Virginia, disclosed the fact that Governor Clark felt
some resentment because Holmes's brigades had been summarily
dispatched to the Richmond front.[23] The War Department
continued its efforts to get troops from South Carolina and from
Alabama as well,[24] but Lee had to abandon his project for an
invasion of Pennsylvania almost as soon as he formulated it. He
determined, however, to send Lawton, upon his arrival from
Georgia, to reinforce Jackson. "We must aid a gallant man if
we perish," said he.[25] Beyond this, he had not decided what
should be undertaken in the valley when, on June 8, he received
an important letter from Jackson. His forces, the valley commander reported, were so disposed that if Shields attempted to
advance and join Frémont, the Federal column would have to
cross his front. If, Jackson went on, his command was required
at Richmond, he could have part of his troops at the railroad
after one day's march. "At present," he said, "I do not see that
I can do much more than rest my command and devote its time
to drilling." [26] Lee reasoned that if this were Jackson's prospect,
reinforcements would be lost on him; consequently he at once
wrote Jackson to rest his men, and to be prepared to move to
Richmond, but meantime "should an opportunity occur for striking the enemy a successful blow, do not let it escape you." [27] The

[22] O. R., 14, 536.
[23] O. R., 14, 528, 534, 535, 536, 538, 539, 540, 541, 548, 549, 560, 567, 569, 603, 613; O. R., 53, 247, 251.
[24] O. R., 14, 558; O. R., 51, part 2, p. 569.   [25] O. R., 12, part 3, p. 907.
[26] O. R., 12, part 3, pp. 906–7. This dispatch was addressed to Johnston.
[27] Ibid., endorsement, and O. R., 12, part 3, p. 908.

93

date on which he might summon Jackson was left open, because the Richmond defenses were not yet completed, and Lee did not intend to undertake an offensive until the works were ready.[28]

The next morning, June 9, there came news that once again changed Lee's plans for the employment of Jackson: under the shadow of the Massanutton Mountain, Jackson had struck Frémont at Cross Keys and had halted him, bewildered. Ere Lee got this report, the other wing of Jackson's army had grappled furiously with Shields's advanced guard at Port Republic and had hurled it back, bloody and crippled, on the main force.[29] As these twin battles of great tactical brilliance definitely gave Jackson the advantage again, Lee instantly decided to make the most of it. He ordered Lawton's brigade and a few North Carolina regiments united at once with Jackson's[30] force and he began immediately to ponder the possibilities of the general situation. McClellan was working on his bridges and his fortifications, but as the roads remained impassable, there was no immediate threat of an advance. Lee still had no way of sending Jackson enough men to undertake the cherished project of a great offensive in Pennsylvania, but he had learned something from the quick recall of McDowell after Jackson had defeated Banks. He had made a discovery, in fact, that was to influence his strategy many times in the next two years and on occasion was to shape it: President Lincoln, he perceived, was easily alarmed for the safety of Washington. Any Confederate movement that threatened the Federal capital would be apt to prompt Mr. Lincoln to call troops from Virginia to its defense. This Lee had found out. Might it not be possible, then, to dispatch to Jackson a few more brigades from the Army of Northern Virginia? With these, might not Jackson undertake a short, sharp offensive that would crush the enemy in his front and so alarm the Northern President that McDowell's army would be summoned to Washington? With the valley cleared, Jackson might then move swiftly to Richmond and join in the attack on McClellan. Even if only a part of McDowell's force were recalled

[28] O. R., 11, part 2, p. 490.
[29] O. R., 12, part 1, pp. 710–11; Jackson to Samuel Cooper; Jackson to Lee, June 9, 1862, MS., Chilton Papers.
[30] O. R., 11, part 3, pp. 584, 585.

to Washington, while the rest joined McClellan, a diversion by Jackson, followed by a quick march of his troops to Richmond, might give Lee sufficient strength to hope for a victory in the field. Such a plan involved risks, of course, but how was Richmond to be saved by a numerically inferior force without taking risks?

Rain came on the night of June 9 and continued through the 10th[31]—a blessed downfall because it meant that the naturally hesitant McClellan would be chained to his positions for several days longer. As the rain poured down, Lee debated the reinforcement of Jackson and by the evening of June 10, he reached his decision: he would send Jackson eight strong regiments besides Lawton's brigade and the North Carolina detachment; with these Jackson could attack and defeat the enemy, and then, by the time the earthworks were finished, he could be near Richmond.

It doubtless was futile to hope that such a large-scale troop-movement to the valley of Virginia could be concealed from McClellan's spies in Richmond; therefore it might as well be capitalized. If the troops moved boldly away, in open daylight, Lincoln would hear of it and would be more alarmed than ever for the safety of Washington. McDowell would be less disposed to move southward, though he would be unable to reinforce the valley in time to check Jackson. McClellan would reason that if Lee could afford to send off two brigades, he was too strong to be attacked.

On June 11, Lee detached Whiting, with eight regiments of that officer's own selection,[32] ordered the men through Richmond to the Richmond and Danville station, and sent a staff officer thither to create the impression that much importance was attached to the speedy departure of the reinforcements in order that an offensive might be launched in the valley.[33] Lest the enemy might suspect the true nature of the ruse, he took pains to see that the Richmond newspapers said nothing, one way or the other.[34] Jackson's orders were explicit: "The object," Lee wrote, "is to enable you to crush the forces opposed to you." This done, Jackson was to leave in the valley his weaker infantry units, his

---

[31] O. R., 11, part 1, p. 46; ibid., part 3, p. 224.
[32] O. R., 11, part 3, pp. 591, 594; N. A. Davis, 42.
[33] Marshall, 84. [34] O. R., 11, part 3, p. 590.

cavalry, and his artillery, in order to screen the movement and to guard the passes. With the rest of his troops, including Ewell, Lawton, and Whiting, he was to move eastward by the Virginia Central Railroad, and was to assail McClellan's right flank while Lee attacked in front.[35]

As the bridges on the Virginia Central Railroad between Richmond and Hanover Junction had been burned by Federal raiders,[36] Whiting moved by way of Burkeville, Lynchburg, and Charlottesville. After his departure, Lee at once turned to preparations for the offensive that was to be undertaken when Jackson arrived. The first step was to procure exact information concerning McClellan's position and line of communications. The Federal left, which was too strong to be turned, had been accurately located. It was covered by White Oak Swamp, a sluggish stream that ran into the Chickahominy through a marshy, overflowed bottom from a point two and a half miles south of Seven Pines.[37] The centre, running northward to the Chickahominy, was in plain view and was also very strong. But there was some doubt how far north of the Chickahominy the Federal right extended. Communications manifestly were maintained with the White House, on the Pamunkey, *via* the Richmond and York River Railroad. It was suspected, moreover, that the right was being supplied by a wagon-train running northward from

[35] *O. R.*, 12, part 3, p. 910. Few of Lee's operations have been more misunderstood than this. Nearly all the early accounts follow the misstatement of *McCabe*, p. 122, that the detachment of Whiting was altogether a ruse and that Lee planned simply to move the troops to the valley and then to bring them back at once without striking at Shields and Frémont. See, for instance, *Cooke*, 68; *Dabney*, 432; *Long*, 170. These narratives were all written, apparently, without knowledge of the dispatch of June 11, containing the significant sentence: "The object is to enable you to crush the force in your front." Nor did these authors know, it would seem, of Lee's dispatch of June 16, quoted below. The mistake of these biographers has been followed by most later writers, who either relied upon the previous statements or else were deceived by the fact that after explaining to Jackson that the reinforcements were to enable him to defeat the enemy in his front, Lee proceeded in the very next sentence of his dispatch of June 11 to say: "Leave your enfeebled troops to watch the country . . . and with your main body . . . move rapidly to Ashland . . . and sweep down between the Chickahominy and Pamunkey . . ." (*O. R.*, 12, part 3, p. 910). President Davis, *op. cit.*, 2, 131–32, and Colonel Taylor in his *General Lee*, 60, avoided the mistake of the others but even they did not state the facts fully. The contemporary newspaper accounts are of little value. *The Richmond Dispatch*, July 9, 1862, p. 2, col. 1, was more nearly correct than the others. The facts, as here stated, are established beyond question by the dispatch of June 16, quoted on p. 104.
[36] C. S. Anderson, war-time conductor, in *Locomotive Engineering*, October, 1892, p. 371; November, 1892, p. 405. For this interesting authority, the writer is indebted to Mrs. Mary Carter Anderson Gardner.
[37] A. S. Webb: *The Peninsula* (cited hereafter as *Webb*), 118.

the White House and thence by the Piping Tree road to the Old Church road and on to McClellan's lines.[38] The existence of these communications needed to be established, and if they were in use, they should be destroyed or, at the least, interrupted.

To ascertain the facts, Lee determined to order a cavalry raid to the rear of McClellan's right, and for this purpose on June 11 called to headquarters Brigadier General J. E. B. Stuart, now at the head of the cavalry. This picturesque young officer had reached the mature age of twenty-nine. He had seen little of his old West Point superintendent during the first year of the war, and as recently as January, 1862, had privately admitted that Lee had "disappointed" him as a general;[39] but now, when Lee explained what was desired, he entered joyfully into the plan for a reconnaissance in the rear of McClellan's army and confided to his chief that he believed he could ride entirely around the Federal forces.[40] Lee was in no position to risk the loss of his cavalry, and after talking with Stuart, he gave him lengthy instructions written in his own hand,[41] explaining the information he desired and cautioning him against too great exposure of his men. ". . . be content," said he, "to accomplish all the good you can without feeling it necessary to obtain all that might be desired." [42] Enough cavalry must be left to serve the army. ". . . and remember," Lee admonished, "that one of the chief objects of your expedition is to gain intelligence for the guidance of future operations." Because of the plans he was already making to bring Jackson from the valley, Lee particularly instructed Stuart to examine the watershed of Totopotomoy Creek, down which Jackson was apt to advance. He intimated to Stuart, also, that a threat against McClellan's communications would probably lead the Federal commander to detach troops to defend them, thereby reducing his front-line strength.[43]

As happily as if starting on a honeymoon, young Stuart picked some 1200 men from his cavalry regiments and disappeared up Brook road with them on the 12th, pretending that he was bound for the valley to support Whiting and to reinforce Jackson. He

[38] *O. R.*, 11, part 3, p. 590.
[39] John W. Thomason, Jr.: *Jeb Stuart* (cited hereafter as *Thomason*), 138.
[40] *O. R.*, 11, part 1, p. 1038.   [41] *H. B. McClellan*, 52.
[42] *O. R.*, 11, part 3, p. 590.
[43] *O. R.*, 11, part 2, pp. 514, 516; part 3, pp. 590-91.

had chosen some of his best lieutenants for the honor of the great adventure—Rooney Lee, now colonel of the 9th Virginia Cavalry, Colonel Fitz Lee of the 1st, and Lieutenant Colonel W. T. Martin of the Jeff Davis Legion. A gigantic German officer of bewildering apparel, Heros von Borcke, rode as aide; Lieutenant James Breathed had a section of the horse artillery under his charge, and a sharp-visaged, wiry young man, John S. Mosby, rode along, half aide, half courier, unattached and uncommissioned, but exhibiting already some of the qualities that were to make him the most renowned of all the partisan rangers. Promising youngsters, all of them, but reckless fellows! There was no telling what they might attempt, once they were on those narrow, sandy roads of Hanover, with the Union cavalry lurking in the woods.

Other concerns now crowded Lee's mind, along with that for Stuart. There were evidences that McClellan was being reinforced. Burnside was known to have joined him, though it was not certain that any of his troops had come with Burnside from North Carolina.[44] Belated word came on the 14th that Federal transports had gone up the Rappahannock to Fredericksburg and that at least one large steamer had descended the river, jammed with soldiers, bound presumably from McDowell to McClellan.[45] Sickness was taking thousands of men from McClellan's lines, according to Lee's information, but the troops from McDowell and other recruits would more than balance the account.[46] Besides, the fickle weather had turned Unionist again. There had been no rain since the 10th. The sun was beating down in a typical Virginia "hot spell," and the roads were drying fast.[47] This meant, of course, that McClellan would soon be able to advance his heavy guns, despite the railway battery, which was not yet ready for service. Whatever was done by Jackson in the valley must be done quickly, for every man that he could spare would soon be needed on the Richmond front.

[44] O. R., 12, part 3, p. 913. Actually, the Rhode Islander was on a visit to discuss future co-operation with McClellan.

[45] O. R., 51, part 2, p. 569. This movement was that of McCall's division.

[46] O. R., 12, part 3, p. 913.

[47] For the weather on the 11th, see O. R., 11, part 3, p. 223; for that of the 12th, see ibid., 225; for the 14th, see O. R., 11, part 1, p. 47; for the "hot spell," see O. R., 11, part 1, p. 1012, and Waldrop in 3 Richmond Howitzers, 39–40. The writer has found no reference to the weather of the 13th, but McClellan's mention (O. R., 11, part 3, p. 229) of the "cessation of the rains a few days past" would indicate that it was clear.

For these reasons, June 14 was a day of anxiety. Before it ended, there arrived an exhausted courier, in the person of Corporal Turner Doswell, with a message from Stuart—the first to be received from that daredevil since he had started on the reconnaissance. And what a message it was! Stuart had ridden to McClellan's rear, had destroyed a wagon-train, had captured some 165 men and more than that number of horses, with only one casualty, and had circled entirely around the rear of the Federal army, precisely as he had said he believed he could do. On reaching the Chickahominy, more than thirty miles below Richmond, he found the ford so deep and so swift that Fitz Lee had nearly lost his life in crossing it. There was no bridge and no other ford close by. Stuart was on the far side of the stream when Doswell left, and all his men were with him. He had, however, been quite confident he would get back to the Confederate lines and he had directed Doswell to request Lee to make a diversion on the Charles City road so that the Federals would not be able to send a force to cut him off as he returned to Richmond.[48] A man less self-controlled than Lee would have sworn because Stuart had taken such chances and he would have resolved inwardly to bring that reckless dragoon to court-martial if he escaped with his life. As it was, Lee said nothing and could do nothing, at that hour, to relieve the raiders. He must wait until morning to make the diversion.

With the dawn of the 15th, Stuart himself rode up to headquarters. His finery was much bedraggled and even his iron frame was weary, but he was triumphant and full of information. After he had sent off Doswell, said Stuart, he had found the skeleton of a burned bridge a mile below the ford, had repaired this and had crossed the entire command. The column, undisturbed, was moving toward Richmond under Colonel Fitz Lee. Stuart had ridden ahead of it to report. During the course of the raid, Stuart went on to say, he had encountered Lee's old regiment, the 2d Cavalry, now the 5th; and his pursuers, who had easily been outdistanced, had belonged to the command of his

<hr />

[48] H. B. McClellan, 64; O. R., 11, part 1, p. 1039; G. W. Beale: *A Lieutenant of Cavalry in Lee's Army*, 24, this last a little-known but excellent account of the raid; R. L. T. Beale: *History of the Ninth Virginia Cavalry* (cited hereafter as *R. L. T. Beale*), 17 ff.

own father-in-law, Brigadier General Philip Saint George Cooke. There was much more, however, than adventure and élan

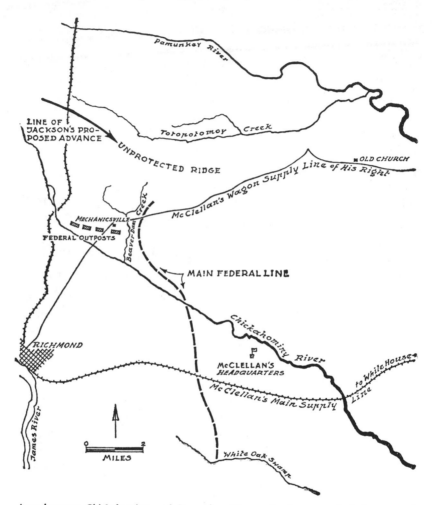

Area between Chickahominy and Pamunkey Rivers, showing watershed (unprotected according to Stuart's report) down which Jackson was to advance.

about the raid. To Stuart's report of the ground and of the Federal dispositions Lee gave instant and serious ear. The roads behind the Federal lines, Stuart said, were worse than those on the Confederate front.[49] That was encouraging, because it meant

[49] *O. R.*, 11, part 1, p. 1031.

that McClellan's movements would be slow. Secondly, Stuart reported, there was no doubt that the Federals were supplying their lines by wagon-trains from the vicinity of the White House, as well as by the railroad.[50] There were no signs of any intention on McClellan's part to change his base to James River. All this indicated, of course, that if the Confederates could turn the Federal right, they might get on McClellan's line of communications Perhaps they might even cut him off from his base. Finally, Stuart had invaluable information concerning the state of affairs on McClellan's right. Beyond the headwaters of Beaver Dam Creek, he had found no Federals on the long ridge that Lee had especially enjoined him to examine. There was nothing, so far as Stuart could see, to keep Jackson from turning Beaver Dam Creek and sweeping on down toward the White House.[51] That was news, indeed! It justified all the risks that Stuart had taken.

Realizing that McClellan might be alarmed by Stuart's raid and might strengthen his right wing, Lee at once had his infantry feel out the Federal front to see if it had been weakened.[52] Finding no evidence of this, Lee's hopes of a successful offensive rose, and with them his satisfaction over Stuart's exploit. He commended Stuart and his troops in general orders,[53] taking good pains not to mention his son and his nephew, whom Stuart had warmly praised and had recommended for promotion.[54] From that time forward, Lee trusted the discretion of Stuart That bold young cavalry commander was to become, in more than a metaphor, the eyes of the army.

[50] The Federals, in reality, were not using this road so much as Stuart believed though they generally had a wagon-train on it. Their first advanced base was at Savage Station, on the Richmond and York River railroad, but they had developed an even larger base at Oak Orchard, or Orchard Station, between Savage Station and Fair Oaks. *Joel Cook*, 231, 232. The *Report of the Committee on the Conduct of the War*, 1, 362, contains an interesting description of Oak Orchard base.

[51] *Marshall*, 82.

[52] *O. R.*, 11, part 3, p. 601; D. H. Hill, Jr.: *North Carolina in the War Between the States, From Bethel to Sharpsburg* (cited hereafter as *D. H. Hill*), 2, 97.

[53] *O. R.*, 11, part 1, p. 1042.   [54] *O. R.*, 11, part 1, p. 1041.

CHAPTER X

A Dusty Horseman Reaches Headquarters

STUART's information about McClellan's position resolved the ground-factor in Lee's equation of an offensive. While Stuart was on the raid, the time-factor was brought closer to an answer. Colonel A. R. Boteler, the unofficial envoy of the Army of the Valley, arrived again at Lee's headquarters on the evening of June 14 with a confidential message and a formal dispatch from Jackson. The message was a renewal of the suggestion that Lee bring up Jackson's strength to 40,000 men so that he could invade the North. This, of course, was now out of the question; but Lee discussed it with Boteler.

"Colonel," he said, "don't you think General Jackson had better come down here first and help me to drive these troublesome people away from before Richmond?"

"I think," Boteler answered, "that it would be very presumptuous in me, General, to answer that question, as it would be hazarding an opinion upon an important military movement which I don't feel competent to give."

"Nevertheless," Lee replied, "I'd like to know your opinion."

"Well, if I answer your question at all," said Boteler, "it must be in the negative."

"Why so?" inquired Lee.

"Because," Boteler explained, "if you bring our valley boys down here at this season among the pestilential swamps of the Chickahominy the change from their pure mountain air to the miasmatic atmosphere will kill them off faster than the Federals have been doing."

"That," said Lee, "will depend upon the time they'd have to stay here. Have you any other reason to offer?"

"Yes," Boteler rejoined stoutly, "and it's that Jackson has been doing so well with an independent command that it seems a pity not to let him have his own way; and then, too, bringing him here, General, will be—to use a homely phrase—putting all your eggs in one basket."

"I see," Lee said with a kindly laugh, "that you appreciate General Jackson as highly as I myself do, and it is because of my appreciation of him that I wish to have him here."

Lee then made some inquiries as to conditions in the valley[1] and examined the dispatch Boteler delivered. Unfortunately, it was a confusing document. Jackson acknowledged Lee's letter of June 8, in which Lee had hinted that he might call him to Richmond, but he said nothing about the letter of the 11th, wherein Lee had told him he was sending him reinforcements so that he could crush the enemy in his front before joining the Army of Northern Virginia.[2] Yet Jackson said, "You can halt the reinforcements coming here if you so desire, without interfering with my plans provided the movement to Richmond takes place." Lee could not tell from this whether Jackson was referring to reinforcements previously mentioned in a general way or to those specifically named in his letter of June 11. Boteler did not know what letters Jackson had received; so, telling the colonel that he would have an answer for him, Lee bade him good-night and began to study anew the condition that "Stonewall" faced.[3]

It was clear from Jackson's dispatch that when he wrote on the 13th, he was at Mount Meridian, close to Port Republic, where he had fought his most recent battle. If Jackson had not moved from there, he certainly could not hope to reach the Federals, to attack them, and to return to the railroad in time to reach Richmond before McClellan was ready to open with his heavy guns. Besides, Jackson said in his letter, "So far as I am concerned my opinion is that we should not attempt another march down the Valley to Winchester, until we are in a condition under the blessing of Providence to hold the country." [4] Obviously Lee could not spare troops to hold the lower valley. If, then, a long offensive was dangerous with the forces Jackson had, and if a short offensive

---

[1] 40 S. H. S. P., 173–74. [2] O. R., 12, part 3, p. 913. [3] 40 S. H. S. P., 174.
[4] Jackson to Lee MS., June 13, 1862. This dispatch, which was long supposed by historians to have been lost, is among some Lee papers acquired by the library of Duke University.

could not be completed within the time allowed, the course to follow was to bring Jackson to Richmond at once.

Lee accordingly wrote Jackson on the 16th: "From your account of the position of the enemy I think it would be difficult for you to engage him in time to unite with this army in the battle for Richmond. . . .[5] If you agree with me, the sooner you can make arrangements [to move on Richmond] the better. In moving your troops you could let it be understood that it was to pursue the enemy in your front. Dispose those to hold the Valley so as to deceive the enemy, keeping your cavalry well in your front, and at the proper time suddenly descending upon the Pamunkey. To be efficacious, the movement must be secret. Let me know the force you can bring, and be careful to guard from friends and foes your purpose and your intention of personally leaving the valley. . . . Unless McClellan can be driven out of his intrenchments he will move by positions under cover of his heavy guns within shelling distance of Richmond. I know of no surer way of thwarting him than that proposed. I should like to have the advantage of your views and be able to confer with you. Will meet you at some point on your approach to the Chickahominy."[6]

Thus was the climax approaching. The army was not wholly unprepared for it. Organization had been improved; officers and men were gaining confidence in their new commander, though he used no magic with them beyond that of energy and manifest ability;[7] the Federal communications were known; the weakest point on McClellan's line had been discovered; such reinforcements as could be had from the valley would soon be on the way.

The next step was to work out the precise details of the offensive. Lee lost no time in doing this. A few hours after he had written Jackson, he left his headquarters with Colonel Long and rode out to the north of the Chickahominy. As far as the out-

---

[5] This is the language which proves conclusively that when Lee detached Whiting and sent Lawton on to Jackson, he contemplated an offensive and was not merely employing a ruse. See *supra*, p. 96.

[6] *O. R.*, 12, part 3, p. 913.

[7] Some interesting but unimportant anecdotes of Lee's dealings with his men at this time will be found in B. Napier: *A Soldier's Story of the War* (cited hereafter as *Napier*), 98; *The Land We Love*, 3, 253; *Battlefields of the South* . . . by an English Combatant (cited hereafter as *English Combatant*). 2. 15–16.

posts of the enemy, he made a careful examination of the country-side that swept in a plateau eastward along the northern bank of the protecting stream. "Now, Colonel Long," he said, "how are we to get at those people?" [8] Long was discreet enough to know that Lee was speaking more to himself than to him, and he had no suggestions to make. There was, of course, no question as to the general wisdom of attacking McClellan's exposed right flank. It seemed providentially extended for a turning-movement. Davis and Lee had agreed, soon after Johnston had withdrawn beyond the Chickahominy, that an attack against this flank was the proper strategic move, and Johnston had been about to commence such an advance when he had deferred his offensive on receipt of the news that McDowell had started back to Fredericksburg.[9] Johnston, however, had intended to attack south of the Chicka-hominy at the same time that he assaulted north of the river. The question now to be decided was whether Lee should launch his drive on both sides of the stream or should maintain a strict de-fensive on the south side of the Chickahominy and transfer the greater part of the Confederate army north of the river to co-operate with Jackson.

Lee said nothing of this to Long, but when he returned to headquarters, Longstreet called and, by odd coincidence, proposed that Jackson be brought down from the valley and be hurled against the Federal right. Lee had no hesitation in confiding to Longstreet that this had already been ordered and he sketched a plan for an attack north and south of the river. From his own painful experience at Seven Pines, Longstreet knew something of the difficulties of bringing the whole Army of Northern Virginia simultaneously into action, and he raised the practical question of what would happen if, for any reason, the frontal attack south of the Chickahominy were delayed when Jackson advanced. Might not the enemy concentrate overwhelmingly against Jack-son and drive him back against the Pamunkey, the fords and bridges of which it was reasonable to assume a vigilant enemy had destroyed? Lee weighed this objection and, on the strength of it, at length decided to move the greater part of his troops north of

[8] *Long,* 168.   [9] See *supra,* p. 66.

the river while a small force defended the works on the south side against a possible Federal attack.[10]

When Lee next met Davis, he laid this plan before him. The President was quick to ask if Lee thought McClellan would quietly permit him to take the initiative north of the Chickahominy and not deliver a counter-attack south of the river against Lee's weakened centre and right? The line south of the river, he said, was much too weak to sustain long assaults. If McClellan was the man he had taken him to be when he had been Secretary of War and had appointed him a member of the military commission to observe the war in the Crimea, McClellan would march into Richmond. If, on the other hand, said Davis, the Federal commander acted like an engineer officer and considered it his first duty to protect his line of communication, then he would not attack, and Lee's plan would work out successfully. Lee fired a bit at the suggestion that engineer officers were likely to make such mistakes and for the moment was in the humorous position of defending his opponent, a fellow-engineer of the old army, but he had a better answer: "If," said he, "you will hold as long as you can at the intrenchment, and then fall back on the detached works around the city, I will be on the enemy's heels before he gets there." [11] This was not bravado, but a well-reasoned conclusion. It was based in part on Lee's knowledge of McClellan. In larger degree, it was founded on the belief that if he could once drive McClellan eastward on the north side of the Chickahominy, till he passed New Bridge, he had nothing to fear on the south side. For New Bridge, which was about three and

[10] *Longstreet*, 120. On the basis of his conversation with Lee, Longstreet after the war claimed credit for originating the plan of campaign employed in the Seven Days' Fight. There was a lively exchange of letters among General Early, General D. H. Hill, and Colonels W. H. Taylor and Charles Marshall in 1876 concerning this claim. Unfortunately, the correspondents were not of one mind regarding what Longstreet took to himself, nor did all of them describe the same incidents in discussing it. Taylor mentioned the matter in his *General Lee*, 59, and some of the correspondence is preserved in the *Taylor MSS*. There probably is no mystery about the affair: Longstreet on June 3 had proposed an attack north of the Chickahominy (*Longstreet*, 114–15), but he was certainly not the first to do so. He may have been author of the suggestion to concentrate heavily there and to maintain a strict defensive south of the river.

[11] 2 *Davis*, 132. It is worth noting that when the writer was once discussing this campaign, on the grounds, with Marshal Foch, that distinguished soldier raised the same objection as Mr. Davis. His idea was that McClellan should of course have attacked south of the river and that Lee could only have held the centre and right by concentrating his artillery there. He was very particular to know how many heavy guns Lee had between the Chickahominy and White Oak Swamp.

a half miles below the crossing of the Mechanicsville Turnpike, was not far from the Confederate lines on the south side of the river. Once in control of that bridge, Lee felt that he could easily reinforce that part of his command south of the river or get in the rear of McClellan's forces there if they attempted an advance on Richmond. The outcome fully justified Lee in this.

By this time, the atmosphere of camp and of city was one of expectancy. Every one in authority had the air of knowing a secret. Hints of an early offensive kept men from being wholly cast down by the news that Fort Pillow on the Mississippi had been abandoned on June 4 and that Memphis had been occupied by the enemy on the 6th.[12] In the lull of waiting for his plan to be executed, Lee found time to write a few domestic letters in his usual playful spirit. In one of them he answered the inquiries of his daughter-in-law about his personal appearance in uniform and beard, assuring her that "an uglier person you have never seen, and so unattractive is it to our enemies that they shoot at it whenever visible to them." He concluded calmly: "Our enemy is quietly working within his lines, and collecting additional forces to drive us from our capital. I hope we shall be able yet to disappoint him, and drive him back to his own country."[13]

This was on June 22. A great part of the next day Lee spent at the Dabbs house.[14] During the forenoon, he sent off couriers with sealed dispatches to three division commanders, Longstreet, D. H. Hill, and A. P. Hill. Then he transacted army business. About 3 P.M., two dusty horsemen rode up the lane on weary, panting horses, and halted at the fence. One of them stiffly dismounted, gave his steed to the other and walked to the house with long strides. It was Jackson.

[12] 1 R. W. C. D., 134–35; Mrs. McGuire, 121.
[13] Lee to Charlotte Lee, June 22, 1862; Jones, 391.   [14] Long, 166.

CHAPTER XI

Lee Seizes the Initiative

AFTER receiving Lee's letter by Boteler, Jackson had elaborately masked his movements and, on the evening of June 17, had left his old battleground. At Charlottesville he had awaited the arrival of his troops. Delayed at Gordonsville all day of the 20th by a report that the Federals were advancing from the Rapidan, he had then moved his men rapidly down the Virginia Central Railroad on ten trains of eighteen to twenty freight-cars each. On Sunday, the 22d, he had arrived at Fredericks Hall ahead of his men and had spent the day attending religious meetings. The first of the trains had proceeded a few miles farther to Beaver Dam, where the regiments had left them. That evening Jackson had gone to the room assigned him by his host, Nat M. Harris, but, without retiring, he had waited till the Sabbath was ended. Then, at 1 A.M., he had left and, on relays of commandeered horses had covered the fifty-two miles to Lee's headquarters in fourteen hours.[1]

Finding that Lee was at work when he arrived, Jackson refused to interrupt him and waited in the yard of the house, leaning heavily against the fence, his head bowed and his cap pulled down over his face as if to conceal his identity. Presently D. H. Hill rode up, for Lee had received advance notice of Jackson's coming and it had been to summon Hill and two other division commanders to a council of war that Lee had sent off couriers earlier in the day. D. H. Hill and Jackson had married sisters[2]

---

[1] O. R., 12, part 2, pp. 649–50; 1 Henderson, 392–96; Dabney, 434 ff., Dabney in 2 B. & L., 349; N. A. Davis, 42–43; F. M. Myers, 71; C. S. Anderson: "Train Running for the Confederacy," Locomotive Engineering, August, 1892, pp. 287, 289, October, 1892, p. 369. On his ride to Lee's headquarters, Jackson was attended by only one courier, Charles Harris (H. H. McGuire to Jed Hotchkiss, March 30, 1896, MS.—McGuire Papers).

[2] This was Jackson's wife by his second marriage.

and they were close friends, but Hill could hardly have been more surprised at seeing him if "Stonewall," in all the new fame of his "valley campaign," had dropped out of one of McClellan's troublesome observation balloons. They talked for a few minutes, and then went in to Lee's private office, the rear of the two rooms on the first floor. Lee was awaiting them and offered the tired Jackson some refreshment, but the traveller would take only a glass of milk.[3] In a short time, Longstreet and A. P. Hill arrived, and Lee closed the door.[4]

Lee had already made the momentous decisions regarding the offensive, but much remained to be discussed in an historic council of war that brought together for the first time all the men who were to direct the opening battle. D. H. Hill was to remain with Lee only a few months. The others were to lead his corps and execute his orders until two of them were killed and only Longstreet remained to say farewell at Appomattox. They afforded an interesting contrast, Longstreet, forty-one, five feet ten inches, heavy, slightly deaf, and strongly self-opinionated; D. H. Hill, of the same age as Longstreet, small, somewhat stooped, critical and caustic but wholly devoted;[5] A. P. Hill, thirty-seven, of nervous, quick temperament, exhibiting excellent qualities as an administrator, but quite recently put at the head of a division and untested as yet in that position; and, finally, the gaunt, bearded Jackson, aged thirty-eight, quiet and soft-spoken, neither able in conversation nor magnetic in manner, and bearing in repose no mark of genius. A month before, to the very day, he had struck Banks at Front Royal in the second phase of his valley campaign, and now, in the glamour of Winchester, Cross Keys, and Port Republic, he was possessed of a greater measure of public esteem than Lee enjoyed. All four of the men were West Point graduates. Longstreet had been a captain and a paymaster when, in 1861, he had resigned from the Union army. A. P. Hill had been a captain in the coast survey. D. H. Hill, like

---

[3] D. H. Hill in 2 *B. and L.,* 347. In *Land We Love,* 2, 465, D. H. Hill gave an earlier account, wrongly stating that the conference opened at 10 A.M. R. A. Shotwell, in 1 *Shotwell Papers,* 233–34, quoted Hill extensively as to the discussion at the council, but as his narrative was second-hand and recorded late, it is not used here.

[4] *Marshall* 84, stated that the council was held upstairs, but Longstreet and D. H. Hill both affirmed that it was in Lee's private office, which Long said was on the first floor.

[5] *Sorrell,* 63–64.

Jackson, had left the service before that time to become a college professor. Lee did not give his lieutenants time to ponder these things. Promptly and briefly, he explained the conclusions to which he had come. These were:[6]

1. Richmond could not be successfully defended in a formal siege.

2. It was necessary, therefore, to prevent a siege by assuming the offensive.

3. The offensive could not take the form of a direct assault on the Federal positions because the attacking troops were inexperienced, the positions were strong, and the Union artillery was too powerful.

4. If there could be no direct assault, there must be a turning movement.

5. This was invited by the fact that McClellan was astride the Chickahominy, with his forces divided by that stream.

6. McClellan's right wing, north of the Chickahominy, could be more readily attacked than his left wing south of that stream.

7. A successful attack north of the river would soon threaten McClellan's line of communications, *via* the York River Railroad, with his base at the White House, because the railroad crossed the Chickahominy at Dispatch Station, which was only twelve miles in rear of McClellan's right. The Federal commander would then be forced either to call his whole army to the north side of the Chickahominy to defend his base, or else he would have to withdraw from the north side of the river and seek a new base on James River.[7]

8. To overwhelm the Union right, north of the Chickahominy, it would be necessary to concentrate very heavily there.

There were only three difficulties in the way. First, as Mr. Davis had pointed out, there was risk that the Federals might attack south of the river while the greater part of the Confederate army was north of that stream. Secondly, if the Federal right rested on Beaver Dam Creek, that would be a difficult position to attack directly. Thirdly, the Unionists were on good ground

[6] It must not be understood, of course, that Lee stated the strategical considerations in this order.

[7] *O. R.*, 11, part 2, p. 490; *Marshall*, 89.

and could dispute the crossing of the Meadow Bridges and the Mechanicsville Bridges, over which Lee would have to pass three of his divisions.

How could these difficulties be overcome? Jackson was to move his army to Ashland, sixteen miles north of Richmond. Then, on the day before the battle opened, he was to march southeast. This would put him above the Chickahominy so that he would not be troubled by that watercourse. Stuart was to cover his left. Very early on the day of the action he was to start a march that would carry him past the head of Beaver Dam Creek, as he moved toward Cold Harbor, en route to attack McClellan's line of communications. In this way he would turn the troublesome stream and overcome one of the three difficulties. The army should not and would not have to fight for the high ground along the creek.[8]

As Jackson s march would be at some distance from the Chickahominy, A. P. Hill, whose division was opposite the Meadow Bridges, was to send a brigade under General L. O'B. Branch up the Chickahominy to a place known as Half Sink. When Jackson started his march on the day of battle, Branch was to move to the enemy's side of the Chickahominy and advance toward Mechanicsville. In this way he would establish contact with Jackson and would brush aside any outposts that might molest Jackson's right flank. And, finally, as he moved down the river, Branch would uncover the Meadow Bridges.

When this was done, A. P. Hill would cross at the Meadow Bridges and would advance on Mechanicsville. He would have sufficient force to clear the enemy from that village, and thereby would open the Mechanicsville Bridges to D. H. Hill and Longstreet. This would complete the removal of Lee's second difficulty.

D. H. Hill would then march past A. P. Hill's rear and form in support of Jackson. Thereupon Longstreet would cross and take position in support of A. P. Hill.

By this time, Jackson would have turned Beaver Dam Creek

[8] This is an important point. Marshall, *op. cit.,* 89, said: "General Lee also told me that he did not anticipate a battle at Mechanicsville or Beaver Dam. He thought that Jackson's march turning Beaver Dam would lead to the immediate withdrawal of the force stationed there. . . ." R. E. Lee, Jr., *op. cit.,* 415, quoted Lee as saying in 1870 that the fight at Mechanicsville was "unexpected." *Cf. infra,* p. 132, n. 44.

on his way to Cold Harbor, and from left to right the advancing force would be *en échelon* as follows:

> *Stuart*
>> *Jackson*
>>> *D. H. Hill*
>>>> *A. P. Hill*
>>>>> *Longstreet*

The attack would progress down the Chickahominy, and would have as its intermediate objective the Federal position in front of New Bridge. When this was stormed, the last of the known difficulties would be removed. Contact with the Confederates on the south side would be re-established and the danger of a successful Federal attack on that bank of the river would be passed. The advancing columns could press on toward the final objective, the York River Railroad.

The two divisions of Huger and Magruder that were to be left in front of Richmond while the rest of the army went to the north side were to demonstrate on the day of battle. If they needed help, they were to call on the commands of General Holmes and General Wise who were on either side the James, and if the enemy withdrew from their front, Huger and Magruder were to pursue vigorously.

Graphically, the various movements are represented on page 113.

Having explained all this, Lee did something he had never done before and was never to do again: He excused himself for a time and left his subordinates to discuss among themselves the proposed movement. Doubtless he felt this was safe, in dealing with four professional soldiers of experience, and perhaps he thought it desirable that they should feel free to analyze and criticise his plan so that each might understand precisely what was expected of him.

When Lee returned, after some time, he was told that the four had agreed to launch the offensive on June 26. It is not certain he was informed that Jackson had first stated that he would be in position to attack on the 25th but had been urged by Longstreet to set the following day for the turning movement.[9]

---

[9] *Longstreet,* 121-22.

The conference adjourned about nightfall and Jackson set out at once to spend another sleepless night in the saddle, returning to his command.[10] His ruse on leaving the valley had served its

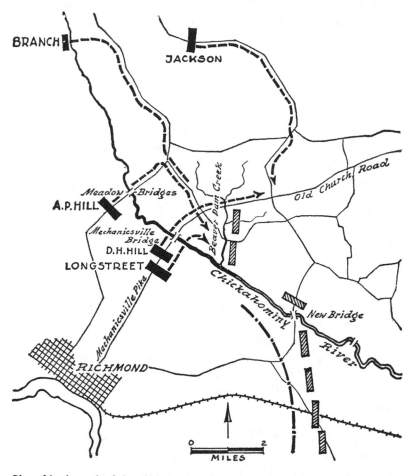

Plan of battle north of the Chickahominy River, as announced by General Lee at the council of war, June 23, 1862.

purpose well in mystifying the Federals in the valley.[11] His ride to Richmond and his departure, the approach of his division and its intended participation in the battle were supposed to be secrets, but a garrulous Confederate quartermaster, however, had

[10] *Taylor's General Lee*, 60–62; *Longstreet, loc. cit.; Marshall*, 84–85; 2 *B. and L.,* 347. [11] *Dabney,* 431 ff.

remarked that all the cars on the Virginia Central Railroad had been sent westward to transport Jackson to Richmond, and in this way the news had reached many people in Richmond.[12] What information McClellan had received, and whether the turning movement by Jackson would surprise him, was, of course, unknown to the Confederates and indeterminable until the day of battle. Lee's hope was that the movement of Whiting and Lawton to the valley had become known but that the advance of Jackson had not been reported to his adversary.

On the 24th Lee personally drafted his general order and had it distributed,[13] for he was determined not to repeat the misunderstandings of Seven Pines by the issuance of verbal instructions to one commander, of which the co-operating officer might be ignorant. Unfortunately, in an effort to condense the language of the order, Lee did not make it altogether unambiguous. He said that A. P. Hill was to cross the Meadow Bridges as soon as the movements of Jackson and of Branch were "discovered." Did this mean that Hill was to cross when he "discovered" that Jackson and Branch had started from their stations or when he "discovered" that they were opposite Meadow Bridge? Again, Lee said: "At 3 o'clock Thursday morning, 26th instant, General Jackson will advance on the road leading to Pole Green church, communicating his march to General Branch." Then he proceeded to explain the crossing of the divisions from the south side. Nothing more was said of Jackson until the order directed that D. H. Hill move to the support of Jackson. Then followed this language:

"The four divisions, keeping in communication with each other and moving en echelon on separate roads, if practicable, the left division in advance, with skirmishers and sharpshooters extending their front, will sweep down the Chickahominy and endeavor to drive the enemy from his position above New Bridge, General Jackson bearing well to his left, turning Beaver Dam Creek and taking the direction toward Cold Harbor."[14]

[12] T. R. R. Cobb in 28 *S. H. S. P.*, 293; *McCabe,* 122 and n.; *Richmond Dispatch,* July 9, 1862, p. 2, col. 1.
[13] *Marshall,* 86.
[14] *O. R.,* 11, part 2, p. 499. The whole text of this important document appears as Appendix II—1.

Was this plain? Would Jackson understand it? Was there danger of two interpretations?

Lee made the disposition of the artillery the subject of special instructions. Whiting had taken only two batteries with him to the valley.[15] The remainder of the artillery of Smith's former division was assigned to Magruder's division, raising his total to thirteen batteries. Lee did not detach any of this ordnance for the offensive, as Magruder had a long line to defend. Huger had six batteries. The reserve artillery of twenty-three batteries was placed under its chief, Brigadier-General W. N. Pendleton, to be used for three purposes, namely, (1) to deal with any emergency; (2) to defend the lines on the south side of the Chickahominy, and (3) to support the attack north of the river, as occasion might require. If none of this reserve artillery had to be sent to the north side, Lee would have 126 guns to hold off any Federal offensive south of the Chickahominy. The attacking divisions, which were not over-gunned, were to carry their regular artillery units with them into action.[16]

A major factor in the operations Lee projected in these orders was the character of the terrain. His field lay between the James and the Pamunkey with the Chickahominy roughly midway between them. All three of the rivers have a general course from northwest to southeast. The average distance from the Pamunkey to the Chickahominy, in this zone, is seven miles, and from the Chickahominy to the James nine miles. The country is flat, in the main, except where the watercourses cut their way. Rain is slow to run off. Along the streams, there are bluffs and wide valleys in some places, and at others the creeks run in narrow, deep ravines. The swamps that gained a sinister name in the campaign were then confined to the valley of the Chickahominy and to a few small creeks or rivulets that lost their way in flats overgrown with a tangle of small trees and bushes. The picture of vast, impassable swamps, with mighty cypress trees and tropical vegetation, was wholly imaginary. In dry weather, when the streams were low, infantry could pass through almost

---

[15] O. R., 11, part 3, p. 594.

[16] The distribution of the artillery is given in O. R., 11, part 2, pp. 483 ff. Lee mentioned in ibid., 490–91, his instructions to Pendleton, who described them more fully in ibid., 553.

any part of the swamps and would only require a foot-bridge. In a wet season, the water filled the bottoms and mired the roads. Two-thirds of the country was wooded, and as the farms were comparatively small, there were scores of narrow roads amid which marching columns could easily lose their way. These roads, little known and poorly mapped, were to prove the chief obstacle to rapid advances and were to explain many things which, if they had occurred in an open country, would have to be written down as inexcusable failures.

Rain had fallen on the 23d and it continued on the 24th, but as the roads had previously dried out, and as the temperature was high,[17] there was nothing to indicate that the weather would hold up the movement. The only pressing duty that remained to be performed was to see that the six excellent North Carolina regiments of Ransom's brigade, then in Petersburg, were brought on to Richmond. Lee decided to employ them with Huger's division on the Williamsburg road, and he could safely assume that they would be in position early on the morning of June 25.[18]

The arrival of these troops gave Lee a total effective strength of about 67,000 men. Jackson would bring 18,500, including Whiting and Lawton, so that Lee hoped to open the battle with about 85,500 soldiers of all arms.[19] Of this number, Lee intended to employ some 56,000, cavalry included, against the Federal right flank north of the Chickahominy. It was a much larger force than, a month previously, it had seemed possible for the Confederates to gather in front of Richmond.

The organization of the army for the movement was to be as follows:

ATTACK DIVISIONS (NORTH OF THE CHICKAHOMINY)

Cavalry (covering the left of the turning column).
J. E. B. Stuart—about 4 regiments, 1800 men.
Left (turning column).
T. J. Jackson's own division, 4 brigades.

[17] Waldrop in 3 *Richmond Howitzers*, 40.
[18] *O. R.*, 11, part 2, p. 791.
[19] There are, unfortunately, no complete returns for the Army of Northern Virginia as of June 20–25. Taylor, in his *Four Years*, 53, estimated the number at 80,762; Alexander, *op. cit.*, 112, put it at about 83,500; Henderson, *op. cit.*, 2, 9, reckoned it at 86,500; D. H. Hill, Jr., *op. cit.*, 2, 94, gave it as 86,152.

R. S. Ewell's division, 3 brigades and the "Maryland Line."
W. H. C. Whiting's division, 2 brigades.
    Total, 9 brigades, 9 batteries, 18,500 men.

Left Support
D. H. Hill's division, 5 brigades, 7 batteries, 9000 men.

Centre
A. P. Hill's division, 6 brigades, 9 batteries, 14,000 men.

Right
James Longstreet's division, 6 brigades, 1 battalion of artillery,
    9000 men.

DEFENSE DIVISIONS (SOUTH OF THE CHICKAHOMINY)

J. B. Magruder's division, 6 brigades, 13 batteries, 12,000 men.
Benjamin Huger's division, 3 brigades, 6 batteries, 9000 men.

DEFENSE DIVISIONS ON JAMES RIVER

North: H. A. Wise's command, 3 regiments, 4 batteries, 1500
men.
South: T. H. H. Holmes's division, 3 brigades, 6 batteries,
6500 men.

RESERVE ARTILLERY

W. N. Pendleton commanding, 23 batteries, 3000 men.

CAVALRY (SOUTH OF THE CHICKAHOMINY)

About 3½ regiments, on the Nine Mile road and the roads
    as far south as James River, 1200 men.[20]

Of the strength of his opponent, Lee had no definite information, though in May or early June he had estimated the Federal
strength at 150,000 or more.[21] He was convinced, in any case,
that McClellan's losses at Seven Poines had been made good, and
that the Unionists heavily outnumbered him. He expected, however, to concentrate on the north side of the Chickahominy a

---

[20] Compiled from *O. R.*, 11, part 1, pp. 483–89. The cavalry is listed as 7 regiments,
one battalion and three detachments from "Legions." The total did not exceed the
equivalent of 7 regiments, about 3000 men.
[21] James Lyons in 7 *S. H. S. P.*, 357.

force superior to that which the Union commander-in-chief had left there.[22]

The 25th dawned with the rain still falling intermittently,[23] but not heavily enough to cause concern for the roads. It was to be a busy day, for Jackson was doubtless on the march, and the divisions of A. P. Hill, Longstreet, and D. H. Hill were to cook three days' rations preparatory to moving that night. Scarcely had routine camp duties been discharged than there came a development not on the schedule. The Federal artillery opened on a wide front, north and south of the Chickahominy. Soon word reached Lee that the Federals were attacking the pickets along the Williamsburg road and were driving them in. What did it mean? Had McClellan learned of the approach of Jackson? Was he launching an attack to spoil Lee's plan? The attack was on Huger's front, and he was not at his quarters. Worse still, the movement was directed, in part, against some of Ransom's troops who had arrived that morning and had never been under fire before.

Reassurance was given Lee later in the morning, with the indications that the Federals were seeking nothing more than to advance their picket-line beyond a no-man's land in the middle of a forest. But Lee was not wholly satisfied, and he rode over to the Williamsburg road to examine the situation for himself. By doing so, he missed a visit from President Davis. Once on the ground, he found, despite the inexperience of some of the units, that the men were fighting admirably. He did not think, however, that the affair had been well handled by the officers in command.[24]

This action raised a question: Should Lee execute his plan for a battle the next day, or should he await the development of the enemy's movement? Studying such information as he had, he concluded that McClellan was not attacking because he was aware of Jackson's advance, but that the Federal commander would certainly assume the offensive very shortly.[25] Ordering General Huger to hold his lines the next morning at any cost and to

---

[22] Actually, McClellan had 117,226 present on June 20, of whom 105,444 were equipped. The force of 10,101 at Fort Monroe is not included (*O. R.*, 11, part 3, p. 238).
[23] Waldrop in 3 *Richmond Howitzers*, 40.
[24] *Lee's Dispatches*, 13.   [25] *O. R.*, 11, part 2, p. 490.

118

advance if possible, Lee let his plan for the offensive stand. It was an audacious decision, but it was based on the belief that the best way to avoid an attack was to deliver one.[26]

Toward evening, the charges and counter-charges on the Williamsburg road ended with the Confederate main line untouched. The artillery-fire, which had continued vigorously on the north side of the Chickahominy, at length fell away.[27] The rain had ceased, too, and as the anxious people of Richmond looked out from the housetops, they saw a rainbow covering the camps of their defenders. It was an omen, the superstitious affirmed.[28] Yet there were many who had no faith in the omen or in the commander of the army. Critics were still to be found on every corner; those who had doubted Lee's qualities of command continued to murmur so dubiously that his admirers had to defend him. At that very hour, perhaps, the editor of *The Richmond Enquirer* was writing for his next day's paper an appeal for confidence in Lee. "Impatient critics," he said, "are still busy with comments upon a policy, the facts leading to which they do not know, and upon which, if they did, they could form no reliable opinion." [29]

Back through the fading rainbow, unmindful of critics, Lee returned to his headquarters. For part of the way he went over the road he and Davis had followed that last night in May, not quite four weeks before, when the President had told him he wished him to assume command of the army. Then the fields and the highways had been full of the wounded, victims of a bungled battle that only the optimist could style a victory. Now, under the summer stars, in the meadows, the men were lighting their camp-fires, and the teamsters were feeding their horses in the knowledge that the cooking of three days' rations meant a new battle.[30] What could Lee have thought as he rode silently

---

[26] *Lee's Dispatches*, 12–14. The dispatch to Davis, No. 4, is wrongly dated June 24. For this affair, known to the Confederates as the battle of King's Schoolhouse, see the reports in *O. R.*, 11, part 2, pp. 95 ff., 787 ff., 804 ff.; H. W. Thomas: *History of the Doles-Cook Brigade* (cited hereafter as *Thomas*), 66–68.

[27] *O. R.*, 11, part 3, p. 252; *Joel Cook*, 295.

[28] *De Leon*, 204. This incident inspired John R. Thompson's poem "The Battle Rainbow."

[29] *Richmond Enquirer*, June 26, 1862, p. 2, col. 1.

[30] *O. R.*, 11, part 2, pp. 623, 647, the latter report being one day wrong in its chronology.

by, and heard the echo of the soldiers' banter, the music of their boyish laughter?

At the Dabbs house, the servants were packing the camp equipage and the office was ready to be abandoned, for, with the dawn, headquarters would be in the field, and none could say where sunset would find them on the morrow. Lee ate his supper, received the last reports, wrote a letter to President Davis, telling him of the affair on the Williamsburg road, questioned the staff once more about the movements of the troops that night, and then sought a few hours' sleep.

The eve of the great struggle for the possession of Richmond; the eve of the first battle Lee had ever directed under the Southern flag! Was everything prepared? Had he forgotten any essential? Would he have the advantage of surprise, or was the enemy at that hour preparing for him? The column that was to make the turning movement was strong enough; the force he would hurl against the enemy's right certainly outnumbered the Federal brigades north of the Chickahominy; the artillery was prudently apportioned; the attacking divisions were well-led; the general staff had done its work carefully; the wagon-train would not be long. If Magruder and Huger put up a bold front, they would be able to hold off the enemy until Lee's advance had passed New Bridge. Then, if the Federals attempted to drive into Richmond, he would recross the river and be on their heels, just as he had promised the President he would be.[31] But . . . was he expecting too much of inexperienced staff officers? The only maps that the engineers had prepared were little more than sketches; would they suffice; were they accurate? Were the roads so narrow and so numerous, in a tangled country, that they would confuse the commanders? Above all . . . was the plan understood? Was it subject to two interpretations in any particular? Was it over-complicated? It provided for the convergence on the heights of the Chickahominy of columns that were to approach by three routes, Jackson's turning column after a long march from the north, A. P. Hill across Meadow Bridges, Longstreet and D. H. Hill by way of Mechanicsville pike. Would they meet at the same time and on the appointed line, or . . . ?

[31] See *supra*, p. 106.

It was getting late; the birds were beginning to stir; that low, continuous sound was the creaking of the complaining wagons on the road; that muffled pulsing, as regular as the beat of an untroubled heart, was the tramp of D. H. Hill's men on the way to their rendezvous. The day of battle had come!

CHAPTER XII

WHERE IS JACKSON?

(MECHANICSVILLE)

DAY dawned fair and pleasant on June 26, one of the flawless mild summer mornings that often follow thunderstorms in eastern Virginia.[1] Lee was early astir. Notice was sent to the President that headquarters would be on the Mechanicsville turnpike,[2] and the Secretary of War, similarly advised, was told to call on the troops guarding the James River water-line if he needed assistance in repelling any attack by the Federal forces south of the Chickahominy.[3]

Bad news came with breakfast. Down the river, opposite New Bridge, artillery fire broke out hotly and lasted half an hour.[4] From Jackson arrived a dispatch explaining that his command had been delayed in its march and had not reached Ashland until the evening of the 25th, whereas the plan had stipulated that the divisions were to camp that night west of the Central Railroad between Ashland and Richmond, about six miles nearer the chosen field of battle. That was a poor beginning for the advance, and it could not be wholly redeemed by the assurance Jackson gave that he would start at 2:30 on the morning of the 26th. At best, Jackson could not cross the railway until 6 o'clock —three hours late.

Jackson reported, also, that his cavalry pickets had been driven in and that the telegraph wire had ben cut near Ashland.[5] That was ominous! Perhaps the plan had been discovered. The attack of the previous day on the Williamsburg road might have been delivered in order to discover whether the Confederate forces on that sector had been reduced for a concentration north of the Chickahominy.[6]

---

[1] 2 B. and L., 327; Waldrop in 3 Richmond Howitzers, 40.
[2] Lee's Dispatches, 17.
[3] O. R., 11, part 3, p. 617; 1 R. W. C. D., 136.   [4] O. R., 11, part 2, p. 746.
[5] Lee doubtless knew already that the telegraph line had been broken as the Federals had been at or near Ashland for several days.
[6] Lee to Davis, June 26, 1862; Lee's Dispatches, 15–16.

Lee's apprehension increased but his purpose was not shaken. He would go on. From the Dabbs house he rode over to the Mechanicsville turnpike, out of which the regiments of D. H. Hill and Longstreet were streaming.[7] The artillery had been sent ahead,[8] and the campfires had been replenished along the front the men had left in order to create the impression that the former lines were still occupied in full strength.[9] By 8 A.M.[10] all the units of the two divisions were in position, masked behind the crest of the hills overlooking the Chickahominy from the south.[11]

Lee rode out to an advanced artillery position and surveyed the verdant panorama.[12] He was on one of the high points of the long heights, which ran roughly from west to east. Half a mile away, in front of him, the two channels of the Chickahominy, so insignificant in drought, so formidable in flood, meandered through a wide, boggy meadow, fringed with trees not so high as those that mar the view today.[13] Straight down from the eminence where Lee stood, across two broken bridges and then northward up the other side, like the shaft of an arrow, ran the sandy Mechanicsville turnpike to the little village whose name it bore, a village perched midway a row of hills almost as elevated as that on which Lee stood.

Mechanicsville was thus in the centre of the scene. It occupied a magnificent site and was an important crossroads,[14] but in itself it was a poor place. Its half-dozen houses, residences, stores, and

---

[7] Most of the units had come up the muddy Williamsburg road to Richmond and then had taken the pike toward the Chickahominy (*O. R.*, 11, part 2, pp. 623, 638, 647, 654, 756).

[8] *O. R.*, 11, part 2, p. 654.

[9] 2 *B. and L.*, 351.   [10] *O. R.*, 11, part 2, p. 756.

[11] *O. R.*, 11, part 2, p. 640. Longstreet, *op. cit.*, 123, stated that no special effort was made to conceal the presence of the troops, but Joel Cook, *op. cit.*, 244, said the trees completely concealed them from Federal view. Marshal Foch once expressed to the writer the opinion that Lee's plan was shaped, in part, by the fact that the foliage at that season made it easy to conceal his troop-movements.

[12] It is probable, though not altogether certain, that his post of observation was on Ravenswood Farm, west of the pike and directly on the crest overlooking the Chickahominy valley.

[13] McClellan gave a very accurate description of the river bottom in *O. R.*, 11, part 1, p. 25.

[14] Southeastward one road ran along the ridge toward Cold Harbor. The Old Church road ran to the northeast, the Mechanicsville and Hanover Courthouse road to the north, and still a fourth road cut to the northwest to join a highway that ran from the Meadow Bridges road, which crossed the Chickahominy, one and three-quarter miles upstream.

saloon had been badly treated by the moving armies. On the west of the turnpike was a grove that had been cleared of under-brush, and in the farther fringe of this grove was a looted and deserted beer-garden. East of the road stood the best and least-damaged house of the village. Flower-beds adorned its front yard; honeysuckle and woodbine ran on a trellis over the porch.

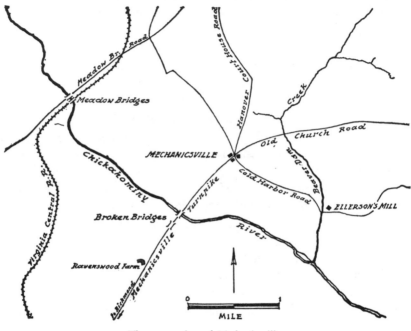

The approaches of Mechanicsville.

From the yard a large vegetable garden stretched toward the river.[15]

On either side of the village, the land formed a slightly rolling plain, clear for a mile to the eastward and for a mile and a half to the westward, except for low thickets along the course of the few small streams that flowed down to the Chickahominy through shallow ravines. North and east of these fields, which the frequent rains had kept green under the summer sun, spread woodlands of oak and of pine, broken here and there by clearings

[15] *Joel Cook*, 231. It is possible that Cook confused his directions and that he re-ferred to the substantial brick house west of the road.

and dotted at intervals with the white dwellings of the planters. West of the village the crossing opposite the Meadow Bridges was hidden by the trees.

About a mile east of Mechanicsville, scarcely observable amid the surrounding growth, was the declivity through which ran the often-mentioned Beaver Dam Creek, where the main Federal position was supposed to be. Fed by several branches that had their source two miles or more up the watershed, the stream wandered through ravines until it found its way into the Chickahominy.

The panorama was as pleasant as could be found in many a mile. At intervals, newly dug parapets stood out from the verdure, for the Federal artillery commanded the hills on the south side.[16] In the village, through strong binoculars, blue-coated infantry could be seen; along the ridge, at intervals, little knots of horsemen might be picked out in the field of the glasses; afar off, McClellan's observation balloons were in the air.[17] But so quiet was the landscape, in the clear morning light, that it was hard to realize that war gripped the countryside, or that thousands of armed men would soon be struggling across it.

Observers on the Richmond side of the valley did not gaze long to the east, or even at the village. Their thought was of Meadow Bridges, where A. P. Hill was waiting. From the woods opposite that point, there might break out at any time the fire of the skirmishers of Branch's brigade. This command, it will be recalled, had been sent to Half Sink. Its instructions were to cross the Chickahominy and to move on Mechanicsville, clearing the road for Hill's crossing at the Meadow Bridges, as soon as the movements of Jackson and of Branch were discovered.[18]

If Jackson were delayed in crossing the railroad, it followed that Branch would be later in marching on Mechanicsville than had been contemplated in orders, but no further word had come from him or from Jackson. It would be afternoon before the village could be taken. Still, the sun did not set until 7:17, and Lee would have at least six hours in which to drive the Federals. Everything depended on Jackson and on Branch. Jackson was a

[16] *Joel Cook,* 228.
[17] R. E. Withers: *Autobiography of an Octogenarian* (cited hereafter as *Withers*), 183.
[18] *O. R.,* 11, part 2, p. 881.

known quantity; Branch was a man of forty-one, a Princeton graduate, a former congressman and not a professional soldier, but he had some knowledge of the country and had acquitted himself well in the action at Hanover Courthouse. It would have

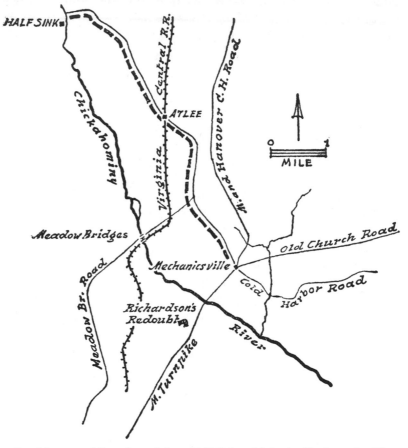

Branch's proposed line of march from Half Sink to Mechanicsville, June 26, 1862.
Branch's route is indicated by the broken line.

been better, perhaps, if the important *liaison* with Jackson had been entrusted to a more experienced officer.

Noon at last by the chiming of far-off Richmond bells; no sound of battle from the north side; no smoke, no dust as of a moving column. Major Richardson on the outermost redoubt south of the Chickahominy and adjoining the turnpike reported that he believed the enemy was leaving the earthworks on the opposite heights, but he was not certain.[19]

Another anxious hour crept by, and another. The President, the Secretary of War, and a number of public men had ridden out.[20] There was enough of conversation and of high company. But to Lee, the suspense must have been akin to that of the tortured morning on the flank of Cheat Mountain, nine months before, when he had waited so long for the sound of the volleys that Colonel Rust had never ordered. The stakes were so immeasurably vaster now! The sun was beginning to slant. The shadows were creeping eastward. Mechanicsville and the whole horizon stood out in sharper relief. Three o'clock was drawing on, and it began to look as if the whole plan might have to be cancelled, for the Federals who had driven in Jackson's pickets had certainly reported his advance by this time. Night would give McClellan opportunity of covering his threatened flank with strong reinforcements from the south side.[21] The fates that thus far had kept Lee from fighting a single battle seemed to be leagued once more against him.

At 3 o'clock—and how long it was in coming!—Major Richardson reported that he was satisfied the enemy was evacuating the gun-positions immediately opposite him.[22] With Longstreet and D. H. Hill, Lee went out on the redoubt to see for himself. Although there was some movement around Mechanicsville, there was nothing definite, nothing to indicate any sudden alarm.

The hour had not long passed when there rolled down the valley a rattle of musketry. It grew into volleys, loud and furious. Every glass was turned upstream. Blue-coated figures began to emerge from the fringe of woods on the far side of the river, below the Meadow Bridges. The attack was being delivered at last! Quickly on the heels of the Federals a Confederate skirmish line appeared. Behind the skirmishers the woods seemed suddenly alive with men, spreading rapidly northward. They halted, formed line of battle, and began to sweep eastward toward Mechanicsville.[23] The effect was electric. The village and the country round about woke up with a start. Bugles echoed.

[19] *O. R.*, 11, part 2, p. 538.
[20] 1 *N. C. Regts.*, 138, 181.
[21] *Marshall*, 91.
[22] *O. R.*, 11, part 2, p. 538.
[23] *O. R.*, 11, part 2, pp. 835, 841.

Horsemen sprang to saddle. A line was quickly formed at Mechanicsville.[24] From the fields behind the earthwork where Lee was watching, the lounging soldiers of D. H. Hill and Longstreet sprang up.[25] Orders rang out. The gunners stood to their pieces, anxiously awaiting the word of command.

The Confederate line on the other side of the river was now moving steadily eastward, almost unopposed by the fleeing Federals. Soon it was evident that some of Hill's artillery had reached the road that led from the Meadow Bridges toward Mechanicsville, for while the road could not be seen, the boom of guns could be heard from beyond the advancing infantry and the smoke of their fire was visible.

There was other smoke, too, across the Chickahominy. Rising faintly over the village and far beyond the Federal line, it was in a most significant position—directly on the line of Jackson's expected advance. His guns must be in action: "Stonewall" and his famous valley soldiers must be close at hand.[26] Late as it was, the plan seemed now to be working out! Hill was coming down the heights to clear the Mechanicsville bridges, and Jackson would soon be turning Beaver Dam Creek. If the summer sun lingered long enough, victory might still be won.

A. P. Hill's advancing line was nearing Mechanicsville now. No Federal batteries remained on the plain to oppose it. The Federal infantry, which manifestly was not strong,[27] was withdrawing rapidly toward the eastward.

But as the Confederates approached Mechanicsville, a heavy artillery fire was opened upon their columns. Evidently the Federals behind Beaver Dam Creek were ready for them. The whole stream seemed to be covered with the smoke of the Union batteries. Hill must not advance too far before Jackson turned the creek. Otherwise he would be torn to pieces. Quickly Lee called to him one of D. H. Hill's volunteer aides who knew the

---

[24] 2 *B. and L.*, 352.

[25] Some of them had been sleeping during the forenoon to make up for their night march (*O. R.*, 11, part 2, p. 647).

[26] *Marshall*, 93.

[27] The village was occupied by the 5th Penn. Infy. and by two companies of the 4th Penn. Cavalry. Six companies of the 1st Penn. Rifles had been on picket near the Meadow Bridges. The 8th Ill. Cavalry was patrolling the roads by which Jackson was advancing. Cooper's battery of six 12 pdr. Napoleons had been at Mechanicsville but had been withdrawn at 3 P.M. (*O. R.*, 11, part 2, pp. 339, 406, 409).

country, Lieutenant Thomas W. Sydnor of the 4th Virginia Cavalry, and ordered him to ride at once to A. P. Hill and direct him to suspend all movement until further orders.[28]

On Hill went to the village, the fire upon him heavier every minute. On his left, the shells were taking his men almost in flank. He began to manœuvre in that direction.[29] The situation was becoming confused. The firmness of the Federal stand on Beaver Dam Creek did not indicate that Jackson was close enough at hand to turn that stream at its headwaters. What was wrong?

Four o'clock found Hill in the village. The turnpike was cleared. D. H. Hill could cross at last and go to support Jackson —if Jackson were there. Longstreet would follow and form on A. P. Hill's right. Down the hill from the south side went D. H. Hill's leading brigade. Lee's outspoken Carolina critic, General R. S. Ripley, was leading it. Soon he reached the first of the two broken bridges over the Chickahominy. A few planks were thrown across it. The troops hurried on. At the second bridge there was a longer delay, but soon the Georgians and North Carolinians were climbing the hill toward Mechanicsville.[30] Ripley's artillery was to follow him before another brigade of infantry took the road. The batteries were ready. They made the first difficult crossing. The second was too much for them. No pioneers were at hand—some one had blundered about that. The gunners had to turn bridge-builders. Half an hour was lost.[31] While the men were still struggling in the water, an insistent cavalcade came down to the bridge and passed on over. At its head was President Davis, riding, as always, to the sound of the firing. With him were excited staff officers, Cabinet members, and politicians.[32]

Lee had waited to see the column well under way. Owing to the delay in repairing the span at the second bridge, it was nearly 5 o'clock before he left Richardson's battery-position to

<hr/>

[28] 2 *Henderson*, 16, on the authority of Sydnor's letter. Henderson did not give the time at which Sydnor was dispatched, but the circumstances and Lee's subsequent orders make it almost certain that the message was sent about 4 P.M., before Lee crossed the river.

[29] *O. R.*, 11, part 2, pp. 835, 841, 877, 899.

[30] *O. R.*, 11, part 2, pp. 647, 657–58.

[31] *O. R.*, 11, part 2, p. 654. Captain A. Burnet Rhett of the leading battery reported that the column started at 3 P.M., but all the other evidence is that it was 4 P.M.

[32] 2 *B. and L.*, 352.

cross the river.[33] When he arrived at Mechanicsville, he found chaos. Hill, he discovered, had not waited till Jackson and Branch were opposite the Meadow Bridges. Instead, Hill had despaired of their arrival, had disregarded his orders, and had moved on his own responsibility.[34] He did not know where Jackson was—did not know when "Stonewall" would turn the creek and force a withdrawal of those fiendish batteries that were tearing his ranks. The village was his. Only Federal dead and wounded remained west of Beaver Dam Creek. But what good did this do? The ground was completely open. The men had no cover. The enemy's fire was on a wide arc. The few guns that Hill could put into position seemed to make no impression on the enemy.[35] Hill had carried out his orders and had formed line of battle for the general advance to the eastward, on a front of about a mile and a quarter.[36] This had availed little. In the face of the continuous fire, some of the regiments had gone forward to the edge of the declivity of Beaver Dam Creek, where there was some cover, even if the ground was within range of the Federal infantry. Where these troops found lodgment a wild, bootless battle was in progress along the creek. Only part of one brigade had been able to cross and it had accomplished nothing.[37] The others barely held the fringe of the thicket facing the stream. Some commanders had halted their men and had made them lie down in line, as they could not hope to storm the Federal position or live in the open. Fortunately the enemy's artillery fire was a little high, else the whole division would have been slaughtered.[38]

All over the plain, the spiteful shells were bursting in fury.

---

[33] *O. R.*, 11, part 2, p. 538.   [34] *O. R.*, 11, part 2, p. 835.

[35] An exciting picture of the handling of a Confederate battery in this phase of the battle will be found in F. W. Dawson: *Confederate Reminiscences* (cited hereafter as F. W. Dawson), 48–49.

[36] Pender was on the right, opposite a bridge that crossed the creek at Ellerson's grist mill. On his left was Field, and on Field's left was Archer, these two occupying approximately the five-eighths of a mile between the Cold Harbor and the Old Church roads. Most, if not all of J. R. Anderson's brigade was north of the Old Church road, holding the extreme left. Gregg was in reserve, and Branch, who had just come up, was in support of the attacking divisions.

[37] *O. R.*, 11, part 2, pp. 491, 836, 877. General Lee stated that this regiment, the 35th Georgia, crossed to communicate with Jackson. A. P. Hill affirmed that it forced its way over in the course of its advance; J. R. Anderson, to whose brigade the regiment was attached, intimated that it was sent over the stream to ascertain the location of the Federal line, which Anderson had believed to be on the near side of the creek.

[38] *O. R.*, 11, part 2, p. 658.

Riders went down; horses were slain; guns were disabled. Many of the green troops were in a frenzy. Lee sat through it all as if he thought he was invulnerable. Nearby, though, was the Presi-

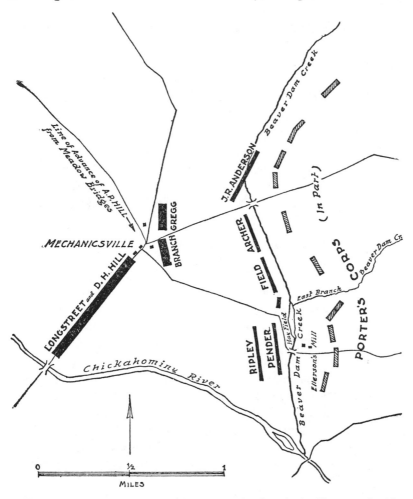

Full extension of Confederate front of attack, Battle of Mechanicsville, June 26, 1862.
(After original of Colonel H. L. Landers, U. S. A.)

dent, with members of his Cabinet and a coterie of politicians. One explosion might kill all of them. They must go to a place of safety.

Lee rode over to Davis. "Mr. President," he asked with a frigid salute, "who is all this army and what is it doing here?"

Davis knew what Lee meant. He squirmed in his saddle. "It is not my army, General," he said.

"It is certainly not my army, Mr. President, and this is no place for it."

Davis was stunned. "Well, General, if I withdraw, perhaps they will follow me." He lifted his hat and rode down the hill. His companions, crestfallen, trooped after him. He disappeared, and Lee did not know till later that Davis had gone only far enough to get out of his sight. Then he halted quickly, but not before a soldier at his feet had been killed by an exploding shell.[39]

Evening was drawing on—what could be done? It was Lee's to decide. He expected Jackson's turning movement against the Federal right to begin at any moment.[40] The whole army was so confident of "Stonewall's" immediate arrival that some of the troops were told that he was already on the flank and in the rear of the enemy. A little later, these troops thought they heard his guns.[41] But what if Jackson did not come up? How could the general plan be saved from ruin? How could McClellan be prevented from attacking on the south side or sending heavy reinforcements to the north side? Quickly Lee dictated an order to Huger, telling him to hold his trenches at the point of the bayonet, if need be, and advising him where he could get help if he required it.[42] A cavalry demonstration on the extreme Confederate right beyond White Oak Swamp was also ordered as a means of ascertaining the enemy's strength and of keeping him from withdrawing troops to the Confederate left.[43]

As for Hill's battle, a direct assault on Beaver Dam Creek was out of the question. The strength of the Federal position was only too well known to Lee and to the senior division commanders. They had never intended to give battle there.[44] The

[39] This story appears in various forms. The writer has used that of Mrs. Burton Harrison, *op. cit.*, 72–73; Mrs. Harrison left the reader to infer that Mr. Davis had just come out from Richmond, but other accounts, already cited, indicate that he had probably arrived on the field before Lee.

[40] *O. R.*, 11, part 2, pp. 491, 835.

[41] *History of the Fourth South Carolina Volunteers*, 97.

[42] *O. R.*, 11, part 3, p. 617. The hour of this dispatch can be fixed approximately by the fact that it was received on the south side at 8:30 P.M.

[43] *Longstreet*, 148; *O. R.*, 11, part 2, p. 526.

[44] See *supra*, note, p. 111, n. 8. Longstreet in May had proposed that the Confederate army make its stand behind the little watercourse. Smith, as already noted, had urged that the attack of May 29 be cancelled because he did not think the creek could be passed

only possible way of winning the position was to turn it. That was what Jackson was to do on the Confederate left—would he never come? If he did not, it was too late in the day to send another column there, even if the slow march of D. H. Hill and Longstreet from across the Chickahominy could be hastened.[45] The only hope was to try the extreme right, where the ridge fell away toward the Chickahominy. The venture would be desperate, but there was no alternative. If Lee halted in front of the Federal position, McClellan might attack on the south side of the Chickahominy the next morning or might reinforce his troops on Beaver Dam Creek overnight and oppose a large force to Jackson. If the Federal right could be turned, the gain was obvious. If the attempt failed, McClellan might at least be kept from sending a heavy column to oppose Jackson.[46]

The decision was made more quickly than the reasoning that prompted it can be retraced. Pender's troops, in some confusion, were already far on the right. Ripley, who commanded the only brigade of D. H. Hill's division that had yet completed the crossing of the Chickahominy, was ordered to move still farther to the right and to turn the enemy's flank. Several messages were

except at great sacrifice of life (*Longstreet*, 82, 85–86; *G. W. Smith*, 148–55). The stream ran southward through a wide and deep ravine, the lofty sides of which, to the east and west, were covered with thick underbrush and woods. The Old Church road crossed the creek a little more than half a mile northeast of Mechanicsville, at a point where high hills on the eastern side of the stream afforded commanding artillery positions, which the Federals had fortified. Three-quarters of a mile downstream from this point, the Cold Harbor road crossed the creek a mile and a quarter southeast of Mechanicsville. Here was located Ellerson's grist-mill, with a hay-field under the hill to the west of the stream. The water had here been diverted into a deep, wide mill-race. The only practicable crossing at Ellerson's Mill was over a narrow bridge, which the Federals had destroyed. On the hill east of the mill was the strong Federal position, with epaulements and rifle pits. The position was not of uniform depth, but on the south side of the road the hill led to a wide plateau, ample for deployment manœuvre. From this eastern hill the Federals could enfilade any direct approach to Ellerson's Mill from the west. Finally, to hold an assaulting column under Federal fire, trees had been felled on the western side of the stream. *Marshall*, 81, 93. For a detailed description of the Federal position, including facts that the Confederates could not have learned at the time, see *O. R.*, 11, part 2, p. 384, and 2 *B. and L.*, 384.

[45] Longstreet stated (*O. R.*, 11, part 2, p. 756) that "some time after dark the rear brigade of my . . . division succeeded in crossing the Chickahominy," but Featherstone, whose brigade was leading Longstreet's division, said it was "about 10 o'clock" when he crossed (*ibid.*, part 2, p. 781). As D. H. Hill's troops arrived, they took up a line of battle under the crest of the ridge, east of the pike (*O. R.*, 11, part 2, p. 640). The movement of the two divisions was slow not only because they had to use the same road, but also because the artillery of each brigade had to follow it up half a mile of a road deep in sand.

[46] *Marshall*, 94; *R. E. Lee, Jr.*, 415, the latter quoting a statement made by General Lee to Cassius F. Lee in 1870.

sent to hurry him forward, one of them by President Davis him-self.[47] Soon Ripley was up; soon he was moving forward. He did not know the ground, of course, and he took the exposed route over which Pender had already moved.[48] Time was lost at the very outset. Casualties were sustained that might have been avoided.

The roar of the artillery continued as twilight came on. The rattle of small arms from the valley of Beaver Dam Creek was ceaseless. Lee waited and hoped, but hoped in vain. For the ambulant wounded, limping back across the fire-swept field, brought news of the failure of Ripley's flank attack. The men of the 1st North Carolina and of the 44th Georgia were not led far enough to the right to get below the hill on the eastern side of the creek when the Federals were making their stand. Instead, the attacking column plunged down a hill, in the very face of the enemy, falling in windrows at every step. The few that reached the bottom found themselves within the easiest point-blank range of the Federal infantry. Those who escaped unhurt cheated death. Rhett's battery, coming up from the Chickahominy, took position within 1200 yards of the Federal guns and somewhat reduced the enemy's fire; another battery added the weight of its metal, but it was in vain.

Darkness settled, and the remnants of Ripley's and of Pender's men were called back from the tangle around the creek and were given such shelter as could be found a few hundred yards from it.[49] By 9 o'clock the infantry action was over. The artillery-duel continued for another hour, and, on some parts of the line until even later.[50] The regiment of Anderson's brigade that had succeeded in crossing the creek, beyond the Old Church road on the Confederate left, was withdrawn to the right bank of the stream.

Lee's first battle was finished. Fought where he had not ex-pected to be engaged, it had carried the Confederates no farther than the prepared position of the Federals, and there it had been

[47] O. R., 11, part 2, p. 623.   [48] O. R., 11, part 2, p. 899.
[49] Later in the night they were relieved by fresh troops (O. R., 11, part 2, pp. 756, 779, 781).
[50] O. R., 11, part 2, pp. 491, 648, 654, 656, 658, 899. For the Federal reports see ibid., 221 ff.

a ghastly failure.[51] With 56,000 men north of the Chickahominy, or crossing it, Lee had been able to get only 14,000 into action and had lost nearly 10 per cent of them, with no other gain than to drive the enemy from the plain around Mechanicsville. The Federal loss could only be surmised, but from the nature of the action, it had to be regarded as trivial.[52] And this was the result of days of hard planning and careful preparation! Where Lee had expected to turn Beaver Dam Creek and to sweep down the Chickahominy, with all the advantage of surprise, something had gone wrong with Jackson, and A. P. Hill had been halted and bloodily repulsed.

The plan, of course, was disclosed to McClellan now. The whole element of surprise was lost. The Federal commander could reinforce his right or attack Richmond on his left. Lee could only hope that Jackson would turn the creek during the night,[53] so that the original battle plan could be carried out. Until 11 o'clock at night he worked to prepare the troops and to make the dispositions for an attack at dawn and then, wearily, he went back across the river to rest.[54] A doubtful mind would have asked if the man who had failed at Cheat Mountain, and failed at Sewell Mountain, and failed at Mechanicsville had in him the stuff of which victory was made. If Lee had such misgivings that clean, starlit June night, he stifled them. It was his duty to go on—and he would!

[51] The gallant 44th Georgia had lost 335 of the 514 with which it had entered the battle (O. R., 11, part 2, p. 656), and the 1st North Carolina had sustained 142 casualties (O. R., 11, part 2, p. 976). Ripley's total killed, wounded, and missing numbered 575 (O. R., 11, part 2, p. 976). The entire cost of the field to the Confederates was around 1350 men (Alexander, 121). As the Confederate casualties during the Seven Days' Battles were not separately reported for the several engagements by all the commanders, it is almost impossible to give accurate figures.

[52] Actually, it was 361. More than one-fourth of these were in the 1st Pennsylvania Rifles, which had supplied the pickets in front of the Meadow Bridges (O. R., 11, part 2, pp. 38–39).

[53] O. R., 11, part 2, p. 491.

[54] Marshall, 96. Marshall did not identify the headquarters for the night other than to say they were in "a house near the Mechanicsville Road, at the top of the hill overlooking the bridge." This may have been Ravenswood.

CHAPTER XIII

Lee's First Victory—at Heavy Cost

(gaines's mill)

Two tasks Lee had on the morning of June 27, 1862. If his plan was not to fail utterly, he must drive the Federals from Beaver Dam Creek, were they found still there, and, secondly, he must pursue them down the north bank of the Chickahominy and either force them to fight away from the cover of their entrenchments and heavy guns or else compel them to retreat.[1] The cloudless sky gave promise of a scorching day. Whatever else happened, rain was not apt to interrupt the army's movements.

Giving orders for his heavy ordnance to move down the valley and to play from across the river on the line of the expected Federal withdrawal,[2] Lee snatched up a hasty breakfast and started for Mechanicsville, whence the sound of renewed infantry and artillery fire was already to be heard.[3] Arriving at the village, while the shell were breaking there,[4] he dispatched Major Walter Taylor to find Jackson and to show him his route, and then he quickly prepared to turn, from the north and from the south, the slaughter-pen on Beaver Dam Creek. Before the turning movement could be organized, the Federals ceased fire and evacuated the position.[5]

Now for the pursuit and the new attack! Repairing quickly the bridge opposite Ellerson's Mill, Maxcy Gregg soon had his brigade across the stream, and in a short time was moving uphill beyond the plain little grist-mill that had won so unhappy a name

---

[1] See *supra*, p. 110.   [2] *O. R.*, 11, part 2, p. 538.
[3] *Marshall*, 97.   [4] *O. R.*, 11, part 2, p. 836.
[5] *O. R.*, 11, part 2, pp. 491, 758, 780, 782, 836. The Confederates assumed that this withdrawal meant that Jackson had just then turned the creek, but in reality orders for a retreat had been received before 2 A.M. and the movement had been under way since that hour. Only a rearguard of one brigade, supported by a few well-handled batteries, had been left to cover the retirement (*O. R.*, 11, part 2, pp. 223, 272, 399–400).

from the battle fought over it on the 26th.[6] The road of Hill's advance, which Gregg was to lead, ran eastward along the heights of the Chickahominy five and a half miles to Old Cold Harbor and thence six miles and a half to Dispatch Station, on the York River Railroad, McClellan's main line of supply. Nearer the

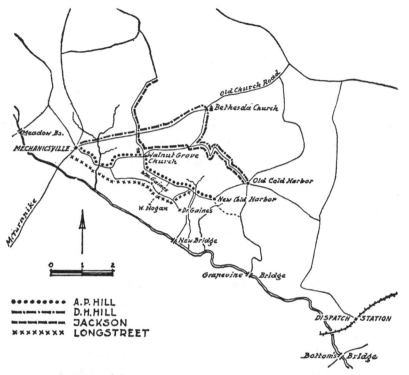

Lines of advance of the Army of Northern Virginia in pursuit of the Federals, morning of June 27, 1862.

Chickahominy, Wilcox, whose brigade was at the head of Longstreet's division, found a broken bridge and beyond it a track that crossed the flats and paralleled the Old Cold Harbor road eastward for three miles.[7] North of the routes by which Longstreet and A. P. Hill were to travel, there were two others by which Jackson and D. H. Hill could advance until they were within two and a half miles of Old Cold Harbor. Then they might have

[6] O. R., 11, part 2, p. 853. For a description of the mill, see *Joel Cook*, 182. The name, indifferently spelt Ellison, Ellyson, and Ellerson in the reports, is correctly Ellerson.
[7] O. R., 11, part 2, pp. 491, 771, 783; *Longstreet*, 125.

to follow the same road. If all went as planned, therefore, the four columns could each move on the heels of the enemy toward the York River Railroad.

By 9 o'clock, A. P. Hill and Longstreet were well under way. D. H. Hill had with him a young lieutenant who had been reared in that vicinity and knew every bypath, but some of Hill's brigadiers and all the commanding officers of Jackson's column were embarrassed from the outset by a lack of competent guides. The maps issued officers proved unworthy of the name, and showed no details of the ground north of the Chickahominy. The route of each division was indicated by a red line which unhappy experience was soon to show the Confederates did not correspond even approximately to the roads they were to follow.[8] The reproduction will illustrate the crudities of the map.

Waiting near Mechanicsville until the last brigade of Longstreet's division was moving, Lee followed the line of march of that command, crossed the lower bridge, picking his way carefully through the ranks,[9] and soon was on ground where burning stores and abandoned supplies evidenced the rapidity of the Federal withdrawal. He had not gone far before he found that contact with the enemy had already been established. In the peachorchard of Fairfield, the home of William Gaines, about a mile eastward, a battery of Federal artillery was blazing away.[10] Hill's advance had brushed the rearguard of the enemy,[11] and, what was equally exciting, had been fired upon by Jackson's artillery.[12] For Jackson was at last on the ground, and the head of his column was near Walnut Grove church, about two miles east of Ellerson's mill, where his route touched A. P. Hill's.

To that little wayside church Lee rode and found Jackson talking to A. P. Hill. After a few minutes, Hill withdrew, and Lee sat down on a cedar stump to confer with the redoubtable commander of the valley army. It was the first time many of Lee's staff-officers had been close to Jackson and they were curi-

---

[8] *Taylor's General Lee*, 65–66; R. Taylor, 86–87; 2 B. and L., 361.

[9] *Morgan*, 134–35.

[10] O. R., 11, part 2, pp. 248–49. For valuable notes on the Hanover homes that figured in this battle, and for constant counsel in solving the problems of this most confused campaign, the author is indebted to his friend J. Ambler Johnston.

[11] O. R., 11, part 2, p. 863.   [12] O. R., 11, part 2, p. 861.

ous to see the man who had dazzled the Confederacy by his victories at Cross Keys and Port Republic, less than three weeks
before. Equally curious were Jackson's aides to have a glimpse of
their new general-in-chief.[13]

There is no record of what passed between Jackson and Lee.
If Jackson made any explanation, it doubtless was to say that on
his march he had enjoyed none of the anticipated advantages of
a surprise. On the contrary, the Federals had acted precisely as
if they had been expecting him, as, indeed, they had.[14] After
leaving Lee on the evening of the 23d, Jackson had rejoined his
command on the 24th. Its march had been slow and difficult on
account of mud, heat, and high water.[15] On the 25th, part of the
army had moved only five miles.[16] Instead of reaching the Central Railroad on the evening of June 25, Jackson had scarcely
made Ashland. He had moved his first division at 3 A.M. on the
morning of the 26th,[17] but many of his men were unaccustomed
to marching in a low country along sandy byways. The officers
knew nothing of the roads. His progress had been so slow that
it had been 9 o'clock before he had crossed the Virginia Central
Railroad.[18] He had at once notified General Branch of that fact.[19]
Not until 3 o'clock had he reached the Totopotomoy Creek, approximately four and one-half miles from the railroad. At that

[13] 2 *Henderson*, 26; 2 *B. and L.*, 353; 9 *S. H. S. P.*, 557.

[14] McClellan had prompt notice of the first dispatch of reinforcements to Jackson
(*O. R.*, 11, part 3, p. 224), but there had been much conflict in reports regarding later
troop-movements and after June 12 there had been a vigorous correspondence among the
Union authorities concerning the transfer of large numbers of men from Lee to Jackson.
This kept up until after Jackson had been engaged at Gaines's Mill (*O. R.*, 12, part 3,
pp. 376, 377, 378, 387, 389, 391, 392, 394–95, 396, 406, 411, 421, 424, 425, 429, 434,
440, 442, 445, 447; *O. R.*, 11, 1, 48, 271; *ibid.*, part 3, pp. 232–33, 234, 238). By June
20, McClellan had been satisfied that Jackson had been heavily reinforced from Richmond, though other Federal authorities still doubted it (*O. R.*, 11, part 1, p. 48). On the
night of the 24th, a deserter had given McClellan news of Jackson's approach (2 *B. and
L.*, 326; *O. R.*, 11, part 1, p. 49). The next day McClellan had been convinced that
Jackson was moving to his right and rear (*O. R.*, 11, part 1, p. 51; part 3, p. 253), and
on the 26th, great clouds of dust, invisible from the south side of the Chickahominy,
had confirmed every suspicion (2 *B. and L.*, 327).

[15] Hotchkiss in 3 *C. M. H.*, 285; G. W. Nichols: *A Soldier's History of His Regiment*,
39. None of Jackson's subordinates had been experienced in handling large bodies of
men and they could not keep the column closed up or speed its movement. His 18,500
troops were spread out on fifteen miles of road (H. H. McGuire to Jed Hotchkiss, March
30, 1896, MS., *McGuire Papers*).

[16] *Diary of B. Y. Malone*, edited by W. W. Pierson, Jr., *James Sprunt Historical Publications*, vol. 16, no. 2 (cited hereafter as *Malone*), 21–22.

[17] *Lee's Dispatches*, 15; *O. R.*, 11, part 2, p. 562.

[18] *O. R.*, 11, part 3, p. 620. Jackson in his report, *ibid.*, part 2, p. 552, said "about
10 o'clock."

[19] *O. R.*, 11, part 2, p. 882.

point, he had found that the Federal pickets had partially destroyed the bridge. Skirmishers had been sent across and Reilly's battery had shelled the woods. It was the smoke of this fire that had been observed from the south side of the Chickahominy just about the time A. P. Hill started from the Meadow Bridges. The engineers having quickly repaired the crossing of the Totopotomoy, Jackson's advance had continued. There had been some alarms and rumors of impending attacks by the enemy. A few obstructions had been encountered in the road. The troops, tired and nervous, had groped their way forward. Jackson had continued his advance to Pole Green church, as his orders had directed, and had gone a little farther to Hundley's Corner, where Ewell's division, which had been moving by roads nearer the railroad, had rejoined the main column. It had then been 4:30 P.M. The sound of A. P. Hill's battle had been audible, and the sun had still been nearly three hours high, but there Jackson had halted and there he had bivouacked, molested only by a few Federal skirmishers who had been driven back after sundown with little difficulty. At least one of Jackson's brigade commanders had thought Jackson should have continued his march,[20] but Jackson had not asked or received counsel from his subordinates.[21] On the morning of the 27th, some of Jackson's units had moved early, but others had not been aroused by their officers when the firing had been resumed in front of Mechanicsville.[22] The march to Walnut Grove church had been but little interrupted by the enemy—and here Jackson was!

He considered that he had discharged the first part of his mission, as far as the conditions permitted, and he made no apologies for halting at Hundley's Corner.[23] Lee, for his part, appears to have raised no question: he simply told Jackson to hasten his march on Cold Harbor. As D. H. Hill was to continue in support, Jackson would have under his command considerably more than half that part of the army on the north side of the

[20] Trimble, *O. R.*, 11, part 2, p. 614.
[21] *O. R.*, 11, part 2, pp. 233, 490, 491, 514, 528, 552–53, 562, 614, 620–21; 2 *Henderson*, 17; *Hood*, 25; W. H. Palmer to W. H. Taylor, July 24, 1905, *Taylor MSS.*; N. A. Davis, 43–44; *Worsham*, 98; H. H. McGuire to Jed Hotchkiss, March 30, 1896, MS.—*McGuire Papers*.
[22] *O. R.*, 11, part 2, pp. 553, 570, 586, 590, 621, 631.
[23] For a critical discussion of Jackson's operations on June 24–26, see Appendix II—2.

river. His advance would turn Powhite Creek, the only nearby stream on which it was believed that the Federals could make a stand while maintaining direct contact with their forces south of the Chickahominy. If this movement did not itself force a Federal retreat, it would put Jackson on the line of the Federal communications with the York River Railroad and in position to fall on the Unionists when A. P. Hill and Longstreet drove them.[24]

The interview over, Jackson rejoined his command, and Lee rode on to the head of Hill's column, which he instructed to press forward and to attack the enemy as soon as located.[25] Then Lee turned into the lane that led to Selwyn, the home of William Hogan, set in a fine grove of trees overlooking the Chickahominy.[26] It was now about noon, and so far as the situation was known to Lee, it was altogether favorable. For just east of the Hogan House was the military road that led down to New Bridge, Lee's intermediate objective. This crossing had been partially destroyed by the retreating Federals, but under orders that Lee immediately issued, it could be reopened at nightfall.[27] Then Lee would be in close touch with Magruder and could quickly reinforce the southside in case McClellan attacked there. The most serious danger in Lee's plan of campaign seemed to be safely overcome.[28] Besides, A. P. Hill and Longstreet were advancing rapidly, and if Jackson and D. H. Hill did equally well, it could not be long before the battle was joined, with every promise of success.

Longstreet and A. P. Hill soon rode up to the Hogan house,[29] and news began to come in that indicated the proximity of the Federals. From across the river, General W. N. Pendleton, chief

---

[24] Lee's orders were verbal, overheard by no one else, and their content has been the subject of much speculation, but Jackson's subsequent movements and Lee's message to Huger from the Hogan house (*Lee's Dispatches,* 18), leave scarcely any ground for doubt as to what Jackson understood his duty to be.

[25] *O. R.,* 11, part 2, p. 853.

[26] *Joel Cook,* 171. Cook confused Selwyn and Fairfield, the home of William Gaines.

[27] *O. R.,* 11, part 2, p. 679; *Marshall,* 97. West of New Bridge was the Federal Upper Trestle Bridge, but as this was in part of pontoons and had a difficult *débouché,* Lee disregarded it.

[28] Magruder, however, later insisted that as the bridge was fully commanded by the Federal guns at Golding's Farm, it was not a practicable crossing until after the enemy evacuated that position (*O. R.,* 11, part 2, p. 662).

[29] *Marshall,* 97; 2 *English Combatant,* 133.

of the reserve artillery, sent word that he could see the enemy in great force east of Powhite, Doctor Gaines's house, which occupied a knoll, three-quarters of a mile down the Chickahominy from Selwyn.[30] The topography of the country made it probable that the Federals would give battle there. Between Doctor Gaines's plantation and the reported position of the enemy, was the watercourse known as Powhite Creek. On the Confederate maps this appeared as a straight stream, flowing from the north into the Chickahominy. Almost directly opposite the mouth of this creek were the Federal lines on the south side of the river. It seemed altogether probable that the Federals held a continuous front, north and south, along Powhite Creek to the Chickahominy and thence across that stream,[31] and were awaiting attack there.

Lee proceeded to make his first plan of the day in the expectation that the battle would be fought on Powhite Creek. Huger was advised of the state of affairs and was urged if the Federals showed any disposition to abandon their front on the south side, to press them hard.[32] Pendleton was told to employ against the Federals the long-range guns that Lee had ordered into action early in the morning and had subsequently directed to cease firing lest they interfere with the pursuit.[33] As Jackson and D. H. Hill were marching toward the Federal rear, turning Powhite Creek, a sharp attack would force the Federals from that stream and would throw them into the very mouth of Jackson's artillery. A. P. Hill was directed to assault as soon as possible, with his full strength. Longstreet's division, which was still coming up, was to be placed in reserve to support Hill in rear and on the right.[34]

The plan, in graphic terms, is shown on the opposite page.

Meantime, about 11 o'clock, D. H. Hill had arrived at Old Cold Harbor, whence led the road to Dispatch Station. He had found the enemy in strength across another road that linked Old Cold Harbor with Grapevine Bridge over the Chickahominy, and about noon, he had attacked hotly along the upper stretch of a

---

[30] *O. R.*, 11, part 2, p. 535. This message was dispatched at 9 o'clock and is here assumed to have reached Lee by noon. Powhite is pronounced Pow-height and took its name from a tribe of Indians that had lived in the vicinity. It was long the home of William Hartwell Macon, father and son.

[31] *Lee's Dispatches*, 18.   [32] *Ibid.*

[33] *O. R.*, 11, part 2, pp. 534, 905.   [34] *Longstreet*, 125.

little stream that ran from east to west.[35] Lee heard nothing and knew nothing of D. H. Hill's affair to the eastward, though he had sent staff officers to hasten Jackson's advance.

The first intimation Lee had that the infantry had come to-

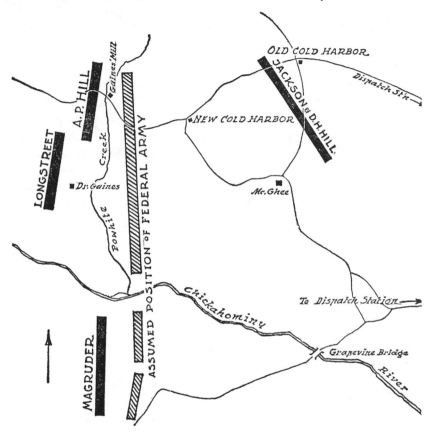

Lee's first, mistaken assumption of the situation as he approached Gaines's Mill, about noon, June 27, 1862.

gether was the sound of rapid volleys about 1 P.M. from the Cold Harbor road on which A. P. Hill was advancing to the east-ward. Riding thither, Lee found that Maxcy Gregg's South Carolina brigade had reached the point where the Cold Harbor road crossed Powhite Creek at Gaines's Mill. The ground there was somewhat similar to that at Ellerson's Mill, and the enemy

[35] *O. R.*, 11, part 2, p. 273.

was perched on the hill east of Powhite Creek to dispute the passage. Gregg, however, moving rapidly, crossed with slight difficulty about 1:30 P.M.,[36] and was soon in pursuit of the enemy.

This was a suspiciously easy beginning if the Federals had really intended to make a stand on Powhite Creek, as Lee had supposed! Why did not the enemy contest the crossing? Why was no artillery in position? Passing uphill from the creek, Lee came to an open plateau, with crops under cultivation, and small woods on the horizon. There was no sign of a Federal line of battle to the east, but there was firing from the south and southeast. Bullets began to fall about Lee. His staff officers suggested that he retire out of range. Instead, he pushed on to a point where Marmaduke Johnson's battery was awaiting orders. At that moment, from a stretch of woods to the southeast, in the vicinity of what was known as New Cold Harbor, some of Gregg's troops began to roll back. Not knowing what had happened, Lee ordered Johnson to unlimber and to prepare to meet an attack. "Gentlemen," he said to his staff and to the officers of the battery, "we must rally those men." He spurred his horse into a gallop and soon was in the midst of the fleeing infantry, calling on them to stop and for the honor of their state to go back and meet the enemy. The panic was local and short-lived. Gregg himself was on the scene in a few minutes and led his men quickly and steadily back into the woods. Soon the fighting there was as hot as before.[37]

The enemy was at bay—and not, as Lee had supposed, on a line running north and south but more nearly on a front extending from west to east, curving widely to the north like the outer side of a drawn bow. Such reconnaissance as was possible under the heavy and increasing fire of the Federals showed the terrain falling away on the south and southeast into a wooded, boggy bottom, through which ran a sluggish little stream known as Boatswain's Swamp.[38] This watercourse was not on Lee's map and its presence explained why McClellan had not stood on Powhite Creek. The position selected by the Federals was stronger

36 *O. R.,* 11, part 2, pp. 278, 854.
37 *O. R.,* 11, part 2, pp. 850, 854, 861; "J. B. M." in 28 *S. H. S. P.,* 95.
38 In the Tidewater section of Virginia, a stream of this sort, as well as the adjacent overflowed land, is styled a swamp.

and more compact than a north-and-south front would have been. Rising on the south of Boatswain's Swamp was a long hill, with steep grades facing the north and the west.[39] In rear of this hill the ground sloped off to the wide flats of the Chickahominy.

This, then, evidently was the main Federal position, and the

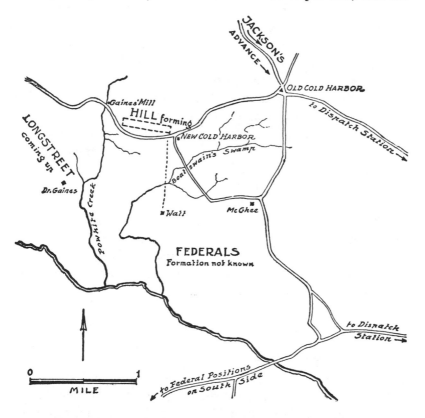

approaches to it were bad. There were only two roads, both narrow. One of them ran straight downgrade from New Cold Harbor to the swamp and thence due south to the home of Mrs. Watt on the crest of the hill. The other road started at almost the same point, went southeast across the swamp and up the hill and then followed the crest eastward, past the McGhee house, to the highway from Old Cold Harbor to Grapevine bridge. Except on these two roads, which ran for part of the distance

[39] The eastern part of this high ground was known as Turkey Hill, and the whole of it was sometimes so designated.

through a thick, high growth and crowding underbrush, the only line of attack was across the fields and through the wooded swamp. It was a terrible position to have to assault. Of the ground on the left, where Jackson was to take position, Lee could see nothing. The heavy thick intervening forest along the Mc-Ghee house road effectually cut off vision.[40] So far as Lee could ascertain, the general topography was as shown on page 145.

The prisoners taken at Mechanicsville and the stragglers picked up along the road all belonged only to Fitz John Porter's V Provisional Corps, but the volume of fire and the calmness of the Federals in taking position and awaiting attack convinced Lee that the greater part of McClellan's army was in his front.[41] In that case, as soon as the Federals discovered that Jackson was on their right, Lee reasoned that they would extend their flank to meet him, as otherwise Jackson would be between them and their base. As Jackson's arrival on the Confederate left was momentarily expected, the Federals were likely to start their shift to the right at any time. If, therefore, Hill engaged them now and Longstreet waited with his fresh troops till the enemy began to move, there was every reason to hope that McClellan, in making for the roads to Dispatch Station, would be trapped by Jackson, as shown on the opposite page.

A. P. Hill made his dispositions with speed. Waiting only long enough to see that Longstreet was coming into position, Hill ordered his men forward at 2:30 P.M., on a front of three and a half brigades, from the woods that fringed the south side of the Gaines's Mill-Cold Harbor road.[42] Most of Hill's troops had never been in action until the previous day, but they did not seem shaken by the reverse at Mechanicsville.[43] In front of Hill's right, west of the road to the Watt farm, was a cleared field surrounding the Parsons house, which had a fenced-in garden. To the south of the house was a small orchard on the brow of the ridge overlooking Boatswain's Swamp.[44] On the left and centre

[40] There is a good general description of the ground in Charles A. Page: *Letters of a War Correspondent*, 4.
[41] *O. R.*, 11, part 2, p. 492. Actually, at this hour only Porter's corps, now 29,600, was in his front.
[42] *O. R.*, 11, part 2, pp. 492, 883. Archer was on the right, then Anderson, then Branch on a half-brigade front, with Gregg on the left. For the location of the woods along the road, see *ibid.*, part 2, p. 272.
[43] *O. R.*, 11, part 2, p. 492.   [44] *O. R.*, 11, part 2, pp. 847, 849.

of Hill's line of advance, open ground led into a wood that ran down to the swamp and beyond it.

At the word of command, Hill's right brigades moved across the field past the Parsons house and to the brow of the ridge.

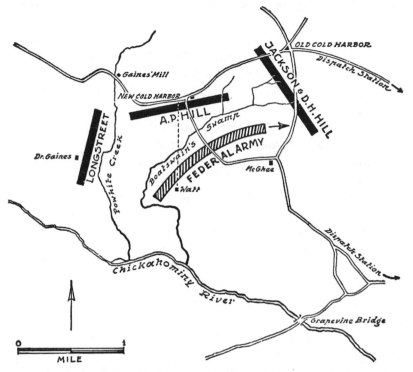

Assumed situation in early afternoon of June 27, 1862, that gave Lee hope of cutting off McClellan's retreat.

Then the Federal artillery from the other side of Boatswain's Swamp opened on them a devastating fire of shrapnel.[45] Men began to fall fast, but the lines swept on and disappeared from Lee's sight as they plunged downward toward the swamp. A moment more and there came the crash of an overwhelming Federal volley, delivered at 500 yards.[46] Right and left the fire swelled along the swamp and echoed against the ridges with a roar that men who were to pass through many battles never forgot to the end of their days.[47] Hill had put three batteries into service to cover

[45] O. R., 11, part 2, p. 282. [46] O. R., 11, part 2, p. 291.
[47] R. L. T. Beale, 24.

the advance, but though they were well served, only Crenshaw's on the left gave any real protection to the attacking force.[48]

It was oppressively hot in the glare of the full afternoon sun.[49] The smoke hung over the hill so heavily[50] that Lee could only judge of the progress of the action by the sound of the firing. On the left, Gregg evidently was advancing. In the centre and on the right, as well as they could be distinguished, the Confederate volleys for a while seemed farther away; then they remained stationary for a time; then they were closer. And soon, with a sinking of heart, observers on the fringe of the wood saw men struggling back over the shell-swept crest. Some were running in panic; some were attempting to hold their formation; others were rallying under their officers and were forming where the grade afforded shelter. In a few moments, the fugitives were back in the woods fronting the Cold Harbor road.[51]

They had a dreadful tale to tell. When they had descended from the ridge, they had found themselves in thick underbrush along the swamp. At some points the swamp was a deep ravine, out of which a man could hardly climb;[52] elsewhere it was sixty feet across, with the stream completely lost in bog;[53] farther down it was a mere ditch, over which a soldier could leap.[54] Behind the ditch, or in the swamp, the Federals had a line, and beyond that a second, at some points close to the swamp and at others, half way up the hill. As far as different men had been able to see this second line, it had consisted of felled timber, of knapsacks against fences, of piled logs—of anything that would stop bullets and give shelter.[55] On the crest of the hill, there seemed to be massed reserves or a third line, with an abundance of artillery. Archer had come within twenty paces of the first line and had been compelled to fall back.[56] J. R. Anderson had made three charges, and one of his regiments had penetrated the line, but when his centre had wavered, he had retreated, and in doing so had confused Field's brigade, which was supporting him.[57] Two of Pen-

48 O. R., 11, part 2, pp. 835, 857, 898, 903.
49 O. R., 11, part 2, pp. 288, 868.
50 And, curiously enough, not over the swamp; McHenry Howard: *Recollections*, 140.
51 O. R., 11, part 2, pp. 849–50.   52 *Worsham*, 100–101.
53 O. R., 11, part 2, p. 272.   54 O. R., 11, part 2, p. 291.
55 O. R., 11, part 2, pp. 290, 296, 301; 2 B. and L., 33.
56 O. R., 11, part 2, p. 897.
57 O. R., 11, part 2, pp. 847, 849, 875.

der's regiments had likewise entered the Federal lines but had been beaten back.[58] Branch's command had been confused.[59] Only Gregg had succeeded in crossing the swamp on the left, where the woods ran well up the flank of Turkey Hill,[60] and there he remained.

Some of the units were rallying, even as the others withdrew, and were now pressing a forlorn, second assault,[61] but it was now nearly 4 o'clock and there was no denying the fact that A. P. Hill had sustained a costly repulse. From the sound of the firing in the swamp, it was believed that the Federals had themselves taken the offensive.[62] This of itself was convincing evidence that there had been no weakening of the Federal left to meet the long-expected movement of Jackson on the right.

Lee had, therefore, to scrap his previous plan of action, and to arrange for a general assault all along the line as soon as the troops could be put in position. Thus far, only A. P. Hill had attacked. If he exhausted himself in futile affrays, there was danger that the tragedy of the 26th would be repeated and that victory would be lost because the whole army could not be thrown into action simultaneously. If, again, Hill were now attacked, his shattered division could not stand. Help must be had at once. Lee kept sending messengers to Jackson, urging him to hurry forward, so that the general assault could be delivered; but as immediate assistance could only be assured on the right, Lee dispatched orders to Longstreet to make a diversion in Hill's favor.[63]

Before Longstreet moved, perhaps before he received Lee's message, Jackson's doughty and eccentric lieutenant, General R. S. Ewell, came down the road from Old Cold Harbor and reported. His division was immediately behind him, he said; Whiting's two brigades and Lawton's Georgians were not far away. D. H. Hill was engaged on the Federal right, Ewell said, and Jackson's

---

[58] O. R., 11, part 2, p. 900.　　[59] O. R., 11, part 2, p. 893.

[60] O. R., 11, part 2, p. 869. For more details of the terrain here, see O. R., 11, part 2, pp. 615–16.

[61] O. R., 11, part 2, pp. 897. It should be noted that the number of assaults delivered by Hill is variously reported at different points along the line. Each account described the attacks on a comparatively narrow front, where quite often the reporting officer wrongly assumed that a general assault was in progress.

[62] O. R., 11, part 2, p. 492. The Federals, in reality, at no point recrossed the swamp after the first assault was delivered.

[63] O. R., 11, part 2, pp. 492, 757; *Longstreet*, 127.

own division, after having been delayed in reaching Old Cold Harbor by taking the wrong road, was coming up.

Lee at once ordered Ewell to support A. P. Hill on the right of the road leading to the McGhee house and directed him to send back staff officers to quicken the march of Whiting and Lawton.[64] As Ewell prepared to throw in two brigades on the ground where A. P. Hill's left had been fighting, Longstreet started a demonstration with four of his brigades, and the second phase of the battle began on a wider front.

Jackson, it now developed, had reached Old Cold Harbor ahead of his division, which had marched very slowly.[65] He had found D. H. Hill engaged hotly with the enemy on the upper stretches of Boatswain's Swamp, with his line drawn east and west, to the left of A. P. Hill but not in contact with him. Jackson knew little of the ground or of the disposition of the Union forces. Expecting that A. P. Hill and Longstreet would drive the enemy across his front, from west to east, in accordance with Lee's first plan, Jackson had become apprehensive that the Confederate attacking force would confuse his own men with the Federals. For that reason, Jackson had ordered D. H. Hill to break off the action and to take a position that would put open ground in front of him. He had not been in that position long, however, before the sound of the firing on the Confederate right gave proof that A. P. Hill was being hard pressed and was facing south. Jackson consequently had ordered D. H. Hill to change front again and he now directed him to advance against the enemy.[66]

Jackson's own brigades, unacquainted with the country, were drifting badly. Some of D. H. Hill's units became confused in reaching their position, and by no means all of them were ready when Ewell went forward on their right; but those who could be brought up emerged from the woods that sheltered them on the western side of the Cold Harbor-Grapevine Bridge road and crossed an open field that led downgrade to a belt of heavy timber.[67] Making their way over the stream, which here was little more than a brook, they reached the southern edge of the

[64] O. R., 11, part 2, p. 605.   [65] McHenry Howard: *Recollections*, 137–38.

[66] O. R., 11, part 2, pp. 348, 361, 553, 624, 641; 2 B. and L., 355. The last-cited authority may be interpreted to mean that D. H. Hill's second position was almost perpendicular to the line A. P. Hill was drawing a mile to the westward.

[67] O. R., 11, part 2, pp. 638, 641.

woods, where the Federals had felled some timber.[68] Beyond
them stretched upward for 400 yards a wide field of young corn.[69]
Then came the first Union line, held by the regular infantry
of Sykes's division, protected in part by the irregularities of the
ground and in part by a fence, and supported by excellent artillery.[70] Well in rear of this line, and so washed and sunken at
points as to afford admirable shelter, was the road that ran across
the crest of the eastern side of the hill past the McGhee house
to the Cold Harbor-Grapevine Bridge highway.[71] The McGhee
house itself was south of the road along the crest and was set on
commanding ground, surrounded by fences, outbuildings, and
an orchard.[72] East of that large property, beyond the Cold
Harbor-Grapevine Bridge road, there was a copse near the Con
federate front, then open ground and a tangle of small, second-
growth pine.[73]

D. H. Hill's progress to the southern end of the woods along
the upper waters of Boatswain's Swamp had been easy, but beyond that point his every attack was met with a quick counter-
thrust.[74] At length, when Garland's and G. B. Anderson's brigades found their progress halted by the fire of a battery near the
McGhee house, Hill ordered the artillery stormed by a separate
column, the 20th North Carolina, while Garland and Anderson
assaulted the infantry. The guns were taken and retaken, but the
two brigades meantime reached the road on the crest in front of
the McGhee house and found shelter there.[75] D. H. Hill was not
so close to victory at this point as he subsequently thought, but he
was in position to co-operate effectively if a general assault was
ordered. Jackson, meantime, was busily employed in bringing up
his own division and in arranging artillery support for D. H. Hill

[68] 2 B. and L., 355.
[69] O. R., 11, part 2, pp. 318, 358, 366, 625, 638, 640.
[70] O. R., 11, part 2, p. 318. One brigade of Sykes's (Warren's) was not composed of
regulars.
[71] O. R., 11, part 2, p. 366.
[72] O. R., 11, part 2, pp. 318, 448, 452.
[73] O. R., 11, part 2, pp. 244, 640.
[74] This was more confidently delivered because the Federals knew that reinforcements
would soon be up. Bartlett's brigade arrived at 4:30 P.M. and went into action at 5
(O. R., 11, part 2, p. 477).
[75] O. R., 11, part 2, pp. 354, 367, 369, 371, 373, 624, 641, 644, 649; 2 B. and L.,
556; History Co. E., 26th N. C. Regiment, 5. The captured guns were Hayden's section
of Edwards's Battery, 3d U. S. Arty. (O. R., 11, part 2, pp. 356, 451; N. W. Curtis:
From Bull Run to Chancellorsville, 120–21).

from guns that had been delayed on the road.[76] As the battle roared toward its climax, Jackson's spirits rose. Sending officers to all his division commanders, he said, "Tell them that this affair must hang in suspense no longer; sweep the field with the bayonet!"[77] When all were on the march to their positions, he rode over toward New Cold Harbor to report to Lee.

By this time Trimble's and Richard Taylor's brigades of Ewell's divisions were feeling the strength of the Federal centre. Ewell's left was not in contact with D. H. Hill nor his right with A. P. Hill. Taylor's brigade was driven off the field, and Gregg's men, who had advanced across the swamp in Hill's major charge, were being forced slowly back. Trimble fared better. His regiments extended their flanks and contrived to keep up a vigorous fire until reinforced a little later by the 5th Texas and a part of Hampton's legion. One private in Trimble's command, finding a loose horse, mounted and rode up and down the ranks at a critical moment, rallying the men, who took him to be an officer of rank.[78]

Beyond Ewell's front, A. P. Hill's survivors were holding on to the crest in front of the Parsons house, facing a fire that was, if anything, stronger than ever.[79] Still farther to the right, Longstreet's demonstration was taking form. Except for his skirmishers, Longstreet had kept his men under the shelter offered by a hill and a small wood[80] during Hill's first attack. Pickett's brigade was on his left, next A. P. Hill and three other brigades, temporarily under Wilcox, were in line on Longstreet's right. As they now began to deploy, they found themselves on difficult ground. A plain, one-quarter mile or more in depth, part of it in wheat, stretched from the eastern bank of Powhite Creek to Boatswain's Swamp.[81] The edge of Boatswain's Swamp was deeply scarped, dammed on its lower stretch, and covered by a belt of partially felled timber much less thick than farther upstream.[82] Where the swamp turned from west to south, into the valley of

---

[76] O. R., 11, part 2, pp. 515, 556, 560.   [77] Dabney, 455.

[78] J. C. Nisbet: Four Years on the Firing Line (cited hereafter as Nisbet), 110; O. R., 11, part 2, pp. 606, 620, 873–74, 888. The private's name was Frank Champion, 15th Alabama.

[79] Newton's and G. W. Taylor's brigades of Slocum's division were coming up (O. R., 11, part 2, pp. 432, 457).

[80] O. R., 11, part 2, p. 757.

[81] O. R., 11, part 2, pp. 344, 757, 772, 785.   [82] O. R., 11, part 2, p. 338.

the Chickahominy, the timber gave way to open fields.[83] Across these fields from the hill occupied by the Federals, and from the heights of the south side of the Chickahominy, there was breaking a cross-fire of shell which no troops could endure.[84] Behind the eastern side of Boatswain's Swamp, on the flank of the hill, were Federal sharpshooters, above them a line of infantry behind felled trees, and at an elevation of about forty feet above the second line, the Federal artillery and reserves were well covered.[85] No sooner did the demonstration disclose the strength of the position in his front than Longstreet saw that a diversion would simply be a waste of life. He could only help A. P. Hill by converting the demonstration into an assault and he accordingly paused to bring up troops for that purpose.[86]

Such was the situation after 5 P.M.—Longstreet preparing for a general assault on the right, A. P. Hill's men on the right centre, delivering a desultory fire, Ewell fighting on the centre with both flanks in the air, Jackson's division, Whiting, and Lawton coming up to plug the holes in the line, D. H. Hill in a favorable position but still encountering stiff resistance, the Federals unshaken and reinforced, their powerful artillery firing fast. If the battle was to be saved, the full weight of the Confederate army must be thrown against the enemy. No time must be lost in hurling Jackson's unemployed troops into the struggle.

At the end of the first phase of the battle, when A. P. Hill had been almost worn out, Ewell had come to his rescue; and now, with the issue still in doubt, down the same road from Old Cold Harbor rode Jackson, dust-covered, with his dingy cadet cap pulled down over his weak eyes, sitting awkwardly on an ugly horse, and sucking a lemon. Lee went up and greeted him.

"Ah, General," said he, "I am very glad to see you. I had hoped to be with you before"—which was a tactful way of saying he had hoped Jackson would have arrived earlier.

Jackson nodded his head quickly and made some brief reply, unintelligible in the deafening din from the woods to the south of them.

"That fire is very heavy," Lee said. "Do you think your men can stand it?"

[83] *Longstreet,* 126; *O. R.,* 11, part 2, p. 757.
[84] *O. R.,* 11, part 2, p. 223, 265.
[85] *O. R.,* 11, part 2, p. 757.
[86] *O. R.,* 11, part 2, p. 757.

Listening a moment, Jackson answered bluntly: "They can stand almost anything! They can stand that."[87]

After a brief conference on the proper disposition of the troops not yet in line, Jackson rode away. Meantime Lawton, with his 3500 Georgians, the largest brigade in the army, had joined Ewell without reporting to Lee, and was making his fire felt. Soon Lee saw up the road his brilliant assistant of Sollers Point, General W. H. C. Whiting, who had been feeling his way to the right from Old Cold Harbor, where the various commands of Jackson's column had been much confused. Lee at once ordered Whiting to support A. P. Hill's right, just as Ewell had been thrown in to relieve A. P. Hill's left.[88]

Ere long the head of Whiting's division was in the road. Lee rode toward it and inquired for General John B. Hood, leading the Texas brigade of that command. Hood came up on his horse and saluted. Briefly Lee told him what had happened—how the troops on the front were fighting gallantly but had not been able to dislodge the enemy. "This must be done," he said quietly. "Can you break his line?"

"I will try," answered Hood, stoutly enough.[89]

As Lee turned his horse's head to ride away, he lifted his hat. "May God be with you," he said.[90]

It would take time for Hood and Law, who commanded Whiting's other brigade, to pass down the road and deploy for action. Meantime, Gregg's men were leaving the swamp, and from the centre and right of A. P. Hill's division, more weary soldiers were seeking the rear. Whiting would help, but Longstreet must not delay. Unless he acted speedily, the day might be lost. Lee hurried a staff officer to Longstreet to tell him so.[91] Anxiously he waited.

Louder and louder the battle roared through a half hour of uncertainty, as the shadows lengthened and twilight began to settle where the woods were thickest. Then, from beyond the

---

[87] *Cooke*, 84; Cooke: *Life of Stonewall Jackson*, 200. Cooke was at this time an officer on Stuart's staff, and he gave this story in detail, but it is plain from his *Wearing of the Gray*, 46–47, that he did not personally witness the meeting. *Mrs. McGuire*, 125, represented Jackson as answering: "General, I know our boys—they will never give back."
[88] *O. R.*, 11, part 2, pp. 563, 614–15.   [89] *Hood*, 25.
[90] J. B. Polley: *Hood's Texas Brigade*, 57.
[91] *Longstreet*, 127, perhaps adorning the tale a bit.

Parsons house came a strange, shrill, sustained cry, as if thousands
of men were calling on the dogs in a fox hunt. It was the "rebel
yell." [92] Whiting's men were going into action. They had established contact with Longstreet, and his brigades also were pressing forward.[93]

From his position, Lee could not see what happened next, but
it was a drama that gave Hood's Texans a place in his heart that
no other command ever won.[94] E. M. Law's brigade was on the
right, next Pickett, who held Longstreet's left. Hood was on the
left of Law. Whiting's orders were that his two brigades should
advance in a double line, straight for the edge of the ridge where
Hill's men still hung on. Then they were to start the double-
quick, trailing arms, and were not to fire a shot. As they went forward, Hood saw a gap and an open field between Law and
Pickett and he quickly moved the 4th Texas across Law's rear
and into this gap. The movement was flawless; the whole division swept onward, the 4th Texas ahead of the others. The
fire grew faster. So did the pace of the men. By the hundred
they fell, but without a break in the alignment. They were passing through Hill's ranks; they were plunging down the grade to
the swamp. A thousand had fallen now, but scarcely a musket
had been fired from the attacking division. The men were
within twenty yards of the Federal front line—within ten—and
then, suddenly, as if the same fear had seized every heart, the
Federals were leaving their works, were running, were throwing
their arms away. Over the second line they swarmed, spreading
panic. Through swamp, in pursuit, the Texans crashed; up the
hill and over the second line they rushed, and then, as the bluecoats spread in a confused mass, the Confederates loosed their
volley, where every bullet reached its mark.[95] A break had been
made. If it could be widened, the enemy would be routed.

The hands on Lee's watch were pointing to 7 o'clock. The
sun was below the forest on the other side of the Chickahominy.[96]

---

[92] 28 S. H. S. P., 96. [93] O. R., 11, part 2, p. 757; Longstreet, 127.

[94] N. A. Davis, 114–15; Reagan, 145.

[95] Hood, 26–27; Law in 2 B. and L., 362; Law in Southern Bivouac, April, 1887,
p. 657; Whiting in O. R., 11, part 2, p. 563.

[96] The time of the different movements of any battle is usually difficult to determine.
Especially is this true of Gaines's Mill, which is perhaps the most confusing of all the
engagements Lee fought. Generally speaking, the hour given by an officer awaiting at-

Lee had in line every man he could hope to place there. It was time for the final thrust. Before he knew the full measure of success that had attended Whiting's assault, he gave orders to A. P. Hill to start a general advance and to communicate the word to right and to left.[97] It was scarcely necessary. The orders given at intervals during the afternoon, the hard riding of the staff officers, and the steady marching of thousands of boys had not been in vain. Longstreet's columns were moving;[98] Lawton had not halted since his brigade had gone into action; Ewell was full of fight, cheering for the Georgians; every one knew that Jackson had arrived; D. H. Hill had seen his opportunity, and his regiments had rushed for the McGhee house about the time the Texans had broken through the swamp.[99] In fifteen minutes, as if some animated jig-saw puzzle had suddenly fallen into place, the full design of the assault showed itself. Through fast-gathering twilight, the Federals yielded slowly and stubbornly in front of the Confederate left, gave ground rapidly in the centre, and on the right, where Whiting had made lodgment, broke wildly, carrying their support with them.[100] A reckless cavalry charge by part of Lee's old regiment and fragments of other units confused the Federal artillery.[101] Fourteen fine guns, foul from firing, some of the very pieces that had balked the Confederates the previous day at Ellerson's mill, were captured after a gallant defense. One brave cannoneer, desperately wounded, dragged himself up by the spokes of a wheel, pulled the laniard and fired into the very faces of the charging Confederates.[102] A battery on the

tack is more apt to be accurate than that reported by the average officer making the attack. A commander who is late, or is called upon to make a complicated movement, usually underestimates the time required and will generally assume the hour is earlier than it actually is. The more hotly an officer is engaged, of course, the less likely is he to consult his watch or to estimate accurately the flight of time. In this battle, Confederate officers on the right state the time with less inaccuracy than those on the left, but there is little agreement among them, and the student has to reconcile their statements as best he can. Although the Federals were on the defensive, their figures differ materially. Porter says it was 2 P.M. when Hill attacked (*O. R.*, 11, part 2, p. 224); Butterfield and Morell say it was 2:30 (*ibid.*, 273, 316). Morell and Butterfield put the second phase of the battle at 5:30; Porter at 6. Butterfield stated the final attack was "shortly after 6," Morell gave 6:30, Colonel R. M. Richardson maintained it was 7:30 (*ibid.*, 327), and Porter wrote that it came "just as darkness was covering everything from view" (*ibid.*, p. 225).

[97] *O. R.*, 11, part 2, p. 837.
[98] *O. R.*, 11, part 2, pp. 757–58; *Longstreet*, 127.
[99] *O. R.*, 11, part 2, pp. 555, 570, 625–26.   [100] *O. R.*, 11, part 2, pp. 70–71.
[101] *O. R.*, 11, part 2, pp. 41–42, 225–26, 273; 2 *B. and L.*, 364.
[102] 2 *B. and L.*, 346.

road to the Watt house discharged a round of double-canister into the attacking column at point-blank range and in the confusion managed to limber up and escape.[103] Two Union regiments were taken on Whiting's front[104] and large detachments everywhere. Small groups of brave men held out here and there; the reserve artillery got away; Sykes's regulars kept their formation, as became their traditions. Cheers rose from the Federal right as the defeated troops met reinforcements.[105] Elsewhere, as darkness settled, the Union troops made for the Chickahominy flats south of the hill, where it was futile to attempt to pursue them.[106]

Lee had won his first victory and promptly dispatched to the President a message in which he prefaced announcement to that effect with the characteristic phrase, "Profoundly grateful to Almighty God." [107] But it was a heavy price he had paid. There had been, Longstreet said, more feats of individual valor than he had seen on any field.[108] The slaughter of officers had been tremendous. The list of the fallen read like a roster of the Southern aristocracy. The 1st Texas had lost nearly 600 of its 800.[109] The 4th Texas had seen all its field officers killed or wounded and had finished the battle under the command of a captain. Its casualties had numbered 252.[110] The total Confederate dead and wounded, though never separately tabulated, could not have fallen below 8000, and in some brigades the slain were so numerous that twenty-four hours scarcely sufficed to bury them.[111] And there might be a like butcher's bill on the morrow!

Nor had the Confederates on the south side of the Chickahominy escaped casualties. Knowing the impetuosity of his army, Lee had apprehended that Magruder's men might not be willing to sit quietly behind their fortifications and see their comrades across the river winning glory at the cannon's mouth. He conse-

---

103 *O. R.*, 11, part 2, p. 284.   104 *O. R.*, 11, part 2, pp. 388, 446.

105 2 *B. and L.*, 358.

106 *O. R.*, 11, part 2, pp. 226, 273, 292, 493.

107 *O. R.*, 11, part 2, p. 622. Worsham, *op. cit.*, 99–100, said Davis was on the field with Lee as Jackson's troops went into action, but there is no other reference to Davis's presence.

108 *O. R.*, 11, part 2, p. 758.

109 *Reagan*, 145.   110 *O. R.*, 11, part 2, p. 569.

111 *O. R.*, 11, part 2, p. 874. The Federal losses were 894 killed, 3107 wounded, and 2836 missing, an aggregate of 6837 (*O. R.*, 11, part 2, p. 41).

quently had taken the precaution in mid-afternoon to order Magruder not to take the initiative except when certain of success and when acting in co-operation with the forces north of the Chickahominy. Through some misunderstanding, however, a reconnaissance had been converted into an attack by General Toombs and some 400 men had been lost in a clumsy and futile operation at Golding's Farm.[112] Lee got the unhappy details late in the evening, but had little time to ponder them.

To plan for the next move, Lee now rode back to Selwyn, the Hogan house, where he conferred with Jackson and Longstreet.[113] It was a night of groaning and of misery for the thousands of wounded, a night of sorrow and of expectancy for the man who issued late orders to his lieutenants and then gave humble thanks to the God of Battles that the grip of the enemy on Richmond had been loosened.

[112] Lee ordered a report made to the Secretary of War, but in the rush of subsequent events the matter was dropped. See *O. R.,* 11, part 2, pp. 661, 689–90, 695–96; J. J. McDaniel: *Diary of Battles, Marches and Incidents of the Seventh South Carolina Regiment* (cited hereafter as *McDaniel*), 6.

[113] A. R. Ellerson in T. N. Page, *Robert E. Lee, Man and Soldier,* 715.

CHAPTER XIV

"A Cloud by Day"

BREAKFAST for General Lee on the morning of June 28 was a matter of snatching up a bit of ham and bread, which he ate as he rode rapidly from the Hogan house at daylight to renew the action.[1] When he reached the battlefield, the ambulance detachments were still at work bringing in a multitude of boys, bloody and prostrate, who had spent an age-long night of misery under the stars. Longstreet's advanced guard was making its way cautiously through the half-light across the hill to locate the enemy.[2] On the left, Jackson was moving in the same way over the fields and down the road toward Grapevine Bridge.

Soon the couriers began to gallop back to Lee, all of them with the same message: the enemy was gone from the north side of the Chickahominy. Jackson's men had met a cavalry detachment, but it had fled at the first fire of the skirmishers. Many prisoners had been taken, among them a soldier much distinguished later, Brigadier General John F. Reynolds, who had slept too long in the woods.[3] Longstreet found only the dead, the wounded, and the straggling in his front. The bridges over the Chickahominy, built with so much skill and patient labor, had all been burned. The enemy appeared to be concentrating on the south side of the river,[4] and apparently had evacuated none of his positions there. All the approaches to the destroyed crossings were under the fire of massed artillery, as if the enemy were prepared to contest pursuit. In effect, the right bank of the river, east of New Bridge, had been made a fortress. At the same time it seemed scarcely conceivable that McClellan, after only one general engagement, had abandoned the railroad by which daily he had been receiving for his great army 600 tons of supplies. He must be preparing to renew

---

[1] G. Wise, who was on duty at the Hogan house, *op. cit.*, p. 75.
[2] *Longstreet,* 129–30.   [3] *O. R.,* 11, part 2, pp. 571, 593.
[4] Longstreet, *loc. cit.*

the battle, somewhere, for the defense of his line of communications, which, it will be remembered, traversed the Chickahominy at Dispatch Station, six miles downstream from the battlefield, and ran thence twelve miles northeastward to the White House, thus:

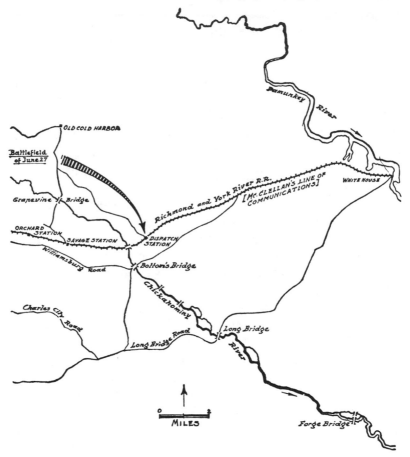

Obviously, if Lee held to his original plan of campaign and destroyed the Federals' rail communications, he would force the enemy to retreat, to change base, or to fight while he subsisted his men with such supplies as were on hand or could be brought up by narrow, threatened roads. Any one of the three courses offered immediate opportunity to Lee.

160

Calling a nearby cavalryman, Lee sent him galloping off to find General Stuart,[5] and when Stuart arrived, Lee directed him to move down the Chickahominy, to destroy the railroad, and to get on McClellan's supply line.[6] Ewell's division was likewise ordered to march in support, on a similar mission, preceded by one regiment of cavalry.[7] General Longstreet was told to bring up such long-range guns as he could collect and to open on the enemy across the river from his position.[8] This was all that could be done at the time. The river stopped reconnaissance; the Federal fire made the rebuilding of the bridges impossible; Magruder could not even feel out the lines in his front, because they were protected by heavy earthworks, felled timber, swamps and woods, and formed an impenetrable screen.[9]

While awaiting developments, Lee rode over part of the ground of the previous day's action, working his way toward the left, look- ing all the while for the Rockbridge Artillery, with which his youngest son was serving as a private. He had heard that the battery had followed Jackson; he did not know whether Robert was dead or alive. Finally, in front of the McGhee house, he found the battery, which had not been engaged in the action of the 27th.[10] A crowd gathered after Lee halted, but Robert was not in it. Search discovered him so soundly asleep under a caisson that calls did not arouse him. Only a vigorous prodding with a sponge staff in the hands of a zealous comrade brought him out, at last, half-dazed. He was well and unscathed, though much the worse for dust and hard marching. Greetings exchanged, Lee rode away, and nobody seemed to think it in any way odd that the son of the commanding general should be serving in the ranks.[11]

Everywhere that Lee moved that morning officers were afield. The men were strolling about or sleeping, the ambulance detach- ments continued to take away the wounded, and the burial squads were at their grim labor. Jackson had ridden over from the left

---

[5] *F. M. Myers*, p. 75.   [6] *O. R.*, 11, part 2, p. 515.

[7] *O. R.*, 12, part 2, pp. 493, 607. General Trimble, in his report, said that he did not move until the 29th (*O. R.*, 11, part 2, p. 617), but his statement of the circumstances of his march and Colonel Nisbet's narrative, *op. cit.*, 115, make it certain that he marched on the 28th.

[8] *O. R.*, 11, part 2, p. 758.   [9] *O. R.*, 11, part 2, p. 494.

[10] *O. R.*, 11, part 2, p. 573.

[11] *R. E. Lee, Jr.*, 73–74. The site of this meeting is fixed by the reference to the prox- imity of the 10th Virginia, for which see *O. R.*, 11, part 2, p. 593.

to examine the ground of Whiting's advance. He seemed fresh and "brisk enough,"[12] though he had been conferring with Stuart long after midnight, and as he examined the obstacles that Hood's Texans had surmounted in their incredible charge, his admiration overcame his reserve. "The men who carried this position were soldiers indeed," he said.[13] It was the first battlefield many of the troops had ever seen. In the enforced halt of the army, after the mad fury of the previous day, its ghastly stillness bewildered them.

As often as they surveyed the bloody battleground, Lee's eyes turned anxiously to the opposite side of the river, where Longstreet's fire had apparently made no impression on the Federals.[14] What was the enemy doing behind those trees that covered the hills above the Chickahominy? How long must the hours of opportunity slip past before Lee would know what move to make? Would McClellan thrust at Richmond? Was he resting and awaiting another attack? Did the woods conceal a retreat? The sun was high and very hot by now;[15] and even where the shade was deep, the roads were drying fast. Ere noon had come, Trimble, of Ewell's division, reported that one of his officers had climbed a tree and had seen the enemy moving southward.[16]

Soon the bright panorama beyond the river-valley began to be obscured. An ever-lengthening cloud began to rise over the tree tops in the calm summer air. It was not the smoke of a silent battle; it was dust, and it could only have been raised by a vast column of laboring horses and marching men. Now there came distant flashes, echoing heavy explosions. Clouds of sulphurous smoke mounted like incense. Magazines were being fired! McClellan was on the move—but why and whither?[17] From youngest recruit to commanding general, the Army of Northern Virginia watched and speculated. The dust cloud lengthened toward the horizon; the explosions multiplied; the smoke of fires spread more widely.[18] "A retreat," jubilant men exclaimed; "a ruse," the pessimistic Whiting contended.[19]

Now a dusty, sweating courier on a frothing horse brought a

---

[12] *Sorrel*, 84. [13] *Hood*, 28. [14] *O. R.*, 11, part 2, p. 758.
[15] W. W. Chamberlaine, *Memoirs of the Civil War* (cited hereafter as *W. W. Chamberlaine*), 21.
[16] *O. R.*, 11, part 2, p. 617.
[17] *O. R.*, 11, part 2, p. 494; 3 *C. M. H.*, 294; *Marshall*, 105.
[18] *N. A. Davis*, 60. [19] 2 *B. and L.*, 362.

message from Stuart: his cavalry had ridden fast and furiously; they had reached Dispatch Station, had cut the telegraph line to the White House, and had torn up a section of the track of the York River Railroad. A force of the enemy had been encountered. It had been compelled to hurry off down the Chickahominy toward Bottom's Bridge. Before doing so—here was what Stuart most desired General Lee to know—it had burned the railroad trestle across the river.[20]

As a later message from Trimble confirmed his earlier report that the enemy was moving southward,[21] there was no misreading the great news: McClellan was so hard hit or so frightened that he was abandoning his base at the White House. He must be doing one of two things: either he was retreating down the Peninsula, by the way he had come, or else he was changing base to the James River, where the Federal sea-power would suffice to refit and revictual him. But which? A retreat down the Peninsula would be an admission of defeat, certain ruin for McClellan's prestige, and a blow to the morale of the North. Militarily easy, it would otherwise be costly. Was McClellan, then, attempting to open a new line of communications from James River while holding his lines close to Richmond? Lee was disposed to believe that McClellan would do this rather than endure the humiliation of a retreat down the Peninsula,[22] but the stake was so large and the uncertainty so great that Lee was unwilling to launch a decisive manœuvre on nothing more substantial than a personal opinion.

If McClellan was establishing a base on the James, the whole of the Army of Northern Virginia should of course be concentrated on the south side of the Chickahominy and should be hurled against the enemy while he was in the confusion of change. But if the Federal commander was preparing to retreat down the Peninsula, there was a compelling reason for keeping a large part of the army north of the Chickahominy: the course of the stream was nearly east and west in front of Lee's position, but below that point

---

[20] *O. R.*, 11, part 2, pp. 200, 493, 516, 607. In their formal reports of the campaign, neither Stuart nor Ewell mentioned the destruction of the bridge, and F. M. Myers, *op. cit.*, 76, thought it was the work of Ewell, but Captain James Brady, 1st Penn. Arty., *O. R.*, 11, part 2, p. 200, stated it was done by him as soon as the Confederates set fire to Dispatch Station.

[21] *O. R.*, 11, part 2, p. 617.   [22] 2 *B. and L.*, 385; 1 *D. H. Hill*, 135.

the river bent more to the southeast and then ran almost south. McClellan was thus in an angle of the Chickahominy, and he could not move down the Peninsula without crossing the river at some of the numerous wagon bridges below Dispatch Station. Were Lee to hurry to the south side in pursuit, McClellan could rapidly move eastward and could put the Chickahominy between him and the Army of Northern Virginia. By crossing once, in pursuit, Lee would have to pass the river again and probably would have to make the second crossing in the face of opposition, perhaps at heavy loss and with considerable delay. By remaining north of the river, Lee had only to march downstream to turn any

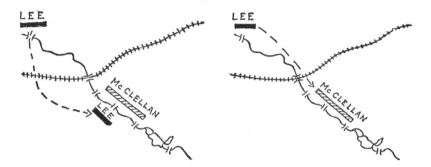

position McClellan might be disposed to take on the left bank of the Chickahominy, preliminary to a withdrawal down the Peninsula.

Risk and probability seemed balanced. As far down the horizon as the dust clouds could be observed, they rose from roads that McClellan would follow whether he was moving his wagon train eastward down the Peninsula or southward toward the James. Not a sign was there of any diminution of strength opposite Lee's own front or opposite that of Magruder and Huger. It was just such a situation as often paralyzes the initiative in pursuit. All that Lee felt he could safely do was to watch and guard the downstream bridges of the Chickahominy, to which McClellan would soon be coming if he were moving eastward. Ewell was ordered along the Chickahominy from Dispatch Station to Bottom's Bridge. The cavalry was sent to observe the lower crossings.[23]

Through the long, hot afternoon, Lee waited for further news

---

[23] *O. R.*, 11, part 2, pp. 493–94; *Marshall*, 105; *cf. Taylor's General Lee*, 72.

from Ewell and from Stuart. Neither reported any activity down the river that suggested the approach of the enemy to the Chickahominy bridges. This silence strengthened Lee's belief that the enemy's objective was the James.[24] He began to shape his plans for a pursuit on the morning of the 29th. In the hope of getting early information of an evacuation of the enemy's works on the south side, he directed that two of General Longstreet's engineers attempt to cross the Chickahominy during the night and make reconnaissance at close range.[25] When General Pendleton arrived with a message from the President during the evening, Lee directed him to return to Magruder's headquarters and to urge the utmost vigilance on the part of that officer's outposts during the night.[26] A little later he reiterated this in a direct message to Magruder, who was exceedingly nervous and apprehensive of an attack on his front.[27]

Thus ended a day that might have changed the whole course of the war if its ample hours of light could have been given to a march on the heels of the enemy. With his orders issued and his plan matured in large part, Lee transferred his headquarters to Doctor Gaines's house, so that he could communicate instantly with Longstreet, who was already established there. By 11 o'clock Lee was in bed and asleep.[28]

[24] *O. R.*, 11, part 2, p. 494.   [25] *O. R.*, 11, part 2, p. 494; *Longstreet*, 130.
[26] *O. R.*, 11, part 2, pp. 494, 536. Lee was not too busy to tell Pendleton that his son had come unscathed through the battle of Gaines's Mill. "A fine young man," he added (*Pendleton*, 194).
[27] *O. R.*, 11, part 2, p. 662.
[28] Jubal A. Early: *Autobiographical Sketch and Narrative of the War Between the States* (cited hereafter as *Early*), 76, 89. Early said Lee's headquarters were at the "Gaines House," but as Longstreet is known to have been at Doctor Gaines's, it is reasonably certain that this, and not William Gaines's home at Fairfield, was Lee's resting-place for the night.

CHAPTER XV

The Pursuit Goes Astray

(SAVAGE STATION)

Soon after sunrise on the morning of June 29, Lee received a message of great import from Major R. K. Meade and Lieutenant S. R. Johnston, the two engineers who had been sent from Longstreet's division to attempt a reconnaissance across the Chickahominy. They had succeeded in making their way over the swamp, and their report sent a thrill through the army: the great, frowning Federal works around Golding's Farm were empty! This was the key position south of the Chickahominy. If McClellan had evacuated Golding's Farm, it could only mean one thing: he had abandoned his attempt to take Richmond.

Lee's spirits rose at the news. What fairer opportunity could any soldier ask than to attack his adversary in retreat and while changing base? The aim of the campaign had been to force McClellan to retire or to come out from behind his entrenchments so that he could be attacked to advantage. McClellan obligingly had done both.

In the midst of the first exhilaration an officer arrived from the southside with the news that Magruder was preparing to attack. The theatrical tone of the announcement aroused Lee's sense of humor. He sent the officer back with his compliments to the General and with the facetious request that in making his assault, Magruder should take care not to injure Major Meade and Lieutenant Johnston, who already occupied the works.[1]

The plan of operations, which Lee had doubtless been maturing on the 28th, now took form rapidly. As no report had been received during the night of any appearance of the Federals on the

---

[1] *O. R.*, 11, part 2, pp. 494, 662; *Longstreet*, 130; 9 *S. H. S. P.*, 567–68; *Jones*, 242. Magruder's message was not so belated, nor was it based upon so scant a knowledge of the situation, as this episode might indicate. At 3:30 A.M. the Federal lines in his front had been held in strength (*O. R.*, 11, part 2, p. 662).

lower Chickahominy, Lee considered it almost certain that Mc-Clellan was making for the James River;[2] but as the enemy might have been delayed in his retreat, Lee could not completely put aside the possibility that his opponent was making for the Peninsula, even though Ewell and Stuart had as yet seen nothing of him. Ewell and Stuart therefore had better be held where they were, guarding the lower bridges of the Chickahominy. The remainder of the army should be put in pursuit of the enemy. Lacking, however, all information as to the line of McClellan's probable withdrawal to the James, Lee had to dispose his forces anew in the most practicable manner to meet his adversary on any route that he might follow. This was a difficult task in detail, but if it were rightly performed Lee believed that he could keep McClellan from reaching the James River.[3]

The distance from Gaines's Mill to the James was too great for the whole army to get in front of McClellan's moving army before nightfall of the 29th. The main battle would have to be fought on the 30th. In his retreat, however, McClellan would have to take his whole army across White Oak Swamp, a troublesome miniature of the Chickahominy that ran from McClellan's left into the larger stream midway between Bottom's Bridge and the Long Bridges. McClellan's leading corps doubtless would be able to reach the south side of White Oak Swamp that day, but if his rear was pressed with vigor part of his army might be cut off north of that stream.

There were, then, two battles to be planned—first the attack on the rearguard that day and a general engagement on the 30th. How was the army to be disposed for these successive operations? Jackson was opposite Grapevine Bridge, which of course must be rebuilt at once. Should it develop, after all, that McClellan was making for the lower crossings of the Chickahominy, Jackson could march down the left bank and support Ewell and Stuart. Otherwise, he could cross the bridge when it was completed and could march down the right bank, available either to support the attack on the rearguard or to cut off the Federals if they were balked at White Oak Swamp and attempted to march on to the lower bridges over the Chickahominy. Magruder could move

<hr>

[2] *Lee's Dispatches*, 21.   [3] *Longstreet*, 148.

down the Williamsburg road. Then, when the Federal rearguard had been cut off, Magruder and probably Jackson also could cross the swamp and again assail the rear. Huger, by going down the Charles City road, would be on the Federals' flank.[4]

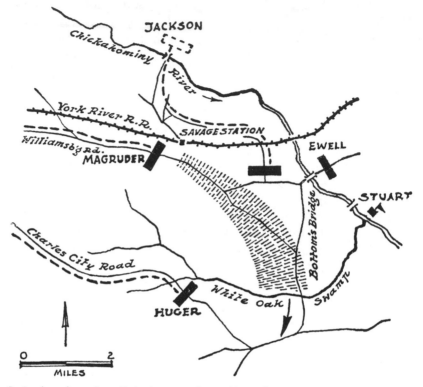

Lee's plan of attack on Federal rearguard at White Oak Swamp, June 29, 1862. The shaded area suggests the crowding of the approaches to White Oak Swamp Bridge as the Federals retreated.

Longstreet and A. P. Hill should be placed well to the south or to the southwest of White Oak Swamp, where they could strike McClellan in flank or in front, according to his position on the 30th.

Based on this reasoning, orders were issued for movements on the 29th as follows:

1. Ewell to remain at Bottom's Bridge, guarding the crossing.[5]

---

[4] O. R., 11, part 2, p. 494.
[5] O. R., 11, part 2, p. 607; R. Taylor, 88. For Federal activities opposite Dispatch Station and Bottom's Bridge, see O. R., 11, part 2, pp. 198–99, 200, 215.

2. Stuart to watch the lower passages of the Chickahominy.[6]

3. Jackson to rebuild Grapevine Bridge and, in the absence of other instructions, to cross and move down the right bank of the Chickahominy, supporting Magruder and moving against the enemy with all speed.[7]

4. Magruder[8] to pursue vigorously the Federal rear down the Williamsburg road and engage it before it reached White Oak Swamp.

5. Huger[9] to follow the Charles City road and to take the Federals in flank at White Oak Swamp or before they reached that point.

6. Longstreet, commanding his own and A. P. Hill's division,[10] to cross the Chickahominy at New Bridge and to take the shortest route to the Darbytown road; thence down that highway into position on the Long Bridge road to intercept the Federal retreat to the James.[11]

The general plan of advance was to be as shown on page 170.

A. P. Hill's and Longstreet's men, having been prepared for immediate movement, were able to start as soon as these orders were received. Lee hurried ahead of them to explain to Magruder and to Huger in person what was expected of them. Crossing New Bridge, he sent Colonel Chilton forward to find Magruder. When Magruder had reported, Lee went forward with him down the Nine Mile road, Lee reviewing the plan of operations. Magruder, however, was greatly excited and much preoccupied with the movement of his own division and, as it subsequently developed, got the impression that Huger was to take the Williamsburg road, whereas Huger was to advance down the Charles City road.[12] Lee

---

[6] O. R., 11, part 2, p. 517. [7] O. R., 11, part 2, p. 687.

[8] 11,500 fresh troops. [9] 9000 fresh troops.

[10] Longstreet, 130; O. R., 11, part 2, p. 837.

[11] O. R., 11, part 2, pp. 494, 662. The crude pamphlet The Seven Days Battle Around Richmond quoted from a Richmond newspaper this simple method of keeping in mind the roads around Richmond. N. A. Davis also reprinted it, op. cit., 44; "Place your [left] hand [palm upward] upon the table with the index finger pointing a little north of east. Spread your fingers so that the tips will form the arc of a circle. Imagine Richmond as situated on your wrist; the outer edge of your thumb as the Central railroad, the inner edge the Mechanicsville turnpike, the first finger as the Nine Mile or New Bridge road, the second as the Williamsburg Pike running nearly parallel with the York River railroad—the railroad running between the two fingers. The third as the Charles City Turnpike (which runs to the southward of the White Oak Swamp) and the fourth as the Darbytown road."

[12] O. R., 11, part 2, pp. 662, 679.

remained with Magruder until they were well inside the former Federal lines at Fair Oaks Station,[13] and then he hastened to General Huger's headquarters on the Williamsburg road. General

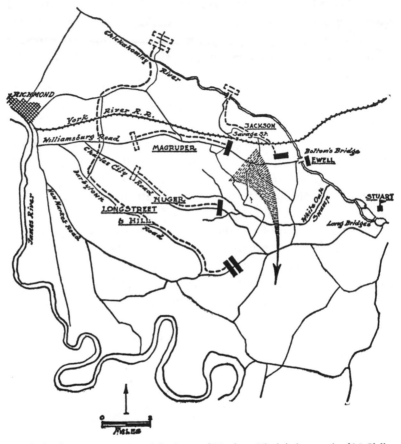

General plan for reconcentration of the Army of Northern Virginia in pursuit of McClellan, as formulated on the morning of June 29, 1862. The arrow suggests the massing of the Federals on their assumed approach to the narrow roads leading to James River.

Huger, he discovered, had been into the evacuated Federal position and had then ridden along the front announcing to his men the news of the Federal retreat. The advance of his troops was under way but seems to have been slow and poorly organized. At length, when Huger went on with his command, Lee decided to remain for the time at Huger's quarters,[14] which were conveniently placed

[13] O. R., 11, part 2, p. 662.   [14] O. R., 11, part 2, p. 789.

for ready communication with Longstreet and A. P. Hill as well as with Huger and Magruder. Lee did not attempt to arrange the tactical details of the expected action against the rear of the enemy, but left these to General Magruder.

Already the day was intensely hot,[15] and as the roads were now dust-covered, the march of the pursuit column would be hard and miserable, but otherwise nothing happened to indicate any miscarriage of plans until there arrived a dispatch from Magruder at Fair Oaks, stating that a strong force was in his front and was moving against him.[16] Lee seems to have discounted this, perhaps attributing the report of an enemy advance to General Magruder's excitement, but as the two rear brigades of Huger's division had not marched far, he ordered them recalled and had them moved over to the Williamsburg road.[17] Fearing, however, that this might involve a halt by the whole division, Lee in a short while sent Huger a note in which he reminded him of the importance of advancing rapidly down the Charles City road. If Magruder did not need assistance, Huger was to move on.[18] Nothing further, it would seem, was heard from Magruder or from Huger for some hours. Lee had no apprehension, for Jackson's advance from Grapevine Bridge would inevitably turn the flank of any Federal column that might have been drawn up across the Williamsburg road to halt Magruder's pursuit.

Smoke climbed high from piles of abandoned stores to which the retreating Federals had set fire during the night. From the east, the dust still rose in a mighty column. Here and there farm houses, barns, and haystacks were smouldering from an incendiary torch. The fields over which the enemy had retreated were littered with accoutrements and arms. By the roadside stood abandoned wagons and broken ambulances.[19] At Lee's temporary headquarters there was the same "fog of war" that somehow had prevailed from the beginning of the campaign. Few couriers came and those few brought little news. Either the majority of the division commanders did not appreciate the necessity of keeping G. H. Q. informed, or else each of them was acting as if he were exercising independent command, and under no necessity of co-

15 O. R., 11, part 2, p. 789. 16 O. R., 11, part 2, p. 680.
17 O. R., 11, part 2, pp. 680, 789. 18 O. R., 11, part 2, p. 789.
19 21 S. H. S. P., 162.

ordinating his movements with the others'. Stuart, who had gone on from Dispatch Station to the White House, reported that base abandoned, vast stores burned, and Rooney Lee's historic home destroyed. The cavalry commander was satisfied that the enemy's movement was toward the James and that McClellan had no intention of retreating down the Peninsula.[20] Word reached Lee, also, that General T. H. H. Holmes, with 6000 of his men, had crossed to the north side of the James by the pontoon bridges at Drewry's Bluff and had been ordered by the War Department to move down the left bank of that river by way of the New Market road to co-operate with Lee—a very welcome reinforcement, nearly compensating for the casualties at Gaines's Mill.[21]

As the day closed, it was believed at headquarters that the enemy might be headed off at the intersection of the Long Bridge and Charles City roads, a place familiar in later campaigns as Riddell's Shop. This was, in reality, most improbable, because so great an army, with its wagon train, could not be crowded into the space between Riddell's Shop and the known rear of the enemy; but Stuart was ordered across the Chickahominy to co-operate in an attack at the point where the head of the column was supposed at the moment to be.[22] Longstreet and A. P. Hill had made a fair day's march, considering the heat and the dust—thirteen miles.[23] Their advance had reached Atlee's farm, on the Darbytown road, though some of Hill's units had been compelled to keep the road until 9 P.M.[24] The two divisions were still seven miles from Riddell's Shop, but, by an early start on the 30th, could get there in time to head off McClellan if he were there. The news from the other commands was far less favorable, and it reached headquarters in a torrential rain that continued far into the night.[25] Huger had done a wretched day. Bewildered by the dispatch of troops to

---

[20] *O. R.*, 11, part 2, pp. 483, 497, 516 ff.; *H. B. McClellan*, 77–79. The White House, where Martha Dandridge Custis had been living at the time of her marriage to Washington, had been spared and guarded by the Federals but had been set afire on the 28th, "by an incendiary . . . a private of the Ninety-Third New York . . ." (*O. R.*, 11, part 2, p. 333).

[21] *O. R.*, 11, part 2, pp. 495, 906–7. For the correspondence regarding Holmes's advance, see *Ibid.*, part 3, p. 613 ff.

[22] *O. R.*, 11, part 2, p. 518.

[23] *Cf.* D. E. Johnston: *The Story of a Confederate Boy*, 112.

[24] Longstreet was not precise regarding this march in 2 *B. and L.*, 399. See *O. R.*, 11, part 2, pp. 759, 775, 874; 3 *C. M. H.*, 295; 21 *S. H. S. P.*, 162.

[25] *O. R.*, 11, part 2, pp. 79, 691; *R. Taylor*, 89.

and from Magruder, he had spent long hours in the road and then had hesitated in the belief that the enemy was still in White Oak Swamp on his flank. He had bivouacked at Brightwell's, not more than six miles from his starting point.[26] If this was the best that could be expected from a fresh division of 9000, it augured ill for the morrow.

Magruder, it developed, had spent several hours at Fair Oaks in placing his troops in line of battle and then had waited for the expected arrival of Huger on his right and of Jackson on his left, in the hope of enveloping the Federal rearguard. Huger, exercising the discretion Lee had given him, had recalled his two brigades because he did not find any need or place for them.[27] Jackson had not arrived. After a long delay, Magruder had attacked and had driven the Federals back to Savage Station, one of their advanced bases on the York River Railroad.[28] Then he had brought into action the railroad battery that Lee early in June had asked the Navy Department to construct.[29] Kershaw's and Semmes's brigades of McLaws's division had assaulted a lightly fortified Federal position and had made some progress in a two-hour battle that had ended with darkness, but they had not routed the Federals or perceptibly hastened the withdrawal of the rearguard. The advance of the column for the day had been only five miles, the casualties had been 441, and the net result was that the Federals had another night in which to complete the crossing of White Oak Swamp, with two roads available to them across it.[30]

Lee was disappointed. He did not know the great strength

[26] *O. R.,* 11, part 2, pp. 789, 797; P. F. Brown: *Reminiscences of the War of 1861–1865,* pp. 17–18. For the movements of Kearny's Federal division, whose whereabouts alarmed Huger, see *O. R., loc. cit.,* 162.

[27] *O. R.,* 11, part 2, p. 789. [28] See *supra,* p. 101, n. 50.

[29] 2 *English Combatant,* 163. The gun had been reported ready for action on June 24. *O. R.,* 11, part 2, p. 615. For its subsequent use, see *O. R.,* 36, part 3, p. 725; *O. R.,* 51, part 2, p. 996.

[30] *Joel Cook,* 326; *O. R.,* 11, part 2, pp. 494, 663 *ff.,* 691, 717, 726; *McDaniel,* 6–7; *History of Kershaw's Brigade,* 128; N. A. Davis, *op. cit.,* 61, described the "railroad Merrimac." The Federals had Sumner's, Franklin's, and Heintzelman's corps on the Williamsburg road, but Heintzelman resumed his march, in the belief that the ground was too crowded to permit the employment of his troops (*O. R.,* 11, part 2, pp. 50, 91; 2 *B. and L.,* 372 *ff.*). Early on the morning of the 30th, the Confederates reached the Federal field hospital at Savage Station and took prisoner 2400 sick and wounded. The fullest account of the destruction of stores, of the hospital at Savage Station, and of the running of an ammunition train down the York River Railroad into the Chickahominy is that of James J. Marks: *The Peninsula Campaign in Virginia* (cited hereafter as *Marks*), 230 *ff.,* 245.

of the force encountered by Magruder, and he wrote him in serious strain. "I regret very much that you have made so little progress today in the pursuit of the enemy. In order to reap the fruits of our victory the pursuit should be most vigorous. I must urge you, then, again to press on his rear rapidly and steadily. We must lose no more time or he will escape us entirely."[34] After this letter had been written, late in the evening, but before it had been dispatched, Major Walter Taylor rode in from an interview with General Magruder, to whom he had carried orders to feel out the enemy during the night.[32] Taylor had a strange tale to tell. General D. R. Jones, commanding one of Magruder's small divisions,[33] had been expecting Jackson's co-operation on his left, next the Chickahominy, but before the action at Savage Station had opened he had received word from Jackson that he could not help him, as he had "other important duty to perform."[34] Magruder had repeated this to Taylor, who had no knowledge of any conflicting orders for Jackson. Taylor had proposed to Magruder that he ride on to Grapevine Bridge, see Jackson, and ascertain what Jackson meant, but as the night was blackness itself and Taylor did not know the road, Magruder sent one of his own officers and Taylor returned to headquarters. Lee was as much in the dark as Magruder concerning Jackson's "other important duty," though he knew, of course, that when he had left the north side of the Chickahominy that morning Jackson had not completed the rebuilding of Grapevine Bridge.[35] So Lee added a postscript to the letter he had previously written Magruder. "I learn from Major Taylor," he said, "that you are under the impression that General Jackson has been ordered not to support you. On the contrary, he

---

[31] O. R., 11, part 2, p. 687.

[32] O. R., 11, part 2, p. 667. In the *McGuire Papers* is a letter from H. H. McGuire to Jed Hotchkiss, April 10, 1896, in which Doctor McGuire stated that on the afternoon of June 29, about 5 o'clock, the rebuilding of Grapevine Bridge was so nearly complete that Jackson crossed and met Lee and Magruder at the Trent house, where Lee gave Jackson his verbal orders for June 30. As Doctor McGuire recorded as a part of this meeting an incident that is known to have occurred early on the morning of June 29, it seems quite certain that he confused both the hour and the place of meeting. The dispatch of Taylor to Magruder late in the day, and Lee's surprise at Taylor's report, are almost conclusive evidence that Lee did not see Jackson or Magruder that afternoon.

[33] Magruder had three—his own, Jones's, and McLaws's, but in the Confederate correspondence of the campaign, the whole are loosely described as "Magruder's division" or "Magruder's command."

[34] O. R., 11, part 3, p. 625.

[35] Jackson had been expected to finish the bridge during the day (O. R., 11, part 2, p. 663).

has been directed to do so and to push the pursuit vigorously." [36]
From Jackson himself, Lee had no words. This, then, was the
position of the army at 10 P.M., June 29:

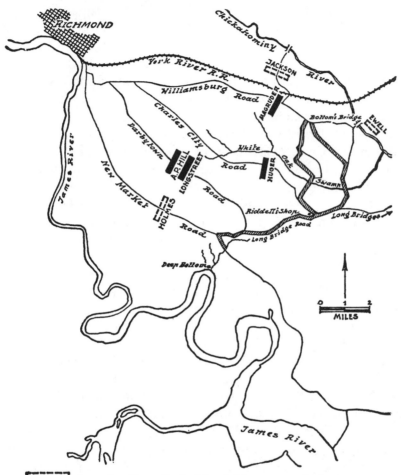

Assumed positions. Roads of heaviest troop movements, June 29–30,
are shaded.

The situation was by no means what Lee had hoped it would be
at the end of the day's operations. The Union rearguard had not
been caught on the north side of White Oak Swamp; the columns pursuing the Federal rear were not yet close to the swamp;

[36] O. R., 11, part 2, p. 687. Cf. ibid., 665.

there was growing improbability that the head of McClellan's column could be in the vicinity of Riddell's Shop. The day's operations had been a failure, not to say a fiasco. Still, the enemy would be within striking distance the next day, if only for that one day. McClellan doubtless was crossing White Oak Swamp and might have the rear of his army across before morning, but he would be strung out along the roads. And he would be bound for the James River. Of that, Lee was now fully satisfied. Had McClellan been moving toward the lower Chickahominy, Stuart and Ewell would certainly have had some evidence of his proximity ere this. They had reported none.

If McClellan was not headed off at the junction of the Long Bridge and Charles City roads, by what route would he make for the river? Lee did not know, and he ordered such cavalry as he had at hand to make a bold scout and to ascertain the enemy's position. The result was a bloody repulse for the Confederate horsemen on the Willis Church road, which led to the James. Little else was established except that the enemy was well to the south of Riddell's Shop.[37]

Was it possible to dispose the Army of Northern Virginia so as to cut McClellan off before he reached the James? As Lee pondered that question, he saw a possibility of attacking the enemy on the move. Then, if he demoralized and defeated the Federals, he would have a chance of enveloping them. Holmes was close to the river and too weak to interpose his division between the enemy and the James, but he could cover the extreme right flank and would be available in case the enemy were broken and fled in disorder toward the James. Longstreet, A. P. Hill, and Huger would be on McClellan's flank. By crossing White Oak Swamp, Jackson's strong column would be in rear of the Army of the Potomac. Magruder could be brought around White Oak Swamp as a general reserve. A great opportunity was presented for a convergence of force in a simultaneous attack on a moving enemy, encumbered with a great wagon train.

Lee determined to make the effort, hopeful of large results. Orders were prepared as follows for the movement of the different columns, beginning on the Confederate right:

[37] *O. R.,* 11, part 2, p. 525.

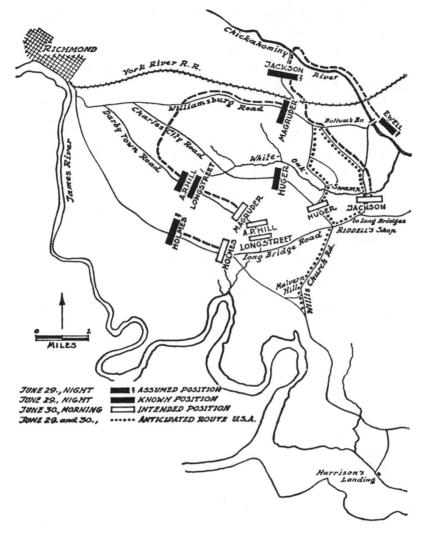

Lines of advance as ordered by Lee on the night of June 29, 1862, for reconcentration and attack on June 30.

1. Holmes to advance down the New Market road and take a strong defensive position at New Market Heights near the junction of his route and the Long Bridge road.[38]

2. Magruder to return from Savage Station, enter the Darby-

---

[38] O. R., 11, part 2, p. 906.

town road by the shortest byway, advance down it, and take position as a general reserve.

3. Longstreet and A. P. Hill to continue down the Darbytown road to the Long Bridge road and to be prepared to attack the Federals when and where located.

4. Huger to march down the Charles City road, and to open with his artillery when he established contact with the enemy.

5. Jackson, with Whiting and D. H. Hill, to march to White Oak Swamp bridge, cross there, and attack the enemy in rear.

6. Stuart's previous orders to stand—to move to the main army and to co-operate as circumstance permitted.

7. The movements at dawn. As Huger was nearest the enemy, the opening of his guns to be the signal for the advance of the attacking columns.[39]

All these orders, except those for Magruder, were issued while the storm was still raging around Savage Station. After it passed, silence settled over the countryside.[40] The only dispatch of any importance that arrived late in the night was one from the sleepless and excited Magruder. Regarding the situation as "by no means satisfactory," he asked for reinforcements, in case Jackson did not arrive. Lee thought them unnecessary and did not send them.[41]

[39] O. R., 11, part 2, p. 495.
[40] Lee's headquarters for the night are not known.
[41] O. R., 11, part 2, p. 665.

CHAPTER XVI

THE ARMY SHOWS ITSELF UNREADY FOR A CANNÆ

(FRAYSER'S FARM)

THE decisive day, June 30, broke "cloudless and calm"[1] upon awakening thousands of confident soldiers who expected McClellan's army to be destroyed ere night fell again over the swamps and forests below Richmond. Lee's first concern was for Magruder. Riding down to Savage Station, he found that Jackson had joined "Prince John" at 3:30 A.M.[2] Jackson, it is recorded by a young artillerist, "appeared worn down to the lowest point of flesh consistent with effective service. His hair, skin, eyes and clothes were all one neutral dust tint, and his badges of rank so dulled and tarnished as to be scarcely perceptible. . . . When [Lee] recognized Jackson he rode forward with a courier, his staff halting. As he gracefully dismounted, handing his bridle rein to his attendant, and advanced, drawing his gauntlet from his right hand, Jackson flung himself from his horse and advanced to meet Lee, Little Sorrel trotting back to the staff, where a courier secured him. The two Generals greeted each other warmly, but wasted no time upon the greeting. They stood facing each other. . . . Jackson began talking in a jerky, impetuous way, meanwhile drawing a diagram on the ground with the toe of his right boot. He traced two sides of a triangle with promptness and decision; then starting at the end of the second line, began to draw a third projected toward the first. This third line he traced slowly and with hesitation, alternately looking up at Lee's face and down at the diagram, meanwhile talking earnestly; and when at last the third line crossed the first and the triangle was complete, he raised his foot and stamped it down with emphasis saying 'We've got him,' then signalled for his horse."[3] There is no further record of

---

[1] *Marks*, 258.   [2] *O. R.*, 11, part 2, p. 665.
[3] Robert Stiles: *Four Years Under Marse Robert*, pp. 98–99.

what passed between the two, but it is certain that Jackson understood the plan of operations and his part in it. Lee doubtless reiterated Jackson's simple instructions "to pursue the enemy on the road he had taken."[4] Jackson hurried on; Lee sought out Magruder. In person he gave "Prince John" his orders to move over to the Darbytown road and supplied him with a guide who knew the terrain.

Then Lee went across the country to the Darbytown road and joined Longstreet's marching men.[5] Before noon the force approached the junction with Long Bridge road. As Longstreet had not ridden up, Lee directed A. P. Hill to take temporary command of his own and of Longstreet's division. Accompanied by R. H. Anderson, Longstreet's senior brigadier, Hill examined the ground with care. As far as could be ascertained, the enemy was in motion southward down the Willis Church road, some two miles to the east of the Confederate van. The Long Bridge road, as it chanced, ran eastward at this point, before turning northeastward toward Riddell's Shop; consequently Hill had only to march "up" the road, in an easterly direction, to approach the enemy. Quickly he formed line of battle on the road, with Longstreet's division in front, supported on the right by Branch's brigade of Hill's own command. The "Light Division" was placed in immediate reserve.[6] Soon the advancing infantry came upon a small force of Confederate cavalry engaged with Federal skirmishers.[7] McClellan evidently was on the alert and had troops west of the road on which he was hurrying southward.

About this time Longstreet arrived in person and, at Lee's order, assumed charge of the field.[8] While the troops moved confidently into position under Longstreet's direction, over ground thickly set with forests and underbrush, Lee sent back to ascertain how Magruder was progressing.[9] He had no word from Jackson. Huger dispatched a messenger to report that his progress was obstructed,[10] but his march was so short that it hardly seemed possible he would be held up long. As, however, there was prospect of

---

4 *O. R.*, 11, part 2, p. 495.
6 *O. R.*, 11, part 2, p. 838.
8 *O. R.*, 11, part 2, p. 685.
10 *O. R.*, 11, part 2, p. 495.

5 *O. R.*, 11, part 2, p. 759.
7 *O. R.*, 11, part 2, pp. 532, 759.
9 *O. R.*, 11, part 2, pp. 666, 675.

some delay on his part in opening the action, Lee sent back to Magruder to halt and rest his men,[11] so that they would not be fatigued when put into action.

Close to 2:30 P.M., there came from the direction of Huger's advance the sound of light artillery fire. It was the signal gun, every one supposed. Lee at once rode forward to join Longstreet. In a little clearing of broomstraw and small pines,[12] he found Longstreet and with him Mr. Davis.

"Why, General," said the President, "what are you doing here? You are in too dangerous a position for the commander of the army."

"I'm trying," Lee answered, "to find out something about the movements and plans of those people. But you must excuse me, Mr. President, for asking what you are doing here, and for suggesting that this is no proper place for the commander-in-chief of all our armies."

Davis was determined that Lee should not send him off as he had done at Mechanicsville, and he answered lightly. "Oh, I am here on the same mission that you are."

They chatted cheerfully, their spirits high, as they waited for Huger's artillery to open in heavier volume to cover the advance of his infantry. Longstreet had sent word for nearby batteries to fire a few rounds in acknowledgment of what he took to be Huger's signal, but almost before the Southern gunners could do so the Federal artillery opened, and its shells began to burst close by.

Just then A. P. Hill dashed up: "This is no place for either of you," he exclaimed, doubtless with a smile that kept his words from being insubordinate, "and as commander of this part of the field, I order you both to the rear."

"We will obey your orders," said Davis, and moved off. Lee had to follow. A short distance away the President halted, still within range. A. P. Hill would not have it. In the same solicitous tone, he inquired: "Did I not tell you to go away from here, and did you not promise to obey my orders? Why, one shot from that battery over yonder may presently deprive the Confederacy of its

---

[11] *O. R.*, 11, part 2, p. 666.   [12] *Alexander*, 139.

President and the Army of Northern Virginia of its commander!"

This time they had to retire, and were fortunate to escape with no fatality.[13]

It was now almost 3 o'clock and the fire from Huger's position did not swell any louder or seem any nearer. Soon R. H. Anderson's brigade of Longstreet's division became lightly engaged with the enemy's infantry, and by 3 o'clock the artillery on both sides was barking viciously, regardless of what Huger and Jackson might or might not be doing.[14]

At his field headquarters, in rear of Longstreet's stout-hearted regiments, a courier handed Lee a note from Colonel Thomas L. Rosser, commanding the 5th Virginia Cavalry, which was operating in front of Holmes, on the New Market road. Lee must have read it with a sudden consciousness that the outlook was not so favorable as it seemed. For Rosser reported that the enemy's column, with much haste and confusion, was then moving southward over Malvern Hill, which was within little more than gun shot from the James River![15]

Lee perhaps remembered Malvern Hill—or, more properly Malvern Hills—as one of the large estates of his grandfather, Charles Carter, but if he had ever ridden over the ground, he had done so long before, in boyhood, at an age when he had no thought of military positions. He knew little or nothing of the sinister strength of its heights. What shook him now from the confidence of victory was the realization that if the enemy was retreating over Malvern Hill, McClellan might already be escaping before the battle was joined. Instead of fighting the decisive battle on the day of his great opportunity, Lee might have in prospect little more than a bootless rearguard action.

It was not a matter about which to take the word of a subordinate. He must see for himself. Apprizing Longstreet of what was reported, and leaving to him the direction of the brewing battle and the employment of Magruder's reserve division, Lee galloped down the Long Bridge road to its junction with the New Market road and hurried eastward, along the New Market or River road.

---

[13] Davis, quoted in 14 *S. H. S. P.*, 451–52; *Longstreet*, 134–35; 2 *B. and L.*, 400; *O. R.*, 11, part 2, p. 838.

[14] 2 *Davis*, 145; *Longstreet*, 135; *O. R.*, 11, part 2, pp. 51, 111, 123, 390.

[15] *O. R.*, 11, part 2, p. 532.

He found that Holmes already was aware of the enemy's movement and was sending forward six guns, supported by a regiment
of infantry.[16] Making his way through these troops, Lee under-

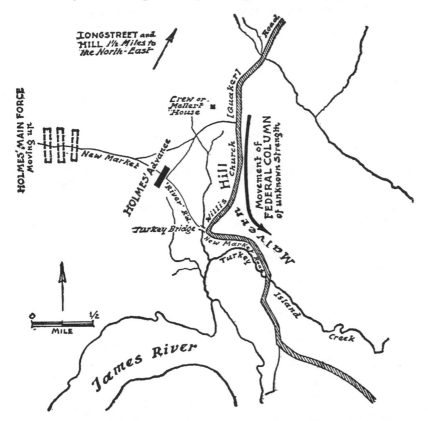

Situation around Malvern Hill, about 3:30 P.M., June 30, 1862, as developed
by Lee's personal reconnaissance.

took a reconnaissance in person, close to the enemy's position. This
soon showed him that Rosser's report was all too true. The Federal
columns were plainly visible on the elevation toward which
Lee was looking.[17]

Returning from his reconnaissance, conscious that opportunity
was slipping through his fingers, Lee met Holmes riding for-

[16] O. R., 11, part 2, p. 907.
[17] President Davis, op. cit., 143–44, believed, on insufficient evidence, that Lee expected the enemy to retreat down the Long Bridge road and that Lee did not know of the
movement down the Willis Church road.

ward and directed him to bring up the rest of his division to support his batteries and then to open fire,[18] in the hope of doing what damage he could to the retreating column.

A little farther on the way back from Holmes's advanced position, Lee again encountered President Davis, who also had heard of the menacing new situation near the river and had ridden down to see what was afoot. For a second time Davis protested that Lee was rashly exposing himself. The General replied, truly enough, that the only way he could get accurate information was by personal examination of the ground. Then he galloped back to the main field of action, whence there rolled an increasing volume of artillery fire. As he rode on, there came ominously from the opposite direction a still louder roar of heavier ordnance: Federal gunboats were in the river and were opening fire across the flats over which Holmes's green troops had to advance. If McClellan's army was already getting under the cover of those guns, the game was up!

When Lee reached the troops on the Long Bridge road he found the artillery blazing away, but the infantry not yet fully engaged. Magruder had been ordered by Longstreet to march to the support of Holmes.[19] Nothing further had been heard from Huger and nothing from Jackson. Neither of them could be attacking successfully, if at all, because such reconnaissance as could be made by Lee showed that the Federal right and centre, which would have been exposed to assaults by Jackson and Huger, were standing staunchly, apparently inviting the Confederates to attack. It was manifest that if Longstreet and Hill waited much longer, the enemy would have passed their front and would have escaped. Dangerous and difficult as it was to order an advance with only two divisions against a force of unknown strength, Lee had either to use the troops he had or else let slip all opportunity of striking McClellan. Without hesitation, though doubtless with deep regret at the weakness of the force he could bring to bear where he had expected to thrust with his full strength, Lee ordered an attack.

As far as the enemy's position had been developed, when this order was given, McClellan, unprotected by earthworks, seemed

---

[18] *O. R.,* 11, part 2, p. 907.   [19] *O. R.,* 11, part 2, p. 667.

to be across the Charles City road and west of the Willis Church road. The two formed an obtuse angle at Riddell's Shop. This angle was bisected by the Long Bridge road, on either side of which Longstreet was advancing. The country was flat, except on the Confederate right, where it was uneven and, at some points, almost

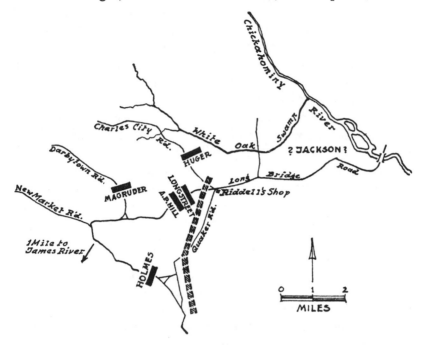

General situation in vicinity of Willis Church road as known to Lee
about 5 P.M., June 30, 1862.

precipitous.[20] Woods covered the whole front, broken at intervals by the clearings of small farmhouses, and at points almost impenetrable because of bogs and underbrush. The nearby settlement was known as Glendale, and the largest property in the neighborhood was Frayser's Farm. The battle was to bear both names.[21]

At the moment the advance began, about 5 o'clock,[22] Branch's

[20] *O. R.,* 11, part 2, pp. 762–65.
[21] For descriptions of the ground, see *O. R.,* 11, part 2, pp. 175, 254, 265, 390, 403, 423, 762–65, 777, 786, 870, 891, 893; D. E. Johnston: *Story of a Confederate Boy,* 113. Frayser's Farm of 214 acres was conveyed by William G. Keesee to Francis Frayser May 20, 1818, *Henrico County Deed-Book,* No. 17, p. 228. In 1849 it was conveyed to Nathaniel Nelson, *et al.* For this information the writer is indebted to Thomas C. Fletcher, Esq. The name is often misspelled Frazier.
[22] *O. R.,* 11, part 2, p. 763.

brigade of Hill's division was on the Confederate right. On its left was Kemper's brigade of Longstreet, then, on its left, R. H. Anderson's brigade, commanded by Colonel Micah Jenkins, as Anderson was temporarily in command of Longstreet's division. Beyond Jenkins, toward the left, was Wilcox's brigade, astride the Long Bridge road. Featherstone was on the extreme left. Pryor was in support of Wilcox. Pickett's brigade, commanded by Colonel Eppa Hunton, was between Jenkins and Wilcox, slightly to the rear, but was soon shifted to the right. All Hill's division, except Branch's brigade, was in immediate reserve.

Kemper's Virginians included many of the earliest volunteers of 1861, who had chafed at the fate that had denied them an active share in the earlier battles of the campaign, and now that they had an opportunity they swept wildly forward. Hurling back the enemy's skirmishers, the men seemed to think they were close to the main Federal position, and without waiting for orders, they raised the rebel yell and broke into the double-quick. Through the wood they rushed, across a little field, through another boggy wood, crowded with underbrush, and into a second field some 600 or 700 yards square.[23] In this they discovered a barricaded log house, surrounded by a crude breastwork of rails.[24] To the left and rear of this place, which was known as the Whitlock house, were two batteries of four guns each, which the Confederates took to be a unit.[25] Undeterred by the fire from the breastwork, the house, and the artillery, Kemper's men stormed onward, overran the house, captured six of the eight guns,[26] and, though their line was irregular, pushed on to the woods east of the clearing. Here they found themselves facing a heavy fire from the front and from both flanks and saw that they had far outrun the brigades on either side of them. Determined to hold their ground, they made the best of their bad position and maintained a vigorous fire,[27] though their right was soon threatened by what seemed to be a strong force.[28]

Branch, on Kemper's right, had no guide and floundered for some time, ignorant of the position of the other units. Then his

[23] O. R., 11, part 2, p. 265.   [24] O. R., 11, part 2, pp. 403, 893.
[25] O. R., 11, part 2, p. 764. Cf. ibid., 100, 425, 429. The batteries were Knierem's and Diederich's, see infra, p. 240, n. 100.
[26] O. R., 11, part 2, p. 265, for the escape of two of Knierem's guns.
[27] O. R., 11, part 2, pp. 763-65.   [28] 18 S. H. S. P., 391-93.

men began slowly to advance.[29] Jenkins, on Kemper's left, had started early, perhaps ahead of Kemper, but for some unexplained reason gained little ground.

Wilcox, next Jenkins, was detained by conflicting orders for more than half an hour after Kemper went forward, but at 5:40 he advanced. Soon he noticed that the Long Bridge road divided his two right regiments from those on his left, but his fine Alabama infantrymen pressed on, through woods, down to a little stream with a dense growth of trees along it, then through another wood, thin on the left of the road and heavy on the right. Here the brigade emerged into open ground and came under rifle fire. In the field could be seen infantry and two batteries, one on either side of the road. There was a cleared tract directly between the attacking force and the left battery, but behind the battery and to the left of it the woods were close enough to shelter the enemy's infantry. The 8th Alabama became engaged with the force in the woods on the left of the battery and could not progress, but the 11th Alabama, facing a very heavy fire, got within 100 yards of the battery before the fierceness of the Federal defense forced it back. The regiment renewed the attack and this time came within fifty yards of the Federal guns, which were being admirably served by Lieutenant Alanson M. Randol. Once more the 11th gave ground, followed closely by the bluecoats. There was a bitter clash, and the Union troops were forced to flee. This time the Alabamians were on their heels, and as the Federal infantry masked Randol's guns, Wilcox's men quickly overran the pieces. Randol's gunners, however, were of stubborn stuff, and after they had reached the edge of the woods in the rear of their battery, they rallied with infantry support and soon delivered a counterattack. The 11th Alabama held its ground. Bayonet crossed bayonet in a fierce mêlée. Captain W. C. Y. Parker felled two Federal officers with his sword, only to fall with three bayonet wounds and with a musket ball through his thigh. Heads were mashed with rifle butts. Primal rage possessed the struggling men. Decimated at last, the Alabamians were driven back to their right into the strip of woods flanking the road.[30]

29 *O. R.*, 11, part 2, p. 883.

30 *O. R.*, 11, part 2, pp. 237–38, 255–56, 391, 403, 421, 776–77. The accounts of this episode differ somewhat in detail. An effort has here been made to reconcile them.

On the other side of the road, the 9th and 10th Alabama had formed for the charge when they saw a Union regiment advancing through the field to attack them. Awaiting this onslaught, the Confederates received one volley, then sprang at the enemy and drove him back on the guns, which belonged to Cooper's battery. Close to these pieces, the Alabamians recoiled but rallied quickly and took the pieces. Soon the Federals attacked again and with so much violence that they compelled the Confederates to retire to the woods on the left, along the Long Bridge road, where the 11th Regiment, driven from Randol's battery, had already sought cover. The Alabamians were still in advance, but they held less than they had sought to gain. The Federals contented themselves with what they had accomplished and did not attempt to recover Cooper's guns, which remained silent in the field, amid writhing horses and dying men.[31]

Pryor's brigade was to have gone into action on the left of Wilcox, and simultaneously with him, but it encountered delay in the woods and did not reach the front until after Wilcox had been driven back from his most advanced position. Finding himself confronted with a heavy fire on front and flank, Pryor called for reinforcements from Featherston, who had been intended as a reserve but had already been ordered forward. Featherston formed on Pryor's left and advanced some distance. The enemy, however, seemed about to launch a flanking movement, so Featherston sent back for help and held on as best he could.[32] Gregg, of Hill's division, was hurried to him.[33]

As sunset approached, the situation grew more serious. Kemper on the right and Wilcox on the centre were spearheads held fast in the heavy blue line. They had inflicted heavy loss and had silenced all the enemy's batteries on a long sector, or had forced the gunners to retreat,[34] but neither brigade could be extricated or pushed farther to reach the vitals of the enemy. Both on the left and on the right, the Federal lines overlapped those of the Confederates and threatened to envelop them. The last brigade of Longstreet's

[31] O. R., 11, part 2, pp. 255, 410, 423, 777–78.
[32] O. R., 11, part 2, pp. 781, 785–86.   [33] O. R., 11, part 2, pp. 786, 867.
[34] Amsden's battery, its ammunition exhausted, had been compelled to withdraw from the line (O. R., 11, part 2, p. 412). Thompson's had been ordered from the field (O. R., 11, part 2, p. 256)

division, that of General Pickett, was being marched to the endangered right. Magruder was out of reach on his way to Holmes. There was nothing to do but to throw in the remaining brigades of A. P. Hill's division in an effort to consolidate and hold the

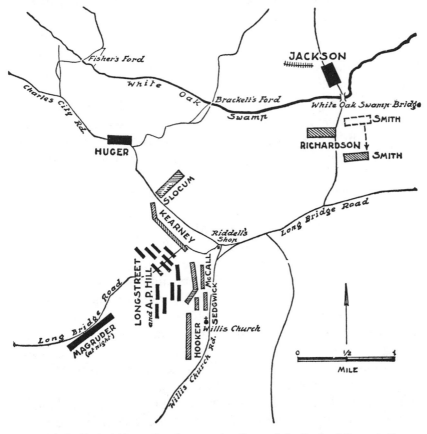

General distribution of opposing forces at the climax of the Battle of Frayser's Farm (Glendale), June 30, 1862. After map by Colonel H. L. Landers, U. S. A.

ground already won. Longstreet, who was still directing the battle, gave orders accordingly.[35]

Forgetful of the slaughter of Mechanicsville and unmindful of their frightful losses at Gaines's Mill, Hill's regiments moved forward at the order of command. Archer was to the right, supporting Kemper and Branch, with Pickett on his right. Field,

[35] *Longstreet,* 136.

supported by Pender, went in to relieve Wilcox's brigade. J. R. Anderson was prudently held back by Hill as a final reserve. About the time this advance began, Branch's slow progress was speeded up and he was drawn closer to the centre.[36] The brigade of Pickett[37] passed through Kemper's lines and reached the Federal batteries of Knierem and Diederich. Strange hesitated a while to employ the guns, believing that other Confederate commands were in his front, but at length he opened effectively on the enemy.[38] The left of the line was threatened anew, as Branch shifted toward the centre, but it was held against a vigorous fire.[39]

On the centre, Field's Virginia brigade divided as Wilcox's had in moving over the same ground, the 56th and the 60th Virginia on the right of the Long Bridge road, and the 40th and the 47th Virginia Regiments and the Second Virginia battalion on the left. The regiments on the right found Cooper's battery deserted but the enemy close behind it. Loading and firing as they advanced, the men reached the guns, recaptured them once more, and then pressed on to the woods in rear.[40] Meantime, on the other side of the road, the 47th Virginia had driven off the Federals, who had recovered Randol's battery and were moving fast toward the woods.[41] Together the three regiments and the battalion pressed on. Finding the Federals in strength, the right regiments charged bayonets and soon were at grips with the enemy. One private of the 60th was confronted by four Federals at the same instant. Although several times stabbed with bayonets, he killed three of his four antagonists. The other was dispatched by his brother.[42] Soon the 56th and the 60th Virginia outdistanced the troopers on the left of the road and found themselves far in front.[43] The 47th, halting near the edge of the woods, protected the flank of the other regiments as best it could and turned one of Randol's guns against the Federal position in the woods to the left.[44] The 40th had drifted off in that direction and soon faced a fiery attack, which

---

[36] *Longstreet,* 138; *O. R.,* 11, part 2, p. 883.
[37] Commanded now by Colonel J. B. Strange, as Colonel Eppa Hunton had dropped from exhaustion.
[38] *O. R.,* 11, part 2, p. 769.   [39] *Longstreet,* 138.
[40] The colonel of the 60th Virginia mistakenly reported this battery as Randol's (*O. R.,* 11, part 2, p. 850).
[41] *O. R.,* 11, part 2, p. 847.
[42] These gallant men were Robert A. and Eli W. Christian (*O. R.,* 11, part 2, p. 851).
[43] *O R.,* 11, part 2, pp. 842, 847, 850.   [44] *O. R.,* 11, part 2, p. 845.

it successfully beat off, though the enemy got within twenty feet.[45] Field now withdrew his right regiments from their exposed position.[46] The enemy, however, by this time was closing in from the right, and was actually in rear of Field, unknown both to him and to the Federal commander, but Pender's fine brigade was in support of Field, and when the enemy, moving from right to left across his front, was within seventy-five yards, Pender opened and quickly scattered it. Ere long, Archer was in touch with Pender on his right.[47]

Still the enemy fought hard.[48] Close as the Confederate front had advanced to the Federal line, its ability to hold on was doubtful. Fortunately, A. P. Hill had followed the changing situation with a clear eye and he had already ordered forward his last reserve, J. R. Anderson's brigade, with instructions to raise the rebel yell in full voice. Through gathering darkness and in precise accord with his orders, Anderson moved up the road on a wide front and delivered a volley at close range. The loud outcry of his troops deceived the Federals into thinking that heavy, fresh reserves were at hand. They broke and ran. In a short time, with night lying black on the field, the infantry action was over. The artillery continued a blind fire until 9 o'clock.[49]

Lee was with Longstreet during this last phase of the battle. While the excitement of the action was still upon them, a mounted officer rode up, surrounded by a guard of weary but proud Confederates: they were of the 47th Virginia and brought to the commander a live Federal general, whom they had bagged when he had ridden into their ranks in search of his scattered infantry.[50] Longstreet recognized him at once as Brigadier General George A. McCall, commander of the Third division of Porter's V Corps, whom he had known in the "old army," as the Confederates always styled the ante-bellum military forces of the United States. Longstreet started to extend his hand as McCall dismounted, but saw instantly that the Federal was in no mood to accept amenities. He contented himself with directing that McCall be escorted to Richmond.[51]

McCall had commanded the Pennsylvania Reserves, who had

[45] O. R., 11, part 2, pp. 178, 844. [46] O. R., 11, part 2, p. 842.
[47] O. R., 11, part 2, p. 901. [48] O. R., 11, part 2, p. 838.
[49] O. R., 11, part 2, pp. 495, 838–39, 879–80. [50] O. R., 11, part 2, p. 845.
[51] 2 B. and L., 401–2.

repulsed A. P. Hill at Beaver Dam Creek and had fought so stubbornly at Gaines's Mill. His presence was the first information Lee had, perhaps, as to the identity of the troops in front of the Confederate centre.[52] There was a certain satisfaction in the knowledge that these stubborn soldiers had been defeated. The fact that their leader had strayed into the Southern lines in the confusion of a retreat was as sure an evidence as the eighteen captured guns that the Confederates had won the field.

But the field was not the battle, and on the battle the campaign had hung. The enemy might resume the fighting at dawn, and even if he did not, it was as certain as anything could be that his wagon train by that time would be safe on the James River. The ambitious plan for the convergence of Jackson, Huger, Longstreet, A. P. Hill, Magruder, and Holmes had failed tragically. Every man of Longstreet's and Hill's 20,000 had been thrown into action, leaving not a soldier in reserve—and more than 50,000 other Southern troops had stood virtually idle within sound of the guns.[53]

Magruder had not been able to bolster Holmes in an offensive below Malvern Hill, whither he had been sent. The advance of Holmes's infantry had raised so much dust that it had disclosed his presence to the enemy. An overwhelming artillery fire had paralyzed Holmes until nightfall, and some of his raw artillery and cavalry had behaved very badly.[54] Magruder, however, could now be recalled to relieve A. P. Hill and Longstreet, though his men had marched so far that they would be well-nigh exhausted when they arrived.[55] Stuart, by this time, should be on his way across the Chickahominy to co-operate.[56] His men would help.

[52] The burden of the fighting at Frayser's Farm was borne on the Federal right by Kearny's Third division of Heintzelman's III corps; on the right centre by McCall's division, which was more roughly handled than any of the others; on the left centre by Sedgwick's Second division of Sumner's II corps; and on the left by Hooker's Second division of the II corps.

[53] All Richmond was agog with reports that McClellan was in full retreat (*O. R.*, 11, part 3, p. 627), or was surrounded (*Mrs. McGuire*, 126).

[54] *O. R.*, 11, part 2, pp. 228, 532, 906 ff.; 2 *B. and L.*, 391. There was much subsequent discussion as to the fate of two of Holmes's guns. Apparently, they were captured and were spiked the next day (*O. R.*, 11, part 2, p. 380; 2 *B. and L.*, 432).

[55] *O. R.*, 11, part 2, pp. 495, 667.

[56] *O. R.*, 11, part 2, p. 518. "A Prussian Officer," quoted in E. A. Pollard: *Second Year of the War*, 321, gave a picture of Lee, "Gloomy and out of humor . . . with a dry, harsh voice," ordering the burial of the dead by Wise and Magruder, who were not on the field. The remainder of this officer's narrative is so replete with errors that the author is not willing to cite him in the text.

But if Magruder's absence was justified and Stuart was accounted for, what of the others? Why had Huger failed to attack on Longstreet's left? What had happened to him? The answer was not given until the next morning and was then as brief as it was unsatisfactory. Huger had started down the Charles City road from Brightwell's at daybreak, very much concerned lest he be attacked on his left flank from White Oak Swamp. He threw Wright's brigade to the north side of the swamp to protect his flank and proceeded cautiously down the south side with the rest of his force. Before he had gone a mile, with Mahone's brigade in advance, he found trees felled across the road. Instead of leaving his artillery and pushing on through the woods, he started to make a new road around the obstructions. As his men chopped away with poor tools, the Federals continued to cut trees along the highway. In this unequal contest between road-making and road-blocking, the greater part of the day was passed. When the Federal rearguard was at length driven in, the main position of the enemy was found so strong that Huger and Mahone reconnoitred with much caution and finally brought up one battery. This opened the fire that Lee assumed to be the signal for beginning the attack on the Long Bridge road. The battery continued its fire until dark, and the supporting infantry sustained seventy-eight casualties, but Huger made no assault. The day's operations ended with the advance less than two miles from its starting-point. After reporting early that his road was blocked, Huger did nothing to communicate with Lee or to reinforce the left of Longstreet and Hill, though there was a woods road on Huger's right that would have carried him, after a march of about one and a half miles, to the ground where Featherston was fighting. It was inexcusable failure to co-operate, the result of extreme over-caution. So far as the records show, however, Lee sent no staff officer with further orders to Huger and did not call upon him to dispatch any part of his idle force to the right. The reason, perhaps, was that Lee was afraid to weaken Huger, as that officer's column afforded a measure of insurance that the overlapping Federal right would not be pushed dangerously far in flanking operations against Longstreet's left.[57]

[57] *O. R.*, 11, part 2, pp. 547, 789–90, 797–98; *W. W. Chamberlaine*, 22–23. For the

And what of Jackson on the Federal rear? Why had he, too, failed to do his expected part? During the afternoon Longstreet had sent Major J. W. Fairfax back across White Oak Swamp to ask Jackson for reinforcements,[58] and though there is no specific record of the fact, it is almost certain that Fairfax returned and, so far as he had seen the situation, reported what had befallen the 20,000 infantry on whose attack at White Oak Swamp Lee had reckoned in his plan of action. Jackson had not moved across the Chickahominy at Grapevine Bridge until after midnight on the night of June 29–30, when he had been awakened by the storm.[59] He did not explain then or thereafter the nature of the "other important duty" that kept him from supporting Magruder, as Lee had ordered.[60] Ewell, meantime, had been ordered back via Grapevine Bridge and was marching in rear of Jackson's column.[61] The advance on the morning of June 30 was so delayed by the collection of discarded Federal small arms and by the capture of more than 1000 prisoners[62] that Jackson himself did not cover the seven miles to White Oak Swamp until about noon, and some of the troops did not come up till late afternoon.[63] Had Jackson been a few hours earlier he would have caught the enemy in the act of crossing the bridge on the main road, for at daybreak Federal stragglers had been wedged in so closely at the approach that for a time they could not move.[64] As it was, the last of the

operations of Slocum's division, the chief Federal force opposing Huger, see *ibid.*, 435. Colonel W. H. Palmer wrote Colonel Walter Taylor, July 24, 1905, that he had gone in 1864 over the ground of Huger's advance down the Charles City road, and that one company could easily have thrown to right and to left the trees that obstructed the road (*Taylor MSS.*).

[58] Wade Hampton, quoted in Marshall, 111.

[59] Mrs. T. J. (Mary Anna) Jackson: *Memoirs of Stonewall Jackson* (cited hereafter as *Mrs. Jackson*), 296–97; *Malone*, 22; *O. R.*, 11, part 2, p. 557.

[60] General Alexander did not so state in his *Military Memoirs*, but he was of opinion that Jackson delayed until Sunday was past and that his "other important duty" was religious worship (E. P. Alexander to W. H. Taylor, Aug. 20, 1902—*Taylor MSS.*). No other explanation has ever been offered, except the obvious one that the reconstruction of Grapevine Bridge took longer than had been anticipated. On this point, General Magruder noted that at noon, or about that time, on the 29th, the completion of the bridge was expected within two hours (*O. R.*, 11, part 2, p. 663).

[61] *O. R.*, 11, part 2, pp. 607, 617–18.

[62] *O. R.*, 11, part 2, pp. 556, 627. For an excellent description of the march and of the debris left by the Federals, see *Dabney*, 460–61.

[63] *O. R.*, 11, part 2, pp. 556, 571, 593, 618, 634. Jackson's chief of artillery, Colonel Crutchfield said the artillery arrived about 9:30 (*O. R.*, 11, part 2, p. 561), but the opposing Federal commander, General I. B. Richardson, stated the Federals did not destroy the bridge until 10 A.M. (*O. R.*, 11, part 2, p. 55).

[64] *O. R.*, 11, part 2, p. 55.

organized rearguard was beyond reach when Jackson arrived. A fine pontoon train was in plain sight on the south side of the swamp and the enemy's wagons were moving slowly up the road toward Glendale, out of range. The bridge had been broken up and burned by the Federals, and the timbers had been thrown into the miry ford, which had thus been rendered almost impassable.[65] A Federal battery was in waiting across the stream,[66] with infantry in support.[67]

It was undeniably a difficult stream to pass in the face of the enemy. Woods came down to the swamp; a thick growth of small timber crowded it. Only the road was clear, and that was commanded from the south bank by high ground on both sides of the crossing.[68] At least one of the Federal generals who had examined the position was of opinion that it could not be forced.[69] Jackson's impulse, as always, was first to employ his guns. Crutchfield cut a road to a good artillery position to the right and rear of the crossing[70] and about 1000 yards from the enemy's battery.[71] At 1:45 P.M. he opened with twenty-three pieces. The fire was overwhelming, according to the testimony of many Federal officers.[72] The enemy fired only four shots in reply and then withdrew, leaving one gun on the ground.[73] A Confederate battery was at once moved into the road to deal with the Federal sharpshooters,[74] detachments were put to work repairing the bridge, and Munford's cavalry, with D. H. Hill's skirmishers, were promptly thrown across. The going was bad, but they were soon on the other side. Jackson and some of his officers also passed over to reconnoitre.[75] Had the infantry followed without delay it might have succeeded in storming the Federal position,

---

[65] H. B. McClellan, 81; Wade Hampton in Alexander, 150.

[66] Marshall, 110.

[67] The Federal defense was in charge of General W. B. Franklin, commander of the VI Corps. He had with him his second division, General W. F. Smith, Richardson's first division of Sumner's II Corps, Naglee's second brigade of Peck's second division of Keyes IV Corps and, for two hours, Gorman's (Sully's) first brigade and Dana's third brigade of Sedgwick's second division of Sumner's II Corps.

[68] Doctor Hunter McGuire in 2 Henderson, 51n.

[69] McCall in O. R., 11, part 2, p. 389.

[70] O. R., 11, part 2, p. 655.   [71] O. R., 11, part 2, p. 561.

[72] O. R., 11, part 2, pp. 58, 464 ff.; Thomas L. Livermore: Days and Events, 86–87. General Franklin said the fire was of a severity "which I had never heard equalled in the field" (2 B. and L., 377–78). The description of the sequence of events in 2 Henderson 50 ff. is confused and in part reversed.

[73] O. R., 11, part 2, pp. 561, 627, 653, 655.   [74] O. R., 11, part 2, p. 561.

[75] O. R., 11, part 2, p. 627; 2 B. and L., 387, 2 Henderson, 51n.

for the enemy at the moment was badly demoralized. Soon, however, the Federal infantry was rallied on a strong second line, and
the United States batteries were moved to the right of the road,
directly opposite the Confederate artillery, out of sight but close
enough to give the longer-range Parrott guns a great advantage
over the Confederate ordnance.[76] Discouraged by this manœuvre,
Jackson returned to the north side of the swamp, and the cavalry
ere long retired also, but the skirmishers remained in the thicket.[77]
The troops reconstructing the bridge were now under a distant,
random fire, and refused to work.[78]

Jackson had been in a "peculiar mood" early in the day, but
had been smiling and hopeful when he had reached the swamp.[79]
During the engagement he was active and energetic.[80] During
the afternoon, however, a strange inertia overwhelmed him. General Wright of Huger's division, who had crossed higher up the
swamp during the morning, arrived at Jackson's position with his
command and reported for orders. Jackson told him to retrace
his steps and to cross the swamp again, if possible, as the enemy
in large force was opposing him at the site of the bridge. The
information as to his situation, Jackson directed Wright to convey
to General Huger.[81] Wright marched back with his troops and
a competent guide, and though he found the nearest ford, Brackett's, guarded by the enemy, he had no difficulty in passing over
White Oak Swamp at Fisher's Ford, only a little more than three
miles from Jackson's artillery position.[82] Jackson neither sent to
see whether Wright could cross nor gave him instruction to report if he found a ford. Nothing further seems to have been done
by Jackson to communicate with the forces on the other side of
the swamp, though General D. H. Hill readily enough found a
way of sending an engineer officer to Huger, requesting him to
attack the force blocking the road at White Oak Bridge. The
officer got back safely with a report on Huger's situation.[83]

---

[76] O. R., 11, part 2, pp. 55–56, 465, 477, 481, 561, 655. "Right" is from the Confederate approach.
[77] O. R., 11, part 2, p. 627.   [78] O. R., 11, part 2, p. 566.
[79] Munford in 2 Henderson, 50.   [80] Doctor Hunter McGuire in 2 Henderson, 55.
[81] O. R., 11, part 2, p. 790.
[82] O. R., 11, part 2, pp. 809–10. For a partial description of these fords, see H. G.
Berry in O. R., 11, part 2, p. 185.
[83] 2 B. and L., 388. Longstreet's aide, it will be recalled, also arrived and presumably
returned (Hampton in Marshall, 111).

General Wade Hampton, meantime, started to reconnoitre on the left, while the artillery continued its blind fire and the infantry waited, ready to move.[84] A short distance from the road, where the swamp was only ten or fifteen feet wide, Hampton found a

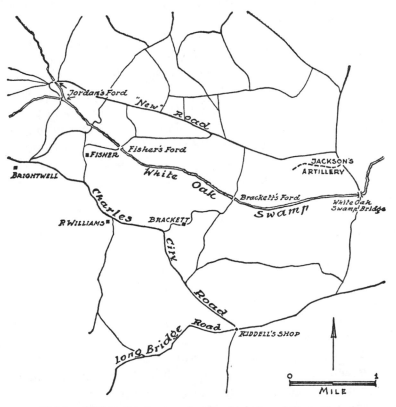

Vicinity of White Oak Swamp, showing the fords and the position of Jackson's artillery, June 30, 1862.

good sandy bottom and shallow water. He rode across the swamp and discovered that he was beyond the right flank of the Federals. They were lying down, at ease, having no guard at the creek and apparently not suspecting that an enemy was at hand. Riding back, Hampton reported his findings to Jackson. Could he build a bridge over the swamp at the point he had described? Jackson asked. Easily for infantry, Hampton answered, but

[84] For a detailed account of the condition of Jackson's men this day, the writer is indebted to the late Lieutenant W. S. Archer.

not for artillery, as the cutting of a road would give the alarm.
Jackson told him to set about it. In a few minutes the bridge
was made, and Hampton went across again. He found the
Federals still unaware of their danger. When he returned,
he again reported to Jackson, who was sitting alone on a log
by the roadside, his cap down over his eyes. Hampton announced that the bridge was ready. Jackson sat silent for a time
and then got up and stalked off without saying a word.[85] No
orders were issued and nothing was done, though the sound of
the opening of the battle at Frayser's Farm ere long was audible.[86]
Instead of reconnoitring in person, Jackson sat down and penned
a letter to his wife describing his loss of rest and advising her
what money she should contribute to the church.[87] At second
hand, it is also said that Jackson fell asleep and either was not or
could not be aroused by his staff officers.[88] Night came. The roar
of the battle at Frayser's Farm continued to crash over White
Oak Swamp. Jackson's artillery ceased firing. The men prepared
to bivouac. The General started to eat supper with his staff but
was so weary that he fell asleep with his food between his teeth.
His sense of duty did not desert him even then. Arousing himself
he said, "Now, gentlemen, let us at once to bed, and rise with the
dawn and see if we cannot do something." [89]

Myths have grown up regarding Jackson's strange lapse that
day, and many theories have developed from endless speculation
—that he was disgruntled at subordination to Lee, that he thought
his weary troops should be spared while the Richmond garrison
did some of the fighting, that he was deterred from seeking another ford because his orders were to cross where he was, that he
did not cross because he could not carry his artillery with him,
and that he did all that could be expected of any man in such a
position, with the enemy commanding the road. The evidence is
not such that a positive choice can be made among these theories
on the basis of determinable fact. Individual opinion of the
weight of probabilities must shape one's conclusion. Most stu-

[85] Hampton gave the same account of this incident to Marshall in 1871, *op. cit.*, 109
ff., and to Alexander, *op. cit.*, 149, many years later.
[86] *Ibid.*   [87] *Mrs. Jackson*, 296–97.
[88] *Long*, 175–76; McHenry Howard, *Recollections*, 148–49; John Lamb in 25 *S. H.
S. P.*, 211, citing Doctor Harvey Black.
[89] *Dabney*, 467.

dents probably will conclude that the most likely explanations are these: either the position, in Jackson's judgment at the time, was so strong that he did not think he could take it without excessive and unwarranted casualties; or else, the none-too-robust frame of Jackson had been exhausted by loss of sleep, on which his physique was especially dependent. Perhaps the two reasons are one: in his normal state of mind, well-rested, Jackson might have stormed the Federal positions.[90]

However this may be, Frayser's Farm was one of the great lost opportunities in Confederate military history. It was the bitterest disappointment Lee had ever sustained, and one that he could not conceal. Many times thereafter he was to discover a weak point in his adversary's line or a mistake in his antagonist's plan, but never again was he to find the enemy in full retreat across his front. Victories in the field were to be registered, but two years of open campaign were not to produce another situation where envelopment seemed possible. He had only that one day for a Cannæ, and the army was not ready for it.

[90] For a detailed discussion of the theories of Jackson's failure, see Appendix II—3.

CHAPTER XVII

THE FEDERAL ARTILLERY PROVES TOO STRONG

(MALVERN HILL)

AT 2 A.M. on the morning of July 1—a year before the battle of
Gettysburg opened, to the very day—Magruder's troops arrived
on the battlefield of Frayser's Farm after their futile march to
the support of Holmes. The regiments had been moving almost
continuously for eighteen hours, without food,[1] but they at once
relieved Longstreet's and Hill's divisions, which were worn with
much fighting. When they groped their way through the woods
to their advanced position, the newcomers found the Federals
still in their front.[2] After an hour, as the dawn was graying, the
skirmishers crept forward and discovered that the enemy was
gone. Soon they established contact with Jackson, who had
crossed White Oak Swamp after the enemy had abandoned the
hill and was advancing, with Whiting's division in front.[3] Shortly
thereafter, Lee sent Major Taylor to bring up Huger. That officer
received in a message from Longstreet his first intimation that
the Charles City road was clear.[4]

The depleted army was now united again for the last stage of
a pursuit that every one felt was well-nigh hopeless. Lee was on
the Long Bridge road when Jackson arrived at the Willis Church.
His disappointment at the outcome of the previous day's failure
to concentrate was apparent to all; his temper was not of the best
and he was feeling unwell, but he bore himself calmly[5] and talked
quietly with Longstreet, A. P. Hill, and Magruder of the battle
of the previous day.

While they were discussing the situation, Surgeon N. F. Marsh
of the 4th Pennsylvania cavalry came up. He explained that
he had been left with Federal wounded at Willis Church, and

---

[1] O. R., 11, part 2, p. 686.
[3] O. R., 11, part 2, pp. 627, 667, 705.
[5] 2 B. and L., 391; Longstreet, 142.

[2] O. R., 11, part 2, p. 667.
[4] O. R., 11, part 2, p. 790.

stated that Jackson had directed him to report to Lee. Protection and supplies for his men, he said, were needed. Lee at once promised such help as he could give and directed Longstreet to write a permit for Doctor Marsh to remain undisturbed with his charges. Longstreet engaged Marsh in conversation. Had the surgeon been in the battle? he asked. Yes, Marsh replied, he had. What troops had participated in it? Longstreet inquired. Marsh answered that he only knew of his own division, McCall's, which had fought over the very ground where they then were. "Well," said Longstreet, "McCall is safe in Richmond; but if his division had not offered the stubborn resistance it did on this road, we would have captured your whole army. Never mind; we will do it yet." [6]

Lee made no comment on this optimistic prediction. Doubtful, in his fatigue, whether he would be able to conduct the day's operations, he asked Longstreet to remain with him[7] and then rode over to the Willis Church. There he found D. H. Hill, who was as pessimistic as Longstreet was hopeful. Hill explained that he had in his command a chaplain, Reverend W. L. Allen, who had lived in that vicinity and knew Malvern Hill well. He repeated a description Allen had given him of the great strength of the hill, and added: "If General McClellan is there in strength, we had better let him alone." Longstreet broke in banteringly: "Don't get scared, now that we have got him whipped." Hill naturally said no more, and Lee did not pursue the discussion.[8]

The orders for the march were then issued. Jackson, who was on the ground, was directed to take up the pursuit at once down the Willis Church road.[9] Magruder had already seen Jackson and had offered to lead the van, but Jackson had insisted on doing so, as his troops were fresher than Magruder's.[10] Word was sent to Magruder, who had not ridden forward with Lee, to take "the Quaker road" and to form on Jackson's right.[11] Huger's division

---

[6] O. R., 11, part 2, p. 397. Doctor Marsh stated that this incident occurred on the New Market road, but his description makes it clear that he was on the Long Bridge road at the time. That day Lee offered to parole all the wounded Federal prisoners if McClellan would receive them (R. E. Lee to Fitz Lee, July 15, 1862, Jones, L. and L., 185), but he did not succeed in effecting such an arrangement till July 10, or about that time (O. R., 11, part 3, p. 315).
[7] Longstreet, 143.   [8] 2 B. and L., 391; O. R., 11, part 2, p. 628.
[9] O. R., 11, part 2, pp. 495, 557.   [10] O. R., 11, part 2, p. 667.
[11] O. R., 11, part 2, p. 667.

was divided. Two of his brigades, those of Armistead and Wright, were to advance, by a track through the woods, southward from the Charles City road to the Long Bridge road and were to move thence southeastward toward Malvern Hill. Mahone and Ransom, leading Huger's other brigades, were to follow Jackson down the Willis Church road.[12] The divisions of Longstreet and A. P. Hill were to remain in reserve. They had done their part and were too weary to resume fighting immediately, unless an emergency demanded their employment. Holmes was to hold his position and co-operate.

It was tactically bad, of course, to send Jackson's three divisions, two brigades of Huger's, and Magruder's three divisions, one behind another, down the narrow Willis Church road, but there was no alternative. As far as Lee knew, there was no other approach to the Federal flank or rear. He may, however, have read an omen of disaster in the crowding of so many bayonetted thousands on one wooded route, for his grip on his temper began to fail him. When General Jubal A. Early came up to be assigned to command and expressed his concern lest McClellan escape, Lee answered grimly and with some impatience, "Yes, he will get away because I cannot have my orders carried out!" His mind could not cease dwelling on the lost opportunity.[13]

A ride of two miles and a half down the Willis Church road with Jackson's division brought Lee to the northern foot of the Malvern Hills. It was a peaceful, sleepy landscape in normal times. Past cleared and cultivated fields, a straight dirt road climbed to the crest of a wide hill. Atop it, set back on either side, were two planters' homes, surrounded with shade trees, bathed a lustrous, shimmering green in the morning sun. At another season, the quiet beauty of the scene would have stirred the nature-loving Lee, but now his anxious eyes could not fail to see that it was just such a position as the Federals had chosen at Ellerson's Mill and behind Boatswain's Swamp. There was a similar difficult approach, through a forest of pines, oaks, and chestnut.[14] A little stream flowed in a swamp and a jungle, so

---

[12] O. R., 11, part 2, pp. 790, 794, 798, 811, 818.

[13] John Goode: Recollections of a Lifetime, 58. Early was placed in command of Elzey's brigade, Ewell's division, as General Elzey had been seriously wounded at Cold Harbor (O. R., 11, part 2, pp. 607, 611).

[14] 18 S. H. S. P., 60.

situated that as the troops marched southward to take position on
the centre and right, they would be jammed together where they

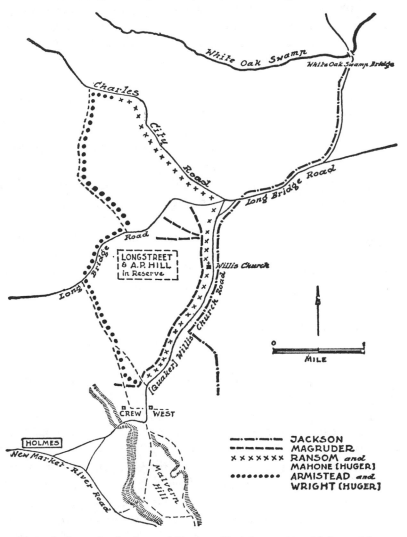

Lines of advance by the Army of Northern Virginia, morning of July 1, 1862.

could be extricated only with the greatest difficulty.[15] Beyond the
swamp, toward the enemy, the slowly rising, open ground afforded an ideal field of defense. The Federals had their guns

[15] Taylor in his *General Lee,* 78, attributed the slow formation of the Confederate
forces to this condition.

massed in a long crescent from west to northeast, with two lines
of infantry in support on that part of their line facing the Southern army. Most of their field artillery was placed in a lane running for a quarter of a mile, from the large, white Crew house
on the upper side of the ridge, eastward to the West house
across the Willis Church road. Beyond the West house other batteries guarded the Federal right. Every avenue of advance was
covered by the guns. On Lee's left the ground sloped gradually
to the rising sun. On his right, beyond the range of his vision,
the ridge fell abruptly away for fifty feet or more from the rear
of the Crew house to a meadow that skirted Malvern Hill for a
mile toward the James. This meadow had been planted in wheat,
which had been cut and placed in shocks, behind which Federal
sharpshooters were lurking. The enemy evidently was confident
that no attack could be successful on that flank, for all the guns,
most significantly, were trailed toward Lee's left.[16] It was, altogether, an exceedingly formidable position. Had the Union
engineers searched the whole countryside below Richmond, they
could not have found ground more ideally set for the slaughter
of an attacking army. It was a miniature Vimy Ridge, a Waterloo
with a protected flank.[17]

One sweep of the field with his glasses was enough to show Lee
the difficulty of attacking such a natural fortress. D. H. Hill had
not exaggerated its strength. Nothing could be accomplished unless the enemy was badly demoralized, and even then an attack
could not wisely be undertaken without a careful reconnaissance
to uncover the vulnerable part of the terrain. This reconnaissance,
of course, should be made at once. As the Confederate troops
were advancing slowly down the Willis Church road and would
certainly be delayed in their deployment, Lee sent Longstreet to
the right to study the ground and started toward the left himself.[18] At the time, however, he did not undertake a detailed examination of the land in that quarter. The reason for his failure to do so is not plain. He may have been too fatigued; he may
have assumed that Jackson would reconnoitre.

[16] *Longstreet*, 143. McClellan's only apprehension was for his right (1 *Report of the
Committee on the Conduct of the War*, 437).
[17] For a fuller description of the ground see Appendix II—4.
[18] *Longstreet*, 142.

In a short time Longstreet came back and reported. Magruder, he said, was far to the right on a road that he insisted was the Quaker road Lee had directed him to follow, when, in reality, Lee had intended him to march down the Willis Church road and take position to the right of it. Magruder was correct, so far as the usual local names of the roads were concerned. Lee had certainly said the "Quaker road," because he had been told that this was the name of the road on which the rest of the army was moving. It was sometimes so styled, but was more generally known as "Willis Church." The error, which was due to poor guides and poorer maps, meant that Magruder would be forced to make another troublesome countermarch. A staff officer was at once dispatched to correct the misunderstanding and to bring Magruder up.[19] As two of the brigades of Huger's division were already close at hand on the Willis Church road, Lee decided to place these brigades on Jackson's right, and he told Chilton to put Magruder in line to the right of Huger, a move of no small difficulty in the morass west of the Willis Church road.[20]

Longstreet reported, however, that on the right of the Confederate position, where Magruder was to form, he had found an admirable artillery position. It was on a little knoll at an elevation equalling that on which the Federal batteries were standing. From that knoll he had observed on the Confederate left a large open field that afforded a direct line of fire to the Union gun positions. Longstreet expressed the opinion that if the Confederate batteries were employed in full force on the knoll to the right and in the field to the left, they would bring to bear on the enemy a converging fire that would demoralize the Northern artillerists and open the way for the Confederate infantry, as shown on page 206.[21]

D. H. Hill had sent all his guns to the rear from White Oak Swamp, as his ammunition was entirely exhausted,[22] but the other

---

[19] *Longstreet,* 143; *O. R.,* 11, part 2, pp. 668, 675–77; 25 *S. H. S. P.,* 212–13. A casual reading of Longstreet, *loc. cit.,* would create the impression that Colonel Chilton was sent to Magruder, but that officer almost certainly went to Magruder later in the day. The "Quaker road" that was followed by Magruder ran southwestward into the New Market road from a point near the Enroughty house, about five-eighths of a mile eastward from the junction of the old Darbytown road with the Long Bridge road.

[20] *O. R.,* 11, part 2, pp. 496, 668.   [21] *Longstreet,* 143; *cf. O. R.,* 11, part 2, p. 496.

[22] *O. R.,* 11, part 2, pp. 653, 655.

divisional batteries were virtually intact and presumably nearby. The large force of reserve artillery, under General Pendleton, had now caught up with the army. It seemed perfectly feasible to con-

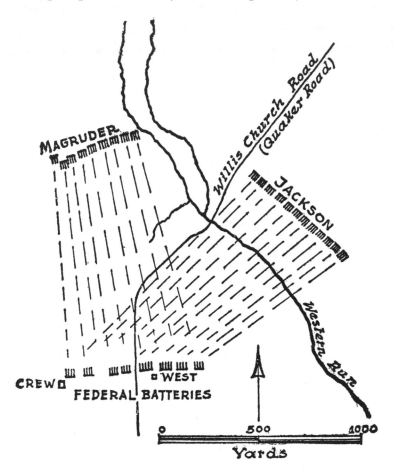

centrate ordnance as Longstreet suggested and to deliver one more blow at an enemy who apparently was inviting further punishment. In the absence of a better method of attack, and with no personal knowledge of conditions either on the Confederate right or on the left, Lee approved the plan. Longstreet was sent back to the right to locate the batteries on that flank; the pioneer corps was dispatched in the same direction to cut a road to the knoll; word was given Jackson to concentrate his artillery on the left.[23] When the Confederate guns had demoralized the enemy, all the infantry were to make a simultaneous assault and were to wrest Malvern Hill from the enemy.

Ere this plan of action had been determined upon, the enemy's artillery had opened all along the front. Very heavy shells were falling far within the right of the Confederate position—shell at first assumed to come from Federal gunboats in the James River but later found to be fired by a battery of Federal siege guns, slightly more than three-quarters of a mile in rear of the front Union artillery position.[24] Under this fire, heightened by that of many fieldpieces, Armistead and Wright of Huger's division, in accordance with Lee's instructions, made their way from the Long Bridge road to the right of the Willis Church road, under the north side of Malvern Hill, and were soon engaged with the enemy's skirmishers.

If the action was to be a heavy bombardment, followed by an assault all along the line, how was the order to be given? As it happened, the position that Armistead had taken was close to the knoll where the artillery was to be placed on the right. Until Magruder arrived, Armistead's brigade was, likewise, to form the extreme right of the front of attack. Its commander would consequently be the first to observe the effect of the proposed converging fire and the logical man to start the advance. Lee accordingly directed that if Armistead found the Confederate fire breaking the Union line, he was to charge with a yell. This was to be the signal for all the divisions to assault together. An order to this effect was prepared by Colonel Chilton.[25] It read as follows:

July 1, 1862.

Batteries have been established to rake the enemy's lines. If it is broken, as is probable, Armistead, who can witness the effect of the fire, has been ordered to charge with a yell. Do the same.

R. H. CHILTON,

Assistant Adjutant General.[26]

---

[23] O. R., 11, p. 558; Longstreet, 143.

[24] The Federal warships fired a few rounds, but their effective range was only 1320 yards (O. R., 11, part 3, p. 196). The ships' fire did as much execution in the Federal as in the Confederate ranks, and was quickly suspended (2 B. and L., 442; Longstreet, 141; 18 S. H. S. P., 64n.; O. R., 11, part 2, pp. 229, 238).

[25] 2 B. and L., 392.   [26] O. R., 11, part 2, p. 677.

This order was issued about 1:30 P.M.[27] and was entrusted to staff officers and couriers who had to wander through an unfamiliar jungle in order to deliver the paper to the division commanders. There was no telling how long it would take to do this, especially as Magruder had not yet returned from his march down the wrong road.

And now to bring up the artillery and to begin the bombardment! In thicket and swamp the infantry waited, some of the units well-covered, others sustaining not a few casualties. Minutes passed in suspense, for every one knew it would be slow work pulling guns through the tangle on the Confederate centre and right. At last, from the knoll behind Armistead, the sound of firing was heard. It was taken up on the left. Before men could do more than ask one another why the fire was so feeble, the Union guns answered with a defiant roar. In roaring crescendo the Federal batteries found their target. The whole of the Union position was billowing smoke. Not a moment's intermission was there in the overwhelming fire.[28] Presently word began to filter down the line that the Confederate guns were fast being silenced in an unequal exchange. Presently only the Union guns and an occasional weak reply from the Confederate side could be heard. On the right, as it subsequently developed, Armistead's guns had been far in the rear and substitute batteries had been called for. Only three had arrived. They had not opened simultaneously,[29] and were quickly blanketed.[30] On the left, where Jackson's chief of artillery was sick, fire had been started when two batteries were in position. One of these had been knocked to pieces; the other had been under shelter and had been able to send its missiles across the hill; two others were employed a little later and were well-fought, though the impression had somehow been created that all the batteries were to be withdrawn.[31] The reserve artil-

---

[27] D. H. Hill received it about 2 o'clock (*O. R.,* 11, part 2, p. 628). Garland was mistaken in saying (*ibid.,* 643) that it did not arrive until "late in the afternoon."

[28] As instancing the vigor of the Federal artillery-fire, it may be noted that Ames's battery of six guns, close to the Willis Church road, used 1300 rounds during the day (*O. R.,* 11, part 2, p. 253).

[29] Grimes's, Moorman's, and what was left of Pegram's (*O. R.,* 11, part 2, pp. 813, 819).

[30] *O. R.,* 11, part 2, pp. 802, 813.

[31] *O. R.,* 11, part 2, pp. 558, 562, 567, 573, 574.

lery did little or nothing.[32] Instead of one hundred guns, not more than twenty had been turned on the Federals at the same time. The preparatory bombardment, in short, was little more than a bloody farce, a futile sacrifice of some of the finest youth of Virginia. The "long arm of Lee," as Colonel Jennings C. Wise has aptly styled the artillery of the Army of Northern Virginia, was paralyzed in one of the most critical hours of need the army had thus far known. If the infantry advance depended on artillery preparation, there could be no general assault!

By 2:30 P.M., the first phase of the battle was over and the situation was this: The Federal artillery had not been shaken, and the Union infantry, except for some of the skirmishers, had not been engaged. Magruder was on the march to the right. He was ignorant of the progress of the battle and had not received Lee's orders about the bombardment or the attack that was to follow it, if practicable. Armistead, on the right of the line, had driven in the enemy's pickets,[33] and was loudly calling for more artillery. The other units that were to form the right centre were slowly untangling themselves from the swamp and baffling woods. Nobody on that wing seemed to know who was in command or whence orders were emanating.[34] Armistead did not realize that he was the ranking officer there. On the centre and the left, D. H. Hill's and Jackson's troops were forming, or in immediate reserve, but had no orders to attack. The few Confederate guns that had not been put out of action were continuing a vain fire. Confusion and uncertainty prevailed everywhere. Longstreet, and perhaps others, got the impression that no assault was to be made because of the strength of the Federal position.[35] But up the Willis Church road, at a pair of gateposts near the house of C. W. Smith, where Jackson had his headquarters,[36] Lee was waiting and pondering and planning. A tenacity

[32] Its commander, General Pendleton, had been sick on June 29 (*Pendleton*, 194), and he reported after the battle of July 1 was over that he spent the morning looking for General Lee, and the afternoon seeking vainly for some position where the heavy guns could be employed. "To remain near by . . ." he said, "and await events and orders, in readiness for whatever service might be called for, was all that I could do" (*O. R.*, 11, part 2, p. 536; E. P. Alexander to W. H. Taylor, Aug. 29, 1902, *Taylor MSS.*; cf. Colonel A. S. Cutts's comment in *O. R.*, 11, part 2, p. 547).

[33] *O. R.*, 11, part 2, pp. 818, 826.

[34] *O. R.*, 11, part 2, p. 697.   [35] *O. R.*, 11, part 2, p. 760.

[36] *O. R.*, 11, part 2, pp. 597, 818; E. A. Moore: *The Story of a Cannoneer under Stonewall Jackson* (cited hereafter as *E. A. Moore*), 89; 2 *B. and L.*, 408.

that he had never before had occasion to exhibit in battle showed itself, a tenacity that was to become one of his strongest military characteristics. He had pursued McClellan too long and at too heavy a cost to permit him to escape without one last challenge. If he had failed with his artillery, he would attempt a turning movement.

Summoning Longstreet, he rode hurriedly to the east to see if there was any point beyond the Federal flank from which he could advance and force McClellan to evacuate Malvern Hill. Arriving on the left, a hurried examination of the terrain convinced him that if high ground in that quarter could be seized he could accomplish his object. Had he looked more closely, he would have found a superb position, undefended by the enemy, where he could dispose his infantry, bring up his artillery and, by a swift, strong movement, not only force the evacuation of Malvern Hill but also, with good luck, cut off the enemy's retreat.[37]

How could Lee make this shift to the left? It was impossible of course, to move any of the troops then engaged with or immediately facing the enemy. But the two divisions of Longstreet and of A. P. Hill were in reserve, weary and with thinned ranks, yet still serviceable. They could be utilized. Quickly Lee ordered Longstreet to move these troops to the left. Longstreet, who seemed cool and unwearied after nearly a week's hard fighting, galloped off to bring them forward.[38]

Whiting with his division had long been waiting under shell fire, but as the ground gave them protection, only their artillery suffered seriously.[39] About this time, close to 4 o'clock, the Federal batteries suddenly ceased firing on Whiting's front. Soon a horseman galloped up from that officer to Lee, who was returning to the centre. Whiting, said the messenger, could see Federal baggage trains and troops in motion, apparently in retreat from the field.[40] Almost simultaneously, it would appear from

---

[37] *Longstreet*, 144. A slightly different version is given by the same author in 2 *B. and L.*, 403. Hood had seen the opportunity earlier in the day and had wished to attack but had been forbidden by Whiting.

[38] *Longstreet*, 144.

[39] *O. R.*, 11, part 2, pp. 557, 566, 593. Ewell's (*ibid.*, 607), and Jackson's divisions (*ibid.*, 557), were close at hand. ready in support.

[40] *O. R.*, 11, part 2, p. 566.

the vague and conflicting reports, Captain A. G. Dickinson brought word that Magruder had arrived on the right, and that Armistead had driven back a heavy force of the enemy and had gained an advantage that could be followed up.[41]

This news put the whole situation in a new light. It did not seem possible that the scattered Confederate artillery fire had broken the Federal line, but it might have demoralized the enemy. Armistead might have delivered a telling thrust on ground of which Lee had seen nothing and knew little. If the enemy was retreating in front of the Confederate left and was being driven on the Confederate right, then the course to follow obviously was to scrap the plan for a turning movement on the left and to attack on the whole front at once. Turning to Dickinson, who was Magruder's aide, Lee gave him verbal orders which the officer immediately wrote as follows:

"General Lee expects you to advance rapidly. He says it is reported the enemy is getting off. Press forward your whole command and follow up Armistead's successes. I will have Mahone's brigade in the place just occupied by Colonel Anderson. Ransom's brigade has gone on to re-enforce General Cobb. . . ."[42]

Similar orders doubtless were sent to the other division commanders unless, indeed, Lee reasoned that when they heard Armistead cheer and saw him start forward they would take this to be the signal for the general assault authorized by the orders of 1:30 P.M. and not countermanded. Longstreet, at least, quickly understood and halted his movement to the left.[43]

The centre of gravity in the battle now shifted to the right. Magruder had arrived there about 4 o'clock,[44] very hot but vigorous and in high spirits.[45] He found that Armistead had not received the additional artillery for which he had called but had repulsed the enemy's skirmishers about 3 o'clock and had then

[41] This message, if written, has been lost. Its content has to be reconstructed from the reply of Magruder's assistant-adjutant general, Captain A. G. Dickinson, who probably was the officer carrying the message to Lee. In *O. R.*, 11, part 2, p. 678, is a dispatch he sent Magruder by Lee's direction.

[42] *O. R.*, 11, part 2, pp. 677–78.

[43] *Longstreet*, 144. General Longstreet always thought (*cf. op. cit.*, 144–45), that the attack on the right originated because the order of 1:30 P.M. had not been countermanded, but he was mistaken. The attack, as the dispatch by Captain Dickinson plainly demonstrates, was formally ordered.

[44] *O. R.*, 11, part 2, p. 814.   [45] *W. W. Chamberlaine*, 25.

thrown forward three of his regiments.[46] Although these Virginians had rashly advanced too far ahead of the main position,
they had found some cover and had stubbornly held their
ground.[47] Sending immediately for his artillery,[48] Magruder, in
great excitement, began a characteristically reckless examination
of the ground. Almost before he could complete it, he received
for the first time the order Lee had sent him about 1:30 P.M., telling him to advance at the sound of Armistead's cheering if the
artillery preparation broke the enemy's line. As this paper did
not carry the time of its dispatch, it was accepted by Magruder as
a current order.[49] He set to work immediately to prepare for its
execution, in the midst of an intensified bombardment, turned on
him from the left as well as from the batteries in his front. Ere
he could complete his dispositions, a courier brought him the
message written a short time previously by Captain Dickinson.[50]

Magruder was fully conscious of the inadequacy of his artillery
and before attacking he was anxious to get into position the guns
for which he had sent, but he did not consider that Lee's repeated
orders justified him in further delay.[51] Making another quick
reconnaissance, he determined to assault the front of the Crew
house hill and, simultaneously, to move troops down the flank of
the hill into the edge of the wheat field so that he could attack
from the west, also, under the brow of the hill. It was a desperately dangerous manœuvre when unsupported by artillery, and it
would never have been approved by Lee if he had seen the
ground, but it seemed to Magruder the only course to follow in
obeying instructions that he regarded as peremptory.

Magruder had at hand Armistead's, Wright's, and Mahone's
brigades of Huger's division. G. T. Anderson's, Semmes's, and
Barksdale's brigades of his own command were within striking
distance on his right. Cobb's brigade was in support of Armistead,
and Kershaw was some distance to the rear. The combined
strength of these troops was around 15,000.[52]

---

[46] The 14th, 38th, and 53d Virginia. The position of the 53d is vague in Armistead's
report, which seems to locate it in two places simultaneously (*O. R.*, 11, part 2, p. 819),
but the report of Colonel H. B. Tomlin, *ibid.*, 828–29, indicated that it shared in this
major skirmish.

[47] *O. R.*, 11. part 2, p. 819. [48] *O. R.*, 11, part 2, p. 669.
[49] *Ibid.* [50] *Ibid.*
[51] *O. R.*, 11, part 2, p 669. [52] *O. R.*, 11, part 2, p. 669.

Wright's brigade from the Gulf states had been skirmishing heavily for some hours and was somewhat scattered. The Virginians of Mahone were fresh, though one of his regiments was temporarily lost.[53] About 4:15 Wright carefully advanced his main line to the position of his skirmishers, under the shelter of the Crew house hill, and at 4:45 he received the order to advance.[54] Up from the depression sprang the sweating troops, with Mahone's brigade in support, full of the ardor of 1862 that made all the Confederates regard an infantry charge on a battery as the supreme glory of war.

Almost as soon as the line started forward the Federal gunners redoubled their fire. Ere long the supporting Federal infantry could make its musketry count. Wright's ranks were torn, Mahone's were thinned. Armistead's men, rallied by the appearance of troops on their right, swept onward.[55] Every foot of advance brought heavier casualties. Still the men kept on until they were within 300 yards of the Federal gunners and in danger of being cut off by a force of Union soldiers that was deploying as if to flank them. Wright halted, changed front, and engaged this new enemy. The fighting was close, and the cross-fire enough to shake the morale of veterans. Every discharge of the nearby Federal guns made the earth tremble under the panting Confederates.[56] Nothing could be seen of other Confederate troops engaged on either flank. Magruder's main line was 1000 yards in rear. To the men of the attacking brigades, it seemed as if they had been sent out alone, to make a futile, unsupported charge, and then to be killed off, one by one, huddled under the edge of the hill.[57] They began to waver as they feverishly loaded and fired. It could be only a matter of minutes before they would break for the rear —to be wiped out as they ran.

Just then there came the roll of nervous musketry on the left, and soon D. H. Hill's division was seen advancing from the Con-

---

[53] *W. W. Chamberlaine,* 25.

[54] *O. R.,* 11, part 2, p. 814. The Federals who were awaiting this attack, confident of the strength of the position, were from left to right, Morrell's first division of Porter's V Corps, Couch's first division of Keyes's IV Corps, Sickles's second brigade of Hooker's second division, Heintzelman's III Corps and Meagher's second brigade of Sumner's II Corps. The artillery was chiefly the army reserve, under Hunt.

[55] 18 *S. H. S. P.,* 65; *O. R.,* 11, part 2, pp. 824, 826.

[56] 18 *S. H. S. P.,* 61–62.

[57] *O. R.,* 11, part 2, p. 800.

federate centre, on either side of the Willis Church road.[58] Hill had heard cheering as Wright and Mahone had advanced, and he had taken this to be the signal for the charge that Armistead was to have initiated in accordance with the original plan of attack.[59] As quickly as might be, in a jungle of forest and vines, swamps and underbrush, where the voice of command could be heard only a few paces,[60] D. H. Hill had pushed all his brigades forward,[61] and now they were advancing up an incline of 700 or 800 yards[62] that designing Nature seemed to have set at that very point to lure on the incautious. The grade was so gradual that it did not discourage the attacking force, but all of it was exposed, and the ground nearest the Federals had been ploughed.[63] The enemy had an almost perfect field of fire.[64]

Inspired by the appearance of Hill's men, Armistead made still another attempt. Wright and Mahone dashed across the shoulder of a ridge and reached a hollow not more than seventy-five yards from the enemy. They were now so near the steep brow of the hill that the men had to kneel to load, and exposed their heads to the enemy every time they rose to fire.[65]

Hill's division by this time was feeling the full, blasting force of the Union shell and canister. The Confederate gunners could not interrupt this fire, much less silence it, because very little of Magruder's artillery, though it was close by, could be brought into position.[66] Garland's brigade, distinguished at Gaines's Mill, covered 400 of the 800 yards to the Federal batteries and then had to lie down and await reinforcements.[67] Colonel John B. Gordon of Georgia, destined to larger fame, led Rodes's brigade forward in the absence of its sick commander, and brought it within 200 yards of the nearest battery—only to be compelled to halt. The colors of the 3d Alabama were both symbol and target in Gor-

---

[58] O. R., 11, part 2, p. 814.

[59] It has been assumed that D. H. Hill ordered his advance when he heard the cheer that Armistead's skirmishers raised when they took their advanced position, but Hill's statement that this was "about an hour and a half before sundown" (O. R., 11, part 2, p. 628), makes it plain that it was the advance of Wright and Mahone, followed by Armistead's attempt at a new charge, that sent D. H. Hill forward. This fits in perfectly with the sequence of events given in Wright's report, ibid., 814.

[60] O. R., 11, part 2, p. 650.   [61] O. R., 11, part 2, p. 628.

[62] Including the southern edge of the wood, which was under fire.

[63] O. R., 11, part 2, p. 643.   [64] O. R., 11, part 2, pp. 635, 643.

[65] 18 S. H. S. P., 66.   [66] O. R., 11, part 2, p. 747.

[67] O. R., 11, part 2, p. 643.

don's advance. Six men were shot down carrying the flag, the staff itself was shattered, and the bunting literally cut to bits. The seventh color-bearer brought off only a part of the staff.[68] Ripley advanced with the other brigades and like them had to stop. Colquitt was brought to a standstill; G. B. Anderson could not reach the batteries that were decimating his North Carolinians.[69]

Lee had gone to Magruder's front soon after the attack began and was now with General McLaws, one of Magruder's division commanders. On receipt of a call from Magruder he undertook to hasten McLaws's men to the support of Armistead, Mahone, and Wright.[70] Could all Magruder's troops be thrown immediately into action, while D. H. Hill's attack was occupying the Federal centre, there was still a chance that the Federal right might be stormed, impregnable though its position seemed. But the chance seemed remote. Most of the reserves on the right were exhausted by hunger and hard marching and had suffered heavily from straggling.[71] Semmes's brigade of McLaws's division could muster only 557 muskets, and Kershaw had only 956. As they advanced from the northwest across Carter's field, the two brigades became separated and lost touch with each other.[72] Cobb's strong brigade of 2700 men had only 1500 left after a day and a half on the road, though it had suffered few casualties.[73] However, they must be thrown into the battle now.

The confusion was maddening. Magruder, unaware of Lee's proximity, thought he was about to be attacked and hurriedly called on Longstreet for reinforcements. Longstreet started A. P. Hill toward him and moved his own division to protect Magruder's right flank.[74] Ransom, who had been attached to Huger, had already been called upon by Magruder for help, but refused for a long time to move without Huger's approval.[75] Barksdale and G. T. Anderson, of Magruder's command, encountered a rain of shell as they attempted to go on.[76] As far as the general advance of this attacking wing of the army could be said to have taken form at this time, it was soon drifting so far to the left that

---

[68] O. R., 11, part 2, p. 635.
[70] O. R., 11, part 2, p. 680.
[72] O. R., 11, part 2, p. 719.
[74] O. R., 11, part 2, p. 760.
[76] O. R., 11, part 2, pp. 705, 751.
[69] O. R., 11, part 2, p. 628.
[71] O. R., 11, part 2, p. 719.
[73] O. R., 11, part 2, pp. 748-50.
[75] O. R., 11, part 2, p. 795.

Lee had to send word to Magruder to press more to his right.[77] This order served only to confuse the excited Magruder still more,[78] though he strove his utmost to change direction.

D. H. Hill, meantime, had called for reinforcements from Jackson, whose men had done nothing all day except support the artillery that was firing on the Federal left. Whiting seems to have felt that the attack was confined to the Confederate right; Jackson apparently regarded the Union position in his front as impregnable.[79] He had, however, already ordered up that part of Ewell's division in reserve and had sent back word for his own division to move forward.[80] But the Willis Church road, the only direct avenue of approach, was crowded with artillery and fugitives and was almost impassable.[81] As General Early tried to carry his brigade toward D. H. Hill's right, by moving in rear of the centre brigades, he encountered so many skulkers and disorganized troops that he lost touch with his own men.[82]

The clear, hot day[83] was about to end. The steady breeze, which had tempered the sun's heat on the Federal position, had cleared the air. Sounds were more distinct, the fighting seemed closer.[84] The mist of evening was beginning to rise from the wheat field on the eastern edge of which Mahone and Wright were still desperately struggling.[85] The last moment was at hand when a Confederate victory could possibly be wrested from the chaos of a costly contest. Would the climax of Gaines's Mill be repeated in a sudden, resistless charge at twilight, with every brigade somehow finding its place in the line of battle?

The confident roar of the unwearied Federal batteries gave a mocking answer. The move on the left that Whiting had taken as a sign of retreat had not weakened the enemy's resistance. Toombs's brigade came up in support of D. H. Hill. It reached the crest of the hill, broke in blood and then flowed back to the woods. Garland had shot his bolt.[86] Even Gordon had retreated. Fire from bewildered troops in their rear was adding to the losses of Ripley and of Kershaw.[87] Winder and Trimble were

77 O. R., 11, part 2, p. 680.   78 O. R., 11, part 2, p. 671.
79 O. R., 11, part 2, pp. 558, 566, 567, 587, 597–98; Hood, 30–31.
80 O. R., 11, part 2, p. 557.   81 O. R., 11, part 2, p. 576.
82 O. R., 11, part 2, p. 612–13.   83 W. W. Chamberlaine, 24; 2 B. and L., 417n.
84 33 S. H. S. P., 116.   85 O. R., 11, part 2, p. 275.
86 O. R., 11, part 2, p. 643.   87 O. R., 11, part 2, pp. 659, 728–29.

pressing their men forward through the woods.[88] Ewell was
crashing furiously in a jungle.[89] All these troops were moving as
rapidly as the ground permitted, but none of them could hope to
reach the line in time to support the assault before night fell.[90]

On the right, by this time, Magruder's weary reserve brigades
were coming into action, but they were now under an artillery
fire that wrecked or demoralized them. Most of them opened
their volleys too soon and too high.[91] Few of them got to grips
with the foe. Semmes's brigade, facing musketry from friends on
its flank, had to withdraw.[92] Only Ransom, late to start in answer
to Magruder's repeated appeals, got close enough to give any real
assistance to Wright and Mahone, and he attacked almost west
of the Crew house, on ground that would have been a slaughter
pen had not the mist somewhat obscured his movement. Unsus-
tained and uninstructed, his men stormed within twenty yards
of the enemy's guns and then fell back to the position from which
they had charged.[93] The gory remnants of Wright's and Mahone's brigades were facing over the brow of the Crew house an
enemy that seemed strong enough to smother them and was, besides, well protected by the undulations of the ground.[94] Armistead, who had advanced before Mahone and Wright and then
had charged with them, delivered three more assaults.[95] There
was a moment when the furious onslaught of these few men
made the issue doubtful. One of the finest of the Union batteries
was forced to limber up when the Confederates got within
revolver range.[96] Griffin's Federal brigade, which had borne the
heaviest of the infantry fight, was compelled to give ground.[97]
An hour more of daylight and a little more vigor on the part of
Magruder's weary troops might have spelled a triumph as incredible as that of Missionary Ridge.[98] But it was too late. Dark-

88 *O. R.,* 11, part 2, pp. 558, 571–72.
89 *O. R.,* 11, part 2, pp. 607, 729.   90 *O. R.,* 11, part 2, pp. 628–29.
91 *O. R.,* 11, part 2, pp. 208, 815.   92 *O. R.,* 11, part 2, p. 724.
93 *O. R.,* 11, part 2, p. 795.   94 *O. R.,* 11, part 2, p. 275.
95 Armistead said four times, Cabell and Bernard said three (*O. R.,* 11, part 2, pp.
824, 826; 18 *S. H. S. P.,* 65. *Cf.* P. F. Brown: *Reminiscences of the War of 1861–1865,*
pp. 19–20).
96 *O. R.,* 11, part 2, p. 357.   97 *O. R.,* 11, part 2, p. 314; *cf. ibid.,* 295.
98 *Cf.* Hunt in 1 *Report of the Committee on the Conduct of the War,* 574: "The battle frequently trembled in the balance. The last attack was made with all their forces and
was very nearly successful. We won from the fact that we kept our reserves in hand for
just such an attack. . . . I cannot say that our victory was so very decisive."

ness had now settled. Hill's division withdrew; Magruder's supporting brigades returned as they had come; only Wright and Mahone clung to their most advanced position. The assault had been "grandly heroic" on the right, as D. H. Hill subsequently wrote in apology for early strictures on Magruder, but "it was not war—it was murder."[99]

The field was in the utmost confusion and the moonless night was red and glowing from the long-continued fire of the artillery[100] when Lee had at last to admit to himself that the day had ended in failure. No one knew where the troops were, or what they would face on the morrow. Only those wounded who were lying close to the Confederate position could be succored, for fear of new collisions with the enemy. When the artillery finally ceased between 9 and 10 P.M., the heart-breaking calls from agonizing boys on the hillside gave the night a ghastly terror rivalling that of the day.[101]

Wearily and with a heavy heart, Lee made such dispositions as he could for the safety of the lines and the comfort of the fallen. He realized fully that he had made a mistake in permitting the right wing of the army to attack a position the strength of which he had not known until he had arrived on that part of the line after the general assault had begun. He probably wondered why Magruder had not sent to him and reported the hopelessness of a charge on that flank. As he rode sadly among the bivouacs he found Magruder, who was just preparing to lie down on blankets that had been spread for him.

"General Magruder," he asked, "why did you attack?"

Magruder answered unhesitatingly: "In obedience to your orders, twice repeated."

Lee said nothing in reply, for there was nothing to say. The orders had been issued and if Magruder had felt it his duty to obey them, without waiting to explain, discipline came before discretion.[102]

---

[99] 2 B. and L., 394.   [100] Dabney, 472.

[101] The confusion on the right was so great that a Federal detachment crept forward to a house and captured a Confederate officer and twenty-three men (O. R., 11, part 2, p. 364).

[102] For Lee's visit to Magruder, see John Lamb in 25 S. H. S. P., 217. Captain Lamb in this paper did not quote the conversation between Lee and Magruder, but in recounting the circumstances to the writer he repeatedly employed the language quoted in the text, and insisted on its literal accuracy. He was with Magruder at the time of this interview

As the night wore on, to the wild accompaniment of the cries of the wounded, Stuart came up after a long ride from the Chickahominy and reported that his cavalry were bivouacked not far from the line of possible Federal retreat down the river. He was ordered to await developments.[103] If any report at all came from Holmes that night, it was to the effect that he had been unable to advance against a Federal position dominated by strong artillery and well-guarded by infantry.[104]

Midnight brought alarums. General Early distinctly heard the rumbling of wheels, indicating a movement of the enemy's artillery.[105] Jackson, who had gone to bed very sleepy, was aroused at 1 A.M. by his division commanders, who wished to know what dispositions to make in case McClellan took the offensive at daylight. Jackson was very indifferent and asked few questions. "No," he said, when asked if he wished to give any orders, "I think he will clear out in the morning." And he went back to sleep.[106] If Lee troubled a weary mind for answer to the same vexing question of the enemy's movement on the morrow, he probably was of like opinion, but with the sickening reflection that though McClellan had been forced to abandon his lines under the very shadows of Richmond's spires, and had been struck hard and often, he had escaped the destruction Lee had planned for him.

as temporary aide, and was arranging the General's blankets while Lee talked with Magruder. It was whispered after the battle that Magruder had been drunk during the action (T. R. R. Cobb in 28 *S. H. S. P.*, 293), but Magruder's surgeon (*O. R.*, 11, part 2, pp. 682–83) and Captain Lamb (*loc. cit.*) both denied this flatly.

[103] *O. R.*, 11, part 2, pp. 497, 518.   [104] *O. R.*, 11, part 2, pp. 908, 914, 915.
[105] *O. R.*, 11, part 2, p. 613.   [106] *Mrs. Jackson*, 299.

CHAPTER XVIII

"The Federal Army Should Have Been Destroyed"

A heavy mist as wet as rain hung over the battlefield when July 2 dawned. From the Confederate side it was impossible to tell whether the enemy still held Malvern Hill or had retired.[1] Lee's brigades were still hopelessly confused. Commanders did not know where their men were; men could not find their officers.[2] As it grew lighter, three thin regiments of Early's brigade were visible near the centre in the open field. To their right lay not more than a dozen weary men, Armistead among them. A little farther around the Crew house hill, with their faces still toward the enemy, were the remnants of Wright's and Mahone's brigades, stoutly holding the ground they had won under the muzzles of the Federal guns.[3] Elsewhere, over the field of the charge, only the victims of the slaughter were to be seen amid the debris of the battle. "A third of them were dead," attested a Federal officer who stood not far away, "but enough were alive and moving to give the field a singular crawling effect. The different stages of the ebbing tide are often marked by the lines of flotsam and jetsam left along the seashore. So here could be seen three distinct lines . . . marking the last front of three Confederate charges of the night before."[4]

On the crest of the hill a mixed Federal force of cavalry and infantry was waiting. It made a show of advance, but drew back at the first fire of scattered Confederates. A few score of Huger's men came up about this time and at Early's instance reported to Armistead. From the woods the ambulance details began to trickle slowly out; officers rode forward; soon an informal truce prevailed and thousands of hungry, restless men emerged from the woods to search for missing comrades or to look for food in the

---

[1] *Dabney*, 474; *Long*, 176; 2 *B. and L.*, 431. [2] *O. R.*, 11, part 2, p. 619.
[3] *Early*, 82–83.
[4] General W. W. Averell in 2 *B. and L.*, 432.

haversacks of the fallen.[5] Shattered bodies were everywhere and dead men in every contortion of their last agony. Weapons and the keepsakes of soldiers, caps and knapsacks, playing-cards and pocket testaments, bloody heads with bulging eyes, booted legs, severed arms with hands gripped tight, torsos with the limbs blown away, gray coats dyed black with boys' blood—it was a nightmare of hell, set on a firm, green field of reality, under a workaday, leaden, summer sky, a scene to sicken the simple, home-loving soldiers who had to fight the war while the politicians responsible for bringing a nation to madness stood in the streets of safe cities and mouthed wrathful platitudes about constitutional rights.

Toward 10 o'clock, after the mist had turned into a cold and drenching rain,[6] the last of the Federals disappeared. At the Poindexter house, where he probably had spent the night, Lee received reports. Once again he had to ask the question, where had McClellan betaken himself? An immediate Federal offensive against Richmond could of course be left out of consideration, inasmuch as the Federals were in retreat. Eliminating that, there were three possibilities: The enemy might be nearby, preparing to refit and again offer battle; he might be retiring farther down the river to take ship and renew the struggle on some other front; or, lastly, he might be about to pass over the James, as he had crossed the Chickahominy, unite with Burnside's army from North Carolina, capture Drewry's Bluff and open the way for his men-of-war to reach Richmond. There had been some disquieting and rather mysterious activity on the James during the battles of the Seven Days. The War Department was concerned, especially as Drewry's had been almost stripped of men when Holmes had been moved to the north side of the James.[7]

Canvassing these possibilities, Lee determined: (1) to send the cavalry immediately in pursuit; (2) to move a part of the army down the James to be at hand if the enemy proved aggressive, and (3) to return Holmes to Drewry's Bluff at once. Orders were

---

[5] O. R., 11, part 2, p. 613; Early, 84; 2 B. and L., 432.
[6] O. R., 11, part 2, p. 383; Early, 85; 2 B. and L., 432; Livermore, 99, W. W. Chamberlaine, 26. McClellan stated (O. R., 11, part 1, p. 72), that where he was, on James River, the storm began at 4 A.M.
[7] O. R., 11, part 3, p. 623 ff.

issued accordingly, and President Davis was so advised by letter.[8]

As Jackson was nearest the line of the Federal retreat and had suffered least in the campaign, he was ordered to leave D. H. Hill's battered division at Malvern Hill and to move against the enemy with the rest of his force.[9] Longstreet and A. P. Hill were to follow.[10] The remaining units of the army were to remain for the time in their positions, burying the dead, caring for the wounded, and collecting arms and accoutrements from the field.[11]

The rain was falling very heavily by the time these orders were issued. Every officer who came to report was streaming. The downpour already was changing the bottom-lands into a miry pond, miles wide.[12] Jackson's men were ready but wet and had been directed to build fires, to cook, and to dry their clothing.[13] Longstreet and A. P. Hill were preparing to make their way through the still-disorganized forces on the Confederate centre. The enemy also must be suffering. Persons in the neighborhood whom Jackson had interviewed earlier in the morning told him that the Federals were retreating down the River road in the greatest demoralization. He so reported to Lee, when he called at the Poindexters'.[14] Stuart's information was to the same effect.[15] The opportunity seemed great if the endurance of the men sufficed and the deluge did not prevent pursuit.

Jackson remained with Lee by the fire in the dining room of the plantation house until his men could take the road. Presently Longstreet came in. Lee was dictating to Taylor at the moment, but he was interrupted by the newcomer.

"General," said Longstreet, brusquely, "are you sending any one to Richmond today?"

"Yes," answered Lee, "an orderly will set out soon; can we do anything for you?"

"Yes, send Mrs. Longstreet word I am alive yet; she is up at Lynchburg."

[8] *Lee's Dispatches*, 22–24. [9] *O. R.*, 11, part 2, p. 559.
[10] *O. R.*, 11, part 2, p. 760.
[11] Longstreet, *op. cit.*, 146, said that Magruder and Huger were to follow Jackson, but there is no confirmation of this. The report of Colonel James D. Nance of Kershaw's brigade, Magruder's division (*O. R.*, 11, part 2, p. 739), and that of General Armistead or Huger's division contain no mention of any orders to move until July 3. The other reports are silent.
[12] *O. R.*, 11, part 2, p. 218. [13] *Dabney*, 474.
[14] *Dabney*, 474–75. [15] *O. R.*, 11, part 2, p. 519.

Lee was a little embarrassed: it did not accord with his ideas of the social amenities to have a message to the wife of a high officer telegraphed by an orderly. "Oh, General Longstreet," he said in his most polished tones, "will you not write yourself? Is it not due to your good lady after these tremendous events?"

Longstreet threw himself into a chair and dashed off a few lines, which he duly delivered.

Lee resumed the conversation: "General, has your morning's ride led you to see anything of the scene of awful struggle of the afternoon?"

"Yes, General, I rode over pretty much all of the line of the fighting."

"What are your impressions?" Lee inquired.

"I think you hurt them about as much as they hurt you."

That was not to Lee's liking: equal losses were not gain. There was a bit of irony, almost a twang, in his voice as he replied, "Then I am glad we punished them well, at any rate."[16]

Longstreet was not cheerful, however, despite his claim. The weather and the condition of the troops both depressed him. After awhile he sloshed out in his wet garments. Lee was left with Jackson and a few officers of their staffs, pondering still the plan of pursuit.

Soon another visitor came in—the President, attended by his brother, Colonel Joseph Davis. The chief executive had been scouring the country in an effort to find whiskey for the wet and exhausted men,[17] and his coming was so unexpected that Lee forgot part of his usual address.

"President," he said (not Mr. President), "I am delighted to see you."

They shook hands; Davis looked about him; his glance rested on Jackson, whom he had never met. "Stonewall" bristled at the sight of the President, because he considered Davis had been unjust to him in the controversy over the Romney expedition. All that Jackson did, after rising, was to stand stiffly at attention.

"Why," said Lee, "President, don't you know General Jackson? This is our Stonewall Jackson."

[16] Memorandum of R. H. Dabney for G. F. R. Henderson, May 7, 1896, MS.—McGuire Papers.
[17] 2 Davis, 149.

Davis saw that the General was not disposed to accept advances, so he merely bowed. "Old Jack" saluted and said nothing.[18]

Sitting down with the President at the table, Lee reviewed the military outlook. When Davis made what seemed to be an impracticable proposal, Lee listened courteously and then explained why it could not be carried out. To Jackson's staff officers, treated to this rare sight of a confidential discussion between the commander-in-chief and the commanding general of the army, it seemed that Lee had an easy ascendancy over the mind of Davis.[19]

As the two talked, the rain continued mercilessly, a heavier downpour than ever. The more the situation was considered, the more confused it appeared. At last Lee and Davis agreed that the weather and the uncertainty of the army made effective pursuit impracticable that day.[20] Jackson sat silent as the reasons for this regrettable decision were canvassed, and when he was asked for his opinion, he only remarked quietly, "They have not all got away if we go immediately after them."[21] But his eyes were flashing and his military instincts were in rebellion.[22] He believed that the enemy could and should be pursued, for his experience with a retreating enemy persuaded him that McClellan was beaten and not merely retiring for new manœuvres.

Undoubtedly Jackson was right regarding the condition of the enemy, but insistence on a swift pursuit, in such weather, was the counsel of perfection.[23] The Army of Northern Virginia, at the close of the action at Malvern Hill, was in the condition in

---

[18] H. H. McGuire to Jed Hotchkiss, May 28, 1896, MS.—*McGuire Papers.*
[19] McGuire Papers, *loc. cit.*   [20] Dabney Memorandum, *loc. cit.*
[21] 2 *Davis*, 150.   [22] McGuire Papers, *loc. cit.*
[23] Had pursuit been practicable, there is little doubt that McClellan might have been subjected to heavy losses, even though the proximity of his gunboats would have prevented any such Confederate triumph as was later pictured by those who were wise after the event. A large part of the Union wagon train was still moving. Many of the Federal troops were badly demoralized. Examination made the next day of the route of their retreat showed greater evidence of disorganization and panic than after any other battle of the Seven Days. The hurrying soldiers trampled flat a field of standing wheat at Shirley, in their haste to avoid delay on the crowded road, and in this same field they threw away 925 rifles (*O. R.,* 11, part 2, p. 739). "It was like the retreat of a whipped army," General Joseph Hooker subsequently testified, ". . . and a few shots from the rebels would have panic-stricken the whole command" (1 *Committee on the Conduct of the War,* 580; *cf. O. R.,* 11, part 2, pp. 629, 678–79). But this was the condition of only a part of the army. Heintzelman's Corps had suffered heavily but it reached the shelter of the guns early on the 2d, without the loss of a wagon (*O. R.,* 11, part 2, p. 103). Although Keyes's wagon train was still exposed, he affirmed that his men were never more formidable than in this last phase of the retreat (*O. R.,* 11, part 2, p. 195). Sumner's

which both it and the Army of the Potomac were to find themselves after nearly every major engagement of the next two years.
The adversary put up so good a battle, winning or losing, that the
opposing army was exhausted and incapable of pursuit. The margin of superiority was so narrow, on either side, that a victory
could rarely be developed into a triumph. The best evidence that
this was the case after Malvern Hill is the fact that Longstreet
and A. P. Hill, who certainly could not be accused of slacking at
any stage of the campaign, were able to make only two miles
across the front through the storm of July 2.[24]

The rain ceased on the morning of July 3,[25] and the pursuit
began down the New Market-River road. It had hardly started
before Lee learned from Stuart that the Federals had already
reached Harrison's Landing, eight miles down the James from
the Confederate position at Malvern Hill. The main road was
muddy, horribly cut up, exposed for part of the way to possible
fire from Federal gunboats in the James, and was said to have
been obstructed by the enemy. From the north, the approach was
so much better in every respect that Lee determined to change his
line of advance, to avoid the New Market-River road as far as possible, and to carry his columns back up the Willis Church road
and then to distribute them over roads leading southward. This
unfortunately threw all the troops on the Willis Church road for
a distance of two and a half miles. Jackson was in advance, with
Longstreet following, but as Longstreet had consistently out-
marched Jackson during the campaign, Lee ordered Jackson to
halt and to give the road to Longstreet.[26]

Lee remained at the Poindexter house to await developments.
Rumors were current that McClellan was preparing a great shift
across the James, but Stuart's dispatches, arriving every few hours,
indicated no such movement on the enemy's part.[27] Lee's judgment was on the side of Stuart's observation. The misgivings he

corps was on the James by daylight on July 1 and only two of his brigades were in action
that day (*O. R.*, 11, part 2, p. 52). Franklin's corps was already safe (*O. R.*, 11, part 2,
p. 431).
[24] *O. R.*, 11, part 2, p. 760. [25] *Early*, 85.
[26] Dabney, *op. cit.*, 475–76, explained the change of route but did not give all the
reasons for it. Longstreet, *op. cit.*, 146, indicated that his march on July 2 was via the
northern roads, but his position on the night of July 2 (*O. R.*, 11, part 2, p. 760) would
make it appear that he was mistaken.
[27] *Cf. O. R.*, 11, part 2, p. 520.

had felt on the 2d disappeared almost entirely, and he concluded that it was hardly possible for McClellan to effect a crossing and to organize a new advance on the south side of the James. However, as it was doubtful whether the whole of the army could be employed against McClellan in his new position, Lee decided to hold most of the troops of Huger, of Magruder, and of D. H. Hill at Malvern Hill, whence they could be moved easily down the James or, if needed, to the right bank of that stream.[28] The reserve artillery was ordered back to positions nearer Richmond.[29] It was useless where it was and could not be convieniently furnished with supplies.

After reporting to the President on the state of affairs, Lee on July 3 made only one or two minor detachments of force. He dispatched a few troops to the vicinity of his mother's nearby girhood home, Shirley, probably in answer to a message from Colonel T. R. R. Cobb of the cavalry, who sent word that, if he were reinforced, he believed he could cut off the rear wagon train of the Federals. Unfortunately, the troops sent to support him did not establish contact with the cavalry.[30] Another detachment was ordered in the same direction to collect the arms the Federals had discarded.[31] Later in the afternoon, Stuart announced that he had held the high ground north of the Federal position until driven off about 2 P.M. by a superior force. He had hoped that Longstreet and Jackson would come up in time to occupy the position in force but they had not arrived.[32] Longstreet, as a matter of fact, had missed his road but he reached the front of the enemy before nightfall. Jackson, following Longstreet, could only cover three miles that day—proof enough that he was mistaken in his belief on the 2d that a rapid pursuit was practicable.[33]

Lee's first care on the morning of July 4 was to send D. R. Jones's division of Magruder's command down the river to Longstreet's support.[34] This done, Lee rode forward to examine McClellan's position. He had not gone far before he received an

[28] *Lee's Dispatches*, 24–25.　　　　[29] *O. R.*, 11, part 2, p. 537.
[30] *O. R.*, 11, part 2, pp. 524, 819.　　[31] *O. R.*, 11, part 2, p. 739.
[32] *Cf. O. R.*, 11, part 2, p. 520.

[33] *Dabney*, 476; *O. R.*, 11, part 2, p. 761. There seems to be no justification for the strictures Hotchkiss makes in 3 *C. M. H.*, 301, on Longstreet's march. Major Hotchkiss was mistaken regarding some of the facts.

[34] *O. R.*, 11, part 2, p. 713; *cf. Longstreet*, 146. In his report, Jones did not mention this advance.

urgent request from Longstreet to join him.[35] On arrival he found part of the army drawn up in line of battle—A. P. Hill on the right and Jackson in the centre, with Longstreet in support. D. R. Jones, as his men came up, was taking position on the left. Longstreet, as senior division commander, had made these dispositions, with the intention of recovering the high ground, known as Evelington Heights, which Stuart had been forced to give up the previous day. The Federal skirmishers had been driven in, but Jackson had protested that his men were in no condition to attack and had requested that the advance be not ordered till Lee could be consulted.[36]

Lee was much disappointed to learn that no opportunity of striking the enemy had been found,[37] and he proceeded at once and on foot to reconnoitre.[38] The Federals' ground had been chosen with the same care that had been displayed in the selection of all McClellan's defensive positions during the campaign. Harrison's Landing was on a long, low promontory extending into the James River. On the west was a small stream known as Kimmage's Creek. From a point about a mile east of this stream, Herring Creek meandered eastward for some three miles through a swamp and thence turned southward into the James. Opposite the low ground, along the two creeks, Federal gunboats lay in the river, with the batteries trained across the meadows. North of Herring Creek the River road[39] ran from east to west across a ridge that dominated the fields where the Union troops were resting. This ridge was Evelington Heights, for the recovery of which Longstreet had prepared his line of battle.[40] Stuart had learned on the night of the 2d that the Federals had incautiously neglected to occupy the heights in strength, and on the morning

---

[35] O. R., 11, part 2, p. 761.

[36] Longstreet, 146. Jackson stated in his report (O. R., 11, part 2, p. 559), that he "arrived near the landing and drove in the enemy's skirmishers" on the morning of the 3d, but this is clearly a lapsus. All the other reports that mention dates give the 4th (cf. O. R., 11, part 2, pp. 568, 587, 588, 590, 607, 619, 622). The reason Jackson protested that his men were not in condition to attack doubtless was that they had been marching since dawn. A hard march was necessary to bring them into position early in the day.

[37] Dabney, 476.

[38] 2 Henderson, 472. Colonel Henderson, following Jackson's report, was one day in error in his chronology.

[39] In his reports, Lee called it the Charles City road.

[40] The best general description of the ground is that of General J. G. Barnard in 1 Report of the Committee on the Conduct of the War, 409 ff.

of the 3d he had seized them. Instead, however, of concealing his
cavalry until the infantry arrived, he had boldly opened fire with
the solitary howitzer attached to his command. This, of course,
had given the alarm without inflicting any appreciable damage
on the enemy. By 2 o'clock Stuart had been driven off. Federals

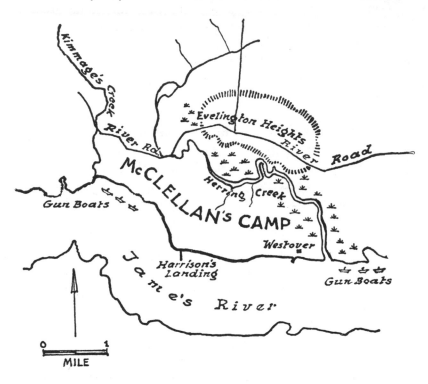

had at once occupied the ridge. Lee now learned all the facts for
the first time, and as he examined the ground he found the
heights crowned with Union artillery and ample infantry support[41] In the light of reality, Stuart's message of the previous
afternoon, announcing his evacuation of the position, took on an
unhappy significance. The only opportunity of winning a decisive victory after the battle of Frayser's Farm had been thrown
away for the pleasure of annoying the enemy with one howitzer!
Longstreet was chafing to attack; Jackson's judgment was

41 O. R., 11, part 2, pp. 295, 519–20, Fitz Lee, 165; Taylor's Four Years, 42–44;
Taylor's General Lee, 82. The defense of Stuart's action will be found in H. B. McClellan,
82 ff.

against it; Lee did not attempt a decision until he had thoroughly surveyed every line of approach. Finding at last that the Federal position was protected on all sides, except for a narrow stretch on the northwest, he concluded most unwillingly that an offensive was not justified.[42] "As far as I can now see," he wrote the President, "there is no way to attack [the enemy] to advantage; nor do I wish to expose the men to the destructive missiles of his gunboats. . . . I fear he is too secure under cover of his boats to be driven from his position."[43]

This decision in reality marked the end of the campaign.[44] Later reconnaissance confirmed Lee's judgment of the impracticability of an attack without heavy loss of life. Mr. Davis concurred in Lee's decision with much inward distress that a *coup de grâce* could not be administered the foe,[45] and on July 5 he issued a congratulatory order that was in itself a recognition that a further development of the Confederate success was not expected.[46]

The aftermath was brief. Lee organized an artillery expedition to bombard the Federal shipping from a point below Harrison's Landing, but achieved no large results.[47] Signs multiplied that the enemy was being reinforced and was digging in at Harrison's Landing, apparently with the intention of remaining there until he decided upon some new plan of action.[48] Lee established headquarters at the Phillips House, near Salem Church, about four miles north of Evelington Heights, and there awaited developments.[49] More than once he was tempted to strike, but, as he told President Davis, "in the present condition of our troops I did not think proper to risk an attack, on the results of which so much depended.[50] If this was the case, nothing was to be gained by keeping the infantry huddled together in front of Harrison's Landing. They could rest and reorganize far more readily away from the strain of close contact with the enemy. On July 7, Lee

[42] *Taylor's General Lee*, 82.   [43] *Lee's Dispatches*, 25–27.
[44] The enemy, however, continued to expect an attack (*O. R.*, 11, part 3, p. 300).
[45] *O. R.*, 11, part 3, p. 362. Richmond had believed on the night of July 1 that McClellan was surrounded, despite the roar of guns (C. S. Anderson in *Locomotive Engineering*, October, 1892, p. 371).
[46] *McCabe*, 168–69.   [47] *O. R.*, 11, part 2, pp. 924–25.
[48] *O. R.*, 11, part 3, p. 635.
[49] Cf. *O. R.*, 11, part 2, p. 635; Heros von Borcke: *Memoirs of the Confederate War for Independence* (cited hereafter as *von Borcke*), 1, 76.
[50] *Lee's Dispatches*, 29.

published his order thanking the army for its service;[51] the next day he prepared for the move, and on July 9, leaving the cavalry to watch McClellan, he put the columns on the march back toward camps near Richmond.[52] His own headquarters were reestablished at the Dabbs house.[53]

The tangible results of the campaign were for every man's reckoning. The whole plan of Federal operations in Virginia had been disrupted after its success had seemed inevitable. On June 26, McClellan's army of 105,000 effectives[54] had been like a sharpened sickle, ready to sweep over Richmond. His outposts, five miles from the city, could see its highest spire. The farthest Union infantry had been less than eight miles from the capitol itself. Now his diminished and disorganized army, with its equipment in chaos, was crowded into an entrenched camp eighteen miles away.[55] Fifty-two fine Federal guns were in Confederate hands. Ten thousand prisoners had been captured,[56] and upwards of 31,000 needed small arms were gleaned from the fields.[57] "The siege of Richmond was raised," Lee reported, "and the object of the campaign, which had been prosecuted after months of preparation at an enormous expenditure of men and money, completely frustrated."[58]

Yet too many Confederate dead were buried between Mechanicsville and Malvern Hill, and too many men lay wretched in the hospitals for Lee to feel any elation. Of the 85,500 men with whom he had opened the campaign, 3286 were dead, 15,909 were wounded, and 946 were missing, a total of 20,141.[59] Half the

[51] O. R., 11, part 2, p. 500.
[52] O. R., 11, part 3, pp. 636–37; Lee's Dispatches, 30–31.
[53] Lee's Dispatches, 31–32; O. R., 11, part 3, p. 637.
[54] His total strength, not including Dix's force at Fort Monroe, was 117,000 (O. R., 11, part 3, p. 238).
[55] On the day when Stuart so imprudently bombarded the camp from Evelington heights, the demoralized McClellan wrote President Lincoln that he doubted if he had 50,000 men with their colors—a panicky underestimate—and that he would need more than 100,000 additional troops if he was to take Richmond and end the war (O. R., 11, part 3, p. 292).
[56] The unwounded prisoners numbered 6053 (Alexander, 171).
[57] O. R., 11, part 2, p. 498. Lee put the small arms at 35,000. The figure here used is that of the ordnance bureau, ibid., 511.
[58] O. R., 11, part 2, p. 497.
[59] Alexander, 171. Alexander computed the casualties for the separate battles—the actual figures not being completely given in O. R., 11, part 2, p. 973 ff.—as follows: Mechanicsville, 1350; Gaines's Mill, 8358; Savage Station, 441; Frayser's Farm, 3305; Malvern Hill, 5590; "other affairs," chiefly the actions of June 25, 27, and 28 on the southside of the Chickahominy, 1124.

wounded, roughly, were doomed to die or to be permanently in-capacitated for field duty. In other words, 11,000 men, the "first line" of the South, had been lost to the Confederacy for all time. Some brigades had been reduced by half their strength. Ripley, for example, had seen 45 officers and 846 men sacrificed in a total of 2366.[60] Those artillerists who had been able to get into action had been decimated. In Pegram's gallant battery, 60 of his 80 men were among the fallen.[61] The loss of officers was staggering. The leading men in every community, the trained, the intelligent and the martial-minded, had been chosen to command in 1861; many of them had been re-elected in 1862. Recklessly charging at the head of their soldiers, they had been slain by scores. Many of those who were already displaying talent that would have made them brigade and division commanders in 1863–64 died on the hills or in the swamps along the Chickahominy. The potential excellence of the field command of the Army of Northern Virginia was impaired in proportion. Federal losses were assumed to be higher,[62] but actually they were less by nearly 4300.[63]

The heavy casualties were not the only reason why Lee viewed the outcome of the campaign without any of the exhilaration of triumph. He had achieved less than he had hoped, less than he believed he should have accomplished. "Under ordinary circumstances," he stated in his report, "the Federal army should have been destroyed." He did not write this until March, 1863, when some of the division commanders of the Seven Days had left the army, and when Jackson had gloriously redeemed his inaction in front of Richmond. This fact, coupled with Lee's unfailing consideration for the feelings of others, prompted him to pass lightly over blunders and omissions that would have explained why the Federal army escaped envelopment and capture. In his official summary of the reasons why complete success was not attained, he merely stated which moves were not completed, without assigning the reasons or placing the blame. Of the wreck of his plan on the critical 30th of June, for example, he simply said, "Huger not coming up, and Jackson having been unable to force

---

[60] Seven of his eleven field-officers had been killed or wounded (O. R., 11, part 2, p. 651). The tabulated summary in *ibid.*, 676–77, put Ripley's loss at 908.
[61] O. R., 11, part 2, p. 843.　　　　[62] O. R., 11, part 2, p. 498.
[63] Killed, 1734; wounded, 8062; missing, 6053, total 15,849 (O. R., 11, part 2, p. 37). About 4000 of the wounded became prisoners of war.

the passage of White Oak Swamp, Longstreet and Hill were without the expected support."[64] He particularized only in one respect concerning the reasons for McClellan's escape: "Prominent among these," he said, "is the want of correct and timely information. This fact, attributable chiefly to the character of the country, enabled General McClellan skillfully to conceal his retreat and to add much to the obstructions with which nature had beset the way of our pursuing columns; but regret that more was not accomplished gives way to gratitude to the Sovereign Ruler of the Universe for the results achieved."[65]

But if Lee did not deem it expedient to state why he failed to destroy the Federal army, the causes were plain and, to the student of war, are the most instructive aspect of the campaign. Many of them are informative and monitory in a different tactical era. "The want of correct and timely information," which Lee emphasized was, first of all, a matter of cartography in a country by nature so difficult for military operations that a leader without an accurate map was almost helpless. The absence of reliable maps proved as serious throughout the campaign as it had been in the instances already cited, at Mechanicsville and at Frayser's Farm. A better knowledge of the country might have shown Lee how he could have avoided the bloody battle of Gaines's Mill by striking directly for Dispatch Station.[66] Unfamiliarity with the roads slowed down the march and confused the division commanders, in particular General Jackson, who was entirely unacquainted with the country.[67] Bad maps put Magruder on the wrong road on July 1, and bad maps delayed pursuit on July 3. D. H. Hill summed up the case when he said, "Throughout this campaign we attacked just when and where the enemy wished us to attack. This was owing to our ignorance of the country and lack of reconnaissance of the successive battlefields."[68]

Nearly all the mistakes due to lack of acquaintance with the country affected seriously the outcome of the campaign. This, therefore, is a pertinent question: To what extent can Lee be held accountable for the failure to procure good maps of the country

[64] *O. R.*, 11, part 2, p. 495.   [65] *O. R.*, 11, part 2, p. 497.
[66] *Cf.* D. H. Hill in 2 *B. and L.*, 361.
[67] Major Hotchkiss noted (3 *C. M. H.*, 287) that Jackson had expected to be supplied with maps and had sent him back to the Valley to prepare a good map of that area.
[68] 2 *B. and L.*, 395. *Cf.* E. M. Law in *Southern Bivouac*, April, 1887, p. 655.

below Richmond? The responsibility is not altogether his, assuredly, for he was not in charge of operations until March, 1862. There were only thirteen engineer officers in the Confederate service who had belonged to the engineering corps of the United States army at the outbreak of the war. Engineers of the Confederate provisional army, who had come from civil pursuits, numbered no more than ninety-three.[69] The field commanders were continually asking for more engineering assistance. Topographical engineers were almost unprocurable. Among all the published documents on the preliminaries of the Seven Days, there is no mention of maps, good or bad. As Lee was himself an engineer, whose experience at Puebla in collecting topographical data had shown him their value, it is inconceivable that he did not realize the necessity of having an accurate map. He doubtless knew that a map was being prepared; he did not know, and he could not know until it was checked on the ground, that the one supplied him was so full of errors as to be worthless.[70] President Davis blamed General Johnston for failure to reconnoitre the roads and attributed to his negligence the embarrassment of Lee,[71] but the conditions that impeded the engineers while Lee was in command applied equally, perhaps even more, while Johnston was responsible for army administration.

Amateurish and incompetent staff work was a second factor in denying the army commanders "correct and timely information." Colonel Wolseley, later Field Marshal Lord Wolseley, who visited Lee's headquarters in the autumn of 1862, remarked that the "staff-organization in the Confederacy was not as well established [during the Seven Days] as it is now. . . . Every one in the South will tell you that McClellan's army was saved, first by General Lee's orders not being accurately executed, and, secondly, by his gunboats . . ."[72] The first part of this statement is a very conservative summary of the case. The campaign will always

[69] IV *O. R.*, 2, p. 259–60. *Cf. O. R.*, 12, part 3, p. 945.

[70] It has been mistakenly assumed, even by so competent an authority as General Maurice, see his footnote in *Marshall*, 117–18, that Lee knew the Cold Harbor district well by reason of his frequent visits to the White House plantation. As a matter of fact, Lee had gone to the White House but seldom and then most probably by the Old Church and Piping Tree roads, rather than via Cold Harbor, if, indeed, he journeyed by Richmond at all.

[71] *O. R.*, 47, part 2, p. 1306.

[72] G. Wolseley: *A Month's Visit to the Confederate Headquarters* (cited hereafter as *Wolseley*), *Blackwood's Magazine*, January, 1863, p. 12.

remain a tragic monument to defective staff work. Following it stage by stage, battle by battle, one gets a singular impression of Lee's detachment. He was responsible for the outcome yet in the dark respecting the most important movements of some of the commanders charged with important duties. There were long hours in the campaign when Lee knew scarcely more of the whereabouts of his troops than McClellan did.[73] The condition was so glaring and so continuous that a detailed list of the errors of the staff would be a review of the campaign. None of the battles began until late afternoon, because the staff could not get the columns up earlier; there was no satisfactory *liaison* between Jackson and Lee or between A. P. Hill and Jackson on June 26; although operating in a friendly country, where almost every farmer was potentially a Confederate spy, Lee's intelligence service was nearly non-existent. He thought, for example, that virtually the whole of the Federal army was in his front on June 27, when, in reality, he faced only Fitz John Porter's corps until nearly the close of the action at Gaines's Mill. The failure of the staff to effect co-ordination in the attack that day speaks for itself. Again, on June 30, Huger's movements for some hours were unreported, either by Lee's staff officers or by Huger's, in spite of the fact that Huger could hear the fire of Longstreet's guns at Frayser's Farm and Lee could hear those of Huger on the Charles City road; the lack of contact with Jackson on June 30 was almost complete; it is not certain that Lee knew of Holmes's advance until late on the 29th of June. As for Malvern Hill, there might as well have been no headquarters staff for all the good it did in seeing that the senior officer on each part of the line was familiar with the general situation and knew what was expected of him.

Some of Lee's staff officers were men of ability, who later were to prove invaluable to him, but in this campaign they functioned simply as the inexperienced staff of the average division commander might have done.[74] The reasons for this were in part a lack of training and in part a bad organization. Lee had brought back with him from South Carolina only Captain Walter H. Taylor,[75] and he had recalled Major T. A. Washington about

---

[73] *Cf. W. W. Chamberlaine,* 135.   [74] *Cf.* Wilson: *John A. Rawlins,* 197–98.
[75] *Taylor's General Lee,* 42; *Taylor MSS.*

April 3[76] and Major A. L. Long in May.[77] Under the act of March 25 which provided him with a staff of a colonel as military secretary and four aides ranking as major,[78] Lee had named Long as military secretary, had retained Taylor,[79] and for the other vacancies had chosen Major Charles S. Venable, Major Charles Marshall, and Major T. M. R. Talcott, son of his old friend Captain Andrew Talcott.[80] Major Washington had left the staff late in April. On assuming command of the Army of Northern Virginia on June 1, Lee had continued Captain A. P. Mason, of Johnston's staff, as assistant adjutant general.[81] On June 4 Lieutenant Colonel R. H. Chilton, a comrade of Lee's Texas days, had reported to Lee as assistant adjutant and inspector general, and had been announced as chief of staff.[82]

At first Lee had somewhat awkwardly called his staff about him every morning, and had distributed routine papers among them, with a verbal outline of the answers, but he had soon discarded this arrangement and had designated Major Taylor as assistant adjutant general, to care for all the regular correspondence.[83] That had been about the extent of the personal staff. Colonel Chilton, a West Pointer, was somewhat of a misfit, more than an aide but less than a chief of staff. Major Taylor was an admirable officer, young and diligent, whose only weakness was a longing for field service. Whenever opportunity offered—at Seven Pines on June 1, on the Rapidan in 1863, in the Wilderness on May 10, 1864, and at Petersburg on March 31, 1865, he took advantage of presence at the scene of action to lead desperate charges with conspicuous valor. Marshall, a Baltimore lawyer, was excellent in drafting papers, Talcott was an able engineer, and Venable a man of most superior intellect, but none of the staff, except Taylor and Long, had been with Lee for more than a few months when this campaign opened, and Chilton had been at headquarters only three weeks. The general staff officers, inherited from Johnston, were more experienced and were strengthened conspicuously on the eve of the campaign by the addition of

---

[76] *O. R.,* 6, 406–7; *O. R.,* 11, part 3, p. 419.
[77] *Long,* 143. He signed as military secretary after May 15.
[78] IV *O. R.,* 1, 1021. Cf. *ibid.,* 997, 998. [79] *Taylor's General Lee,* 42.
[80] *O. R.,* 51, part 2, pp. 548, 554; *Marshall,* 3, 8. [81] *Taylor's General Lee,* 55.
[82] *O. R.,* 11, part 3, p. 574. [83] *Taylor's General Lee,* 56.

Lieutenant Colonel James L. Corley, assistant quartermaster general,[84] but these officers were not in close touch with the commanding general. Lee, for that matter, was scarcely more adept in handling a staff at this time than the officers were in serving him.

In the sense, then, that General Randolph B. Marcy acted for McClellan, Lee had no chief of staff. A comparison between Chilton and Marcy is typical of the difference in the staff work of the two armies as a whole during this campaign and measures Lee's burden in this respect with approximate accuracy. The Federals in 1861 had the immense advantage of beginning the war with all the divisions of the staff organized and operating. Except in their intelligence service, which was wretched, the Union armies were still enjoying this advantage at the time of the Seven Days' battles. The Federal staff work during the change of base was well-nigh flawless. McClellan had felt it necessary to maintain troops north of the Chickahominy to defend the Richmond and York River Railroad[85] but his eyes had been opened by Stuart's raid of June 13–15 to the possible necesisty of having to abandon the base at the White House and on June 18 he ordered transports and supplies up the James.[86] Until the afternoon of the 27th the activity of Lee's army on the south side of the Chickahominy was so deceptive that McClellan was not certain where the major blow would fall.[87] That day, while the battle was raging at Gaines's Mill, Marcy hinted at a change of base in a dispatch to Secretary E. M. Stanton.[88] The same evening it was determined upon, after brief consideration of the alternative of an advance on Richmond up the south side of the Chickahominy, which on June 23 had been discussed.[89] At 2 A.M., June 28, General Morrell marched his weary, shattered brigades across the Chickahominy.[90] From that time until the morning of

---

[84] O. R., 51, part 2, p. 576.

[85] 1 Report of the Committee on the Conduct of the War, 624.

[86] 2 B. and L., 178.

[87] 2 B. and L., 181; O. R., 11, part 3, p. 264; McClellan's Own Story, 419.

[88] O. R., 11, part 3, p. 265.

[89] O. R., 11, part 2, p. 98; ibid., part 3, p. 247; Comte de Paris: History of the Civil War in America, 2, 105–6; 1 Report of the Committee on the Conduct of the War, 355, 592.

[90] O. R., 11. part 2, p. 274.

July 3 some part of the army was continuously on the road with an immense train that included 3450 wagons, 2518 beef cattle, fifty-two field batteries, and all the reserve artillery.[91] Much was destroyed before the retreat began and much was thrown away by the soldiers on the march, but the withdrawal was orderly except at White Oak Swamp bridge on the night of June 29 and on the road from Malvern Hill to Harrison's Landing, July 1–2. It is hardly too much to say that McClellan owed his escape primarily to the excellence of his staff and to the inefficiency of Lee's. If McClellan had not relied upon an intelligence service that was immeasurably worse than none, deceiving him with wild lies and wilder guesses regarding the strength of the Confederate forces opposing him, the difference in the two staffs might have been the difference between failure and success, despite the strategy of Lee and the almost incredible timidity of McClellan.

But Lee's lack of "correct and timely information" was due, in part, to something besides poor maps and bad staff work. A third and not inconsiderable factor was the faulty employment of the cavalry during the closing days of the operations. At the outset the mounted men were well located and handled. Stuart was most needed to cover Jackson's advance, and was most successful in doing so. No fault can be found with the tactical use of the cavalry on June 26. The next day brought little opportunity for employing that arm in the wooded country around Cold Harbor. When McClellan "sealed the front" of the Chickahominy on June 28 it was proper to send Stuart down the left bank to see if the Army of the Potomac intended to cross that stream in a withdrawal down the Peninsula. Again, the discovery that communications with the White House had been abandoned by the enemy made it desirable that the cavalry destroy the supplies at the base. This was done. But from that time until the morning of July 1 Stuart was useless to the army. His troopers remained beyond the Chickahominy, resting and observing the crossings, when they could have been scouting or assailing the wagon trains moving southward. Had the cavalry been divided on June 29 and half of it returned to Lee, it is not likely that the line of the enemy's retreat to the James would have been in doubt, or that

[91] 2 *D. H. Hill*, 131; *McClellan's Own Story*, 423.

237

the prospect of a concentration at Malvern Hill would have gone unreported.[92]

Aside from these three conditions, that cost Lee "correct and timely information," there were other reasons why the Army of Northern Virginia failed to achieve the full triumph Lee believed it should have won. The poor use made of the Confederate artillery, in comparison with the admirable employment of that arm by the Federals, was one of these reasons. To this was due the prolongation of several of the battles when speed might have enlarged a victory. Costly casualties were piled up in infantry charges on batteries that massed artillery preparation might have silenced. "It was one of the greatest errors of the early days of the Confederacy," wrote Captain Francis W. Dawson, "that batteries were allowed to be knocked to pieces in detail when, by massing a dozen batteries, the enemy could have been knocked quickly out of time and many lives saved."[93] Gun for gun the Confederate ordnance was far inferior to the Federal in range and in precision. Lee's one hope of winning equality, not to speak of gaining superiority, depended on better tactical employment. Yet what were the facts? At Mechanicsville the few Confederate batteries that got into action made no impression on the well-placed Federal guns; A. P. Hill used little artillery at Gaines's Mill, and Jackson could not mass his pieces soon enough to protect his infantry; at Frayser's Farm the Confederate artillerists had little opportunity; Malvern Hill was comparable only to Sharpsburg, the Southern gunners' hades. Only in Jackson's operation at White Oak Swamp bridge was there any effective massing of ordnance—and the temporary advantage gained there was not followed up soon enough by a strong infantry attack.

Some of the circumstances responsible for this poor showing by the Confederate artillery were of a sort not easily overcome: the Federals had chosen and had prepared the better positions. The actions at Mechanicsville and at Gaines's Mill had been joined before the artillery could be brought up in adequate strength. Unknown roads, troublesome marshes, and dense forests had to be passed before the faithful gunners could bring

[92] Stuart's report is in *O. R.*, 11, part 2, p. 515 *ff*. A good critique of the cavalry in the campaign appears in *Dabney*, 480 *ff*.
[93] *F. W. Dawson*, 48.

their poor pieces to bear on the excellent Federal batteries. The reserve artillery rendered little service. Apart from all this, how-ver, as the campaign is reviewed, one feels that Lee and all his division commanders except Jackson failed to put a proper valuation on the co-ordination of the infantry and the artillery. Reliance was placed, at cruel cost, on the naked valor of the infantry.[94]

General Pendleton had not shone in the Seven Days, but he appraised the failure of his arm with absolute candor in his report: "Too little was thrown into action at once," he said, "too much was left in the rear unused. . . . We needed more guns taking part, alike for our own protection and for crippling the enemy. With a powerful array opposed to his own, we divide his attention, shake his nerves, make him shoot at random, and more readily drive him from the field worsted and alarmed. A main cause of this error in the present case was no doubt a peculiar intricacy in the country, from the prevalence of woods and swamps. We could form little idea of positions, and were very generally ignorant of those chosen by the enemy and of the best modes of approaching them." [95] The Federals were conscious of their advantage, despite the loss of fifty-two guns. One newspaper correspondent went so far as to say, "Our superiority in artillery has saved the army from annihilation." [96]

Another reason for Lee's failure to win a decisive victory during the campaign was his disposition to rely too largely on subordinates, some of whom failed to measure up either to their responsibility or to their opportunities. Longstreet realized this. Self-opinionated as he was and vain as he became, he wrote after the war, "Lee depended almost too much on his officers" for the execution of his orders.[97]

Here again the explanation is fairly simple. Lee had been trained in the school of Scott, who conceived it to be the function of the commanding general to devise the strategic plan, to bring the troops on the field at the proper time and place, and then to leave tactics and combat to the division commanders. Lee rarely

---

[94] For a full and intelligent discussion of the employment of the Confederate artillery in this campaign, see *Wise*, 1, 207 ff.

[95] *O. R.*, 11, part 2, p. 537.

[96] C. A. Page: *Letters of a War Correspondent*, 22.   [97] 2 *B. and L.*, 405.

departed in this respect from his practical instruction in Mexico. In the second place, Lee's consideration for the sensibilities of others, that refined quality so often mentioned in these pages, made it temperamentally difficult for him to dominate a field. Moreover, it must again be remembered that he was a newcomer among commanders who had an *esprit de corps* of a kind and were jealous of their authority. In the case of Jackson, his popular reputation at the time was higher than that of Lee himself. The victor of Cross Keys and Port Republic had to be treated deferentially. Had the personal equation been different—had Lee been disposed to deal sternly—it is doubtful if the staff could have functioned to see that his orders were promptly and literally enforced. Besides, the troops he led during the Seven Days were not a united force, accustomed to working together, but consisted of four separate armies, met together for the first time on the field of battle—Johnston's old Army of the Potomac, the Valley army of Jackson, Huger's command from the Norfolk front, and Magruder's brigades, which might be styled the Yorktown army.[98] One result of this conglomerate organization was that Mechanicsville was A. P. Hill's battle, Savage Station was Magruder's, and Frayser's Farm was Longstreet's. Malvern Hill was nobody's. Only at Gaines's Mill, and then only for part of the day, was the action really Lee's own.

Finally, the campaign did not lead to the destruction of the enemy because Lee faced an army that was so handled on the field of battle as to make the most of its excellent personnel. Writing long after the war, with most of the essential evidence before him, Colonel Walter Taylor placed high among the causes preventing a more complete victory "the character and personality of the men behind the guns on the Federal side." He added: "The army under General McClellan was made up largely of the flower of the manhood of the Northern and Eastern states, and his lieutenants were men and soldiers of a very high type." [99] This is no more than justice.[100] In nearly every clash during the

---

[98] Holmes's division might have been counted a fifth army, but most of its units had originally come from Johnston in northern Virginia.

[99] *Taylor's General Lee*, 84.

[100] It was indicative of the spirit of the Army of the Potomac in June 1862, that officers and men scarcely concealed their contempt for Diederich's and Knieriem's artillery which gave so poor an account of themselves at Frayser's Farm (see *supra*, p. 186). Al-

Seven Days, when infantry was matched against infantry, the already terrible footmen of the Army of Northern Virginia showed their superiority, but it was not by a wide margin, nor was it with the aid of superior tactical dispositions on the part of their general in chief. Lee showed no genius of this sort at any time during the Seven Days. Mechanicsville was not tactically well fought from the Confederate point of view. At Gaines's Mill, for a multitude of reasons, Lee's numerically superior forces were very poorly fed into action and some of his units were in danger of being destroyed in detail. Malvern Hill was tactically about as bad as it could have been. In the intelligent employment of the forces at hand, Frayser's Farm was the best battle of the Confederates waged during the campaign, futile though that action was. And there, it must in candor be recorded, the guiding hand was not Lee's but Longstreet's.

To summarize, then, the Federal army was not destroyed, as Lee had hoped it would be, for four reasons: (1) The Confederate commander lacked adequate information for operating in a difficult country because his maps were worthless, his staff work inexperienced, and his cavalry absent at the crisis of the campaign; (2) the Confederate artillery was poorly employed; (3) Lee trusted too much to his subordinates, some of whom failed him almost completely; and (4) Lee displayed no tactical genius in combating a fine, well-led Federal army.

When these four factors are given their just valuation, the wonder is not that an honest commander had to admit that he had failed to realize his full expectation. Rather is the wonder that so much of success was attained. In the face of obstacles and failures, how was Lee able to break the grip of McClellan on Richmond and to pen up that splendid Federal army in the entrenched camp at Harrison's Landing?

There would seem to be three major explanations. The first, of course, was the fundamental soundness of Lee's strategy. It has been developed stage by stage in these chapters and it need not be recapitulated here. The campaign may well be cited as a

though the men who served those ill-fated guns were native-born Pennsylvanians of German extraction, the ardent Union soldiers of native stock looked down on them as the "Dutch batteries." The time was to come within a year when there were entire "Dutch divisions" in the army of the United States.

241

text-book example of the manner in which the highest type of strategy, if consistently followed, will sometimes overcome difficulties and atone for tactical blunders.

Secondly, Lee accomplished the major object of his campaign because the valor of his infantry was neither shaken by losses nor impaired by long campaigning. The reckless courage of Ripley's green troops at Mechanicsville, the steady advance of Lawton's Georgians, the charge of the 20th North Carolina, and the magnificent behavior of Hood's brigade at Gaines's Mill, the persistence of the struggle for Randol's and Cooper's guns at Frayser's Farm, the desperate determination of Wright's and Mahone's men in clinging to the hillside at the Crew house even after a great assault had failed to materialize at Malvern Hill—these and like achievements show that Lee had magnificent material at the outset, however much he improved its morale by his successful and brilliant strategy. Through the worst hardships of the campaign, the men remained wholly confident of victory and convinced that they would soon end the war.[101]

The final explanation of the outcome of the campaign was the singular temperament of Lee's chief opponent. It is beside the purpose of this biography to discuss whether McClellan or the administration was chiefly to blame for the exposure of the right flank of the Army of the Potomac at Mechanicsville after all immediate hope of reinforcement by McDowell was past. Neither is it necessary to argue here whether Fitz John Porter was right in affirming that if McClellan had not moved to the James, after the battle of Gaines's Mill, he would have had no alternative to hasty abandonment of his attack on Richmond, with a retirement by the route he had followed up the Peninsula.[102] These and the intriguing questions of what a different man would have done on the morning of June 28, or how he would have moved after he had repulsed Lee's attack at Malvern Hill, belong to the general military history of the War between the States. What is of bearing here is that though General McClellan was certainly the ablest organizer and probably the best military administrator developed in the North during the war, possessing his men's

---

[101] Chaplain Marks (*op. cit.*) noted this time and time again as he conversed with Confederate soldiers while watching over Federal wounded.

[102] *O. R.,* 11, part 2, p. 22.

affection as did no other Federal general in chief, he was not far from panic during the Seven Days. This may have been due to the feeling that the clique opposed to him had wrought his ruin by withholding McDowell. It may have been that in dealing with Lee he was still a lieutenant of engineers in Mexico. Perhaps the main reason was that he had been deceived by his incompetent spies into believing that Lee vastly outnumbered him.[103] It is impossible to state the precise cause or combination of causes for his condition. Whatever it may have been, it aided Lee to a degree past all reckoning. On the night of June 27 McClellan was so convinced he had to make a general and immediate retreat that he contemplated issuing an order for the destruction of officers' baggage and perhaps of camp equipage, calling on the men at the same time to endure privation for a few days.[104] On the evening of the battle of Frayser's Farm he telegraphed Stanton, "If none of us escape, we shall have done honor to our country."[105] During most of the retreat he was in advance of the army, seeking defensive positions and a safe refuge for his men. Yet on July 2 he was boasting to President Lincoln that he had lost only one gun and one wagon,[106] and on July 9 he jubilantly reported to Washington that the enemy was in "full retreat."[107] His private letters, even after he had edited them for publication, were a curious medley of fears and bravado.[108] Lee could not have asked for a more favorable state of mind on the part of his adversary, or for a temper more certain to bewilder an administration that had to deal with such a man.

So appears the campaign after seventy years. At the time, it provoked conflicting opinions. Hostile critics of President Davis and of General Lee, balancing successes against failures, professed disappointment with Lee's generalship and with the results obtained. Said *The Charleston Mercury,* "Much as we praise the strategy, projected as we hear, by General Johnston, some time since, by which McClellan has been beaten on the Chickahominy, the blundering manner in which he has been allowed to get away, the desultory manner in which he has been pursued by

---

[103] Cf. *Joel Cook,* 302, 347.
[104] I *Report of the Committee on the Conduct of the War,* 592.
[105] *O. R.,* 11, part 3, p. 280.   [106] *O. R.,* 11, part 3, p. 287.
[107] *O. R.,* 11, part 3, p. 309.   [108] *McClellan's Own Story,* 441 ff.

divisions instead of our whole force, enabling him to repulse our attacks, to carry off his artillery, and, finally, to make a fresh stand with an army reinforced are facts, we fear, not very flattering to the practical generalship of General Lee." [109] Some of General Johnston's friends jealously grumbled that their hero would have made a better showing than Lee if he had been supported by the administration in concentrating as large an army as Lee had.[110] Robert Toombs wrote Vice-President Stephens that Lee was "far below the occasion." [111] And so for other critics less distinguished.

But the public saw the successes, not the shortcomings. Especially in Richmond, press and people did not judge the Seven Days as a series of close battles but in their proper light, as a campaign of strategy that began with the first move to transfer Jackson from the Valley and ended when McClellan was caged and impotent at Harrison's Landing, with his plan of operations hopelessly shattered. They remembered the panic of May; they did not forget how they had seen the glow of bombardment and had heard above the anxious beating of their own hearts the defiant challenge of the enemy's guns. And in the contrast between June 1 and July 4, they read a mighty achievement. "The people at large," one observer testified, "greeted Lee as the author of a great deliverance worked out for them." [112] Some were most eulogistic. "The operations of General Lee . . .," *The Richmond Dispatch* affirmed, "were certainly those of a master. No captain that ever lived could have planned or executed a better plan. . . . Its success places its author among the highest military names." [113] A correspondent of *The Richmond Enquirer* insisted, "Never has such a result been achieved in so short a time and with so small cost to the victors. I do not believe the records of modern warfare can produce a parallel when the battle is considered in this aspect." [114] Lee, said *The Richmond Whig,* "has amazed and confounded his detractors by the brilliancy of his genius, the

[109] *Charleston Mercury*, July 8, 1862. *Cf.* 1 R. W. C. D., 141.

[110] For Johnston's own view, see *Johnston's Narrative*, 145–46, fully answered in 2 *Davis*, 156.

[111] *Toombs, etc., Correspondence*, 601.   [112] *Cooke*, 96.

[113] *Richmond Dispatch*, July 9, 1862, p. 2, col. 1.

[114] "Justice," quoted from *The Enquirer* of July 1, 1862, in *The Richmond Whig,* July 2, 1862, p. 2, col. 2.

fertility of his resources, his energy and daring. He has established his reputation forever, and has entitled himself to the lasting gratitude of his country."[115] Thoughtful men saw in the outcome a vindication of the President's policy[116] and the hope of a long period of successes in arms.[117]

More important, far, than popular acclaim was the confidence and admiration aroused among the soldiers in the ranks. Within a month the "King of Spades" became the father of his men, trusted and idolized. He gave them the *causerie de bivouac* that Napoleon considered essential to the morale of a victorious army. Stories of his simplicity, of his devotion, and of his humility began to go the rounds.[118] The troops already felt that he was superior to the best general the enemy had, and that their lives and their cause were safe in his hands. After this first campaign, their faith in him was unbounded.[119]

Back in his old headquarters at the Dabbs house, Lee gave little time and less thought to the reading of the newspapers that were discounting his performance or sounding his praises. The many evidences of the good-will of the army and the marked deference now shown him by officers who had been slightly superior in manner wrought no change in his treatment of them. He had passed through the most fruitful period of his military education, barring perhaps those months under Scott in 1847 on the road to Mexico City, and he was determined to profit by it in correcting his own mistakes and in overcoming, so far as he could, the defects his subordinates had disclosed. His immediate task was to reorganize the army for the campaigns he knew were before him. The most pressing part of that task, of course, was to provide better divisional leadership. Longstreet had emerged as the most dependable man, at the moment, among his lieutenants.[120] He did not fail to put a high estimate on his opinions and he did not hesitate to express his theories of strategy, but he had exhibited, as yet, no stubbornness. His movements had been prompt and

---

[115] *Richmond Whig*, July 15, 1862, p. 1, col. 1.
[116] *O. R.*, 51, part 2, p. 587. [117] 1 *R. W. C. D.*, 142.
[118] *Cf.* the anecdote in *Jones*, 162–63, of the manner in which he was said to have moved his headquarters during one of the battles of the Seven Days in order to give place to the wounded.
[119] *Eggleston*, 42.
[120] *Cf.* Robert Toombs to A. H. Stephens, July 2, 1862; *Toombs, etc. Correspondence*, 601.

his discipline good. In battle, he had displayed a brusque cheer-
fulness and a quick understanding of troop-movements and positions. More fully than any other division commander he had
shown himself worthy of trust with a larger command. D. H.
Hill was caustic and critical, but in action he had been admirable.
A. P. Hill was too impetuous, but he had marched well and had
fought hard. His conduct at Frayser's Farm had been above
criticism. A little more seasoning under the guidance of a steadier
man would make him an efficient divisional commander. Magruder, brave and loyal for all his pompous manner, was too
excitable for such fighting as lay ahead. Fortunately, the question
of disposing of him had been solved in advance: he had been
offered command in the Trans-Mississippi department, was
anxious to go there, and waited only long enough to defend himself against whispered imputations of poor generalship at Malvern
Hill.[121] His large force was promptly broken up: D. R. Jones's
division was placed with Longstreet's command, and Magruder's
own small division was consolidated with McLaws's, under the
command of McLaws.[122] Neither Jones nor McLaws had yet
been sufficiently tested to show his qualities. Huger's failure had
been unrelieved and was irredeemable. Circumstances and perhaps design had placed most of his troops under Magruder during
the action at Malvern Hill. Quietly and with the utmost consideration, he was now named inspector of artillery and ordnance
for the army of the Confederacy and was to appear no more with
Lee. His division was assigned to R. H. Anderson of South
Carolina, who was promoted major general. His abilities were
good and his weakness for strong drink was believed to have been
overcome.[123] This was a change that Lee had desired to make
before the opening of the campaign.[124] Holmes had not exhibited
brilliance and was slow and deaf, besides, though a competent
routine administrator. Like Magruder, he was given command
in the Trans-Mississippi department.[125] D. H. Hill was assigned
in his place, with an eye to semi-independent service in his native
North Carolina.

[121] O. R., 11, part 2, p. 674 ff., ibid., part 3, p. 630; O. R., 13, 845.
[122] O. R., 11, part 3, p. 630.
[123] O. R., 11, part 3, pp. 640, 642; Lee's Dispatches, 10.
[124] Lee's Dispatches, 14.   [125] O. R., 9, p. 713; O. R., 13, pp. 855, 860.

There remained Jackson—what should be done about him? By every test, Jackson had failed throughout the Seven Days. He had not turned Beaver Dam Creek, though he had fulfilled the letter of his orders. At Gaines's Mill he had done no more than others, if as much. His failure to support Magruder at Savage Station had been inexplicable, and the reasons for his failure to cross White Oak Swamp were at best debatable. In the battle of Malvern Hill his division had achieved little. Although the army was so much elated that there was little disposition to find fault,[126] ugly tales about Jackson were in circulation. He was reported to have said he did not intend his men should do all the fighting.[127] Without stopping to ask whether the figures might not have some other explanation, critics may have thought this rumor was verified by the fact that Jackson's and Ewell's divisions, the original Army of the Valley, had sustained less than 6 per cent of the casualties of the campaign.[128]

Had Jackson fought as hard and done as well as Longstreet and A. P. Hill, there would have been a different tale to tell. Lee may have felt this. He never had the slightest doubt concerning Jackson's ability, his discretion, or his daring independent command, but he may have feared that Jackson was ambitious and ill-disposed to fight under another. A certain letter that will be quoted in describing the reorganization of the army after the battle of Sharpsburg gives color to this view. Yet Jackson had done well during the early months of the war, as Lee well knew, and he had to his credit the amazing campaign in the Valley that had shown of what he was capable. Lee could not overlook past performance. He may have been aware, also, of Jackson's physical condition.

There is not a line in any letter, or a hint in the gossip of the time, so far as it has been preserved, to indicate that Lee criticised Jackson, much less that he considered quietly disposing of him, as he did of Huger, of Holmes, and of Magruder. He retained his faith in Jackson, but he made a significant change in the organization of the army. He left Lawton's brigade to fill out

---

126 W. H. Taylor to E. P. Alexander, Aug. 26, 1902—*Taylor MSS.*
127 *Alexander,* 152.
128 Excluding Lawton's brigade and Whiting's division which had not fought in the Valley, Jackson's casualties were 1195 (*O. R.,* 11, part 2, pp. 973 *ff.*).

Jackson's old division and he retained Ewell under the control of Jackson. Thus, if required for separate use, the Army of the Valley was intact. Whiting's division was joined with Holmes's former force under D. H. Hill. The rest of the infantry, Longstreet's, A. P. Hill's, D. H. Hill's, R. H. Anderson's, and McLaws's divisions were entrusted to Longstreet. In short, Jackson fought the Seven Days with fourteen brigades; in the reorganization, he was allotted seven. Longstreet had carried six brigades across the Chickahominy; he soon had twenty-eight. The changes were made gradually and quietly, and seem to have attracted little or no attention,[129] especially as D. H. Hill's subordination to Jackson had been recognized as temporary and due solely to the arrangement made on June 27 for the pursuit of McClellan. Nevertheless, the disproportion in the size of Longstreet's and Jackson's command must reflect, to some extent, Lee's belief at the time regarding the comparative willingness of the two men to co-operate. If Jackson was to return to independent command, his great abilities could of course be trusted, but if he was to remain with the Army of Northern Virginia and was to prove recalcitrant, his power to thwart the general strategy of the army was to be limited. This seems a safe inference from the facts.

What did Jackson think of all this? He never told any one, so far as the records show, that he felt he had failed to do his part in the campaign. His report, when written months afterward, contained no apologies. If he did not blame himself, however, it is certain he did not blame Lee or criticise the distribution of force. The one reference he is known to have made to his chief immediately after the campaign was as full of praise as it was sincere: ". . . His perception is as quick and unerring," he said of Lee in a conversation to be quoted more fully in Chapter XX, on page 261, "as his judgment is infallible. . . . So great is my confidence in General Lee that I am willing to follow him blindfolded."[130]

The subject of this encomium was as quick to apply one of the lessons of the campaign to himself as he was to protect the army

---

[129] Compare the organization as of June 26, 1862, *O. R.,* 11, part 2, pp. 483 *ff.,* with that of July 23, 1862, *ibid.,* part 3, pp. 648 *ff.*

[130] Colonel A. R. Boteler, in 40 *S. H. S. P.,* 181. The same remark in substance is quoted in *Jones,* 156 and in *Cooke,* 264–65.

against errors by incompetent subordinates or possible mistakes by men of whom he was not yet certain. He abandoned the "grand strategy" of converging columns and envelopment for simpler methods that inexperienced brigade commanders and a green staff could be expected to employ more readily. Here, again, there is no direct evidence to cite. Lee's determination is to be read in what he did thereafter, not in what he then said. He was learning the duties of his position, as his subordinates were learning theirs—by experience. Never again did he attempt any such complicated manœuvring as that by which he had tried to trap McClellan at Frayser's Farm. Flank attacks, quick marches to the rear, and better tactics took the place of great designs of destruction.

Beyond this, Lee did not go in correcting the weaknesses the campaign disclosed. So far as the records show, he had no official part in urging the preparation of maps. Little was done in this respect during 1862.[131] No reorganization of the artillery was undertaken. The general staff was not modified, and Lee's personal staff was not changed. As Colonel Chilton failed to develop the qualities of an efficient chief of staff, Lee came gradually to act as his own chief staff officer. Perhaps, as an engineer who had worked almost alone on many projects, it was both his impulse and his preference to do this. Increasingly, after the Seven Days, Lee personally drafted his important dispatches to the President. Where they were not strictly confidential, he had them copied in his official letter-book. Many of the most important of those addressed to the President were forwarded without being transcribed.[132] It seems strange, at first glance, that a man so mindful of the value of military details should have done so little to prepare maps, to make his artillery more efficient, and to build up the staff. Perhaps more might have been done. Lee, however, had already realized that Confederate success depended on utilizing the means at hand, without waiting to perfect them in competition with an enemy whose resources were so much greater than those of the Confederacy that the North would be certain to gain most by delay. Conditions had changed since 1861 and the

---

131 IV O. R., 2, p. 262.
132 Most of those sent in this manner found their way into the De Renne collection and were issued in 1915 under the title Lee's Dispatches, edited by D. S. Freeman.

early spring of 1862: whatever the Southern States could hope to do must be done quickly. Lee had to leave much to chance and more to the accumulating experience of the army, as he prepared for a dramatic new stage of the war in Virginia.

CHAPTER XIX

A Domestic Interlude

GENERAL LEE saw little of his family during the desperate weeks that raced relentlessly to the bloody climax of Malvern Hill. When in March, 1862, he came back to Richmond, Mrs. Lee was at the White House, with her daughter-in-law, Charlotte. The girls were visiting,[1] Rooney was with his command in the field, Robert was still at the University of Virginia, and only Custis was in the city, acting as an aide to the President. The General had his quarters at the Spotswood Hotel in Spartan loneliness. His duties kept him for long hours at the War Department building and gave him few opportunities for social life. He went daily to morning prayer-meeting at 7 o'clock,[2] but he did not find time to visit even his old rector of boyhood days, now the Bishop of Virginia, Right Reverend William Meade. On the evening of March 14, Bishop Meade sent for Lee, who hurried at once to see him. The distinguished cleric was nearing his end, feeble and in great pain, but rational and resigned. In an affecting farewell, the bishop gave him his blessing. "God bless you! God bless you, Robert!" he said, "and fit you for your high and responsible duties. I can't call you 'general'—I must call you 'Robert'; I have heard you your catechism too often."

"Yes, Bishop, very often," Lee said, choking with tears and pressing his hand.[3]

That night the venerable cleric died. "'I ne'er shall look upon his like again,'" Lee sorrowfully quoted.[4] "Of all the men I have ever known," he wrote after the war, "I consider him the purest."[5]

That evening, after Bishop Meade expired, Robert Lee came to

---

[1] Annie, however, joined her mother before the end of March. Annie Lee to Agnes Lee, May 2, 1862, MS., Duke University.

[2] *Charleston Mercury*, April 22, 1862.   [3] *Jones*, 436; *Cooke*, 47.

[4] Lee to Mrs. Lee, March 14, 1862; *R. E. Lee, Jr.*, 67.

[5] Lee to Right Reverend John Johns, March 7, 1866; *Jones*, 436.

town, intent on entering the army.[6] His father had opposed this in April, 1861, but had weakened in September[7] and now he was reconciled to it. He did not believe the boy would study at college and he did not wish him to attend simply to claim the military exemption allowed students. "I must leave the rest in the hands of our merciful God," Lee told his wife. "I hope our son will do his duty and make a good soldier."[8] The next day he went with Robert to get his outfit, with which the boy left in a few days to join the Rockbridge Artillery as a private. It was in that capacity Lee next met him, on the field of Gaines's Mill.[9]

Lee left it to Mrs. Lee to decide whether she would remain for the time being at the White House or would come to Richmond, though he reminded her that "in the present condition of affairs no one can foresee what may happen, nor in my judgment is it advisable for any one to make arrangements with a view to permanency or pleasure."[10] Mrs. Lee elected to continue at the White House, and there she stayed until the Federals were close at hand. Her impulse doubtless was to hold the plantation against McClellan and all his army, for she had the finest of courage; but she was prevailed upon to seek refuge at the home of a neighbor. Prior to May 11, she left,[11] but not until she had penned and had attached to the front door this appeal:

"Northern soldiers who profess to reverence Washington, forbear to desecrate the home of his first married life, the property of his wife, now owned by her descendants.

"A GRAND-DAUGHTER OF MRS. WASHINGTON."[12]

A few days later, two Federal officers with an escort rode up to her new shelter and asked for her. One introduced himself as Captain Joseph Kirkland, aide to General Fitz John Porter. The other was Doctor George H. Lyman, medical director of Porter's corps. They had come, they explained, with a message from

[6] Annie Lee to Agnes Lee, May 2, 1862; MS., Duke University.
[7] Lee to Mrs. Lee, Sept. 9, 1861; R. E. Lee, Jr., 43–44.
[8] Lee to Mrs. Lee, March 15, 1862; R. E. Lee, Jr., 68.
[9] See supra, p. 161.   [10] Lee to Mrs. Lee, March 14, 1862; R. E. Lee, Jr., 67.
[11] National Intelligencer, May 13, 1862, p. 3, col. 2. The Intelligencer's correspondent says Mrs. Lee was "stopping with a physician a few miles in advance." If he was correct in this, then Mrs. Lee must have been at Mt. Prospect, the home of Doctor William Hartwell Macon.
[12] Cooke, 61; N. M. Curtis, From Bull Run to Chancellorsville, 104–5; Jones, 982.

General Porter, to acquaint her with "his desire to assure her proper care and protection with as little of constraint to her wishes and movements as might be compatible with her position" inside the Federal lines. Mrs. Lee feared no Federal from commanding general to foraging private, and she proceeded to give the abashed officers a piece of her mind. It was an indignity, she said, to be confined to a house with sentinels posted about, especially at the order of General Porter, who had often been a guest at Arlington. Kirkland and Lyman protested that Porter was acting under McClellan's orders and that the wish of all was to show her every possible protection until she could be passed through the lines.[13] Mrs. Lee broke in with an emphatic announcement that she did not want to "pass through the lines"; she wished to return to the White House, "if not yet in ruins." The puzzled Federals told her that if she desired to do so, she could journey there or anywhere else, as long as she had an escort. That did not suit her: she would not go to the White House or make any move if she had to have bluecoats buzzing about her. The officers diplomatically explained that an escort was for her protection, not for espionage, and that it was necessary if she intended moving about where ignorant soldiers might not be considerate of her sex and station. This somewhat mollified her. "The visit was finally terminated with much more courtesy on her part," Doctor Lyman subsequently wrote, "than our reception promised." [14]

Soon thereafter Mrs. Lee shook the dust of the Federal camps from her creaking carriage-wheels and journeyed up the Pamunkey to Marlbourne, the estate of Edmund Ruffin, the famous agricultural experimentalist, who had fired the first gun on Fort Sumter. There she remained for some weeks—only to find the onmarching Federals, ere long, at nearby Old Church. Again she was "within the enemy's lines," with a suspicious colonel confident she would soon report the movements of his command to the Confederates.[15]

[13] McClellan was criticised by Northern extremists for posting a guard at the White House. *McClellan's Own Story*, 406.

[14] G. H. Lyman: *Some Aspects of the Medical Service in the Armies of the United States during the War of the Rebellion*, 13 *Papers of the Military Historical Society of Mass.* (cited hereafter as *M. H. S. M.*), 193–94. Lyman's account is merely paraphrased in the text. There is no other report of the interview.

[15] *O. R.*, 11, part 3, pp. 202, 203.

This time, Mrs. Lee decided that if she was to leave the company of the Federals, she would go where she did not believe they could follow her—to Richmond. Lee arranged with McClellan for her to pass through the lines, and not long before the opening of the Seven Days, he sent Major W. Roy Mason to meet her. Mason awaited her at McClellan's headquarters, where the General himself received her with due honors. Thence the carriage took her across the Meadow Bridges to Gooch's farm, a mile and a half from the Chickahominy. There General Lee welcomed her. It was the first time he had seen her since he had kissed her good-bye at Arlington on April 22, 1861, fifteen months before. Physically she had changed much for the worse during that time, as she always seemed to do in their long separations. Travel, arthritis, and suspense had aged and crippled her. Only with great difficulty was she able to walk at all.[16]

During the first weeks after Mrs. Lee's return to Richmond, the General was rarely with her, but when the Seven Days lay behind him, he could occasionally come into the city for a few days and could taste a little of the domestic life he so well loved. Robert got a furlough on account of minor sickness, and the girls fluttered home. The quiescence of the enemy temporarily lifted from his heart the burden of his responsibility. "He was the same loving father to us all," Robert remembered, "as kind and thoughtful of my mother . . . and of us, his children, as if our comfort and happiness were all he had to care for. His great victory did not elate him, so far as one could see." [17] He told his wife, "Our success has not been so great or complete as we could have desired, but God knows what is best for us. Our enemy met with a heavy loss, from which it will take him some time to recover, before he can recommence his operations." [18]

16 For many years it did not seem possible to fix the date of Mrs. Lee's arrival at Marlbourne or that of her coming to Richmond. She was at Marlbourne on May 30 (*O. R.,* 11, part 3, p. 202), and as she passed McClellan's headquarters before they were moved to Doctor Trent's house, south of the Chickahominy, it was manifest that she entered the Confederate lines prior to June 12, the date McClellan transferred headquarters. That was about all that could be established until recently when, through the kindness of Miss Susan Elizabeth Latané of Richmond, the writer was granted access to the diary of Robert G. Haile and to a letter written by this Confederate officer on June 10, 1862. These show that Mrs. Lee passed the outposts on June 10. For information on the stay of Mrs. Lee at Marlbourne, the writer is indebted to the late Mrs. Mary Sayre Johnston of Richmond. Capt. R. G. Haile's diary gives the date as June 10.

17 *R. E. Lee, Jr.,* 74.   18 Lee to Mrs. Lee, July 9, 1862; *R. E. Lee, Jr.,* 75.

It was not for long. Robert rejoined his command, Mrs. Lee and some of the girls went to Hickory Hill, the Wickham home in Hanover County, and thence to the Warren County springs in North Carolina;[19] and soon the rumble of artillery, the clatter of cavalry, and the haunting tramp of ill-shod infantry were echoing again through the streets of Richmond. The army was moving northward to still bloodier fields, and Lee must lead it there.

[19] *R. E. Lee, Jr.,* 75; Mrs. A. C. W. Byerly to Senator H. T. Wickham, Jan. 29, 1931, *Wickham MSS.*

CHAPTER XX

Enter General John Pope

During the six weeks following his hard battles around Richmond, Lee sought to rest, refit, reinforce, and reorganize the Army of Northern Virginia—a labor in the four r's of campaign aftermath. The infantry having been entirely withdrawn from in front of McClellan, and observation of the Federals having been left to a brigade of cavalry, which was changed at intervals,[1] most of the troops had only routine duties to perform, and even these were suspended on Sunday.[2] From captured and imported arms, now abundant, each regiment was uniformly armed.[3] Worn shoes and ragged jackets were replaced. Leisure and decent rations quickly restored the health of men removed to clean camps from the malarial swamps.

Reinforcement was more difficult. Except for Drayton's and Evans's brigades, which could be spared by the end of July from Charleston,[4] no additional units could be expected. For maintaining the strength of his army, Lee had to rely on the flow of conscripts, on the return of wounded men, on the prevention of absence without leave, and on the stoppage of wasteful details.[5] The signing on July 22 of a cartel for the general exchange of prisoners helped, also.[6] All these measures did not suffice, however, to swell the muster-rolls of the Army of Northern Virginia to the number present for duty at the opening of the Seven Days' battles.

Reorganization was necessary to fill the places of officers slain in battle and to restore the efficiency of regiments left under the command of incompetent captains, but it was retarded by slow

[1] O. R., 12, part 2, pp. 119, 176.   [2] J. W. Jones: *Christ in Camp*, 49.
[3] O. R., 11, part 3, pp. 40–41; IV O. R., 2, 48.
[4] O. R., 11, part 3, pp. 642, 644; O. R., 12, part 2, p. 637.
[5] O. R., 11, part 3, pp. 638, 639, 640; *ibid.*, 12, part 3, pp. 923–24, 928; IV O. R., 2, 7.
[6] II O. R., 4, 266.

256

action on recommendations for promotion[7] and, except for the cavalry, was dangerously far from completion when the army again entered on active operations. The mounted arm was taken vigorously in hand. It needed centralized direction and it got it. Stuart was given command of all the horse; two brigades were created; Wade Hampton was put at the head of one of them, and Fitz Lee, the General's nephew, was assigned the other, though not without some grumbling at the rapid advancement of the Lees.[8] The reorganization of Jackson's cavalry was deferred.[9]

Bickerings interfered with the work of welding semi-independent divisions into an efficient army. General Toombs felt that D. H. Hill had impugned his courage and challenged him to a duel;[10] Colonel H. L. Benning argued with so much vehemence against the constitutionality of the conscript act that he was in danger of arrest.[11] Longstreet became piqued at the praise of A. P. Hill in *The Richmond Examiner* and had his adjutant general rejoin with a letter in *The Richmond Whig* that led Hill to refuse to have either personal or military dealings with that officer, whereupon Longstreet put Hill under arrest and gave command of the division for the time to Hill's senior brigadier, Joseph R. Anderson.[12] Lee himself was not exempt from attack, despite the praise heaped upon him by the public. A cabal that was alleged to be seeking to "undermine the confidence of the army and of the country in his capacity" was denounced in the press.[13] As usual, Lee made no reply, but the multitude of vexations that were daily encountered drew from him a characteristic confession to his wife. Said he: "In the prospect before me I cannot see a single ray of pleasure during this war; but as long as I can perform any service to the country, I am content." [14]

While Lee was meeting these conditions as best he could, the Federals were not idle. Three hundred thousand volunteers had been called for on July 1, with the promise of a bounty of one

[7] *O. R.*, 11, part 3, pp. 669, 671.
[8] *O. R.*, 11, part 3, p. 657; R. E. Lee to S. S. Lee, July 31, 1862; Jones, *L. and L.*, 188; T. R. R. Cobb to his wife, July 28, 1862, 28 *S. H. S. P.*, 294.
[9] *Lee's Dispatches*, 42–43.   [10] 28 *S. H. S. P.*, 294.   [11] 28 *S. H. S. P.*, 294.
[12] *O. R.*, 11, part 3, pp. 639–40; *ibid.*, 51, part 2, p. 590; *Sorrel*, 87 ff.
[13] *Richmond Whig*, July 22, 1862, p. 4, col. 1.
[14] July 28, 1862; *White*, 173.

hundred dollars for each man.[15] Defeat stiffened the determination of the North. By July 10, besides the main force under Mc-
Clellan at Harrison's Landing, Lee had to watch three Federal
armies. The shattered divisions of McDowell, Banks, and Frémont had been organized into a new "Army of Virginia."
Frémont had retired and had been succeeded by Brigadier General Franz Sigel.[16] All these troops had been placed under Major
General John Pope, who, in the West, had won some reputation
for activity. Lee did not know whether these forces had been
consolidated or where they were located, but he assumed them
to be in the general vicinity of Manassas.[17] A second additional
column was known to be around Fredericksburg. Like the Army
of Virginia, its strength had not been reported, but Lee's earlier
reports had indicated that it was large.[18] The third force, likewise of undetermined numbers, had come from Burnside in
North Carolina and was on transports off Fortress Monroe.[19]

These troops were disposed strategically. If Burnside's men
joined McClellan, they would presumably make good, or almost
make good, his losses during the Seven Days. If they moved to
Fredericksburg, they might be strong enough to duplicate the
movement projected for McDowell in the spring and advance
southward from that point to Richmond or, at the least, trouble
communications between Richmond and western Virginia, via
the Virginia Central Railroad. And if, finally, the force from
Burnside or the Fredericksburg garrison, or both of them, should
reinforce Pope, that officer would be dangerously strong and
could cut the Virginia Central Railroad, march eastward toward
Richmond, or force Lee to make so large a detachment to meet
him as to put Richmond in danger of capture by McClellan. It
was, in some respects, potentially as dangerous a state of affairs
as that which had confronted Lee when he took command. He
had then been taxed to bring together all available troops in front
of Richmond to meet a concentration there by the enemy. Now,
with a superior force still immediately in his front, he had to
decide this difficult question: should he continue his concentra-

---

[15] III *O. R.*, 2, 198 *ff.*
[16] 2 *B. and L.*, 513; *O. R.*, 12, part 3, p. 435.
[17] Lee to Jackson, *O. R.*, 12, part 3, p. 916.   [18] *O. R.*, 12, part 3, p. 916.
[19] This force had arrived on July 7; *O. R.*, 11, part 3, p. 305.

tion, so as to checkmate McClellan, or should he disperse his forces in order to protect his communications and to prevent a still more dangerous reinforcement of his principal adversary?

Lee did not meet this situation with any large strategic plan, quickly conceived and steadfastly executed. His initial planning was not a matter of prescience or even of precision. Knowing comparatively little of the intentions of his opponents, he had to shape his plan, step by step, as his information accumulated.[20] The starting point was the fact that the battles for Richmond had given to the retention of that city a moral value out of all proportion to its importance as a railroad junction or even as a munitions centre. The occupation of the capital, despite all attacks to capture it, became so much a matter of prestige that it formed the basis of Lee's strategy during the months that were to follow, without any formal declaration of military policy to that effect. As early as July, 1862, the chief Virginia city was symbolically the Verdun of the South.

If Richmond was to be held, then, of course, it must be fortified further, especially on the front where it would be most exposed to combined land-and-water attacks. To this work Lee now gave himself as assiduously as he had to the construction of the light defensive line early in June. At Drewry's Bluff, on the north side of the river opposite that point, and across the roads paralleling the James, heavy works rose steadily. Ere long, these were entrusted to Lieutenant Colonel J. F. Gilmer, a most capable engineer.[21] The faithful creator of the first defenses, Colonel W. H. Stevens, was sent to Petersburg to prepare that city for possible investment.[22]

---

[20] This assertion is abundantly proved by the facts that follow in the text. It is proper to state, however, that it is contrary to the contentions of nearly all General Lee's early biographers. Writing before the publication of the *Official Records*, or else neglecting the all-important correspondence accompanying the reports in that vast storehouse, and unfamiliar, besides, with Lee's dispatch of August 30, 1862, these writers read into General Lee's quick detachment of troops an intention, on his part, from early in July, to threaten Washington and thereby to force McClellan to withdraw from the James. See *Taylor's Four Years*, 57; *Long*, 183; *Marshall*, 122; *Fitz Lee*, 173; *Taylor's General Lee*, 85. The writer has not found one line of evidence to support this claim, and a multitude of facts to disprove such a contention. It is noteworthy that General Maurice avoided error in this particular and that Colonel Henderson laid little emphasis on Lee's alleged purpose at this time to play on Lincoln's fears for the safety of Washington.

[21] *O. R.*, 11, part 3, pp. 639, 646, 658, 664; *O. R.*, 12, part 2, p. 176; *O. R.*, 51, part 2, pp. 589, 592, 600; *Lee's Dispatches*, 40.

[22] *O. R.*, 11, part 3. p. 663.

Improvement of the Richmond fortifications, while of high importance in protecting the city against McClellan, would of course make it less difficult for Lee to detach troops in case the forces in northern Virginia seriously threatened an advance. Jackson, who was now rested and full of ardor, was for an immediate offensive that would sweep past Pope's army and carry the war into the enemy's country. Lee listened patiently, but as he had known Pope casually in the old army and had no very high estimate of his abilities,[23] he was for some days less alarmed than was "Stonewall," and would not commit himself on Jackson's proposal.[24] With McClellan still dangerously close to Richmond and at the head of an army larger than his own, Lee was averse to weakening himself, at least until he knew what Pope would attempt to do.

Jackson was not satisfied. At the first opportunity, he sought out Colonel A. R. Boteler, who was a member of Congress as well as an acting member of his staff.

"Do you know that we are losing valuable time here?" Jackson began.

"How so?" Boteler replied.

"Why, by repeating the blunder we made after the battle of Manassas, in allowing the enemy leisure to recover from his defeat and ourselves to suffer by inaction. Yes"—and he became excited as he went on—"we are wasting precious time and energies in this malarious region that can be much better employed elsewhere and I want to talk to you about it."

He then explained that as McClellan was beaten, he would have to reorganize and reinforce his army before it would be in fighting trim, and that this assured the safety of Richmond. Advantage should be taken of this to invade the North. He wanted Boteler to go forthwith to see the President, to urge this course on him, and to say for Jackson that he was not making this proposal in any spirit of self-seeking, but, on the contrary, would serve under any one Davis designated.

"What is the use of my going to Mr. Davis," Boteler asked, "as he'll probably refer me again to General Lee? So why don't you yourself speak to General Lee upon the subject?"

[23] 2 B. and L., 513. [24] Dabney, 486–87.

"I have already done so," Jackson said.

"Well, what does he say?"

"He says nothing." And then he added carefully, "Don't think I complain of his silence; he doubtless has good reason for it."

"Then," Boteler inquired, half-curiously, "you don't think that General Lee is slow in making up his mind?"

"Slow!" exclaimed Jackson with much energy. "By no means, Colonel! On the contrary his perception is as quick and unerring as his judgment is infallible. But with the vast responsibilities now resting on him, he is perfectly right in withholding a hasty expression of his opinions and purposes."

He paused for a moment and then he said: "So great is my confidence in General Lee that I am willing to follow him blindfolded. But I fear he is unable to give me a definite answer now because of influences at Richmond, where, perhaps, the matter has been mentioned by him and may be under consideration. I, therefore, want you to see the President and urge the importance of prompt action." [25]

Boteler duly called on Mr. Davis and stated Jackson's views. He subsequently thought that it was on this representation that Jackson was moved,[26] but he was mistaken in this. The first shift in the army was brought about by the receipt of news on July 12 that the Federals had occupied Culpeper Courthouse that morning.[27] Culpeper was on the Orange and Alexandria, now the Southern Railway. It is only thirty-five miles northwest of Fredericksburg and just twenty-seven miles north of Gordonsville. And Gordonsville lay on an exposed bend of the Virginia Central Railroad,[28] the only direct line of rail communication between Richmond and the Shenandoah Valley. A serious threat in that quarter was an immediate menace to an indispensable line and had to be met at any cost. Desirable as it was to await the development of the enemy's plan, Lee did not feel that he could delay in defending the line of the Virginia Central, now that Pope was moving southward. On the 13th, therefore, he ordered Jackson with his own and Ewell's division, to proceed by train to Louisa,

[25] 40 *S. H. S. P.*, 180–81.   [26] *Ibid.*, 182.   [27] *O. R.*, 51, part 2, p. 590.
[28] C. S. Anderson in *Locomotive Engineering*, September, 1897, p. 678.

and, if Pope had not anticipated him, to proceed to Gordonsville.[29] Part of Jackson's cavalry was sent to Hanover Junction.[30]

This was the first time Lee had been called upon to apply in Virginia a principle he doubtless had learned in South Carolina— that "it is easier to defend a railroad by massing troops at salient

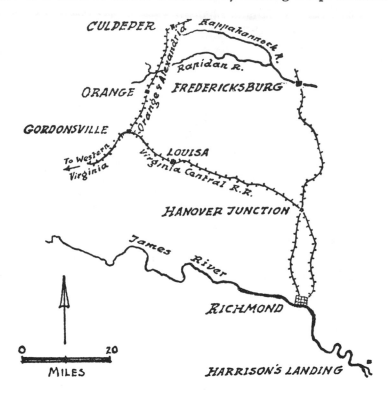

and commanding points to repress the attack of the enemy and strike him if he advances, than to extend the force along the whole line."[31] He did not scatter infantry along the railroad, which was perpendicular to the line of Pope's advance and consequently exposed for a long distance. Instead, he kept Jackson's troops together to strike the invader as he approached the railway.

[29] O. R., 12, part 3, p. 915. Four supplementary batteries were dispatched the next day (O. R., 51, part 2, pp. 591–92). For a vivid account of the difficulties encountered in moving these troops, see C. S. Anderson in Locomotive Engineering, April, 1893, p. 177.

[30] O. R., 12, part 3, p. 916. See supra, vol. I, pp. 630–31.

[31] Lee quoted by Davis, O. R., 14, 594.

Against cavalry raids he had to guard as best he could with his own horse, but he kept this equally concentrated, except for outposts and videttes. When Jackson was forced to withdraw his cavalry from Hanover Junction, Lee replaced it by part of Stuart's command, though not in time to prevent a dash by Federal cavalry to Beaver Dam Station on the Virginia Central Railroad on July 20.[32] The raid yielded the Federals nothing of consequence except the person of a young cavalry captain, who was taken prisoner while waiting for a train.[33] He was to prove a very costly capture.

Arrived at Gordonsville, Jackson could learn little of his adversary's strength and movements, but thought the Federals were withdrawing from Fredericksburg to concentrate against him. As Lee was not positive as to the size of the force at Fredericksburg, he directed Stuart to scout in that direction and to find out what was afoot.[34]

While Stuart was undertaking this, Pope brought his new Army of Virginia before the Confederate commander in a novel fashion by the issuance of an extraordinary series of orders. On taking command, he assured his troops that he was accustomed to see only the backs of his enemies, and he admonished his soldiers to dismiss from their minds "certain phrases," which, said he, "I am sorry to find so much in vogue amongst you. I hear constantly of 'taking strong positions and holding them,' of 'lines of retreat' and 'bases of supplies.' Let us discard such ideas. . . . Let us study the probable lines of retreat of our enemies, and leave our own to take care of themselves." [35] This bombast aroused only ridicule—as much in the North as in the South. His later orders were more serious. One of them directed his army to live off the country in which it operated and to reimburse only loyal citizens.[36] Another order put on each community the expense of making good the damage done by guerrillas and threatened the instant destruction of any house from which any soldier was shot.[37] A third mandate provided for the arrest of all male noncombatants within the Federal lines and for the expulsion of those

---

[32] O. R., 11, part 3, p. 330.
[33] O. R., 12, part 2, p. 119; ibid., part 3, p. 916.
[34] O. R., 12, part 3, p. 916.   [35] O. R., 12, part 3, pp. 473–74.
[36] O. R., 12, part 2, p. 50.   [37] O. R., 12, part 2, p. 51.

who refused to take the oath and to give security for their good behavior. Any person who returned after being sent away, as well as any person within the lines who communicated with the enemy, was liable to the penalty of death.[38] A mother who wrote her son a letter could be treated as a spy under this order. One of Pope's subordinates, Brigadier General A. von Steinwehr, outdid his chief in arresting five citizens of the town of Luray, with the announcement that whenever a guerrilla killed a soldier of his, one of these hostages would be shot unless the guerrilla was forthwith delivered to the Federal commander.[39]

Lee had felt that McClellan had been brutal in destroying the medicine needed for the sick and wounded left behind at Savage Station,[40] and now his wrath rose hotly at these orders of Steinwehr and Pope. To all strategic considerations for driving Pope back from the vicinity of the Virginia Central Railroad, there was added in Lee's mind a strong desire to relieve the civil population of an alleged form of mistreatment previously unknown in the war. Lee twice wrote that Pope must be "suppressed"—a word that seems to have reflected his state of mind with precision.[41] In one of his dispatches he referred to him as the "miscreant Pope,"[42] and in a private letter, when he mentioned his nephew Louis Marshall, who had sided with the North, he remarked, "I could forgive [his] fighting against us, but not his joining Pope." [43] For no other adversary in the entire war did Lee have anything that approached the contempt and personal dislike he had for Pope. He was in entire accord with the orders he received from the President to notify the Federal administration that the Confederacy would be compelled to retaliate if the offensive orders were enforced.[44]

---

[38] *O. R.,* 12, part 2, p. 52.

[39] Text in *McCabe,* 182.

[40] *O. R.,* 11, part 2, p. 494; Alfred Bagby: *King and Queen County, Virginia,* 163.

[41] *Cf. Lee's Dispatches,* 38–39; *O. R.,* 12, part 3, p. 919.

[42] *O. R.,* 11, part 2, p. 936.

[43] To Mrs. Lee, July 28, 1862; *R. E. Lee, Jr.,* 77.

[44] II *O. R.,* 4, 329, 362; 2 *Davis,* 315; 19 *S. H. S. P.,* 105; *Cooke,* 105–6; *McCabe,* 190 ff.; *Lee's Dispatches,* 45. General Halleck refused to receive Lee's letter on the ground that it contained insults to the government of the United States, but Pope's "pillage order" was materially modified on Aug. 14, and Steinwehr was rebuked for the conduct of his troops (*O. R.,* 12, part 3, pp. 573, 577). The effect of the orders, however, was demoralizing. (See a correspondent of *The New York World,* quoted in *McCabe,* 185–88.) In one instance mentioned by Miss Brock (*op. cit.,* 156–57), Pope's orders were made a basis of false accusation.

Thus far Lee had developed only two of the fundamentals of a new campaign, namely, to strengthen the Richmond fortifications so as to make a detachment of force possible, and, secondly, to guard his communications with the Valley. Pope was quiet for some days after reaching Culpeper, but Burnside's troops remained aboard transports off Old Point, as if preparing for another voyage, and on July 22 the Army of the Potomac began to show signs of activity.[45] Lee was not immediately alarmed by these stirrings in the camps of McClellan, for experience had taught him the Federal commander was slow to complete preparations for an offensive. Anticipating that he would have a period of grace before McClellan felt himself ready to strike, Lee began to study the third step in the development of a new plan: he began to ask himself whether he could send enough men to Jackson to defeat Pope, and then return them to Richmond in time to meet McClellan, precisely as he had hurried Whiting to Jackson early in June.[46]

Such a move manifestly depended on being able to meet three conditions: First, Pope must be near enough to permit Jackson to reach him without detaining too long the additional troops dispatched from Richmond;[47] second, McClellan must not meantime receive sufficient reinforcements to undertake a speedy offensive; and, third, enough troops must be left at Richmond to protect the city from capture in case Lee underestimated the time McClellan would require for a resumption of the offensive. This last was a serious matter. After Jackson's departure, Lee had only 69,732 men present for duty, including Holmes's former command that had been returned to the south side of the James.[48] He had to assume that his adversary was far stronger than that.

From July 23 to July 27, Lee wrestled over the logistics of this aspect of his plan. McClellan's activities increased. Longstreet was compelled to move an infantry force to New Market Heights, which were on the line of the shortest advance from Harrison's Landing to Richmond.[49] Lee was uncertain whether McClellan was demonstrating to deceive him, or testing out the strength of

---

[45] Lee to Jackson, July 23, *O. R.*, 12, part 3, pp. 916–17.
[46] *O. R.*, 12, part 3, pp. 916–17.   [47] *Ibid.*
[48] *O. R.*, 11, part 3, p. 645.   [49] *O. R.*, 51, part 3, pp. 595–96.

the Confederates in his front, or preparing for a serious advance. In any case, unless some decision was soon reached and put in execution, both Lee and Jackson might be assaulted. So reasoning, Lee reached this solution: The two brigades that were coming from South Carolina would arrive on July 28. They would number 4000 men.[50] Lee would incorporate them in his army and would send 18,000 veterans forthwith to Jackson for a blow against Pope. This would leave 56,000 men on the James. Lee would take his chances of holding Richmond with that number. To discourage and delay McClellan's advance, he would organize a diversion on the south side of the James against McClellan's base and would endeavor to interrupt the transport of supplies to McClellan by employing artillery on the lower James.[51] In this way, Jackson might be strong enough to dispose of Pope, and McClellan might be held back until this was done, or, if McClellan advanced, a sufficient force would be at hand to maintain a good defensive on the newly fortified Richmond front.

Who should go to Jackson? Not Longstreet, because he would be needed at Richmond. The next man in ability and equipment was A. P. Hill. But he was still under arrest, and his senior brigadier, L. O. B. Branch, was as yet too inexperienced, in Lee's opinion, to be entrusted with a division.[52] Hill must be restored to duty. Longstreet's theory of discipline, which had inspired that officer's arrest, must be subordinated to the army's necessity. There was, however, another possible embarrassment. The commander of the "Light Division" was high-spirited and sensitive. Jackson played a lone hand, was stern in his discipline and was secretive in his methods. There was danger that Hill and Jackson might not work well in harness. Lee determined to provide against this in the most direct manner. In a letter to Jackson, he dropped a hint that was as positive as it was diplomatic:

"A. P. Hill you will, I think, find a good officer, with whom you can consult, and by advising with your division commanders as to your movements much trouble will be saved you in arrang-

---

[50] *O. R.*, 14, 575–76.   [51] *O. R.*, 11, part 3, p. 647.

[52] *Lee's Dispatches*, 38–39. General Jos. R. Anderson, who had been Hill's senior brigade-commander, had resigned on July 19 to manage the Tredegar Iron Works, the munition-plant of which he was the chief proprietor.

ing details, as they can act more intelligently. I wish to save you trouble from my increasing your command." [53]

All this being arranged, Lee anticipated by one day the arrival of the two brigades from South Carolina and, on July 27, took the third step in the development of his plan: A. P. Hill, with his division and the Louisiana brigade, was ordered to Gordonsville.[54] "I want Pope to be suppressed," Lee repeated.[55] Hill's men moved quietly away on the day their orders were received. The Army of Northern Virginia was reduced by 20 per cent. Yet there is missing from Lee's correspondence the tension observable when he had faced the converse of the problem two months before and had been feeding troops to the Richmond line. Although Lee did not minimize his difficulties or display any rashness, his dispatches were calm and most of his movements assured. Three reasons may be advanced for this. First, he had acquired some experience in the quick transfer of large bodies of men on the interior lines; second, he was confident of the fighting qualities of his army; and third, he was beginning to read with more assurance the minds of the men who opposed him. Pope he never took very seriously; McClellan he respected but understood.

But for these psychological factors, the situation would have seemed most unpromising, with Pope strong on the upper Rappahannock, a force of unknown numbers at Fredericksburg, Burnside presumably still on his transports off Fort Monroe, and the Army of the Potomac in the entrenched camp at Harrison's Landing, supported by a navy that had undisputed command of the sea. McClellan was believed to have received an accession of numbers[56] and was known to have a force much larger than Lee's. If, therefore, Burnside should reinforce McClellan, after Hill's departure had left Lee with only 56,000, an advance on Richmond would be a serious matter. On the other hand, if Burnside should join Pope, he would give the Army of Virginia

[53] O. R., 12, part 3, p. 918.

[54] O. R., 12, part 3, pp. 917-19. It is possible that Lee was influenced in his decision by a rumor that Burnside was returning to North Carolina (O. R., 11, part 3, p. 656), and by two spies' report that there was only a small force at Fredericksburg (Lee's Dispatches, 36-37), but in none of his rather full dispatches of this period is there any reference to these factors.

[55] O. R., 12, part 3, p. 919.   [56] O. R., 12, part 3, p. 917.

a number of men in excess of the 30,000 to 36,000 that Lee calculated Jackson would have on Hill's arrival.[57] Burnside's movements consequently became of the utmost moment to Lee, who
watched them at the end of July with more immediate concern
than he felt either for Jackson or for his own army.[58]

The junction of Burnside and McClellan was a risk that had to
be taken. Nothing could be done to prevent it. If it happened at
once, only the completion of strong defenses and the stubbornest
sort of fighting would negative it. If it were delayed, Jackson and
Hill might meantime dispose of Pope and again be available for
duty on the James.[59] Meantime, Lee pushed the work on the
fortification of Richmond and developed his plan to delay and
interrupt McClellan's offensive preparation by the projected
operation against his shipping. As Lee studied this diversion, he
became impressed with its possibilities. He believed that if he
could bring a heavy fire to bear on Harrison's Landing and could
assail from the river banks the Federal supply vessels ascending
the James, he could anchor McClellan to his base. This might
make it possible to detach still more troops to Jackson, and thereby
to drive, if not to destroy Pope.[60] It was as Lee dwelt on the great
results he might achieve if he could further reinforce Jackson that
the first glimpse of the next stage of his larger strategy is to be
had.

The details of the operation against McClellan's entrenched
camp and supply line were assigned to Generals S. G. French and
D. H. Hill. The concentration of artillery was entrusted to
General W. N. Pendleton. Preparations were made with some
care. Coggin's Point, on the south side of the James, opposite
Harrison's, was chosen as the most favorable position. Forty-three
guns, large and small, were secretly concentrated there. On the
night of July 31–August 1, a violent bombardment of the Federal
entrenched camp was begun. It caused much confusion but
inflicted slight damage, and before daylight it was abandoned as
the guns had to be withdrawn to avoid capture.[61] Lee determined
to persist in annoying his opponent,[62] but when McClellan made

---

[57] O. R., 12, part 3, p. 918. [58] Marshall, 122–23.
[59] O. R., 12, part 3, pp. 918–19. [60] O. R., 11, part 2, p. 936.
[61] O. R., 11, part 2, pp. 939 ff.; O. R., 12, part 2, pp. 176–77; S. G. French: *Two
Wars* (cited hereafter as *French*), 148 ff.
[62] O. R., 11, part 3, p. 938.

the obvious countermove, by sending a force across the James and occupying Coggin's Point on August 3,[63] Lee had to admit his inability to drive him away. The whole operation was written down as a failure, except, Lee thought, as it might delay the start of McClellan's offensive a few days,[64] at a time when every day might count.

If it was impossible to interfere materially with McClellan's occupation of Harrison's Landing, there was nothing at the moment that Lee could do except to prepare to resist McClellan's expected advance as vigorously as he might, and, in case of necessity, to recall Jackson and Hill, leaving Pope to do his worst against the Virginia Central Railroad. Meantime, the idea that had occurred to him while he was projecting the Coggin's Point expedition must have shaped itself in an insistent question: Was there any way by which he could strengthen Jackson so as to assure the destruction of Pope?

About this time there arrived as an exchanged prisoner of war the young captain who had been made prisoner on July 20 at Beaver Dam Station by the Federal cavalry in their raid. This officer was none other than John S. Mosby, subsequently head of the famous "Rangers" that bore his name. Mosby had been sent to Fort Monroe, and, while awaiting exchange, had kept his eyes open and had shrewdly questioned his guards. He had concluded from what he had seen and heard that Burnside's expedition was about to sail to Fredericksburg to join Pope's army, and he hastened to communicate to Lee that conclusion and the reasons for it.[65] If Mosby was correct, his news manifestly was of the greatest moment and made it seem highly probable that the next major effort of the enemy was to be in northern Virginia.

But on August 5 the evidence seemed to indicate that the long-awaited offensive by McClellan was under way: the Confederate cavalry reported a heavy force advancing up the left bank of the James toward Richmond. Lee set himself for a shock. He put

[63] *O. R.*, 11, part 1, p. 76. [64] *O. R.*, 11, part 3, p. 660.
[65] *Cooke*, 109; Cooke: *Wearing of the Gray*, 116; Cooke: *Life of Stonewall Jackson*, 256. It has not been possible to establish with certainty the date of Mosby's arrival at Lee's headquarters, but it is a reasonable inference from Lee to Jackson, Aug. 4, 1862, *O. R.*, 12, part 3, pp. 922–23, that Lee did not have information on that day that Burnside was moving to support Pope, and it is clear from Lee to Jackson, Aug. 7, 1862, *O. R.*, 12, part 3, pp. 925–26, that he knew by Aug. 6 that Burnside was in Fredericksburg. Mosby, therefore, must have reached Lee on Aug. 5 or 6.

three divisions in motion the next day and found McClellan drawn up at Malvern Hill, on the very ground occupied by the Federals on July 1. This time there was no hurried, blind attack by the Army of Northern Virginia. Instead, the Confederate lines were deliberately drawn. Arriving on the ground in person, Lee directed that the Confederate left be extended toward the Willis Church road, to command the routes that led to McClellan's rear. The Confederate right skirmished briskly with the Federals; there were many signs of approaching battle. Then, on the morning of August 7, when a clash seemed certain, an amazing situation was disclosed: the Federals had gone as they had come, and soon were back at Harrison's Landing![66]

What did this mean? Obviously, if McClellan had any immediate intention of moving on Richmond, he would not occupy the strongest approach and then evacuate it overnight. But what was up? Why had he advanced at all? Lee concluded that his opponent must have made the demonstration to cover an advance on the part of Burnside in northern Virginia. Had Burnside really gone up the Rappahannock to Fredericksburg? Was he already there? If so, what was his objective? Stuart reported rumors that there were 16,000 infantry in Fredericksburg, and that 6000 cavalry which he had dispersed had undertaken a raid on Hanover Courthouse.[67] Were these troops a part of Pope's command, or were they from Burnside? The surest means of dealing with them and with Pope's main force was, of course, for Jackson to advance. If Jackson would do that, and Pope were not strong, Pope would be apt to draw to his support the troops at Fredericksburg, provided they were under his command. But if Pope were strong and if the Fredericksburg troops were Burnside's, there was danger that they would be employed disastrously against Jackson's communications via the Virginia Central Railroad. The only way safely to ignore the force at Fredericksburg and at the same time to protect the railroad against raids, would be to send Jackson enough men for a speedy and successful blow at Pope. Then the force at Fredericksburg would have to fall back. But was it possible to strengthen Jackson further with McClellan where he was, strong and preparing, perhaps, to take

---

[66] O. R., 11, part 3, p. 356; ibid., 12, part 2, p. 177; ibid., 51, part 2, p. 603.
[67] O. R., 12, part 3, pp. 924–25.

a new position, even though his withdrawal from Malvern Hill indicated plainly that he was not yet ready for an offensive?[68]

Thus the argument in Lee's mind pursued a circle, caution bringing him back to the waiting policy from which his desire to suppress Pope and his concern for the Virginia Central Railroad constantly were drawing him. In his dilemma he did the only thing he could do at a distance from a situation he could not fathom—he gave discretion to Jackson. On August 7 he wrote him fully. Explaining that he did not know whether he could promise the reinforcements Jackson required, he urged him not to count on them, though if possible he would send them. Then he reviewed the contingencies and especially cautioned Jackson not to attack the strong positions of the enemy but to turn them so as to draw the Federals out. "I would rather you should have easy fighting and heavy victories," he said. He concluded with *carte blanche:* "I must now leave the matter to your reflection and good judgment. Make up your mind what is best to be done under all the circumstances which surround us, and let me hear the result at which you arrive. I will inform you if any change takes place here that bears on the subject." [69]

Granting discretion to Jackson did not mean any evasion of his own responsibilities. Neither did it lead him to relax for a moment his efforts to find additional troops with which to reinforce Jackson. On the same day that he told Jackson to stand or to advance as his judgment dictated, he urged D. H. Hill to hurry the completion of the works at Drewry's Bluff, as it might soon be necessary to withdraw his division for service in the field.[70] The next day, moreover, he ordered Hood to prepare to move to Hanover Junction, where he could protect the Virginia Central Railroad or move, if necessary, to Jackson's support.[71]

Jackson did not wait for the discretionary orders Lee sent him. Having learned that a part of Pope's troops were moving southward in advance of the main army, he notified Lee of his intention to attack them and set out accordingly.[72] On the afternoon of August 9 he found the Federals on Cedar Run in the vicinity of an eminence that bore the sinister name of Slaughter Moun-

[68] *O. R.,* 12, part 3, pp. 925–26.
[69] *O. R.,* 12, part 3, pp. 925-26.
[71] *O. R.,* 11, part 3, p. 667.
[70] *O. R.,* 11, part 3, p. 666.
[72] *Cf. O. R.,* 12, part 3, p. 926.

tain. He attacked viciously and after suffering a temporary reverse on part of his line, swept forward and drove the Federals from the field. His losses were 1276.[73] It developed that the troops with whom he had been engaged were those of his old opponent of the Valley, General N. P. Banks.

Lee was delighted at Jackson's success and sent him a message of warm congratulation.[74] The success justified the confidence that Lee had retained in Jackson even after the Seven Days. It showed that Jackson was himself again. Jackson, however, soon realized that he had met only the vanguard of Pope's army and that the remainder was rapidly coming up. Very prudently, on the night of August 11, he decided to withdraw closer to Gordonsville, there to await reinforcements.[75] This move decided Lee on his course of action. The road to the Virginia Central was open. There was no longer any prospect that Jackson would be able to cripple Pope and return to Richmond in time to help in disposing of McClellan. Whatever the risks meantime, Jackson must be strengthened to strike a blow at his adversary and to save the railroad. On August 13, therefore, Lee ordered Longstreet with ten brigades to move to Jackson's aid.[76] In dispatching Longstreet, Lee sketched a plan of advance for that officer's study on the ground.[77]

Scarcely had these orders been issued than Lee received a report that Burnside had left Fredericksburg and had joined Pope. Although the details were not wholly convincing, Lee believed the report to be correct,[78] and he immediately directed Hood to carry out the projected movement of his division of two brigades to Hanover Junction. There he could cover the railroad and, as Burnside advanced, he could parallel him and join Longstreet.[79]

By one of the curious chances of war, on the very day when Lee decided that he must face the risk involved in these further

[73] O. R., 12, part 1, pp. 179–80.
[74] O. R., 12, part 2, p. 185. Jackson's original dispatch, announcing the victory, is in the Chilton Papers in the Confederate Museum, Richmond.
[75] O. R., 12, part 2, p. 185.   [76] O. R., 11, part 3, p. 675.
[77] Longstreet, 159; O. R., 11, part 3, p. 676.
[78] O. R., 11, part 3, pp. 674–75; O. R., 12, part 3, p. 928.
[79] O. R., 11, part 3, pp. 674–75. It has generally been supposed that Longstreet was sent to Jackson on receipt of the report of Burnside's advance and that the orders to Hood were issued simultaneously, but Lee to Longstreet, O. R., 11, part 3, p. 676, makes it certain that the movement of Longstreet was ordered prior to the report of Burnside's advance, and that Hood's advance was ordered subsequent thereto.

detachments from the James, it developed that the risk might not be so great as he had previously believed. Ever since the end of July there had been rumors that McClellan was reducing his force at Harrison's Landing,[80] but nothing definite was reported until August 13, when an English deserter came into the Confederate lines and stated that part of McClellan's army had embarked for a move. Deserters' stories were notoriously unreliable, but this one impressed Lee as being true. He immediately instructed D. H. Hill to send scouts down the right bank of the river to ascertain the facts.[81] The next day, August 14, D. H. Hill reported there was no doubt that Fitz John Porter had left McClellan. Three deserters from Burnside's army averred that he had reached Fredericksburg with 12,000 men and after arriving there had been reinforced by twenty-one regiments.[82]

This was news of the greatest moment. Lee quickly interpreted it to indicate that a part of the Army of the Potomac was being withdrawn to support Pope.[83] That officer would soon present a most formidable front on the line of the Virginia Central Railroad. Unless Jackson were still further reinforced he would be overwhelmed, even with Longstreet's support. But, along with a great danger, a large opportunity was presented. If Lee could take advantage of the interior lines and concentrate against Pope before any troops from the Army of the Potomac could reach him, a great victory might be won. But it would be a race, perhaps a close race, between Lee's reinforcements, already moving by rail to Gordonsville, and McClellan's detachments, hurrying by water down the James and up the Rappahannock or the Potomac, and thence overland. Whoever won that race might win the war. No time was to be lost. Lee acted with the utmost decision and dispatch. He immediately decided to go to Gordonsville himself, and he sounded out the President on the dispatch thither of R. H. Anderson's division, which was then at Drewry's Bluff.[84] Lee had to be diplomatic in his approach, because Mr. Davis was sensitive to any danger to Richmond. For his own part Lee was convinced that the changed situation justified a further reduction of force on the Richmond front. The great

---

[80] *O. R.*, 51, part 2, p. 602.   [81] *O. R.*, 11, part 3, p. 674.
[82] *Lee's Dispatches*, 47–49.   [83] *O. R.*, 11, part 3, pp. 675–76.
[84] *Lee's Dispatches*, 47–49.

questions in his mind were these: How large a part of McClellan's army was on the move? How many of the Confederate troops still on the James could be sent northward? How much of a lead did McClellan have?

Some time could be saved by delivering the attack on Pope as soon as the troops were at hand. To assure that, Lee arranged for a council of war with Longstreet and Jackson, to be held as soon as his train reached Gordonsville. As a preliminary, he telegraphed Longstreet that he inclined to attack by the right flank, and he renewed a suggestion made before Longstreet left Richmond—that Stuart move around Pope's army, get in rear of it, and attack its communications.[85]

G. W. Smith, who had returned from sick leave on June 10,[86] was put at the head of the three divisions to be left behind, and was instructed to speed the completion of the Richmond defenses and to hold them to the last extremity.[87] In anticipation of the President's approval of the detachment of R. H. Anderson, Lee directed that officer to prepare for a movement to Gordonsville with no surplus wagons.[88]

So crowded was the 14th day of August with these arrangements that Lee did not have time to ride into Richmond and say farewell, though, with his usual care in such matters, he sent in his straw hat and a surplus undershirt to be saved for calmer summers.[89] At 4 o'clock on the morning of August 15, the first stage of the transfer of the army to the new front having been completed, he took train. "I go to Gordonsville," he told Custis. "My after movements depend on circumstances that I cannot foresee." [90]

Such, then, was the chain of circumstances that prompted Lee to hurry troops away from Richmond with even greater speed and secrecy than he had displayed in concentrating them there two months before. First had developed the sentimental necessity of holding Richmond as the symbol of Southern resistance after the battles of the Seven Days. This had found its immediate

[85] O. R., 11, part 3, p. 676.   [86] O. R., 11, part 3, p. 671; G. W. Smith, 256–57.
[87] O. R., 11, part 3, p. 677. The land-defenses at Drewry's Bluff were expected to be completed in another week's work, ibid., 679.
[88] O. R., 11, part 3, pp. 677–78.
[89] R. E. Lee to G. W. C. Lee, Aug. 14, 1862; Jones, L. and L., 189.
[90] Ibid.; Lee's Dispatches, 48; Marshall, 124; O. R., 11, part 3, p. 676.

expression in a strengthening of the city's defenses, and this, in turn, had made it possible for him to detach Jackson when the arrival of Pope at Culpeper had raised fears for the safety of communications with the valley of the Shenandoah via the Virginia Central Railroad. Pope's hard orders had next aroused Lee's indignation and had been a major factor in disposing him to send A. P. Hill to strengthen Jackson for a blow at Pope as soon as he had received two brigades of reinforcements from South Carolina. To hold McClellan inactive while Jackson struck Pope, Lee had organized the Coggin's Point expedition. Although this had failed, Lee's desire to dispose of Pope had steadily increased, and McClellan's advance to Malvern Hill had convinced him that Burnside was planning either to join Pope or to threaten Jackson's communications. Lee had just prepared to send Hood to guard the railroad when the withdrawal of Jackson from Cedar Run had still further increased his concern and had prompted him to dispatch Longstreet to Gordonsville. This had been followed by the discovery that McClellan was reducing force to strengthen Pope. Thereupon Lee concluded that he had to run a race to attack and destroy Pope before McClellan's troops could reach the new Federal commander in northern Virginia.

These events were not spectacular in themselves, but they are of interest to the student of war in two particulars, and first as an illustration of the manner in which sound military judgment must sometimes supplement the fullest information that can be procured of the movements of an adversary. Lee had more to do than interpret his intelligence reports: he had to read in them and through them the intentions of four separate forces, and on the validity of his conclusions he had to stake the safety of Richmond and the life of his army. Above all, he had to act with promptness. Delay, as so often happens, might mean disaster.

How correct were his conclusions? To answer that question, in a case of so much complexity, is, at this period of his career, to take the measure of Lee as a strategist, in a very important respect.

Lee had learned of Burnside's movement to Fredericksburg, it will be recalled, on August 5 or 6. That officer had not landed there until the night of August 3 and did not report all his troops ashore until August 9.[91] It was on August 13 that Lee was convinced that troops from Burnside's command were moving to reinforce Pope; the first troops to depart, King's division, which had been at Fredericksburg before the arrival of Burnside, had actually left on August 9–10,[92] and the major reinforcement, Reno with twelve regiments, started on the evening of August 12.[93] As for McClellan, he had passed through a long controversy with the administration over the removal of his army from the James.[94] Aside from his wounded, the first troops that he sent off were some batteries and 1000 cavalry needed for Burnside, who had only a few mounted men. These left on August 11.[95] Two days later Lee was informed that McClellan was reducing force. The news of the departure of Fitz John Porter's corps was received by Lee before Porter's column had crossed the Chickahominy on its march down the Peninsula.[96] As Lee took the train for Gordonsville, confident that he could safely diminish the troops guarding Richmond, McClellan's army was cooking rations for its departure from Harrison's Landing.[97] Lee's record in interpreting the plan of his opponents thus speaks for itself. It is the more

[91] Cf. O. R., 12, part 3, pp. 523, 528–29, 554.

[92] O. R., 12, part 3, pp. 553, 556.   [93] Cf. O. R., 12, part 3, pp. 565–66.

[94] After McClellan reached Harrison's Landing, he recovered a measure of his self-confidence, though he still believed that Lee outnumbered him two to one (O. R., 11, part 3, p. 315). On July 25, he received a visit from Major-General H. W. Halleck, who had assumed command as general in chief two days previously. Halleck was for the withdrawal of the Army of the Potomac to northern Virginia; McClellan was for remaining where he was. He stated that if Halleck would give him 30,000 additional men, he could attack Richmond with a good chance of success. Halleck explained that only 20,000 could be supplied. The next day McClellan agreed to resume the offensive if the 20,000 were forthcoming, but he was not sanguine of success. He still insisted that Lee had 200,000 men (O. R., 11, part 3, pp. 337–38). "My opinion," he wrote Mr. Lincoln on the 28th, "is more and more firm that here is the defence of Washington" (O. R., 11, part 1, p. 75; cf. ibid., 11, part 3, p. 342). Halleck, however, was convinced that the Federals were dangerously disadvantaged with Lee's army between McClellan and Pope, and as he had the ear of Mr. Lincoln and of Mr. Stanton, he prevailed upon them to order the abandonment of the plan of operations to which General Grant was compelled to return, in effect, before he could capture Richmond. On Aug. 3, Halleck sent McClellan orders to prepare to move to Aquia Creek as soon as possible, and to begin immediately the removal of his sick and wounded by transport (O. R., 11, part 1, pp. 80–81). The evacuation of invalids and casualties was a slow process, provoking much tart correspondence between Halleck and McClellan (O. R., 11, part 1, p. 84; O. R., 11, part 3, p. 377). McClellan obeyed orders, it would appear, as promptly as circumstances allowed, but he held to the view that the transfer to northern Virginia was not in the public interest, and as late as Aug. 12, he argued that he could attack to advantage as Lee's army had been much weakened by detachments (O. R., 11, part 3, pp. 372–73).

[95] O. R., 11, part 3, p. 369. It is not certain from the reports when the artillery embarked. It may have been on the 10th, possibly on the 9th.

[96] O. R., 12, part 3, p. 579.

[97] O. R., 11, part 3, p. 377.

remarkable when one remembers that his intelligence service, at this time, was still crude.

The transfer of Confederate units from James River to Gordonsville is the second point of interest in this period, because it is an admirable example of the manner in which rapid troop movements could be conducted secretly during the War between the States. General King, at Fredericksburg, had heard a rumor of Jackson's departure from Richmond three days before the men were put on trains, and he had promptly reported it,[98] but no attention had been paid to it. Not until July 16 had there been further intimation that Jackson's "foot-cavalry" had left the James,[99] and then, for a week, conflicting stories had circulated as to Jackson's whereabouts and strength.[100] After it had become reasonably sure that Jackson and Ewell were in the vicinity of Gordonsville, the Federals had not been in agreement as to the size of the Confederate force in their front. Estimates ran from 15,000 to 80,000.[101] Hill's arrival at Gordonsville had been unobserved and had occurred at a time when the Federals had been satisfied that the Virginia Central was operating irregularly, if at all.[102] It was August 3 before Pope was certain that Hill had joined Jackson.[103] Longstreet arrived with equal secrecy. As late as August 20, only when Lee was ready to launch his offensive, were the Federals satisfied that Longstreet was on the move.[104]

Of the accuracy of his deductions, the secrecy of his troop movements and the confusion of his foes, Lee knew little when, on the morning of August 15, he "took the cars" for Gordonsville. It was the first time he had travelled on that railway since he had returned from West Virginia in November, 1861. What a change that brief period had wrought! "Granny" Lee, the butt of all the sarcasm of the street-corner strategists, had become "the King of Spades" to his grumbling trench-digging soldiers; and now, as the "first captain of the Confederacy," the "saviour of Richmond," he was leaving a delivered capital with the confidence of the South. Daring marches, thrilling victories, and heart-breaking

[98] *O. R.,* 12, part 3, p. 463.   [99] *O. R.,* 12, part 3, p. 476.
[100] *O. R.,* 11, part 3, pp. 327, 328, 329; *O. R.,* 12, part 3, pp. 476, 481, 482, 486, 487, 488, 491, 494, 495, 499, 500.
[101] *O. R.,* 11, part 3, p. 334; *O. R.,* 12, part 3, pp. 505, 506, 509, 514, 516, 521.
[102] *O. R.,* 12, part 3, pp. 503, 525.   [103] *O. R.,* 12, part 3, p. 527.
[104] *O. R.,* 12, part 3, pp. 560, 561, 569, 590–91: *O. R.,* 11, part 3, p. 380.

disappointments lay ahead, but the worn rails over which he was moving were to be, in a singular sense, a new frontier. South of the line of the Virginia Central he was not to permit the main army of the enemy to pass again for twenty-one bloody months.

CHAPTER XXI

GENERAL POPE RETIRES TOO SOON

THE little town of Gordonsville, where Lee arrived on August 15, is set in a lovely country that seemed in 1862 to invite great adventure. Then as now that section of Virginia was known as Piedmont, the "foot of the mountains" that rose in the lofty, tree-clad Blue Ridge. Westward, beyond the range, lay the Shenandoah Valley, already made forever famous in war by Jackson's battles. East of the mountains, which run roughly north and south, were long, low ridges, covered with grass or growing crops and broken here and there by rounded eminences, exalted with the name of mountains. Heavy forests were few. Swamps were rarely encountered along the clear-cut streams. The briar did not flourish. There was little underbrush to cover skirmishers or to confuse an advancing column. Firmer roads ran closer to the surveyor's straight line than in eastern Virginia, and were not as confusingly numerous. The possibilities of bold military operations were limited only by the scarcity of cover, which made it difficult to hide large bodies of troops for such strategy as Lee employed.[1]

Thanks to Jackson's forethought, when Lee sat down in council with him and Longstreet on the 15th, he had a good map and adequate intelligence reports. The Rapidan River on the south and the Rappahannock on the north form a great "V" laid on its side with its apex to the east, where the two rivers unite, about nine miles west of Fredericksburg. Across the open end of this "V," at an average distance of twenty miles from the confluence of the streams, ran the Orange and Alexandria Railroad, which constituted Pope's line of supply. Into the angle between the two rivers, before Burnside had sent reinforcements, Pope had brought a force which Jackson estimated at 45,000 to 50,000. Pope's front was to the Rapidan. Behind him lay the Rappa-

[1] Cf Hotchkiss in 3 C. M. H., 317.

279

hannock. Twenty thousand men, Lee estimated, had reached Pope from Burnside and from King, the latter being now first identified as in command at Fredericksburg before the coming of Burnside. These accessions, the Confederates computed, made Pope's full strength 65,000 to 70,000 men. No troops were coming down the railroad from Alexandria, escaped civilians said, but all the supplies of Pope's army were moving by that line and across

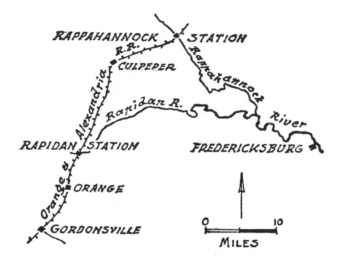

a bridge that spanned the northern river at Rappahannock Station.

Pope's ignorance of Lee's movements had caused him incautiously to present his adversary as fair an opportunity as ever a soldier was offered. If the infantry of the Army of Northern Virginia could be concentrated close to the Rapidan, the cavalry could be dispatched quickly to burn the bridge at Rappahannock Station, and then the veteran brigades from the Peninsula could be hurled across the Rapidan. Pope would thus be caught within the "V" between the two rivers and might be destroyed.

But this must be done quickly, for General French telegraphed on the morning of the 16th that 108 vessels had gone down the James in less than twenty-four hours and that only eight had come upstream. Moreover, Lee had received a copy of *The Philadelphia Inquirer,* in which its correspondent from Fort Monroe

280

affirmed that a movement of the whole or a part of McClellan's army was to be expected. Adding these scraps to the information he already possessed, Lee concluded that the whole instead of merely a part of McClellan's army was probably, though not certainly, moving to reinforce Pope and that it would arrive as rapidly as the men could be transported. Both the stakes and the participants in the race might be even greater than Lee had assumed. "It may be," he wrote the President on the 16th, "that this part of the country is to be the scene of operations." [2]

The situation had sufficiently developed on the 15th for Lee to ask that R. H. Anderson's division be sent forward immediately— a request that Davis honored with dispatch.[3] On the 16th, Lee recommended that the rest of the troops left at Richmond, except the garrison and the reserve artillery, be ordered to join him, not only because he would need them but, also, as he diplomatically told the President, because their discipline would be improved if they were removed from the vicinity of the city.[4] He could not wait for their arrival, however, if Mr. Davis consented to release them. He must strike while the opportunity was open, and before Pope became alarmed and put the Rappahannock between him and the Army of Northern Virginia. Forced to the utmost effort in June to prevent a Federal concentration on Richmond, Lee must now be equally diligent to forestall a concentration away from Richmond.

The only questions to be decided were when and on which flank the attack should be made. Longstreet was all for a movement by the Confederate left, to give the army the vantage-ground of the long ridges and high hills. Lee reasoned that it was sounder strategy to assail Pope's left, so as to interpose between him and any fast-moving force from McClellan that might advance by way of Fredericksburg.[5]

And what was the earliest date at which the army could cross the Rapidan? Jackson, who had been in the country long enough to organize his transportation and to accumulate provisions, had moved on the 15th to Mount Pisgah Church, five miles northeast of Orange Courthouse.[6] He advocated crossing the Rapidan on

[2] *Lee's Dispatches*, 51; *O. R.*, 11, part 3, p. 680.
[3] *O. R.*, 11, part 3, pp. 678–80. [4] *Lee's Dispatches*, 51.
[5] *Longstreet*, 159. [6] *O. R.*, 12, part 2, p. 641.

the 16th, to give battle on the 17th. Some of "Stonewall's" ad-mirers have affirmed that Longstreet insisted on having more time to provision his men, though Jackson offered to loan him enough hard bread for the march.[7] This may be true, for Long-street had moved to Gordonsville so hurriedly that his com-missary doubtless was disorganized.[8] If the claim be true, it should in fairness be remembered that Longstreet's only previous experience with Jackson's logistics had been during the Seven Days. At the conference of June 23, Jackson had announced that he would be in position to turn Beaver Dam Creek on June 25. At Longstreet's instance, the opening of the attack had been delayed until the 26th, and even then Jackson was late.[9] Long-street might readily have been forgiven if, after that experience, he argued for more time. Had Longstreet in the later case been both wrong in his estimate of Jackson and wrong in demanding delay for victualling his men, this could not have been the only reason why Lee did not order an advance on August 16–17. The cavalry operation against Rappahannock Bridge was an essential part of Lee's plan, and the cavalry was not then concentrated and could not be by the night of the 16th, certainly not with the horses in condition to undertake a long and exacting raid. Later developments proved this all too clearly.

The decision, then, was to approach the fords of the Rapidan on the 17th and to give battle to Pope on the 18th, between the Rapidan and the Rappahannock. Orders to this effect were issued on the 16th, within approximately thirty hours after Lee reached Gordonsville. If busy Major E. P. Alexander of the engineers knew of these orders and timed them, one is disposed to wonder if he remembered that ride with Colonel Ives, soon after Lee had assumed command, when he had somewhat skeptically asked Ives if Lee had the measure of audacity the necessities of the Southern cause demanded.

From Gordonsville, Lee had changed his headquarters on the evening of the 15th to the plantation of Barton Haxall, and on the 16th he went to the Taylor farm, near Orange Courthouse.[10]

---

[7] *White*, 177.

[8] Lee in *O. R.*, 12, part 3, p. 940, mentioned provisions as one of the reasons for de-laying the advance.

[9] See *supra*, p. 112.

[10] Walter H. Taylor to his sister, Aug. 17, 1862, *Taylor MSS.*

There, on the 17th, though his information from the Richmond front was not very detailed, Lee concluded that McClellan's withdrawal involved the whole of McClellan's army, and from that time he gave himself no further immediate concern for the capital. His only comment to Mrs. Lee was: "I suppose [McClellan] is coming here too so we shall have a busy time."[11] Through the adjutant general, he ordered General G. W. Smith to follow R. H. Anderson with another division, so that he would have ample troops for immediate operations, though he did not accept the camp estimate that Pope already had 92,000 men.[12]

Stuart reached Orange Courthouse by train on the afternoon of the 17th, and came out to Lee's headquarters. He reported that he had moved Fitz Lee's brigade from Hanover Courthouse on the 16th to the vicinity of Beaver Dam, and had left him there with orders to march on the 17th toward Raccoon Ford on the Rapidan, where Stuart expected to cross the river. Nothing was said that indicated any doubt in Stuart's mind concerning the arrival of Fitz Lee at the designated point that day. Hampton's cavalry brigade had been left on the Richmond front and could not possibly join the army in time to participate in the first stages of the new campaign.[13] Fitz Lee's command, therefore, was all that Stuart had, except one battery of horse artillery, for the arduous task Lee had assigned him in dealing with the numerically superior Federal cavalry, which were showing vast improvement.[14] To strengthen Stuart and to assure unified command of the cavalry, Lee now placed under Stuart's control the cavalry previously attached to Jackson, known as Robertson's brigade.[15] This created no friction, as Jackson had not been satisfied with the handling of his cavalry and had the highest opinion of Stuart.

Preparations went on apace all day of the 17th. The army was in excellent spirits, confident of its ability to defeat Pope.[16] There was no sign, as yet, that the Federals were aware of the thunderbolt Lee was forging for them. Everything pointed to an early and an overwhelming victory ere Pope could draw to him a single

[11] *White*, 178. [12] *White*, 178.
[13] *O. R.*, 12, part 2, p. 725. [14] 2 *Henderson*, 82–83.
[15] *O. R.*, 12, part 2, p. 725; *O. R.*, 11, part 3, p. 934.
[16] *R. E. Lee, Jr.*, 77; W. H. Taylor to his sister, Aug. 17; *Taylor MSS.*

man of McClellan's hurrying thousands, or seek refuge behind the
high-banked Rappahannock.

But when the morning of the 18th came, the army was not
prepared. Anderson's division was arriving from Richmond and
was not in position.[17] There was no news from Stuart as to his
whereabouts and none as to the arrival of Fitz Lee from Beaver
Dam Station. The cavalry on the Confederate left was not disposed to suit Lee.[18] The commissary did not have enough hard
bread on hand to serve for the move to the Rapidan and for the
march beyond it as well. Lee consequently had to defer the
crossing of the river until the 19th.[19]

Even had all else been ready, Fitz Lee's cavalry would not
have been at hand for its important work. For, as Lee learned
later in the day, Stuart had been the victim of a curious mis-
adventure that morning. Late in the afternoon of the 17th he
had ridden thirteen miles eastward from Orange to the little
hamlet known as Verdiersville, where he expected Fitz Lee to
halt for the night on his way to the rendezvous at Raccoon Ford.
The quiet people of the slumbering countryside had answered
with blank looks Stuart's questions regarding the location of the
Confederate cavalry camp. They had seen no cavalry, they said.
Much puzzled, Stuart had sent his assistant adjutant general,
Major Norman Fitzhugh, down the road to find Fitz Lee and to
hurry him on. Then Stuart and his aides had lain down on the
porch of a private house to await the arrival of the belated
troopers. As day was breaking on the 18th Stuart saw a body
of horsemen some 400 yards away and heard the clatter of advancing hoofs and the groaning of wheels. He asked Captain
Mosby and Lieutenant Gibson to inquire if the column was Fitz
Lee's. There was a moment's wait, loud voices, a shout of "Yankee cavalry," a few nervous shots—and in an instant more Stuart
was up, mounted, over a fence and dashing for the nearby woods,
while his aides were scattered and galloping off with a Federal
patrol in avid pursuit. Fortunately, all the staff escaped except
Major Fitzhugh, who had been captured while looking vainly

---

[17] O. R., 12, part 3, p. 934.
[18] Ibid. The 2d Virginia Cavalry of Jackson's command was detached (O. R., 12,
part 2, p. 726).
[19] Ibid.

for Fitz Lee, and had been an unhappy spectator of his chief's hurried flight.[20] The Federals rode triumphantly off with Stuart's hat and coat and left him wondering how they had stolen across the Rapidan. As he subsequently discovered, the explanation was simple: finding that Fitz Lee had not arrived on the evening of the 17th, Longstreet had ordered two of his infantry regiments to guard the road from Raccoon Ford, but these men had been ordered away by their brigadier, General Robert Toombs, who had denied Longstreet's authority to move his men without his consent. A Federal scouting party, finding the road open, had promptly moved southward and was returning when Stuart saw it. For permitting such a thing to happen, Toombs was promptly put under arrest, but that, of course, did not save Stuart's pride or restore his lost plumage.[21]

It probably was late in the morning of the 18th when the general in chief heard from Stuart of this mishap, and still later when he received a telegram from Fitz Lee reporting where he was. Either because his orders had been carelessly drawn, or else because he had misinterpreted them, Fitz Lee had not understood that he was to press on to Raccoon Ford by the evening of the 17th.[22] If he had known that the opening of the attack depended on his arrival at that time, it is inconceivable that he would not have covered the thirty-two miles from Davenport's Bridge to the rendezvous.[23] As it was, he had gone by way of Louisa Courthouse, where he had issued rations to his men and had replenished his ammunition. His telegram showed him still on the road[24] with small prospect of reaching Raccoon Ford before the night of the 18th. Had he pushed ahead on the 17th, as Stuart had expected him to do, he would have had to cover sixty-two miles in two days. Now that he was behind schedule and was following a longer road, it was certain that his mounts would require a day's rest. So, regretfully, the commanding general was forced to postpone the crossing of the Rapidan one day more, until the morning of the 20th.[25]

[20] O. R., 12, part 2, pp. 725–26; 1 *von Borcke*, 105 *ff.*; *H. B. McClellan*, 89 *ff.*; *Thomason*, 222 *ff.*
[21] *Longstreet*, 161; *Sorrel*, 100 *ff.*; 2 B. and L., 526.
[22] *Fitz Lee*, 182.   [23] *H. B. McClellan*, 91.
[24] O. R., 12, part 3, p. 934.   [25] O. R., 12, part 3, p. 934.

Stuart charged Fitz Lee with dereliction of duty,[26] and Long-street, who had a post-bellum controversy with him, insisted years afterwards that Fitz Lee's failure to arrive at Raccoon Ford on the 17th lost the war to the South.[27] But all early criticism of the young cavalryman curiously enough leaves out of account the fact that the commanding general had postponed the offensive before he heard that Fitz Lee was late. The fault was one of organization rather than of an individual, and the delay in launching the offensive probably would have occurred even if the cavalry had arrived. The army had not yet learned the difficult art of a quick and sure co-ordination of all the arms of the service.[28]

Lee must have realized this. To his disappointment over his inability to strike Pope in his exposed position at the time he had appointed, there was added on the 18th a fear that the enemy had discovered his presence despite his efforts to conceal the army.[29] He learned that the Federals at daylight had raided a signal station that Jackson had established on a fine eminence known as Clark's Mountain, overlooking the valley of the Rapidan and the country northward toward the Rappahannock, where Pope had his camps. There was no way of telling what the enemy had seen before he had been driven back, or what records he had found.[30]

Before nightfall the worst apprehensions seemed realized in reports from the lookouts that the Federals were breaking up their camps and retiring toward Culpeper Courthouse,[31] but the magnitude and meaning of this move were not wholly apparent then. Nor was there very definite news early on the morning of the 19th. Lee went ahead with his preparations. He had summoned the reserve artillery from Richmond on the 18th,[32] and he now revised his orders for the advance on the 20th.[33] In

---

[26] O. R., 12, part 2, p. 726.   [27] Longstreet, 196.

[28] It is proper to note that this statement of the events of Aug. 17–18 is contrary to all the previous accounts, which have taken the traditional view that Fitz Lee's delay held up the offensive. It is enough to say in justification of the interpretation here put upon the events that none of those who placed the full burden of blame on Fitz Lee ever offered any explanation of Lee's dispatch to Stuart of Aug. 18, 1862, written, as the internal evidence shows, before he had learned what had happened to Fitz Lee. This dispatch (O. R., 12, part 3, p. 934), began with the significant sentence: "I hope to be prepared today to cross tomorrow."

[29] O. R., 12, part 3, p. 940.   [30] O. R., 12, part 3, pp. 544, 649.

[31] O. R., 12, part 3, p. 728.   [32] O. R., 12, part 3, p. 965.

[33] O. R., 12, part 2, p. 729.

person he drafted new instructions for Stuart, whom he cautioned to rest his troops and to report how he was progressing in his concentration of the cavalry for the operations in rear of Culpeper Courthouse.[34]

The air, of course, was tense. The men knew that an advance was immediately in prospect. All private strategists of the camp messes were busily explaining what should be done to confound the foe. Before noon the signal station announced another movement by the enemy. Without waiting for particulars, Lee sent for Longstreet and rode with him to the crest of the mountain. "From its summit," wrote Longstreet, "we had a fair view of many points, and the camp-flags, as they opened their folds to the fitful breezes, seemed to mark places of rest. Changing our glasses to the right and left and rear, the white tops of army wagons were seen moving. Half an hour's close watch revealed that the move was for the Rappahannock River. Changing the field of view to the bivouacs, they seemed serenely quiet, under the cover of the noon-day August sun. As we were there to learn from personal observation, our vigilance was prolonged until the wagons rolled down the declivities of the Rappahannock. Then, turning again to view the bivouacs, a stir was seen at all points. Little clouds of dust arose which marked the tramp of soldiers, and these presently began to swell into dense columns along the rearward lines. Watching without comment till the clouds grew thinner and thinner as they approached the river and melted into the bright haze of the afternoon sun, General Lee finally put away his glasses, and with a deeply-drawn breath, expressive at once of disappointment and resignation, said, 'General, we little thought that the enemy would turn his back upon us thus early in the campaign.' " [35]

It was all true, just as they had seen it. Unknown to Lee, a copy of one of his orders to Stuart, showing something of the whereabouts of the army, had been found on Major Fitzhugh when he had been captured, and this document had been sent to Pope.[36]

[34] O. R., 12, part 2, p. 728.

[35] Longstreet, 161–62. Oddly enough, General Longstreet misdated the events of Aug. 18–19 and placed them on Aug. 17–18. A very fine description of the view from Clark's Mountain will be found in 2 Henderson, 111–12, cf. ibid., 116 and Long, 187.

[36] O. R., 12, part 2, p. 29. Pope said this order was dated at Gordonsville, Aug. 13. As Lee was not at Gordonsville on Aug. 13, either the place or the date was wrong. Most probably the date was Aug. 16, and the order that first issued for the advance.

A spy, moreover, on the morning of August 18, had reported the Confederate preparations to General McDowell.[37] General Reno had also discovered the Confederate dispositions.[38] At 1:30 P.M. on the 18th Pope had started to withdraw from the trap in which he found himself.[39] What Lee witnessed from Clark's Mountain was not the first but the final phase of the retreat of the gentleman who had exhorted his soldiery to concern itself with the enemy's line of retreat and to leave its own to take care of itself.

But whither was Pope withdrawing? As far as Lee could make out, he was moving by the road to Fredericksburg, but that road led into the narrow part of the "V" formed by the Rappahannock and Rapidan, where his condition would be worse than before. It was obvious that the Federals must intend to cross the Rappahannock and go northward. As the course of the Orange and Alexandria Railroad was from southwest to northeast beyond Culpeper, Pope could cross well down the Rappahannock and still not be at a dangerous distance from his communications.

It was too late to begin pursuit on the afternoon of the 19th, and if the men started that night they would not be fresh for battle the next day. Lee consequently decided to give troops and horses a little rest and to cross the Rapidan at 4 A.M., with the rising of the moon. Stuart's proposed raid against Rappahannock Station would, of course, be futile if the enemy had already crossed the river, so his orders were amended, and he was instructed to sweep well to the eastward, covering Longstreet's right flank. Then he was to negotiate the Rappahannock at Kelly's Ford.[40] Longstreet, in command of the right wing, was to cross the Rapidan at Raccoon Ford, where Lafayette once had met the waters of the Rapidan. Longstreet's objective was to be Culpeper Courthouse. Jackson, leading the left wing, was to pass over the river at Somerville Ford and was to move in the same direction. Anderson, following Jackson, was to form the general reserve.[41] The rest, in Lee's mind, was with God and with circumstance.

[37] *O. R.*, 12, part 2, p. 329.
[38] *O. R.*, 12, part 3, p. 592.
[39] *O. R.*, 12, part 3, p. 591.
[40] *O. R.*, 12, part 2, p. 729.
[41] *O. R.*, 12, part 2, p. 729.

CHAPTER XXII

By the Left Flank Up the Rappahannock

In the dim light of a wasted moon, on the morning of August 20, 1862, the Army of Northern Virginia crossed the undefended fords of the Rapidan. Its seven divisions and two unattached brigades of infantry numbered about 50,000 men. The cavalry division and the artillery brought the total effectives to some 54,500.[1] Lee had already asked that the divisions of D. H. Hill and McLaws be sent from Richmond to the North Anna River, near Hanover Junction, to guard against a reported Federal movement in that direction.[2] If these 17,000 troops were not detained there by the enemy, they might be counted as in three days' support of the main army on the Rapidan. There were no others nearer than Richmond.

The known strength of the Federal horse and the uncertainty as to the movements of the enemy's infantry made it desirable, at the outset, to modify the orders for the employment of the Confederate cavalry. Fitz Lee was directed to cover the front and right flank of Longstreet's wing. Stuart went with Robertson in advance of Jackson. The detached regiment of Robertson's brigade remained on Jackson's left flank. Fitz Lee met with no opposition until he was close to Kelly's Ford on the Rappahannock. There he ran into the rear of the retiring Federals and had a brush. Stuart found the enemy cavalry in force between Stevensburg and Brandy Station and after some manœuvring drove them close to the Rappahannock, where they had shelter under the fire of Federal batteries on the north side of the river. Two regiments of Fitz Lee's, summoned from Kelly's Ford, arrived promptly with Pelham's horse artillery to support Robert-

[1] In 2 *D. H. Hill*, 220, the various estimates of Lee's strength are given. Rhodes's, the lowest, is 49,000; Henderson's, the highest, is 55,000.

[2] *O. R.*, 12, part 3, pp. 936–37. D. H. Hill on the 20th was returned from departmental to divisional command because of the shortage of competent officers.

son, but not in time to prevent the passage of the river by the Federal troopers, unpunished.

Following the cavalry, the infantry had an undisturbed march. Longstreet ended the day with his advanced guard close to Kelly's

Situation on the evening of August 20, 1862.

Ford and his rear five miles to the south. Jackson covered the distance from Somerville Ford to Stevensburg, with his van not far from Brandy Station. Lee, moving with Jackson's column, established his headquarters and bivouacked for the night near Brandy.[3]

It was apparent to Lee that the whole of Pope's army was above the Rappahannock, with the fords heavily guarded. The ground

[3] O. R., 12, part 2, pp. 552, 727, 745-46; 1 von Borcke, 115.

on Lee's right was lower than that occupied by the Federals on the other side of the river. To effect a crossing without excessive losses, Lee had to move up the Rappahannock, by his left flank.[4] Fortunately, this did not appear to be a difficult operation because, while few bridges spanned the stream, the fords were numerous, easy, and close together.

Accordingly, on the morning of the 21st, Robertson's brigade advanced up the right bank of the Rappahannock, crossed above Beverley Ford,[5] and began to reconnoitre downstream on the left bank. Stuart proceeded to Beverley Ford, which was less than two miles above Rappahannock Bridge, and waited until the infantry arrived and joined him. Jackson put his rear division in front and set out from Brandy for the same ford, while Longstreet completed his movement to Kelly's Ford and extended his left flank up the river to establish contact with Jackson's right.[6]

After Taliaferro's division of Jackson's command reached Beverley Ford it began a hot artillery action with Federal batteries on the opposite bank. Under cover of this fire, Stuart moved over the river and made some minor captures. Robertson, coming down the left bank from higher up the river, got in touch with his chief and reported the enemy nearby in strength. This meant, of course, that the passage of the infantry was apt to be costly. Lee carefully examined the ground, weighed the chances of success, decided not to attempt a crossing, and recalled Stuart to the south bank.[7] Longstreet was ordered to advance up the south bank of the Rappahannock from Kelly's Ford to Beverley Ford— a march that was started in the late afternoon, attended by a sharp and picturesque rearguard action with a Federal force that ventured to the right bank of the river.[8]

The presence of the enemy near Beverley Ford did not mean that the turning movement up the Rappahannock was to be abandoned. On the contrary, Lee was more intent upon it than ever. From his imperfect information of the enemy's movements, he concluded that part of Pope's army was moving toward Fredericksburg and part toward Warrenton,[9] and he considered it

[4] O. R., 12, part 3, pp. 940–41.   [5] Sometimes called Cunningham's Ford.
[6] Lee's Report, O. R., 12, part 2, p. 552, and C. M. Wilcox, ibid., pp. 596–97.
[7] O. R., 12, part 2, pp. 552, 655, 730.
[8] O. R., 12, part 2, pp. 563, 595–96.   [9] O. R., 51, part 2, p. 609.

desirable on every count to attack and dispose of the force nearest him.

But the extension of his left flank up the Rappahannock would hourly carry Lee a greater distance from Richmond and might even put Pope between him and that city ere the Federals were flanked. Was this safe? Could the capital be held if he ventured farther into northern Virginia? The question, he felt, was one that should properly be referred to the President, so he telegraphed the facts and asked Davis's opinion.[10] The answer came back promptly. The President said that he had not contemplated any lengthy offensive operations north of the Rappahannock, and that he had no definite information of a retreat by McClellan beyond New Kent Courthouse. The two divisions en route to Hanover Junction must be held there to co-operate as needed, and the five brigades immediately in front of Richmond must be retained.[11]

This was not all that Lee could have desired. Still, the presence of two divisions at Hanover Junction would secure his communications.[12] Moreover, the information of the War Department confirmed his belief that the whole of the Federal army was leaving the Peninsula.[13] He would press up the Rappahannock, move his army over the first undisputed ford, and give battle. Stuart was to proceed ahead, cover the occupied fords, and permit Jackson to pass upstream with the infantry until he could effect a crossing. Longstreet was to follow.

This operation to turn the flank of an enemy who might be expected to advance by parallel lines on the other side of the river was reduced to its simplest and safest form by considering the forces of Stuart, Jackson, and Longstreet as separate but co-operating units. In moving by the left flank up the Rappahannock, no commander was to leave any ford unguarded till the column next in rear had occupied ground opposite it. The enemy must not be allowed to cross the stream and get between the columns. Tactically, such an operation is familiar, but the opportunities it offers and the difficulties it involves were rarely so well illustrated as in this instance.

Still another possibility was presented. The plan to break up

[10] O. R., 51, part 2, p. 609. [11] O. R., 12, part 3, pp. 938–39.
[12] Taylor's General Lee, 97. [13] O. R., 12, part 3, p. 938.

Pope's communications by destroying the bridge at Rappahannock Station had been abandoned when the Federal commander had retreated behind the river; but his railroad supply line was most temptingly exposed to a cavalry raid, for the Orange and Alexandria crossed several small streams on wooden spans that daring men might wreck, to the great discomfiture of General Pope. Stuart had proposed a raid to demolish the bridge at Catlett's Station, and Lee now had this under advisement. He delayed a decision probably because he wished to see whether the developing situation imposed other compelling duty on the cavalry the next day.

The news that came to headquarters on the morning of the 22d was not particularly encouraging. There was no word from the vicinity of the North Anna as to the arrival there of D. H. Hill or of McLaws, and no information concerning the whereabouts of the force that Lee was still of opinion Pope had detached from his left and had moved toward Fredericksburg. Nothing could be learned concerning the position of the van of McClellan's army, which must be hurrying at the utmost speed to join Pope. Worse still, the enemy seemed fully apprized of Lee's purpose to turn his right by outflanking him up the Rappahannock. When Stuart that day reached the next good crossing, Freeman's Ford, there were the Federals, strongly placed on the opposite bank, as if defying the Confederates to force a passage. Jackson duly arrived and relieved Stuart, but had to continue his march up the river, searching for an undefended crossing.

The operation was becoming tedious. Wherever Lee moved, there was Pope, apparently confident and fully the master of the situation. Lee decided that something must be done to shake and demoralize the enemy. No means at Lee's disposal so readily promised this as the quick dash that Stuart had asked that he be permitted to make, with torch and carbine, against the Federal rear at Catlett's Station. Orders to prepare for the raid were accordingly issued as soon as the situation at Freeman's Ford was disclosed. They reached Stuart while he was still engaged with the enemy opposite that crossing.[14]

To cover this ford, as he continued his march up the Rappa-

---

[14] *O. R.*, 12, part 2, p. 730.

hannock on the 22d, Jackson left Trimble's brigade behind him. Trimble had not been in position more than two hours when he learned, about noon, that the Federals had done what Lee had been careful to guard against. They had thrown a force across the river and were attacking the divisional wagon train. Trimble, an excellent soldier, beat off the enemy from the wagons, but finding that Federal reinforcements had been brought up, he prudently decided to wait until the head of Longstreet's column arrived. When Hood's Texans and Law's stout brigade came on the ground, Trimble took the combined force and drove the Federals beyond the Rappahannock with some loss.[15]

Jackson, meantime, marched seven miles upstream on the afternoon of the 22d until he was opposite Warrenton Sulphur Springs, a modest summer resort. The bridge across the river at this point had been burned, and there were signs that the Federals could not be far distant; but observation failed to show any blue-coats immediately at hand. Here, at last, was an opportunity to effect a passage unopposed, the opportunity the army had been seeking in its long march up the river. Jackson at once moved a regiment through the ford[16] to hold the ground on the opposite side, and then he started Ewell's division across. Early's brigade and eight guns, using a dilapidated dam as a roadway, got safely over,[17] but their passage was very slow. Before it had been completed, night fell and a heavy storm broke, such a storm as always means in the foothills of the Blue Ridge that streamlets will be torrents, creeks past fording, and every minor watershed an island. The passage of the Rappahannock had to be halted, and Mars had to await the pleasure of Jupiter Pluvius. On the left bank, General Early was soon cut off from the rest of Jackson's command.[18] Longstreet, *ad interim,* had completed his withdrawal from Kelly's Ford and was concentrated around Rappahannock Station, with his left advanced to Freeman's Ford.

The rainy night of the 22d settled, then, in unrelieved blackness on a situation that was still unpromising. Stuart had started off on a raid against Catlett's Station with all except two regi-

---

[15] O. R., 12, part 2, pp. 605, 719.
[16] Styled Sulphur Springs Ford in some of the reports.
[17] O. R., 12, part 2, pp. 642, 705.   [18] O. R., 12, part 2, pp. 642, 705.

ments of the cavalry.[19] Jackson, at Warrenton Springs Ford, had eight small regiments and two batteries, under Early, cut off by the raging Rappahannock. Longstreet and Anderson, downstream, were facing superior artillery. All that was known of

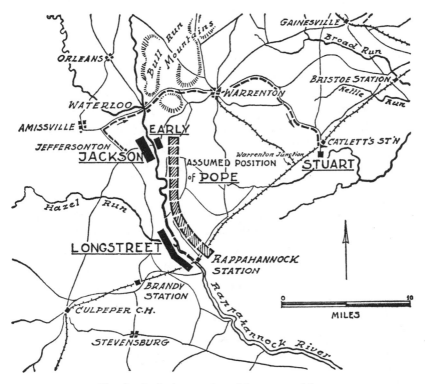

Situation in the late evening of August 22, 1862.

Pope was that he was conforming to the Confederate left-flank movement and was holding, or else was close, to all the fords the army had tried. During the night it was reported, also, that a force had recrossed to the south side of the river at Rappahannock Bridge.

Manifestly, if the enemy was strong in front of Early on the left bank of the river, the flank movement had to be extended farther up the Rappahannock, but this would depend on developments at Warrenton Springs Ford. On the evening of the 22d, nothing

[19] The 3d and 7th Virginia, O. R., 12, part 2, p. 730.

definite could be planned for the next day beyond a strong artillery demonstration at Rappahannock Bridge for the double purpose of driving back the Federals at that point and of creating the impression, if possible, that the Confederates intended crossing there.

At dawn on the 23d of August, as Longstreet's artillery was brought up to demonstrate at Rappahannock Station, a heavy mist overhung the river.[20] When this lifted, the batteries opened. A small force of Federals that was found to hold a little redoubt on the south side of the river was promptly forced to seek the north bank, and the opposing Federal guns were silenced.[21]

While Longstreet was making this demonstration, Jackson was trying to rebuild the burned bridge at Warrenton Springs Ford and was instructing Early regarding the defense he was to make in his threatened position. If attacked heavily before the bridge was finished, Early was to retreat up the left bank of the Rappahannock and cross where he could.[22] Luckily, the hours passed without an assault on Early, but before the anxious day ended, word was passed back to Lee that the Federals seemed to be massing opposite the ford. This seemed a reasonable probability, because Pope naturally would conclude that the high water lower down the river would keep the Confederates from turning his left and for that reason would hasten to strengthen his right. As a countermove, Lee directed that Longstreet waste no more time and powder at Rappahannock Bridge, but join Jackson forthwith.[23]

Much more important than these happenings of the 23d was the news from Stuart. After receiving his orders on the 22d, that officer had ridden to Catlett's Station in the blackness of what he described as the darkest night he had ever seen. A friendly Negro had guided him to Pope's headquarters, which happened to be nearby. The commander of the Army of Virginia had been

---

[20] O. R., 12, part 2, p. 569.

[21] O. R., 12, part 2, pp. 567, 569, 573, 628. The Macbeth battery, which took the position vacated by the Federals, had the curious experience of finding itself on a bare hilltop, exposed to a concentric fire, in a redoubt so small that the pieces could not be shifted. Needless to say, the battery withdrew quickly (O. R., 12, part 2, pp. 569–70).

[22] O. R., 12, part 2, pp. 705 ff.; Early, 107 ff. G. H. Gordon in his History of the Campaign of the Army of Virginia (cited hereafter as G. H. Gordon), 66–67, insisted that Early's position was by no means so critical as Early thought it was.

[23] O. R., 12, part 3, p. 942.

absent at the time, but his uniform coat had been in his tent, and several of his staff had been there, including Lee's nephew, Louis Marshall. A miscellaneous mass of Pope's military papers, including a dispatch book, had been carelessly placed where the Confederates could seize them. They had been gathered up and brought off, together with General Pope's quartermaster, who had subsequently done some indiscreet talking. The railroad bridge had been too wet to burn and too heavy to cut down in the darkness, but failure in that particular was quite forgotten when the nature of the captured correspondence was discovered.[24]

Lee's first information of all this merely covered what Stuart had accomplished and what the captured quartermaster had said. This loquacious officer affirmed that Cox's army in western Virginia had been ordered to move to Wheeling and then to join Pope. Without waiting for the arrival of Pope's papers, Lee advised the War Department of this news and urged that General Loring's little force, which had been watching Cox, should be sent to cut the Baltimore and Ohio Railroad, against which he had already dispatched a small cavalry column from the Appalachian district.[25]

Late on the 23d or early in the morning of the 24th, Lee received a few of the more important of Pope's papers.[26] From these he discovered that Pope had 45,000 men on August 20, exclusive of the reinforcements from Burnside and that he had not detached any of these eastward toward Fredericksburg, as Lee had thought on the 21st. Pope's expectation, he read, was to hold the line of the Rappahannock until McClellan could join him from the vicinity of Fredericksburg. This movement, Lee found, was

---

[24] For the raid, see *O. R., 12*, part 2, p. 731.

[25] *O. R., 12*, part 3, pp. 936, 937, 940 *ff.*

[26] It seems impossible to determine from evidence now available precisely why Lee received Pope's correspondence in instalments, and after so long a delay, unless it was because the papers had been seized by different men in the ranks and had to be collected. He certainly had not received any of it when he wrote Davis on the 23d (*O. R., 12*, part 3, pp. 940–41). He had Pope's letter to McClellan, dated July 4, at hand when he addressed Randolph and Loring later in the day (*ibid.*, 940, 941–42), but apparently he did not then have the entire file. His letter of Aug. 24, which seems to have been written during the forenoon, shows that he had examined by that time Pope's letter of Aug. 20, 1862, to Halleck, printed in *O. R., 12*, part 3, p. 603. As von Borcke stated (*op. cit.*, 1, 133), that he went to Lee's headquarters with the bulk of Pope's papers, it is manifest that Lee did not have all of them until after Jackson had been sent off on his movement to Pope's rear. Lee's letter to Randolph, Aug. 25, indicates that he had so recently received the documents that he had only been able to examine them "in a very cursory manner" (*O. R., 12*, part 3, p. 943).

already under way, and Porter's corps, the advanced unit of Mc-
Clellan's army, was to march from the vicinity of Fredericksburg
to Pope's left flank.[27]

The reading of the dispatches containing this information
showed that the race between Lee and McClellan to reach Pope
was getting dangerously close. That knowledge was the turning-
point of the campaign. All that followed, until the second battle
of Manassas, was based upon what Lee learned at this time of his
adversary's plans and numbers. His first reaction was one of
wariness. He now knew, as he had already suspected, that Pope
was numerically superior to him, besides having a great advantage
in artillery.[28] As soon as McClellan's divisions joined Pope, the
odds against the Army of Northern Virginia would be hopeless,
even if the conclusive evidence of McClellan's withdrawal from
Richmond made Mr. Davis willing to strip the defenses of the
capital and to send Lee all the units still around the city. If,
luckily, a part of Pope's army could be caught, it would of course
be attacked, but an offensive leading to a battle between the whole
of the two armies would entail losses to the Confederates that
could not then be replaced, even if a victory were gained. A
general engagemen* was therefore to be avoided.

What, then, could Lee do? Obviously, he could ask Davis to
forward the troops on the North Anna and those around Richmond, and thus reduce the disparity of forces. But beyond that,
what? Should he retire, should he advance, or should he remain
where he was? He had reached a part of Virginia from which
the Federals previously had been drawing supplies. If he remained there he could subsist his men on supplies the Federals
would otherwise devour, and to that extent he would be saving
the rest of the South from a drain on its resources.[29] It was desirable, then, to remain north of the Rappahannock and, if possible, to go still farther into the territory occupied by the enemy.
But, once again, how? There was only one way, and that was to
continue manœuvring. Every mile that he could lead Pope away

---

[27] O. R., 12, part 3, pp. 603, 942.   [28] O. R., 12, part 3, p. 942.
[29] Cf. Lee to Davis, Aug. 23, 1862, O. R., 12, part 3, p. 941: "If we are able to change
the theatre of the war from James River to the north of the Rappahannock we shall be
able to consume provisions and forage now being used in supporting the enemy. This will
be some advantage and prevent so great a draft upon other parts of the country." Cf.
ibid., p. 942.

from Fredericksburg was another mile to be covered by the units from McClellan before they could form a junction with Pope; every square mile that could be cleared of Federals before it was cleared of provisions meant to the Confederacy so many more bushels of grain and so many pounds of bacon that, by any other military policy, most certainly would feed the enemy.

If the proper course was to avoid a general engagement and to force Pope away from McClellan and out of the fat agricultural districts of northern Virginia, what form of manœuvre would accomplish the largest result in the shortest time? As Lee looked at his map for the answer, he of course fixed his eye on the Orange and Alexandria Railroad. He had hoped to cut that supply line at Rappahannock Bridge but had been thwarted by Pope's swift retreat; he had essayed it with Stuart's cavalry at Catlett's Station but had been balked by the rain that had wet the timbers of the bridge. He would try again at a greater distance, to insure a larger success and a longer retreat. In doing so, he might be able to put part of his army between Pope and Washington. Once before, when he had been anxious to keep McDowell from joining McClellan, he had sent Jackson to the Potomac after the battles of Cross Keys and Port Republic, and had found the Federals quick to rush troops to defend their capital. It was worth while to try the same strategy now. If it failed, he would still be close to the mountains and, if need be, could enter the Shenandoah Valley, which led to the upper Potomac. And the Potomac was the lane to the back door of Washington.[30]

This, then, was the course dictated by a reading of the dispatches that General Pope's clerks had patiently copied into his dispatch book, with little thought that they were preparing an intelligence report for General Lee: A general engagement with a stronger adversary army was to be avoided, because the losses could not be replaced; instead, there must be manœuvre to lengthen the distance between Pope and McClellan and to feed the Confederates in territory the enemy otherwise would strip. This manœuvre must be undertaken with one eye to cutting Pope's railroad, and with the other eye on Washington.[31]

[30] *Marshall*, 129-30.
[31] The writer is aware, of course, that this explanation of Lee's plan runs counter to the views set forth in all the previous biographies of Lee and in all the accounts of the

And now to the details: During the early morning of August 24, Early returned to the right bank of the Rappahannock, without loss, over the bridge that Jackson had reconstructed at Warrenton Springs Ford.[32] The Federals were beginning to appear in great strength on the opposite side, as if anticipating an attempt by the Confederates to cross there. A. P. Hill's artillery was massed to confront them but held its fire until the Union infantry appeared, about noon. Then it opened and broke up the deployment.[33]

Lee now wrote Davis of his discoveries from Pope's correspondence and tactfully ordered the remaining units of the Army of Northern Virginia to rejoin him. He added that if the President did not approve of this, he could countermand it.[34] Then, while Hill's guns were roaring, Lee sent for Jackson to come to his headquarters, which had now been moved to the quiet little village of Jeffersonton.[35]

The conference that followed between the two was one of the most important Lee ever held. Briefly he told Jackson that he wished him to take his command, to march up the Rappahannock, to get in rear of Pope's army, and to cut his communications with Washington. There is no evidence that he mentioned Manassas Junction as the point at which the road was to be cut, and it is more than likely that he left the specific objective and the line of advance to Jackson.[36] Jackson was much excited at the prospect,

campaign prior to that written by General Maurice. But the writer does not believe that the evidence made available in *Lee's Dispatches* and in Colonel Marshall's *An Aide de Camp of Lee* keeps the question in any sort of doubt, especially when considered in the light of Lee's statement to President Davis that he wished to subsist his troops in territory the Federals would otherwise occupy. Colonel Marshall (*op. cit.*, 129–30) gave the view here presented. He wrote prior to the discovery of Lee's dispatch of Aug. 30 to Davis, and probably he had no knowledge of the existence of that paper, but he precisely bore out Lee's statement therein, viz., "My desire has been to avoid a general engagement, being the weaker force, and by maneuvering to relieve the portion of the country referred to" (*Lee's Dispatches*, 56).

[32] *O. R.,* 12, part 2, p. 707.

[33] *O. R.,* 12, part 2, pp. 650, 673–74. Lee was justified in his conclusion that the Federals moved to Warrenton Springs Ford in the belief that he intended to cross there. Pope, at 6:30 P.M., Aug. 24, advised Halleck that the enemy's movement would be on Warrenton, via Sulphur Springs (*O. R.,* 12, part 2, p. 58).

[34] *O. R.,* 12, part 3, p. 942.

[35] Jefferson on some of the maps and in some of the reports.

[36] Lee said in his report (*O. R.,* 12, part 2, pp. 553–54): "In pursuance of the plan of operations determined upon, Jackson was directed on the 25th to cross above Waterloo and move around the enemy's right, so as to strike the Orange and Alexandria railroad in his rear." Jackson said (*ibid.,* 642–43): "Pursuing the instructions of the commanding general, I left Jeffersonton on the morning of the 25th to throw my command between

and as he and Lee stood together, he drew with his boot on the ground a rough diagram of the manœuvre. Lee, listening, nodded approval.[37]

Why did Lee choose Jackson for this movement, after Jackson's failure in front of Richmond? The explanation is simple. Jackson was now a very different person from the exhausted general of the Seven Days. He was conveniently on the left; he knew the country; he shone best on detached service; his men were inured to long, fast marches in just such country as that which they were to traverse. These considerations, or some of them, doubtless account for Lee's choice.

Jackson would carry with him in his three divisions, Taliaferro's, Ewell's, and A. P. Hill's, approximately 23,000 men. That would leave Lee only some 32,000, until the arrival of the reinforcements the President might forward from the North Anna and from the Richmond front. Such a division of force in the face of an enemy of known superior strength, apt to be reinforced at any time, was, of course, a violation of the strategic canon of concentration in the face of the enemy. Lee deliberately violated that canon in this instance. He did not do so because of contempt for Pope, as has been alleged,[38] for the truth was that after the initial blunder of placing himself between the Rapidan and the Rappahannock, Pope had made no mistake. On the contrary, his dispositions had been prompt and soldier-like and had offered Lee no opening. The reason for Lee's division of force has already been given. It was that an attack on Pope's line of communica-

Washington City and the army of General Pope and to break up his railroad communications with the Federal capital." The only direct suggestion that Manassas was originally chosen as the objective is the statement of Jackson's engineer, Captain J. K. Boswell (*ibid.*, 650), that Jackson sent for him at 3 P.M., on Aug. 24, and thereupon ordered him to select "the most direct and covered route to Manassas." Jackson, however, did not strike for Manassas, but for Bristoe Station, presumably to destroy the railroad bridge over Broad Run. He stated in his report (*ibid.*, 642), that after he reached Bristoe on the evening of Aug. 26, he learned that the enemy had collected "at Manassas Junction, a station about 7 miles distant, stores of great value" and he left the inference that it was only when he ascertained this fact that he determined to move to Manassas. It is possible that Jackson mentioned Manassas to Boswell because he knew, from his previous service in northern Virginia, that the only road over the mountains, north of those leading to Warrenton, ran in the direction of Manassas. There is likewise the possibility that his sense of the military value of secrecy led him to conceal his real objective even from his military engineer.

37 Doctor Hunter McGuire in 2 *Henderson*, 123–24. This incident led Doctor McGuire to believe that Jackson originated the proposal. No other writer on the campaign has made any such claim for Jackson.

38 *Cf. G. H. Gordon*, 72.

tions seemed to be the only means of manœuvring into a retreat an opponent whom he did not feel strong enough to fight. Had he any intention to give battle, it is unlikely that Lee would have adopted such a dangerous course. Even as it was, he did not

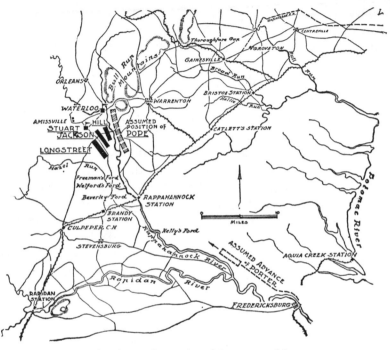

Situation on the evening of August 24, 1862.

intend that Longstreet should be separated from Jackson longer than was necessary to mask Jackson's advance.[39] Years afterwards, when told that his move had been criticised as over-rash, he said: "Such criticism is obvious, but the disparity . . . between the contending forces rendered the risks unavoidable." [40]

The orders for the afternoon of August 24 and for the 25th were, then, as follows:

1. A. P. Hill to continue his demonstration at Warrenton Springs Ford until dark on the 24th.

2. Longstreet to replace A. P. Hill after nightfall and to cover

[39] O. R., 12, part 2, p. 554.
[40] William Allan: The Army of Northern Virginia in 1862, p. 200.

the Rappahannock as far as Waterloo Bridge, four miles above Warrenton Springs Ford.

3. Jackson to move at dawn on the 25th, with three divisions in light marching order, carrying only his ordnance train and ambulances, and a herd of cattle for subsistence; to cross the Rappahannock above Waterloo Bridge, in order to cut Pope's communications via the Orange and Alexandria Railroad and thereby to put himself between Pope's army and Washington.

4. Stuart to continue on reconnaissance to guard Waterloo Bridge until relieved, and to make ready to follow and to support Jackson upon receipt of orders.

Jackson's men received the familiar instructions to prepare three days' cooked rations—the usual preliminary to a hard march—and after Hill's artillery fire died away, they gossiped over their camp fires about their probable movements; but on neither side of the now-subdued Rappahannock, flowing calmly within peaceful banks, was there an intimation of the tremendous events that were to follow Jackson's departure with the dawn.

CHAPTER XXIII

GREAT NEWS COMES ON A HARD MARCH

LONGSTREET's van relieved A. P. Hill after nightfall on the 24th, and the rest of his gray regiments came over the green hills opposite Warrenton Springs Ford while the last of Jackson's "foot-cavalry" filed off about daybreak on August 25. The Federals were still in position on the other side of the Rappahannock and were known to have extended their right flank far upstream, because Stuart's sharpshooters had been forced to ram and fire fast the previous day to keep the enemy from crossing at Waterloo Bridge.

All the morning and most of the afternoon of the 25th the artillery exchanged its challenge across the river, but the demonstrations ended in smoke and sound. The infantry were not engaged. Lee had time for study of his situation and for his correspondence. Pope's defiant strength led him to suspect that part of McClellan's army had come up, so he hurried off a courier to Rapidan Station with a telegram for the President. This set forth his views and urged speed in the dispatch of the reinforcements of whose advance he had heard little.[1] General Gilmer was directed by letter to hasten the completion of the Richmond defenses, so that still more troops could be withdrawn from them,[2] and the Secretary of War was asked to locate and to send forward a regiment of cavalry reported idle in North Carolina. "Cavalry is very much needed in this region," Lee told General Randolph; "the service is hard and the enemy strong in that arm." [3]

In the evening General Stuart rode over to headquarters at Jeffersonton to report and to get his orders. Lee gave him detailed

[1] *Lee's Dispatches*, 53. [2] *O. R.*, 12, part 3, pp. 944, 944–45.
[3] *O. R.*, 12, part 3, p. 944.

304

instructions for his march in support of Jackson, and in the knowledge that Jackson's operation required an abundance of cavalry, Lee authorized Stuart to take all his troopers with him, an overgenerous act for which he was soon to pay.[4] The day ended with a visit from Rooney. Lee had not seen him for some

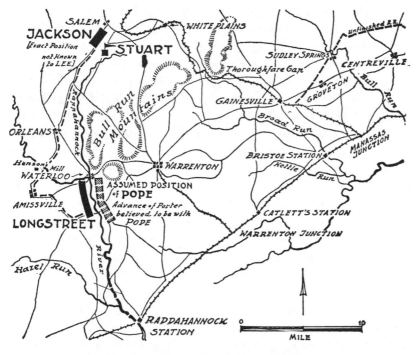

Situation on the evening of August 25, 1862.

time and had heard little from his family since he had left Richmond. Rooney told his father of his adventures with Stuart, a tale that stirred the heart of the whilom colonel of the 2d United States Cavalry. At first opportunity, he wrote Charlotte about the pleasant moments with his son, and could not forbear expressing a measure of pride over Rooney's part in the raid on Catlett's Station. "He is very well," he told her, "and the picture of health. . . . In the recent expedition . . . he led his regiment,

[4] *O. R.,* 12, part 2, p. 733.

during a terrible storm at night, right through the camp of the enemy, capturing several hundred prisoners and some valuable papers of General Pope. I am so grateful to Almighty God for preserving, guiding, and directing him in this war: Help me pray to Him for the continuance of his signal favor." [5]

There was something suspicious about the movements of the enemy the next morning, August 26. The bridgehead was still occupied and the fire was strong, but the bustle was not that of a foe expecting to receive or intending to deliver an attack. Soon Lee interpreted what was happening across the river as an indication that the enemy was beginning to move away. Did this mean that Pope had discovered that Jackson had left, and was he hurrying to protect his rear and to crush the "foot-cavalry" while Lee's forces were divided? [6] Lee could not answer the question, but he did not hesitate over his dispositions. If Pope was moving away from the Rappahannock, he would soon be within striking distance of Jackson, even if he had not already had wind of the march of "Stonewall." The Army of Northern Virginia must, therefore, be reunited. Calling to him the stocky, hardheaded Longstreet, who was already known to his men as "Old Pete," Lee told him he intended to join Jackson as soon as possible. Would Longstreet prefer to force the crossings of the Rappahannock and take the shorter route, or did he think it better to follow the longer but safer road that Jackson had chosen? Longstreet deliberated and then announced that as there were several strong positions where Pope could oppose him between the Rappahannock and Warrenton, he would rather advance as Jackson had gone, via Orleans and Salem.

Orders were issued accordingly. R. H. Anderson was told to cover Warrenton Springs Ford, and the "right wing," that was soon to be the famous "First Corps," stole quietly away during the afternoon under cover of the hills and headed north.[7] Passing over a branch of the Rappahannock at Henson's Mill,[8] it covered eleven honest miles before it bivouacked for the night. Everywhere, as it marched on, the country people doubtless told

[5] Letter of Aug. 26, 1862; *Jones,* 392.   [6] *Marshall,* 134; 2 B. and L., 517.
[7] *O. R.,* 12, part 2, pp. 555, 564; 2 B. and L., 517.
[8] On the maps as "Hinson's" and so spelled in most of the reports, probably because the dialect of that section of Virginia sometimes gives "e" the spoken value of "ĭ."

how Jackson's column had passed the day before, swinging fast
in the cool of the morning, while Jackson grimly urged them on
with the oft-repeated words, "Close up, men, close up."

As Lee and his mess were preparing to eat their meagre evening meal by the roadside near Orleans, an invitation, as pressing

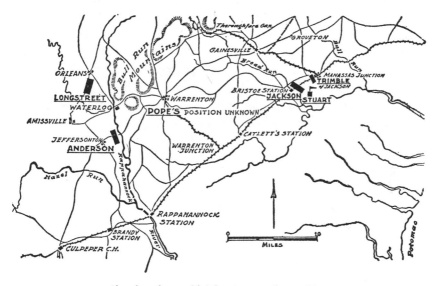

Situation about midnight, August 26–27, 1862.

as gracious, came for the General and his staff and Longstreet
and his military household to have supper at the nearby home of
the Marshalls. Lee was careful never to stay at private homes
in a country where the subsequent appearance of the enemy might
bring embarrassment to his hosts or provoke reprisals on them;
but in this instance, as it seemed unlikely that the Federals could
soon return, he accepted. A glorious meal in the lavish Virginia
style was followed by a pleasant evening of social conversation,
during which even Longstreet unbent. Before retiring, Lee told
Mrs. Marshall that his party would have to start so early the next
morning that he could not possibly accept her invitation to breakfast. The hostess, however, was not to be outdone in courtesy, and
at dawn a bountiful breakfast was announced. Not knowing
when or where they again would taste such cookery, the staff

ate heartily, and with many thanks rode off, blessing the honored name of Marshall.[9]

At the head of the long, long column, which was marching doggedly on at the route step, Lee and his officers on the morning of August 27 covered the ten miles to the vicinity of the little village of Salem, now known as Marshall. There a halt was made for a short rest. Hungry and thirsty soldiers in the leading regiments walked ahead to see if the stores and wells offered refreshment. Soon a quartermaster came dashing back down the road, crying loudly, "The Federal cavalry are upon us!" And on his heels galloped a bluecoated squadron. Only his staff and a few couriers were with Lee, who was directly in the line of the advancing troopers. There were shouts and hasty appeals to General Lee to hurry to the rear. Holsters were unstrapped with nervous fingers, swords were bared; the little cavalcade spread itself across the road, determined at any price to delay the enemy until the General could make off. An anxious half-minute passed; then the Federals halted, looked for an instant, mistook the mounted men for a strong cavalry column, and retired as they had come. It was the first close escape Lee had experienced since that day in western Virginia when a detachment of Union cavalry had swept past without seeing him in the woods.[10]

Who were the Federals, and what did their presence signify? Lee had no cavalry to whom he could look for an answer. The whole column had to wait until the neighbors could be questioned as to the direction from which the bluecoats had come and the numbers they had displayed. The conclusion was that they had moved from the vicinity of Warrenton and that they were not strong enough to threaten the column; but time was lost, valuable time, in trying to ascertain what a regiment of cavalry could have established in half an hour. So much for the mistake in detaching the whole of the cavalry to help Jackson.[11]

Even when the army at length moved forward again, the men on the lookout for the Federals unconsciously slowed their pace. The only tangible evidence of enemy depredation found by the ad-

[9] *Long*, 191–92.
[10] *Marshall*, 134; *Long*, 192; W. M. Owen: *In Camp and Battle with the Washington Artillery of New Orleans* (cited hereafter as *Owen*), 111; *Napier*, 118; *G. Wise*, 94.
[11] *Marshall*, 135; *Longstreet*, 170.

vanced files was of a singular sort. Directly in the middle of the road on which Longstreet was moving, stood a deserted family carriage, its horses gone and its occupants fled. When Lee rode up and inquired about this odd spectacle, he was told that the owner, a lady of the neighborhood, had taken refuge in a nearby house with her daughters. Characteristically, he cantered over to ascertain what had happened. He learned from the matron's regretful lips that she had heard of his approach and had ridden out with her daughters to see him. On the way the Federals had overtaken them, and, deaf to the ladies' remonstrances, had unceremoniously taken her span of bay horses and had gone off with them. Lee administered such comfort of words as he could and expressed his regret that he could not replace the lost team. The lady was pleased at his civilities and felt that she had at least accomplished the object of her errand, but she was compelled to admit thereafter that two matched carriage horses were a rather heavy price to pay, even for a chat with General Lee.[12]

The march continued in sickening heat and stifling dust. The road was so narrow that the column was strung out for miles, and water was so scarce that the thirsty men drank dry the stagnant mud holes. It was in vain that Lee, to save them from exhaustion, asked if there were no other, shorter roads his men might follow.[13]

Two and a half miles from Salem the weariness of the march was broken by the arrival of a courier. He had come over the Bull Run Mountains, and he brought from Jackson a dispatch that made every heart beat faster.[14] By an astounding two days' march Jackson had covered fifty-four miles, and the previous evening had reached Bristoe Station. There he had captured two trains, though two had escaped. Then, while some of their men had been tearing up the track, Trimble with two regiments and Stuart with part of the cavalry had gone seven miles farther up the Orange and Alexandria Railroad to Manassas Junction, where Jackson had heard that the Federals had accumulated vast stores. The junction had been taken with slight opposition, and all its treasures were the Confederates'. The dispatch modestly announced the occupation of Bristoe and Manassas, but the army instantly

[12] *Long,* 193.   [13] *Napier,* 126.
[14] *Marshall,* 134; *Lee's Dispatches,* 54.

acclaimed the operation one of the greatest feats of the war. Jackson was precisely where Lee wanted him to be—in rear of the Federal army and between it and Washington.[15] Not only so, but at the time Jackson had written, there had been little evidence that the Federals were massing to meet him. With good fortune, the two wings of the army could unite again before Pope's retreat, which was now inevitable, brought him in superior force to Manassas.

Lee saw possibilities of high manœuvres from Jackson's position, if more men were forthcoming, and in customary manner he wrote of the next move as he read of the last. In a dispatch to the President, conveying the good news, he urged once again that reinforcements, particularly Hampton's cavalry brigade, be sent forward with all speed.[16] Somewhere on the way, the messenger that carried this dispatch to the telegraph station at Rapidan probably passed a courier bound from that place with a message from Davis. In this, the President told Lee of the advance of the troops already sent to his assistance. With a mind to the criticism that would certainly overwhelm him if Richmond were taken because it was stripped of its defenders, the President concluded: "Confidence in you overcomes the view which would otherwise be taken of the exposed condition of Richmond, and the troops retained for the defense of the capital are surrendered to you on a new request." [17]

Reinforcements coming, Jackson between Pope and Washington, the railroad cut, the enemy's advanced base destroyed—it was enough to strengthen men to endure even the torture of that endless day's groping through dust that burned eyes and parched throats. Yet, though the troops marched cheerfully, there was a definite lessening of tension, and the pace was slower. Lee did not have the heart to push the men when there was nothing in Jackson's dispatch to indicate that his situation demanded a forced march. Headquarters were established late in the evening at the home of James W. Foster, near White Plains.[18] Some of

[15] O. R., 12, part 2, pp. 643, 670 ff., 720–21, 748; 13 S. H. S. P., 10; 2 Henderson 125 ff.
[16] Lee's Dispatches, 54.
[17] O. R., 12, part 3, p. 945. This dispatch is dated Aug. 26 but it could not have reached Lee before the 27th.
[18] Later known simply as The Plains, G. Wise, 94.

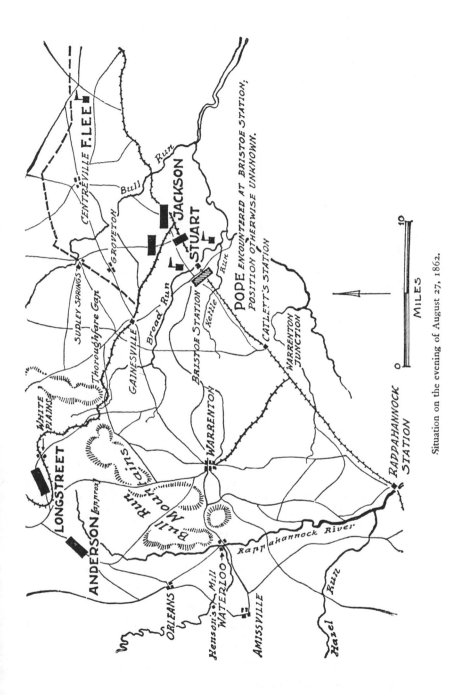

Situation on the evening of August 27, 1862.

the rear units kept the road until 2 A.M. and then lay down where they halted.[19] Even then the stinted rest of exhausted bodies was broken when "an old gray mare" belonging to one of the Texas regiments dashed frantically through the sleeping ranks. "Some one gave the alarm," General Hood subsequently wrote, "crying with a loud voice, 'Look out!' and the brave men who had fought so nobly at Cold Harbor sprang to their feet, deserted their colors and guns, and ran down the slope over a well-constructed fence, which was soon levelled to the ground, and had continued their flight several hundred yards before they awoke sufficiently to recover their wits, and boldly marched back, convulsed with laughter." [20]

Lee was now on the watershed of the Potomac, the dividing line between the Union and the Confederacy. If Jackson was still at Manassas, the remainder of the Army of Northern Virginia, on the morning of August 28, was just twenty-two miles from him, a long but not an impossible day's march. There was only one natural obstacle in the way—Thoroughfare Gap. The road from the plains led up Bull Run Mountains to this pass, paralleling the Manassas Gap Railroad and a little stream that flows finally into Occoquan Creek. The gap itself was not so formidable as its name implied—nor so much of a cañon as some writers have represented it to be.[21] With good tactics it could be wrested from a small opposing force; but if the enemy by any evil chance of war held the gap in strength, there would be trouble! At the moment there seemed little prospect of this. All the news was reassuring. Couriers arrived at intervals during the morning from Jackson, passing unhindered through the gap. They brought the cheering and important tidings that Jackson had left the exposed position at Manassas, and was resting his men, undisturbed and apparently unobserved, at a place called Groveton, seven miles northwest of Manassas. This move put him nineteen miles from Lee and not twenty-two, as had been supposed.[22]

Confidently, then, the tired soldiers rose on the morning of August 28 from their short night's broken slumber and moved

---

[19] 2 B. and L., 517; O. R., 12, part 2, pp. 555, 564.
[20] Hood, 32.
[21] It is curious to note that even Longstreet (op. cit., 174), writing many years after the war, exaggerated the strength of the gap.
[22] 2 B. and L., 517; Longstreet, 173.

through a beautiful country toward Thoroughfare Gap. The highest ground was reached before the gap was visible, and the down grade began; but the progress of the wagon train was slow and the day was hot, despite the elevation. The morning had dragged to noon, and the noon to 3 P.M. before the head of the column approached the gap. Lee was disposed to call a halt and give the men twelve hours' sleep, so that they would be fresh the next morning to descend the Bull Run Mountains and to join with Jackson in a new manœuvre that would throw Pope back on Washington. As a precaution, however, Lee determined to send forward Longstreet's leading division, that of D. R. Jones, to occupy the pass against possible seizure by the Federals, who by this time might be close at hand.[23]

Jones went briskly forward, with G. T. Anderson's brigade of Georgians in the lead. Soon from the echoing sides of the defile[24] there rolled the sound of an angry fire. Presently the message of all messages that Lee least wished to hear was glumly brought back: The enemy in undetermined strength held the pass and commanded it from a ridge at the opposite side. Jackson had been interposed between the Federals and Washington; now the Federals stood squarely between the two wings of the Army of Northern Virginia. Bad news, indeed! For if the Union force in the mountains was large enough and stubborn enough, Longstreet could be held off while the rest of Pope's army demolished Jackson. Then the united force of Pope and McClellan could fall upon Longstreet.

So reasoned the strategists in the ranks and some of those in command, as the report swept swiftly rearward. But if Lee shared these fears, he gave no outward sign. Quietly he rode forward to the summit of the hill west of the pass and there he dismounted. Slowly and without a tremor he put his glasses to his eyes and studied the gap closely. Then he calmly put his binocular back into the case, returned to his mount and went back down the hill.[25] Perhaps he knew enough of Jackson's position to realize that if "Stonewall" learned that Longstreet was in difficulties, he could skirt the northern end of the Bull Run Mountains and join him. Perhaps, again, Lee's quick eye for

[23] *Longstreet*, 173.   [24] Sorrel, *op. cit.*, 97, noted the singular resonance of the pass.
[25] Cooke, an eye-witness, *op. cit.*, 119–20.

313

topography and his experience in Mexico and western Virginia convinced him that Thoroughfare Gap was not so formidable as it was reputed to be—that there must be trails or minor passes by which resolute men could turn the position of the enemy. He gave his orders briskly:[26] D. R. Jones was to press the enemy on either side of the gap. Hood's division was to search for a nearby route over the mountain, and Wilcox, temporarily commanding three brigades, was to move them quickly to the northward and to try Hopewell Gap, three miles to the left. While these dispositions were being made, Lee went to dine at the nearby Robison home, the hospitable owner of which pressed an invitation on him and his staff; and "this meal," wrote an officer who had a good memory for gustatory delights, "was partaken of with as good an appetite and with as much geniality of manner as if the occasion was an ordinary one, not a moment in which victory or ruin hung trembling in the balance." [27]

It must have been about the time Lee finished dinner, in the late afternoon, that the troops who were climbing and crawling over the barren rock and through the tangled mountain laurel heard in the intervals between the slow Federal artillery fire a low and ominous mutter far from the eastward—gunfire, artillery, a battle undoubtedly in progress in the distance. It must be Jackson, found and assailed by the enemy who might, ere this, have been joined by some of those hard-hitting volunteers from the Army of the Potomac! It seemed a critical hour. At the gap, the Federals now pushed forward their artillery and swept the defile. Jones put one brigade on the cliffs to the left, and another, with two regiments of a third, to the right. Two regiments were held in reserve. As Jones could not bring his batteries to bear, his unprotected men had to force their way from rock to rock, firing as they came closer to the Federals. Finally, one of Jones's regiments, the 1st Georgia regulars, got within effective range. It made its fire count. An attempt by the enemy to hurl back the Georgians was quickly repulsed.

Twilight began to fall in the pass, but the fire continued, as if the Federals, in confident possession of a dominating position, were determined to hold off the Confederates until Jackson was finished. The situation gave every promise of a long, ugly fight.

[26] Long, 194.   [27] Long, 194.

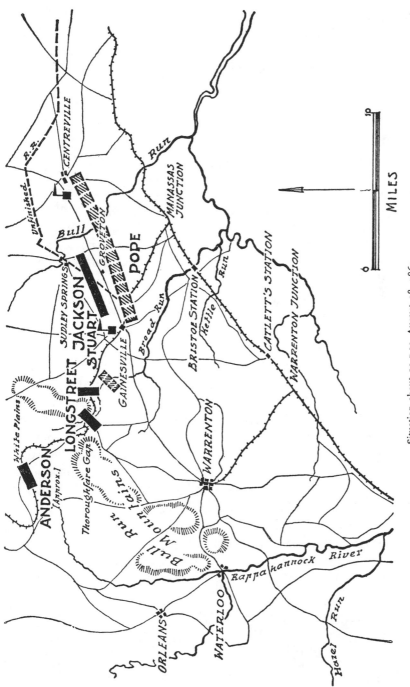

MILES

Situation about 10 P.M. August 28. 1862.

Map labels: CENTREVILLE, R.R., Unfinished, Bull, Run, MANASSAS JUNCTION, GROVETON, POPE, SUDLEY SPRINGS, JACKSON, STUART, Broad Run, Kettle Run, BRISTOL STATION, CATLETT'S STATION, WARRENTON JUNCTION, GAINESVILLE, LONGSTREET, ANDERSON, [Approx.], White Plains, Thoroughfare Gap, Bull Run Mountains, WARRENTON, Rappahannock River, WATERLOO, ORLEANS, Hazel Run

Law's brigade, however, had been sent a little farther to the left by General Hood, under the guidance of a man who professed to know a trail. When the end of this was reached, Law found a cleft in the rock through which his men could go forward, one at a time. Ere long, his skirmish line was formed on the crest, and as it descended, Law breathed in immense relief; for, looking down, he could see that he was beyond the flank of the Federals facing the gap! Resolution, speed, and good tactics might drive the enemy, even if only that one brigade could be thrown against him. Quickly Law's line was formed to turn the enemy's batteries; anxiously the men started forward. Before they got in range, the Union batteries limbered up and dashed to the rear. Law was for pushing on, and he frothed with rage a few minutes later when peremptory orders came for him to retire. Most unwillingly his men returned as they had come, tramping in the half-darkness over dangerous ground.

But the threat of the advancing Confederates had already had its effect, and there was no reason for exposing the brigade. The enemy was preparing to retreat. Jones waited a while and then boldly marched his division unopposed through the pass. Wilcox, hurrying to Hopewell Gap, found evidence that the Federals had been there during the day, but they had left at nightfall, and by 10 P.M. he started on his unmolested march to the eastern face of the mountains. When the anxious day ended, the danger was past, as if by some miracle. Lee sent a courier to Jackson, announcing the outcome of the fight at the gap,[28] and two stout divisions of the Army of Northern Virginia slept on their arms with their faces toward "Stonewall's" battleground. Since the forenoon they had heard nothing directly from him, except the growl of his guns, which had continued until 9 P.M. But there was hope in their hearts. Only the open road lay before them now, and they were determined that all the might that Pope could muster should not halt them on the morrow.[29]

28 *McCabe,* 221.
29 *O. R.,* 12, part 2, pp. 555–56, 579, 594, 598; Law in 2 *B. and L.,* 527–28. The 1st New Jersey cavalry alone had defended the gap until 3 P.M., the approximate hour of the arrival of the head of Longstreet's column. At that hour, Ricketts's 2d Division of McDowell's III Corps had arrived. Ricketts had not had time to make his dispositions and had been satisfied that his flank was being turned from left and from right. He withdrew during the night in a state close to panic, satisfied, as he reported, that his position was "critical" (*O. R.,* 12, part 2, p. 384).

CHAPTER XXIV

"MY DESIRE HAS BEEN TO AVOID A GENERAL ENGAGEMENT

(THE SECOND BATTLE OF MANASSAS)

THE road to the eastward led to Jackson's position on the morning of August 29, 1862, but south of that road, nine miles away, lay Warrenton, where Pope, by the latest report, had a large force.

A Confederate column marching eastward to Groveton by way of Haymarket would expose its right flank to an attack from Warrenton and must guard itself accordingly. Cavalry was needed for this purpose, and as Lee had none, he had to improvise them. Fortunately, during the early morning, a detached cavalry company rode into the lines at Thoroughfare Gap. Lee took this company, collected all available mounted men from the different commands, placed them under Stuart's quartermaster, Major Samuel H. Hairston, who happened to be with the infantry, and sent them off, 150 strong, to ascertain if any Federals were still in the vicinity of Warrenton.[1]

Before Hairston could set out, the infantry were on the road. Hood's division was in advance, and picked Texas riflemen acted as skirmishers. Contact was soon established with the rearguard of the Federals who had held the gap the night before, but they fled fast and soon disappeared altogether.[2] The steady tramp of Longstreet's regiments was uninterrupted. The dust was thick and the air already hot by the time Haymarket was reached and passed. A pleasant rolling country, half pastoral, half agricultural, was opening before the army. From high points a wide and inspiring panorama was spread out. At intervals green forests cut off the view.

---

[1] This is an obscure incident, mentioned only in Major Hairston's report (*O. R.*, 12, part 2, p. 753). None of the other reports of the cavalry commanders—they are not very numerous or very full—identify the company which Major Hairston said, "General Lee had halted at Thoroughfare and turned over to me when he ordered me to go on the expedition."

[2] *O. R.*, 12, part 2, p. 605.

Soon, on the left, in the edge of a wood, horsemen were seen. Lee's staff turned their glasses on them to ascertain whether they were friends or foes. There was a moment's scrutiny, and then the breeze rippled the blue cross against the red field of the flag the troops were carrying. The cavalry at the same moment decided that the marching column was Longstreet's and they started for it. As their leader galloped ahead, his flowing beard and familiar garb identified him as Stuart.

"Well, General," Lee inquired, the instant Stuart had ridden up and had exchanged greetings, "what of Jackson?"

"He has fallen back from Manassas," Stuart answered, "and is holding the enemy at bay at Sudley's Ford."

"We must hurry on and help him," said Lee. "Is there no path by which we may move our tired men and get them out of the heat and dust?"

There was no other road. Stuart had to advise that the infantry keep to the main highway till Gainesville was reached and then turn to the left into the Warrenton-Gainesville-Centreville turnpike.[3] This would bring Longstreet to Jackson's right flank.

The arrival of the cavalry was most reassuring, because it could guard the exposed right of Longstreet's column from sudden attack based on Warrenton. The infantry were halted in the road so that the cavalry might cross to the south for this purpose. Refreshed by the rest this pause afforded them, the regiments took up the march and soon were close to Gainesville. The sound of desultory artillery fire had beaten an uncertain accompaniment to the tramp of the troops for several miles, and now it swelled in faster time. The pace grew swifter, the banter died away.[4] Lee's mind was busy. How strong was the enemy, and how disposed? Was Jackson's line secure? Could contact be established easily? Had the Army of Northern Virginia won the race to Pope? If not, how much of McClellan's army was with the general whose headquarters were "in the saddle"? Lee had not

---

[3] *O. R.*, 12, part 2, p. 740. There is a conflict of testimony between Napier, *op. cit.*, 127, and W. M. Owen, *op. cit.*, 114, whether it was Stuart or General Beverly H. Robertson who met Lee, but as the two witnesses give almost precisely the same conversation, and as Stuart affirmed (*O. R.*, 12, part 2, p. 736) that he met Lee, the version given in the text has been preferred.

[4] *Longstreet*, 180; *Marshall*, 136.

intended to bring his campaign of manœuvre to an issue, but there, ahead of him, Jackson was waging a defensive battle. Could it be broken off? Should it be broken off? Or was there a prospect of victory, beyond the ridge where the smoke was rising?

As Lee pondered, the head of the column reached Gainesville. The Manassas Gap Railway and the road followed by the army continued to the southeast; the Warrenton-Gainesville-Centreville turnpike ran to the northeast, like the course of an arrow in still air. The leading regiment of Hood's division turned to the left into the turnpike,[5] and Jackson, who had been watching the advance, rode out for a moment and spoke to Hood.[6] The time, which was subsequently disputed in the trial of Fitz-John Porter, was around 10:30, perhaps a little earlier.

Lee came up shortly thereafter and established his headquarters on a little hill about 400 yards south of the turnpike in rear of the ground where Hood's men were quietly forming their line of battle. He sat down on a stump to await reconnaissance.[7] Presently there galloped up from the left a solitary courier, sent by General William E. Starke, to ascertain whether the troops who were taking position with so much composure were Federals or the long-awaited divisions of Longstreet. The courier paused only long enough to make sure and then he returned as fast as spurs could force his jaded horse toward the waiting and weary captors of Manassas. "It's Longstreet," he cried joyously, so that every listening ear caught the words. A mighty cheer went up, and Jackson's men knew for the first time that the worst danger was past, that the Army of Northern Virginia was united again.[8]

Jackson's "foot-cavalry" had reason both to rejoice and to be proud, for their performance from the time Lee had heard of their arrival at Bristoe Station and at Manassas had been almost as splendid as their march to Pope's rear. On the morning of the 27th, after Trimble and Stuart had seized the base at Manassas Junction, Hill's and Jackson's divisions had marched to that

[5] O. R., 12, part 2, pp. 556, 564.   [6] Hood, 33.
[7] Marshall, 137. Colonel Marshall took much pains at a later time to identify the exact location. A detail map was carefully studied by him at the Porter Inquiry and an "L," marking Lee's headquarters, inserted. See Proceedings and Report . . . in the Case of Fitz-John Porter, Washington, 1879, 3 vol. edition (cited hereafter as Porter Inquiry), 2, 933.
[8] 32 S. H. S. P., 85–86; 130–31.

point, leaving Ewell at Bristoe, to dispute the Federal pursuit and, ere retiring, to burn the railroad bridge over Broad Run. Taylor's Federal brigade had come up from Alexandria and had attacked near Manassas Junction in the belief that it was encountering only a raiding party. Jackson had tried to save the New Jersey troops from slaughter by demanding their surrender, but they had rushed on and had been wrecked.[9] Unhindered thereafter, Jackson's men had sacked the immense stores. Many had found clothing and shoes; others, feasting freely, had thought only to supply the inner man.[10] All had been allowed to help themselves, because as Jackson had only his ambulances with him, there had been no hope of removing much of the plunder.[11] While the men of Hill and of Taliaferro[12] had been thus pleasantly engaged, Ewell had been holding off a threatening attack at Bristoe Station.[13]

During the night of August 27–28, Taliaferro had marched to a new position, northwest of Manassas; the rearguard had destroyed the base and two miles of loaded freight-cars;[14] and then, after Ewell had broken off the fight at Bristoe, first Hill and then he had moved to join Taliaferro.[15] Jackson had most admirably chosen his new position. Moving to the northwest, he had occupied a long ridge at Groveton, where he would be able to withdraw to Thoroughfare Gap, or north of the Bull Run Mountains if hard pressed, yet where he commanded a long sweep of the Gainesville-Centreville turnpike, in case an unwary foe should move across his front.

In seeking to locate Jackson, Pope had lost much time in mistaken manœuvres.[16] Jackson, waiting quietly, had let Pope wear out his men at hide-and-seek, until the late afternoon of the 28th when he had hurled his right wing, 8000 men, against King's division, which he had assumed to be the flank guard of a passing army corps.[17]

---

9 Fitz Lee, 187; Mrs. Jackson, 319; 2 B. and L., 529.
10 13 S. H. S. P., 12; 2 B. and L., 533.   11 2 B. and L., 529.
12 Brigadier-General W. B. Taliaferro had commanded Jackson's old division after the death of Brigadier-General Charles Winder at Cedar Run.
13 O. R., 12, part 2, pp. 644, 708–9; Early, 115 ff.
14 O. R., 12, part 2, pp. 670, 679.   15 O. R., 12, part 2, p. 644.
16 2 Henderson, 141–42; Long, 196.
17 2 Henderson, 145. Jackson's own explanation of this attack (O. R., 12, part 2, pp. 644-45) is not altogether clear. Henderson, loc. cit., interpreted it to mean that Jackson

The enemy had resisted with great stubbornness and had not been driven off the field until 9 o'clock on the evening of August 28. Jackson's loss had been heavy and had included two of his three division commanders, Ewell and Taliaferro. Ewell had lost a leg and would be absent for months. Taliaferro's wounds were not serious,[18] though they temporarily incapacitated him. The vigil of the night had been relieved, despite these losses, by the knowledge that the rest of the army was near at hand. The cannonading at Thoroughfare Gap had been heard on Jackson's lines.[19]

On the morning of the 29th, Jackson had found the Federals farther to his left, interposed between him and Washington. He had slightly changed position to conform, and had drawn his line along and close to the cut of the so-called "unfinished railroad," which was an excavated grade intended to give the Manassas Gap Railroad direct connection with Alexandria, instead of by way of Manassas Junction.[20] Jackson's division, now under Brigadier General Starke, had been placed on the right, where Longstreet was expected to join him. Ewell's division, commanded by Brigadier General A. R. Lawton, had been put in the centre, and Hill had been given the left, the post of greatest danger. These dispositions had been made and two vigorous artillery exchanges had occurred, when word had been passed down the line that Longstreet had come up. The whole operation, from the start at Warrenton Springs Ford to the moment of Lee's arrival on the scene, had been conducted on Jackson's part without a serious mistake of any sort. His troops were weary and were sadly deficient in senior officers, but their spirit was high, and when they saw their old comrades of the Seven Days file into position, they turned again defiantly to the enemy, who was massing on the front as Longstreet came up.[21]

believed the enemy was moving by way of Manassas, instead of along the turnpike toward Alexandria "and if Pope was to be fought in the open field before he could be reinforced by McClellan, he must be induced to retrace his steps."

18 *O. R.,* 12, part 2, pp. 645, 656–57, 679, 700, 735; 2 *B. and L.,* 508, 511; *Taylor's General Lee,* 103.

19 *Long,* 195.   20 *O. R.,* 12, part 2, p. 645.

21 *O. R.,* 12, part 2, pp. 645, 670. As illustrating the shortage of officers in Jackson's command, it may be noted that none of the brigades of Jackson's (Taliaferro's) division was under a general officer. One of them was commanded by a major (*O. R.,* 12, part 2, p. 641). After General Trimble was wounded on the 29th, command of his brigade devolved temporarily on a captain (*O. R.,* 12, part 2, p. 712).

Longstreet's line was formed promptly. Hood's division was placed perpendicular to the turnpike, with its left close to the right of Jackson's line. Evans was in immediate support. Three brigades under Wilcox were put in rear of Hood's left, and three others under Kemper were behind Hood's right. D. R. Jones's division was sent to the right of Hood, where his flank rested on the Manassas Gap Railroad.[22] It was an admirable position in which to meet an attack, though not quite so good for hurling quickly the full weight of the army in assault. Communication from one flank to the other was open. With Jackson extending to the northeast, along the unfinished railroad, Longstreet's line was shaping itself southward. The whole front formed an angle of approximately 160 degrees, strongest at the apex, which was near the Gainesville-Centreville road, looking east.

Hood's batteries, which had taken position immediately upon arrival, were now strengthened by some of Longstreet's already famous companies of the Washington Artillery. Their brisk and well-directed fire quickly caused the enemy to shift his line opposite Jackson's right.[23] As Anderson's division, which had followed Longstreet from Warrenton Springs Ford, was known to be close enough to share in any general engagement, Lee had at hand all the troops he could hope to put into action, whereas troops arriving from McClellan might so strengthen Pope that he could seize the initiative. Lee's martial instinct and his military judgment alike told him that the thing to do was to attack at once. He so informed Longstreet.[24] But "Old Pete" was not satisfied. He believed, as Maurice has aptly said, that the recipe for victory was to manœuvre the army into a position where the enemy would have to attack disadvantageously,[25] and he asked for time in which to examine the ground more fully and to ascertain what force was gathering on his right.[26] Reluctantly Lee consented. Longstreet rode off to the southeast, near the flank of Jones's division, and climbed an eminence there.[27] Lee waited. The artillery duel continued. The Federals seemed to be moving away to concentrate against Jackson's left.[28]

After a while, Longstreet returned. He was full of misgiving.

---

[22] O. R., 12, part 2, pp. 556, 579.
[24] Longstreet, 181; 2 B. and L., 519.
[26] 2 B. and L., 519.
[28] O. R., 12, part 2, p. 556.

[23] O. R., 12, part 2, pp. 556, 565, 571.
[25] Maurice, 143.
[27] 2 B. and L., 519.

The Federals extended far to the south of the turnpike, he said. The terrain was not inviting. Besides, there was no telling what force the enemy might be bringing up from the direction of Manassas Junction. An attack might send the Confederate right flank squarely into a strong Federal column.[29] Lee was disappointed. It would be possible, he said, to send troops beyond the Federal left and to seize the strong ground of which Longstreet spoke.

As the two debated, a message arrived from General Stuart, who was on reconnaissance down the road leading from Gainesville to Manassas. Stuart said that a column was approaching from that direction. Another force, reckoned as a full army corps, was advancing on the road from Bristoe to Sudley Springs, and if not halted would strike Longstreet's flank. He had an excellent artillery position, Stuart stated, and was having men drag the road from Gainesville toward the Federals, to raise a dust and create an impression that troops were moving out to meet the Federals, but if the ground was to be held, reinforcements had to be dispatched to that quarter immediately.[30]

Wilcox's three brigades were at once ordered to move from the centre, in rear of Hood's left, around to the right of Jones.[31] Longstreet hurried off to see the situation for himself and to dispose Wilcox's men as they came up on the right. Again Lee had to wait. As he studied the woods and ridges in front of him, while the artillery still thundered on the centre and the dust-clouds rose from the direction of Bristoe and Manassas to the southeast, Jackson rode up, weary and dishevelled. It was the first time Lee had seen him since they had ended their memorable council at Jeffersonton on the afternoon of the 25th, and their brief conversation must have been of Jackson's march, of his battle with King on the 28th, and of the ominous movement of the Federals to his left flank. As they talked, Longstreet returned. This time he was somewhat reassured. The force opposite his right was hardly large enough as yet to threaten his flank, he said, but there was more dust down the road toward Manassas. Further troops might be moving in that direction.[32]

[29] 2 *B. and L.*, 519; Longstreet in 1 *Porter Inquiry*, 552.
[30] *O. R.*, 12, part 2, pp. 556, 736; *Longstreet*, 182; 2 *B. and L.*, 519.
[31] *O. R.*, 12, part 2, p. 598.   [32] *Longstreet*, 128.

"Hadn't we better move our line forward?" Lee asked, with the deference it had become his habit to show his division commanders, especially Longstreet, in all matters of tactics on the field of battle.

"I think not," Longstreet answered cautiously; "we had better wait until we hear more from Stuart about the force he has reported moving against us from Manassas."

Jackson said nothing.[33] Lee hesitated to order an attack where the man who was to deliver it was opposed to it, so he unwillingly consented to await developments a while longer. Jackson rode off, for the fire from the left of his line was growing in volume. Soon Stuart arrived, to confirm what Longstreet had said of a movement up the road from Manassas.[34] The troops that were coming up were almost certainly Porter's corps. Pope's command was being reinforced still further by the Army of the Potomac—dark news! The last lap of the race to Pope was being run on the field of battle. Lee determined now to ascertain the facts for himself. Leaving Stuart at headquarters, he made a personal reconnaissance. This satisfied him that the Confederate line outflanked the Federals, whose numbers did not seem to exceed 10,000.[35] After an hour, he rode back to the hill. His first inquiry was for Stuart.

"Here I am, General," Stuart answered instantly, rising from the ground where he had been sleeping calmly throughout the whole of his chief's absence.

"I want you to send a message to your troops over on the left to send a few more cavalry over to the right."

"I would better go myself," said Stuart, and he rode off singing loudly his favorite "Jine the cavalry." [36]

For the third time Lee declared himself for an attack. He believed that a drive along the Gainesville-Centreville turnpike would certainly dislodge the force on the right at the same time that it would relieve Jackson, whose troops were now furiously engaged on the extreme left. Longstreet was obdurate. The day was nearly done, "Old Pete" argued. An advance would get

---

[33] *W. M. Owen,* 117.   [34] *Longstreet,* 183.

[35] Lee to Fitz John Porter, Oct. 31, 1867, and July n. d., 1870: 1 *Porter Inquiry,* pp. 510, 551.

[36] 2 *B. and L.,* 525.

nowhere and might be disastrous. It would be far better to make a reconnaissance later in the evening. Then, if an opening were found, the whole army could be thrown against the enemy. Lee hesitated. Judgment and consideration for the opinion of his subordinate were at odds. At length, though unconvinced, he assented. His decision was reached after far too little deliberation and probably was expressed in a very few words, but the moment was an important one in the military career of Lee, important less in its effect on the outcome of the battle than in its bearing on Lee's future relations with Longstreet. In all the operations since Lee had taken command of the Army of Northern Virginia he had not shown any of the excessive consideration for the feelings of others that he had exhibited in West Virginia in his dealings with General Loring; now it appeared again. The seeds of much of the disaster at Gettysburg were sown in that instant—when Lee yielded to Longstreet and Longstreet discovered that he would.

Longstreet, satisfied, set about preparing Hood's division for a reconnaissance in force.[37] Wilcox was ordered back from the right to be ready to support Hood, with whom Evans was to move.[38]

The roar from the left now told of such a battle as even the Army of Northern Virginia had seldom fought. Hill, on Jackson's left flank, had his six brigades in a double line from right to left as follows: Field, Thomas, and Gregg in front, with Branch, Pender, and Archer in support. They were along or close to the cut of the unfinished railroad,[39] on ground where the artillery could do little to protect the infantry or to drive back the enemy. Gregg's South Carolinians, on the extreme left, occupied "a small, rocky, wooded knoll, with the railroad cut on the east and north fronts, and a cleared field to the northwest."[40] Against this line, now swinging to the right and now to the left, Pope threw his troops in successive charges from 3 o'clock

[37] *Longstreet*, 183–84.

[38] An interesting question is raised by this shift: Would it have been better to make the proposed diversion on the right flank, rather than on the centre? The artillery could readily have held the centre; a diversion on the right would have clarified the obscure situation there and might have facilitated the advance on the 30th. But would it have led Pope to become alarmed for his right and so to strengthen it during the night of the 19th–30th as to outflank Longstreet on the 30th?

[39] *O. R.*, 12, part 2, pp. 652, 670. [40] *O. R.*, 12, part 2, p. 679.

until 6.[41] On some parts of the front the ammunition was exhausted after the second Federal assault, and the men had to meet the enemy with the bayonet.[42] On Thomas's front the enemy gained the cut and was driven back from it.[43] Gregg, with the cartridge-boxes of his men empty, sent word to his division commander: "Tell General Hill that my ammunition is exhausted, but that I will hold my position with the bayonet." [44] And when the Federal general, Cuvier Grover, threw his men into a gap in the line between Thomas and Gregg, in what a philosophical colonel styled "the consummation of the grand debate between Massachusetts and South Carolina,"[45] Gregg rallied them for a last stand. Weary and deaf, he walked up and down his thinned line with an old Revolutionary scimitar in his hand. "Let us die here, my men," he said, "let us die here!" The enemy was across the railroad cut, and the survivors of the regiments that had fought in the swamp at Gaines's Mill were preparing to meet them with steel, when there was a shout behind them. Thinking that they were surrounded, they turned in dread—and saw the familiar gray of Early's brigades and a part of Lawton's, comparatively fresh.[46] There was a brief, wild encounter; then the Federals were repulsed once more and were forced to retreat beyond the line of the unfinished railroad.[47]

Of all this, of course, Lee could see nothing, but as he received no call for assistance from Jackson, he knew that all was well. About sunset, Hood was sent forward along the turnpike to make the reconnaissance that Longstreet had favored. He had not gone far before he encountered a Federal force advancing to attack him. A quick, fierce clash occurred in gathering darkness. Wilcox was hurried to support Hood's left, and Hunton, with a brigade of Kemper's, formed on the right of Hood.[48] Together they swept on into the Federal positions and were engulfed by twilight.

[41] O. R., 12, part 2, p. 671.   [42] O. R., 12, part 2, p. 700.
[43] O. R., 12, part 2, pp. 702–3.   [44] O. R., 12, part 2, p. 671.
[45] 13 S. H. S. P., 30.
[46] O. R., 12, part 2, pp. 680–81. See also ibid., 684–90—one of the most thrilling battle-reports in the Official Records; dramatically revised in 13 S. H. S. P., 34–35. Colonel Edward McCrady, Jr., who wrote this report and narrative, stated that the troops who relieved him were Fields's and Pender's brigades. Field filed no report and Pender's mentioned no such episode. Early's account makes it clear that he and Lawton were responsible.
[47] O. R., 12, part 2, pp. 671, 711–12; Early, 124–25.   [48] O. R., 12, part 2, p. 565.

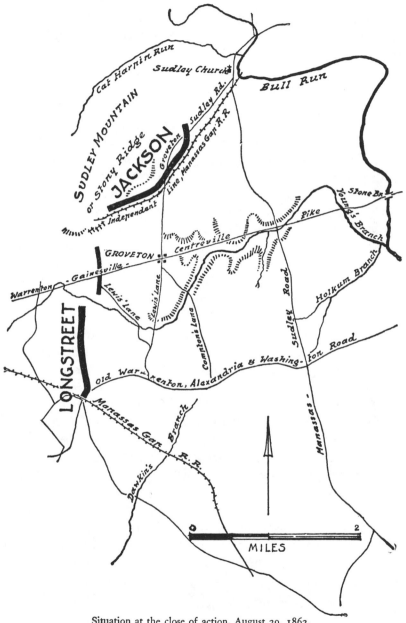

Situation at the close of action, August 29, 1862.

It was late when Hood came back to Lee and Longstreet and reported that he had advanced so far that he could not distinguish bluecoat from gray. He advocated a withdrawal to his original line. More than that, he had made, at Longstreet's instance, as careful a study as possible of the enemy's position. His conclusion was disconcerting, almost disheartening. The ground held by the enemy was very strong, he said. An attack the next morning would be dangerous. General Wilcox, who made a separate report, was of the same opinion.[49] By Lee's order, Hood immediately began to withdraw. On the way out he met R. H. Anderson's division, which had completed the long march as rearguard from Warrenton Springs Ford, and, undirected, had pushed forward almost into the enemy's lines.[50]

The information supplied by Hood and Wilcox threw Lee back on his original plan to avoid a general engagement and to rely on manœuvre in forcing Pope from northern Virginia. He sent off a dispatch to the President, recounting what had happened,[51] and then he retired to a little cabin some 400 yards to the left of the turnpike, about three-quarters of a mile behind Hood's lines, there to await the returning sun.

Day broke clear and bright on the morning of the fateful 30th of August,[52] and in a stillness that did not suggest a renewal of the enemy's attacks. On some parts of the line scarcely a gun was fired as the sun began to climb upward, while the hungry men stirred in the nearby cornfields to find for themselves the rations the commissary could not supply.[53] Lee was satisfied that if the enemy dared to attack, he would be repulsed in two hours,[54] but such slight movements as could be observed from headquarters, which were re-established on the ridge where they had been located on the previous evening, suggested a withdrawal rather than an assault. The feeling spread that the enemy might escape.[55] When Lee sat down to write an early-morning dispatch to the President, his mind was not on an offensive battle but on the possibility of further manœuvres to clear the enemy from

[49] *Longstreet*, 184.   [50] *O. R.*, 12, part 2, pp. 557, 565, 605; *Hood*, 34–35.
[51] *Lee's Dispatches*, 55.   [52] *McCabe*, 224.   [53] *G. Wise*, 96.
[54] S. G. Welch: *A Confederate Surgeon's Letters to His Wife* (cited hereafter as *Welch*), 27.
[55] 2 *B. and L.*, 520.

fruitful northern Virginia. "My dispatches," he said, "will have informed you of the march of this portion of the army. Its progress has been necessarily slow, having a large and superior force on its flank; narrow and rough roads to travel, and the difficulties of obtaining forage and provisions to contend with. It has so far advanced in safety and has succeeded in deceiving the enemy as to its object. The movement has, as far as I am able to judge, drawn the enemy from the Rappahannock frontier and caused him to concentrate his troops between Manassas and Centreville. My desire has been to avoid a general engagement, being the weaker force, and by maneuvering to relieve the portion of the country referred to. I think if not overpowered we shall be able to relieve other portions of the country, as it seems to be the purpose of the enemy to collect his strength here. . . ." [56]

By the oddest chance, and in the most ironical contrast, General Pope a few minutes before had telegraphed to General Halleck his appraisal of the situation. "We fought a terrific battle here yesterday," he reported. . . . "We have lost not less than 8000 men killed and wounded, but from the appearance of the field the enemy lost at least two to one. . . . The news just reaches me from the front that the enemy is retreating towards the mountains. . . ." [57]

About 8 o'clock the enemy's batteries opened a slow fire, but this caused no apprehension. For at dawn, Stephen D. Lee's battalion of reserve artillery, eighteen guns, had come up and had taken the position occupied by the Washington Artillery on the 29th—a ridge near the centre and somewhat in advance of the infantry, a quarter of a mile in length and facing open ground in front for a distance of about 2000 yards. [58] "You are just where I wanted you," General Lee said to the alert young colonel, "stay there." [59] With these guns so advantageously placed to support the batteries attached to the infantry commands, Lee felt that he had little to fear in an artillery engagement, even from the superior ordnance of the Federals, though his ammunition was so low that he had to urge economy in its expenditure. [60]

[56] *Lee's Dispatches*, 56–58.   [57] *O. R.*, 12, part 3, p. 741.
[58] *O. R.*, 12, part 2, p. 577.
[59] 6 *S. H. S. P.*, 63; Royal W. Figg: *Where Men Only Dare to Go* (cited hereafter as *Figg*), 27–28.
[60] *O. R.*, 51, part 2, p. 613.

The fire kept up for about an hour; then it died away in a silence more profound than before.[61] Lee began to formulate the details of the next move in his campaign of manœuvre. Studying the map, he decided that if the Federals made no assault during the day he would demonstrate along the line in the afternoon, then slip across Bull Run in the vicinity of Sudley Springs after nightfall, and endeavor once again to get in Pope's rear.[62]

Straining ears heard the distant rumbling of artillery wheels about noon, and anxious eyes ere long saw rising clouds of dust on the left.[63] General Stuart reported that from a perch in a great walnut tree, one of his men could see the Federals gradually massing in three heavy lines opposite Jackson.[64] Perhaps Pope intended to attack, after all! Couriers were dispatched to put the troops on the alert. Jackson joined Lee and Longstreet at head-quarters. Stuart was summoned and came up quickly.[65] Over the field there passed the expectancy that always lights the eyes of the brave and makes them look to their arms ere "the long roll" is sounded and the grim "Fall in" is shouted. Preparations were complete, the generals reported. D. R. Jones had been advanced slightly on the right[66] and Jackson had sheltered his men in the woods northwest of the railroad cut,[67] both to rest them and to mystify the Federals. Unless still more of McClellan's troops had come up during the night to swell Pope's numbers to invincible odds, Lee had only to fear that the army would run out of ammunition or that Jackson's thinned regiments would be overborne.[68]

Jackson returned to his command. Longstreet still had some doubt whether the Federal army really would take the offensive, so he went off toward Hood's position to prepare for the demonstration intended to precede the movement that was to be made to Sudley Springs that night,[69] in case the Federals did not attack. Stuart galloped away to make his dispositions. As Lee, at head-

---

[61] *Long*, 197.
[63] *G. Wise*, 96.
[65] 1 *von Borcke*, 153.
[67] *Alexander*, 212.

[62] *Longstreet*, 186.
[64] *O. R.*, 12, part 2, p. 736.
[66] *Longstreet*, 186.

[68] Some of Jackson's regiments had been almost wiped out by sickness, hard marching, and casualties. The 2d Virginia had carried only about 100 men into action on the 29th (*O. R.*, 12, part 2, p. 659). The 4th Virginia had less than 100 left on the 30th (*ibid.*, 662), and the 27th Virginia had only forty-five including officers (*ibid.*, 663). All these regiments belonged to the "Stonewall Brigade."

[69] *Longstreet*, 186.

quarters, waited and watched, there arrived an unexpected visitor in the person of General Pendleton. He was sick and travel-worn, but along with dispatches from President Davis he brought the good news that the rest of the reserve artillery was on the march to Lee and that D. H. Hill's division was at Rapidan Station. On the next move, whatever it might be, Lee would have reinforcements. That meant much.[70] He sent General Pendleton off to rest and turned to ascertain the meaning of the fire that was now rolling heavily from Jackson's front.

The Federals had begun a new attack.[71] At first it was heaviest on Jackson's right. Opposite the second brigade of Jackson's old division, the enemy got so close to the cut that the opposing flags were only ten yards apart. When the ammunition of the Confederates was exhausted, they took up rocks from the embankment and beat back the enemy with these. One officer, having no arms with him, fought throughout with stones. For half an hour the battle raged here;[72] then it appeared to be directed chiefly against the left flank, as on the previous afternoon.

Lee turned to his signal officer, Captain J. L. Bartlett, who had established his station near headquarters, and had him flag to Jackson, two miles off, "What is the result of the movements on your left?" Presently the answer came back: "So far, the enemy appear to be trying to get possession of a piece of woods to withdraw out of our sight." [73]

But "Old Jack" was wrong. Quickly the Federals returned in force that made their first assault seem as nothing more than a skirmish. Hill's men, fighting hard, began to waver at one point in the line, and Jackson quickly sent word to Longstreet and to Lee, asking for reinforcements.[74] Lee immediately forwarded an order to Longstreet to hurry a division to Jackson. Longstreet received this message while standing on high ground near the centre, whence he could see the left flank of the Federals who were then renewing their assault on Jackson's right at the same time they were pounding his left. As the Federal left was within easy artillery range of his guns, Longstreet reasoned that a well-

---

[70] *Pendleton*, 209; *O. R.*, 12, part 3, p. 948.
[71] The time is variously given at from 1 to 4 P.M., but the attack probably started in force about 3 o'clock.
[72] *O. R.*, 12, part 2, pp. 666–67.   [73] *O. R.*, 12, part 2, p. 563.
[74] 6 *S. H. S. P.*, 59; *Longstreet.* 186–87.

directed fire would break up the attack before he could possibly march a division to Jackson's relief. He had noticed, as he had ridden up, that the battery commanders, with instincts surer in this case than his own, had been anticipating an order to advance and had their horses harnessed and the men standing to the guns. It now took him only a minute to send an aide dashing back to bring up these batteries. Samuel Chapman's company, the first to arrive, went quickly into action; Captain Robert Boyce followed; Captain James Reilly's six-gun battery swept up with foam-covered horses. Stephen D. Lee's eighteen guns were ready.[75]

Across the road, at his field headquarters, Lee was waiting. All around him officers were aquiver, but the General did not move a muscle. As some wagons passed to the front, he turned to a subordinate and said calmly, "I observe that some of those mules are without shoes. I wish you would see to it that all of the animals are shod at once." A moment later he heard the loud crash of Longstreet's guns. The expression of his face did not change in the slightest.[76] Taking the fire to mean that Longstreet had probably decided on some other measure of relief than the dispatch of reinforcements, Lee sent Longstreet word that if he saw anything better to do than to reinforce Jackson, he should do it.[77] Perceiving soon the effect of Longstreet's fire, Lee signalled Jackson: "Do you still want reinforcements?"[78] and, as the Federal flank began to melt away, he saw that a great opportunity had come. Instantly he seized it: Let R. H. Anderson move from reserve to support Longstreet; order Longstreet to attack at once with his full force; pass the word to right and to left for a general assault; throw every man in his army against Pope. Quick action would engulf the whole of the Federal left and left-centre.[79]

As the lines prepared to move forward, the answer to Lee's signal came back from Jackson, half an hour after it had been sent. "No," Jackson said, he did not need reinforcements, "the

[75] *Longstreet*, 187; *O. R.*, 12, part 2, pp. 607, 640; 6 *S. H. S. P.*, 60, 64–65.

[76] G. T. Lee: "Reminiscences of General Robert E. Lee," in *South Atlantic Quarterly*, July, 1927, pp. 247–48. Major Lee got this story from General R. F. Hoke, and understood that Hoke was an eye-witness, but as General Hoke was far around on the left, fighting with Lane's brigade, Hoke himself must have heard of the incident from some one who was present. There seems no reason for doubting its substantial accuracy.

[77] 2 *B. and L.*, 524.　　　　[78] *O. R.*, 12, part 2, p. 563.

[79] *O. R.*, 12, part 2, pp. 557, 565–66; 2 *B. and L.*, 524.

enemy are giving way." [80] Hill's men had rallied; Pender and Brockenbrough had been advanced; the Federals had been repulsed in their front.[81]

Longstreet had anticipated the order to attack; his lines were about to move forward when Lee's messenger reached him.[82] The battle smoke drifted back to headquarters; the roar of the guns shook the hills. There was victory in the air. "General Longstreet is advancing," Lee signalled Jackson; "look out for and protect his left flank,"[83] for Longstreet's left would have to advance almost across the front of Jackson's right, unless Jackson could advance simultaneously.

Were the troops all ready—A. P. Hill there on Jackson's left, Early in the centre, and then Jackson's division? On Longstreet's line, did Wilcox, next Jackson's right, understand what was expected of him? Was Hood on the right of Wilcox, with Evans and R. H. Anderson in support? Was Kemper, with three brigades, flanking Hood and D. R. Jones, properly disposed on the extreme right?

Northeast for Longstreet's right; east for the troops on his left; Jackson's direction would be east and southeast. What if there was a measure of convergence between left and right, apt to cause piling-up of the troops nearest the centre along the Gainesville-Centreville turnpike? It was a small matter compared with the possibilities that the break on Pope's right-centre presented. A general advance on the ridges occupied by the Federals might hurl the foe back to the famous old stone bridge across Bull Run, with the prospect of a confused slaughter there. Forward, then!

The assault began with far greater precision than at Gaines's Mill or at Malvern Hill. Instead of the wasteful attacks in detail, nearly the whole of the right went forward simultaneously. The spearhead, as on June 27, was the Texas brigade, vigorously supported by Law, then by Evans and later by R. H. Anderson. Hood met the Federals within 150 yards of his position.[84] Very soon the resistance was stiff and the field confused. Jackson's division did not come up promptly. The advance of Longstreet's left was exposed to an enfilading fire from batteries that had been

80 *O. R.*, 12, part 2, p. 563.
82 *O. R.*, 12, part 2, pp. 557, 566.
84 *O. R.*, 12, part 2, pp. 605–6.
81 *O. R.*, 12, part 2, p. 671.
83 *O. R.*, 12, part 2, p. 563.

placed in front of Jackson's right. Time was lost in silencing these guns,[85] though Lee hurried orders to Jackson to hasten his advance. In the face of this opposition, Wilcox was directed to move his brigade to the right to support Hood.[86] On Wilcox's departure, Featherstone, who was slow in starting,[87] and Pryor, who commanded the third of Wilcox's brigades, became bewildered and ere long drifted to the left, where they fought under Jackson. Off on the right of Longstreet, G. T. Anderson faced a very heavy fire[88] and lacked the support of Drayton's brigade, which was held up, without authority, on a false report from the cavalry that the enemy were moving to turn the extreme Confederate right flank.[89]

Despite these checks and complications, the line swept on. "The easy rounded ridges," General Sorrel later wrote, "ran at right angles to the turnpike, and over these infantry and artillery poured in pursuit. The artillery would gallop furiously to the nearest ridge, limber to the front, deliver a few rounds until the enemy was out of range, and then gallop again to the next ridge."[90] Far in front, the Fifth Texas saw nothing of Kemper's supporting column on its right,[91] but it did not relax its pace. The color-bearer, Private Jimmy Harris, insisted on rushing ahead, waving the flag, until he was sixty or seventy yards in front of the line; then he would halt, turn toward his comrades and shout, "Come on." When he was shot down, another man seized the colors, only to fall within 200 paces. Then a captain took the standard and bore it onward, to pass it at length into the hands of a private who seemed to have a charmed life.[92] Hood's men were well blown when they halted at the Chinn house, near which Toombs, on the right, was troubled by a persistent enfilading battery.[93] But Dick Anderson was up now and mingled his men with Hood's in a continued pursuit.[94] Jackson's thinned line was moving, also; the enemy was in general retreat except where stubbornly resisting at strong points opposite the Confederate right.

But the end of the pursuit had to come before the objective was

---

85 *Longstreet*, 189.
86 *O. R.*, 12, part 2, p. 600.
87 *O. R.*, 12, part 2, p. 599.
88 *O. R.*, 12, part 2, p. 595.
89 *O. R.*, 12, part 2, p. 579.
90 *Sorrel*, 98.
91 *O. R.*, 12, part 2, p. 617.
92 *O. R.*, 12, part 2, p. 620.
93 *O. R.*, 12, part 2, pp. 583–84. Toombs, who had been put under arrest for withdrawing his troops from the Raccoon Ford road (see *supra*, p. 285), was restored to command by Longstreet on the battlefield.
94 *Longstreet*, 189.

reached. Scattered by their advance of more than a mile and a half, weakened by losses and confused by strange ground, Longstreet's men were overtaken by darkness as they approached the ridge of the Henry house. The sky had become overcast. Visibility was low. A storm was threatened. There was danger that a farther advance would throw Federal and Confederate so close together that the Southerners would fire into their own ranks. The Fifth Texas "slipped the bridle," as Hood put it,[95] and made a last wild attack, but gradually the infantry became disengaged or were halted, and only the artillery, firing blindly, kept up the sound of battle. Through a rain that soon began to fall, the Federals surged back across Young's Branch and the Stone Bridge at Bull Run, protected in their flight by a few regiments that held the hill of the Henry house with magnificent resolution.[96]

Lee had not been able to remain at headquarters, in the unparticipating rear, while his troops were making the most triumphant advance their banners had ever shone upon. When the infantry had started, he had followed fast with his officers, and during the time when Longstreet's left had been exposed to an enfilade, he would have ridden straight into the fire had not "Old Pete," after pleading in vain for Lee to turn back, guided him under cover of a cross-ravine. Freed after a short time from the protesting voice of Longstreet, Lee had ridden forward over the dead-strewn field, before the merciful darkness had hidden any of its horrors. He had reached the most advanced artillery position just after the order to "cease firing" had been given, and from the crest of the ridge, astride Traveller, he studied the ground in front with his binoculars. Not fifteen feet from him was a silent gun.

"General," said Captain Mason of the staff, when Lee at last dropped his glasses, "here is some one who wants to speak to you."

Lee looked and saw a powder-blackened gunner, his sponge staff in his hand. Ever since he had been asked for a chew of tobacco by the raw private in western Virginia, he had been accustomed to receive all manner of complaints and requests at unexpected places from unknown members of the voluntary association known as the Army of Northern Virginia; so there was

[95] *Hood*, 37.   [96] *Longstreet*, 189–90.

no surprise in his voice when he said, "Well, my man, what can I do for you?"

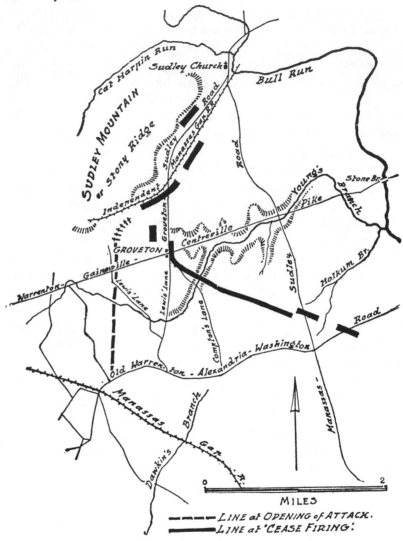

Advance of the Confederate right at Second Manassas, August 30, 1862.

"Why, General," said the cannoneer in aggrieved and familiar tones, "don't you know me?"

It was Robert.[97]

[97] *R. E. Lee, Jr.*, 76–77.

JEFFERSON DAVIS, PRESIDENT OF THE CONFEDERATE STATES OF AMERICA
After the painting in the Westmoreland Club, Richmond.

MECHANICSVILLE, VIRGINIA, SCENE OF LEE'S FIRST BATTLE

This photograph was taken in April, 1865, from the field across which Ripley and Pender advanced.

THE CRUDE MAP OF THE VICINITY OF RICHMOND, USED BY THE CONFEDERATE HIGH COMMAND DURING THE SEVEN DAYS' BATTLES OF 1862

The errors and inadequate detail of this map were responsible for some of the failures of Lee's initial operations to prevent the threatened siege of Richmond by McClellan. *After an original in the Confederate Museum, Richmond.*

LIEUTENANT GENERAL JAMES LONGSTREET—"OLD PETE"—AFTER A
PHOTOGRAPH TAKEN PROBABLY IN 1863 OR 1864
At the time of the Seven Days' battles, he was still a Major General.

THE WRECK OF GAINES'S MILL AFTER THE OPERATIONS OF 1862 AND 1864

The initial brush in the battle that took its name from this structure occurred on the dam of this mill.

GRAPEVINE BRIDGE OVER THE CHICKAHOMINY RIVER, AS IT APPEARED IN 1862

Across this unstable structure General McClellan moved a part of his army on the night of June 27, following the defeat of his right wing at Gaines's Mill. There were several crossings of branches of this stream in the vicinity. Collectively, they were called "Grapevine" because of their tortuous course.

RUINS OF THE "STONE BRIDGE" ACROSS BULL RUN

After this photograph was taken in March, 1862, the bridge was rebuilt but was destroyed on the night of August 30, 1862, by the Federal army to delay pursuit.

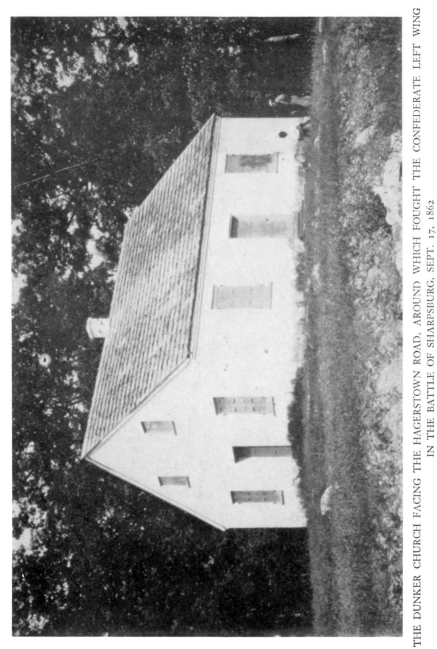

THE DUNKER CHURCH FACING THE HAGERSTOWN ROAD, AROUND WHICH FOUGHT THE CONFEDERATE LEFT WING
IN THE BATTLE OF SHARPSBURG, SEPT. 17, 1862

In this contemporary photograph, the marks of many projectiles are visible on the white-washed walls.

BURNSIDE'S BRIDGE ACROSS THE ANTIETAM, NEAR SHARPSBURG, MARYLAND

Looking from the Union left front of attack toward the high ground held on Sept. 17, 1862, by the Confederate right wing.

FEDERAL PONTOON BRIDGES BELOW FREDERICKSBURG, AS SEEN FROM THE RIGHT BANK OF THE RIVER, WITH PART OF STAFFORD HEIGHTS IN THE BACKGROUND

This photograph was taken in June, 1863, but the bridges then in use were in every respect similar to those thrown across the river in December, 1862.

GENERAL LEE IN 1863 AT THE HEIGHT OF HIS MILITARY SUCCESS

He rarely wore his sword and scarcely ever his sash. Both Lee's sword and his sash,
however, are preserved in the Confederate Museum, Richmond.

Reproduced from an original negative, now in the possession of H. P. Cook, Richmond.

THREE OF THE DAUGHTERS OF GENERAL LEE

Centre: Mary Custis, the General's eldest daughter; *left:* Agnes, the third daughter; *right:* Mildred, the youngest. No well-authenticated picture of Annie, the second daughter, is known to exist.

From photographs, now in the Confederate Museum, Richmond, taken shortly after the War between the States.

TWO SONS OF R. E. LEE WHO BECAME MAJOR GENERALS IN THE CONFEDERATE ARMY

Right: G. W. Custis Lee, the eldest of the three sons of the General; *left:* W. H. F. ("Rooney") Lee, the second son. Both these photographs, the originals of which are in the Confederate Museum, Richmond, were made a few years after the War between the States.

"STONEWALL" JACKSON—THE "WINCHESTER PHOTOGRAPH"

Taken in the winter of 1861–62, when he was a major general and only a few months before the famous "Valley Campaign." Mrs. Jackson regarded this as the best likeness of her husband.

THE COTTAGE ON THE CHANDLER FARM, NEAR GUINEY'S STATION, VIRGINIA, WHERE "STONEWALL" JACKSON DIED

The general was sheltered in this plain structure because of the danger of infection in the main residence, where several soldiers had succumbed to erysipelas. The early photograph from which this illustration was made is in the Confederate Museum, Richmond.

DEATH MASK OF "STONEWALL" JACKSON, MADE IN RICHMOND, MAY, 1863, BY
FRED VOLCK; AFTER THE ORIGINAL IN THE VALENTINE MUSEUM

Copyright, 1934, by the Valentine Museum and published by permission.

Headquarters for the night were established in an open field, and a fire of boards was lighted for the reading of dispatches. These were unanimous in asserting a victory on every part of the field. Lee's spirits rose and his gratitude to God increased as the good news continued to come in, especially when the commanders were able to report that though many a good man had fallen, the losses of the day had not been excessive. Presently Hood rode up, weary and proud. Lee greeted him cordially. What, he asked, had become of the enemy? Hood answered enthusiastically that Pope's army had been driven across Bull Run almost at the double-quick. It had been a beautiful sight, he said, to see the Confederate battle flags dancing after the retreating Federals.

"God forbid," said Lee, "I should ever live to see our colors moving in the opposite direction." [98]

Colonel Long came after a full reconnaissance and told how the Federals had vanished.[99] Stuart wrote that Robertson's cavalry had pursued the foe across Bull Run, [100] while Fitz Lee had been scouting as far in the enemy's rear as Fairfax Courthouse. Stuart was anxious to get permission to organize a night attack with the help of Armistead's brigade of infantry, which had been acting with him, but Lee would not approve.

In this atmosphere, Lee sat down to compose his victory dispatch that would have to be carried all the way back to Rapidan before it could be telegraphed to Richmond and announced to the anxious Southern people. Here is what he wrote:

Groveton, 30 Aug. 10 o'clock P.M.

Presdt Davis: This Army today achieved on the plains of Manassas a signal victory over combined forces of Genls. McClellan and Pope. On the 28th and 29th each wing under Genls. Longstreet and Jackson repulsed with valour attacks made on them separately. We mourn the loss of our gallant dead in every conflict yet our gratitude to Almighty God for his mercies rises higher and higher each day, to Him and to the valour of our troops a nation's gratitude is due.

R. E. LEE.[101]

98 *Hood*, 38.   99 *Long*, 199.
100 *O. R.*, 12, part 2, pp. 737, 746–47, 748.   101 *Lee's Dispatches*, 59–60.

When a short night's rest ended with daylight on August 31, the rain was still falling, a sharp wind was blowing, all the roads except the turnpike were heavy with mud, and Bull Run, rising fast, was in danger of becoming impassable.[102] Although Lee was satisfied with the results of the previous day's fighting, he said little[103] and he did not minimize the difficulties that still confronted him. The stone bridge was down. Pursuit would be slow, if possible at all. Reports indicated that the enemy was at Centreville, doubtless in the works the Confederates had labored the previous winter to render impregnable.[104] Worse still, Fitz Lee wrote that Franklin's and Sumner's corps, from McClellan's army, together with Sturgis's and Cox's divisions, had arrived at Centreville.[105] Pope had not been defeated a day too soon. Even now, heavy odds had to be faced by an army that was at this time almost without provisions,[106] and incapable of sustained action until the commissary could find food. This paralyzing shortage of food was, perhaps, the most serious condition of all, for even the Army of Northern Virginia travelled on its belly. The caissons and ordnance train, moreover, were almost empty.

Clad in rubber overalls and with a rubber poncho over his shoulders, Lee rode out early on a short reconnaissance across Bull Run accompanied by Jackson, to see the situation at first hand.[107] Soon he came under fire of the enemey's pickets. Pope evidently was still close at hand. Returning, Lee was satisfied that his only possible course was to continue to manœuvre and, if possible, once more to interpose his army between Pope and Washington or so to threaten Pope's flank as to force him into a further retreat. Lee explained this to Longstreet and to Jackson and gave his orders for the day: Jackson, being nearest the exposed flank of the enemy, was to take his entire command and cross Bull Run at Sudley Springs. He was to move north until he struck the Little River turnpike. Then he was to turn southeast again. If all went well, this would put Jackson on the enemy's line of retreat and would force the evacuation of Centreville. To aid Jackson, Stuart and his cavalry, supported by a brigade of infantry, were to pass over Bull

---

102 *Taylor's General Lee*, 115; 1 *von Borcke*, 161; *Longstreet*, 191.
103 2 *B. and L.*, 524.   104 *Longstreet*, 191.
105 *Fitz Lee*, 193; *cf. O. R.*, 12, part 2, p. 16.
106 Lee in 1870, quoted in *R. E. Lee, Jr.*, 416.   107 1 *von Borcke*, 165.

Run and create a diversion. Longstreet was to remain on the battlefield, looking after the wounded and burying the dead, until Jackson had a good start. Then Longstreet was to follow, and D. H. Hill, when he arrived from the South, was to complete the gruesome work Longstreet left unfinished.[108] The plan was as simple as it was bold, and it appealed to Jackson. "Good," said he, when Lee had finished, and without another word, he set out to put his part in execution.[109]

Later in the day, after Jackson left, and while Longstreet was preparing to place some of his units in line of march, Lee again rode over a section of the field. He was with his staff when he came upon a sergeant of the 16th Mississippi, who had been into the woods to relieve a dead Federal of a pair of Northern shoes, wherewith to cover his bare feet.

Lee hailed him: "What are you doing here, sir," he said, "away from your command?"

The sergeant, who had no idea of the identity of his inquisitor, answered gamely: "That's none of your business, by God."

"You are a straggler, sir, and deserve the severest punishment."

"It's a damned lie, sir," the sergeant returned hotly. "I only left my regiment a few minutes ago to hunt me a pair of shoes. I went through all the fight yesterday, and that's more than you can say; for where were you yesterday when General Stuart wanted your damned cavalry to charge the Yankees after we put 'em to running? You were lying back in the pine thickets and couldn't be found; but today, when there's no danger, you come out and charge other men with straggling, damn you."

Lee had to laugh, and, finding no ready answer, rode subdued on his way. He probably did not hear one of his officers ask the sergeant if he knew to whom he was talking. "To a cowardly Virginia cavalryman," the offended N. C. O. stoutly answered.

"No, sir, that was General Lee."

"Ho-o-what? General Lee, did you say?"

"Yes."

"And his staff?"

"Yes."

[108] *Longstreet*, 191.   [109] *Ibid.*

"Scissors to grind, I'm a goner!" and with no more ado, he
started running down the road as fast as he could.[110]

The "cowardly Virginia cavalryman" rode on, ere long, to
Stewart's farm[111] and dismounted in a thick wood to make some
dispositions. He was standing by Traveller, with the reins on the
animal's neck. Suddenly a cry was raised, "Yankee cavalry!"
Traveller started at the sudden commotion, and Lee stepped forward to catch the bridle. As he did so he tripped in his long overalls and fell forward. He caught himself on both hands and was
up in an instant, but it was soon apparent that he was hurt. The
scare of Union cavalry proving unfounded, the nearest surgeon
was sent for. He found a small bone broken in one hand and the
other hand badly sprained. Both had to be put in splints and
treated with a liniment.[112] As this of course kept Lee from riding,
he had, much against his will, to enter an ambulance. Reports
that Lee had been wounded in battle spread quickly and, in the
North, were coupled with fictitious accounts of how it had happened.[113]

To the injured General, as he waited for Jackson's rear to clear
the muddy road for Longstreet's advance, General Pope sent a
message asking for a truce. Lee consented that the Federal ambulances should enter the lines to remove the wounded but he
would not agree to a suspension of hostilities.[114] At 2 P.M., he set
Longstreet in motion[115] and left his old headquarters. A band
cheerfully saluted him with the strains of "Dixie." [116]

The road the army had to follow to Sudley Springs on Bull
Run was narrow and muddy. Progress was almost as slow as on
that wet 2d of July when the same troops had fought through
equally tenacious mud in their effort to overtake McClellan's retreat from Malvern Hill. Night found Longstreet not yet across
Bull Run. Jackson was on the Little River turnpike with his front

110 "Personne" [F. G. de Fontaine]: *Marginalia* (cited hereafter as *Marginalia*), 86–
87. The time is fixed, approximately, by the fact that Lee was riding his horse and therefore had not received the injury that crippled his hands.

111 H. W. Thomas: *History of the Doles-Cooke Brigade* (cited hereafter as *Thomas*),
469.

112 *Longstreet*, 192; *Sorrel*, 103; Thomas, *op. cit.*, 469, said that the injury was
dressed by Surgeon N. S. Walker of the 44th Georgia, but the writer has been unable to
verify this from available records.

113 *Sorrel*, 103.   114 *O. R.*, 12, part 2, p. 779.

115 *Longstreet*, 192; *O. R.*, 12, part 2, p. 566.   116 2 *B. and L.*, 527.

toward Fairfax Courthouse, but his weary men had not been able to move fast enough to get in rear of Pope.[117] Stuart had been hovering on the enemy's flank and had employed his horse artillery against a wagon train that crowded the road of the enemy's retreat, but he had accomplished no substantial result.[118] In a word, the exhaustion of the hungry men and the condition of the roads cost Lee virtually the whole advantage he had hoped to gain on the critical first day after the victory.

The rain had ceased falling on the morning of September 1, but the army was still hungry. Jackson's column, though covered by Stuart's cavalry, moved very slowly. Not until late afternoon did it reach the vicinity of the friendly mansion of Chantilly, which Lee remembered with the affection of his boyhood days. It was then apparent that the enemy was fully aware of the threat to his flank and was prepared. At Jackson's order, Hill sent forward Branch's and Brockenbrough's[119] brigades to feel out the enemy. The rest of Hill's division was placed on the right of the line, with Ewell's troops in the centre and Jackson's own division on the left. All these troops were on the right of the road, with the artillery massed on an eminence to the left. A heavy thunderstorm had set in as the troops had approached Chantilly,[120] and as the two brigades went forward the rain beat in the men's faces, almost blinding them. The Federals met the attack with vigor. Massing on the flank and front of Branch, they drove him back on his supports, along with Brockenbrough; and when three more brigades of Hill's division were thrown into the battle, they, too, were roughly handled. The battle soon engulfed a part of Ewell's division in the midst of almost continuous thunder that drowned the roar of the guns.[121] Night was falling before there was any wavering in the Federal line and even then it was darkness rather than defeat that led the enemy to withdraw slightly. Longstreet by this time had come up in support of Jackson, but as the battle had died away there was nothing for him to do.[122] The rain, in

---

[117] O. R., 12, part 2, pp. 566, 647.   [118] O. R., 12, part 2, pp. 737–38, 743–44.
[119] Colonel J. M. Brockenbrough of the 40th Virginia Infantry had succeeded on the 29th to the temporary command of the brigade of General Charles W. Field, who was severely wounded (O. R., 12, part 2, p. 671).
[120] G. Wise, 105.   [121] 3 C. M. H., 333.
[122] O. R., 12, part 2. pp. 566, 647, 672; Longstreet, 193–94.

fact, was so heavy that the whole field was in confusion and the final withdrawal of the enemy was unobserved. A little later, scouting parties reported that the Federals were still in great strength a short distance down the road.

Lee himself had no part in this action, which sometimes is styled Chantilly and sometimes Ox Hill. He had established his headquarters in a little farm house where he had no more exciting experience than to be challenged by his own sentinel when he returned from a brief walk with Colonel Marshall.[123] He had one sombre report, however: In the closing minutes of the fight, a Federal officer had unwittingly ridden into the Confederate lines and, when observed, had quickly turned his horse and had attempted to gallop off. He had fallen before the fire of some Confederates who later picked up his dead body and brought it into the lines. With the regret that soldiers always feel at the death of a brilliant and gallant foe, he was identified as Brigadier General Phil Kearny, commander of the First Division of Heintzelman's corps. When they told Lee of the incident he must have had a sudden picture of the old days in Mexico, especially of the battle of Churubusco, when young Kearny had led his pursuing troopers under the very walls of Santa Anna's capital. Lee had the corpse prepared for burial, and the next day sent it into the lines with a brief note to General Pope: "The body of General Philip Kearny," he wrote, "was brought from the field last night, and he was reported dead. I send it forward under a flag of truce, thinking that the possession of his remains may be a consolation to his family." [124]

When the skirmish line went forward later in the morning over the same road that the bearers of the flag followed, it was found that the enemy had evacuated his position both at Centreville and in front of Jackson. Stuart's cavalry went in pursuit, only to discover that the long Federal columns were moving steadily toward the Washington entrenchments, whither it would be futile to pursue them.[125]

About the hour Lee realized from these reports that this phase of his campaign of manœuvre was at an end, President Davis was

[123] L. W. Hopkins: *From Bull Run to Appomattox*, 50.
[124] *O. R.*, 12, part 3, p. 807.   [125] *O. R.*, 12, part 2, pp 558, 744–45.

sending to the Confederate Congress the recent dispatches from Lee, including the message written on the field of Second Manassas after the battle of the 30th. It had been received in Richmond on September 1,[126] and its content was of course known ere this to the Congress, but there was pride and jubilation in Davis's closing sentence. "Too much praise," said he, "cannot be bestowed upon the skill and daring of the commanding general who conceived, or the valor and hardihood of the troops who executed, the brilliant movement whose result is now communicated." [127]

The words did not exaggerate the fact, nor did they even touch upon the contrast between the situation Mr. Davis described and that which had existed three months previously to the very day. On June 2, Lee's first full day in command of the Army of Northern Virginia, McClellan had been in front of Richmond, Jackson was being pursued up the Shenandoah Valley by three strong forces, western Virginia was completely in the hands of the Federals, and the North Carolina coast was overrun. Now, western Virginia was almost evacuated, Confederate cavalry were soon to cross into Ohio at Ravenswood,[128] Winchester was about to be abandoned,[129] the North Carolina coast was safe, and the wrecked Army of Virginia, together with most of the Army of the Potomac, was in full retreat on Washington. Despairing officials in the Federal capital had given orders to ship all movable government property to New York. The government clerks were called out to share in the anticipated defense of the city.[130] Except for the troops at Norfolk and at Fort Monroe, the only Federals closer than 100 miles to Richmond were prisoners of war and men who were busily preparing to retreat from the base at Aquia Creek.[131]

This amazing transformation had been wrought at a time when the Confederates on other fronts had been able to do nothing to relieve the pressure on Virginia. It had been the work, and ex-

---

[126] 1 R. W. C. D., 151.

[127] O. R., 51, part 2, p. 615. Lee had been voted the thanks of the Confederate House of Representatives on Aug. 22 for his operations in front of Richmond; the senate had not acted (*Journal of the Congress of the Confederate States of America*, vol. 2, pp. 234, 442, 443; vol. 5, p. 306).

[128] O. R., 12, part 2, p. 759.   [129] O. R., 12, part 2, p. 765.

[130] O. R., 12, part 3, pp. 802, 807.   [131] O. R., 12, part 3, pp. 813–14.

clusively the work, of the Army of Northern Virginia, with the assistance of such units as had been brought from the Carolinas and Georgia. And what the Army of Northern Virginia had executed, with numbers pitifully inferior to the combined strength of the forces it had confronted, General Lee had planned.

His operations had improved in excellence as they had developed. By every standard, Second Manassas was better than the Seven Days. Staff work was incomparably superior. The artillery had been more effectively employed. So had the cavalry. The intelligence service was much improved. The superiority of the tactics was attested by the relative losses. From the crossing of the Rapidan to the final pursuit of the Federals into the Washington defenses, Confederate casualties had been 9112,[132] and an exceptionally large percentage of these were men but slightly wounded.[133] Pope's casualties August 16 to September 2 were 14,462,[134] including 4163 prisoners. The losses in the campaign thus were, roughly, four and a half Confederates to seven Federals. During the seven days they had been five Confederates to four Federals.

Like his tactics, Lee's strategy was better at Second Manassas than around Richmond. It was better because it was somewhat simpler, and, still more, because it placed responsibility in the hands of fewer men. There were no more attempts to bring six commands, under six semi-independent generals, together on the field of battle, as at Frayser's Farm. Divisions remained, as did divisional commanders, but the responsibility of executing Lee's strategical plan was placed on three men—Jackson, Longstreet, and Stuart.

This concentration of authority was one reason for success. Another reason was the excellent logistics. Lee's troop movements had been prompt and rapid. It will be remembered that Longstreet had left the Richmond front to reinforce Jackson before the Federals had evacuated any except the sick and wounded from Harrison's Landing. While the first units of Porter's corps were landing at Aquia Creek, the Army of Northern Virginia was crossing the Rapidan.[135] Jackson was marching for Manassas as

132 *O. R.*, 12, part 2, pp. 560 ff., 566, 648, 810–14.
133 *O. R.*, 12, part 2, p. 657.   134 *O. R.*, 12, part 2, p. 262.
13b For the movement of Porter, see *O. R.*, 12, part 3, pp. 594, 599, 600 602.

Franklin was hunting for transportation and waiting for cavalry around Alexandria.[136] Longstreet was in line of battle when Porter marched on the field on the 29th. The race to Pope had been won, but three days' delay in sending Longstreet from Richmond, or a wait of even twenty-four hours more in crossing the Rapidan might have made victory at Second Manassas impossible. On the other hand, greater speed in hurrying Franklin forward, cavalry or no cavalry, might have saved Pope. Delay in some stage of every campaign is of the very nature of war. The thrifty soldier saves by prompt starts and speedy moves the time he may later have to spend in delays he cannot avoid.

Lee's strategic plan succeeded, thirdly, because at nearly every stage of the campaign his reasoning from his evidence was sounder than his adversary's. He had not known when Heintzelman joined Pope,[137] nor had he been aware that Franklin and Sumner were debarking at Alexandria for their advance to the support of Pope. In neither of these instances, as it happened, was his lack of information costly. As for the essential facts, he had drawn the right conclusion concerning the movement and destination of McClellan's army, and he had been correct to the very day in his calculation of when Pope received his first substantial reinforcements from the Army of the Potomac.[138] General Pope had not been so fortunate either in procuring news of the enemy's moves or in reading the mind of his opponent. His original plan had been to move to Gordonsville and Charlottesville and then to advance on Richmond from the west, but he had halted in a mistaken estimate of the strength of the troops Lee first sent to confront him. Not until August 18, it will be recalled, had he been aware of the threat against him. The import of the shift to the Confederate left had escaped him altogether. After he was relieved of command, on September 5, he professed that he had known all the while of Jackson's flank movement and had ignored it because he had relied on the promise of troops to protect Manassas;[139] but his own correspondence shows that he had

---

[136] Cf. O. R., 12, part 3, p. 689.

[137] Heintzelman left the peninsula Aug. 20–21 (O. R., 12, part 2, p. 612; ibid., part 3, p. 412), and had his whole command in the vicinity of Warrenton Junction on the 26th (O. R., 12, part 3, p. 412).

[138] Aug. 25: Lee's Dispatches, 52; O. R., 12, part 3, p. 651 ff.

[139] O. R., 12, part 2, p. 13; 2 B. and L., 461.

believed the Confederates were marching to the Valley.[140] **When**
he had received accurate information of Jackson's position, some-
time before noon on August 26,[141] he had not drawn the proper
inference. Apparently he had not learned of Longstreet's march
to join Jackson until the 29th[142] and his confused handling of his
troops on the 27th and 28th had more than justified Lee's conservative observation that General Pope "did not appear to be
aware of his situation." [143] No blame could be attached to the
personnel of Pope's army or to the divisions from McClellan.
They had borne themselves well. "The Yankees fought as if in
earnest," Lee's adjutant general wrote.[144] The defeat, the withdrawal to Washington, and the temporary demoralization were
essentially the result of Lee's good strategy, executed with rapidity.

Only three reasonable criticisms can be made of Lee's handling
of operations from the time he reached Gordonsville until the Federals disappeared from his front on the morning of September 2.
The first, that he should have crossed the Rapidan earlier than the
20th, is based on the valid assumption that if he had been able to
catch Pope between the Rapidan and the Rappahannock, he could
have destroyed him. But this criticism leaves out of account the
shortage of provisions, a subject about which, unfortunately, there
is little specific information. Insofar as this criticism is applied
solely to the failure of the cavalry to concentrate on the 17th of
August, it takes for granted that if Fitz Lee had come up, the
movement across the Rapidan could have been launched on the
morning of the 18th. The facts already cited make it doubtful
whether the horses would have been in condition for pursuit.
The only way of assuring the advance at any time prior to the
20th, with horses fit for long, hard marching, would have been
to move Fitz Lee's cavalry from Hanover Courthouse not later
than August 15, better still on August 14. This would not have

[140] *O. R.,* 12, part 2, p. 67; *cf. G. H. Gordon,* 69–70.
[141] *O. R.,* 12, part 2, p. 70. [142] *O. R.,* 12, part 3, p. 729.
[143] *Cooke,* 117. When Pope thought Jackson was cornered, his self-confidence returned (see his dispatch of Aug. 29, quoted in the text, p. 329 *supra*). But when he was
beaten and in retreat toward Washington, he plumbed the depths of despair. "Unless
something can be done to restore tone to this army it will melt away before you know
it," he telegraphed Halleck early on the morning of Sept. 2. ". . . The enemy is in very
heavy force and must be stopped in some way. These forces under my command are not
able to do so in the open field, and if again checked I fear the force will be useless afterwards" (*O. R.,* 12, part 3, p. 797).
[144] *Taylor MSS.,* Aug. 31, 1863.

been justified by the information Lee had. Viewed in another light, Lee's consideration for his horses was rewarded. Stuart was able to keep his troopers in the field until Pope retreated on Washington. Pope's cavalry, though numerous, well led, and superior in every way to that which McClellan had commanded on the Peninsula, was so overridden that it was almost useless by August 30.

The second criticism is that Lee should have forced Longstreet to attack on the afternoon of August 29, instead of permitting him to delay until the 30th. Had Longstreet attacked successfully on the 29th, Lee would have been able to pursue on the 30th in clear weather, instead of having to encounter on the 31st a rain that paralyzed his army. The gain would have been substantial and might conceivably have resulted in very heavy losses to Pope. This criticism, to be sure, takes three things for granted: first, that an attack would certainly have been successful on the 29th, though Porter and McDowell were hovering on Lee's right flank; second, that the army would have been fresh enough on the 30th to pursue with vigor across Bull Run in the face of superior artillery; and, third, that the objections Longstreet raised to attacking on the 29th were of a sort that should have been overruled by the commanding general.[145] All these points must be given due weight. Lee knew he was not omniscient and he did not believe he could be omnipresent. He held to his theory of the high command. Having put the army under the best officers at his disposal, he felt that on the field of battle he should trust their discretion. "You must know our circumstances," Lee told a German observer, Scheibert, "and see that my leading in battle would do more harm than good. It would be a bad thing if I could not then rely on my brigade and division commanders. I plan and work with all my might to bring the troops to the right place at the right time; with that I have done my duty. As soon as I order the troops forward into battle, I lay the fate of my army in the hands of God." [146] This is a sound general rule. In the study of war it is

---

[145] For a hostile summary of the case against Longstreet, see Early in 5 *S. H. S. P.,* 275.

[146] J. Scheibert: *Der Bürgerkrieg in den Nordamerikanischen Staaten,* 39. Cf. *ibid.,* 181, quoting Lee: "I strive to make my plans as good as my human skill allows, but on the day of battle I lay the fate of my army in the hands of God; it is my generals' turn to perform their duty."

futile to canvass what cannot be decided, and for that reason it cannot positively be asserted that Lee should have given Long-street a peremptory order to attack or would have been sure of a greater victory if he had. His yielding to Longstreet probably had a less disastrous effect on the battle than on the mind of that officer; it cost little, perhaps, at Second Manassas but it cost much at Gettysburg. For it is a dire thing in war for a subordinate to believe that if he is stubborn enough in holding out against his superior's orders he can have his own way. There can be little doubt that after Second Manassas, Longstreet thought he could dominate Lee, and that added a new and indeterminable factor to the full execution of Lee's plans. On the other hand, Longstreet's judgment had been so good and his diligence had been so much above challenge during the Seven Days that Lee had acquired a high respect for him. As the wisdom of attacking on the afternoon of the 29th manifestly presented a close question, this respect for Longstreet's ability as a soldier undoubtedly weighed with Lee and saved his act from being mere weakness. Lee was more nearly justified in yielding to Longstreet at Second Manassas, after the Seven Days, than he could ever be after Second Manassas, when dissent had become a habit with Longstreet.

The third criticism is that Lee should have organized a prompt pursuit of Pope. In part, of course, the answer to this depends on the judgment one forms of the second criticism. If Lee should have compelled Longstreet to attack on the afternoon of the 29th, and if Longstreet had gained an advantage that afternoon without exhausting the army, then manifestly the whole of the army should have been moved in pursuit of Pope on the 30th. As it was, rapid pursuit on and after August 31 was impossible. The mud was paralyzing. Lee did not know, of course, that Franklin's and Sumner's corps, strong and fresh, were close at hand, but he did know that McClellan's army was coming up and he had every reason to assume that the Washington defenses were well-manned and strong.[147] These circumstances and the hunger of his own men deterred him. Talking in 1870 with his cousin Cassius F. Lee, who lived near the fortifications on the south side of the

[147] Some 27,000 Federals, ready for duty, were in and around Washington (O. R., 12. part 3, p. 781).

Potomac, General Lee said in explanation of his failure to pursue, "My men had nothing to eat." Pointing to Fort Wade, he went on, "I could not tell my men to take that fort when they had had nothing to eat for three days."[148] To have moved a hungry army through the mud against heavy defenses, readily manned, would have been to flirt with ruin. Behind these facts, compelling in themselves, was the large consideration of the purpose of the campaign of which Second Manassas was the second and not the final phase. Manœuvre, his prime aim, was still possible if the army kept the field, but manœuvre would be impossible and starvation might threaten if the army were committed to a siege at a long distance from its base. Lee's thought was of the next manœuvre, not of a bootless investment of Washington, as he saw the rearguard of Pope's army fade into the horizon on the morning of September 2.

[148] R. E. Lee, Jr., 416.

CHAPTER XXV

"My Maryland"—or His?

LEE's manœuvring after the second battle of Manassas had to be extensive and not a mere matter of shifting a few miles in this direction or in that, because Fairfax County, in which the army had halted, had already been stripped of food and of forage. The scant and overworked wagon train could not be relied upon to bring from Richmond an adequate supply of provisions, much less of horse feed.

Likewise, manœuvre had to be prompt. The Federals, Lee reasoned, had been weakened and demoralized by recent defeats, but his information was that 60,000 replacement troops had already been received at Washington and would soon be embodied. Quick action opened advantage and might deter the Federals from aggressive moves until the coming of winter, but delay would place in front of the Army of Northern Virginia a larger force than it had yet encountered. The weaker side could not wait. In this respect, September, 1862, was to Lee what March, 1918, was to Ludendorff.

If manœuvre had to be undertaken promptly in a country where the army could be subsisted, whither should it be directed? Not eastward, for that would carry the army under the very shadow of the Washington defenses. Not southward to any great distance, for that would take the army into a ravaged land and would bring the war back toward Richmond. Withdrawal a slight distance southward, to Warrenton, for instance, might be considered. That would put the Army of Northern Virginia on the flank of any force advancing to Richmond, and would give it the advantage of direct rail communication with the capital, once the bridges across the Rapidan and the Rappahannock were reconstructed.[1] Carrying the army westward would put it in the Shenandoah Valley, a terrain of many strategical possibilities, but

[1] O. R., 19, part 2, p. 593.

350

one in which a retreat would force the army steadily back toward the line of the Virginia Central Railroad.

By elimination, then, destiny beckoned northward, across the Potomac. And not by elimination only did Maryland and Pennsylvania invite the next stage of manœuvre. They offered positive advantage. The enemy could be drawn away from the Washington defenses. With Maryland occupied, Virginia would be free. No Federal army based on Washington would dare advance on Richmond so long as Lee was north of the Potomac.[2] Secure in western Maryland or in Pennsylvania, the Army of Northern Virginia would be able to harass if it might not destroy the Federals, and while the farmers of Virginia harvested their crops, untroubled by the enemy, Lee could await with equanimity the arrival of cold weather.

Political not less than military advantage seemed to be offered in Maryland. The South believed, from events which seemed to justify belief, that strong sentiment for the Confederacy existed in Maryland and would have exhibited itself in extensive volunteering and possible secession had it not been repressed with the overwhelming power of a Federal Government that was charged with brushing aside constitutional rights. What meant the Baltimore riots of April, 1861, if not this? Why had legislators and prominent private citizens been arrested and detained in defiance of *habeas corpus?* Was not the devoted service of the many Maryland soldiers in the Army of Northern Virginia a pledge of what thousands of others would do if opportunity were theirs? The presence of a large Confederate force above the Potomac, Lee reasoned, would not assure revolt against Federal authority, but it would give the people of Maryland what they had never had—a chance to express their will. The possibility that invasion might lead to an uprising which would surround the Northern capital by hostile territory would be an added reason why the Federals would not dare move south while the Confederate army was north of the Potomac.[3]

There were risks, of course, in undertaking promptly an extensive manœuvre for the sake of the military and political ad-

---

[2] "As long as the army of the enemy are employed on this frontier I have no fears for the safety of Richmond . . ." (Lee to Davis, Sept. 3, 1862; *O. R.*, 19, part 2, p. 591).
[3] *Cf.* Lee in *O. R.*, 12, part 1, p. 144; *ibid.*, part 2, pp. 592, 593.

vantages that the occupation of Maryland and perhaps of Pennsylvania would offer. The army was not equipped for it. Uni-
forms were in rags. Thousands of men were shoeless. The horses
of many of the cavalrymen were so exhausted that they could not
be employed in any forward movement.[4] Scanty as was the train,
it was apparent that some of the wagons would have to be left at
Manassas to supplement the ambulances in evacuating the wounded.[5] Ammunition must be replenished from Richmond, and if the
line of supply was to be kept safe from Federal raiders, it must of
necessity be shifted westward to the district of the Shenandoah.[6]
The Federals were still in the lower Valley, lingering at Winchester and garrisoning Harpers Ferry and Martinsburg, and would
have to be driven out before a line of communications could be
opened there, though it was reasonable to assume that when the
army crossed into Maryland these posts would be evacuated.[7]

More serious than any of these military difficulties was the question of a legal method of procuring subsistence north of the
Potomac. The rich valleys of Maryland were untroubled by war.
On its well-stored cities the hand of the quartermaster had never
fallen. But could the army be fed in Maryland without recourse
to wholesale seizures such as Pope had countenanced, to the indignation of right-minded people, North and South? This aspect
of the question stuck in Lee's mind. He discussed it with Longstreet, who reminded him that in Mexico the troops to which
Longstreet had been attached had subsisted for three days on corn
and green oranges. The corn was now ripening in the rows,
Longstreet reminded him, and with "roasting-ears" to feed them,
the men would not starve.[8]

A final risk there was, of course, that from some unexpected
quarter in some unanticipated way, the Federals might be able to
throw a strong army to the James and capture Richmond. Lee
regarded this, however, as more a psychological than a military
risk. The danger was less in the might of the enemy than in the
mind of Mr. Davis. In addition to believing that the Potomac was
the best line for the defense of the Southern capital, General Lee
hoped that the new ironclad *Richmond,* the "second Merrimac,"

[4] *O. R.,* 19, part 2, p. 589.
[5] *O. R.,* 19, part 2, pp. 593, 606.
[7] *O. R.,* 19, part 2, p. 594.

[6] *O. R.,* 12, part 3, pp. 593-94.
[8] Longstreet in 2 *B. and L.,* 663. Cf. 14
S. H. S. P., 102.

would soon be completed and would be able to clear the James of the enemy's fleet.[9] With the river line closed to the Federals, he considered the danger to Richmond slight. He could send troops back to the city as quickly as the enemy could march them thither.[10]

Weighing necessity, advantage, and risk in the scales of his judgment, Lee virtually decided on September 3 to enter Maryland, and that day he set the army in motion for Loudoun County, where he could feed it temporarily while threatening the Shenandoah Valley and debating further the advantages of an invasion of the North.[11] The next day he was fully persuaded of the benefits to be gained, and wrote the President that he would proceed unless Mr. Davis disapproved.[12] He was already looking, indeed, beyond Maryland, and he told the chief executive that if the results justified, he intended to enter Pennsylvania.[13] If he were forced to fall back, Warrenton was his second choice of a position,[14] and with that place in mind he urged the prompt rebuilding of the railway bridges over the Rapidan and the Rappahannock.[15]

One important point remained to be settled: Where should he enter Maryland, east of the Blue Ridge or west of it? His conclusion, promptly reached, was to advance east of the mountains, because this would be regarded by the Federals as a direct threat to Washington and to Baltimore. The administration, he reasoned, would at once call to the north of the Potomac all the forces operating on the south side of that river. This would remove all danger both to his supply line and to the troops collecting the arms and caring for the wounded on the field of Manassas. Having prompted the Federals to evacuate northern Virginia, he planned to move westward in Maryland to Hagerstown. There he would be on the straight road into Pennsylvania and in direct line with his communications up the Shenandoah Valley.[16]

[9] O. R., 19, part 2, p. 591.
[10] General Lee's explanation of his reason for invading Maryland, though often misunderstood, was fully given in documents of different dates, as follows: (1) His contemporary dispatches of Sept. 3, 4, and 5 (O. R., 19, part 2, pp. 500 ff.); (2) his formal report of his campaign, dated Aug. 19, 1863 (ibid., part 1, p. 144); and (3) his letter of April 15, 1868, to William M. McDonald (Jones, 266), elaborated in a conversation with William Allan (quoted in Marshall, 248–49). There is remarkable consistency among these accounts, though the last was written six and a half years after the first.
[11] O. R., 19, part 2, p. 590; Long, 204.   [12] O. R., 19, part 2, pp. 591–92.
[13] Ibid.   [14] O. R., 19, part 2, p. 593.   [15] Ibid.
[16] O. R., 19, part 1, p. 144; ibid., part 2, p. 604.

These questions decided, the march into Loudoun County to provision the troops became merely a halt on the way to Maryland. The greater part of the Army of Northern Virginia moved on from Dranesville to Leesburg, where Lee, overwhelmed with social attentions,[17] had his headquarters for two days, most of the time at the home of Henry Harrison.[18] From Leesburg, the army tramped to White's Ford on the Potomac, eleven miles south of Frederick.[19]

On September 5–6, the head of the columns prepared to cross the river. The drama of invasion lacked nearly all the stage properties calculated to impress observers with the might of conquest. There was no rehearsal on the south bank; no pageant was shaped to fire the ardor of Marylanders. The first dusty troops to reach the Potomac halted, stripped, or pulled frayed trouser legs high over aching knees, and plunged into the shallow water of the boundary river. As they clambered up the northern bank they cheered in the proud knowledge that they had carried the war into the enemy's country. The few and battered bands played "Maryland, My Maryland," and the soldiers cheered the more. They were confident of their ability to win new victories, confident of their cause, and confident of their commander.

The country people seemed glad to see them,[20] but they must have wondered how such an army could have won the victories blazoned on its faded flags. Lank and lagging horses bore tattered riders ahead of the ragged columns of dirty, unshaven, and cadaverous infantrymen, neat in nothing but the well-tended rifles they carried. Scarcely a shining button or a trim uniform was to be seen, even in brigades the very names of whose officers had the ring of iron discipline. Hats hung in battered brims; shocks of hair stuck through the holes; caps had lost their color. Toes gaped from flapping shoes and naked feet limped in protest at the hardness of Maryland's stony roads. Smoke-covered caissons rattled; dilapidated wagons groaned; the worn wheels that carried the lean guns of the artillery complained. Men who had beheld the army in the mud of the Chickahominy Valley and in the dust

---

[17] *Owen*, 130.
[18] *O. R.*, 19, part 2, pp. 591, 593; *Taylor's General Lee*, 118; 1 *von Borcke*, 183.
[19] *O. R.*, 19, part 1, pp. 814, 835, 839, 885, 952, 965; *O. R.*, 19, part 2, p. 588.
[20] *Napier*, 129.

of the road to Thoroughfare Gap had to confess that never had they seen it so filthy, so ragged, or so ill-provided for. "Ireland in her worst straits," one Federal correspondent wrote in disgust, "could present no parallel."[21] A boy who saw them march by remembered: "They were the dirtiest men I ever saw, a most ragged, lean, and hungry set of wolves. Yet there was a dash about them that the Northern men lacked. They rode like circus riders. Many of them were from the far South and spoke a dialect I could scarcely understand. They were profane beyond belief and talked incessantly."[22]

As Lee himself approached the river, after the first troops had passed over, he came upon some of Hill's troops, prone in the road, awaiting their turn. A. P. Hill was with him at the time and he said, "Move out of the road, men."

"Never mind, General," Lee broke in immediately, "we will ride around them. Lie still, men." And he turned his horse out of the road.[23]

Once in Maryland, Lee rode with the infantry straight for Frederick, within two miles of which he established his headquarters on September 7.[24] His tents were pitched near those of Longstreet, in a beautiful grove of oaks,[25] which soon became the objective of many curious visitors. The more outspoken Southern sympathizers showered him with invitations, which he declined. It would go hard with his hosts, he explained, after the army moved on and it became known that they had entertained him.[26] He made only one exception, so far as is known. Going to dinner in a private home, he found among the guests a very young and exceedingly bashful corporal of the Rockbridge Artillery. The gilded staff officers ignored this young man from the ranks, but the General went up to him, put a crippled hand on his shoulder and spoke with pride of the fine service the boy's battery had rendered.[27]

The first impressions made by the army on the people of Maryland were not wholly unfavorable. Firm discipline was en-

---

[21] *Mason*, 136; 10 *S. H. S. P.*, 508.
[22] Leighton Parks: "What a Boy Saw of the Civil War" (cited hereafter as *Leighton Parks*), *Century Magazine*, vol. 70, No. 2, p. 258 *ff*.
[23] Thomas Hartman, in 30 *Confederate Veteran*, 45.
[24] *O. R.*, 19, part I, p. 139.   [25] *Owen*, 131.   [26] Leighton Parks, *op. cit.*
[27] Reverend J. P. Smith in *Richmond Times Dispatch*, Jan. 20, 1907.

joined on the army. Sentinels were posted at the stores in Frederick, and the soldiers were forbidden to enter the town, though many of them contrived to purchase necessities with Confederate money and soon began to take on a less bedraggled appearance.[28] Those who had to march through the town had a varied reception. Some women brought out food; others held their noses and waved the Union flag.[29]

Dispositions were made promptly. The cavalry was stationed at Urbana, seven miles southeast of Frederick, on the main road to Washington.[30] The infantry and artillery were encamped around Frederick, with the exception of Early's division, which was moved a few miles southward with instructions to destroy the bridge over the Monocacy River at the junction of the main line of the Baltimore and Ohio Railroad with the branch to Frederick.[31] It was known that McClellan had replaced Pope in general command, and that was not pleasant news, for Lee regarded McClellan as the ablest of the Federal commanders;[32] but there were no signs of any advance on the part of the restored leader.[33] The populace showed no disposition to rise, though making no resistance to the purchase of supplies, which for a few days were to be had in abundance.[34] Lee's plan was to wait at Frederick until the people showed their sentiments or until McClellan appeared in his front,[35] and he hoped for the arrival of ex-Governor Enoch L. Lowe of Maryland, an ardent Southern supporter, who was believed to have great influence with the people of that part of the state. Governor Lowe not arriving, Lee decided to issue a proclamation to the people of Maryland.[36] This appeared on September 8, and read as follows:

"It is right that you should know the purpose that brought the army under my command within the limits of your State, so far as that purpose concerns yourselves. The people of the Confederate States have long watched with the deepest sympathy the wrongs and outrages that have been inflicted upon the citizens of

28 *Grayjackets*, 273; W. H. Taylor to his sister, Sept. 7, 1862, *Taylor MSS.*
29 *McDaniel*, 10–11.
30 *O. R.*, 19, part 1, p. 815.   31 *O. R.*, 19, part 1, p. 966; *Early*, 135.
32 *R. E. Lee, Jr.*, 416.   33 *O. R.*, 19, part 2, p. 600–601.
34 *O. R.*, 19, part 2, pp. 596–97.   35 *Long*, 207.
36 *O. R.*, 19, part 2, p. 605. The address doubtless was written by Col. Charles Marshall, a Marylander.

a commonwealth allied to the States of the South by the strongest social, political and commercial ties. They have seen with profound indignation their sister State deprived of every right and reduced to the condition of a conquered province. Under the pretence of supporting the Constitution, but in violation of its most valuable provisions, your citizens have been arrested and imprisoned upon no charge and contrary to all forms of law. The faithful and manly protest against this outrage made by the venerable and illustrious Marylander, to whom in better days no citizen appealed for right in vain, was treated with scorn and contempt; the government of your chief city has been usurped by armed strangers; your legislature has been dissolved by the unlawful arrest of its members; freedom of the press and of speech has been suppressed; words have been declared offences by an arbitrary decree of the Federal Executive, and citizens ordered to be tried by a military commission for what they may dare to speak. Believing that the people of Maryland possessed a spirit too lofty to submit to such a government, the people of the South have long wished to aid you in throwing off this foreign yoke, to enable you again to enjoy the inalienable rights of freemen, and restore independence and sovereignty to your State. In obedience to this wish, our army has come among you, and is prepared to assist you with the power of its arms in regaining the rights of which you have been despoiled.

"This, citizens of Maryland, is our mission, so far as you are concerned. No constraint upon your free will is intended; no intimidation will be allowed within the limits of this army, at least. Marylanders shall once more enjoy their ancient freedom of thought and speech. We know no enemies among you, and will protect all, of every opinion. It is for you to decide your destiny freely and without constraint. This army will respect your choice, whatever it may be; and while the Southern people will rejoice to welcome you to your natural position among them, they will only welcome you when you come of your own free will.

R. E. Lee,

General, Commanding." [37]

---

[37] *O. R.,* 19, part 2, pp. 601–2. President Davis had sent Lee instructions as to the scope of the proclamation, but these did not arrive in time (*O. R.,* 19, part 2, pp. 598–99).

Lee looked to something more than recruits. It seemed to him that the military situation had been so changed that the Confederacy should make a peace proposal, based on the recognition of its independence. On the day that he issued his statement to the people of Maryland, he suggested to the President a move to this end. "Such a proposition," he wrote, "coming from us at this time, could in no way be regarded as suing for peace; but, being made when it is in our power to inflict injury upon our adversary, would show conclusively to the world that our sole object is the establishment of our independence and the attainment of an honorable peace. The rejection of this offer would prove to the country that the responsibility of the continuance of the war does not rest upon us, but that the party in power in the United States elect to prosecute it for purposes of their own. The proposal of peace would enable the people of the United States to determine at their coming elections whether they will support those who favor a prolongation of the war, or those who wish to bring it to a termination, which can but be productive of good to both parties without affecting the honor of either." [38]

This was Lee's first and almost his last adventure in "foreign relations" while in the army of the Confederacy. It proved futile because of the quick turn of events, but it was prompted by a desire to see the end of a war that wrung his heart, and it illustrates his confidence at the time that nothing was likely to happen to his army that would make a move for peace appear as the plea of a beaten people.

There were, indeed, only two circumstances that seemed in any wise to cast doubt on the continued ability of Lee to manœuvre in Maryland and in Pennsylvania as he had in northern Virginia. One of these was the unexpected development of a dangerous degree of straggling in the army. Many of the men were accustomed in civil life to ride on horseback and very rarely to walk. The constant marching and hard fighting of August had exhausted hundreds of faithful soldiers, particularly those whose shoes had worn out. Bruised feet could not long endure the pace that had carried the army from the Rapidan to the Monocacy in eighteen days.[39] Some there were who had

[38] O. R., 19, part 2, p. 600.
[39] R. Taylor, 36. L. W. Hopkins noted (op. cit., 51) that straggling began before

been ardent in battling for their homes, yet were unwilling to wage offensive warfare against the North. Lee had brought only some 53,000 troops into Maryland,[40] and he was deeply concerned to see his ranks thinning. He promptly appealed to the President for the appointment of a military commission to move with the army and to act through a strong provost-marshal's guard.[41]

The other evil portent was the approaching exhaustion of supplies in the country around Frederick.[42] Lee could not supplement them adequately by maintaining his line of communications via Culpeper Courthouse, because that line was so much exposed to attack from the direction of Washington that he was already preparing to abandon it.[43] When he carried out his original plan and moved westward to Hagerstown, he would still have no guarantee of sufficient food for his army and would have to draw from Virginia, whence, also, his ammunition must come. His proposed new line would run down the Shenandoah Valley directly by Martinsburg and within sixteen miles of Harpers Ferry. And there was the rub. Winchester had been occupied by the Confederates on September 3,[44] but the Federals were still at Harpers Ferry and at Martinsburg in strength.

The desirability of reducing these posts had suggested itself strongly to Lee during the early stages of the advance into Maryland, even when it seemed probable that both would be evacuated as soon as McClellan knew that the Army of Northern Virginia was in Maryland. Longstreet, however, had argued so warmly against a division of force that Lee had determined to wait and see if the Federals would not voluntarily abandon the towns.[45] Now there seemed no alternative to sending a force to take them. Nor did the risk seem greater, in dealing with a deliberate opponent like McClellan, than the risk that the weaker army always must take to win advantage. By every test of known temperament and previous behavior, McClellan would organize thoroughly before advancing at all, and then would move so slowly and cautiously that the troublesome posts could be taken

the army crossed the Potomac and that Lee left his bodyguard from the 6th Virginia cavalry at the ford to turn stragglers back to Winchester. *Cf.* 13 *S. H. S. P.,* 13.

[40] *O. R.,* 19, part 2, p. 639. [41] *O. R.,* 19, part 2, p. 597; *Cf. ibid.,* 143.
[42] *O. R.,* 19, part 2, p. 602. [43] *O. R.,* 19, part 2, pp. 600–601.
[44] *O. R.,* 19, part 1, p. 139. [45] Longstreet in 2 *B. and L.,* 662.

and the detached forces returned to the army at Boonsboro or at Hagerstown before a battle had to be fought, if, indeed, one could not be avoided altogether. Once the army was reunited and its line of communications clear, dazzling possibilities of manœuvre

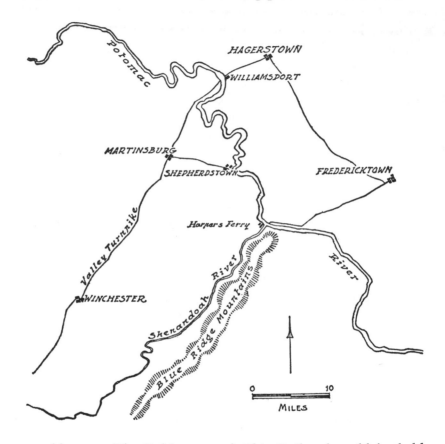

would open. The Baltimore and Ohio Railroad could be held or destroyed, and the army could move from Hagerstown to Harrisburg, a distance of only seventy-one miles. West of Harrisburg, the Susquehanna bridge of the Pennsylvania Railroad could be broken. Then the East would be cut off from the West, except for the slow and circuitous route by the Great Lakes. Lee would be left free to deal with McClellan, assured that no reinforcements could reach his adversary from the West. A march on Philadelphia, Baltimore, or Washington would be practicable, and the war might be won. Such an opportunity justified the danger incident to dividing the army.[46]

If Harpers Ferry and Martinsburg were to be cleared of Federals before these great manœuvres were undertaken, then Jackson was the man to do the work. He was perfectly familiar with the country by reason of his long service there.[47] Lee called him to headquarters, on or about September 9, closed the flap of his tent and began a discussion of the best way to accomplish his object. While they were talking, Longstreet's voice was heard outside. Lee immediately invited him to share their council. Longstreet was not sympathetic with the project, and sulked at the decision, but as he saw it had been determined upon, he made no other suggestion than that, if Jackson should be detached, the remainder of the army should be kept together.[48]

Harpers Ferry, as already noted,[49] is one of the most vulnerable of positions. Lying on the west bank of the Shenandoah, at the junction of that stream with the Potomac, it is in a flat dominated from three directions. In rear of the town stand the Bolivar Heights. Eastward, across the Shenandoah, rise the Loudoun Heights. From the northward, on the other side of the Potomac, the lofty Maryland Heights look down. From any one of these positions artillery could rake the town and make it untenable. But if the garrison was to be captured along with the place the task was not easy. An enemy attacked from the Virginia side could quickly escape across the Potomac bridge. Assailed from the Maryland side and from Bolivar Heights, a vigilant commander could slip a short distance up the Shenandoah from Harpers Ferry to fords which offered a retreat to the Loudoun Heights. Lee reasoned that the garrison should be taken along with the post, and to effect this he had to close all the exits by organizing three columns to converge simultaneously—one on Loudoun Heights, one on Maryland Heights, and one from the rear of Harpers Ferry on Bolivar Heights. The last of these three columns could readily force the Federal troops at Martinsburg

---

[46] It is curious that this plan, which was plainly set forth in Lee's conversation with General J. G. Walker (2 *B. and L.*, 604–5), should have been overlooked in published accounts of General Lee's reasons for dividing his army.

[47] Hotchkiss in 3 *C. M. H.*, 338.

[48] 2 *B. and L.*, 663.

[49] See *supra*, vol. I, pp. 472, 484.

to retreat to the ferry. For the occupation of Loudoun Heights, Lee chose the small but fresh division of Brigadier General John G. Walker, who had come from Richmond with D. H. Hill. To seize Maryland Heights from the north, a troublesome advance through a very difficult country, he selected McLaws's and R. H. Anderson's divisions of Longstreet's command. And for the most serious part of the work, cutting off the retreat of the garrison from in rear of Harpers Ferry, so that it would surrender to McLaws, Lee designated the whole of Jackson's "left wing of the army." As he moved forward, Jackson could tear up the Baltimore and Ohio Railroad. Each of these forces was carefully proportioned to the nature and magnitude of the task assigned it.

Walker's line of advance would carry him close by the mouth of the Monocacy River, which the Chesapeake and Ohio Canal crossed. This aqueduct of the canal could be demolished *en route* so as to destroy that line of communication with the west. That Walker might know precisely what was expected of him, Lee summoned him to headquarters, went over the plan in detail, with a map before them, and then told him of his intention to march from Hagerstown to Harrisburg.

Walker could not conceal his astonishment. Lee observed it. "You doubtless regard it hazardous to leave McClellan practically on my line of communication, and to march into the heart of the enemy's country?"

Walker had to admit that it seemed so to him.

"Are you acquainted with General McClellan?" Lee inquired.

Walker had served with McClellan in Mexico but had not been close to him since that time.

"He is an able general," Lee said, "but a very cautious one. His enemies among his own people think him too much so. His army is in a very demoralized and chaotic condition, and will not be prepared for offensive operations—or he will not think it so—for three or four weeks. Before that time I hope to be on the Susquehanna." [50]

No time was to be lost in launching the enterprise. The main army was to be moving toward Hagerstown while the detached columns were on their mission. The work of destroying the

[50] 2 *B. and L.*, 605-6.

Baltimore and Ohio and the canal was to be an integral part of the operations against Harpers Ferry, but was to be preliminary to it. Harpers Ferry itself was to be captured Friday, September 12. Then the army would be ready to reconcentrate at Hagerstown or at Boonsboro, and to advance into Pennsylvania.

All these details were covered by Special Orders No. 191, issued on September 9, and destined to have a memorable place in American military history.[51] Copies were made at general headquarters for all those division commanders who were to participate in the movement, and as D. H. Hill was not formally attached either to Jackson's or to Longstreet's "wing," the text was delivered directly to him from general headquarters. Jackson, however, had never been notified that D. H. Hill had been taken from under his control, so he also sent the paper to that officer. This copy from Jackson Hill carefully preserved. The other, being superfluous, was used by some staff officer of Hill's— the world will never know by whom—to wrap up three cigars against the time when the owner should want them.[52] It was to prove the costliest covering ever used for such a purpose.

The routes set forth in these orders were as follows:

1. Jackson in advance: Frederick to Middletown to Sharpsburg, passing the Potomac at a ford of his selection, taking possession of the Baltimore and Ohio on the morning of September 12, capturing Martinsburg and cutting off the retreat of the enemy from Harpers Ferry.[53]

2. McLaws, with R. H. Anderson: Frederick to Middletown to Harpers Ferry, occupying the Maryland Heights on Friday morning, September 12, and endeavoring to capture the garrison there.

3. Walker to complete the destruction of the Monocacy aqueduct, then across the Potomac at Cheek's Ford, to occupy Loudoun Heights.[54]

4. Longstreet, with part of the wagon trains: Frederick to Boonsboro.

[51] Cf. Long, 264.
[52] Taylor's Four Years, 67 and n.; Shotwell Papers, 327; 2 D. H. Hill, 345–46 and n.
[53] Jackson changed his route and went from Boonsboro to Williamsport and not by Sharpsburg (O. R., 19, part 1, p. 953).
[54] Walker, finding the route by Cheek's Ford commanded by Federal artillery, moved by Point of Rocks (O. R., 19, part 1, p. 913).

5. D. H. Hill, preceded by the rest of the wagon trains and the reserve artillery, to follow Longstreet as a rearguard.

6. Stuart, detaching a squadron each for the columns of Jackson, Longstreet, and McLaws, to cover the route of the army and to round up all stragglers.

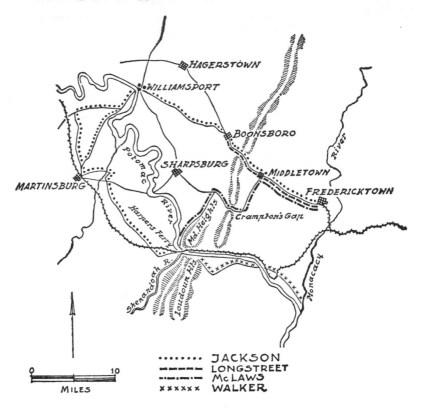

.... JACKSON
▬ ▬ ▬ ▬ LONGSTREET
▬·▬·▬·▬ McLAWS
x x x x x WALKER

7. All movements to begin the morning of September 10.

8. Jackson, McLaws, and Walker, on completion of their mission, to rejoin at Boonsboro or at Hagerstown.[55]

Graphically, the actual routes, slightly modified from those set forth in the orders, were as shown above.

At the designated time, the march began. Lee remained with Longstreet until time for that officer to move and then rode westward with him. The advance carried him through a quiet,

[55] *O. R.,* 19, part 2, pp. 603–4.

rolling country toward South Mountain. This low and beautiful range, running almost with the meridian at this point, is part of the familiar Blue Ridge chain in Virginia, and forms an impressive barrier between Frederick and Hagerstown. As the veterans of Longstreet's hard-hitting brigades passed through Turner's Gap in the mountains, reminiscent of the highlands through which they had tramped to Manassas, every soldier must have reflected that the nearby heights would make a good fortress from which to defy McClellan. But as Lee expected the speedy conclusion of the Harpers Ferry expedition, he had no thought of holding the mountain pass. On the contrary, it seemed more to his advantage to draw McClellan westward beyond the range, so that he would have to negotiate it in victualling his army.[56] At the least, Lee intended to move on to Boonsboro, two miles and a half from the crest of the mountains. From that point he could observe the progress of the operations against Harpers Ferry, and could advance quickly if the Federals at the Ferry eluded McLaws and tried to join McClellan.

Before the 10th of September ended, a rumor reached Lee that a Federal force was moving southward on Hagerstown from the direction of Chambersburg, Penna. This had not been reckoned upon. If it were a fact, the Federals could cross in front of Lee's column and play havoc with his communications or interrupt the operations against Harpers Ferry. Hagerstown must be secured. Longstreet was therefore directed to proceed thither the next day, instead of remaining at Boonsboro.

Lee was loath, however, to abandon altogether the strategic position at Boonsboro until he was certain that the Federals at Harpers Ferry had been bagged, for there was no other point from which he could move so quickly toward Harpers Ferry in case of emergency. Besides, Stuart might need infantry support closer than Hagerstown. Reasoning in this way, Lee determined to leave D. H. Hill at Boonsboro while Longstreet went on to Hagerstown.[57] This meant splitting the army into five detachments—Jackson en route to Martinsburg, McLaws moving toward Maryland Heights, Walker on his way to Loudoun Heights, Longstreet advancing to Hagerstown, and D. H. Hill remaining

[56] *O. R.,* 19, part 1, p. 145.   [57] *O. R.,* 19, part 1, p. 145.

at Boonsboro, while the cavalry, as yet, was east of South Mountain. Still, so long as McClellan lingered under the shelter of the Washington defenses, a dispersion of force that violated all the canons of war might serve the needs of the situation and involve no undue risks.

Lee rode on with Longstreet to Hagerstown on the 11th. He found no signs of any Federal advance from Pennsylvania and nothing to create alarm. The reception of the army was more sympathetic than at Frederick,[58] but the stiffest discipline was maintained among the men for the protection of hostile civilians in accordance with the spirit of Lee's proclamation. When a woman insisted on singing "The Star-Spangled Banner" under his very nose as he rode through the town, Lee lifted his hat to her and gave orders that nobody was to molest her in any way.[59] In the towns and from the country round about some supplies were procured, but no bacon was to be had. The advantage of maintaining the supply line south of the Potomac seemed more apparent than ever, for it was certain Lee would have to continue to draw provisions from Virginia.[60]

The 12th did not bring the news of the capture of Harpers Ferry that Lee had hoped to receive. Instead, Stuart reported through D. H. Hill that the enemy was advancing on Frederick. Except that a part of Burnside's corps was included, Stuart was unable to say what strength the Federals had.[61] This intelligence was most disquieting. Why was the deliberate Federal commander on the move? He who was so careful to prepare everything in advance—how could he be stirring, much less pushing boldly forward, so soon after the defeat at Manassas? McClellan was not running true to form! What had happened to him?

The next morning, September 13, there was still no information of the capture of Harpers Ferry. Jackson was known to have reached Martinsburg, whence the Federal garrison, estimated at 2500 to 3000, was said to have fled to Harpers Ferry. "Stonewall" was expected to be in front of the latter position by noon of the 13th, but McLaws had not sent Lee a word concerning his progress. As it was reasonable to suppose that the advancing Federals

---

[58] 10 S. H. S. P., 511; 31 ibid., 39. [59] Mason, 137.
[60] O. R., 19, part 2, p. 605. [61] O. R., 19, part 1, p. 816.

had occupied Frederick, Lee warned McLaws to watch the road from Frederick to Harpers Ferry.[62]

The outlook was vaguely darkening. Lee was increasingly conscious of the weakness produced by straggling. In answer to a letter from Davis, who proposed to visit the army,[63] Lee wrote: ". . . so much depends upon circumstances beyond [the army's] control and the aid that we may receive, that it is difficult for me to conjecture the result. To look to the safety of our own frontier and to operate untrammeled in an enemy's territory, you need not be told is very difficult. Every effort, however, will be made to acquire every advantage which our position and means may warrant." [64]

During the evening of the 13th, intelligence arrived that justified, and more than justified, the cautious tone of this dispatch. Through D. H. Hill, who outranked him, Stuart reported the alarming news that the Federals at 2 P.M. had driven him from the gap in the Catoctin Mountains, a minor range that lay about seven miles east of South Mountain.[65] McClellan, still contrary to all expectation, was pushing on—and shrewdly. For the gap from which Stuart had been forced by the enemy was on the road from Frederick to Boonsboro. Once the enemy covered the distance from the Catoctin Gap to Turner's Gap, in South Mountain, the whole situation would be changed. The Federals would be in rear of McLaws on the Maryland Heights and he might be compelled to retreat quickly to escape capture. If the Federals still held out at Harpers Ferry, when McLaws was forced to retire, they might cross the Potomac bridge and join the main Union army.[66] Lee would then have to face McClellan, with Jackson and Walker detached and with McLaws's fate uncertain. It was a prospect so serious that there was but one thing to do—to hurry D. H. Hill back to South Mountain, which Lee had not intended to defend, and to hold off McClellan at that point until Harpers Ferry fell or McLaws, at the least, was out of danger. The situation is shown on page 368.

Lee at once dispatched a messenger to D. H. Hill with orders

---

[62] O. R., 19, part 2, p. 606.
[63] Cf. O. R., 19, part 2, p. 603.
[65] O. R., 19, part 1, p. 817.

[64] O. R., 19, part 2, pp. 605-6.
[66] O. R., 19, part 1, p. 146.

to defend Turner's Gap.[67] Longstreet was called to headquarters and arrived while Lee was studying his map. He told "Old Pete" of the state of affairs, and, after discussing it, instructed him to leave Toombs at Hagerstown with one brigade as a guard for

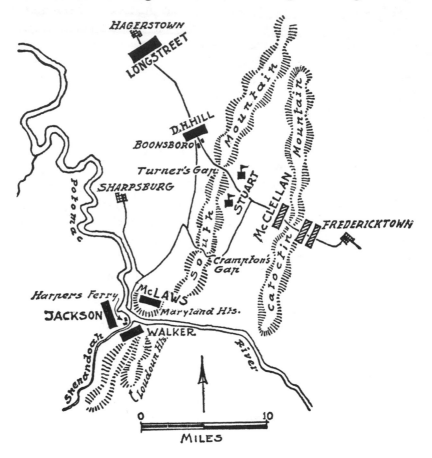

the trains and with the rest of his command to march at daylight the next morning, September 14, to support D. H. Hill.[68] This did not appeal to Longstreet. Arguing that his troops would arrive at the gap too tired to make any effective defense, he insisted that the proper course was to withdraw to Sharpsburg and to reconcentrate all the army there. Lee listened, but this time

[67] Often called Boonsboro Gap in the dispatches (*O. R.,* 19, part 1, pp. 146, 1019).
[68] *O. R.,* 19, part 1, p. 140.

he did not yield to Longstreet. On a question of strategy, rather than of combat, he held to his opinion, doubtless because he did not feel it wise to leave McLaws unprotected against an attack on his rear from South Mountain.[69] At 10 P.M., Lee sent warning to McLaws of his danger. He urged him to proceed with all speed to take Harpers Ferry and then, if he received no contrary orders from Jackson, to move as rapidly as possible to Sharpsburg, where he would be out of danger.[70] Later in the night, after Longstreet had left, Lee received from him a note again urging that the defense of South Mountain be not attempted, but that the army be moved to Sharpsburg.[71] Lee did not change his plan.

In the darkest uncertainty as to the situation, Lee on the morning of the 14th renewed his instructions to McLaws and told him of the position of the other troops. Stuart, he said, with support from D. H. Hill, was holding Turner's Gap, and Munford and Hampton, with their cavalry, were at Crampton's Gap in South Mountain, seven miles south of Turner's Gap.[72] This dispatch sent off, Lee joined Longstreet in his advance to the support of D. H. Hill at South Mountain. He was able by this time to ride Traveller again, but he could not use the reins sufficiently to guide him over rough ground, though he had become so weary of the ambulance that he would no longer use it.[73]

As the column approached the mountain, D. H. Hill could be

---

[69] 2 B. and L., 665–66; Longstreet, 219–20.

[70] O. R., 19, part 2, p. 607. Longstreet, op. cit., 220, in the face of the easily accessible text of this dispatch, made the statement that "no warning was sent to McLaws to defend his rear. . . ."

[71] 2 B. and L., 666.

[72] O. R., 19, part 2, p. 608. It was asserted by William Allan (op. cit., p. 345) that Stuart notified Lee during the evening of Sept. 13 that a citizen of Frederick had come to him and had reported that McClellan had found a copy of Special Order No. 191 in Frederick. Nearly every writer has repeated this assertion and has assumed that Lee knew that evening that McClellan was in possession of his plans. The contrary is almost certainly the case. If Stuart had received such intelligence, he would surely have mentioned it in his report. Longstreet said nothing of it. Neither did Taylor. Marshall (op. cit., 160) flatly asserted that "Lee did not become aware of the cause that led to the sudden advance of the Federal army after he had left Frederick until the official report of General McClellan was published some months later." Lee mentioned in his official report the discovery of the order, but he did not write the report until the summer of 1863, when the facts had become generally known. Colonel Allan was not at Hagerstown on the night of the 13th, as far as the records show. Although he is justly rated as one of the most accurate and painstaking writers on the campaigns of 1862, in this instance he must have accepted hearsay.

[73] Cf. Taylor's General Lee, 115–16.

heard, furiously engaged. Ere long there came a dispatch from
Hill to Longstreet asking that the reinforcements come forward
with all speed, as he was hard-pressed by a greatly superior force.[74]
Lee joined with the subordinate officers in urging the men to
quicken their march.[75] About three o'clock, just after he had
passed Boonsboro, Lee drew to the side of the road and watched
the men go into action. Soon the Texas brigade passed by. It
was ready for a fight, but it had a grievance because its commander, General John B. Hood, had been put under arrest at
Manassas for insubordination growing out of a quarrel with
General N. G. Evans over some captured ambulances.[76] "Give
us Hood," the Texans yelled, as they saw the commanding general. Lee raised his hat. "You shall have him, gentlemen." [77]
Presently when Hood came up—he had been permitted to remain
with his command—Lee sent for him.

"General," he said, "here I am just upon the eve of entering
into battle, and with one of my best officers under arrest. If you
will merely say that you regret this occurrence I will release you
and restore you to the command of your division."

Hood stoutly refused and began to argue his case.

Lee pressed him. Hood stood out. "Well," said Lee, "I will
suspend your arrest till the impending battle is decided." Hood
rode off. His men received him with a shout and filed off to the
right of the road to take position.[78]

Reinforcements had not come an hour too soon for Hill's necessity. He had been fighting since early in the morning with five
small brigades against a much stronger force in a position of
extreme difficulty. Overlooking the northern side of Turner's
Gap there are two high ridges, one to the east and one to the
west. Two similar ridges dominate the gap from the south. On
the Confederate left, as the troops faced eastward, the old
Hagerstown road mounted a ravine, about a mile from the main
highway, and then ran along the crest back to the pass. On the
Confederate right, the former Sharpsburg road paralleled the
highway and then turned to the southwest. There were in addition two other rough roads up the mountainside—a total of five

[74] O. R., 19, part 1, p. 140.   [75] Owen, 137.   [76] Hood, 38–39.
[77] J. B. Polley: Hood's Texas Brigade, 114.   [78] Hood, 39.

including the main highway, that Hill had been required to defend.[79] Placing Rodes on the left, with Colquitt astride the main road, he had stationed G. B. Anderson and Ripley on the

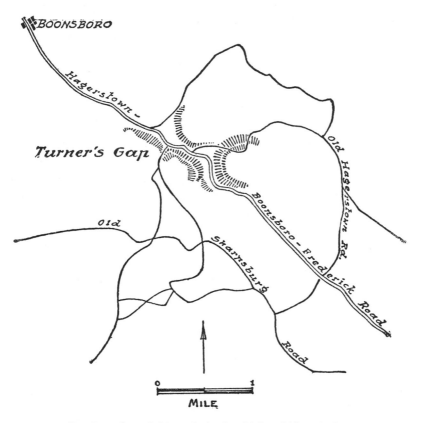

Crossings of South Mountain in the vicinity of Turner's Gap.

right to support Garland's brigade, which had been thrown in early and had been demoralized after its commander had been killed in a most brilliant defense.[80] The right had held thereafter, but at the time Longstreet came up it was evident that the Federals were massing heavily to turn the Confederate left, maintained with much stubbornness and skill by Rodes's brigade.[81]

[79] O. R., 19, part 1, pp. 48, 1020.
[80] O. R., 19, part 1, pp. 146, 1020, 1039.
[81] O. R., 19, part 1, p. 1020.

Lee sent his staff officers forward to ascertain the situation[82] and placed the reserve artillery as it came up,[83] but in his crippled condition he did not attempt to direct the battle. Longstreet took it in hand without consulting D. H. Hill[84] and threw in his troops before he familiarized himself with the terrain. In a short time Longstreet sent back word to Lee to prepare to retire that night as it would not be possible to hold South Mountain against the forces then pressing forward.[85] The troops, however, were determined not to yield their ground before darkness came to their relief. D. R. Jones and Evans on the left,[86] and Hood on the right, gallantly seconded Hill's men in contesting obstinately every foot of the rough mountain, weary though they were from their hurried march. On the right, the situation was stabilized;[87] on the left, Rodes was driven back on his supports, but with Colquitt's aid and some assistance from Longstreet's men, he was able to keep the enemy from the main road.[88]

When nightfall ended this battle of South Mountain, as it was subsequently called, some 1800 Confederates and a like number of Federals lay dead or wounded on the ridges, and the greater part of Garland's brigade had been captured.[89] The Federal lines extended beyond both flanks of the Confederates. It was manifest that unless the Army of Northern Virginia was reinforced, the pass would be stormed the next morning. And there was no prospect of reinforcement.[90]

The hours that followed were among the most anxious Lee had known. Never before in his campaigning had the situation changed so often or so perplexingly as between dark on the 14th and dawn on the 15th. Rarely thereafter did the events of any ten hours present so many contradictions. Lee looked squarely at the facts: the day had been bad; the morrow might be worse. The enemy's advance through the mountains would put him di-

[82] *Long*, 215.
[83] *O. R.*, 19, part 1, p. 830.
[84] *O. R.*, 19, part 1, p. 1021.
[85] 2 *B. and O.*, 666.
[86] *O. R.*, 19, part 1, p. 885, 939.
[87] *O. R.*, 19, part 1, p. 922.
[88] *O. R.*, 19, part 1, pp. 1021, 1034.
[89] Federal losses were 1831; the Confederate casualties were not separately computed. D. H. Hill (2 *B. and L.*, 579) estimated the loss in his five brigades as 934. Livermore places the gross casualties in the Army of Northern Virginia, including 800 prisoners, at 2685—probably too high a figure. All the reports appear in *O. R.*, 19, part 1. A useful study of the battle is George S. Grattan: *The Battle of Boonsboro Gap or South Mountain.*
[90] *O. R.*, 19, part 1, p. 147.

rectly in rear of McLaws. The Federals at Harpers Ferry, across the Potomac from McLaws, would command the bridge, if they still held out in the face of Jackson's and Walker's attack. Longstreet, Hill, and Stuart might be able to keep McClellan off McLaws's rear for a few hours, but they could not succor him. McLaws must get across the Potomac as soon as possible, by some ford that the Federals did not command. There was no alternative. McLaws's retreat, however, would leave only the three divisions and the few scattered brigades then with Lee on the north side of the Potomac to contend alone against the full strength of the army of McClellan on the 15th, in hopeless numerical inferiority. All the high hopes of manœuvre had to be abandoned. All the air castles that had been built around Harrisburg and the Susquehanna bridge had to be vacated. The Army of Northern Virginia, being unable to reconcentrate on the north side of the Potomac, must seek the friendly soil on the south side of the river, and await a new opportunity. So reasoned Lee. At 8 P.M. he dictated this dispatch to McLaws and sent it off at once by courier:

"General: The day has gone against us and this army will go by Sharpsburg and cross the river. It is necessary for you to abandon your position tonight. Send your trains not required on the road to cross the river. Your troops you must have well in hand to unite with this command, which will retire by Sharpsburg. Send forward officers to explore the way, ascertain the best crossing of the Potomac, and if you can find any between you and Shepherdstown leave the Shepherdstown Ford for this command. Send an officer to report to me on the Sharpsburg road, where you are and what crossing you will take. You will of course bring Anderson's division with you." [91]

Then Longstreet and D. H. Hill arrived with their reports of the situation at the end of the battle. Hood came also. Their opinion was unanimously in concurrence with that which Lee had already formed: The army must retreat. It could not hold South Mountain the next day. Lee did not tell his subordinates that he intended to recross the Potomac at once. Perhaps he

[91] O. R., 51, part 2, pp. 618–19.

deemed it best to withhold announcement of that unpleasant necessity from men who were weary from the strain of battle.

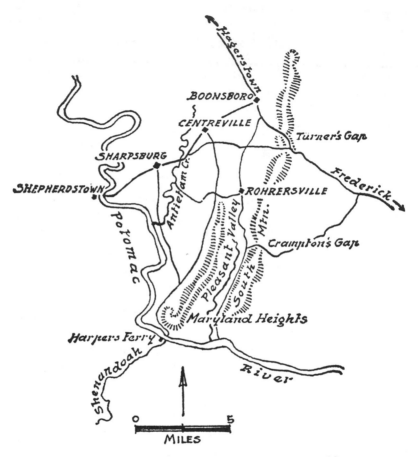

Sketch to illustrate Lee's operations, September 14–15, 1862.

They left with no other instruction than that they were to march to Centreville,[92] on the road to Sharpsburg. There they would be able to give some measure of temporary protection to McLaws's rear.[93] Fitz Lee's brigade of cavalry would cover the retreat.

Not long after this council of war, bad news confirmed Lee's decision to withdraw: The Confederate cavalry sent to defend

[92] Called Keedysville in most of the Confederate reports.
[93] *Longstreet,* 227; Hill in 2 *B. and L.,* 571; *Fitz Lee,* 205; *Hood,* 41.

Crampton's Gap had lost it; the Federals were pouring through directly in McLaws's rear.[94] This, of course, aggravated the danger of McLaws being cut off. More than that, it gave the enemy a short and direct road to Sharpsburg, past which town Lee expected to move on his way back to Virginia soil. The army manifestly must lose no time in reaching Centreville, both to protect McLaws and to guard its own line of retreat.

On the heels of the messenger bringing this grim news of the occupation of Crampton's Gap, a report from Jackson reached headquarters. It was not specific in promise—that was not Jackson's way—but it led Lee to believe that Harpers Ferry would fall the next morning.[95] That suggested a possibility of retrieving the situation. If Jackson took Harpers Ferry, his orders were to rejoin the army and he could be counted on to do so promptly, perhaps at Sharpsburg, which was only twelve miles from Harpers Ferry by the most direct road. If, moreover, McLaws could find a way out of his trap and, instead of marching into Virginia, could also get to Sharpsburg, the army could be reunited on the north side of the Potomac and might be able to resume its campaign of manœuvre. It was, however, a prospect that hung on many contingencies, and if the gamble were lost, then the army must return to Virginia, and must secure the fords as a precaution.

With this analysis of the situation, Lee issued instructions as follows:

1. The main army was to march to Centreville to protect McLaws's rear, as decided at the council of war, and to cover the road to Sharpsburg.

2. McLaws was to cross into Virginia if he must, but was to seek a road over the mountains or follow the road up the river, and if he could march on Sharpsburg, was to notify headquarters, which would be established at Centreville.[96]

3. The cavalry that had fought at Crampton's Gap were to cover McLaws's rear, holding Rohrersville on the main road from Boonsboro to Maryland Heights, and were to assist McLaws in finding a road to Sharpsburg.[97]

---

[94] *O. R.,* 19, part 1, pp. 140, 147, 826, 854.
[96] *O. R.,* 19, part 2, p. 608.
[95] *O. R.,* 19, part 1, p. 140.
[97] *O. R.,* 19, part 2, p. 609.

4. Jackson's and Walker's orders to rejoin the army were to stand.[98]

5. One battalion of reserve artillery was to remain with the army at Centreville; the rest was to recross the Potomac at once and cover the fords[99] in case a retreat across the river became necessary.[100]

These decisions did not end the responsibilities of a night of foreboding. Rumor spread from the outposts on the mountain that the Federals were withdrawing. For a moment Lee hesitated over his own retreat, but fortunately a prisoner was brought in who stated that Sumner's corps was coming into position, fresh for an attack with the dawn. This confirmed Lee in his decision. The army was set in motion,[101] preceded by the wagon trains. The dead and the seriously wounded had to be left behind.

On the road, Lee sent another urgent note to McLaws,[102] from whom he had heard nothing and to whom he doubted if his earlier messages had been delivered. He told McLaws to move to Harpers Ferry it it had fallen by the time McLaws received his dispatch. Then, making still another change of plan, Lee decided it would be better to march direct to Sharpsburg than to halt at Centreville. He reasoned that if his main force were at Sharpsburg he would be able to render McLaws almost as much assistance as at Centreville, if McLaws, meantime, had not crossed to Harpers Ferry. The remainder of the army could be stationed on good ground at Sharpsburg. Further, the columns could more readily be transferred from that point than from Centreville to the south bank of the Potomac in case "Stonewall" and the other commanders of detached columns could not reach Lee in time.

---

[98] Cf. O. R., 19, part 2, p. 604.   [99] O. R., 19, part 1, p. 830.

[100] Lee's dispatch of 8 P.M. to McLaws (O. R., 51, part 2, pp. 618–19), which seems to have been overlooked by all writers on this campaign, except White and Hotchkiss, contains the only direct mention of Lee's intention to recross the Potomac after the battle of South Mountain. It raises a number of rather difficult questions, but it certainly fits in with Lee's dispatch of 11:15 P.M. to McLaws and also with the instructions to Pendleton concerning the withdrawal of the reserve artillery to the south side of the river. The explanation given in the text seems to conform to all the known facts and to run counter to nothing that has been found in the sources. The late J. C. Ropes and Colonel Walter H. Taylor had some correspondence regarding the little-known order of 8 P.M. Mr. Ropes's letter is not in the Taylor MSS., but Colonel Taylor's answer advanced the view that Lee intended to remain on the north side of the Potomac if he could reconcentrate his whole army there, but that he intended to recross to the south bank if full reconcentration was not possible. Colonel Taylor added, however, that he was not with General Lee at the time and could not speak finally on the subject.

[101] O. R., 19, part 1, p. 140.   [102] O. R., 19, part 2, pp. 609–10.

"MY MARYLAND"—OR HIS?

As the army marched at daylight to the low hills around the undistinguished little town of Sharpsburg, which it was to make forever renowned, these alternatives, then, must have been uppermost in Lee's mind: Was it retreat or manœuvre that awaited him, a bloody anti-climax to the Seven Days and to Manassas, or a new success?

CHAPTER XXVI

With Eyes on the Harpers Ferry Road

SHARPSBURG appeared in the morning light of September 15, 1862, as a quiet, substantially built little town lying under one of a series of ridges between the sluggish Antietam Creek and the winding Potomac. The course of the river is from north to south until it reaches a point about three miles southwest of Sharpsburg, where it turns almost directly east. The meandering Antietam runs almost due south into the river. The average depth of position between the creek and the river is about three miles. The ground Lee had chosen for his concentration was thus a peninsula between the Antietam and the Potomac, reasonably strong but dangerously shallow in case of disaster. In rear of it was only one good ford, about a mile and a half below Shepherdstown.[1]

Slowly and doggedly Longstreet's and D. H. Hill's divisions tramped down from Centreville, by way of the Boonsboro and Sharpsburg road, crossed the creek, and took positions on either side of the road. Their first dispositions were nearly parallel to the Antietam and east of the town. All the morning the dusty veterans moved toward the town and turned to right and to left before they reached it.[2] Lee personally helped to put the last of them into position. "We will make our stand on those hills," he said, as he told the men where to go.[3] They were only 18,000, all told—such had been the price of Lee's dispersion of force—and they seemed a pitifully small command with which to face the army they knew was in pursuit. Most of the soldiers were hungry, too, for the commissary had broken down, and few rations were to be had by the roadside.

About noon[4] a courier galloped up the road from Shepherds-

---

[1] Plates XXVIII and XXIX in the *Atlas* of the *Official Records* offer the best maps, except for the remarkable and detailed *Atlas of the Battlefield of Antietam*, prepared under the direction of the Antietam Battlefield Board (1904).

[2] *Longstreet*, 233.   [3] *Morgan*, 141.   [4] *Long*, 216.

378

town and came to Lee's temporary quarters. He brought a message from Jackson, written in the familiar, unsoldierly handwriting of "Stonewall." General Lee broke the seal and read:

Near 8 A.M., September 15, 1862.

General: Through God's blessing, Harper's Ferry and its garrison are to be surrendered. As Hill's troops have borne the heaviest part in the engagement, he will be left in command until the prisoners and public property shall be disposed of, unless you direct otherwise. The other forces can move off this evening so soon as they get their rations. To what place shall they move? I write at this time in order that you may be apprised of the condition of things. You may expect to hear from me again today after I get more information respecting the number of prisoners, etc.

Respectfully

T. J. JACKSON,

Major-General.[5]

"That is indeed good news," said Lee, "let it be announced to the troops." [6] Quickly the word was passed; the men seemed charged with new courage when they heard it. The worst danger from the division of the army would soon be over: for Lee, of course, immediately ordered Jackson's stout-hearted brigades to rejoin the main army as soon as possible. McLaws and Walker, likewise relieved from detached duty by the capture of Harpers Ferry, would also proceed promptly to Sharpsburg. This prospect of an early reconcentration of his whole army seemed to answer the question Lee had asked himself at dawn. He could now afford to invite attack on the Maryland side and need not forego the advantage of prospective manœuvre in the enemy's country or take a chance of losing what Jackson had captured at Harpers Ferry.

Lee was over his map at 2 P.M., studying troop positions and roads,[7] when a message from Fitz Lee advised him that the enemy was approaching the Antietam.[8] Soon the Union troops began to

[5] *O. R.*, 19, part 1, p. 951.   [6] *Owen*, 139.   [7] *White*, 211.

[8] Fitz Lee had skillfully delayed the enemy's advance after the blue columns had begun to stream down Turner's Gap at 8 A.M., and at this time he was retiring slowly before them (*O. R.*, 19, part 1, p. 148).

appear. Steadily through the afternoon, moving clouds of dust, far-off flags and glimpses of blue on distant hills showed that the Federals were coming up in great strength. They made no attack, however. Only their fine, long-range artillery warned the Confederates of what was in store for them.[9] Lee watched guns and moving columns with apparent unconcern. Jackson would surely be up the next day with all his force, and McClellan was not a man to attack hurriedly. So confident was Lee of this that he did not hesitate to express the opinion that the next day would pass without a battle.[10]

Before the 15th ended, Stuart the ubiquitous rode over from Harpers Ferry with fuller news of what had befallen Jackson. He had a tale to tell of successes that more than counterbalanced the losses at South Mountain. Moving by Williamsport, Light's Ford, and Martinsburg, Jackson had come in sight of Bolivar Heights, in rear of Harpers Ferry, about 11 A.M. on the 13th.[11] Walker had failed to destroy the aqueduct at the mouth of the Monacacy but had reached Loudoun Heights on the afternoon of the 13th.[12] McLaws had encountered some opposition from the strong Federal positions on Maryland Heights but had managed to get his troops on the crest by 4:30 P.M. the same day. On the 14th Jackson had made his dispositions very skillfully and had seized commanding ground behind the town.[13] McLaws had been gravely threatened that day when the Federals had broken through Crampton's Gap, but with some help from Stuart he had drawn his lines to face the enemy in his rear. He had been in as instant danger as Lee had supposed on the night of the 14th, but fortunately he had not been pushed.[14] By the morning of the 15th, the Federals at Harpers Ferry had been so completely under the Southern artillery that the garrison had surrendered. Only a small cavalry command had escaped. More than 11,000 men, 73 guns, about 13,000 small arms, and vast miscellaneous stores had been captured.[15] When Stuart had left, the way had been clear

[9] O. R., 19, part 1, p. 844; Longstreet, 234.
[10] Owen, 139.   [11] O. R., 19, part 1, p. 953.
[12] O. R., 19, part 1, p. 913.   [13] O. R., 19, part 1, p. 954.
[14] O. R., 19, part 1, pp. 826, 854–55, 862–64, 870; McDaniel, 11; History of Kershaw's Brigade, 147 ff.
[15] O. R., 19, part 1, pp. 954–55.

for McLaws to cross to Harpers Ferry. As the garrison at Martinsburg had fled to Harpers Ferry and had been included in the capitulation, the line of communications via the Shenandoah Valley was clear, the roads were open, and the detached units could rejoin the Army of Northern Virginia as soon as they could cover the ground from Harpers Ferry to Sharpsburg. The situation was immensely bettered. But for the rapid and unexplained advance of the Federals, all Lee's misgivings of the night of the 14th–15th would have been dissipated by the news Stuart brought, and the campaign of manœuvre could have swept northward according to the original plan.

Refreshed by sound sleep, Lee on the morning of September 16 exhibited no fear of the fast-swelling mass of Federals in front of him. "If he had had a well-equipped army of 100,000 veterans at his back," wrote a comrade who saw him that day, "he could not have appeared more composed and confident." [16] He had as yet only the 18,000 infantry who had marched from South Mountain. The great bends of the Potomac behind his lines were like the coils of a snake waiting to envelop him. But not once did he hint of any withdrawal across the Potomac. He had to allow time for the removal of the booty taken at Harpers Ferry; he was dealing with a cautious adversary who had never yet fought an offensive battle; he would soon have together all the units of an unbeaten army that had established its superiority over Pope's greater host only a little more than a fortnight before. A quick withdrawal in the face of his proclamation to the people of Maryland would mean the definite and probably the permanent loss of that state to the Confederacy. The considerations that brought him across the Potomac kept him there: if McClellan should attack and could be defeated, all the promising manœuvres Lee had projected at Frederick might still be executed, whereas retreat would restore the morale of the Army of the Potomac and would carry the war back into the strife-swept counties of Virginia, ever nearer and nearer to Richmond.

So, on the 16th, Lee waited. When the sun was at its highest, dust along the road from the Potomac heralded the approach of a column. A little after 12 o'clock, Jackson and Walker rode up

[16] General J. G. Walker in 2 B. and L., 675.

to headquarters and reported that their troops were behind them, en route to Sharpsburg. Lee shook the hands of the two generals and congratulated them on the outcome of the operations at Harpers Ferry. With their aid, he said, he felt he could hold his ground until the arrival of the three missing divisions of A. P. Hill, R. H. Anderson, and McLaws, which he expected to come up during the day.[17] Jackson's troops, on arrival, were directed to the left.[18] Walker's men, who had marched behind Jackson,[19] were given some rest and, at 4 P.M. received instructions to move before light the next morning and to occupy the extreme right of the Confederate position.[20]

The artillery had been active most of the forenoon. As Lee had gone through Sharpsburg, unconscious of danger and leading Traveller by the bridle, he had cautioned passing gunners not to waste their ammunition in an idle duel with the Federal batteries but to save it for the infantry,[21] which was crossing the Antietam, out of range, and was massing opposite the Confederate left. About sundown, the Union artillery quickened its fire on that part of the front. Soon there came to Lee's ears the rattle of musketry and the shouts of engaging troops. The enemy was attacking, but as his advance was against Hood's veteran division, which had never yielded ground, Lee probably felt no concern. The attack ended with darkness and left the opposing wings about where they had stood when it commenced.[22]

At headquarters, during the evening, Lee waited in vain for the arrival of the three divisions that Jackson had left on the south side of the river. Their absence began to be serious, for everything indicated that the enemy would attack the next day. It would be a difficult matter to hold off the whole of the Army of the Potomac if three divisions were missing. A hurried message was dispatched to A. P. Hill to hurry forward with all speed.[23] Soon Stuart rode up for orders and was sent to the Confederate left, where the ground seemed to offer some opening for a possible counterstroke.[24] Hood came, also, with a report that his

---

[17] *O. R.*, 19, part 1, p. 141; 2 *B. and L.*, 675.　　　[18] *O. R.*, 19, part 1, p. 955.
[19] *O. R.*, 19, part 1, p. 148.
[20] 2 *B. and L.*, 675; *O. R.*, 19, part 1, p. 914.
[21] *Owen*, 141.
[22] *O. R.*, 19, part 1, pp. 148, 923; *Hood*, 42.
[23] *O. R.*, 19, part 1, p. 981.　　　[24] 1 *von Borcke*, 229.

men had received only half a ration of beef in three days. They were exhausted, he said, and should be relieved from the front line in order that they might rest and cook rations. Lee was sensitive to their distress but in the absence of A. P. Hill, Anderson, and McLaws, he had to admit to Hood that he did not have a division to put in his place. He could only suggest that Hood go to Jackson and ask if he could send part of a division to man the front Hood had occupied. Hood went and found Jackson willing to help him but so conscious of the odds the army would have to face on the morrow that he exacted a promise from Hood to bring his troops back into line if Jackson needed them in the morning.[25] At 10 o'clock Hood's men slipped silently to the rear, and Lawton and Trimble of Ewell's division moved into their places.[26] A gentle rain was falling then, but the tired veterans would have slept on in spite of it had not a nervous picket-firing swept often and loudly along the long, dark lines that lay across the hills. It was a brief last night of earth for hundreds of the soldiers, such a night as the army had not known since the field of Seven Pines. Always before, the graycoats had expected to attack; now they must stand on the defensive. Odds they had always faced, and with confidence; this time, the odds were appalling. Both because of straggling and because of the arrival of the enemy before the whole army had been reconcentrated, they numbered less than 25,000, artillery and cavalry included. Twenty-four brigades faced forty-four,[27] with strong Federal reserves close at hand. Even if all the troops engaged in the Harpers Ferry operations could be brought up, Lee would have less than 40,000 with which to face twice that number.

The bivouac of this ghost of an army was just to the east of a road that starts at the Potomac and runs northward to Sharpsburg and thence in the same direction toward Hagerstown. The road is roughly parallel to the Antietam on the east and to the Potomac on the west; it defends the hills around Sharpsburg from an attack across the Antietam and covers the crossings of the river. From the highway, rounded ridges go down to the Potomac. The ravines among them are not generally precipitous but

---

[25] *Hood*, 42; *Longstreet*, 237. [26] *O. R.*, 19, part 1, p. 149.
[27] *Taylor's Four Years*, 73; 2 *D. H. Hill*, 407.

they were to have a singular influence on the action that was soon to open. For these ridges and ravines segmented the battlefield so completely that men on the right could not see what was happening on the centre, nor those on the centre all that occurred on the left. The Antietam, in fact, offered not one battleground, but three, on each of which, ere another day passed, the dead were to lie in hecatombs.

Beginning at a point about a mile and a half south of the town, the right extended to the road that runs from Boonsboro to Sharpsburg. With a small cavalry force on the flank, the southern end of this part of the front, which was strongly defended by hills overlooking the creek, was to be occupied at daylight by J. G. Walker's division of 3200.[28] On his left, extending as far as the Boonsboro-Sharpsburg road, already was D. R. Jones's division of Longstreet's command, only 2430 effectives, well supported by artillery.[29] Flanking the Boonsboro-Sharpsburg road on either side was Evans, with his own and G. T. Anderson's brigades, some 2600 men.[30] North of the road from Boonsboro to Sharpsburg was a strong artillery force on high ground, and then D. H. Hill's division, reduced by straggling and by losses at South Mountain to hardly more than 3000 men. Its line extended irregularly northward from the road for slightly more than a mile and a quarter. Most of the division was on a little farm road subsequently bearing the sinister name of "Bloody Lane." The left brigade of D. H. Hill under General Ripley, was about a quarter of a mile south of a grove known after the battle as the East Wood. Hill's line faced slightly east of north and had in support the admirable artillery of Stephen D. Lee, in a fine position just southeast of a whitewashed Dunker church that was a landmark on the Sharpsburg-Hagerstown road.

Opposite the East Wood, in advance of Ripley, was Lawton's scratch command, consisting of his own and Trimble's brigades. The front held by these units bent sharply to the westward opposite the East Wood, so that Lawton's brigade faced almost due north. Beyond Lawton's left was Jackson's old division under Brigadier General J. R. Jones, plus Early's brigade of Lawton's

---

[28] O. R., 19, part 1, p. 914; *Taylor's Four Years*, 72.   [29] O. R., 19, part 1, p. 886.
[30] O. R., 19, part 1, p. 939; *Taylor's Four Years*, 71–72.

division.[31] On J. R. Jones's left was Stuart's cavalry, with its artillery. The distance from Lawton's right, where it covered

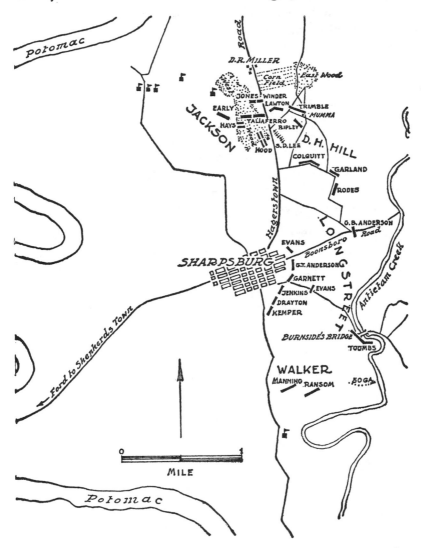

Position of that part of the Army of Northern Virginia in the immediate vicinity of Sharpsburg at daylight, September 17, 1862.

Ripley, to the extreme left flank of the infantry was about three-quarters of a mile. Approximately 5000 infantry were on this

[31] Lawton was temporarily commanding Ewell's division.

sector, and beyond them about 3000 cavalry,[32] with Hood's 2400 infantry in immediate reserve.[33] This was not a heavy concentration, but it was the best that Lee could present, despite the fact that McClellan had incautiously, almost ostentatiously, massed troops in that quarter during the afternoon of the 16th as if to advertise his intention of attacking there.[34] Lee had no breastworks on any part of his line.[35] About 50 batteries, slightly more than 200 guns and 3000 men, were on the field, though some of them were in exposed positions where they could not cope with the heavier metal of the enemy. Except for Hood's division, which was subject to call by Jackson at any time, no reserves were at hand and none could be expected until McLaws and R. H. Anderson arrived in advance of A. P. Hill. They were expected hourly—but when would they come up?

[32] *Taylor's Four Years*, 71.

[33] The line of Longstreet, from the heights above the Antietam to the vicinity of the Boonsboro-Sharpsburg road, is regarded as the right. The centre is here treated as the front from Longstreet's left to the point where Trimble's brigade stood, close to the East Wood, at the beginning of the engagement. The left extended from Trimble to Stuart.

[34] Palfrey: *The Antietam and Fredericksburg*, 60, 62, 73.

[35] Clarke in 5 *N. C. Regiments*, 73.

CHAPTER XXVII

The Bloodiest Day of the War

(SHARPSBURG)

It was still black night on September 17 when the sporadic fire of the skirmish lines far off on the Confederate left broke into the steady rattle of an approaching general engagement.[1] At his headquarters, Lee must have heard the sound with some satisfaction, for it meant that McClellan was about to attack where the two best combat divisions of the army, Jackson's and Hood's, had been placed. Still, with three divisions not yet reported from Harpers Ferry, the dangers of a prolonged battle begun at daylight were apparent, and the possibilities of an enforced retreat were not to be burked. Lee accordingly took the precaution, at 4:30 A.M., of warning General Pendleton, who had moved his batteries across the Potomac, to guard well the fords with part of the reserve artillery.[2] The rest was ordered up.[3] Fortunately, too, General J. B. Kershaw rode up about daylight and reported that McLaws and R. H. Anderson, after a slow and straggling hard march from Harpers Ferry, were approaching Sharpsburg.[4]

The heavy fire of the skirmishers was taken up by the artillery as soon as it was light enough for the guns to be sighted. Not only on the Confederate left but from the Federal positions across Antietam Creek, as well, the 20-pounder Parrotts of the enemy swept the ground of the attack. The Confederate batteries answered quickly. Soon the volleys echoed down the Hagerstown road.

By 6 o'clock news began to filter back to headquarters. Soon thereafter, at the point where the Confederate left crossed the Hagerstown road, about a mile and a half north of Sharpsburg, a powerful Federal force, later identified as Hooker's corps, struck

---

[1] O. R., 19, part 1, pp. 845, 928.   [2] O. R., 19, part 2, p. 610.   [3] Ibid.
[4] O. R., 19, part 1, p. 865. The 8th S. C. Infantry of Kershaw's Brigade carried only forty-five men into action (O. R., 19, part 1, p. 866).

furiously. Lawton's brigade was wrecked. Trimble and Hays, who had been moved to the east of the road, were hurled back. Jackson's old division, containing the survivors of the Valley cam-

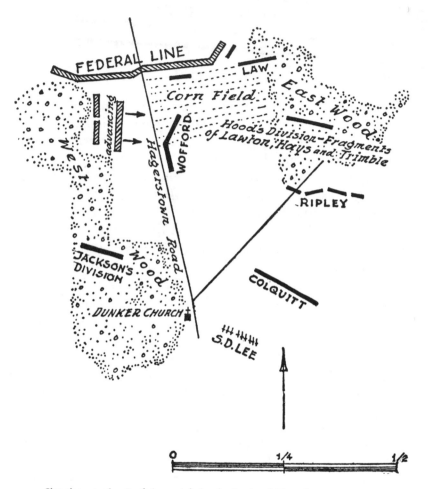

Situation on the Confederate left in the battle of Sharpsburg, 7:20 A.M., September 17, 1862.

paign, was swept aside. A great gap was torn in the Confederate flank between Early's brigade, supporting the cavalry on the extreme left, and D. H. Hill's line on the centre. The enemy was reported to be streaming down the Hagerstown road and through the West Wood, close to the dominating ground of the Dunker Church. Hood's division had already been called up and was advancing to meet the wave.[5] The situation is shown on page 388.

This was a threat of immediate disaster. Still, if the line could be held until McLaws and Anderson were brought up and thrown into action, the day might be retrieved. But was it possible to maintain the left of the line against such concentrated fire and such heavy assaults as were being delivered in that direction by the Federals? Lee had justified faith in the gallant infantry of Hood, who were moving into the gap or standing stubbornly on either side of it, but with the odds so heavy and the stake so great they must have help, and speedily. Whence could it come? Only from the right, where thus far there had been nothing more serious than skirmishing and artillery exchanges. At any time the Federals might open an attack there. But in war, all risks are relative. It was far better to take the chance of having the right assailed than of having the left broken. So, before 7:30 Lee sent orders to Colonel G. T. Anderson, commanding a brigade on the Boonsboro road, east of Sharpsburg, to march at once to support Hood.[6] About an hour later he directed General J. G. Walker to take the two brigades of his division to Jackson.[7] This meant that he was to employ thirteen of his twenty-four brigades and most of his cavalry on about one mile of his four and a half miles of front. On the right flank he left only seven brigades to defend one and a half miles, with one of these brigades, that of General Toombs, to defend the important crossing at the lower bridge over the Antietam. The centre of the line, held by D. H. Hill's 3000, was already engaged and "in the air" on its left. To state these facts is to measure the emergency.

Anderson and Walker moved promptly, but as their strength was small and the danger great, Lee promptly ordered McLaws, who was now resting his men near the town, to start to the sector through which the enemy had broken. R. H. Anderson, with his small division, was sent to strengthen D. H. Hill. In short, all the reserves that had come up were promptly moved into action, with no assurance that they would stem the tide.

[5] O. R., 19, part 1, pp. 956, 975, 976, 1022, 1032; *Alexander*, 252; *Hood*, 42.
[6] O. R., 19, part 1, p. 909.   [7] O. R., 19, part 1, p. 914.

To see the situation for himself, Lee rode to the left, profoundly concerned for the safety of that flank. On the way he met his cousin, Captain T. H. Carter of the artillery. He directed him to move his battery and such other artillery as he could collect to defend the ridge about three-quarters of a mile northwest of Sharpsburg, in the hope that this would keep the enemy from turning the left even if the troops he was now moving up could not halt the Federals' advance.[8] It probably was at this time, when his nerves were tense, that Lee met a straggler who, in some fashion, had found and killed a pig which he was carrying to his camp. Straggling, in Lee's mind, was largely responsible for the plight of the army, and at the sight of the man, his wrath rose. He completely lost grip of himself for a moment and sternly ordered that the soldier be sent to Jackson with orders to have him shot as a warning to the army.[9]

Almost as quickly as he lost his temper, Lee recovered it. As he rode on toward the firing, Colonel Stephen D. Lee, who had been fighting magnificently with his battalion of reserve artillery near the Dunker Church, reported from General Hood. The Texans and Law's brigade, he said, had plunged into the gap created by Hooker's attack. By the fiercest of fighting they had driven back the Federals almost to the point where the battle had opened. D. H. Hill had given gallant support by moving up his brigades from the right, and Early, with some fragments of Jackson's men, held the line on the left of the gap. At the moment of their farthest advance, a second Federal onslaught had been made with an overwhelming force of fresh troops.[10] Hood's ammunition had been exhausted, and his weary men had been forced to give ground. The left of D. H. Hill's division had been heavily engaged. The gap had been opened a second time as far as the

[8] *O. R.,* 19, part 1, p. 1030.

[9] *Long,* 222. Jackson decided that it was better to let the enemy act as executioner, so he sent the straggler into the hottest of the battle. The man fought so well that his offense was forgiven him when he emerged unscathed from the fire. Long remarked that the straggler lost his pig but saved his bacon. At another time during the battle, Lee challenged a straggler who was going to the rear and demanded why he was leaving the field. "I have been stung by a bung," said the man, who probably was having his first acquaintance with shell, often called "bombs" by the illiterate recruits, "and I'm what they call demoralized." Lee let him go (*Marginalia,* 94). It is proper to add that the sequence of Lee's movements on September 17 is very difficult to establish. In this instance the time of the episode is hypothetical.

[10] Mansfield's corps.

Dunker Church. Walker had then gone in; G. T. Anderson had reinforced D. H. Hill; the line had been restored in part and the Federals had been driven back once more from the ground they had taken.[11] Already, however, the Federals were preparing for a third assault with troops that had not been previously employed. The left of D. H. Hill's line was being slowly pushed back, and he was urgently calling for reinforcements.[12]

All this Stephen Lee reported and added that General Hood was afraid the day would be lost unless supports were sent in. The commanding general listened quietly and answered in an even voice, "Don't be excited about it, Colonel; go tell General Hood to hold his ground, reinforcements are now rapidly approaching between Sharpsburg and the ford." Soon McLaws's division, a long gray line, appeared over the hill.[13] Then Lee rode on to post the artillery that Carter was to bring up.[14]

By this time Walker had shot his bolt. His command had swept forward into the open until it had reached a stout post-and-rail fence, where it had been exposed to a devastating fire of infantry and artillery. Unable to cross the fence, the men had halted and then had fallen slowly back.[15]

It was now McLaws's turn. In the lull that came while that officer deployed his men for the third counterattack of the morning, Lee turned back from the left, and rode toward the centre in anticipation of an attack there. He found R. H. Anderson's division, less than 4000 men, arriving to support D. H. Hill. Soon Hill joined Lee. Together they rode down the line. Lee told the regimental officers he met that they must prepare themselves for an attack at any moment and he encouraged them as best he could. As he spoke to some of Rodes's brigade, which had fought so admirably and had suffered so much at South Mountain, the colonel of the 6th Alabama, John B. Gordon, answered him with words as cheering as his own: "These men are going to stay here, General," he said, "till the sun goes down or victory is won." [16]

Ere long "Old Pete" came up to Lee and D. H. Hill and went

[11] O. R., 19, part 1, pp. 149, 909–10, 914–15, 923, 938, 1022–23.
[12] O. R., 19, part 1, p. 1023.
[13] S. D. Lee, quoted in White, 218.   [14] O. R., 19, part 1, p. 1030.
[15] Walker in 2 B. and L., 678; O. R., 19, part 1, pp. 915, 918, 920.
[16] John B. Gordon: Reminiscences of the Civil War (cited hereafter as Gordon), 84.

with them to a little eminence, whence they could see an ominous concentration on their left. Lee dismounted, and Longstreet, an unsmoked cigar in his mouth, did the same thing. Hill sat astride his horse. "If you insist on riding up there and drawing the fire," Longstreet banteringly said, "give us a little interval so that we may not be in the line of the fire when they open upon us." Hill did not get down, but, like the other two, studied the dispositions of the enemy to the left. Presently, as Longstreet changed the field of his glasses, he noted a puff of smoke. "There is a shot for you," he cried. A few seconds later the ball struck Hill's horse and carried off the forelegs of the animal. It was with some difficulty that Hill dismounted, as the horse stood shivering in anguish on his knees.[17]

Ere that shot, McLaws's troops had attacked with splendid *élan*. Cobb's brigade moved at too wide an angle to the right, lost contact with the rest of the division, and joined the left of Rodes's brigade. Semmes, on the left of McLaws, was obliqued to the left by Jackson's order to support Stuart's cavalry, whose artillery under Pelham was plastering the Federal right.[18] The brigades of Kershaw and Barksdale, sweeping splendidly forward, drove back from the woods a strong Federal force that proved to be a part of Sumner's corps—the third corps that had been hurled against the Confederate left that day. The pursuit carried McLaws to the fence where Walker had been halted by the enemy's fire. There McLaws's men, too, had to stop, unable to throw down or to climb over the barrier. In a few minutes they had in turn to fall back to the edge of the West Wood. But this time they were not followed. Anything might happen where three assaults had been delivered with so much pertinacity, but for the moment it looked as if the worst were over on the left.[19]

But on the centre, the segmented centre, the intense bombardment and the massing of distant blue lines could mean only that the enemy was about to open the second battle of the day and was to assail the thin line of D. H. Hill. His left, which had held the right of the gap at the angle in the line, had already been roughly handled. Three of his five brigades had been demoralized. The

[17] 2 *B. and L.*, 671.   [18] *O. R.*, 19, part 1, p. 874.

[19] *O. R.*, 19, part 1, pp. 858, 865, 871–72, 874–75, 883; *History of Kershaw's Brigade,* 155; *McDaniel,* 14–16.

brunt of the attack would have to be borne by Rodes's and George B. Anderson's brigades, which stood in a sunken road, aptly styled thereafter "The Bloody Lane," that formed a minor salient in the line, approximately one mile northeast of the town. The suspense was not long. Soon the troops of Franklin's corps began to stream forward in heavy masses.[20] They were met with resolution and were hurled back. Again they attacked and again met a repulse. A third assault had the same fate, thanks alike to the valor of the infantry and to the enfilading fire of some guns that Hill brought up.[21]

The attacks on the centre seemed about to die away when a lieutenant colonel of Rodes's brigade reported that a force of the enemy had worked around to a point of vantage whence it could enfilade a part of the sunken road. Rodes at once ordered one flank drawn in, but the officer understood that this was to involve the withdrawal of the whole brigade. Before Rodes looked up from caring for one of his aides, who had been wounded at that instant, the whole of his line retired. General G. B. Anderson held his brigade together for a short time, but he too was enfiladed and fell mortally wounded. His men broke and came across the road. Soon the enemy was in hot pursuit and was within a few hundred yards of the high ground on which stood the Dunker Church. R. H. Anderson's division by this time was fighting hard and incapable of giving D. H. Hill any support. A gap yawned in the centre as ominously as the one that had been made on the left earlier in the action. And there were no troops to fill it. Disaster seemed at hand, but D. H. Hill refused to admit that the day was lost. He found Boyce's battery near by and set it firing furiously with grape and canister. Personally, Hill gathered a few men together and led them against the enemy. About 200 other soldiers, collected by a few diligent officers, were launched against the right of the Federals who were pouring into the gap. There was wild confusion for a time and then, most mysteriously, the enemy halted, though his artillery continued to pour its fire against a line that had almost disappeared.[22]

[20] *O. R.*, 19, part 1, p. 1023.   [21] *O. R.*, 19, part 1, p. 1923.

[22] *O. R.*, 19, part 1, pp. 1023–24, 1037–38, 1047–48. General Sumner, it was subsequently learned, had met Franklin, whom he outranked, and had advised against a renewal of the attack.

Despite this pause, a renewal of the attack on the centre seemed so nearly certain of success that Lee had to undertake some movement to lessen the pressure on D. H. Hill. He had no reserves on

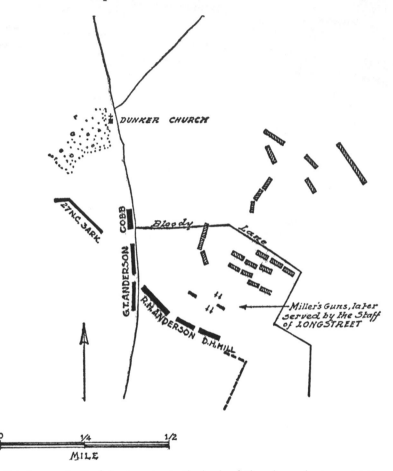

Situation on the Confederate centre in the battle of Sharpsburg, about 12:15 P.M., September 17, 1862.

the field, though A. P. Hill was supposed to be on a forced march from Harpers Ferry. The roar of guns from the right told of an impending attack that forbade the withdrawal of troops from that flank. He must create a diversion and the one point at which he could attack with any promise of success was on his left, where the assaults of the enemy had not been renewed. Orders were at

394

once sent to Jackson to attempt to turn the enemy's right near the Potomac, with the assistance of Stuart, while Walker brought his worn regiments together and renewed the offensive on the Hagerstown road, at the point where the line bent to the left.[23]

Before Jackson could deploy, the action on the Confederate right became so heavy that Lee had to ride in that direction to see what had befallen D. R. Jones's division. That command had been holding the whole of the line south of the Boonsboro-Sharpsburg road, for a distance of more than a mile, since Walker and G. T. Anderson had been ordered away. The right of D. R. Jones's position, which faced a bridge and two fords across the Antietam, had been defended by three regiments of the brigade of Robert Toombs, with the help of a few scattered companies. Toombs had placed his men close to the creek and had engaged early the Federal skirmishers and sharpshooters. After 10 o'clock four attacks had been delivered on him. Fortunately for Toombs, these were directed against the bridge, the approach to which was along a road that paralleled the creek for a few hundred yards and was exposed to the fire of the Southern batteries. Each time the Federals had been repulsed bloodily by the 2d and 20th Georgia regiments. Now, about 1 o'clock, the Federals massed opposite the fords below the bridge in such numbers that it was manifest Toombs's weary men could no longer prevent a crossing.[24] The best that could be hoped was that they could retreat and hold the high ground west of the fords and south of Sharpsburg until A. P. Hill came up. If he arrived in time, the enemy might be pressed back to the creek. If he were delayed, nothing could prevent the Federals from pushing forward until they got in rear of Longstreet's left. They might even sweep on until they cut off the retreat of the army to the Potomac in the vicinity of Shepherdstown. Either advance would certainly mean ruin, unless Jackson meantime turned the Federal right flank.

As Lee waited in the streets of Sharpsburg, where every wall echoed the roar of the guns, Captain Thomas M. Garnett, of the 5th North Carolina, Garland's brigade, approached and asked for orders. His brigade, he said, had been driven from the centre, and his regiment was badly scattered. That sounded as if the centre

[23] *O. R.,* 19, part 1, pp. 151, 956; *White,* 221.   [24] *O. R.,* 19, part 1, p. 890.

had been broken at the same time that the right was about to give ground, but as yet there was no sign of a general retreat on D. H. Hill's front, so far as Lee could observe. He ordered Garnett to

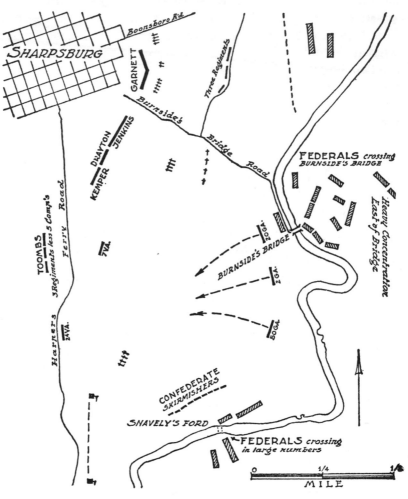

Situation on the Confederate right in the battle of Sharpsburg, about 1 P.M., September 17, 1862.

support Evans, the nearest command, in the outskirts of the town, facing the Antietam.[25] Then he rode to an eminence west of the town, where he watched Toombs's men form with the rest of

[25] *O. R.,* 19, part 1, p. 1042.

D. R. Jones's division for a last stand on the ridge to which they had by this time skillfully withdrawn.

Soon, from the Confederate left, there crept the shattered wreck of a battery—two disabled guns and one piece that seemed still serviceable. A handful of begrimed and staggering cannoneers followed the exhausted horses. The captain of the battery, with a few of his men, came up to Lee for instructions. The officer in command proved to be Captain W. T. Poague, in whose battery Bob Lee was serving. The boy himself was among the survivors. Lee listened to Poague and then ordered him to take the remaining gun and the best horses and return to Jackson's front, to share in the offensive that "Stonewall" was preparing.

"General," said Robert, as Poague turned to go, "are you going to send us in again?"

"Yes, my son," he answered, "you all must do what you can to help drive these people back." [26]

It was now nearly 2 o'clock. No new attack had been delivered against the Confederate left since McLaws had fallen back. On the centre, D. H. Hill's shattered line was making a grisly bluff to conceal the weakness of the front. Longstreet's staff, finding a battery whose gunners had been decimated, were serving two of the pieces themselves, while "Old Pete" looked after their horses.[27] Colonel Chilton, who was sent forward to ascertain the state of affairs, brought back the astonishing report that Longstreet said he was holding a stretch of the line with two guns and one regiment, and the regiment did not have a cartridge. As a matter of fact, the survivors of Cobb's brigade and two stout-hearted regiments were still in position, the 27th North Carolina, Colonel John R. Cooke, and the 3d Arkansas, Captain John W. Reedy. When word was sent to Cooke that he must keep his position at any cost, he grimly told the staff officer that his command was "still ready to lick this whole damn outfit"—language that General Lee would not have approved, however much he would have applauded the sentiment.[28] Cooke continued to wave his flag; Longstreet's amateur cannoneers kept their two guns hot; other nearby

[26] R. E. Lee, Jr., 78. This incident, here quoted almost in the language of the young man, appears in many versions.

[27] 2 B. and L., 669; Sorrel, 113; O. R., 19, part 1, pp. 849–50.

[28] Sorrel, 114; 2 N. C. Regiments, 436 ff.

artillery added its fire.[29] Such a day of suspense and instant danger Lee had never known, and now, while the September sun seemed to stand still at the bidding of a Northern Joshua, crisis piled on crisis. Jackson reported that the enemy's guns so completely commanded the Confederate left that he could not turn the Federal right.[30] Lee's immediate hope of a counterstroke vanished at the word. He had only one recourse—the concentration of all available artillery to hold the Federals in check. As he found batteries, he had them put in action on the right, firing over the heads of the Confederates and into the ranks of the enemy, who, by this time, had brought across the creek some guns that were supporting the Union left with vigor. Against such odds as now faced Longstreet's right, even the stubborn spirit of the Army of Northern Virginia could not stand much longer. The strongest were near collapse. Men walked like ghosts and fought like automatons. In many brigades ammunition was exhausted, and the soldier had to supply himself from the cartridge boxes of the fallen. Caissons were well-nigh empty. Regiments were commanded by captains, brigades by junior colonels. Divisions were confused. The smoke-filled streets of the little town were crowded with agonized wounded and with bewildered refugees. Still the concentration against the Confederate right grew; still the Federals hammered at the centre. An army that had never known defeat was perilously close to it.

Then, at 2:30, when the very seconds seemed to be ticking doom, from the south a group of officers rode up at the gallop on frothing horses. A. P. Hill had come at last! Starting from Harpers Ferry at 7:30, only an hour after he had received Lee's order to move to Sharpsburg with the utmost speed, Hill had covered seventeen miles in seven hours by pushing his troops to the utmost limit of their endurance.[31] He had only 3000 men and they were an hour and more behind him, panting on the road. They would arrive—but would they be too late? The roar of the Federal guns seemed to give an ominous answer.

Half an hour passed. The situation grew tenser. Then, at 3

---

[29] 2 *B. and L.*, 669–70. The stand made by the 27th N. C. and the 3d Arkansas was believed by many to have saved the day (H. M. Wagstaff, ed.: *The James A. Graham Papers*, 1861–1884, p. 132; 1 *N. C. Regiments*, 187–88).

[30] *O. R.*, 19, part 1, pp. 151, 956.   [31] *O. R.*, 19, part 1, p. 981.

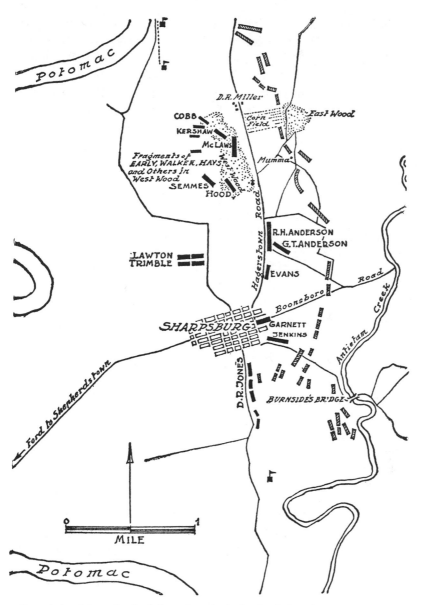

General situation on the Confederate front in the battle of Sharpsburg, about 4 P.M.
September 17, 1862.

o'clock, the threatened attack on the right broke in fury. Up the hill came the Federals, disdainful of losses. On to the confused ranks of D. R. Jones's division they fought their way. The Southern lines bent and shifted and almost broke as the weary men slowly gave ground. Everything now depended on the speed with which the four brigades of A. P. Hill[32] could reach the field and go into action. Until they could form, D. R. Jones's men must fight as best they could, and the artillery must dispute the Federals' advance. A retreat would be fatal—but was it inevitable? Had the left thrice closed the gap at the angle in the line, at desperate cost, to have the right doubled up? Along the front of McLaws and down to D. H. Hill's position a new attack was sweeping, bitterly contested by the survivors of Hill's regiments with the support of R. H. Anderson and of Hood, who was called back into the line for the third time that day. The field was close to chaos; the enemy was perilously near a victory. In the thickest of the action Lee at one time thought the Federals had the whole of Sharpsburg.[33] Steadily the Northerners advanced; stubbornly for an hour the Confederates resisted. The approximate situation along the front about 4 o'clock is shown on page 399.

The concentration against the Confederate right was overwhelming. It could only be a matter of minutes before the line must break. As Lee watched the columns that were plunging toward D. R. Jones's little division under a pall of smoke, a section of the Rowan Artillery passed by on its way to the front. Noticing that its commander, Lieutenant John A. Ramsay, had a telescope, Lee pointed to a distant column and asked, "What troops are those?"

Ramsay offered him the glass.

"Can't use it," Lee said, holding up his still bandaged fingers.

The lieutenant focused the telescope: "They are flying the United States flag."

Lee pointed to the right, where another line was now visible. He repeated his question—a fateful question, for the troops at which he looked were where they could flank Jones quickly.

Ramsay looked, looked for an instant that must have seemed an æon.

[32] Thomas's brigade had been left at Harpers Ferry to care for the captured property.
[33] 16 S. H. S. P., 395.

"They are flying the Virginia and Confederate flags," he reported. Lee did not move a muscle, though the words spelled salvation.

"It is A. P. Hill from Harpers Ferry," he said quietly, and, with no other word of explanation, he hastened to tell Ramsay to open on the enemy he had first sighted.

"General Lee," said Ramsay, "as soon as we fire we will draw the enemy's fire."

"Never mind me," the General answered.

The first shot of the battery exploded in the Federal ranks. Soon the column halted and then got out of range.

"Well done," said Lee. "Elevate your guns and continue to fire until those troops"—and he pointed again to Hill's vanguard, which was almost at right angles to the Federals—"come near your line of fire. Then change your position to the ridge on the right of the line and fire on the troops beyond the creek."[34]

With that he rode off to witness Hill's advance.[35] It came late, but it came with explosive power. Archer's brigade was on Hill's left as the division formed line of battle. Quickly his men were hurled against a Federal column that had overrun McIntosh's battery, sent to the field ahead of Hill's infantry. Raising a defiant rebel yell, Archer's troops swept forward without a halt, recovered McIntosh's guns, and continued to press the enemy. Gregg and Branch, on the right of Archer, awaited the Federal advance, repulsed it, and then followed steadily the swift retirement of the enemy. Pender was brought up from A. P. Hill's extreme right, but before he could engage, the bluecoats were surging back from the edge of the town and over the ridges to the shelter of the stream bank. Toombs and D. R. Jones joined in the pursuit, and Toombs was for pressing the advance beyond the creek.

The Federal artillery continued to challenge the hills; the heavy blue columns could still be glimpsed in overmastering strength across the creek and far around to the Federal right, where D. H. Hill and R. H. Anderson and McLaws and Walker and Jackson himself were counting the army of the dead. But the enemy had enough. The fine divisions of Burnside's corps—for he it was who made the attack on the Confederate right from across

[34] 1 *N. C. Regiments*, 575.   [35] *O. R.*, 19, part 1, p. 988.

the bridge that has since borne his name—were content to find such cover as they could away from the avenging rifles of A. P. Hill's infantry. Shining as red as if it reflected the blood on the Maryland hills,[36] the September sun set at last, and the battle was abruptly over, within an hour and a half after A. P. Hill's division had gone into action. Three thousand men, only 2000 of whom had been engaged in the final counterstroke, had saved Lee's army from almost certain destruction.

As quick darkness fell on the ghastly ridges, Lee found that he had fought three battles, one on each of the three segments into which the field was divided by nature. Hooker had attacked Lawton's and the Stonewall division on the Confederate left and had first opened the gap; Hood had closed it but had withdrawn before Mansfield's assault; Walker had arrived in time to drive Mansfield off, only to find himself hurled back to the Dunker Church by Sumner; then McLaws had charged and had ended the first battle. Sumner's attack, extending down the line of D. H. Hill, had opened the second battle of the day and had been followed by the repeated assaults of Franklin's corps. Before Franklin had worn himself out, Burnside had attacked on the Confederate right at the bridge and the third engagement had opened.

Each of the three battles had taken heavy toll. The dead were everywhere. The lanterns of the ambulance corps on both sides were soon flickering like the fireflies on a Southern river, but they did not reach all the corners of the fields or penetrate the shadows in the woods and under the rocks where the dead stiffened and the wounded cried in vain for water. Of the 36,000 infantry or thereabouts,[37] that Lee had in action from sunrise to nightfall, more than 10,000 were casualties.[38] Some units had been almost wiped out.[39] The dead included two of Lee's general officers—

---

[36] 2 B. and L., 684.

[37] Taylor's first estimate in his Four Years, p. 73, was 35,255. In 24 S. H. S. P., 272, he revised this to 36,175. Lee said (O. R., 19, part 1, p. 151) he had "less than 40,000 men."

[38] Lee's heavy casualties, as mentioned in note 89, p. 372, were not separately reported for the different battles of the Maryland campaign. The total, as computed by Alexander, op. cit., 274, was 13,609. Allowing 2900 for Boonsboro, Crampton's Gap, and the Harpers Ferry operations, the Southern casualties at Sharpsburg appear to have been around 10,700. Of the 87,176 that McClellan had at hand—though he had employed only a little more than half of them—his losses were 12,410 (O. R., 19, part 1, p. 200).

[39] The Texas brigade lost 560 of 854 (O. R., 19, part 1, p. 929). The 1st Texas lost 182 of 226 (ibid., 933). The 7th South Carolina lost 140 of 268 (ibid., 866).

L. O'B. Branch and William E. Starke. A third, G. B. Anderson, was mortally wounded.[40]

Grievous as the losses had been, and desperately as the outcome had hinged, time after time, on the arrival of Lee's scant reinforcements, what could the morrow hold except disaster more nearly complete? Every division was in line; in all northern Virginia there were no troops except Thomas's brigade at Harpers Ferry that could possibly be called upon, even in the direst emergency. Another series of attacks like those that had been delivered all day would certainly drive the army into the Potomac.

So, at least, thought nearly all the officers who made their way during the evening to the headquarters Lee had established in an open field west of the town. Jackson came, and both the Hills, and Hood and Early and D. R. Jones. Lee walked among them and got their reports of losses and weakness, but he was calm and as nearly cheerful as a man could be with almost a third of his army dead on the field or tortured with wounds. Not one word did he say of the thing that was uppermost in the minds of most of his officers—a retreat that night across the Potomac.

"Where is Longstreet?" Lee asked anxiously, after he had conversed with each of the others.

"I saw him at sundown, all right," said Major Venable.

At that moment "Old Pete" rode up. He had stopped in Sharpsburg to render what help he could to a group of ladies whose home was on fire, and he still had his unsmoked cigar in his mouth. Lee walked over to him as Longstreet dismounted.

"Ah," he said grasping his hand, "here is Longstreet; here is my old war horse." And he began a conversation in a low tone.[41]

When the last of the reports had been received, Lee concluded that an offensive was out of the question the next day, but he was confident that the army could and would defend its position if McClellan again attacked.[42] Artillery was to be placed to cover the bridge across which Burnside had attacked;[43] rations were to be cooked and delivered to the men who slept on their arms almost where the battle had opened; guards were to be sent back

[40] Two Federal corps commanders, Mansfield and Reno, and two divisional commanders, Richardson and Rodman, had also been slain.

[41] *Owen*, 156. General Sorrel (*op. cit.*, 116), represented Lee as saying, "Here comes my old warhorse from the field he has done so much to save!"

[42] 2 *B. and L.*, 671–72.   [43] *O. R.*, 19, part i, p. 1031.

to collect stragglers between the lines and the Potomac. After all this had been arranged without a touch of the theatrical, the division commanders were allowed to return to their troops, some of them frankly amazed at Lee's daring. What manner of man was he who would elect after that doubtful battle against vast odds to stand for another day with his back to the river?[44]

[44] From 1896, or thereabouts, General Stephen D. Lee was wont, when in reminiscent mood, to give a very dramatic picture of this meeting at Lee's headquarters on the night of the 17th. He said that the commanding general asked each subordinate in turn, "How is it on your part of the line?" Longstreet, according to General Stephen Lee, answered "As bad as bad can be." D. H. Hill said, "My division is cut to pieces." Jackson replied, "The greatest odds I have ever met—losses terrible." All advised a retreat, but Lee, rising more erect in his stirrups, said, "Gentlemen, we will not cross the Potomac tonight. You will go to your respective commands, strengthen your lines; send two officers from each brigade towards the ford to collect stragglers and get them up. Many others have come up. I have had the proper steps taken to collect all the men who are in the rear. If McClellan wants to fight in the morning, I will give him battle again. Go!" General Stephen D. Lee gave a written account of this incident to Hotchkiss, who quoted it in 3 *C. M. H.*, 356–57. White, *op. cit.*, 223–24, accepted it, as did David Knowles in his *American Civil War*, 107–8. Hotchkiss's version is printed, also, in 1 *N. C. Regiments*, 626. Despite the splendid character and standing of General Stephen D. Lee, whom he much admired, the writer has been unable to accept this account of the incident for these reasons: (1) Although there was a large company of officers present at headquarters, no one else mentioned any such conversation, as some at least would have been almost certain to do if it had been as dramatic as S. D. Lee represented it to have been; (2) neither Owen nor Sorrel, who saw Longstreet ride up, referred to any formal council of any sort; (3) Longstreet himself stated he reached headquarters after the others had reported, whereas Stephen D. Lee had him the first to answer Lee's question; (4) S. D. Lee said that General R. E. Lee was on his horse, which the other witnesses deny; (5) it was not Lee's custom to hold councils of this sort, nor to ask opinions of his generals as a group, in the presence of a large coterie of staff-officers. Major Hotchkiss, though he printed the story, took pains to attribute it to Stephen D. Lee and carefully eliminated Jackson's answer, which did not seem to him to have the ring of authenticity. Colonel Walter H. Taylor likewise believed that the story had been embellished with much telling, though he stated that he was unwilling to contradict what General Stephen D. Lee asserted as a fact. The writer believes that the version given in the text is substantially what happened.

CHAPTER XXVIII

SHARPSBURG IN REVIEW

THE seemly silence of a vast cemetery lay over the green ridges on the morning of September 18. The Confederate line had been drawn in about 200 yards on the centre; elsewhere it remained where it stood at the close of the battle. Numerous stragglers had come up during the night.[1] For the first time in days, meat and bread were eaten in reasonable abundance by all.

Nowhere on the long front did the enemy stir.[2] Reconnaissance showed that he had massed his artillery on the east bank of the Antietam, as if expecting an attack.[3] Encouraged by this, Lee ordered another examination of the left, to see if it would be possible to break through the enveloping lines on that flank and to resume manœuvre. He rode there himself to prepare for the move,[4] but to his manifest disappointment, Jackson had to confess that the enemy's guns were too strongly posted.[5]

Deprived of his only hope of a turning movement, Lee was still confident that he could resist successfully a Federal attack and he waited expectantly.[6] Noon brought no action by an enemy whose front had been aflame ere daybreak on the 17th. Most of the wounded had been evacuated. The spirit of the men was reviving somewhat. Still, the strength of the army was too low for Lee to consider an immediate offensive on so shallow a field.[7] Every sign indicated the early arrival of very substantial Federal reinforcements to take the place of the fallen.[8] If Lee could not attack where he stood, and if the enemy would not do so till fresh troops came up, it was the policy of prudence for the army to retire across the Potomac and to choose some new line of ad-

[1] *O. R.*, 19, part 1, p. 151.
[2] *McDaniel*, 16.
[3] *O. R.*, 19, part 1, p. 841.
[4] 1 *von Borcke*, 237.
[5] *White*, 225; *O. R.*, 19, part 1, p. 820.
[6] Cf. *O. R.*, 19, part 1, p. 151: "We awaited without apprehension the renewal of the attack."
[7] *O. R.*, 19, part 1, p. 151.
[8] *O. R.*, 19, part 1, p. 151.

vance for a continuance of the campaign of manœuvre. So, at 2 o'clock, Lee notified Longstreet of his intention to withdraw that night. He began quiet preparations[9] without repining. For there were other fords and other roads, surely, by which he could re-enter Maryland as soon as he was ready for new adventures there.

The day ended as quietly as it had opened and witnessed no challenge of the Confederate position. After midnight of the 18th–19th, Longstreet led the way over the Potomac and formed line of battle on the right bank.[10] Stuart crossed with part of the cavalry at Shepherdstown and advanced up the Potomac in order to return into Maryland again and vex the Federal flank if the retirement of the army was contested.[11] Fitz Lee was to remain and to cover the temporary retreat. Steadily through the night and into the morning of the 19th the gray columns passed back into Virginia at the ford a mile and a quarter below Shepherdstown. Lee himself took post at the crossing, to give directions to the teamsters,[12] and when Walker's division was over and its commander reported that only his wagons with his wounded and a single battery of artillery remained behind, Lee voiced an audible "Thank God." [13] Not so reverent were the men. When going northward, they had sung "My Maryland." Now, to quote one who waded the river, "all was quiet on that point. Occasionally some fellow would strike that tune, and you would then hear the echo, 'Damn my Maryland.'" [14]

Safely on Virginia soil again, Lee had only to fear a strong and vigorous pursuit by the Federals. They attacked Fitz Lee on the morning of the 19th as he guarded the rear[15] and they might attempt to force a crossing. To guard against this possibility, Lee directed General Pendleton to cover with his reserve artillery the ford by which the army had passed. To support the guns, Lee left Pendleton two infantry brigades, which, however, numbered only 600 bayonets.[16] The remainder of the tired army moved a

---

9 *O. R.*, 19, part 1, p. 841.   10 *O. R.*, 19, part 1, p. 841.
11 *O. R.*, 19, part 1, p. 151.   12 *Figg*, 57.   13 2 *B. and L.*, 682.
14 John H. Lewis: *Recollections from 1860 to 1865* (cited hereafter as *John H. Lewis*) 46.
15 *O. R.*, 19, part 2, p. 151.   16 *O. R.*, 19, part 2, pp. 613, 831 *ff*.

short distance back from the river and spread itself out on the hills to rest from its battles. Darkness on the 19th found Lee and his staff bivouacked under an apple tree, supperless but fed with the promise of long-desired silence.

About midnight Lee was awakened by an urgent visitor, none other than General Pendleton, whom he had left at the ford. That bewildered officer had a startling tale to tell. The Federals, he said, had silently crossed the river above the point he was guarding. His infantry support had been driven back, and . . . and all the guns of the reserve artillery had been captured.

"All?" asked Lee in amazement.

"Yes, General, I fear all."

One of Lee's staff officers, awakened by the conversation, heard Pendleton's confession and was so outraged that he sprang up and ran off to conceal his feelings. And well he might. To permit the enemy to cross the river unhindered and capture all the reserve artillery, some forty guns, was to threaten Virginia with new invasion and the army with ruin. Lee was, of course, much disturbed, but he said little; and as it was futile to attempt a counterattack in the dark, he decided to do nothing until daylight.[17]

When Jackson heard the news he showed more anxiety than he had ever exhibited during the war.[18] He rode back at dawn to the ford to supervise the operations of A. P. Hill, whom he directed to move up troops and drive the enemy into the river. Lee sent him two anxious messages during the morning of the 20th and was immensely relieved when Jackson characteristically answered his second note, "With the blessing of Providence, they will soon be driven back."[19] He was as good as his word. Hill's men attacked with the vigor they had shown at Sharpsburg and forced the enemy to abandon the south bank. Some two hundred were captured, many were drowned in attempting to recross, and the Virginia side of the stream was clear again. Instead of capturing the whole of the reserve artillery, as Pendleton in his alarm had feared, the Federals had taken only four pieces.[20] Mc-

[17] Mason, 151; Pendleton, 214; O. R., 19, part 1, pp. 142, 831 ff.
[18] Mrs. Jackson, 345.　　　　　　　[19] Ibid.
[20] O. R., 19, part 2, pp. 834, 957, 982. In Ham Chamberlayne, Virginian, edited by Churchill G. Chamberlayne, pp. 111, 115–16, 118, 134, a young artillerist in contemporary letters very tartly criticised General Pendleton's behavior on this occasion. It was re-

Clellan made no further attempt to pursue the Southern army.

Lee withdrew his command on September 20 to the vicinity of Martinsburg,[21] in order to manœuvre to the westward, to pass over the Potomac again at Williamsport, to move on Hagerstown, and to defeat McClellan.[22] If that could not be done, his plan was to occupy the enemy on the frontier, and, should the occasion require, to enter the Shenandoah Valley.[23] But it could not be. Even with the stragglers who had come up, he had only 36,418 infantry present for duty on September 22.[24] Absentees were scattered through a wide country. Thousands had no shoes, no blankets, and scarcely any garments.[25] Lee called vigorously for clothing and footgear and urged stern measures against straggling,[26] but for the time his initiative was paralyzed. He had to forgo all his plans for further manœuvre in Maryland in order to collect stragglers and refit the ragged faithful. What might be termed the "Maryland phase" of the campaign—it should not be regarded as a campaign in itself—was at an end.

Judged by comparative losses, Lee had given a good account of the men entrusted to him. He sustained a total of 13,609 casualties during the whole of the Maryland operation. The Federals lost in killed, wounded, and prisoners, including the Harpers Ferry and Martinsburg garrisons, 27,767.[27] A commander who disposes in thirteen days of enemy forces exceeding 50 per cent of his entire army is not usually charged with failure. The seventy-three guns and the 13,000 small arms captured at the Ferry were rich prizes. The 11,000 prisoners, duly exchanged, compensated for

ported to Jackson's staff-officers that Lee was greatly excited when he heard of the Federal advance, and that he was about to order the whole army to fall back on the line held by Longstreet. Jackson's quick action, his officers believed, saved Lee from a move that would have meant a speedy pursuit. Major R. H. Dabney, on the authority of D. H. Hill, so stated in his *Life of Jackson*, but when General Lee reviewed the MS. of that work, at the instance of Mrs. Jackson, he insisted that Dabney was in error. Dabney, forced to accept either D. H. Hill's statement or Lee's, struck out his own language and substituted Lee's words in quotation marks without citing his authority (*Cf. Dabney*, 577–78; R. H. Dabney: *Memorandum for Col. G. F. R. Henderson*, May 7, 1896—*McGuire Papers*).

[21] *O. R.*, 19, part 1, p. 152.

[22] *O. R.*, 19, part 2, pp. 626–27; W. H. Taylor to his sister, Sept. 28, 1862, *Taylor MSS.*

[23] *O. R.*, 19, part 1, p. 143.   [24] *O. R.*, 19, part 2, p. 621.

[25] S. G. Welch to his wife, Sept. 24, 1862, *Welch*, 31.

[26] *O. R.*, 19, part 1, p. 143. *Ibid.*, part 2, pp. 614, 617–19; cf. 1 *R. W. C. D.*, 157.

[27] *Alexander*, 273–75.

Lee's losses. He was not pleased, of course, at having to leave Maryland,[28] but he was gratified at what the army had achieved, and in time he became prouder of Sharpsburg than of any other battle he directed, because, as he believed, his men there faced the heaviest odds they ever encountered.[29] "History," he wrote Mr. Davis, "records but few examples of a greater amount of labor and fighting than has been done by this army during the present campaign." [30] In his congratulatory orders to the troops, issued on October 2, he praised the "indomitable courage [the army] has displayed in battle and its cheerful endurance of privation and hardship on the march." [31] The letters of one of his aides, Major Walter H. Taylor, contain a more detailed appraisal of the results and reflect the spirit of the command immediately after the return to Virginia. "Don't let any of your friends sing 'My Maryland,'" Taylor wrote, "—not 'my Western Maryland' anyhow." Harpers Ferry, Taylor went on, was compensation for all the trouble they had experienced. "The fight of the 17th," he said, "has taught us the value of our men, who can, even when weary with constant marching and fighting, and when on short rations, contend with and resist three times their own numbers. . . . We do not claim a victory. . . . It was not decisive enough for that. . . . If either had the advantage, it certainly was with us. . . . Congress must provide for reinforcing us, and then we will be enabled to realize their sanguine expectation. Give us the men and then talk about invading Pennsylvania. Our present army is not equal to the task, in my opinion. You see, the Federals get 3000 or 4000 new troops a day; and though we have done wonders, we can't perform miracles." [32]

Although this was fair judgment, by no means all historians have confirmed it. The three weeks covered by the Maryland expedition have been the most criticised of Lee's entire military career. His strategy in invading Maryland has been assailed; his division of his army for the capture of Harpers Ferry has been condemned as rash and unsoldierly; his dispatch of Longstreet to Hagerstown instead of keeping him with D. H. Hill on the march westward from Frederick has been held responsible for

[28] 2 B. and L., 674. [29] Andrew Hunter in 10 S. H. S. P., 503.
[30] O. R., 19, part 2, p. 633. [31] O. R., 19, part 2, pp. 644-45.
[32] W. H. Taylor to his sister, Sept. 21, 1862, Taylor MSS.

failure at Boonsboro; his decision to accept battle on the 17th, and, still more, his determination not to leave Maryland the night after the battle have been said to exhibit an infirmity of judgment he disclosed at no other time.

When biography becomes defense, it descends to special pleading and forfeits all confidence. The facts must speak for themselves. The duty of the biographer is discharged when he has arrayed them in their proper place and order. The informed reader who follows the successive steps of Lee's planning must himself be the judge of the fairness of these criticisms; but the reader, at the same time, must examine all the circumstances in their relation to the desperate leadership of a desperate cause.

If this be done, the unsuccessful outcome of the operations in Maryland will be found to hinge upon the unexpected rapidity and assurance of the Federal movements on and after September 13. A Union army that had suffered demoralization at Second Manassas, and was now under a commander who was deliberation incarnate, suddenly began to march swiftly on Lee. A new McClellan seemed to emerge, a McClellan who divined the movements of his opponent. Lee did not understand this at the time and did not know the explanation until the publication of McClellan's official report.[33] Then he learned that at Frederick, on the 13th, McClellan had received from the hands of a soldier, who had picked it up in the streets, a package of three cigars, wrapped in a headquarters copy of Special Orders No. 191, covering the movement to Harpers Ferry and the march of all the units of the army.[34] This information had dissipated the "fog of war," had galvanized McClellan and had made it possible for him to advance in full knowledge of where Lee was and of what Lee intended to do. If the Maryland operations be hypothetically reconstructed on the assumption that McClellan had not received a copy of these orders, the division of the army for the capture of Harpers Ferry appears as a move that the fast-marching Army of Northern Virginia was justified in making when the slow McClellan was on the eastern side of the mountains and had

[33] McClellan's preliminary report, dated Oct. 15, 1862, merely stated that he received at Frederick "reliable information of the movements and intentions of the enemy" (O. R., 19, part 1, p. 26). His full report, of Aug. 4, 1863 (ibid.. p. 36), quoted the "lost order."
[34] See p. 369, n. 72, supra. For the finding of the "lost order," see 2 B. and L., p. 603.

hardly ventured from the Washington defenses. It was not that Lee was reckless but that McClellan was lucky. To justify this criticism of dispersion of force it is necessary, therefore, to argue a fundamental that Lee subsequently expressed, namely, "It is proper for us to expect [the enemy] to do what he ought to do." [35] In other words, Lee can be condemned only on the assumption that he should have assumed that McClellan would discover the Confederate army was divided.

While Lee, then, is not reasonably censurable for detaching part of his troops to capture Harpers Ferry, he may be criticised for venturing into Maryland without reducing that post. He likewise erred in his logistics in that he underestimated by two days the time required to force the capitulation of the town. Still again, he made a mistake, if a very natural mistake, in dispatching Longstreet to Hagerstown, while D. H. Hill was left at Boonsboro. This final division of force was made on mistaken information that Federals were marching southward from Pennsylvania toward Hagerstown. Lee, of course, should have investigated this report, and he should have had cavalry at hand for that purpose. Small as was his mounted force, he should have had enough of it in advance to have ascertained the falsity of the report without having to send off infantry. He had made a like mistake in separating himself from his cavalry, though with less serious results, when he moved Longstreet to Groveton the previous month.

Turning now from those criticisms that concern the dispersal of force, it is necessary to inquire to what extent Lee was responsible for the straggling of his army, responsible, that is, in the sense that he might have prevented this loss of strength. No student can read of Sharpsburg and not have a shock when he learns that an army which numbered 53,000 just before it entered Maryland mustered less than 40,000 in the critical hour of combat, though it had not sustained heavy battle losses during the preliminaries. Lee himself was conscious of failure here, for he told Alexander, "My army is ruined by straggling." [36] There had never before been anything like it in the Army of Northern Virginia, and it never was repeated until the very end of the war.

[35] *O. R.,* 25, part 2, p. 624.   [36] 13 *S. H. S. P.,* 13.

There can be no sort of doubt that Lee underestimated the exhaustion of his army after Second Manassas. That is, in reality, the major criticism of the Maryland operation: he carried worn-out men across the Potomac. As for the specific reasons for excessive straggling, these have already been given in part. Many soldiers fell out from weariness and some because they were unwilling to invade the North, being concerned only with the defense of their own homes. At bottom, the greater part of the straggling was due to bad shoes and good roads. The footgear of many of the men had been worn thin by their stern, fast marching from the Rapidan to the Potomac. The hard Maryland roads completed the ruin of their shoes, slowed down their marching, and cut their feet horribly. Surgeon S. G. Welch, who examined many of the men after their return to Virginia, bore witness to the suffering sustained by men who were accustomed to soft dirt roads.[37] Straggling diminished as soon as the men's feet healed, and in the next phase of the campaign it was scarcely mentioned.

There remain but two criticisms to review. The first is that Lee should not have stood at Sharpsburg, but should have withdrawn to Virginia from South Mountain. The reasons that have been assigned in these pages for Lee's decision to fight at Sharpsburg are the only answer that can be made—perhaps all that need be made—to this contention. The second and final criticism is that, if Lee was justified at all in fighting at Sharpsburg, he should have retreated on the night of September 17 and should not have remained north of the Potomac on the 18th. This overlooks important facts. Lee needed time to secure the booty at Harpers Ferry, needed time to evacuate his wounded, and time to collect his stragglers. He could have done none of these things if he had retreated with an exhausted army on the night of the 17th. Believing that he could repulse McClellan's attacks the next day, he was willing to give battle to restore his army, to save his booty, and to care for his prisoners. The result vindicated his decision.[38]

[37] Welch, 31. Cf. Colonel Edward McCrady, Jr., in 13 S. H. S. P., 13.

[38] Most writers on this campaign have contended that the chief reason Lee did not retire was that he did not believe McClellan would attack. This is contrary to the spirit of Lee's remarks and preparations when he met his generals on the evening of the 17th, and contrary to other direct evidence. After the war, Lee stated to J. William Jones, "I

On the positive side, the Maryland phase of the campaign of manœuvre was important in the development of the army and in the training of its commanders. The operations demonstrated, in the first place, the fine quality of the Army of Northern Virginia in defensive fighting, with which it had previously had little or no experience, except that acquired by Jackson's command at Second Manassas. Lee had felt that he could usually count on the army to capture a position; Sharpsburg satisfied him that he could always rely on it to hold one.

The staff and the division commanders, in the second place, learned other new lessons in co-operation at Sharpsburg. In a few reports there were complaints that supports did not arrive or that troops on the flank did not do their part, but far more often even the ambitious generals, jealous of the fame of their own commands, paid tribute in their reports to the units in the line that gave them assistance. To read the official narratives of the Seven Days and to follow these with a close scrutiny of the official narratives of Sharpsburg is to marvel at the progress the army made during a little more than three months in welding itself into an effective weapon. No longer could it be called a congeries of regiments.

At Second Manassas the artillery had given a far better account of itself than in the swamps and thickets along the Chickahominy and the James. At Sharpsburg the artillery was much criticised by D. H. Hill,[39] and some of the gun positions were faulty and exposed, but many of the batteries had shared to the fullest the losses and laurels of the infantry.[40] This was the more to their credit because, from the Confederate side, Sharpsburg was rightly styled an "artillerists' hell." The Southern guns, well-served, were outranged along the whole front by the heavier, rifled metal of the Federals. The 20 and 24 pounder Parrott guns

remember distinctly that at Sharpsburg we held a large part of the battlefield, we remained in line of battle the whole of the next day, expecting—and in fact hoping for—an attack, and that we only withdrew upon information that the enemy was being largely reenforced" (*Jones*, 240). In his dispatch of Sept. 20, 1862, to President Davis, Lee explained why he had recrossed the river. He said, *inter alia* . . . "finding the enemy indisposed to make an attack on that day . . . I determined to cross the army to the Virginia side."

[39] *O. R.*, 19, part 1, p. 1026.

[40] S. D. Lee's battalion of 300 men had eighty-six casualties (*O. R.*, 19, part 1, p. 846).

redeemed many a Federal mistake on that red field, so much so that when Lee was back in Virginia, one of his first appeals to the ordnance department was to prepare ammunition and forward four 24 pounder Parrotts captured at Harpers Ferry. At the same time he directed that two-thirds of future issues of ammunition should be for the long-range or rifled guns.[41] Valor was not enough: the army could only stand on its guns. This was the third lesson learned at Sharpsburg.

Perhaps the greatest development of the Maryland operations was in Lee himself. He did not abandon his view that the chief duty of the commanding general was performed when he brought the troops into position on the field of battle. He continued to leave the tactical details of action to the brigade and division commanders. But in the emergency of the day at Sharpsburg, when every general had been occupied on his own front, the larger tactical direction of the action had fallen to Lee and he had discharged it flawlessly. Walker had been moved from the right to the left at precisely the right moment: McLaws had been directed to that part of the line where he was most needed; R. H. Anderson had been at hand to support D. H. Hill when that officer's own division had been shattered; A. P. Hill had been sent to precisely the place where his timely arrival, and only his arrival, could save the day. In a word, Sharpsburg was the first major battle that Lee had completely directed, and if he had ever believed, deep in his own heart, that his ability as a tactician was less than his skill as a strategist, Sharpsburg must have given him new confidence. For that action remains a model in the full employment of a small force for a defensive battle on the inner line.

[41] *O. R.*, 19, part 2, p. 613.

CHAPTER XXIX

MATCHING WITS WITH CHANGING OPPONENTS

PRECISELY two months after the exhausted survivors of the Maryland operations dragged themselves back across the Potomac they were marching swiftly in long, confident columns to meet the enemy on the Rappahannock. Never, except during the dreadful last retreat to Appomattox, was the army more disorganized than when it returned to Virginia on September 19, 1862; never, unless after Chancellorsville, was its spirit so high or assured as when it was moving on November 19, 1862, from the hills around Culpeper to the heights at Fredericksburg. It was a recovery in every respect as remarkable as that which in less than three weeks turned the defeated host of Pope into the storming columns that carried McClellan's flags to the walls of the Dunker Church. Perhaps it was a more extraordinary feat when the ability of the North to supply unlimited stores and abounding reserves after Second Manassas is compared with the feeble resources of men and *matériel* the Confederacy could command in making good the losses sustained in Maryland. This transformation of his army between Sharpsburg and Fredericksburg was essentially the work of Lee. The measures he took to refit and inspire it anew constitute a lesson that may some day be helpful to the commander of an American army who finds his ranks ragged and depleted after an indecisive battle.

Rest, food, refitting, and discipline—that was Lee's prescription. Rest was largely the gift of General McClellan, who was slow to start across the Potomac for a renewal of the campaign. Lee made the most of this adversary's delay. Except for necessary operations in destroying railroads and watching his opponent, he left the infantry as long as he could in untroubled camps. Most of the divisions, with little marching to do, got five full weeks for recuperation in a beautiful country, which was then very dry.[1]

[1] *Pendleton*, 228, 230.

Food he procured in an enlarged ration[2] by using nearby mills and by collecting cattle. It was not an easy task. Increasingly he had to devote his time to commissary duty. Before he left the Blue Ridge for the lower Rappahannock Valley, he received notice from the War Department that provisions were scarce and that a cut in the army ration seemed inevitable.[3] It was the first serious warning of the shortage of food that was ultimately to make near-starvation almost as potent a foe as the Army of the Potomac.

Refitting was a large undertaking because the army was in tatters, but Lee continued the appeals he made immediately after his return from Maryland. Ere long clothing and blankets in considerable quantities were forwarded to the army. A temporary shortage of arms was reported from Jackson's command, where 3000 men were without weapons, but this was promptly covered by the issue of captured rifles. As late as the battle of Fredericksburg, however, a few men were still supplied with smooth-bore muskets,[4] which they threw away for the better Federal arms they found on that field.[5]

The army's greatest lack was shoes and horses. On November 15 more than 6400 men in Longstreet's command were barefooted, and in that condition had to march to Fredericksburg.[6] The shoes that were supplied some of the units were mere strips of untanned hide, stitched crudely together as moccasins and so long that the men could scarcely walk in them.[7] The army mounts, which had seen very hard service, were greatly reduced, and in November suffered much from an outbreak of foot-and-mouth disease. Lee did what he could to conserve them by humane treatment and by the consolidation of small artillery units that used an unnecessary number of animals. He proposed, also, to transfer dismounted cavalrymen to the infantry and to offer cavalry service to foot

---

[2] *O. R.*, 21, 1016.

[3] *O. R.*, 19, part 2, pp. 623, 672 ff., 699–700, 716; *ibid.*, 21, 1018.

[4] *O. R.*, 19, part 2, p. 646; *O. R.*, 21, p. 568.

[5] Cf. *Wolseley:* "Officers have declared to me, that they have seen whole regiments go into action with smooth-bore muskets and without greatcoats, and known them in the evening to be well provided with everything—having changed their old muskets for rifles."

[6] *O. R.*, 19, part 2, p. 718. These figures do not include Ransom's division, which was detached and made no report. Some men went as long as two months without shoes (*cf.* Richard Lewis to his mother, Nov. 20, 1862; *Camp Life of a Confederate Boy*, 35).

[7] *John H. Lewis*, 53–54.

soldiers who would procure mounts. The War Department was urged to bring horses from Texas, where they were still abundant. The utmost vigilance on Lee's part, and Stuart's success in capturing some 1200 horses in Pennsylvania in October,[8] scarcely sufficed to keep the wagons rolling and the cavalry in the field. The final exhaustion of the horse supply, which was destined to cripple the army in the winter of 1864–65, was ominously forecast as early as the autumn of 1862.[9]

Lee's disciplinary measures were incident to his effort to increase the army's strength and were of three sorts—the collection of stragglers, recruitment, and reorganization under competent officers. Continuing his efforts to procure stern legislation for dealing with stragglers, he had the nearby country combed for them. J. R. Jones reported from the Shenandoah Valley that he had sent back between 5000 and 6000 by September 27, and on October 8 Secretary Randolph noted with satisfaction that the strength of the army had increased by 20,000 in eight days.[10] Convalescents were forwarded in considerable numbers. Under the conscription law, the vigorous enforcement of which Lee warmly urged,[11] new recruits were sent in a constant if small stream. These men, however, so generally fell sick that Lee asked the War Department to detain them at camps of instruction until they had passed through the communicable diseases which were then prevalent in the ranks.[12] By October 10, Lee had 64,273 present for duty; by October 20 he could count 68,033; and according to the tri-monthly return of November 10 he had 70,909,[13] though he did not then consider that he had half enough men to resist the enemy on even terms.[14]

Besides the consolidation of the weaker artillery companies, which encountered some legal difficulties,[15] Lee's scheme of reorganization involved the division of the cavalry into four brigades. His son Rooney was promoted to the command of one of these, with the rank of brigadier general.[16] Another step in

---

[8] See *infra*, p. 423.
[9] *O. R.*, 19, part 2, pp. 642–43, 647, 709, 716.
[10] *O. R.*, 19, part 2, pp. 625, 629, 640, 656–57, 679, 722.
[11] *O. R.*, 19, part 2, pp. 625, 626 *ff.*
[12] *O. R.*, 19, part 2, pp. 643, 657, 679; *Welch*, 34; 1 *R. W. C. D.*, 168.
[13] *O. R.*, 19, part 2, pp. 660, 674, 713.   [14] 1 *R. W. C. D.*, 187.
[15] *O. R.*, 19, part 2, pp. 632, 646 *ff.*, 656.   [16] *O. R.*, 19, part 2, p. 712.

reorganization was the choice of the better qualified officers for the commands that had lost their leaders,[17] though little progress was made in applying the new law Congress had passed for the demotion of incompetent officers.[18] A vigorous effort was made, at the same time, to strengthen the Texas units,[19] which had now become Lee's favorite shock-troops.

The most important step in reorganization was the division of the armies into two corps, the first under Longstreet and the second under Jackson. Congress had passed an act providing for the appointment of lieutenant generals, and Davis had written for recommendations.[20] Lee unhesitatingly endorsed Longstreet. In advocating like rank for Jackson, Lee employed language which records the final dissipation of all his doubts as to "Stonewall's" willingness to co-operate. Lee said: "My opinion of the merits of General Jackson has been greatly enhanced during this expedition. He is true, honest and brave; has a single eye to the good of the service, and spares no exertion to accomplish his object." [21] The formal announcement of these promotions was not made until November 6.[22] Had Lee thought it necessary to divide the army into three corps, he would have recommended the promotion of A. P. Hill, whom he ranked next after Longstreet and Jackson.[23]

Lee sometimes confided to his staff officers that he wished some capable brigadier headed a division commanded by a mediocre major general;[24] but in this instance he declined to recommend promotions for the vacated places of the new lieutenant generals. "I believe you have sufficient names before you," he told the President, "to fill the vacancies. Your own knowledge of the

---

[17] Cf. O. R., 19, part 2, pp. 639, 683, 705.   [18] McCabe, 280.

[19] Lee wrote General Lewis T. Wigfall: "I rely upon those we have in all tight places, and fear I have to call upon them too often . . . with a few more such regiments as Hood now has, as an example of daring and bravery, I could feel much more confident of the campaign" (N. A. Davis, 114–15). Despite an unfavorable inspection report of Hood's division (O. R., 19, part 2, p. 718), Lee was unwilling to disturb the command to give place to General W. H. C. Whiting, who had returned from furlough (O. R., 19, part 2, p. 681).

[20] O. R., 19, part 2, pp. 633–34.

[21] O. R., 19, part 2, p. 643.   [22] O. R., 19, part 2, pp. 698–99.

[23] O. R., 19, part 2, p. 643. Hill at the time was under charges of neglect of duty, preferred by Jackson, with whom Hill was at odds, precisely as he had been with Longstreet. Lee sought to allay this bad feeling and declined to bring Hill to trial (O. R., 19, part 2, p. 729 ff.). The "charges and specifications" have disappeared from the records.

[24] Taylor's Four Years, 147.

claims and qualifications of the officers will, I feel assured, enable you to make the best selection." [25] This was dangerous deference, for the responsibility would rest on Lee and the price might be the lives of hundreds of men, if the President erred in his choice. Lee probably refrained because he knew the embarrassments of the President at the time. A growing jealousy of the Virginia generals was being voiced by those who felt that the soldiers of the Old Dominion were being unduly advanced. There was much insistence on "recognizing" the different states in the distribution of military honors. Politicians of a certain stamp put residence above merit. Graduates of the United States Military Academy, also, were regarded with disfavor by some ardent patriots who had no military education.[26]

Such were Lee's methods in refitting and reorganizing the army for the next struggle. It was a work he had been called upon to perform after the Seven Days, a work to which he had to give himself at the close of nearly all his subsequent campaigns. While he labored in this manner to raise the efficiency of his forces, two other influences, very different in their nature, operated on individual soldiers. By proclamation of September 23, President Lincoln announced that he would emancipate on January 1, 1863, all slaves in districts where the people were "in rebellion against the United States." [27] This confirmed the belief of Southerners that the election of Lincoln was a conspiracy against the Constitution. A new sense of justification showed itself in the resistance of the South. A little later there began in the army a "revival of religion" that spread from division to division for more than a year. This improved discipline and helped to give the army the quality that Cromwell desired when he said he wanted only such men as "made some conscience" of what they did.[28]

Straggling ceased altogether.[29] By October 12 an observant

[25] *O. R.,* 19, part 2, p. 643.
[26] *Cf.* T. R. R. Cobb, Oct. 9, 1862: "Let me but get away from these 'West Pointers.' . . . Never have I seen men who had so little appreciation of merit in others. Self-sufficiency and self-aggrandizement are their great controlling characteristics" (28 *S. H. S. P.,* 297).
[27] III *O. R.,* 2, p. 584.   [28] *Long,* 230. See *infra,* p. 496.
[29] *Cf.* A. P. Hill in his report on Fredericksburg, *O. R.,* 21, 647: "The absence of straggling was remarkable. . . ."

officer could write: "Our army is in splendid condition. It has been rapidly increasing during the last three weeks by conscripts and convalescents who have been coming in. If the enemy cross the Potomac to begin the offensive, we shall, I think, have another great battle . . . , and I feel sure that it will be a splendid victory for us." [30] At headquarters, Major Walter Taylor echoed the same opinion.[31] Colonel Garnet Wolseley, later Field-Marshal Lord Wolseley of the British army, who visited Lee at this time, observed no signs of demoralization. "I never saw [an army]," he wrote after he left, "composed of finer men, or that looked more like *work* than that portion of General Lee's army which I was fortunate enough to see inspected." As for Lee, "he spoke," Wolseley attested, "as a man proud of his country, and confident of ultimate success under the blessings of the Almighty, whom he glorified for past successes, and whose aid he invoked for all future operations." [32] It may have been Wolseley whose face betrayed some surprise when he saw how ragged were the breeches of Hood's men after their first files had passed in review. "Never mind the raggedness, Colonel," Lee said quietly, "the enemy never sees the backs of my Texans." [33]

The first stages of the reorganization were passed while Lee was still handicapped by the injury he had received on August 31. All his correspondence had to be conducted with one or another of his staff officers as amanuensis. It was not until approximately October 12 that he was able to dress and undress himself with his left hand, and, with his right, to sign his name.[34] Trying as were the times, and hard as were his duties, he did not forget the amenities. There was a note of regret in his reference to the death of his "old engineering comrade, General Mansfield," his superior officer more than thirty years before at Cockspur Island, who had been killed at Sharpsburg.[35] When General Kearny's widow applied for the mount and horse furnishings that had been captured when that gallant Federal had fallen at Ox Hill, Lee had them appraised, paid for them himself, and sent them

---

[30] *Memoir and Memorials, Elisha Franklin Paxton* (cited hereafter as *Paxton*), 66 The quotation is from a letter to his wife.

[31] W. H. Taylor to his brother, Oct. 15, 1862, *Taylor MSS.*

[32] *Wolseley*, 21, 24.　　　　　　　[33] Polley: *Hood's Texas Brigade*, 239.

[34] *R. E. Lee, Jr.*, 79.　　　　　　　[35] *Mason*. 148.

to Mrs. Kearny, pending adjustment by the War Department.[36]

The last days of his convalescence were brightened by a visit from Custis, who came from Richmond to see him,[37] but within a few weeks he was dealt a personal blow far worse than a physical injury. His second daughter, Annie, had gone to the Warren White Sulphur Spring, North Carolina, and had been stricken ill there. On October 20, she died. Lee had known of her illness and had been most apprehensive, but he was not prepared for her death when he received the announcement of it. After he got the letter, he pulled himself together and went over the official correspondence of the morning in Major Taylor's company, without revealing his loss or showing his emotion. After Major Taylor left, he took out the letter again and as he read its pathetic details of the passing of the girl—she was only twenty-three—he could no longer repress his grief. When Taylor unceremoniously re-entered the tent a few minutes later, Lee was weeping. As soon as he could control himself, he sent word to his sons in the army. "I cannot express the anguish I feel at the death of my sweet Annie," he wrote Mrs. Lee. "To know that I shall never see her again on earth, that her place in our circle, which I always hoped one day to enjoy, is forever vacant, is agonizing in the extreme. But God in this, as in all things, has mingled mercy with the blow, in selecting that one best prepared to leave us. May you be able to join me in saying, 'His will be done' . . ."[38] To his brother, Charles Carter Lee, he wrote in the same spirit. God "has taken," he said, "the purest and best; but his will be done."[39] His grief hung long and heavily upon him. From Fredericksburg, the next month, when every day threatened battle, he wrote to his daughter, Mary: "In the quiet hours of the night, when there is nothing to lighten the full weight of my grief, I feel as if I should be overwhelmed. I have always counted, if God should spare me a few days after this Civil War was ended, that I should have her with me, but year after year my hopes go out, and I must be resigned."[40]

Meantime, the tragedy was shaping itself again to a bloody

---

[36] O. R., 19, part 2, pp. 645, 654–55.   [37] R. E. Lee, Jr., 79.
[38] Lee to Mrs. Lee, Oct. 26, 1862, R. E. Lee, Jr., 79–80; Taylor's Four Years, 76.
[39] Oct. 26, 1862; 31 Confederate Veteran, 287.   [40] R. E. Lee, Jr., 80.

climax. Lee knew too well the weakness of Harpers Ferry to attempt to hold it. On September 22 it was occupied by Sumner's corps.[41] Anticipating no early attack from this vanguard, Lee set a large force to work destroying twenty miles of the track of the Baltimore and Ohio west of the town.[42] While maintaining his own line of communications down the Shenandoah Valley by means of his wagons,[43] he proceeded, also, to break up the railway between Harpers Ferry and Winchester, so as to retard an advance by the enemy in that direction.[44] Before the wrecking of the Baltimore and Ohio was well under way, he retired with the greater part of the army a few miles higher up the valley pike, with his left at Bunker Hill and his right near Winchester.[45] His headquarters were established at Falling Waters.[46]

Federal activity in North Carolina and signs of an advance from Norfolk up the south side of the James River about this time created some alarm in Richmond and led to an agitation for the return of the Army of Northern Virginia.[47] Lee was not unmindful of the safety of the capital, but he believed that McClellan's first advance would be toward the Virginia Central Railroad, which he thought he could protect by manœuvring on the flank of the enemy.[48] However, in order to ascertain what the enemy was doing and at the same time to delay and demoralize him, he ordered Stuart on October 8 to undertake a cavalry raid into Maryland and Pennsylvania. He outlined Stuart's route in some detail and set the destruction of the bridge over the Concocheague at Chambersburg as his main object. If this could be done, the Cumberland Valley Railroad would be cut and McClellan would be forced to bring up his supplies over the Baltimore and Ohio westward from Baltimore.[49]

Stuart left camp with 1800 men and four guns on October 9, crossed the Potomac at McCoy's Ford, between Williamsport and Hancock, on the morning of October 10, reached Chambers-

[41] O. R., 19, part 1, p. 69.
[42] O. R., 19, part 2, p. 623; Grayjackets, 176; Early, 163.
[43] O. R., 19, part 2, p. 627.
[44] O. R., 19, part 2, pp. 673–75. This work was completed Oct. 23.
[45] O. R., 19, part 1, p. 152. The best map for this area is O. R. Atlas, Plate XXVII.
[46] 1 von Borcke, 288; Wolseley, 20–21.
[47] O. R., 19, part 2, p. 634; 1 R. W. C. D., 170, 174.
[48] O. R., 19, part 2, pp. 641, 644, 646.
[49] See his orders to Stuart in O. R., 19, part 2, p. 55. The Cumberland Valley Railroad then had its southern terminus at Hagerstown.

burg, Penna., that night, and sent a detachment to destroy the bridge. Unfortunately, the structure was found to be of iron and defied the wreckers. Riding fast from Chambersburg to escape the Federal cavalry, Stuart passed through Emmitsburg and Hyattstown and recrossed the Potomac at White's Ferry, near Poolsville, on the morning of October 12. He brought off 1200 horses, leaving 60 of his own jaded mounts on the road, and escorted into the Confederate lines some thirty Federal office-holders as hostages. In twenty-seven hours he had covered eighty miles with no casualties except one man wounded and two miss-ing. The Federal cavalry that followed him lost nearly half their men from straggling and were useless for days as a result of their mad riding.[50]

Stuart's observations on this Chambersburg raid convinced Lee that McClellan was not withdrawing troops eastward,[51] but Lee did not interpret this to mean that the Army of the Potomac had abandoned all hope of moving on the Confederate capital. Although he considered that Richmond was in no immediate danger, he believed that if McClellan found it impossible to ad-vance southward to the Virginia Central Railroad, he would later move against Richmond from the south side of the James. Mean-time, the longer the Army of Northern Virginia could delay the enemy on the frontier, the shorter the period McClellan would have for field operations.

This last consideration became the major factor in Lee's plan of campaign. Whatever was done and whatever had to be risked, Lee reasoned that he must fight for time. A junction with his ally, winter, was his main objective.[52] Temporarily, to create a diversion and to interrupt McClellan's communications with the West, he had considered an advance by Loring from the Kanawha Valley to the line of the Baltimore and Ohio, but the lateness of the season and a threat by the enemy in the Kanawha district compelled him to forgo this.[53]

On October 16 word reached headquarters that a mixed Federal force of some size had crossed the Potomac and was making its

---

[50] O. R., 19, part 2, p. 52 ff.; H. B. McClellan, 136 ff.; Thomason, 297 ff.
[51] O. R., 19, part 2, p. 51.
[52] O. R., 19, part 2, pp. 659, 662–63, 669, 675, 680, 681, 682.
[53] O. R., 19, part 2, pp. 625–26, 637–38, 665, 666.

way southwestward from Shepherdstown toward the Confederate front. Lee hoped that if McClellan were advancing, he would move up the Valley of the Shenandoah, but his reports during the day favored the view that McClellan was merely feeling out the Confederate lines in force. Stuart opposed the enemy's progress and fell slowly back before him. To strengthen Stuart against eventualities, A. P. Hill was ordered in support. Early in the morning of the 17th, when couriers reported the enemy still advancing on the road that led from Kearneysville on the Baltimore and Ohio to Smithfield,[54] Lee issued precautionary orders[55] and rode out in person to examine the situation. Finding the division commanders on the alert and the enemy hesitant in his movements, he did not linger long at the front. With a few staff officers and couriers, he rode back toward headquarters. Ten minutes after he crossed the Kearneysville-Smithfield road, a small Federal scouting party galloped by on its way to Smithfield. It was Lee's closest call since the August morning when he had met a similar Federal cavalcade near Salem, on his march to join Jackson at Groveton. Before the day was over, the enemy returned the way he had come. The alarm was past for the time, and the army settled down once more to await McClellan's next move.[56]

Convinced that the blow would fall soon, Lee made his preparations with care. He ordered the routes through the Blue Ridge examined,[57] and on October 22 he directed General J. G. Walker to take his division eastward over the mountains to Upperville to check raids in that district and to observe the enemy.[58] Stuart was directed to place cavalry on the eastern flank of Walker, and Colonel John R. Chambliss, commanding a small cavalry force around Fredericksburg, was told to connect his pickets with those of Walker. In this way Lee put a screen between himself and the enemy all the way from Martinsburg to Fredericksburg, a distance of approximately ninety-five miles.[59]

[54] Smithfield is about five miles west of Charlestown.
[55] O. R., 19, part 2, p. 670.
[56] O. R., 19, part 2, p. 82 ff.; 1 von Borcke, 309 ff.; B. W. Crowninshield: History of the First Massachusetts Cavalry, 83.
[57] Pendleton, 231.
[58] General Walker, assigned other duty, was relieved on Nov. 7 by Brigadier General Robert Ransom, Jr. (O. R., 19, part 2, pp. 703-4).
[59] O. R., 19, part 2, pp. 675, 676, 678.

Four days passed. Then, on October 26, the outposts reported that the Federal army was crossing the Potomac, apparently in full strength. More than a month had been gained; the gray regiments were rested and ready; and Lee, though conscious of the odds, faced his old antagonist with steadfast heart. On the very day of McClellan's crossing he wrote his brother: "I am glad you derive satisfaction from the operations of the army. I acknowledge nothing can surpass the valor and endurance of our troops, yet while so much remains to be done, I feel as if nothing had been accomplished. But we must endure to the end, and if our people are true to themselves and our soldiers continue to discard all thoughts of self and to press nobly forward in defence alone of their country and their rights, I have no fear of the result. We may be annihilated, but we cannot be conquered. No sooner is one army scattered than another rises up. This snatches from us the fruits of victory and covers the battlefields with our dead. Yet what have we to live for if not victorious?" [60]

In this spirit Lee once more asked himself the vexing old question: What will the enemy do? McClellan had two routes of immediate advance open to him. First, he could move southward down the Shenandoah Valley toward Staunton. By holding all the gaps of the Blue Ridge this would be a reasonably safe move, but it involved the maintenance of lengthy communication by wagon train. Further, as Jackson had demonstrated, the Shenandoah Valley afforded excellent ground for strategic defensive manœuvre, especially in the vicinity of the Massanutton Mountain. The other route open to McClellan was Pope's old road east of the Blue Ridge, with Gordonsville and the seizure of the Virginia Central Railroad as the first objectives. This line was much less protected than that of the Shenandoah Valley, but it had the great advantage of offering railway communication *via* the Orange and Alexandria Railway. The two routes appear on the accompanying sketch.

From the time of his return to Virginia after the Maryland expedition, Lee had hoped that McClellan would enter the Shenandoah Valley, but he considered it more likely his foe

[60] To Charles Carter Lee; 31 *Confederate Veteran*, 287.

would move southward on the eastern side of the Blue Ridge, and he had to provide for either contingency. He did so without delay. On October 28 he ordered the army divided. Jackson was to withdraw a few miles up the Valley to the road from Berry-

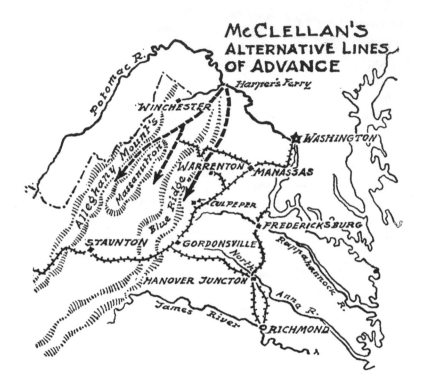

McCLELLAN'S ALTERNATIVE LINES OF ADVANCE

ville to Charlestown, where he would have better forage and would be nearer the passes of the Blue Ridge. Semi-independent command was given "Stonewall," with instructions to act at discretion when he could not readily communicate with army headquarters. Longstreet was to march for Culpeper, accompanying Lee.[61] The two corps were to keep in touch with each other, so that they could be united on either side of the Blue Ridge as McClellan's manœuvres might require. If the enemy advanced up the Valley in force, Jackson was to delay him, retire before

---

[61] From Culpeper, rail communications to the Virginia Central could be opened, as the destroyed bridge at Rappahannock station was replaced and ready for use on Oct. ₇ (O. R., 19, part 2, p. 637).

him, and then make for the gaps through which, if necessary, he might form junction with Longstreet. In case the enemy marched southward east of the mountains and gave him an opening, Jackson was to move on the rear of the Unionists and cut their communications. Longstreet was to defend the direct line of advance east of the Blue Ridge. The cavalry was to be divided between the corps, and one brigade was to operate on the flank and in front of McClellan.[62]

At this stage of his preparations Lee was called to Richmond, which he had not visited since he had left on August 14 to join Jackson at Gordonsville. The reason for the summons was the desire of the President to discuss with him the size of the reinforcements that could be sent Lee from southern Virginia and eastern North Carolina, where some believed the enemy had abandoned all thought of an early offensive. The question was a delicate one, for opinion as to the intentions of the Federal garrisons on the coast was divided. Lee was in Richmond on November 1[63] and conferred with the President and General S. G. French, who was in immediate command of the threatened area. At the "Gray House," Lee asked French what was the least number of men he would require to hold his line for a short time. After reflecting, French said 6000. "That's reasonable," Lee answered. "When you return, order all above that number to report to me." French remembered this as an example of Lee's consideration in not strengthening his army at the expense of other officers charged with heavy responsibility.[64]

By November 6, Lee was back at Culpeper, where he established his headquarters in a pine thicket.[65] He found the situation developing fast. The enemy was advancing with some vigor between the Blue Ridge and the Orange and Alexandria Railroad and was holding all the passes on his right flank and in rear of his right. It seemed for the time as if McClellan were seeking to interpose between Jackson and Longstreet, though Lee did not believe his cautious antagonist would venture far southward on the eastern side of the mountains, so long as Jackson remained potentially on his flank. Neither did he believe McClellan would

---

[62] *O. R.*, 19, part 2, pp. 685–86, 687, 689.   [63] 1 *R. W. C. D.*, 179.
[64] *French*, 150.   [65] 2 *von Borcke*, 61.

try to descend on Jackson unless he felt able to make an over-whelming detachment of force for that purpose. His first hope was to turn McClellan's columns near the Blue Ridge. Concluding that this was not possible, he suggested to Jackson that he move up the Valley so that he could quickly unite with Longstreet through Swift Run Gap in case of emergency.[66]

Lee learned on the 7th that the advance of the enemy had reached Warrenton and that his cavalry was on the Rappahannock.[67] During the next few days he was apprized of the arrival of further units around Warrenton. The cavalry was active, and there were some indications that the enemy, after all, might be planning to march into the Shenandoah Valley, in which case Lee intended to throw Longstreet against his line of communications.[68] But nothing happened. To the surprise of many, the general advance stopped. On the 10th, within twenty-four hours after the reason for this halt became known to the Army of the Potomac, it was reported to Lee: McClellan had been superseded on the 7th by Major General Ambrose E. Burnside and on the 9th had transferred command.[69]

The news was received by the Confederates with regrets and rejoicings curiously mingled. Lee was sorry that his old associate of the Mexican War was no longer to oppose him. "We always understood each other so well," he said to Longstreet. "I fear they may continue to make these changes till they find some one whom I don't understand." He was sorry, too, that a man who had always conducted operations with science and humanity was supplanted by one whose respect for principle he had no means of determining until Burnside should begin field operations.[70] Longstreet was glad of the change, because he thought McClellan was developing as a general and, if left in command, would have given the Army of Northern Virginia no further breathing spell.[71] Others reasoned that the change was to the advantage of the South, since Burnside was regarded as less able than "Little Mac."[72] Some of the officers of the army insisted

---

66 *O. R.*, 19, part 2, pp. 695, 696, 697, 698, 701–2, 703, 704, 705, 710.
67 *O. R.*, 19, part 2, p. 701.
68 *O. R.*, 19, part 2, pp. 705–6, 706–7, 711; R. E. Lee to Custis Lee, Jones, *L. and L.*, 199.
69 *O. R.*, 21, 83.
70 2 *B. and L.*, 70; *Longstreet*, 291.
71 *Longstreet*, 291.
72 *Mrs. McGuire.* 170.

that the removal of McClellan would demoralize the troops of his former command, who had held him in high esteem[73]—a feeling that was echoed in Warrenton by many of the retiring leader's old lieutenants.[74]

McClellan left to return no more. Lee did not cross swords with him thereafter and never saw him again. To the last manœuvre, in this final phase of McClellan's operations, Lee had reasoned rightly as to his opponent's intentions. Just as Lee had believed, McClellan had moved southward in the hope of striking at Gordonsville. If that proved impossible, McClellan's plan was to shift to Fredericksburg and to advance on Richmond by that line or preferably to move the army by sea to James River.[75] McClellan had not been confident that his proposed advance on Gordonsville was practicable. His partial success at Sharpsburg had not lessened his secret feeling of inferiority to Lee, whose strength he overestimated in November as in June. Even as stout a soldier as George Gordon Meade had not been hopeful of out-manœuvring the Confederates. "They are so skillful in strategy," he bluntly confessed.[76] Besides, Meade did not believe that the Orange and Alexandria Railroad could handle more than one-third of the supplies the army would require.

On November 12, Lee began to suspect that the change of commanders would involve a change of plan. Although the only definite evidence he had of this was the failure of the Federals to move southward, he thought it likely that the enemy might turn down the Rappahannock to Fredericksburg. He sent warning to Jackson that such a move might require his immediate junction with Longstreet and he told him to be prepared to start on a moment's notice.[77] The next day Stuart reported that the enemy seemed to be moving his right flank away from the mountains. Elsewhere there was no activity, but the Federal cavalry outposts were found along the Rappahannock River.[78] The morning of the 14th brought no new developments, yet Lee was more than ever inclined to think the enemy's advance was down the river toward deep water and the Richmond, Fredericksburg and Potomac Railroad. Again he warned "Stonewall" that he must soon

73 T. R. R. Cobb in 28 *S. H. S. P.*, 299.   74 *Cf. Recollections of John Gibbon*, 96.
75 *O. R.*, 19, part 1, p. 87.   76 1 *Meade*, 324.
77 *O. R.*, 19, part 2, p. 715.   78 *O. R.*, 19, part 2, p. 716, 717.

be ready to start over the mountains.[79] "We will endeavor to confuse and confound [the enemy] as much as our circumstances will permit," he told Jackson.[80] Lee had at that time one regiment of cavalry, four companies of Mississippi infantry, and a battery at Fredericksburg, and he now ordered the commanding officer there to destroy the railroad between that point and Aquia, where the Federals had a landing-place directly off the Potomac. On the 15th, hearing that the enemy was beginning to move from Warrenton toward the Orange and Alexandria Railroad, Lee directed a second battery and a regiment of infantry to the Rappahannock town.[81] Another day of suspense passed. Then, on the 17th, there were doubts in his mind for a few hours whether or not Fredericksburg was the enemy's goal;[82] but while he weighed evidence and argued probabilities, scouts reported that three brigades of the Union infantry were moving against the city and that several Federal transports and gunboats had entered Aquia Creek.[83]

This virtually decided the question in Lee's mind. He gave orders for one division of Longstreet's corps to take the road toward Fredericksburg, and he determined to send the rest of the corps after it the next morning if the news of the Federal march was confirmed.[84] Jeb Stuart undertook a forced reconnaissance across the Rappahannock on the 18th to see if the enemy had left Warrenton; Jackson was advised to move at least a part of the Second Corps to the mountains, preparatory to rejoining the main army; the leading division of Longstreet's command was ordered to continue its march toward Fredericksburg.[85] The reserve artillery also was put on the road.[86] It was a day of immense activity in the camps and at headquarters.

Lee had no desire to make a stand on the south bank of the Rappahannock at Fredericksburg. The position had no depth and was dominated by the heights on the north bank, which the enemy was certain to occupy. The Federal line of communica-

[79] O. R., 19, part 2, pp. 717, 720, 721.
[80] O. R., 19, part 2, p. 721.   [81] O. R., 21, 1013, 1014, 1017.
[82] O. R., 21, 1014–15.   [83] O. R., 21, 550.
[84] O. R., 21, 1016; ibid., 51, part 2, p. 646; Long, 234.
[85] Longstreet, 293; O. R., 21, p. 1019; ibid., 51, part 2, p. 647.
[86] O. R., 21, 1019.

tions was short. Strategically, it was far preferable to withdraw to the line of the North Anna, where the enemy's communications would be more extended and where, as Lee then believed, the nature of the ground would make a counterstroke possible.[87] It was with this object in view that he ordered a division of Longstreet's corps, early on the 18th, to make for the North Anna.[88] But during the day of the 18th one of his spies reported that the force advancing toward Fredericksburg consisted of Sumner's corps only. Lee decided that if no other force were moving to Fredericksburg he should endeavor to hold Sumner on the line of the Rappahannock until Burnside's purpose was disclosed. It might even be possible to surprise Sumner in an attempt to cross the river.[89] The prudence of standing on the Rappahannock seemed the stronger when Jackson reported some movements of the enemy that suggested a possible advance from Harpers Ferry up the Shenandoah Valley.[90] Most particularly, Lee decided to oppose Burnside on the Rappahannock because he could not afford to lose the supplies in the lower valley of that river or to open to the enemy territory south of Fredericksburg which the Federals had not previously pillaged.[91]

For these reasons the division that had been ordered to the North Anna was directed temporarily to take position midway between that river and Fredericksburg.[92] The rest of Longstreet's corps was ordered to move for Fredericksburg on the 19th. The same day Lee broke up his headquarters at Culpeper and started to the new scene of action,[93] confident that the enemy was preparing to advance via Fredericksburg on Richmond.[94] At the instance of Jackson, who was hoping for the opportunity of a counterstroke in the Valley, Lee did not issue peremptory orders for the Second Corps to rejoin immediately, but he again cautioned Jackson to put himself in position to reinforce Longstreet whenever ordered to do so.[95] Jackson's correspondence is missing from the *Official Records,* and consequently it is not possible

[87] Cf. O. R., 21, 549; ibid., 51, 1021; Longstreet, 293. Subsequently Lee discovered that the position on the right bank of the North Anna was no better than that on the Rappahannock.

[88] O. R., 51, part 2, p. 648.

[89] Longstreet, 293.

[90] O. R., 21, 1017, 1018–19.

[91] O. R., 21, 549.

[92] O. R., 51, part 2, p. 647.

[93] O. R., 21, 1020, 1021; ibid., 51, part 2, p. 648.

[94] O. R., 21, 1021.

[95] O. R., 21, 1021.

to say with assurance why he was so anxious to remain far down the Shenandoah Valley near Winchester in the face of Lee's repeated suggestions that he should retire up the Valley and rejoin the army. Apparently Jackson hoped that he might be able to repeat the manœuvre of Second Manassas and to get in rear of the enemy. Lee had considered this possibility. Although he does not seem to have put great faith in it, he had withheld positive orders as long as possible.[96] He was now beginning to shape a plan whereby Jackson would lie off the enemy's flank near Culpeper and discourage a southward move across the Rappahannock.

As Lee rode toward Fredericksburg, through the gloomy "Wilderness of Spottsylvania" that was to be the scene of some of his bloodiest fighting, Burnside was hurrying his troops forward by the roads on the opposite side of the Rappahannock. Lee, in fact, had anticipated the movements of his new opponent with a precision that was almost prescience. The transfer of Longstreet from Richmond to Gordonsville, while McClellan was preparing to reinforce Pope, was scarcely more remarkable. On the very day that Lee had first suspected the Army of the Potomac might shift by the left flank to Fredericksburg, General Burnside had been stubbornly arguing for such an advance in the face of the opposition of General Halleck, who had come to headquarters at Warrenton for a conference. On the 14th, when Lee had been strengthened in his belief that Fredericksburg was the enemy's objective, Burnside had been authorized to advance thither; the first units of Sumner's corps had started for Fredericksburg on the 15th, the very day on which Lee ordered the first small reinforcement there.[97] With all the advantage that the initiative normally offers, the Federals had a start of only one day.[98]

---

[96] 2 *Henderson*, 297–99.
[97] Sumner had started at daylight; Lee's orders were dated 7 P.M.
[98] For the timing of Burnside's movements, see *O. R.*, 21, 83–84.

CHAPTER XXX

Two Signal Guns End Long Suspense

THE gracious little city of Fredericksburg, to which Lee came through a rising storm on November 20,[1] is among the fairest and most ancient of Virginia. Lying at the fall line, it had been settled before the end of the seventeenth century. Across from it George Washington had spent his boyhood, and in a simple house on one of its shaded streets his mother had breathed her last. Paul Jones had climbed its hills. Hugh Mercer had practised physic on its kindly folk. From the Fitzhugh mansion at Chatham, Lee himself in youth had looked upon its gardens. Along the river, among the shops and warehouses, lived humble people; terraced above them were the seats of the socially mighty; still higher, ranged along the western hills that sheltered the town, were a few great homes, proud and separate in the architecture of Jefferson. Aristocrats who remembered the Revolution had built these fine houses, had covered handsome panels with old portraits, and had stored deep cellars with comforting Madeira. Their leisured sons had grown gray reading their fathers' books and holding fast to their politics and their religion. It was a place of respected names and long memories, of tinkling church bells and of children's laughter—proud, brave, patriotic.

As Lee saw it through a rain that had whipped the last of the leaves from the oaks and maples, his eye swept swiftly over its beauties to the Stafford Heights. There they were—the encampments and the fires of the enemy, the batteries and the hurrying dispatch bearers. A demonstration, which the Confederates had taken for an attempt to force a crossing,[2] had been made on the 17th, but otherwise the enemy had been content to await reinforcements.

[1] O. R., 21, 551; McCabe, 305. Lee's first dispatch from Fredericksburg is dated Nov. 21, but the tri-monthly return of Nov. 20 gives the town as his headquarters (O. R., 21, 1025, 1026).

[2] O. R., 21, 85, 103, 551; A. M. Scales: Battle of Fredericksburg (cited hereafter as Scales), 8–9.

Scarcely had Lee made his preliminary dispositions on the 21st, with the storm still raging, than a flag of truce with a message for the mayor of the town was reported on the river front. The flag came from Brigadier General M. R. Patrick, commanding General Burnside's provost guard, and was delivered to Lee. In a letter, General E. V. Sumner, commanding the Right Grand division of the Army of the Potomac, demanded the surrender of Fredericksburg on the grounds that his troops had been fired upon from the streets, while the manufactories had been used to assist the Confederate cause. Capitulation was demanded by 5 P.M. that day, under penalty of a bombardment at 9 A.M. on the 22d.[3] Lee was determined, of course, to protect the civilian population of Fredericksburg. At the same time he could not afford to have the place occupied by the enemy, nor could his batteries in rear of the town prevent a bombardment by the long-range Federal artillery across the Rappahannock. To save the town from destruction, if possible, Lee informed Mayor Slaughter that he would not occupy Fredericksburg or use its factories, though he could not consent to an occupation by the enemy. The mayor immediately dispatched General Sumner a letter of dignity and candor, telling him what Lee had said and reminding him that it was impossible to remove the non-combatant population within the time limit, which was only sixteen hours from the moment of writing.[4] Later in the evening, Lee was told that Sumner had notified the mayor that he would accept the assurances given him and would not begin to shell the town the next morning. Beyond that he made no promise, except to say that General Patrick would meet at Chatham a delegation from Fredericksburg the next day at 9 o'clock.[5] Welcome as was this reprieve to the defenseless townspeople, Lee felt that a collision was likely at any time and that the non-combatants would inevitably suffer if they remained where they were. With a heavy heart he had to advise them to evacuate the town as promptly as possible.

Although the storm was still at its height, the brave women and the old men accepted his advice without a murmur. That night and the next morning a long, dolorous procession moved

[3] *O. R.*, 21, 783.   [4] *O. R.*, 21, 785.
[5] *O. R.*, 21, 785. Chatham was known in the neighborhood as the "Lacy House" and is so styled in much of the official correspondence.

out from Fredericksburg. Those who possessed means and had friends to the southward took the train, which the enemy shelled; the less fortunate had to seek shelter in the woods and farmhouses behind the Confederate lines. Old family carriages were hitched to aged, lame, and blind horses; by Lee's orders the wagons and the ambulances of the army were placed at the disposal of those who had no conveyances;[6] the outraged soldiers shared their poor rations with the hungry.[7] Many of the civilians had neither food, transport, nor protection against the rain of November 22.[8] Not a few mothers were seen, wearily carrying infants, while older children walked at their side through the mud and over frozen ground. Yet such was their spirit that when these women met soldiers, they often greeted them, not with tears or hysterical appeals for succor, but with a stout-hearted "God bless you." [9] As Lee met these brave townsfolk his admiration rose. One little group of children that he saw from the roadside he had his troopers take on their horses and carry to a place of safety.[10] Months later, when he was writing his report, he echoed the tribute expressed in the letters written at the time. "History," said he, "presents no instance of a people exhibiting a purer and more unselfish patriotism or a higher spirit of fortitude and courage than was evinced by the citizens of Fredericksburg. They cheerfully incurred great hardships and privations, and surrendered their homes and property to destruction rather than yield them into the hands of the enemies of their country." [11] The Federals themselves must have been touched by the fortitude and suffering of the women and children, for at a conference held on the afternoon of the 22d, General Sumner gave written guarantee that as long as no hostile demonstrations were made from Fredericksburg the town would not be shelled.[12] Before many days were passed some of the shivering people imprudently crept back to their desolate homes and remained there even when walls were toppling and the streets were fire-swept.[13]

When no advance followed the threatened bombardment of

6 *O. R.*, 21, 1026.   7 *McCabe*, 306.   8 For the weather, see 1 *Meade*, 330.
9 Goolrick: *Historic Fredericksburg* (cited hereafter as *Goolrick*), 40; 1 *R. W. C. D.*, 194; T. R. R. Cobb to his wife, Nov. 22, 1862, 28 *S. H. S. P.*, 299; *Scales*, 10–11.
10 5 *Confederate Veteran*, 18–19.
11 *O. R.*, 21, 551. *Cf.* Lee to Mary Lee, Nov. 24, 1862; *R. E. Lee, Jr.*, 85–86. *Cf. ibid.*, 87.
12 *O. R.*, 21, 789.   13 *Goolrick*, 40.

Fredericksburg, Lee was puzzled. The rebuilding of the wharfs at Aquia Creek seemed to indicate that Burnside intended to use that admirable landing as a base for an advance on Richmond;[14] but there remained a possibility that he might be screening a movement southward to the James.[15] Lee had to shape his defense for either eventuality and had at the same time to hold to the major plan he had adopted against McClellan after Sharpsburg, that of delaying the enemy until the winter halted his advance.

His dispositions were characteristic. General G. W. Smith at Richmond was told of the possibility of an advance to the James and was directed to make every possible effort to discover the plans of the Federals at Norfolk.[16] A battalion of the reserve artillery, under Major John W. Moore, was ordered to Richmond to strengthen the city's defenses, but on second thought was directed to go to the North Anna, where it could defend from a cavalry raid the principal bridge on Lee's line of communications, which was now established by way of the Richmond and Fredericksburg Railroad.[17] If no raid was threatened, this artillery, of course, could be moved in a day either to Richmond or to Fredericksburg.

The most important orders that Lee issued, when he found that Burnside did not follow up his threat to bombard Fredericksburg, were directed to Jackson. Lee at this time had with him less than 31,000 infantry, about 1300 artillerymen, and approximately 7000 cavalry.[18] He assumed he had in front of him, or marching through the autumn fields toward Stafford Heights, virtually the whole Army of the Potomac, fully three times his numbers.[19] Anxious as he was to strengthen himself against these odds by calling up Jackson's 34,000, Lee concluded that for a short time at least Jackson might be of more use to him on the enemy's flank than in the Shenandoah Valley or across the Rappa-

---

14 *O. R.*, 21, 1026.   15 *Cf. O. R.*, 21, 1038.   16 *O. R.*, 18, 784.
17 *O. R.*, 21, 1027, 1028, 1039.   18 *O. R.*, 21, 1025.
19 Actually, Franklin's Left Grand division was at Stafford Courthouse, Hooker's Central Grand division was encamped along the railroad between Aquia Creek and the Rappahannock; Sumner's Right Grand division was on Stafford Heights. This gave Burnside 118,000 troops within nine miles of Fredericksburg. Sigel's corps, an additional 15,000, was at Fairfax courthouse, within two days' march, and Heintzelman had 46,000 in the Washington defenses. Lee did not credit reports that Burnside had 200,000 in his front (*O. R.*, 21, 1053).

hannock from Burnside. He reviewed the situation in a dispatch he wrote Jackson on November 23, and at the end of it he indited a paragraph that perfectly illustrates the relations between the two men and the faith Lee now imposed in the discretion of Jackson. Lee said: "Under this view of things, if correct, I do not see, at this distance, what military effect can be produced by the continuance of your corps in the Valley. If it were east of the Blue Ridge, either in Loudoun, Fauquier or Culpeper, its influence would be felt by the enemy whose rear would be threatened, though they might feel safe with regard to their communications. Another advantage would be, provided you were at Culpeper, that you would be in railroad communication with several points, so that the transfer of your troops would be rendered certain, without regard to the state of the weather or the condition of the roads. If, therefore, you see no way of making an impression on the enemy from where you are, and concur with me in the views I have expressed, I wish you would move east of the Blue Ridge, and take such a position as you may find best." [20] In a word, Lee held to his previous belief that with Jackson at Culpeper, Burnside would hesitate to make any general advance or to detach large forces for operations elsewhere. Even in this belief, he left that move to the discretion of Jackson and, at the same time, had so much confidence in the fighting qualities of Longstreet's corps and in the strength of its position that he was willing to keep the army divided a few days longer and to face the Army of the Potomac with less than 40,000 men.

By November 23, Jackson was on the march from the vicinity of Winchester. Burnside remained mysteriously quiet and even drew back slightly from the Rappahannock. This created some new doubt in Lee's mind as to whether his adversary was not covering a transfer of troops south of the James, but he felt that the Army of the Potomac by this time was so definitely committed to the line of the Rappahannock that a further change of base would be regarded in the North as equivalent to a defeat. "I think, therefore," he said, "he will persevere in his present course, and the longer we can delay him, and throw him into the winter, the more difficult will be his undertaking." [21]

[20] O. R., 21, 1027.   [21] Lee to Davis, Nov. 25, 1862; O. R., 21, 1029.

The probability of a general offensive on the Rappahannock increased as three days, four days, five days passed, and with it grew the desirability of uniting the army. Still Lee had faith in the advantage of holding Jackson on Burnside's flank.[22] It was not until he found that the next storm would probably make the roads almost impassable and would cause a march on Culpeper to be inhumanly severe on Jackson's men that he finally, on November 27, abandoned his plan of keeping the Second Corps on the right of Burnside's army and definitely urged Jackson to move to Fredericksburg and take position close to Longstreet. Even then he left the advance to the discretion of "Stonewall." [23]

On the evening of November 29, while the snow was falling heavily outside his headquarters tent at Hamilton's Crossing,[24] Lee heard some commotion and, on going out, saw the familiar figure of Jackson, who had ridden ahead with one aide to report the advance of his corps.[25] Lee greeted his incomparable lieutenant warmly and after a friendly exchange of good wishes, gave him and his companion supper and then confirmed the directions he had already issued that Jackson place his corps to the right and rear of Longstreet.[26] For Lee was beginning to suspect that Burnside would not dare assault the strong position directly at Fredericksburg, and that, if the Federals crossed the Rappahannock at all in that vicinity, it would be below the city.[27] For this reason he ordered Jackson to establish himself on the Richmond and Fredericksburg Railroad around Guiney's Station, whence he could easily move to support Longstreet, to extend the right, or to face an advance from farther down the Rappahannock.[28]

In accordance with these directions Jackson's troops began to take their position on December 1. Many of them had marched

---

[22] O. R., 21, 1029, 1031, 1031–32.   [23] O. R., 21, 1033, 1034, 1035.
[24] Long, 240.
[25] J. P. Smith in Richmond Times-Dispatch, Jan. 20, 1907. The date of Jackson's arrival is not given in official reports. Captain Smith, who accompanied Jackson, stated that it was Saturday, Nov. 26 (See 43 S. H. S. P., 24). Since Saturday was the 29th, not the 26th, Doctor Smith was mistaken either in the day of the week or in the date, and as he remarked in another connection that the following day was Sunday (ibid., 25), it is certain that the arrival was on the 29th. This fits in with Lee's correspondence, which shows a letter written on the 27th to Jackson, who had not then joined him (O. R., 21, 1035). According to this letter, Jackson had been at Madison Courthouse on the 26th.
[26] J. P. Smith in Richmond Times-Dispatch, Jan. 20, 1907.
[27] O. R., 21, 1037.   [28] See the map, p. 449.

175 miles in twelve days,[29] and though some were barefooted, the physical condition of the whole corps was good and its spirit was high.[30] Their commander did not like his new position, and protested against it to Lee. "We will whip the enemy," Jackson told D. H. Hill, "but gain no fruits of victory."[31] D. H. Hill himself was sent as far down the Rappahannock as Port Royal. Lee felt that he should protect a wide front, but he was fully conscious of the tactical limitations of the position at Fredericksburg and, it will be recalled, had first planned to make his stand against Burnside on the North Anna. Now, in addition to the earlier considerations that had decided him to stand on the line of the Rappahannock, others had arisen. The government at Richmond was concerned over Federal preparations that seemed to indicate a new offensive in the South, and General G. W. Smith, commanding at Richmond, was more apprehensive than ever of a Federal advance up the south side of the James.[32] Lee was willing to withdraw nearer to the capital when the President thought such a move necessary;[33] yet he felt that a retreat from the Rappahannock would bring the enemy close to Richmond, where a further Federal concentration might be effected; and he knew that such a movement would cost the Confederacy the supplies he was then drawing from the lower valley of the Rappahannock. He urged that troops from the South be brought to Richmond, if possible, and that Smith, if attacked, make the best defense he could. In case of emergency he could march to Smith's support.[34] Meantime, he told Smith, "I think it important to keep [Burnside] at a distance [from Richmond] as long as possible,"[35] even if that of necessity involved a battle where a victory could not be followed up.[36]

Fortunately, Lee's intelligence service was now working admirably—even better than when Burnside, at Warrenton, had frankly told the War Department that Lee's means of getting information were "far superior" to his.[37] Confederate spies were

[29] *Welch*, 36. [30] *Paxton*, 73.
[31] *Dabney*, 595; *Cf. Longstreet*, 299, and 3 *B. and L.*, 72.
[32] 5 *Rowland*, 384–85; *O. R.*, 21, 1052. [33] *O. R.*, 21, 1050.
[34] *O. R.*, 21, 1050, 1052. [35] *O. R.*, 21, 1052.
[36] These facts dispose of the contemporary gossip that Lee was compelled by a timid administration to remain on the Rappahannock when he desired, to the very last, to withdraw to the North Anna.
[37] *O. R.*, 21, 99. Burnside's own intelligence service, it should be added, had also been much improved. See 1 *Shotwell Papers*, 368; *Wolseley*, 2.

439

on both flanks of Burnside's army north of the Rappahannock and on the Potomac as well.[38] Another spy had visited the North and had returned with an excellent budget of information.[39] The Federal newspapers, which Lee read assiduously, afforded much of high value.[40] Three days after the arrival of the pontoons by which Burnside intended to cross the Rappahannock, Lee was apprized of the fact.[41] Assured that he would be notified of any movement of consequence,[42] Lee made the best of the time allowed him by Burnside's unexpected delay.

"I tremble for my country," he said, "when I hear of confidence expressed in me. I know too well my weakness, and that our only hope is in God." [43] But there was not lacking in his preparations the calm poise of a man who relied on his own military judgment and on the valor of his army. On the hills around Fredericksburg the reorganization begun after Sharpsburg was completed. Regiments were shifted;[44] Lee's proposal to place in the infantry ranks those cavalrymen who had lost their mounts was at length approved;[45] an incompetent general was tactfully disposed of, and another was sent to seek command elsewhere;[46] pleasant relations were established with the new Secretary of War, James A. Seddon, who on November 15 had succeeded Randolph on the resignation of the latter.[47] When Captain A. P. Mason left him to rejoin General Johnston, Major Walter H. Taylor was formally named acting assistant adjutant general in his place.[48] Refitting went on, despite a threatened breakdown of the railroad to Richmond.[49] Provision was made for recasting the smaller guns into 12-pounder Napoleons;[50] arms were pro-

[38] O. R., 21, 1052.   [39] O. R., 21, 1052.

[40] For Lee's constant and careful study of Northern newspapers, see the admirable monograph of James G. Randall, in 23 American Historical Review, 303 ff.

[41] O. R., 21, 87, 1038. For an excellent example of the fullness and accuracy of the reports made by Lee's spies, see O. R., 21, 1034.

[42] Cf. Lee to Smith, Dec. 6, 1862: The spies "must be very negligent of their duty if any movement is made without my knowledge" (O. R., 21, 1052).

[43] Lee to Mrs. Lee, Dec. 2, 1862, Fitz Lee, 234–35.

[44] O. R., 21, 1033–34.   [45] O. R., 1040–41, 1045, 1048, 1051.

[46] O. R., 21, 1029–30, 1032, 1036–37.

[47] IV O. R., 2, 178. Jones had noted on Oct. 2 that Lee had "razed the [war] department down to a second-class bureau, of which the President himself is chief" (1 R. W. C. D., 162). For the circumstances attending the resignation of Randolph, see 2 English Combatant, 208–9; Memoir of Jefferson Randolph Kean.

[48] O. R., 21, 1026, 1028. Mason had been named assistant adjutant general on Oct. 28, when Colonel Chilton had been made inspector general (O. R., 19, part 2, p. 688).

[49] O. R., 21, 1054.   [50] O. R., 21, 1046–47; 1 R. W. C. D., 207.

vided for Jackson's convalescents;[51] shoes were somehow found for those stalwarts who required footgear larger than the government issued;[52] further supplies of warm clothing were issued for at least some of the men.[53] The fine spirit of the army mounted higher and higher;[54] the men began to indulge in snowball battles for lack of more serious hostilities[55] and, as one pious brigadier remarked, their natures seemed so changed that they bore in patience "what they once would have regarded as beyond human endurance."[56]

Active preparations for the inevitable battle went on apace, in weather that made war impartially against the armies.[57] On the hills back of Fredericksburg, artillery positions were chosen and the ranges set.[58] Possible crossing places below Fredericksburg were examined;[59] some troublesome gunboats in the vicinity of Port Royal were· driven off;[60] cavalry reconnaissances to feel out the enemy were safely conducted;[61] the railroad from Fredericksburg to Hamilton's Crossing was torn up;[62] and absentees were brought into the ranks until, on December 10, Lee had 78,511 men with the colors.[63]

Only two things were left undone, so far as Lee could direct: The army continued on a long, sprawling front of twenty miles, from Fredericksburg to Port Royal, unconcentrated; and, secondly, to the surprise of some officers,[64] only a few earthworks were thrown up. These seeming omissions were undoubtedly deliberate. The occupation of the Port Royal sector seemed necessary to prevent a turning movement that would give the enemy an easy line of advance on Richmond. The position directly at Fredericksburg was so strong that elaborate fortifications would have convinced any antagonist that it was impregnable, especially if the whole Army of Northern Virginia had crowded the heights above the intrepid little town. It doubtless was better, in Lee's

---

[51] *O. R.*, 21, 1040.
[52] *Welch*, 37; *O. R.*, 21, 1041.
[53] *G. Wise*, 126–27.
[54] *Cooke*, 174–75.
[55] 2 *von Borcke*, 82 *ff.*
[56] *Paxton*, 74.
[57] There were four inches of snow on the night of Dec. 5–6. The weather on Dec. 6 and 7 was very cold. On the 8th the snow was still unmelted and the Rappahannock was frozen over (28 *S. H. S. P.*, 300).
[58] *Long*, 236; *Longstreet*, 300; *O. R.*, 21, 564.
[59] *O. R.*, 21, 1042–43.
[60] *O. R.*, 21, 35–36, 563, 564, 642.
[61] *O. R.*, 21, 15, 27.
[62] *Cf. O. R.*, 51, part 2, pp. 651–52.
[63] *O. R.*, 21, 1056.
[64] *E.g.*, *Sorrel*, 132.

opinion, to invite attack by seeming negligence, than to discourage it by a show of complete preparation.

Ten dark December days passed. Headquarters labored to meet the attack when it should come. Axes rang ceaselessly in the woods as the soldiers chopped firewood to keep from freezing.[65] The night of December 10 arrived and a rumor spread through some of the camps that a Southern woman had crept down to the river bank that evening and had called across to the shivering gray pickets that the Federals had received a large issue of rations with orders to cook them at once.[66] The Confederate in the ranks had learned to read the signs of operations that close-mouthed officers sought to keep secret, and he knew that the cooking of extra rations almost invariably meant an army movement on the morrow.

Would the attack come with the dawn? Was Burnside about to pass the river and challenge the confident Army of Northern Virginia on the heights? At every camp fire the questions were argued. They doubtless were still vaguely ranging in the sleeping minds of the soldiers when, about 4:45 o'clock on the morning of December 11, there came from Marye's Heights, behind the town, the roar of a cannon, then of another, and then silence. Two guns . . . signal guns . . . the agreed warning that the enemy was attempting to force a crossing of the Rappahannock.

[65] *Paxton,* 74.   [66] 10 *S. H. S. P.,* 385.

CHAPTER XXXI

"It Is Well That War Is So Terrible . . ."

(FREDERICKSBURG)

By the dim light of a half-obscured moon at 2 o'clock on the morning of December 11, through a rising haze the Confederate pickets in Fredericksburg had observed the first preparations of the Federal engineers to throw their pontoons across the Rappahannock.[1] Word had reached General McLaws about 4:30 that General William Barksdale, who commanded in the town, would open fire as soon as the *pontoniers* were within easy range. A few minutes later McLaws sent a courier to General Lee and ordered Captain J. W. Read's battery of reserve artillery to fire the signal guns.[2]

As Lee rode forward from his headquarters at Hamilton's Crossing, in answer to McLaws's summons, the haze lay thick in the valleys and reduced visibility to less than 100 yards,[3] but he took pains to examine all the artillery positions he passed. Finding one battery badly placed, he asked its captain who put him there. "Colonel Chilton," the officer answered. The back of the General's neck grew red, a sure sign that he was angry, and he jerked his head higher, another familiar omen of an inward battle. "Colonel Chilton takes a lot upon himself," he said and touched his horse.[4] To the sharp accompaniment of musketry from the river bank, he climbed an eminence about a mile and a half southwest of the lower end of the town, an eminence known from that day as Lee's Hill.[5] There he learned

---

[1] *McCabe*, 309. The moon, nearing the last quarter, had risen at 11:41 P.M.

[2] *O. R.*, 21, 578; 3 *B. and L.*, 86. Longstreet, *op. cit.*, 301, was mistaken in saying the signal was given at 3 A.M., and was mistaken, also, in stating in 3 *B. and L.*, 73, that it was fired by the Washington Artillery.

[3] 10 *S. H. S. P.*, 386.

[4] Statement of Colonel T. M. R. Talcott to the author.

[5] Farther to the south the high ground on the ridge was known as Howison's Hill, which has caused some writers mistakenly to assume that Howison's Hill and Lee's Hill were the same.

that the Federals were attempting to throw pontoon bridges across the Rappahannock at three points—the first at the foot of Hawk Street in the town, the second just below the railroad bridge, and the third near the mouth of Deep Run. The location of these bridges is shown with the numerals 1, 2, and 3 on the map on page 445.

The first and second bridges were within effective range of the artillery on the long ridge west of the town, but they could not be bombarded without danger to the houses and population of Fredericksburg. To delay the construction of these two cross-ings, therefore, Lee had to rely on infantry. The third bridge was within range of the better guns on that part of the line, but the ground in front of it on the right bank of the river was open and so dominated by the Federal artillery on the left bank that the Confederate infantry would be too exposed to offer effective resistance.[6] Nevertheless, as Jackson's corps had not been brought up, the crossing had to be delayed as long as practicable at all three points. The following map shows the ranges from the ridge, which fell away in elevation and had a wider plain in its front south of the city.

Opposite the first and second bridges General McLaws had posted Barksdale's Mississippi brigade. The third bridge, near Deep Run, was in front of General Hood's lines. From the outset it was apparent that Hood could not prevent the laying of the bridge. The action and the outcome were largely in the hands of Barksdale's men, who were already engaged hotly when Lee rode to the front. As the haze hung long over the town, and was thickened by the smoke from Barksdale's rifles, little could be seen from Lee's Hill. The commanding general had to rely on reports that came regularly and told confidently of continued success in beating off the engineers. The determined Federals would rush to their farthest boat and and would attempt to throw another into position—only to meet a sharp and accurate fire from the Mississippians. Down would drop the tools, back would run the Federals, and the same drama would be repeated in all its parts. By 9 o'clock the line of boats was almost complete to the

---

[6] For good descriptions of the ground, see *Early*, 167-68, and H. C. Cabell in *O. R.*, 21, 585.

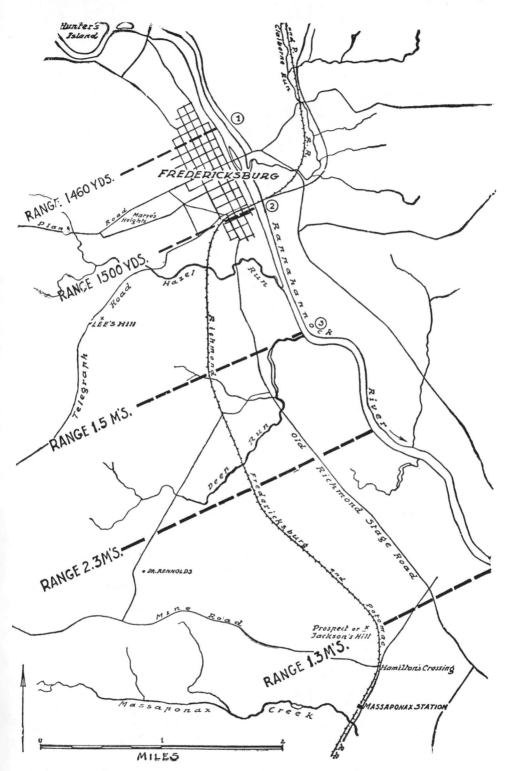

Artillery ranges from the Confederate positions in the battle of Fredericksburg, December 13, 1862.

southern side of the river, opposite Deep Run, but the work on the upstream bridges had progressed scarcely at all since dawn.

A little later the fog began to lift, and the impatient Federals on the Stafford Heights could make out the houses from which the Mississippi volunteers were sharpshooting. At 10 A.M., the whole opposite shore line blazed with fire and a mighty roar echoed against the face of Lee's Hill.[7] A hundred guns were soon in action, pouring their fire indiscriminately into the buildings occupied by the soldiers and into those where only trembling children and anxious mothers were. The cruelty of it aroused Lee's wrath. "These people," he said with emotion, "delight to destroy the weak and those who can make no defense; it just suits them!"[8]

From Lee's Hill there soon was disclosed a spectacle the magnificence of which made men catch their breath. Only the spires of the churches, rising in protest against such godless war, were visible above the mist that seemed, from the Confederate side, still to cling protectingly over the little town. Breaking over this blanket of haze and rising from it were the white spheres of exploding shell. Across the river the high ground was billowed in smoke, along which ran endless tongues of flame from battery to battery. Behind the active batteries could be glimpsed long waiting lines of blue infantry, parked wagon trains, and a multitude of guns with champing horses, ready at the bugle note to hurl new pieces into action or to bring limbers and caissons bouncing down the hillsides to the pontoons. The roar was continuous, and like the bed of some vast volcano, the haze seemed to bubble with the smoke of explosion. Ere long, darker clouds of smoke began to rise from houses set afire by the shell. In the still air these clouds mounted up and up, as if from rival altars kindled to the god of war. At a high elevation, a breeze caught them and spread them in a long streamer over the landscape. Riding untroubled over all were two great balloons, the eyes of the Federal army.[9]

Fifty rounds per gun, 5000 shell, the Union batteries fired,

[7] Longstreet, in 3 *B. and L.*, 75, gave the hour as 1 P.M., and Alexander, *op. cit.*, 290, said 11 A.M. McLaws fixed it at 10 A.M. (3 *B. and L.*, 87), and Walton (*O. R.*, 21, 573) put it at 7 A.M. Hunt (*O. R.*, 21, 182) did not mention the time. As McLaws was in immediate command, and should have known the facts, his statement is accepted here.
[8] *Cooke*, 177.   [9] *Alexander*, 290–91.

446

while frightened women prayed in cellars and the riflemen of Barksdale's brigade found such shelter as they could behind shaking walls in smoke-stifled streets. Then the fire slackened until only the slow gunners were left, shame-faced, to count their final rounds. Soon the artillery ceased altogether, for the Confederates had not wasted their all-too-scant ammunition in practice beyond their range. But the silence lasted only a few minutes. Out from their cover rushed the bridge builders once more. Selected batteries covered their renewed attempt to complete the crossings, and from the houses along the waterfront echoed again the defiant fire of the Mississippians. Under good leadership, they had suffered little during the bombardment, and now, at the first and second pontoon bridges, they were ready as ever to dispute with their rifles the passage of the river. Already they had gained half a day and seemed as fresh in their fire as they had been at dawn. Lee had listened to it all and had watched as much as was visible from his station. Busy artillerists had brought to the hilltop two new 30-pounder Parrott guns from Richmond and numbers of lighter pieces.[10] Longstreet, Stuart, and others of rank had come, observed, rejoiced, and departed as their several duties demanded. Reports from the town continued at short intervals. And each time that Barksdale proudly announced that a new attempt had been beaten off, Lee's countenance lighted up.[11]

A double pontoon bridge near Deep Run was completed by 11 o'clock, though the infantry did not attempt to pass over.[12] Still Barksdale's men hung on. Six, seven, eight, even nine times they drove back the detachment of engineer troops.[13] Before noon, Barksdale was notified by Longstreet that the disposition of the defending force was complete, and that he could retire when he thought proper, but he continued to dispute the crossing.[14] About 1 o'clock Federal infantry streamed down the heights and leaped into waiting batteaux, which immediately put out, with strong arms at the sweeps. If they could not build the bridge, with Barksdale's men to oppose them, the Federals evidently were de-

---

[10] *O. R.*, 21, 1058; 10 *S. H. S. P.*, 387. Pendleton (*O. R.*, 21, 564) misdated the placing of these guns and fixed it on the 12th.
[11] *H. B. McClellan*, 191; 2 *von Borcke*, 98–100.
[12] *O. R.*, 21, 448–49.   [13] *O. R.*, 21, 578.   [14] *Longstreet*, 302.

termined to cross the river, drive off the Mississippians, and establish a bridgehead. As the purpose of the enemy became plain,
the riflemen quickened their fire. In every batteau bluecoats began
to drop, but the stream was narrow, the oarsmen numerous, and
soon the first contingent sprang ashore and deployed.[15] Others
followed quickly.

The game was up. Weary now from their long fight and too
widely scattered to offer instant resistance, the Confederates
slipped away from their posts, withdrew to streets farther from
the shore, and rallied there. Nothing material was to be gained
by prolonging the action in the town, but the fighting blood of
the men was aroused and they contested the enemy's advance
stubbornly and skillfully. It was 7 o'clock that evening before the
last of them crossed the open ground between the town and the
ridge and left Fredericksburg to its captors. By that time both
the upper bridges had been completed.[16]

Meanwhile, of course, Jackson had been notified to prepare to
bring up his troops,[17] if it should develop that the enemy was not
attempting to cross the river farther downstream. After nightfall Barksdale's brigade was relieved by T. R. R. Cobb's Georgians;[18] the force on Marye's Heights was strengthened;[19] and
A. P. Hill was ordered up from Yerby's and Taliaferro from
Guiney's, to move to the right of the line, so that Hood could
draw in his extended flank.[20]

At the hour when these orders were dispatched to A. P. Hill,
Jackson's corps was widely scattered, as the sketch shows.

There was much, in fact, to suggest the situation at Sharpsburg
when Lee had faced McClellan with Jackson's entire command,
McLaws, R. H. Anderson, and Walker detached; yet Lee did not
hurry Early from Buckner's Neck or D. H. Hill from Port Royal.
The reason was simple. He could hardly believe he was to have
the good fortune of receiving Burnside's attack at Fredericksburg.
It did not seem credible that the whole Federal army was to be
hurled against the heights where Longstreet was waiting, with
his ranges set and his infantry at ease. Commanding so vast

---

[15] Cf. 3 B. and L., 121.
[16] Sorrel, 137; 36 S. H. S. P., 20 ff.; O. R., 571, 578, 601, 607.
[17] Pendleton, 240.   [18] O. R., 21, 579.
[19] O. R., 21, 625   [20] O. R., 21, 645.

an army, Burnside had ample men to make a strong feint at Fredericksburg while undertaking a major turning operation down the river, say, in the vicinity of Skinker's Neck, where some

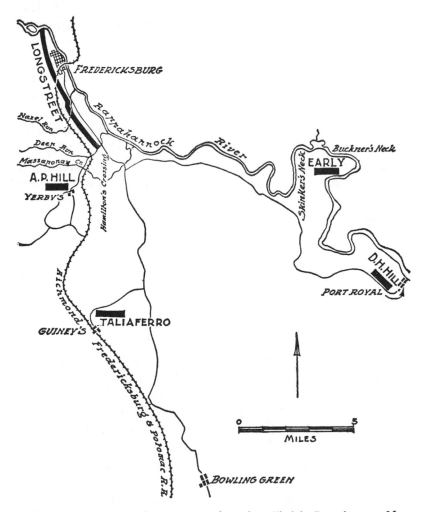

Distribution of the Second corps, Army of Northern Virginia, December 11, 1862.

signs of Federal activity had been observed. If Burnside assaulted at Fredericksburg, with only a part of his army, the arrival of Taliaferro and A. P. Hill would give Lee enough men to defeat him. In case the new Union commander planned simultaneously

449

to cross farther down stream, there must be a sufficient force in his front to delay him there until the rest of the army could be drawn back to the line of the North Anna. Pending the disclosure of the Federal plan, it was the course of wisdom to leave Early and D. H. Hill where they were. Concentration, one of the rules of war, could be neglected for a day in dealing with an adversary who seemed about to defy all the rules.

Haze again covered the river valley on the morning of the 12th and screened the movements of the enemy from the expectant army. The Federals ineffectively shelled the Confederate positions during the morning with their long-range guns across the Rappahannock;[21] but little of the Southern artillery could reach the farther shore, and as Lee had no thought of changing his decision to refrain from firing on the town,[22] it was a one-sided bombardment. The Confederate batteries answered only when the enemy showed himself on exposed ground.[23]

About noon, when the fog had lifted below Fredericksburg, Lee rode to the right, where he was joined by Jackson and, a little later, by Major von Borcke of Stuart's staff. Von Borcke bore a message from Stuart, reporting the rapid concentration of the Federals in front of the Confederate right, and he said he had been within a few hundred yards of the enemy's advanced units. At Lee's instance, he led him and Jackson to the vantage point. First they rode to a barn, where they dismounted. Then the three crept forward along a ditch that carried them to an eminence on which stood two old gateposts. They were now within 400 yards of the enemy, so close that when they used their glasses, they could distinguish the features of the men opposite them. As they carefully examined the enemy's line, everything indicated a general advance. Across one of the two pontoon bridges columns of bluecoats were marching, regiment on regiment, while over the other bridge, sheeted wagons and flawlessly equipped batteries were moving. Immediately in front, Federal picks were flying and stout arms were shovelling dirt for a line of rifle pits that swept along the riverside as far as eye could reach. At one point, thirty-two field guns were already in battery. Slowly and curiously Lee and Jackson scrutinized men and

---

[21] 10 S. H. S. P., 392; 3 B. and L., 97.
[22] McCabe, 313.   [23] 10 S. H. S. P., 392; O. R., 21, 574.

weapons, while von Borcke bent his giant's shoulders in the ditch and asked himself what would happen to the Southern cause if sharpshooters should pick off the two observers or if a sudden rush of cavalry should take them prisoner. Finally Lee put up his glasses and crept back as he had gone, Jackson following him.[24]

Lee had seen enough to convince him that this was a major advance, and not a feint. The Federals evidently intended to make their main effort there, and not farther down the river. Moreover, the activity of the enemy indicated that an attack would probably come the next day. D. H. Hill and Early, therefore, must be recalled at once from Port Royal and Buckner's Neck and the army must be made ready for the morrow. Jackson left to draft orders for D. H. Hill and Early.[25] Taliaferro and A. P. Hill were already coming up.[26] As Lee rode back to the centre of the line he was more than satisfied at the outlook, even though all the signs indicated that the Federals were massing to attack at his weakest point, his right flank. It was better to have them there than farther down the Rappahannock. "I shall try to do them all the damage in our power when they move forward," he said simply.[27]

Night brought a cold and biting wind,[28] and on the picket line, where no fires were allowed, the men suffered cruelly. As the bitter night wore on the wind died like a sullen Fury, and in its place the freezing fog rose from the ground where the un-thawed snow remained in spots the feeble December sun of the previous week had not reached. One soldier died of exposure,[29] and when the late dawn came at last, men rejoiced at the prospect of a battle whose horrors could not be worse than those of the night.

The fog at daybreak was so thick that nothing was visible beyond fifty or sixty yards,[30] but by the time Lee reached his observation post the camps were astir. Crouching over their fires, the men ate their rough rations, wiped the moisture from their rifles, and looked at one another with the forced gaiety that

[24] 2 *von Borcke*, 109–10.
[25] 2 *von Borcke*, 110; H. B. McClellan, 192; O. R., 21, 643, 1060.
[26] O. R., 21, 645, 675.   [27] O. R., 21, 1060.
[28] *History of Kershaw's Brigade*, 182.   [29] O. R., 21, 588.
[30] G. Wise, 128; *Longstreet*, 306; O. R., 21, 612.

soldiers always show when in their hearts they ask themselves which of them will gather again at the next mess and which will be lying in convulsed death on the battlefield. Quickly they were in position along the heights, shivering and excited. The invisible enemy was astir, too, for up the hillside drifted the echo of phantom voices, the roll of drums, snatches of bugle calls and, ere long, the music of bands in well-remembered tunes.[31]

General officers began ere long to ride up with reports and re-assurance. Early had arrived on the right. D. H. Hill's long march from Port Royal had put him in position. The entire army was concentrated to the last regiment. Longstreet's front spread from the high ridge opposite Beck's Island[32] to a point beyond Deep Run; Jackson's corps extended thence to the vicinity of Hamilton's Crossing. On Longstreet's left, R. H. Anderson defended the high ground almost to Marye's Heights, where Ransom was in reserve. McLaws covered the foot of Marye's Heights in a sunken road that was from that dread day to be forever renowned. From the southern end of this sunken road[33] Mc-Laws's line wound past Howison's mill, across Hazel Run and over Lee's Hill to a point beyond the home of the historian Howison. There Pickett took up the line and followed the curve of the ridge nearly at right angles until he reached the vicinity of Doctor Rennolds's[34] house. From that point Hood's line stood on the ridge. His right joined the left of A. P. Hill, who held the front almost to Hamilton's Crossing. Between Hill and the river was the Richmond, Fredericksburg and Potomac Railroad. In his rear were Early and Taliaferro in a second line. D. H. Hill was behind them. Stuart was at hand and was hovering beyond the right flank. Every rifle that the Army of Northern Virginia could muster was at Lee's instant command. Three hundred and six guns were in position.[35] Seventy-eight thousand men were ready for the worst that Burnside's 125,000 could do.[36] Here was Lee's line:

[31] *Taylor's General Lee,* 146.   [32] Now called Hunter's Island.

[33] Some writers mistakenly have assumed that the sunken road ran along the whole of Lee's front. Its southern end, in reality, was under the present National Cemetery. For a detailed description of the road, see *infra,* p. 458.

[34] Wrongly spelled Reynolds on maps of the war period.

[35] *Longstreet,* 300. For a description of the artillery, see 10 *S. H. S. P.,* 387–88.

[36] *O. R.,* 21, 1057, 1121. Burnside's gross strength of 201,000 was reduced to 125,-000 by the Washington garrison and sundry detachments.

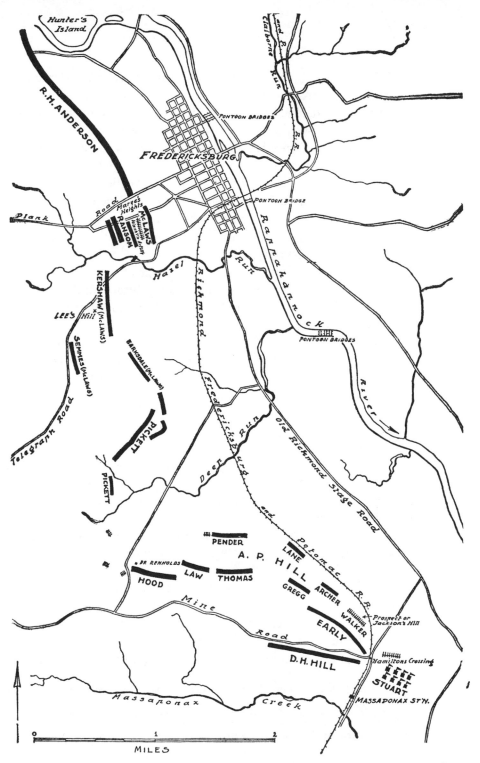

Position of the major units of the Army of Northern Virginia at the opening of the battle of Fredericksburg, December 13, 1862.

Presently came Jackson, apparelled in unwonted splendor—a new uniform coat, a hat adorned with shining braid—mounted on a well-caparisoned and magnificent horse. Even though they knew that the swelling fire of the skirmishers would soon break into battle, the comrades of the grim "Stonewall" could not repress questioning as to the source of so much splendor, and when Jackson confessed in his low voice that he believed it was some of his friend Stuart's doing, badinage overwhelmed him.[37] Stuart was as proud and as pleased as if he had coaxed one of Jackson's blue-stocking clerical aides to join in the most riotous rondel of his banjo-player Sweeny.

Jackson was for business, despite his dress-parade attire. There must be no defensive, said he, but instant attack under cover of the fog, which would keep the Federals from employing their artillery across the river. Stuart seconded him. But Lee said no. He would meet the Federals where he stood, wear them down, let them break their fine divisions in hopeless assaults on his position, while he held back and conserved his strength. Then, when their losses had reduced their numbers nearer to parity, *then* he would strike, but not sooner.[38]

Longstreet's spirit, as always, was aroused at the prospect of battle, and his graceless humor found its usual butt in the grave Jackson. "General," he said, "do not all these multitudes of Federals frighten you?"

"We shall see very soon whether I shall not frighten them," Jackson retorted calmly.[39]

Jackson now started to rejoin his command, but Longstreet pursued his jest: "Jackson, what are you going to do with all those people over there?"

"Sir," answered Jackson, as he mounted, "we will give them the bayonet." [40]

Longstreet had reported early that the orders of command which he had heard through the fog confirmed the general belief that the attack would be on the right.[41] Jackson was of the same

---

[37] *Dabney*, 610; 1 *von Borcke*, 295–96; *Mrs. Jackson*, 365–66; 43 *S. H. S. P.*, 28–29; *Sorrel*, 138.

[38] 2 *von Borcke*, 114; Lee to Mrs. Lee, Dec. 25, 1862; *R. E. Lee, Jr.*, 89; Lee to W. M. McDonald, April 15, 1868, *Jones*, 267.

[39] *Dabney*, 611.   [40] *Sorrel*, 138.   [41] *O. R.*, 21, 570.

mind.[42] As soon, therefore, as he could dispose of details that awaited his decision, Lee rode in that direction. Attended by Jackson and Stuart he covered the whole of the long flank. Everywhere he was received with cheers, but there was great hilarity and some misgiving over the appearance of the much bedizened "Stonewall." Said the soldiers as he went along, "Old Jack will be afraid of his clothes and will not get down to work." [43]

Leaving Jackson in his glory and confusion, Lee crossed with Stuart to a field on the flank of the Federals, and there he tried to ascertain if the enemy was moving. He could hear the vague hum of many voices but he could see nothing distinctly. The fog, however, was beginning to fade, for soon sharpshooters' bullets began to hum about the little group and a few shadowy forms could be glimpsed, as if the Federal outpost had seen the party and was deploying to capture it. Lee took his time, regardless of the Federal riflemen, and did not retire until it was apparent that further reconnaissance in the fog would yield no result.[44]

Back to his post of observation he galloped in a whirlwind of cheers. Had his mind been less occupied with the task before him, he might have recalled his old study of Napoleon and might well have compared his position with that of Archduke Charles in May, 1809, when the emperor had crossed the Danube and had challenged the Austrians. Aspern had been Napoleon's Hamilton's Crossing and Essling his Fredericksburg. Two days' hard fighting had made the battle of Aspern–Essling the first defeat for the invading Corsican—*adsit omen!*

Imperceptibly the baffling fog began to dissipate after Lee resumed his lookout. By 10 o'clock it was manifest that the Confederate positions on the ridge could now be made out by the unseen enemy in the valley, for the impatient captains of a few enterprising Union batteries opened a desultory fire on the right.

Then the white steeples of Fredericksburg's churches were visible above the gray mist. The blurred outlines of the Stafford Heights could be vaguely seen. Vision widened. Drab daylight began to soften into gold under the rays of a mounting sun. A

[42] *Dabney*, 610.   [43] *Fitz Lee*, 227.
[44] *Cooke*, 182. Cooke evidently was present.

few minutes later the ready war god rang up the curtain on the scene set for slaughter, and against the vast back-drop of the gun-studded hills of Stafford, the whole stage was disclosed from the upper fringe of Fredericksburg streets to the distant gray meadows in front of Hamilton's Crossing. Then as now, distances must have been deceptive. It must have seemed incredible that a mile and more, a distance too great to be covered by the short-ranged guns in the Southern batteries, separated the observing audience on the crest of the ridge from the massed multitudes of actors on the far-sweeping plain below.[45] Fifty-five thousand Jackson reckoned in his front, with guns past counting. Hidden in the streets of Fredericksburg must be other thousands. Never had the might of the potent North been so fully displayed before the eyes of the ragged soldiery of the South.

"Test the ranges on the left," Lee ordered at 10:30, and soon a quick blaze of fire swept from Marye's Heights northward.[46] The enemy seemed to take it for a challenge. Almost at once, Lee saw long, heavy blue lines begin an advance against the lower part of the ridge on the right, where waited the veterans of A. P. Hill, who had saved the day at Sharpsburg. Scarcely had the Federals started forward than white smoke-puffs could be seen on the enemy's left. They were from two of Pelham's horse artillery, only two, set boldly out in the field. Soon it was apparent that their fire was enfilading the approaching column. The lines halted. The men sought such cover as the undulation of the open ground offered.[47] Busy batteries could be seen hurrying to silence Pelham. Four of them opened quickly on him. It seemed certain that he would be destroyed. One gun was disabled, but through the gathering smoke, a few minutes later, he shifted his other rifle and put the enemy off his range. Again and again he moved, one piece against sixteen, but he was not silenced. The Federal attacking column remained where it was. The whole army waited, as if to watch the single combat of the paladin gunner. Lee's judgment told him that Stuart had opened too soon,[48] but his admiration for Pelham's fine fighting

---

[45] *Longstreet*, 307; *O. R.*, 21, 631; 3 *B. and L.*, 76; *Long*, 239; *F. W. Dawson*, 85.
[46] *Longstreet*, 308.
[47] For the unevenness of the plain, see H. C. Cabell, in *O. R.*, 21, 586.
[48] *H. B. McClellan* 193.

rose with each round. "It is glorious to see such courage in one so young," he exclaimed.[49] Stuart had thrice to recall Pelham before the young artillerist abandoned the unequal fight.

When at last he withdrew, the Federal artillery began to plaster the front of A. P. Hill's division spitefully. Not a gun answered them. "Old Jack" was unwilling to show his hand for the small stakes his hidden batteries might claim. Soon Lee saw the Federals marching undisturbed down the Richmond stage road to extend their left flank. Presently they halted and faced about. It was a splendid deployment, worthy of Lee's brother-engineer, George Gordon Meade, who had stood with him on the deck of the tiny *Petrita,* fifteen years before, when Scott had made his hazardous reconnaissance of the sea-front at Vera Cruz.

No sooner were the Federals in position than they surged forward in a long line for their first attack. Steadily they came on, their well dressed lines plainly visible from Lee's lookout. Still the ridge in their front sent no challenge. For all the opposition they encountered, they might have been recruits in some training manœuvre, far from the field of action. They had narrowed their distance to 1000 yards, to 900, and were only 800 yards away when, in a single crash, Hill's artillery swept their lines. The startled troops halted, wavered at the second salvo and then in confusion fell back as they had come.[50] A first repulse: the enemy must try again!

Longstreet on the left had opened his batteries at 11 o'clock to create a diversion, in the belief that the attack on the Confederate right was a major assault. His fire swept across Fredericksburg and played on the bridges. The 30-pounder Parrott and the smaller guns on Lee's Hill added their metal. The explosions shook the ridge and filled the air around the commander's lookout with the intoxicating smoke of battle. The artillery had a commanding field of fire. Lee's Hill reaches an elevation of 210 feet. Marye's Heights rise to 130. Between them flows Hazel Run. On a line from north to south, Lee's Hill is about four-

---

[49] *Cooke,* 183; Cooke: *Wearing of the Gray,* 133; Jones, *L. and L.,* 209; Philip Mercer, *The Gallant Pelham,* 135 *ff.* Later in the day Lee said to Jackson, "You should have a Pelham on each flank" (*White,* 244). In his preliminary report of the battle Lee mentioned the young artillerist as the "gallant Pelham" (*O. R.,* 21, 547).

[50] *O. R.,* 21, 631. This fire had been heaviest from Prospect Hill, later called Jackson's Hill, which appears on the map p. 453.

tenths of a mile farther westward from Marye's Heights, which stood out like a promontory. So wide and so open was the zone of fire in front of Lee's Hill that no troops could hope to endure shelling long enough to reach the sides of the hill from the plain below. Marye's Heights were closer to the enemy and seemed to be easier. The town gave cover for massing the assaulting columns. In front of the heights, diagonally from left to right, ran a deep ditch that offered good shelter at a distance varying from 330 to 900 yards. Between this ditch and the heights the ground rose gradually, with one "dip" about midway that was not under direct fire. But from this "dip" the incline was steady and open, though not very steep, to the Telegraph road. This road turns sharply from the west at the southeast corner of Marye's Heights and runs thence northward. It had been cut from the lower part of the ridge to a width of about twenty-five feet and had stone retaining walls on either side. The road itself was sunken, scarcely visible from the town side. The outer retaining wall was four feet high and constituted a perfect parapet for infantry. Above the sunken road were the guns.[51] The general position is shown on the map printed on page 453. The sketch of the front of attack, on the opposite page, shows it in more detail with contour intervals of ten feet.

Behind the stone wall in the sunken road stood a North Carolina regiment of Cooke's brigade[52] and a Georgia brigade, commanded by General T. R. R. Cobb, a publicist of distinction who had been very critical of Lee during the early part of the campaign of 1862 but had been completely won by Lee's kindness. The batteries behind them were the well-equipped Washington Artillery, with Ransom's division of two North Carolina brigades in support.

The heights and the sunken road, in a word, constituted a death trap; were the Federals foolish enough to venture into it? The Confederates speculated and doubted until, at 11:30 o'clock the incredible answer came. Out from the streets poured the Federal infantry, headed straight for Marye's Heights, precisely as Lee had hoped, yet scarcely had dared hope. General Burnside most obligingly was preparing to waste in costly assault the great

---

[51] *O. R.*, 21, 589; *Longstreet*, 298.　　　　[52] *O. R.*, 21, 625.

odds his country had given him. Not only so, but he was deploying in the most injudicious manner, "right in front," instead of "double columns in the centre." [53] The Unionists did not even

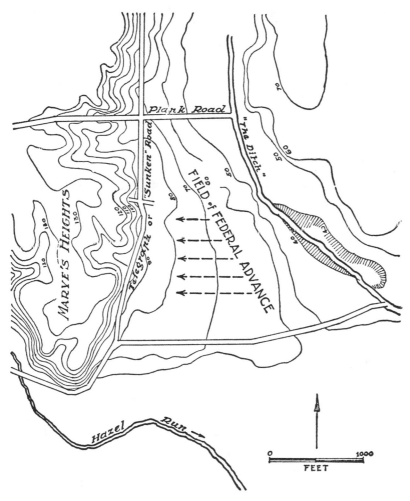

choose the weakest part of Marye's Heights for their assault. Instead of attacking farther to the northward, where the Confederate artillery was less numerous and less advantageously placed,[54] they made their advance against the steepest part of the heights and directly against the sunken road. "It was magnificent,

[53] 10 *S. H. S. P.*, 450.   [54] 10 *S. H. S. P.*, 448.

put it was not war." On they came, plainly visible to Lee, completing their deployment as they advanced. They planted three standards defiantly, but in the very act received the full blast of the artillery almost in their faces. So intense was the fire and so perfectly laid that the ranks thinned at the very first round and soon were melting back to the ditch in blue and blood. The Confederate infantry had scarcely anything to do in repulsing this first advance. Shellfire sufficed.[55]

First blood for Longstreet as for Jackson—but every indication that heavier assaults against both positions were to be delivered speedily! On the right, as 1 o'clock approached, Lee could see the stout columns slowly massing. Almost on the hour, the Stafford Heights broke into flames, as if the door of a furnace had been thrown wide, and with a shout the Federal left wing swept forward against Jackson. It was a major assault this time, and manifestly it was to be delivered in a gigantic effort to take the ridges and turn the right of Lee's line. Quickly the Confederate batteries opened in reply. Gaps were cut in the charging columns. Windrows of dead were left behind. In a long volley the Confederate infantry opened, claiming grievous toll in every regiment. A minute more and the fire was so heavy as almost to drown the nearer batteries on Marye's Heights, against which the Federals were beginning to form for another assault.

The advance was slower now on the right but it seemed resistless. Gradually it concentrated on a neck of woodland that extended from the Confederate front across the railroad. Soon the roar centred there. More and more of the enemy were drawn into the woods, as into a vortex. Presently the fire was closer to the ridge, and whenever the sound of the enemy's cheers could be heard in the din, they were pitched to a note of triumph. Something had gone amiss. The Federals had found an opening. They might be breaking the line. From Lee's Hill it was impossible to tell. Ere long, keen eyes with good field glasses could distinguish figures making their way to the rear in garb of a different color from the blue dots on the plain. Prisoners! Some disaster had overtaken Hill.

The enemy was farther into the woods now—was Jackson being

[55] *O. R.*, 21, 580, 608.

whipped? Advanced batteries had been withdrawn. The guns on Prospect Hill which had broken up the first Federal advance could not bear on the woods where the Federals entered.[56] There was fury and confusion, and, on Lee's Hill, wonder and misgiving. More prisoners, wounded streaming back; but no withdrawal. If the Union troops were not advancing they were at least holding their ground. In front of Marye's Heights they had formed again by this time, were advancing and were being hurled back over their own dead and wounded—but there on the right, what was happening? South of the neck of woods, they were beaten back, and from the line of the railroad were firing uselessly in their front; still they struggled through the woods and on toward the ridge.[57] On the left of the thicket, also, an advance to the railroad was under way.

The Federals with their overmastering artillery were plastering the whole front. A shell buried itself close to Lee under the parapet but did not explode.[58] Through the smoke, Lee found himself looking across the Valley of the Rappahannock to see if he could locate in the yard at Chatham the old tree under which he had wooed Mary Custis.[59] As his thought and vision ranged, officers came and went, reports were received and orders sent to the strange music of the 30-pounder Parrott in the redoubt. Round after round it roared on in excellent practice until after the gunners had rammed home their thirty-ninth charge. Then there was a discordant explosion, a rending sound, and the breech of the gun split into a dozen fragments that fell to the ground. Lee was nearby, as were Longstreet and Pendleton, but none of these and not one of the artillerists was touched.[60]

Suspense was now at the highest. Reports from the right told only that the enemy had made his way between the brigades of Lane and Archer and was fighting savagely. Another column had crept up the ravine of Deep Run and had engaged the left of Pender's brigade. At last, above the deep roar of the artillery,

---

[56] O. R., 21, 636.   [57] O. R., 21, 646.   [58] Longstreet, 312.
[59] Statement of Captain J. P. Smith to the author. For Lee's memories of Chatham see Lee to Mrs. Lee, Dec. 8, 1861; R. E. Lee, Jr., 57.
[60] Sorrel, 140; O. R., 21, 566; 10 S. H. S. P., 453n; Morgan, 149–50; McDaniel, 17. The second 30-pdr.-Richmond Parrott, to the right of Lee's Hill, exploded about the fifty-fourth round, during one of the charges by Humphrey's troops (Longstreet, 313). Pendleton (O. R., 21, 567) was vague as to the time this happened.

there came the echo of the high, quavering rebel yell, an "unearthly, fiendish yell, such as no other troops or civilized beings ever uttered," as a Federal chaplain reported.[61] It must be a Confederate countercharge. A few minutes later, as anxious eyes and ears were strained, the Federals began to run out of the wood they had entered. The very trees seemed to discharge them, limping, crawling, retreating in the confusion or stubbornly and slowly falling back, firing as they went. Louder swelled the rebel yell, faster rolled the fire, until, with a gasp of excited joy, the observers on Lee's Hill saw the familiar ragged men in butternut burst from the wood and down Deep Run in all the passion of pursuit. On they went, close after the Federals, valiantly forming line, only to lose it again as the fleet of foot sought to overtake the laggard Federals.

Lee's eyes flashed as he saw them, and the blood of "Light-Horse Harry" fought in his veins with the calmer strain of the peace-loving Carters. Turning to Longstreet he revealed the whole man in a single brief sentence: "It is well that war is so terrible—we should grow too fond of it!"[62] As he uttered the words, he seemed in the eyes of a British correspondent who stood by to have about him an "antique heroism." [63]

Out into the plain the Confederates pursued, heedless of their officers' commands. Soon they were under fire and began to drop fast. At length those who had come from the neck of woods turned back in good order, but those who had repulsed the attack at Deep Run rushed on until their officers in desperation had almost to beat down their muskets. Finally, after they had sustained needless losses, they too retired. But not in content of mind. They were Carolinians and they felt humiliated that they had been denied the honor of charging their foe to the very banks of the river. Some were weeping in their vexation, and some were swearing at General Hood as they stumbled back over Federal corpses to their own line. "It's because he has no confidence in Carolinians," they protested. "If we had been some of his Texans, he would have let us go on!" [64]

Whatever had happened on the right—and Lee did not know

61 J. C. Gregg: *Life in the Army*, 60. For other descriptions of the rebel yell, see *Morgan*, 70, and *R. L. T. Beale*, 192.
62 *Cooke*, 184.   63 Lawley, quoted in *McCabe*, 315.   64 *Dabney*, 617.

—it had been rectified, the front had been restored and the enemy had been driven back. It was not yet 3 o'clock, and the enemy might renew his assaults in that quarter, but there was scarcely time for speculation on this, because the enemy was again madly hurling his brigades against Marye's Heights in a third attack. General Cobb had been mortally wounded by an enfilading fire from some buildings on the left,[65] and as the cartridges of his gallant brigade ran low, Kershaw's men and two more regiments of Cooke's North Carolinians had been sent down to the sunken road.[66] Kershaw had assumed command there just as this third attack was taking form and he had his troops in line four to six deep, practically filling the road;[67] but they were so composed in the confidence of victory, that each line fired in turn, or else those in front passed their empty rifles to the men behind them and took their loaded pieces.[68] Not one was injured by the fire of those in the rear ranks.[69]

The third attack was repulsed, but it had been pushed so far and with so much vigor that Lee began to wonder if the troops were numerous enough to hold the ground. "General," said he to Longstreet, "they are massing very heavily and will break your line, I am afraid."

Longstreet answered proudly, "General, if you put every man now on the other side of the Potomac in that field to approach me over the same line, and give me plenty of ammunition, I will kill them all before they reach my line. Look to your right; you are in some danger there, but not on my line." [70]

It was not an empty boast on the part of "Old Pete." Again, and with fresh troops, the Federals came forward, and again they were hurled back before a single man could reach the stone wall. Attack followed attack until the soldiers in the sunken road lost count of the number. Their ammunition was exhausted as they poured volleys into the advancing enemy at intervals of only a few seconds, so they took the cartridge boxes from the dead and from the wounded. They had no medical relief closer than the field hospital behind the hill, and the only house into which even the nearest could be removed was that of Mrs. Stevens, facing the

[65] O. R., 21, 590.
[67] O. R., 21, 589.
[69] O. R., 21, 589.
[66] O. R., 21, 574, 580, 588, 625.
[68] History of Kershaw's Brigade, 187.
[70] 3 B. and L., 81.

road. Mrs. Stevens herself was there, having refused to abandon the place, and in a ceaseless hail of bullets she bound the wounds of such soldiers as could reach her shelter. Her very petticoats she tore up for bandages, while the Federals seemed to make her house a target. When Lee heard of what had happened there, his wrath rose, as it always did when non-combatants suffered. "I wish those people would let Mrs. Stevens alone!" he exclaimed hotly.[71]

About 3:30 there came a lull in front of Marye's Heights, while new brigades were prepared for the slaughter. On the right, as on the left, though the artillery continued to roar, there were no infantry charges. The enemy had enough of Jackson's fire. His battle was over, with his lines completely restored. Taking advantage of the pause in the infantry assaults, Colonel Walton on Marye's Heights asked that his Washington Artillery, the caissons of which were almost empty, be relieved by other batteries. Word was quickly sent to Alexander to bring up fresh guns. His shortest road to the Heights was across the front and up a ravine. Without hesitating he hurried his pieces forward in the very face of the enemy. "Down the Telegraph road," wrote one of the men who stood behind the stone wall, "the battery came, their horses rearing and plunging, drivers burying the points of their spurs deep into the flanks of the foaming steeds; riders in front bending low upon the saddle bows to escape the shells that now filled the air, or plowed up the earth beneath the horses' hoofs." One gun was overturned and the column was delayed, but the piece was quickly righted and the wild rush began again, "the men on the caissons clinging with a death-like grip to retain their seats, the heavy wheels spinning around like mad and bounding high in the air." Officers shouted and urged the men on; the batteries turned up the grade, exposed to the full fury of the fire, reached the crest, swung to the right, and unlimbered.[72] Then, and not till then, did Walton's exhausted men drag their scorching, smoke-covered guns to the rear. The Federals saw the withdrawal and, noting the cessation of fire, assumed that a retreat was begin-

[71] Goolrick, 51.
[72] History of Kershaw's Brigade, 188–89; Alexander, 306n; 10 S. H. S. P., 455; O. R., 21, 574, 576.

ning. With a shout, they sprang forward again.[73] But Alexander's guns opened instantly, the infantry in the sunken road were well warmed to their bloody work, and the combined fire repulsed the enemy once more, his casualties added to the writhing army on which the attacking columns trampled as they passed forward and as they retreated.

The day was nearly done, but the bewildered Burnside stubbornly pushed in fresh troops in a mad determination to achieve the impossible by the weight of his numbers and the immensity of his sacrifices. To meet him, Lee ordered Jenkins's brigade from the right to support McLaws and directed Kemper to reinforce Ransom.[74] Two regiments of Kemper's brigade were sent down into the sunken road to relieve the 24th North Carolina, which had been there two days.[75] On the enemy came, with strong supports. If one brigade faltered and lay down, another pressed over it; when one fell back, a second dashed forward. The whole field seemed alive with a blue that by this time was beginning to blend into the twilight on the chill ground. Each time the folly of the blind assault seemed more criminal. One man, presumably an officer, made his way unscathed to within thirty yards of the sunken road and there fell dead. Behind him a few scattered bodies lay at intervals, but few got closer than one hundred yards. Beyond that distance, the bleeding forms were piled man on man in ghastly barricades. Still the gallant columns pressed on toward the stone wall. It was nearly 7 o'clock when the final assault withered in the face of artillery that now was firing by the flashes of the Federal small arms.[76]

On the centre, between Lee's Hill and the left of A. P. Hill's line, there had been no infantry assaults.[77] Late in the afternoon, on the right, Jackson thought he observed preparations for a renewal of the attack, and when this did not materialize he deployed for the offensive, only to find that his advance came under such a heavy fire of artillery that nothing but slaughter could be expected.[78] Out of this brief and abortive deployment

---

[73] O. R., 21, 576, 589. [74] Longstreet, 311.
[75] O. R., 21, 626. [76] O. R., 21, 576, 581, 589; 10 S. H. S. P., 451.
[77] Cf. Scales, 15–16; W. H. Stewart: A Pair of Blankets, 74, quoting J. B. Magruder to his father, Dec. 20, 1862.
[78] O. R., 21, 634, 666; Early, 177–78.

developed the myth that Jackson planned a night attack, which Lee vetoed.[79] Before the final attack on Marye's Heights had been repulsed, any general counterattack would have been dangerous; after that time it was impossible, even if Jackson's experience had not proved that the commanding Federal artillery would have swept the Southern lines precisely as the Confederate batteries had mowed down the Federals in their front. As far as is known, Lee did not consider such a thrust. No one who studies the ground can justly criticise him for failing to do so.[80]

When the artillery at last died away in black night, the very skies seemed to reflect the blood that had been spilled to no purpose in front of the sunken road. First there was a dim, ghostly light beyond the horizon that grew in brightness until it covered a wide arc of the horizon; then it broke into the mysterious shafts of such an aurora borealis as the soldiers from the far South had never seen.[81] It was, in their eyes, a warning of what the morrow would bring forth, for nearly every one expected Burnside to renew the attack.[82] Despite his losses, the Federal commander assuredly would try his strength again in a more intelligent manœuvre against the Confederate position.

At headquarters, whither Lee rode under the glow of the aurora, his generals were all but unanimous in expressing this view. Only Hood insisted that Burnside would not resume the battle. Lee himself was of opinion that Burnside would make his major attack the next morning. In the highest spirits he predicted that further Federal assaults would be repelled and that the Army of Northern Virginia would then assume the offensive.[83] He voiced the expectation of a renewal of the battle in the first telegraphic report of the day's action, sent the Secretary of War at 9 P.M.[84] He believed that his opponent would not throw away his troops again in attacks against Marye's Heights, but would manœuvre for a turning movement. Nothing more was to be gained by luring the enemy to unfortified hills. Consequently he ordered the entire line strengthened, so

---

[79] *Taylor's Four Years*, 81–82.   [80] *Maurice*, 172; *Early*, 180 ff.; *Scales*, 19.

[81] James H. Wood: *The War*, 110. General Alexander in 10 *S. H. S. P.*, 461, stated that this aurora was on the night of Dec. 14.

[82] 2 *von Borcke*, 132.   [83] *Hood*, 50; *O. R.*, 51, part 2, p. 662.

[84] *O. R.*, 21, 546.

that he could hold it with part of his force and have the rest of the army free to manœuvre. Before midnight his judgment seemed to be confirmed by the capture of a messenger bearing a memorandum of Burnside's plan for the next day's fight—the last fight of the Army of the Potomac, as many of the Confederates confidently believed.[85]

There was much to hear and much to do as the night wore on. In particular, Jackson was reminded tactfully to replenish his ammunition,[86] and new reports of a threatened movement against James River were carefully sifted.[87] Lee learned, also, in some detail, of what had happened on the right at 1 P.M., when he had seen the enemy mysteriously enter the neck of woods that extended across the railroad, opposite A. P. Hill's front. It developed that this was a bit of marshy ground, which Hill had thought impassable[88] and had not protected, though von Borcke had suggested that the timber be felled[89] and General Lane had specifically pointed out the danger the position presented.[90] Archer's brigade had been on the right of this gap and Lane on the left, with Gregg in the second line, behind the gap.[91] Finding the weak spot, the Federals had poured in. Two regiments on Archer's left and the whole of Lane's brigade had given ground, but Archer had changed front on his right and had stubbornly resisted.[92] When the Federals had penetrated the woods, they had surprised one regiment of Gregg's brigade, and Gregg himself had mistaken the enemy for a retiring Confederate force. In the mêlée, Gregg had fallen and some of his men had been roughly handled, but Lawton's brigade under Colonel E. N. Atkinson, Trimble's under Colonel R. F. Hoke, and Early's under Colonel J. A. Walker had come up quickly from the second line and had pushed the enemy back. As Hoke's men had rushed forward in pursuit, Gregg had pulled himself up by a sapling and, though dying and unable to speak, had cheered the men onward by waving his hat.[93] The troops who had charged the enemy on the railroad and had then pursued

[85] *Longstreet*, 316.
[86] *Jones*, 155; *White*, 250–51; 39 *S. H. S. P.*, 1; 43 *ibid.*, 32–33.
[87] *O. R.*, 14, 711; *ibid.*, 21, 1061.   [88] *O. R.*, 21, 676.
[89] 2 *von Borcke*, 106.   [90] *O. R.*, 21, 653–54.
[91] *O. R.*, 21, 631–32.   [92] *O. R.*, 21, 632, 656–57.
[93] *Scales*, 14.

them into the plain had been Atkinson's and Hoke's. Thomas's men and two regiments of Lane's had restored the front that Lane had held.[94] The only other point where the enemy had reached the railroad had been on the left of Pender, along Deep Run, and there he had been driven back by a countercharge of a part of Law's brigade.[95] This action at Deep Run and on Hill's front had cost Lee 3054 casualties,[96] and, though it had ended without disaster, it had not been altogether satisfactory. Longstreet had felt that Hood should have attacked more heavily while the fighting was under way near his position.[97]

A brief and troubled night broke in heavy fog on the morning of December 14.[98] Riding early to the front, Lee was pleased to find that the fatigue parties had done their work well in fortifying the heights. "My army," he said, "is as much stronger for these new entrenchments as if I had received reinforcements of 20,000 men."[99] He kept the diggers at their work, and hour by hour he saw the parapets rise higher.[100] Confident of his ability to throw Burnside back a second day, Lee had only one concern: his ammunition was low, and his chief ordnance officer reported that a railway train then on its way contained all the reserve supply from Richmond. Lee could only hope for thrifty gunnery that day, while he urged the War Department to speed the manufacture of more shell.[101]

As the weather was clear, the sun quickly scattered the fog and gave to the expected new battle the setting of a perfect winter's day.[102] When the field became visible, the enemy was seen holding the ditch in front of Marye's Heights, but the men were flat on the ground and showed no disposition to stir.[103] The ends of the streets facing the Confederate positions were barricaded, and the walls of many of the houses were loop-holed for infantry.[104] Manifestly, Burnside did not intend to resume the attack on Marye's Heights, and as no reports came of any activity farther to the left, Lee concluded that the offensive would

94 *O. R.*, 21, 632, 645–46, 653, 657, 663, 667, 672. 95 *O. R.*, 21, 623–24.
96 *Alexander*, 301.
97 *Longstreet*, 307, 317; *O. R.*, 21, 622–23. 98 *O. R.*, 21, 566.
99 2 *von Borcke*, 132–33; *cf.* 10 *S. H. S. P.*, 461.
100 *Longstreet*, 316. 101 *O. R.*, 21, 546.
102 *G. Wise*, 129.
103 *O. R.*, 21, 571, 576. 104 10 *S. H. S. P.*, 459.

not be renewed on that wing. Sending fresh long-range artillery to Jackson,[105] Lee rode to the right and, with "Stonewall" and Hood, went to Prospect Hill, the eminence from which Lindsay Walker's artillery had broken up the first demonstration on the morning of the 13th. "We had a magnificent view of the Federal lines on their left, some seven in number, and each, seemingly, a mile in length," Hood wrote. "General Jackson here turned to me, and asked my estimate of the strength of the enemy then in sight and in our immediate front. I answered fifty thousand, and he remarked that he had estimated their numbers at fifty-five thousand. Strange to say, amid that immense assemblage of Federal troops, not a standard was to be seen; the colors were all lowered. . . ."[106]

What did all this mean? Was it a trick, or could it be possible that the enemy had abandoned the offensive? With the question puzzling him, and almost unwilling to believe the evidence before his eyes, Lee returned to his own post of observation and examined the ground again. The Union troops were burying the dead within their lines and were carrying off such of the wounded as they could reach. Now and again the skirmishers engaged in angry exchanges, and the Federal batteries fired a few half-hearted rounds. That was all.[107] Noon and afternoon brought no change. The waiting Confederates were surprised, then disappointed, then depressed. Lee's amazement grew. "General," he said to Longstreet, "I am losing faith in your friend General Burnside," and he put down the captured memorandum, outlining operations for the 14th, as a *ruse de guerre*.[108] Evening came, and not a man had been engaged at close range. Still, it did not seem credible that so great an army was ready to abandon so elaborate a manœuvre after only one day's partial engagement of his forces. When Lee sat down at night to write his preliminary report of the battle, he could only describe the situation. He did not attempt to forecast its development.[109]

On the morning of the 15th, with his own line still further

---

[105] Lane's six-gun battery, less his 12-pdr. Whitworth (*O. R.*, 21, 566; 10 *S. H. S. P.*, 387).

[106] *Hood*, 50–51.

[107] *O. R.*, 21, 547.

[108] 3 *B. and L.*, 82.

[109] *O. R.*, 21, 546–48.

strengthened, Lee observed that the enemy had dug rifle pits and had thrown up fortifications on the outskirts of the town, as if to repel attacks.[110] He saw a ghastly sight besides: The Federal dead that still remained between the lines had changed color. They no longer were blue, but naked and discolored. During the night, they had been stripped by shivering Confederates, many of whom now boasted overcoats, boots, and jackets for which the people of the North had paid. It was ghoulish business, reprobated by the enemy but excused by the beneficiaries, who asked whether it was better for them to freeze or to take clothing the former owners would not miss.[111]

Jackson came during the morning for a conference,[112] but so far as is known there was no discussion of a counterstroke. How could there be one, when the Federal lines were now well fortified, and the superior artillery was still in position on the plain and across the river to blast the Confederate lines? Lee's spirits sank. If the Federals did not intend to renew the attack, the victory would be barren, save for the losses inflicted. It was a heavy price to pay for having to defend the line of the Rappahannock in order to procure supplies from the lower valley of the river. The strategy of the commissary might be unescapable but it was disheartening.

During the afternoon of the 15th, Burnside sent out a flag of truce for the burial of the dead and for the relief of such of the wounded as had survived forty-eight hours on the ground without even the poor comfort of a canteen of water.[113] Lee readily consented to a truce on that part of the front where the Federals had fallen.[114] Soon the surgeons, the ambulance detachments, and the burial details mingled with the Confederates in the field. The horror of the scene was far greater at close range than it had appeared from the lines. In the space of an acre or so were 1100 dead Federals, some of them piled 7 or 8 deep,[115] "swollen," as one horrified witness has observed, "to twice their natural size, black as Negroes in most cases, lying in every conceivable posture, some on their backs with gaping jaws, some

---

[110] 10 *S. H. S. P.*, 461.
[111] Richard Lewis to his mother, Dec. 19, 1862; *Camp Life of a Confederate Boy*, 37
[112] *O. R.*, 21, 567.
[113] 3 *B. and L.*, 100.
[114] 10 *S. H. S. P.*, 460.
[115] *G. Wise*, 130.

with eyes as large as walnuts, protruding with glassy stare, some doubled up like a contortionist, here one without a head, there one without legs, yonder a head and legs without a trunk, everywhere horrible expressions, fear, rage, agony, madness, torture, lying in pools of blood, lying with heads half buried in mud, with fragments of shell sticking in oozing brain, with bullet holes all over the puffed limbs. . . ."[116] A fifth of them had been killed by artillery; the *minié* balls from the heights and from the sunken road had accounted for the rest.[117] There could be no reasonable computation of the gross casualties. Not until months afterward was it known that the Federals had lost 12,653, compared to 5309 on the Confederate side, many of the latter having trifling wounds.[118] In front of Marye's Heights, where 9000 Federals had fallen, McLaws had lost only 858—in Cobb's brigade but 235—and Ransom's casualties had been 534.[119] The toll on the entire Confederate left, from McLaws's division to the end of the line, including Kemper's and Jenkins's brigades, had not exceeded 1676.

Light as were the losses of the Confederates, contrasted with those of the Federals, the sight of so much human woe would have been intolerable had it not been relieved by episodes that made the burial details laugh even as they shuddered. One Confederate private, who had picked up a fine Belgian rifle that lay on the ground among the dead, was reprimanded by a Federal major. Nobody, the Union officer said, could salvage arms during a truce. The Confederate continued on his way, heedless of the officer, until his eye chanced to light on the Federal's fine boots. "Never mind," he said, "I'll shoot you tomorrow and git them boots."[120]

Another Confederate stooped on the field to take a pair of shoes from the feet of a Federal who lay prone and apparently dead. While he was removing one shoe, he was startled to see the man lift his head reproachfully. The Confederate carefully put the man's foot back on the ground. "Beg pardon, sir," he said, "I thought you had gone above."[121]

---

[116] 1 *Shotwell Papers*, 430–31, with the author's strange punctuation adapted to current usage.
[117] *O. R.*, 21, 587.
[118] *O. R.*, 21, 142; *Alexander*, 313.
[119] *O. R.*, 21, 584, 629.
[120] *Marginalia*, 21.
[121] *Taylor's General Lee*, 149.

By the time this polite ghoul and his comrades had come back into the lines, Lee was suspicious that Burnside was about to retire in order to undertake a new advance somewhere else on the Rappahannock, but still he could not convince himself that an adversary who had done so much boasting and had made so many preparations could afford to withdraw.[122] Lee waited on the lines till a south wind sprang up and a rain began to fall during the evening. Then, in frank perplexity, he returned to his headquarters at Hamilton's Crossing.[123]

The rain was still falling and the morning was dark when he started to the front again on the 16th.[124] As on the previous mornings since Burnside had advanced across the Rappahannock, the haze was so thick that nothing of the enemy's whereabouts could be seen,[125] not even when Lee rode to the right once again to reconnoitre from Jackson's front.

With "Stonewall," he went out to the eminence near the railroad whence he had observed the silent army resting on the morning of the 14th with not a single flag flying. D. H. Hill was on the ground, talking with Colonel Bryan Grimes. Hill met them with the announcement that the enemy had disappeared from his front.

"Who says they are gone?" Jackson demanded.

"Colonel Grimes," Hill said.

"How do you know?" Jackson asked the colonel.

"I have been down as far as their picket line of yesterday," Grimes answered, "and can see nothing of them."

"Move your skirmish line as far as the line," Jackson ordered, "and see where they are."

Lee said nothing, but Grimes observed how deep was the chagrin and humiliation with which he and Jackson received the news.[126]

The report was true. Under cover of the darkness, with the south wind shutting off all sound from the Southern lines, Burnside had retreated and had removed his bridges. It had been an easy task and Lee felt that it could not have been pre-

122 Lee to Mrs. Lee, Dec. 16, 1862, *R. E. Lee, Jr.*, 87. 123 *Dabney*, 625.
124 *G. Wise*, 130. 125 *O. R.*, 21, 581.
126 *Extracts of Letters of Maj.-Gen. Bryan Grimes to His Wife* . . . Compiled by Pulaski Cowper (cited hereafter as *Grimes*), 27.

vented.[127] "Had I divined that was to have been his only effort," he said of Burnside, "he would have had more of it." [128] And again, in disappointment: "[the enemy] suffered heavily as far as the battle went, but it did not go far enough to satisfy me. . . . The contest will have now to be renewed, but on what field I cannot say." [129] He was deeply depressed that he had not been able to strike a decisive blow. "We had really accomplished nothing; we had not gained a foot of ground, and I knew the enemy could easily replace the men he had lost"—thus he reviewed the campaign months afterwards.[130] The army and the country shared his chagrin.[131]

Although there were some signs that the Federals were moving for the Potomac,[132] Lee's expectation was that Burnside would soon cross the river again, probably at Port Royal, in which case he planned to reconcentrate in the enemy's front and to give battle anew. If the Federals slipped over the line of the Rappahannock unopposed—and that would not be difficult on so long a line—then Lee intended to withdraw to the North Anna and meet him there.[133]

That was all. There was no pride in the quick discovery of Burnside's plan to move from Warrenton to Fredericksburg, no boasting that an army of 78,000 had blocked the advance of 125,000 Federals on the Confederate capital, and had captured 11,000 stands of arms,[134] no rejoicing that the great preparations of the enemy had been set at naught with casualties nearly two and a half times those the Army of Northern Virginia had sustained. There was only regret that more had not been done.[135]

---

[127] Lee to W. M. MacDonald, April 15, 1868, *Jones*, 267.

[128] Lee to Mildred Lee, Dec. 25, 1862, *R. E. Lee, Jr.*, 89. *Cf. Marshall*, quoting William Allan, 249.

[129] Lee to Mrs. Lee, Dec. 16, 1862, *R. E. Lee, Jr.*, 87.

[130] 4 *S. H. S. P.*, 153.   [131] *De Leon*, 248; 2 *von Borcke*, 147.

[132] *O. R.*, 21, 1063.   [133] *O. R.*, 21, 548, 548–49.

[134] *O. R.*, 21, 568.

[135] As Burnside's report was not written until November, 1865, Lee did not learn for several years, if indeed he ever knew, all the reasons for Burnside's strange actions. The crossing of the river was delayed because the necessary pontoons were slow in arriving (*O. R.*, 21, 86 *ff.*). The attack on the Confederate right had been entrusted to Franklin's Grand division, but owing to vagueness of orders and to Burnside's lack of a definite plan, it was delivered by only three divisions, Meade's, Gibbon's, and Doubleday's, though Franklin had 60,000 men at his command. The first assaults in front of Marye's Heights were made by French's division of Sumner's command, followed by the rest of Couch's II corps, then by Willcox's IX corps, and finally by parts of Hooker's III and V corps. The final attacks were by Getty's 3d division of the IX corps and by

Slowly and sorrowfully, by the now familiar road, he made his way back to headquarters on the 16th and sat himself down to write Mrs. Lee about the battle and to discuss with her their plans for helping the Arlington Negroes whom he was soon to manumit under the will of Mr. Custis.[136]

Humphreys's 3d division of the V corps. Burnside planned, as Lee anticipated, to renew the attacks on the 14th, but was dissuaded by some of his subordinates. By Dec. 20, the Confederates had a reasonably accurate report of the protests of the Federal commanders against a renewal of the battle. *Cf.* J. B. Magruder to his father, Dec. 20, 1862, in W. H. Stewart: *A Pair of Blankets,* 76. The best Southern account of the battle is Alexander's, *op. cit.,* 285 *ff.* The fullest Northern accounts are F. W. Palfrey's *The Antietam and Fredericksburg,* 136 *ff.* and J. C. Ropes, *op. cit.* William Allan contributed an excellent paper on Fredericksburg to 3 *M. H. S. M.,* 122 *ff.*

[136] Lee to Mrs. Lee, Dec. 16, 1862, *Fitz Lee,* 235. General Lee had repeatedly referred to plans for releasing these slaves and was anxious to do so as promptly as possible. *Cf.* Lee to Custis Lee, Jan. 4, 1862, Jones, *L. and L.,* 157; and same to same, Nov. 22, 1862, *MS., Duke Univ.*

CHAPTER XXXII

THE FIRST WARNINGS OF COMING RUIN

(THE WINTER OF 1862–63)

BURNSIDE's withdrawal across the Rappahannock left Lee in doubt as to the future intentions of his adversary, though he was satisfied that the Army of the Potomac would soon advance again.[1] When a week passed without any movement by the enemy, he sent Stuart and 1800 of his cavalry to scout on the north side of the river, to assail the enemy's communications and to ascertain his dispositions.[2]

While Stuart was away, the army passed a bleak Christmas in such shelters as the men had been able to find on the heights and in the woods. Lee spent the forenoon in writing letters. "My heart," he told Mrs. Lee, "is filled with gratitude to Almighty God for His unspeakable mercies with which He has blessed us in this day, for those He has granted us from the beginning of life, and particularly for those He has vouchsafed us during the past year. What should have become of us without His crowning help and protection? Oh, if our people would only recognize it and cease from vain self-boasting and adulation, how strong would be my belief in final success and happiness to our country! But what a cruel thing is war; to separate and destroy families and friends, and mar the purest joys and happiness God has granted us in this world; to fill our hearts with hatred instead of love for our neighbors, and to devastate the fair face of this beautiful world! I pray that, on this day when only peace and good-will are preached to mankind, better thoughts may fill the hearts of our enemies and turn them to peace. . . ."[3] To his daughter Mildred he wrote in less serious strain, with a touch of homesickness in his heart, but he concluded with the assurance, "I am . . . happy in the knowledge that

[1] *O. R.*, 21, 548, 1068.   [2] *O. R.*, 21, 731, 1076.   [3] *R. E. Lee, Jr.*, 88–89.

475

General Burnside and his army will not eat their promised Christmas dinner in Richmond today."[4]

For his own dinner he went by invitation to Jackson's headquarters, where the doughty "Stonewall" entertained him, Pendleton, and their staffs. Jackson had received many presents of food from admirers and was able to spread a sumptuous table, not forgetting to have his waiters appear in white aprons. This fastidious touch, in such a setting, appealed to Lee's sense of humor. He had much jest at the lavishness of Jackson's entourage. Jackson and his lieutenants, he said, were playing at soldier. They must come and dine with him to see how real soldiers lived. His great lieutenant, of course, was both pleased and confused at Lee's comments.[5]

The last week in December passed uneventfully, except for fatigue duty in strengthening the fortifications on Marye's Heights.[6] On the 29th, Lee executed the deed of manumission for the Custis slaves, taking pains to include all the Negroes he could remember.[7] Two days later, on the last day of the year, he published to the army his congratulatory order on the outcome of the battle of Fredericksburg. In this he warned the men that new duties lay ahead. "The war is not yet ended," said he. "The enemy is still numerous and strong, and the country demands of the army a renewal of its heroic efforts in her behalf. Nobly has it responded to her call in the past, and she will never appeal in vain to its courage and patriotism. The signal manifestations of Divine mercy that have distinguished the eventful and glorious campaign of the year just closing give assurance of hope that, under the guidance of the same Almighty hand, the coming year will be no less fruitful of events that will insure the safety, peace and happiness of our beloved country, and add new lustre to the already imperishable name of the Army of Northern Virginia." This final flourish showed the hand of Major Charles Marshall rather than that of Lee.[8]

The year had, indeed, been one of victory in Virginia, at least during the seven months Lee had commanded the army. Port Re-

---

[4] R. E. Lee, Jr., 87.
[5] Mrs. Jackson, 379; J. P. Smith in Richmond Times-Dispatch, Jan. 20, 1907.
[6] O. R., 51, part 2, p. 666.
[7] R. E. Lee, Jr., 99; MS. deed of manumission, from the records of the Hustings Court, Part I, of the city of Richmond, Va., Confederate Museum.
[8] O. R., 21, 550.

public, Cross Keys, Mechanicsville, Gaines's Mill, Savage Station, Frayser's Farm, Malvern Hill, Cedar Mountain, Second Manassas, Boonsboro, Harpers Ferry, Sharpsburg, and Fredericksburg— thirteen battles great and small—had been fought during that time, and the Confederates had remained masters of the field in every instance except at Boonsboro and at Sharpsburg. Leaving out of account the actions at Cross Keys, Port Republic, and Cedar Mountain, which were tactically Jackson's though Lee had a part in the general strategy, the troops under Lee's command had this account of gains and losses: They had sustained 48,171 casualties and had inflicted 70,725.[9] They had taken from the enemy approximately 75,000 small arms and had yielded scarcely more than 6000. With the loss of 8 cannon, they had secured 155. The infantry practically had been rearmed with improved, captured rifles, and half the batteries boasted superior ordnance that had belonged to the Army of the Potomac.

The morale of the Army of Northern Virginia was vastly higher than it had been when Lee took command, yet there was a consciousness in the ranks, though not in the Richmond executive offices, of the persistent, determined spirit of an enemy who could replace every fallen soldier, make good every captured arm, and supply every necessity of the Army of the Potomac from ample manufactories and open ports. Richmond was fearful of military defeat but refused to admit the inevitable consequences of economic attrition. The Army of Northern Virginia was confident of victory in the field but fearful of economic disaster behind the lines. Before the winter was to end, the danger of starvation and of immobility, resulting from a collapse of transportation, was to be plain to every private in the ranks.

The improvement in organization wrought after July was amazing. Gone were the excitable Magruder, the slow Huger, the gloomy Whiting, and the deaf Holmes. Gone was the cumbersome old arrangement of divisions, operating as if they had been independent armies. In its place were two well-administered corps, commanded by officers of proved capacity. The divisions and brigades were becoming conscious of their relation to the military machine, and were led, in most instances, by men who relied

---

[9] Included in these figures were 4077 prisoners lost and 29,370 captured.

on sound tactics and good discipline, rather than on the costly valor of untrained soldiers. Fifteen of the brigadier generals who had entered the Seven Days' Battle with Lee were no longer present to issue his congratulatory order to their men on the last day of 1862. Some of the best of the fifteen had been killed, notably Garland, Gregg, and Winder, but the incompetents had in part been supplanted and the political generals had been sent elsewhere—and all so quietly, so tactfully, that few realized how the army had been transformed by the time the men tumbled out of their blankets and wished one another a Happy New Year at roll-call on the morning of January 1, 1863.

Stuart came back from his raid that first day of the month, bringing with him about 200 prisoners and some plunder. He had stories of gallant encounters near Dumfries and around Occoquan to tell, but he had no definite news of the enemy's dispositions or plans.[10] Uninformed, in the midst of bitter weather,[11] Lee had to await the next move of his adversary and, meantime, had to give serious thought to the threatened development of a new attack in North Carolina. The Federals had, at that time, a small force at Suffolk, Va., sixteen miles west of Norfolk, and an army of unknown strength in eastern North Carolina. On December 11, 1862, Major General John G. Foster, Federal commander of the Department of North Carolina, had left New Berne with 10,000 troops and had occupied Kinston on the 14th. After driving back a small opposing Confederate force, he had pushed on to Goldsboro, which he reached on the 17th. He had burned an important railroad bridge on the Weldon and Wilmington line and had torn up four miles of track. Although he had retreated promptly to New Berne,[12] his raid had created profound apprehension not only in eastern North Carolina but in Richmond as well. It was feared that he might cut the communications between the capital and the south, and, if reinforced, might move on Richmond from the south. There was a suspicion, also, that the operations against Goldsboro were a feint and that the main objective might be Wilmington.[13] This was Lee's opinion.[14]

To afford immediate protection, he started Ransom's division

[10] O. R., 21, 731–35.
[11] R. E. Lee to Custis Lee, Jan. 5, 1863; Jones, L. and L., 225.
[12] O. R., 18, 54 ff.   [13] O. R., 18, 815.   [14] Lee's Dispatches, 70.

southward on January 3 and decided to place Major General D. H. Hill at the disposal of the government in rallying the people of North Carolina.[15] There was a demand that Lee visit the state to study the enemy's movements,[16] but he did not feel that he could leave the Rappahannock until General Burnside's intentions were more fully disclosed. In case Burnside retired, he believed it would be practicable to send part of his army to North Carolina and, with the rest, to clear the Valley of Virginia, where he had consolidated the command under Brigadier General W. E. Jones, who had one brigade of cavalry.[17]

On January 14, Lee ordered D. H. Hill to Richmond,[18] and on the 16th he went there in person, at Mr. Davis's request, to confer on the situation.[19] He found the administration concerned over the immediate outlook but confident that the war should soon be won, an optimistic delusion he did not share.[20] At the instance of the President, he agreed to detach two brigades for service in North Carolina.[21]

Before any further decision was reached, Lee was hurriedly recalled to Fredericksburg by the news that Burnside's army was on the move and seemed to be threatening to cross the Rappahannock.[22] When he reached headquarters on the 18th, Lee found Jackson and Longstreet at odds concerning the disposition of the army for the expected attack.[23] Quickly settling this, he spent two busy days riding to the left and to the right of the line, and concluded, in the end, that the enemy's effort would be on the upper Rappahannock, above Fredericksburg.[24] Meantime, of necessity, he had suspended the movement of the two brigades that were to be sent to North Carolina, though he assured Mr. Davis that he would dispatch them if the President thought there was greater need of them in North Carolina than with the Army of Northern Virginia—a position he always assumed when calls were made on him for troops.[25]

Signs multiplied by January 20 that the enemy again was preparing to adventure across the Rappahannock.[26] In a heavy rain,

---

[15] O. R., 18, 819; 1 R. W. C. D., 233–34. [16] O. R., 21, 1088.
[17] O. R., 21, 1080, 1086, 1091–92. [18] O. R., 21, 1093.
[19] 1 R. W. C. D., 239. [20] 3 B. and L., 84.
[21] O. R., 21, 1095; T. J. Jackson to R. H. Chilton, Jan. 17, 1862; Chilton Papers.
[22] 1 R. W. C. D., 239. [23] Longstreet, 323.
[24] Taylor's Four Years, 82–83; O. R., 21, 1097. [25] O. R., 21, 1097.
[26] O. R., 21, 1101.

the shivering Confederate troops remained on the alert. Lee him-self was anxious about the enemy's movements and was not hopeful that he would be able to prevent a crossing at some point on his long, exposed line. In case Burnside eluded him he would hold to his plan of withdrawing toward the North Anna in order to reconcentrate his army, a course that Mr. Davis was anxious that he avoid if possible.[27] Two days, three days passed without action. There were new signs of activity below Fredericksburg,[28] and then once more above the city.[29] At length, following a heavy snow storm on January 27-29,[30] all Federal activity ended, and Lee con-cluded that because of the weather or for other reasons, Burnside's attempt had been frustrated.[31] He was correct. The Federal com-mander had contemplated a general offensive, but had found the roads so nearly bottomless that his advance had degenerated into what his disgusted army styled a "Mud March." [32]

During the five weeks that had separated the beginning of the "Mud March" from Burnside's defeat at Fredericksburg, Lee had been fortifying the entire front of the Rappahannock.[33] After the "Mud March" he had this work continued on the whole line of twenty-five miles from Banks's Ford to Port Royal.[34] "The world has never seen such a fortified position," one enthusiastic artillerist wrote after the system of defense had been completed. "The fa-mous lines at Torres Vedras could not compare with them. . . . They follow the contour of the ground and hug the bases of the hills as they wind to and from the river, thus giving natural flanking arrangements, and from the tops of the hills frown the redoubts for sunken batteries and barbette batteries *ad libitum*— far exceeding the number of our guns; while occasionally, where the trenches take straight across the flats, a redoubt stands out defiantly in the open plain to receive our howitzers. . . ." [35] These fortifications marked a definite stage in the evolution of the field defenses that were to be one of Lee's most historic contributions

---

[27] *O. R.*, 21, 1103, 1108. [28] *O. R.*, 21, 1111.

[29] Lee to Longstreet, Jan. 25, 1863, *MS.*, Annamary Brown Memorial, *Brown Univer-sity*; *O. R.*, 25, part 2, p. 597; *ibid.*, 51, part 2, p. 673.

[30] *Taylor's General Lee*, 153.

[31] Lee to Mrs. Lee, Jan. 29, 1863; *Fitz Lee*, 237-38.

[32] For Burnside's brief report of this operation, see *O. R.*, 21, 68-69.

[33] *Longstreet*, 323.

[34] Hotchkiss and Allan: *Chancellorsville* (cited hereafter as *Hotchkiss and Allan*), 15-16.

[35] A. S. Pendleton to his family, April 26, 1863; *Pendleton*, 256-57 n.

to the science of war. The ease with which some of the Fredericks-burg defenses were thrown up and the adequacy of the cover they afforded the army were not forgotten. From this type of work there was only one step to field fortification.

While the dirt was flying and the lines were daily growing stronger, Lee was warning an overconfident administration that the next few months might be decisive. "The enemy," he said, "will make every effort to crush us between now and June, and it will require all our strength to resist him." [36] He renewed his perennial appeal for the completion of the Richmond defenses;[37] he had the line of the North Anna examined by officers, who reported against a prolonged defense there;[38] he exhausted his arguments and almost exhausted his patience in trying to end wasteful details and to bring men into the ranks.[39] At no time during the war was his language more vigorous. "More than once," he wrote the Secretary of War, "have most promising opportunities been lost for want of men to take advantage of them, and victory itself has been made to put on the appearance of defeat because our diminished and exhausted troops have been unable to renew a successful struggle against fresh numbers of the enemy. The lives of our soldiers are too precious to be sacrificed in the attainment of successes that inflict no loss upon the enemy beyond the actual loss in battle. . . . In view of the vast increase of the forces of the enemy, of the savage and brutal policy he has proclaimed,[40] which leaves us no alternative but success or degradation worse than death, if we would save the honor of our families from pollution, our social system from destruction, let every effort be made, every means be employed, to fill and maintain the ranks of our armies, until God, in His mercy, shall bless us with the establishment of our independence." [41] Congress's failure to act aroused to indignation even a nature that had been disciplined from boyhood to respect civil authority. "Our salvation will depend on the next four months," he said prophetically, "and yet I cannot get even regular promotions made to fill vacancies in regiments, while Congress seems to be laboring to pass laws to get easy places for some fa-

---

[36] *O. R.*, 51, part 2, p. 677.   [37] *O. R.*, 51, part 2, p. 679.
[38] *Long*, 247–48.   [39] *O. R.*, 25, part 2, p. 639.
[40] The reference is to Milroy's assessments; see *infra*, p. 482.
[41] *O. R.*, 21, 1086; *cf. ibid.*, 51, part 2, p. 680.

vorites or constituents, or get others out of active service. I shall feel very much obliged if they will pass a law relieving me from all duty and legislating some one in my place, better able to do it." [42] Again he wrote hotly: "What has our Congress done to meet the exigency, I may say *extremity,* in which we are placed? As far as I know, concocted bills to excuse a certain class of men from service, and to transfer another class in service, out of active service, where they hope never to do service." [43]

Regardless of the remissness of the lawmakers, Lee's apprehension of a new crisis kept him from resting, inactive, behind his cavalry outposts, which were extended by this time from Beverley's Ford on the upper Rappahannock far down the river to the watershed between the Rappahannock and the Pamunkey.[44] With the energy that always surged under his calm exterior, he now turned his attention to General R. H. Milroy. That officer, or some one misusing his name, was putting into effect in parts of western Virginia a system of organized blackmail, almost unique in character. Southern sympathizers were notified that loss had been inflicted on Union supporters and that an assessment had been levied against them to make this good. Formal notice of the assessment was accompanied by extracts from an official order of General Milroy, announcing that if the recipient did not pay, his house was to be burned, his property seized, and himself shot. Under this arbitrary system, it was believed that $6000 had been wrung from Southern sympathizers in Tucker County alone.[45] In addition, General Milroy had issued an order requiring all citizens to notify him of the approach of Confederate troops on pain of death and the destruction of their houses.[46] General Lee had protested to General Halleck against these orders, which Halleck had disavowed,[47] but Lee was anxious that the author of such threats be driven from Virginia.[48] From Confederates there came complaints that Brigadier General W. E. Jones, whom Lee had named to command in the Valley, had not been active in dealing

---

[42] Lee to Custis Lee, Feb. 12, 1863; Jones, *L. and L.,* 226.
[43] Lee to Custis Lee, Feb. 28, 1863, Jones, *L. and L.,* 227.
[44] *Hotchkiss and Allan,* 7.
[45] II *O. R.,* 5, 808–11; III *O. R.,* 2, 944–45; III *O. R.,* 3, 14.
[46] III *O. R.,* 2, 944.
[47] *O. R.,* 21, 1102; III *O. R.,* 3, pp. 10, 15–16; *Lee's Dispatches,* 70.
[48] *O. R.,* 21, 1086, 1104.

with Milroy's raiders.[49] Lee had defended Jones, whose difficulties he understood,[50] and he now resolved to detach Fitz Lee's brigade of cavalry to reinforce Jones for an attack on Milroy.[51]

Just at the time when this expedition was moving through the mud toward the Valley on February 14, a fleet of Federal transports, loaded with men, steamed down the Potomac. The troops were suspected to be the IX Corps and their probable destination, Lee thought, was Charleston, where he now expected the next Federal blow to fall, instead of at Wilmington.[52] There was, however, probability that the destination might be southeastern Virginia and the objective Richmond or the railroad leading to it from the south. Lee had already discussed with the President the advisability of sending troops to the exposed railway line of communications through North Carolina,[53] and on call from Richmond he now ordered Pickett with his division of the First Corps to start for Richmond on the 15th. Hood was put on the alert to follow Pickett.[54] Not knowing whether the Federal movement presaged a change of base, Lee directed Stuart to make a reconnaissance when the column intended for the Valley reached Culpeper. If Stuart then discovered signs of any general retirement of the Federals, he was to operate at once on their lines of communication and was to suspend the expedition into the Shenandoah area.[55]

As reports immediately indicated a concentration at Newport News, Lee ordered Hood to follow Pickett to Richmond, and, after he was informed, on the 17th, that a third corps was moving down the Potomac, he directed Longstreet to proceed southward and take command of the two detached divisions. He left the disposition of these troops to the War Department, but he directed them temporarily to camp near Richmond until the plan of the enemy should be more fully disclosed.[56]

The departure of Longstreet left Lee with a total force not exceeding 62,600 officers and men, of whom only 58,800 were on the

49 *O. R.*, 21, 1080; III *O. R.*, 3, 12–14.
50 *O. R.*, 21, 1092; *ibid.*, 25, part 2, p. 604, 641.
51 *O. R.*, 25, part 2, pp. 606, 621, 622.
52 *O. R.*, 14, 766; 1 *R. W. C. D.*, 255; *O. R.*, 25, part 2, pp. 622, 623, 624.
53 *O. R.*, 14, 762, 763, 1019.   54 *O. R.*, 25, part 2, 623.
55 *O. R.*, 25, part 2, p. 623–24.
56 *O. R.*, 25, part 2, pp. 624–25, 630, 632; 1 *R. W. C. D.*, 260, 261; *Longstreet*, 324; *Sorrel*, 159; *Hood*, 51.

line of the Rappahannock.[57] Yet Lee's chief regret was that he could not take the offensive against the diminished Federal command opposing him. He wrote the President: ". . . the most lamentable part of the present condition of things is the impossibility of attacking them with any prospect of advantage. The rivers and streams are all swollen beyond fording; we have no bridges, and the roads are in a liquid state and nearly impracticable. In addition, our horses and mules are in that reduced state that the labor and exposure incident to an attack would result in their destruction, and leave us destitute of the means of transportation." [58]

General Joseph Hooker had now replaced General Burnside in command of the Army of the Potomac—a change that Lee accepted with complacency. In his personal letters he jested mildly over the apparent inability of Hooker to determine on a course of action. "General Hooker is obliged to do something," he wrote one of his daughters on February 6. "I do not know what it will be. He is playing the Chinese game, trying what frightening will do. He runs out his guns, starts wagons and troops up and down the river, and creates an excitement generally. Our men look on in wonder, give a cheer, and all again subsides *in statu quo ante bellum*." [59] Later in the month, when a foot of snow brought new hardship to the men, he complained to Mrs. Lee, "I owe Mr. F[ighting] J[oe] Hooker no thanks for keeping me here. He ought to have made up his mind what to do." [60]

By February 26, Lee concluded that Hooker had decided to do nothing on a large scale until the weather improved.[61] Rest in winter quarters became more of a reality, though the army was not free of all activity. Lee held to his rule not to embarrass private families by crowding himself and his staff into nearby homes.[62] He usually camped near Longstreet in order to hasten the movements of that leisurely general,[63] and after Longstreet left for southside Virginia, he remained in the little clearing in the woods

---

[57] The remainder, 3800, were with W. E. Jones in the Shenandoah Valley (*O. R.,* 25, part 2, p. 650).
[58] *O. R.,* 25, part 2, p. 627; *cf. ibid.,* 658.
[59] Lee to Agnes Lee, *R. E. Lee, Jr.,* 92.
[60] Feb. 23, 1863; *R. E. Lee, Jr.,* 93.   [61] *O. R.,* 25, part 2, pp. 642–43.
[62] For an amusing instance of this, see *Long,* 227.
[63] *White,* 234.

on the Mine Road to Hamilton's Crossing.[64] His tents were few in number and had nothing to indicate that they were the headquarters of the army, except for a flag in front of the tent of Major Taylor.[65] The wagons stood unparked; the horses were tethered in good weather or sheltered in crude bowers against the storms. No sentinel stood at Lee's tent except when he was engaged.[66] Inside were his Spartan camp equipment, his military desk, and a small stove. His most frequent guest was a hen that requited his hospitality by laying an egg regularly under his cot.[67] Other guests of different species were numerous. Robert came more frequently than before, bringing reports, for he had been promoted lieutenant and had become aide to Rooney, his brother. As the brigade he commanded was usually at a distance, Rooney came rarely.[68] The sons and other guests, formal and familiar, were entertained occasionally at dinner, but with no pretense of a well-furnished table. In December, 1862, when Lord Hartington, Colonel Leslie, and Francis Lawley of *The London Times* had been delayed by Jackson's hospitality and had arrived at Lee's quarters long after the hour set for a repast in their honor, they found that the General had finished his simple meal and was relieved, rather than fretted, because they had come late. "Gentlemen," he said, "I hope Jackson has given you a good dinner, and if so, I am very glad things have turned out as they have, for I had given the invitation without knowing the poor state of my mess provisions, and should scarcely have been able to offer you anything." [69]

Whether entertaining or visiting, inspecting or in council, Lee sought during that stern winter to set an example of good cheer and to keep high the spirits of his lieutenants. From no other period of the war have so many diverting stories survived. He was very fond of teasing his messmates and the handsome young officers whom he met on his rounds.[70] Once, in the fall, when he had heard Stuart's famous banjo player, Sweeny, amusing a company of

<hr>

[64] *Cooke,* 205.   [65] *F. W. Dawson,* 88.   [66] 2 *B. and L.,* 524.

[67] *Long,* 241; *R. E. Lee, Jr.,* 85; Wolseley, *loc. cit.,* 20–21. Wolseley visited Lee at Falling Waters early in October, it will be recalled, but his description was applicable to headquarters in almost every campaign.

[68] *R. E. Lee, Jr.,* 81. Rooney and his wife had lost a baby early in December, 1862. General Lee wrote Charlotte, characteristically, in loving sympathy (*Jones,* 395; *Jones, L. and L.,* 202).

[69] 2 *von Borcke,* 166.   [70] *Taylor's General Lee,* 157; 43 *S. H. S. P.,* 41–43.

officers in front of his tent, he had come out to express his thanks, and had observed a jug of liquor sitting rather conspicuously on a boulder. "Gentlemen," he had said, "am I to thank General Stuart or the jug for this fine music?" [71] One day, a little later, when a similar vessel had been observed in his own tent, he had come out to ask his staff if they would "like a glass of something." Willingly and expectantly they followed him inside. He had his mess steward, Bryan, place glasses on the table, and then he told him to serve the officers. Bryan obediently pulled the cork, while lips were smacked expectantly. With the air of one who might have been dispensing a king's best Burgundy, he solemnly poured out to each a glass—of buttermilk.[72] Complaints of hard living he turned off with a jest. When a young officer protested that the biscuits were unconscionably tough, Lee looked at him reassuringly. "You ought not to mind that," he said, "they will stick by you the longer." [73] Major von Borcke, of Stuart's staff, had been compelled, after Fredericksburg, to buy a carriage in order to get a span of horses he had admired. Being thrifty, von Borcke sought to make the carriage do duty as a baggage wagon. Lee rarely met the German Goliath that he did not ask, "Major, where's your carriage?" A little later, when von Borcke chanced to be with him while a minor engagement was in progress, Lee remarked dryly, "If we only had your carriage, what a splendid opportunity to charge the enemy with it!" [74] Hood was another with whom Lee liked to joke. From his nearby camp, Hood called one day when the General chanced to be talking with Colonel Chilton about the depredations of the soldiers in burning fence rails and stealing pigs. Hood, somewhat self-righteously, felt called upon to defend his division against such a charge. Lee let him finish, and then he said, "Ah, General Hood, when you Texans come about, the chickens have to roost mighty high." [75]

It was Jackson, however, that Lee, in common with Jeb Stuart and Longstreet, was most prone to tease. Going to the vicinity of Hayfield with Jackson, he called on its mistress, his kinswoman, Mrs. W. P. Taylor. Two young ladies were present with Mr. and

[71] *Long,* 229.
[72] *Long,* 240–41. Lee had a similar jest at the expense of General John G. Walker. (*D. H. Maury,* 239).
[73] *R. E. Lee, Jr.,* 91.　　[74] *2 von Borcke,* 161.　　[75] *Hood,* 51.

Mrs. Taylor to welcome him and his companions. Lee announced that he had brought his great generals along for the young ladies to see and had allowed the young officers to come along in order that they might see the ladies. To Mrs. Taylor he confided in that officer's presence, that Jackson was one of the most cruel and inhuman of men. At the battle of Fredericksburg, he went on, it had been all he could do to keep Jackson "from putting bayonets on the guns of his men and driving all those people into the river." Mrs. Taylor forthrightly answered that she had always heard that General Jackson was a good Christian man, and that she hoped if "those people" ever crossed at Hayfield, General Lee would not do anything to keep General Jackson from driving them back.[76]

One of the little children at a river plantation sometimes visited by Lee considered him her confidant. She would always come up to kiss him and at last whispered to him that she wanted to kiss General Jackson, too. When Lee repeated this, "Stonewall" was as much confused as if a dazzling Richmond belle had threatened to embrace him. On another visit, when the same little girl came up to greet him, Lee suggested that she would show better taste if she kissed one of the younger officers. "There is the handsome Major Pelham," he said, pointing to Stuart's renowned young artillerist, who blushed in a manner to rival Jackson.[77]

Much as Lee delighted to tease his comrades, he was sensitive to their hardships and unfailing in his consideration for them. Stuart's staff had not forgotten how sympathetically he had talked with Mrs. Stuart in November when he had heard of the loss of her little boy,[78] and almost every officer had some special kindness to cherish. In the midst of a snow storm, answering a summons from Lee, Jackson rode over one night, accompanied by an aide, Captain J. P. Smith. Lee was almost angry that Jackson had exposed himself and Smith to the rigors of the weather when nothing would have been lost by waiting until the storm was over. After Jackson had gone with him into his tent, Lee came out several times to be sure that his staff officers were making Captain Smith comfortable.[79]

[76] 43 *S. H. S. P.*, 41–43; J. P. Smith, the same writer, in *Richmond Times-Dispatch*, Jan. 20, 1907.
[77] *Cooke*, 306.   [78] 2 *von Borcke*, 63.
[79] *Mrs. Jackson*, 380; J. P. Smith, in *The Richmond Times-Dispatch*, Jan. 20, 1907.

Stuart was a constant concern to Lee because his reckless courage led him to expose himself needlessly. Lee depended on him more than on any one else for information as to the enemy's movements; no other officer seemed to have quite the same ability to peer at a distant column from a hilltop, and to say how strong it was and whither it was bound. Such a man was irreplaceable, and Lee knew it. Often he ended official letters to Stuart with warnings against unnecessary risks. A characteristic conclusion to his orders for a hazardous enterprise was, "Commending you to a kindly Providence and your own good judgment. . . ." [80]

Lee's own staff officers shared his sympathy precisely as they had to endure his teasing. One of their number was not especially diligent, and his disposition to take his duties lightly increased the labor of the others. Occasionally some of them felt that the General was inclined to put the burden on those who would bear it and to allow the shirker to go unrebuked. Lee's known aversion to spending time over routine official papers occasionally created unpleasant situations. During the autumn before Fredericksburg, Major Taylor had come into Lee's tent when the General had been in a bad humor. Before the work had fairly begun, Lee had been jerking his head and neck in the familiar manner that showed rising anger. Taylor petulantly had thrown the paper down at his side and had silently defied his chief. Instantly Lee had gripped himself and in perfect calmness, with measured tones had said, "Major Taylor, when I lose my temper, don't let it make you angry." [81]

There was much to do at winter quarters besides keeping the officers in good spirits. Correspondence was heavy. Lee not only wrote out in person most of his confidential dispatches,[82] but also penned many brief papers to save the time and labor of others. He acknowledged in his autograph every present sent him, from a mattress[83] to a prayer book.[84] With pains and sympathy, he addressed, besides, numerous friends whose kinsmen had fallen in the army. One such letter from Hamilton's Crossing was to his old companion, Doctor Orlando Fairfax, whose magnificent young

[80] Cf. O. R., 21, 1076; ibid., 25, part 2, p. 621.   [81] Taylor's Four Years, 77.

[82] Sometimes, as already noted, he did not retain copies of these dispatches, probably because he did not wish even his aides to see them.

[83] Calendar of Confederate Papers, 315; cf. supra, Vol. I, p. 616.

[84] R. E. Lee to Laura Chilton, Dec. 28, 1862; Chilton Papers, Confederate Museum.

son had fallen at Fredericksburg, a private in the ranks.[85] Another similar letter went to Howell Cobb on the death of the brother who had commanded in the sunken road at Marye's Heights. Still a third was sent to Governor F. W. Pickens of South Carolina on the loss of General Gregg. "The death of such a man," Lee said, "is a costly sacrifice, for it is to men of his high integrity and commanding intellect that the country must look to give character to her councils, that she may be respected and honored by all nations." [86]

The never-ending tasks of reorganization likewise consumed much time in winter quarters. The campaigns of 1862 had developed some friction between Jackson and Lee's headquarters staff[87] and had shown a number of weaknesses in the law governing staff organization. The chairman of the Senate committee on military affairs, which was seeking to amend the act, wrote Lee to ask his opinion of the proposed legislation. Lee answered in detail and, knowing the sensitiveness of the President, took care to outline to him in a separate letter his views of the necessary changes. He did not attempt to draw a legal line between the general staff and the personal staff of officers in the field. Instead, he explained that the aides of a general officer need not be numerous, as the general staff could usually assist on the field of battle, when the duties of the aides were heaviest. At other times, the officers of the general staff were busier than a general's aides. His main insistence was twofold. First he argued for equality of rank for the heads of the various staff bureaus serving with a given army unit. Each division of the staff, he argued, in the second place, should be "a complete organization in itself, so that it can manœuvre independently of the corps or division to which it is habitually attached and be attached with promptness and facility when required. . . . If you can then fill these positions with proper officers, not the relatives and social friends of the commanders, who, however agreeable their company, are not always the most useful, you might hope to have the finest army in the world." [88]

[85] Jones, 437; Mrs. Burton Harrison, 96–97; P. Slaughter: Sketch of . . . Randolph Fairfax.
[86] O. R., 21, 1067.
[87] Cf. T. J. Jackson to R. H. Chilton, Jan. 2, 1863; R. H. Chilton to T. J. Jackson, Jan. 5, 1863; Taylor MSS.
[88] IV O. R., 2, 446–48.

The legislation, which was shaped substantially as Lee recommended, was not adopted until June, 1864,[89] but as far as existing statutes permitted, Lee anticipated it and proceeded to reorganize the army staff during the winter of 1862–63.[90] The benefits were soon observable, though he did not succeed in destroying the nests of nepotism that some of the division and brigade commanders had established at their headquarters.

The artillery was reorganized along with the staff. Lee had long doubted the wisdom of attaching batteries permanently to the smaller units, and in February, 1863, he had General Pendleton work out a plan for the establishment of artillery battalions of four batteries each. These battalions were to be assigned to the corps, not to the brigades or to the divisions, and were to be employed as needed. The general reserve was to be reduced to six batteries. At the head of the whole force, which amounted to 264 guns,[91] was to be an army chief of artillery reporting directly to the commanding general. Over the battalions attached to each corps was to be a chief of artillery for that corps. A much-emphasized feature of the plan was the provision of two field officers for each battalion, one a lieutenant colonel and the other a major. Lee assumed that one of these officers would be busy in the general direction of the unit, and that the other would be needed to place the guns. As he explained to President Davis, "If you do not have an officer of judgment and experience to send forward [to] select the position, prepare the way, etc., the captains have to leave their batteries or lead them blindly forward. A captain should always be with his battery." [92] The plan was approved, and the choice of men was debated with much care and not without some heat on Jackson's part. A new statute, enacted to facilitate the reorganization, allowed a brigadier general for each eighty guns, or three for the army. Lee was not satisfied that his friend Pendleton had all the qualifications for army chief of artillery. Instead, he recommended that General Arnold Elzey, if his health and habits permitted, should be chief, that Pendleton should become head of the artillery of the Second Corps, and that Colonel A. L. Long of

[89] *Statutes at Large*, 1st session, Second Congress of the Confederate States, Chap. 58, 1864.
[90] *Hotchkiss and Allan*, 14–15.
[91] *O. R.*, 25, part 2, p. 651.   [92] *Lee's Dispatches*, 76.

his staff, who had shown great skill in handling ordnance, should be promoted chief of artillery of Longstreet's corps, though he recognized the difficulties involved in promoting a staff officer to that position.[93] The President preferred not to disturb the existing assignments and deferred action on the selection of three brigadier generals for the artillery. The battalion organization, however, became effective before the opening of the campaign of 1863. The management of the artillery arm was much improved by the change.[94] The exchange of six-pounder guns for new twelve-pounders, in accordance with a plan of recasting that Lee had formulated in the autumn of 1862, also contributed much to improve the artillery.[95]

Far more serious than reorganization of staff and gunners was the shortage of horses and the danger that lack of forage would cause the death of many of those that had survived the long campaign from Mechanicsville to Fredericksburg. Every horse with the army had to be conserved and additional animals had to be provided, because the heavier cannon would demand larger teams.[96] The spectre of a paralyzing shortage of horses was already haunting the mind of Lee. He mentioned the condition of the animals as one of the chief reasons why he could not take the offensive after the detachment of troops from the Army of the Potomac in February,[97] and from the labor he expended in trying to save the army's horses during the winter of 1862–63, there can be little doubt that even then he saw in the prospective failure of the horse supply one of the most serious obstacles to the establishment of Southern independence. Some 600 or 700 mules had been purchased in the Trans-Mississippi Department and were being wintered at Alexandria, La.[98] Four hundred artillery horses had been procured in Georgia but had not been brought nearer than North Carolina, because they could not be foraged with the army.[99] These were all that could be counted upon to supplement the gaunt and jaded animals with the trains, except, of course, for such additional horses as could be picked up in the unplundered sec-

[93] *Lee's Dispatches*, 78 *ff.*
[94] For the reorganization, see *O. R.*, 25, part 2, pp. 614 *ff.*, 625, 629, 633 *ff.*, 644, 651, 655, 729; *Wise*, 1, 412 *ff.*; *Lee's Dispatches*, 73 *ff.*
[95] *O. R.*, 25, part 2, p. 695.
[96] *O. R.*, 25, part 2, p. 695.
[97] See *supra*, p. 484.
[98] IV *O. R.*, 2, 417.
[99] *O. R.*, 25, 2, 618.

tions of nearby states. The country immediately adjacent to the army had been so completely swept of fodder that as soon as the first threat of a new offensive had passed after the battle of Fredericksburg, he had ordered the whole of the artillery to the rear, except twelve batteries.[100] All the draught horses that could possibly be spared thereafter were sent back from the Rappahannock, some of them as far south as Brunswick County, which lies on the North Carolina border.[101] When Pickett and Hood went to Richmond, Lee was so fearful the artillery horses would break down that he suggested the guns be forwarded by train and the animals be led through the country.[102] The quartermaster of the artillery scoured the line of the Virginia Central for fodder and grain,[103] to increase the limited supply brought by rail from Richmond.[104] Rooney Lee's cavalry brigade was foraged miles from the right of the line, in Essex and Middlesex Counties, though it had to get its meat from the Northern Neck counties across the Rappahannock.[105] The transportation of the army was reduced to the absolute minimum,[106] but even then it was admitted that many of the horses would have to suffer.[107] As the late spring held back the grass,[108] Lee was compelled on April 6, when the advance of the enemy was only a matter of days, to warn Pendleton not to bring up his teams from the south more rapidly than he could find feed for them.[109]

The danger to the cavalry from the shortage of feed was every whit as serious as the threatened paralysis of the artillery. The army would be feeble without artillery but it would be blind without cavalry. The superiority of the Confederate mounted forces, a potent factor in the operations of 1862, was not only challenged, but was in danger of being lost completely. Hampton had been detached and sent southward to recruit, primarily because his horses could not remain with the main army and be supplied.[110] The position of W. E. Jones and that of Rooney Lee

[100] O. R., 21, 1077; 1 R. W. C. D., 228.
[101] O. R., 25, part 2, pp. 618, 709; ibid., 51, part 2, p. 679; Lee's Dispatches, 71–72.
[102] O. R., 25, part 2, p. 632.   [103] O. R., 25, part 2, p. 599.
[104] O. R., 25, part 2, p. 709.   [105] O. R., 25, part 2, p. 703.
[106] O. R., 25, part 2, pp. 681, 726–28, 739, 749.
[107] O. R., 25, part 2, p. 618. R. E. Lee to R. M. T. Hunter, Feb. 12, 1863; Martha T. Hunter: A Memoir of Robert M. T. Hunter, 120.
[108] O. R., 25, part 2, p. 750.   [109] O. R., 25, part 2, p. 709.
[110] O. R., 25, part 2, pp. 711, 740.

have been described. Fitz Lee, who contrived to subsist his men and horses where Hampton's had been in danger of starvation, covered the left flank of the army from the Blue Ridge to the Rapidan.[111] These two brigades were all that Lee had with him during the late winter. Repeatedly through the dark months, by letter and in person, he asked for reinforcements, and as the time for the opening of the campaign approached, he besought the President to find him two more brigades,[112] though he could not graze their mounts and therefore could not order them up until the spring opened, even if they were made available.

Tragic as it was to see the faithful animals of the army die for lack of forage, and bitter as were the unescapable reflections of Lee on what might happen the next winter, he had daily to face a worse condition in the hunger of his own men. Provisions came to the Rappahannock from Richmond by a single-track railroad that was far from regular in its delivery of cars.[113] The nearby country supplied almost nothing. Because of the condition of the horses, only a limited number of wagons could be sent into distant counties to collect provisions there.[114] As early as January 5, Lee doubted whether starvation might not prove a more potent foe than the Army of the Potomac,[115] and thereafter he had to resort to every expedient to keep even a few days ahead of actual hunger in the ranks.[116] Colonel Cole, the chief commissary, went to Richmond to plead with the authorities and brought back many promises but no provisions.[117] Such beeves as were sent forward were generally so thin that Lee had to ask that they be kept to fatten in the spring, and that salt meat be issued instead.[118] Cavalry were used to supplement the government agents in collecting cattle; the commander of a proposed expedition to cut the B. & O. Railroad was told that the meat he might bring back was as important as the damage he might inflict;[119] wagons were furnished to haul to the railroad the wheat purchased by the commissary;[120] appeals to the public were urged on the President by

111 O. R., 25, part 2, p. 740.   112 O. R., 25, part 2, pp. 738, 740, 1047.
113 O. R., 21, 1110; 1 R. W. C. D., 290.   114 Hunter, loc. cit.
115 R. E. Lee to Custis Lee, Jones, L. and L., 225.
116 Cf. O. R., 25, part 2, p. 597.   117 O. R., 25, part 2, p. 599.
118 O. R., 51, part 2, p. 669; 1 R. W. C. D., 242.
119 Hunter, loc. cit.; O. R., 25, part 2, pp. 598, 711, 712.
120 O. R., 25, part 2, p. 612.

Lee;[121] the dispatch of men to collect grain along the James River and Kanawha Canal was suggested;[122] the War Department was importuned to send men southward along the railroads to hasten the movement of supply trains;[123] a report that there was beef in Florida was instantly hurried to the President.[124]

Scurvy began to appear; at the first signs of spring in the woods the soldiers were sent out to collect sassafras buds, onions, and other wild vegetation.[125] Vigorous warning was issued that the men must not damage growing crops on which their subsistence might depend.[126] At a time when 100 cars of sugar, intended for the army, were reported to have stood more than a fortnight on sidings in North Carolina, the soldiers went without that item of food for ten days. "Their ration," Lee wrote Seddon, ". . . consists of one-fourth pound of bacon, 18 ounces of flour, 10 pounds of rice to each 100 men about every third day, with some few peas and a small amount of dried fruit occasionally as they can be obtained. This may give existence to the troops while idle, but will certainly cause them to break down when called upon for exertion." [127] This was only two weeks before the beginning of the Chancellorsville campaign. Still later, when any day, any hour, might see the Federals on the move, Lee had to write the secretary, "I am painfully anxious lest the spirit and efficiency of the men should become impaired, and they be rendered unable to sustain their former reputation, or perform the service necessary for our safety." [128]

Lee's appeals and warnings alike failed to do more than to keep the army alive. Admitting that the shortage of food was due chiefly to a lack of railroad transportation, or to the right use of it,[129] Mr. Seddon was unable to overcome the gloomy contrariness of the commissary general, Colonel L. B. Northrop. This strange man, though he had the full confidence of Mr. Davis, had the singular faculty of keeping every army commander in a state of constant indignation. He is, in fact, one of the few functionaries of the period whose letters, read after seventy years, irritate if they do not actually outrage the historian. Convinced that his own

---

[121] 1 R. W. C. D., 246. [122] O. R., 21, 1110; 1 R. W. C. D., 246.
[123] O. R., 25, part 2, p. 612; cf. ibid., 693, 735–36.
[124] O. R., 25, part 2, p. 737–38. [125] O. R., 25, part 2, p. 687.
[126] O. R., 25, part 2, p. 708. [127] O. R., 25, part 2, p. 730.
[128] Lee to Seddon, April 23, 1863, O. R., 25, part 2, p. 744–45.
[129] O. R., 25, part 2, p. 692.

methods were right and were thwarted by the stupidity or opposition of the generals in the field, he took refuge in interminable letters of explanation when he was asked why the army was starving. He seemed satisfied if he could demonstrate that he was on record as predicting what had come to pass. By his own enigmatic code, he had rather be consistent than efficient. Lee corresponded with him no more frequently than necessity compelled, but he was angered by the mismanagement of the bureau more than by any other obstacle he encountered in his fight against ever-mounting odds. Northrop, for his part, had a grudge against Lee, first because the General would not reduce the army ration as Northrop desired and, secondly, because Lee had failed to accord an interview to a civilian whom Northrop had sent to his headquarters with a scheme for collecting supplies by utilizing the transportation of the army. Whatever the dereliction of which he was accused, no matter how desperate the plight of the Army of Northern Virginia, Northrop rarely failed to hark back to one or the other of his grievances against Lee. The months brought no better understanding.[130] Any experienced soldier could see by this time that war-weariness and the unhindered misdirection of an essential bureau by such a man as Northrop, regardless of other factors, might ultimately bring defeat at the hands of a stronger adversary. In Lee's letters of the winter of 1862–63 there is, however, not a hint that he knew he was championing a hopeless cause. Doubtless he shut his mind to speculation on the outcome and sought simply to do his duty while leaving the rest to God.

The cruel shortage of provisions was sharpened by the severities of an unusually bleak and frigid winter.[131] For a part of the men blankets were lacking even in January. Shoes were bad, especially those of English manufacture.[132] Yet the men somehow contrived to keep from freezing. Many built huts for themselves with chimneys of sticks and mud; others found a way to make themselves decently comfortable in tents by erecting chimneys or by procuring a stove, as Lee did.[133] There were snow battles for excitement,[134] theatricals for amusements, and religious meetings for spiritual

---

[130] For typical instances of his attitude, see *O. R.*, 21, 1088 *ff.*, 1110–11; *ibid.*, 51, part 2, pp. 674–75.
[131] *History of Kershaw's Brigade*, 205; *McCabe*, 327.
[132] *O. R.*, 21, 1097; *Alexander*, 318; *Sorrel*, 133.
[133] *Welch*, 41; *R. E. Lee, Jr.*, 92.   [134] Cf. *Early*, 190.

comfort. The revival that had begun in the lower Valley after the return of the army from Maryland spread from brigade to brigade. Religious leaders from the southern cities joined with the chaplains in preaching to men whose religious impulses had been awakened by the nearness of death. General Lee took deep interest in these meetings, conferred often with the chaplains and attended service whenever he could.[135] As a low churchman, there was nothing alien to him in the emotional evangelism that marked most of the discourses. On the contrary, he and Jackson, sitting side by side on a log, were moved to tears one Sunday by the affecting eloquence with which Reverend B. T. Lacy described the homes from which the army had been drawn.[136]

Music added its cheer. Most of the Confederate bands were notoriously bad, but they were industrious.[137] It was while the two armies were close together, not long after the battle of Fredericksburg, that an excellent Federal band came down to the river bank "and began," as General Sorrel has written, "playing pretty airs, among them the Northern patriotic chants and war songs. 'Now give us some of ours!' shouted our pickets, and at once the music swelled into 'Dixie,' 'My Maryland,' and the 'Bonnie Blue Flag.' Then, after a mighty cheer, a slight pause, the band began again, all listening: this time it was the tender melting bars of 'Home, Sweet Home,' and on both sides of the river there were joyous shouts, and many wet eyes could be found among those hardy warriors under the flags." [138]

Humor had its place with religion and music. Along with pranks and *bons mots,* the standing joke of the Confederate army did hourly duty in a hundred forms: "A 'cavalryman' comes rejoicing in immense top boots, for which in fond pride he has invested full forty dollars of pay; at once the cry from a hundred voices follows him along the line: 'Come out of them boots! Come out! Too soon to go into winter quarters! I know you're in thar!—see your

135 A chaplain who attended a review during the winter in his surplice was much laughed at, but when he approached Lee, the General took off his hat and said: "I salute the Church of God" (*Mason,* 375). Miss Maude Wadell informed the writer that the chaplain to whom this remark was addressed was Reverend Charles Curtis.

136 J. P. Smith in *The Richmond Times-Dispatch,* Jan. 20, 1907. The course of the revival is traced in detail in J. W. Jones, *Christ in the Camp,* 283 ff., and in W. W. Bennett: *A Narrative of the Great Revival* . . . , 231 ff.

137 *Wolseley,* 23.

138 *Sorrel,* 141. This is the incident that inspired John R. Thompson's "Music in Camp," conveniently accessible in *The Home Book of Verse.*

arms sticking out.' A bumpkin rides by in an uncommonly big hat, and is frightened by the shout: 'Come down out o' that hat! Come down! 'Tain't no use to say you ain't up there; I see your legs hanging out!' A fancy staff officer was horrified at the irreverent reception of his nice-twisted moustache, as he heard from behind innumerable trees: 'Take them mice out o' your mouth! Take 'em out. No use to say they ain't thar!—see their tails hanging out!' Another, sporting immense whiskers, was urged to 'come out of that bunch of har! I know you're in thar! I see your ears a working!' " [139]

Lee's consideration for the rights of the private soldier strengthened the morale which the unfailing humor of the troops expressed. If a man were caught within the enemy's lines and unjustly accused of being a spy, the General would exert himself to the utmost to save him from execution.[140] He was always willing to request information regarding a prisoner or the return of a dead captive if the family desired it.[141] During the winter, a court martial condemned to death a private who had deserted on receipt of a distressing letter from his wife. When he reached home and his wife found that he had come without leave, she sent him back. Lee confirmed the sentence of death but had the man pardoned promptly. The circumstances, which appealed to the imagination of homesick boys, redounded as much to Lee's popularity as to the credit of the soldier, who, tradition has it, subsequently fell mortally wounded in action, the last survivor at his gun.[142]

Instead of blaming Lee for their hunger, the troops felt that he was struggling with the administration in their interest, and their reverent affection for him grew daily. "His theory, expressed upon many occasions," wrote an officer who saw him frequently during the winter, "was that the private soldiers—men who fought without the stimulus of rank, emolument, or individual renown—were the most meritorious class of the army, and that they deserved and should receive the utmost respect and consideration." [148] He vetoed a plan for a battalion of honor because he did not believe

[139] *McCabe*, 278, quoting a letter from Jackson's corps.
[140] *Cf.* Lee to Burnside, Dec. 19, 1862, *MS.*, Collection of Edward T. Stuart, Philadelphia, Pa., courteously placed at the writer's disposal by Mr. Stuart. This case concerned John W. Irvine, 9th Virginia Cavalry.
[141] *Cf.* Lee to Burnside, Dec. 28, 1862, *MS.*, Collection of Edward T. Stuart, case of Captain E. P. Lawton.
[142] *Thomas*, 593–95; *La Bree*, 99–101; 8 *S. H. S. P.*, 31.   [148] *Cooke*, 203–4.

it could contain all the men who had distinguished themselves,[144] and to every private who appealed to him he gave a sympathetic hearing. One day he saw a man in uniform standing near his tent.

"Come in, Captain," he said, "and take a seat."

"I'm no captain, General," the soldier replied. "I'm nothing but a private."

"Come in sir," Lee replied, "come in and take a seat. You ought to be a captain." [145]

That was Lee's attitude. Officers and men alike requited it with a confidence that was half of victory. "It does not seem possible to defeat this army now with General Lee at its head," a surgeon wrote.[146] Later, the same observant man told his wife: "You need have no apprehension that this army will ever meet with defeat while commanded by General Lee. General Jackson is a strict Presbyterian, but he is rather too much of a Napoleon Bonaparte in my estimation. Lee is the man, I assure you." [147] A private wrote long afterwards: "It was remarkable what confidence the men reposed in General Lee; they were ready to follow him wherever he might lead, or order them to go." [148]

In this spirit, during a March that was as tempestuous as February, the army passed through a series of alarms and preparations, while Hooker kept his balloons in the air as if he were expecting an attack.[149] An expedition into northwest Virginia by two columns to burn bridges on the B. & O. and to collect supplies was made ready with much interchange of correspondence between the chiefs of the co-operating forces;[150] and a change of commanders in the valley district had to be considered at the instance of the War Department.[151] Attention to these details was interrupted by a call to Richmond for consultation with the President on the military situation.[152]

This visit, like that in January, was ended by a report that the en-

---

144 O. R., 25, part 2, p. 601.   145 Gordon, 136.
146 Welch, 39.   147 Welch, 47.
148 D. E. johnston: Story of a Confederate Boy, 174. Cf. Wolseley, 21, writing as of October, 1862: The soldiers had a "calm confidence of victory when serving under him. . . ."
149 R. E. Lee to Charlotte Lee, Jones, 396–97.
150 O. R., 25, part 2, pp. 652–53, 656, 658, 659, 661, 684, 685, 692, 705, 707, 710, 716, 722, 728, 733.
151 O. R., 25, 641, 654.
152 O. R., 25, part 2, p. 664; ibid., 51, part 2, 683; Lee's Dispatches, 80–81.

emy was massing cavalry, this time at Kelly's Ford. Assuming that this was the beginning of a general offensive, Lee ordered Longstreet's detached divisions to rejoin, but when he reached headquarters on the 18th,[153] he found that the enemy had not attempted to move any infantry across the river and had withdrawn his cavalry after a spectacular battle between 3000 Federal horse and Fitz Lee's mounted brigade. A fire from rifle-pits along the river had somewhat delayed the Federal crossing, and the Confederate cavalry had worsted superior forces with much gallantry. The victory, however, had been dearly bought in the death of Major John Pelham of the Stuart Horse Artillery, probably the most promising artillery officer in the entire army, with the single exception of E. P. Alexander.[154] Lee cancelled the order for the movement of Hood and Pickett, and joined with the rest of his forces in mourning the "knightly scion of a Southern home," who "dazzled the land with deeds." [155]

The wise employment of Longstreet's force, thus left undisturbed south of the James, was becoming a matter of serious moment to Lee. By the detachment of the two divisions of the Second Corps, his strength had been dangerously reduced. The return of convalescents and lightly wounded did not raise his army in the middle of March above 63,000,[156] including Jones's cavalry in the Valley. Longstreet had 44,000 effectives[157] in his department, which was shortly afterward enlarged, under Lee's general supervision, to include the Richmond area, Virginia south of the James, and the whole of North Carolina.[158] The force opposing Longstreet was

---

[153] O. R., 25, part 2, p. 675.
[154] O. R., 25, part 1, pp. 47 ff.; H. B. McClellan, 202 ff.; Mercer: The Gallant Pelham, 156 ff.
[155] J. R. Randall, "The Dead Cannoneer." Two other excellent poems were written on Pelham's death, one anonymously, in The Southern Bivouac, for March, 1884, and the other, contemporaneously, by John Esten Cooke. This begins:

> Oh, band in the pine-trees cease!
> Cease with your splendid call;
> The living are brave and noble
> But the dead are bravest of all!

For the order suspending the recall of Hood and Pickett, see O. R., 18, 927; O. R., 25, part 2, p. 672.
[156] It was 64,800 on March 31 (O. R., 25, part 2, 696).
[157] O. R., 18, 916.   [158] O. R., 18, 953.

not accurately known but was estimated to be about equal to his own.[159]

Obviously, if Longstreet had opportunity of striking at the Federals, he might reasonably hope to defeat them. But was it wise to force the fighting on that front? In attempting to answer that question, Lee had to take two facts into account. First, he could not afford to permit Longstreet to move Hood and Pickett too far from the railroad, because if Hooker advanced on the Rappahannock, Lee might require them speedily. In the second place, the Army of Northern Virginia badly needed supplies, and if it was able to assume the offensive, it must have a reserve of food. Longstreet, as it happened, was within reach of eastern North Carolina, where a large volume of provisions, especially of bacon, was known to be available, but could only be collected with army wagons. Which meant more to the cause—a commissary campaign by Longstreet or a military campaign at a time when Lee might have desperate need of the best units of Longstreet's command?

It was a difficult choice. Lee sought to adjust the use of Long-street's troops to all contingencies. He desired Hood and Pickett held as a reserve, either to support Longstreet, if that officer could take the offensive, or to rejoin the Army of Northern Virginia, should their presence become necessary. Meantime, Longstreet was to employ his force to collect all supplies within that part of his department where the enemy seemed to be weak.[160] Lee wrote Longstreet on March 16 that one corps, and not three, as previously reported, had left the Rappahannock front. He concluded: "As our numbers will not admit of our meeting [the enemy] on equality everywhere, we much endeavor, by judicious dispositions, to be enabled to make our troops available in any quarter where they may be needed [and] after the emergency passes in one place to transfer them to any other point that may be threatened."[161]

Longstreet was of little assistance to his chief in making a wise

---

[159] Actually it was 55,000 at the end of February (O. R., 18, 546). For Longstreet's later estimate, see ibid., 926.

[160] O. R., 18, 906–7, 921–22, 933. The dispatch in ibid., 906–7, is dated March 3, but is attributed by the editors to March 30. The original MS., which is in the collection of the New York Historical Society, has the date corrected in pen. It is either March 30 or March 31.

[161] O. R., 18, 922.

decision as to the employment of his troops. He professed a desire to attack,[162] but he was on his first independent command, and his habitual caution battled with his vanity and his desire to win a victory.[163] He interpreted the restraining orders on Pickett and Hood as a bar to action, and in a wordy correspondence with Lee, repeatedly asked for more men as a prerequisite to taking the offensive and collecting the supplies. With long-range cocksureness, he expressed conviction that Lee could hold Hooker on the Rappahannock, or, if need be, could advantageously withdraw to the North Anna in order to let him have additional troops.[164] Lee did not feel that at so great a distance from Longstreet's lines he could insist on a definite plan. Almost despairing of substantial results in southside Virginia, he left the case to Longstreet's discretion,[165] though urging an offensive. He dismissed the appeal for more regiments with the statement that if he were further weakened, he would have to withdraw to the line of the Annas, which he considered undesirable for reasons he took pains to explain.[166]

While this correspondence was progressing, General Lee received, on March 28, a report that Burnside's Ninth Corps was moving westward by rail, presumably to Kentucky.[167] At first, Lee was not disposed to credit this report,[168] but inquiry convinced him by April 1 that it was well founded.[169] Now, Burnside's corps had been at Newport News. The reinforcement it had afforded the Federals in southern Virginia and North Carolina had been the principal reason for dispatching two of Longstreet's divisions to that section. If, therefore, Longstreet had been deterred from attacking because of the strength of the enemy in fortified positions, the withdrawal of Burnside greatly bettered Longstreet's prospects.

But the solution was not as simple as that. Larger strategic con-

---

[162] *O. R.*, 18, 923-24.

[163] Captain F. W. Dawson, *op. cit.*, 87, quoted gossip of the camp that Longstreet was drinking during the winter of 1862-63.

[164] *O. R.*, 18, 924-25, 926-27, 932, 933-34, 943, 950.

[165] *O. R.*, 933-34.

[166] *O. R.*, 18, 943. In the Confederate correspondence, the North and the South Anna Rivers are often mentioned together as "the Annas."

[167] *O. R.*, 25, part 2, p. 691.   [168] *O. R.*, 25, part 2, p. 691.

[169] *O. R.*, 18, 947, 948, 950, 954. Burnside moved Sturgis's and Willcox's divisions; Getty's was left in Virginia (*O. R.*, 18, 562 *ff.*).

siderations had to be weighed. Kentucky at that time was lightly held by the Federals, chiefly to protect the Louisville and Nashville Railroad, which formed the chief line of communications with General Rosecrans's army, then around Murfreesboro, Tenn. General John Pegram and General Humphrey Marshall were raiding in Kentucky, chiefly for provisions. Any large dispatch of Federal troops to the Ohio not only would put a quietus on these raids but might mean the reinforcement of Rosecrans, whose odds against the Confederate army under Bragg it was important the enemy should not be allowed to increase.

How, then, could the Army of Northern Virginia prevent the dispatch of more troops from the Army of the Potomac to the western front? If Longstreet could strike, that might prove a diversion; if Longstreet reinforced Lee, then as soon as the weather permitted, Lee could draw Hooker out and perhaps so threaten Washington that all troop movement westward would stop. In any case, if Longstreet's two absent divisions rejoined the Army of Northern Virginia, then Lee would be able to make a better resistance and, if he gained a victory, to follow it up. The involvements were thus of the greatest moment to the whole Confederate cause.

At this juncture, when a right decision on Lee's part might affect the outcome of the war, the fates that had so often conspired against the Confederacy at critical hours again intervened on the side of the Union. For the first time during the war, and for the first time since he had been at Sollers Point in 1849, Lee fell ill. He had not been sleeping well,[170] and in some way he contracted a serious throat infection which settled into what seems to have been a pericarditis. His arm, his chest, and his back were attacked with sharp paroxysms of pain that suggest even the possibility of an angina. On March 30, he had to be moved from his bleak winter quarters to Yerby's and put under the care of the medical director of the army, Doctor Lafayette Guild.[171] When Guild was himself taken sick, Lee was attended by Doctor S. M. Bemiss, a

[170] As he often lay awake at night he asked that when he did fall asleep early, he be not awakened before midnight, unless the occasion demanded it. He said that to him, one hour's sleep before midnight was worth two hours' after that time (*Taylor's General Lee,* 155).

[171] Lee to Margaret Stuart, April 5, 1863, in D. S. Freeman: "Lee and the Ladies," *Scribner's Magazine,* vol. 87, p. 462.

distinguished New Orleans physician, then a surgeon with the forces.[172] Lee's illness kept him in bed for some days, with the doctors, as he said, "tapping me all over like an old steam boiler before condemning it." [173] The weather, which was worse in early April than at any time during the winter,[174] contributed to keeping him a captive.

His first impulse was to have Longstreet take the offensive against the diminished forces in his front while he drove the Federal cavalry from the Valley and thereby played once more on Mr. Lincoln's fears for the safety of Washington.[175] But the roads made immediate operations in the Valley impossible, and in view of Longstreet's representations of the strong earthworks of the enemy on his front, Lee did not feel able to do more than once again to trust to Longstreet's discretion. "You are . . .," he wrote Longstreet at the beginning of his illness, "relieved of half the force that has been opposed to you. You will therefore be strong enough to make any movement that you may consider advisable; but, as stated in former letters, so long as the enemy choose to remain on the defensive and covered by their intrenchments and floating batteries I fear you can accomplish but little, except to draw provisions from the invaded districts. If you can accomplish this it will be of positive benefit. I leave the whole matter to your good judgment." [176]

On April 6, after Lee's sickness had begun to abate somewhat, the Secretary of War sounded him out on something that meant even more than the detention of Hood and Pickett in southern Virginia: Would it be possible, the secretary asked, to dispatch part of Longstreet's command to Tennessee to reinforce Bragg?[177] This question was put when Longstreet was still calling for more troops,[178] and when threatening demonstrations against Charleston led to the belief that the forces at Wilmington, N. C., would have to be reduced to reinforce that city.[179] Lee was willing, as always, to release troops if the demand in Tennessee was greater than elsewhere, but, sick as he was, he put forward a bolder plan:

[172] *Pendleton*, 256; 1 *R. W. C. D.*, 296; S. M. Bemiss to his children, *Bemiss MS. Memoirs and Letters*, kindly placed at the writer's disposal by S. M. Bemiss of Richmond.
[173] Letter to Margaret Stuart, *loc. cit.*   [174] *Welch*, 46.
[175] *O. R.*, 18, 954; *O. R.*, 25, part 2, pp. 700–701.
[176] *O. R.*, 18, 954.   [177] *O. R.*, 25, part 2, 708–9.
[178] *O. R.*, 18, 959, 960.   [179] *O. R.*, 18, 972 ff.

On April 9—a date that was to be black with woe in 1865—he wrote the Secretary of War: "Should Hooker's army assume the defensive, the readiest method of relieving the pressure upon General Johnston and General Beauregard would be for this army to cross into Maryland. This cannot be done, however, in the present condition of the roads, nor unless I can obtain a certain amount of provisions and transportation. But this is what I would recommend, if practicable." He went on to explain what Longstreet was doing in the collection of supplies in North Carolina: "Longstreet," he said, "does not think he has troops enough for the purpose, and has applied for more of his corps to be sent to him, which I have not thought advisable to do. If any of his troops are taken from him, I fear it will arrest his operations and deprive us of the benefit anticipated from increasing the supplies of the army. I must, therefore, submit your proposition to the determination of yourself and the President." [180] Meantime, to prepare for eventualities, he called for pontoons to be employed in crossing rivers if he took the offensive.[181]

A week passed. Lee's symptoms moderated still more and he suffered no discomfort except from occasional twinges of what his physicians considered rheumatism, but his condition was enfeebled and he had to take more rest, which the enemy seemed little disposed to allow him. The Federal cavalry was active.[182] There were rumors that Hooker was planning to duplicate McClellan's great manœuvre of March, 1862, and transport his army to the James.[183] Lee did not credit this camp gossip, because he did not believe the enemy would uncover Washington. Expecting the campaign to open in northern Virginia, he made his preparations to carry out the plan he had outlined to Seddon. If Hooker did not seize the initiative before May 1, Lee intended first to sweep Milroy from the Valley. Then, with the provisions he hoped could be accumulated there by the projected raid into northwestern Virginia, he intended to carry the war again into Maryland in the hope of relieving thereby the pressure on the other Confederate armies. But there was one immediate difficulty. Even to move the army on the first leg of its advance toward the Potomac,

---

[180] O. R., 25, part 2, pp. 713–14.   [181] O. R., 25, part 2, pp. 715, 735.
[182] O. R., 25, part 2, pp. 721, 724.   [183] O. R., 25, part 2, p. 725.

Lee must have the supplies from North Carolina, and to collect those supplies, Longstreet must be kept there as long as practicable.[184] This was the reasoning that led him, at the last, to leave Longstreet south of the James and to take the risk of facing Hooker with inferior forces if the Federal commander assumed the offensive.[185]

That risk increased hourly, for the Federal cavalry remained on a wide front. They displayed so much more strength and energy than during the campaign of 1862 that Lee renewed applications he had made earlier in the winter to the President for an increase in his own mounted troops.[186] Lee took the demonstration of the cavalry to mean that Hooker was trying to draw him to the upper Rappahannock in the hope of discovering his strength or of throwing his pontoons across the river and seizing Fredericksburg.[187]

For a few days thereafter, all was quiet. The Federals kept their balloons in the air continually and seemed to be expecting rather than preparing an offensive.[188] Then, on the 23d, evidence began to multiply that Hooker had no intention of waiting until Lee could take the situation in his own hands after Longstreet had collected his bacon and had rejoined the army. A raid was made on Port Royal on April 23.[189] It ended with the return of the Federals to the north bank of the river before they could be assailed, but it was a suspicious affair. Lee took it to be a feint, a warning that the campaign was soon to open,[190] and he notified the troops on the Confederate left to be on the alert, "for," he told Jackson, "I think if a real attempt is made to cross the river, it will be above Fredericksburg."[191] Stuart reported a concentration of Federal cavalry on the upper Rappahannock a few days later[192] and spies informed Lee that all the troops in rear of Hooker's lines had been brought up.[193] Lee watched every development in-

184 O. R., 25, part 2, p. 725–26.
185 For a discussion of the effect of this decision on the outcome of the Chancellorsville campaign, see *infra*, Vol. III, Chap. I.
186 O. R., 25, part 2, pp. 738, 740–41, 748; O. R., 18, 1019.
187 O. R., 25, part 2, p. 730.   188 O. R., 25, part 2, pp. 730, 736–37, 738.
189 O. R., 25, part 2, pp. 744, 749; Pearson: *James S. Wadsworth*, 175.
190 O. R., 25, part 1, p. 796.
191 3 B. and L., 233.   192 O. R., 25, part 1, p. 1045.
193 O. R., 25, part 2, p. 752. Although Lee reported that his spies were having the greatest difficulty in reaching the Federal lines (*cf. O. R.*, 25, part 2, p. 700), General G. K. Warren, Federal Chief of Engineers, insisted that the Confederate "spy system was

tently. He was satisfied that if Hooker delayed until the army could be reunited, he could defeat him. "Should he attempt such a movement when the army is able to operate," he said in characteristically unboastful language, "I think he will find it very difficult to reach his destination." [194] But with the army divided, the horses feeble and provisions low, he doubted his ability "even to act on the defensive"—to quote his words—"as vigorously as circumstances may require." [195] Still, when Longstreet reported that he was getting all the provisions out of North Carolina as rapidly as possible, the bacon of that state seemed so important to the half-starved army that Lee merely inquired how soon Longstreet could finish his task and rejoin. [196]

Sunday morning, April 26, Lee went with Jackson to a religious service, attended by a throng of soldiers, and during the afternoon, he went to call on Mrs. Jackson, who was visiting at Yerby's. [197] That evening, on both sides of the Rappahannock, regimental adjutants were beginning to put together the returns of the personnel of the army, due on the 30th. Hooker's officers had a magnificent total to compile—138,378 present for duty. [198] Spies' reports and a study of the incautious Northern newspapers had led the Confederate signal corps to believe that the number was as high as 150,000 to 160,000, a figure that Lee thought much exaggerated. His own strength cannot be stated with absolute certainty, as events were to prevent the completion of the returns, but the total, excluding Jones's little force of cavalry in the Shenandoah Valley, was not much, if any, in excess of 62,500 of all arms—less than half the force his powerful adversary commanded. [199] Except on the day before the battle of Sharpsburg, he had never faced such

so perfect" that an important move could not be kept from him (*O. R.*, 25, part 1, p. 195). Lee was suffering also from the activity of spies. He had to warn Seddon to employ a cipher (*O. R.*, 14, 763–64), and he rigorously excluded unsponsored civilians from his lines (*O. R.*, 25, part 2, p. 629).

[194] *O. R.*, 25, part 2, p. 745. [195] *O. R.*, 25, part 2, p. 752.
[196] *O. R.*, 18, 1024–25; *O. R.*, 25, part 2, p. 752.
[197] *Mrs. Jackson*, 411. [198] *O. R.*, 25, part 2, p. 320.
[199] The return for April 30, 1863, which is summarized in IV *O. R.*, 2, 530, gave 64,799 including Jones and Hampton, but excluded the artillery of the Second Corps. As Jones was detached in the Valley, with 3402, and as Hampton had around 1800 absent to recruit and refit, the net strength of all the army was about 59,500, plus the artillery of the Second Corps. This artillery was about 1000, bringing the total to 60,500. The totals of the April return are the same as those of March, *O. R.*, 25, part 2, 696; consequently it is probable that the absentees who returned in April should be added. Allowing the liberal figure of 2000 to cover these, the total is around 62,500. Taylor, in *Four Years*, 86, estimated Lee's actual strength at 57,112.

crushing odds, yet he had been planning to take the offensive **if** Hooker did not!

Before daybreak on the morning of April 29, Lee was aroused by a distant roll that he took to be gunfire, but he was overtaken again by drowsiness and was soon asleep once more. Presently he was awakened by some one calling his name. Opening his eyes, he saw the grave face of Jackson's aide, Captain James Power Smith, bending over him. "Captain," said he teasingly, "what do you young men mean by waking a man out of his sleep?"

In a few soldierly words Smith announced that Jackson had sent **him** to inform the General that under cover of the fog Hooker had thrown his pontoons and was crossing the Rappahannock in force.

"Well," said Lee, "I thought I heard firing and was beginning to think it was time some of you young fellows were coming to tell me what it was all about. You want me to send a message to your good general, Captain? Tell him that I am sure he knows what to do. I will meet him at the front very soon." [200]

It was dawn, but it was close to the high noon of the Confederacy.

[200] Captain Smith printed three versions of this episode—in 3 *B. and L.,* 203, in 43 *S. H. S. P.,* 44, and in *Richmond Times-Dispatch,* Jan. 20, 1907. The words here attributed to Lee are a composite of the quotations in the three versions and may not be literally correct, but as Doctor Smith was a man of great accuracy, the differences in language are not material.

CHAPTER XXXIII

JACKSON DISAPPEARS IN THE FOREST

WHEN Lee rode through the fog to the front early in the morning of April 29, 1863, he found that the Federals had very quietly pushed their boats over the Rappahannock just below the mouth of Deep Run, close to the point where the second bridge had been placed on December 11. The Confederate pickets there had seen nothing and had heard nothing until the boats were actually grounding. Retreating before superior forces, the outposts had no information except that the enemy was on the Confederate side of the river and had already completed a pontoon bridge. Farther downstream, opposite the Pratt homestead, Smithfield,[1] another Union column had attempted to cross but had been fired upon by the guards and had been delayed. The Federals were clearing the ground at this point and were throwing their bridge, which, however, they did not complete until after 11 o'clock.[2] The troops that reached the Confederate side did not attempt to advance immediately but sheltered themselves under the bank of the river, covered by the artillery that lined the Stafford Heights. A very large supporting force was in sight on the other shore, as if waiting its turn to move forward. Everything indicated that the Federals were launching a general offensive. This view was confirmed by reports that heavy columns had been seen marching up the Rappahannock toward the Confederate left.[3]

The reasons that had prompted Lee in December not to attempt to resist the enemy in the plain along the river applied with equal weight now. Orders were given to prepare on the ridges to meet the attack, as in the first battle on that terrain.[4] For the moment, Lee could do no more. There was no way of telling where the

---

[1] Now (1933) part of the property of the Mannsfield Hall Country Club.
     Early, 193.   [3] *O. R.*, 25, part 1, p. 796.
     [4] *O. R.*, 25, part 1, p. 796. A typographical error in the report gives April 28 as the date for this crossing.

main blow would fall.[5] Observing that there were no signs of any effort to place pontoons directly opposite Fredericksburg,[6] Lee rode up the Rappahannock to see what was afoot there, but as he found no definite evidences of an attempt to force a crossing, he soon returned and conferred with Jackson on the proper dispositions.[7] President Davis was notified and was asked to send forward any available reinforcements from the south side of the James,[8] though Lee had no expectation that Longstreet could return to him in time for the coming battle, or that any other help on a large scale could reach him speedily.[9] Jackson's own command was ordered up from Port Royal;[10] the artillery in the rear, around Guiney's,[11] was put on the alert and, a little later, was directed to move forward.[12]

Before noon on the 29th, Stuart reported that a force of about 14,000 infantry with six guns and some cavalry had crossed below Kelly's Ford on the upper Rappahannock and apparently was moving towards Gordonsville. Lee reasoned, from other reports, that Stoneman's cavalry would cross in the vicinity of the Warrenton Springs. These forces might readily destroy the Virginia Central and might perhaps reach Lee's supply line, the R. F. and P. Railroad,[13] yet Lee determined not to attempt to detach any infantry from the Army of Northern Virginia to oppose them. Convinced that he must not release any part of his small army for lengthy operations at a distance from him, he had to content himself with informing the President of the new development, with the suggestion that if troops could be found in southside Virginia and in North Carolina, they be sent to Gordonsville.[14]

During the afternoon, a telegram arrived from Stuart[15] announcing that he had engaged the enemy at Maddens, nine miles east of Culpeper and had captured prisoners from the V, XI,

[5] O. R., 25, part 2, p. 757.   [6] O. R., 25, part 1, p. 796.
[7] Cooke, 257.   [8] O. R., 25, part 2, p. 757.
[9] O. R., 18, 1028, 1029, 1049; ibid., 25, part 2, p. 765. Davis promptly ordered the return of such part of Longstreet's command as could be brought together.
[10] O. R., 51, part 1, p. 699.
[11] Subsequently styled Guiney's Station and later Guinea. Doctor J. A. C. Chandler, whose father lived nearby, wrote the author, Aug. 9, 1926, that he had been told in childhood that the place had been named Guiney's after a family that resided a mile and a half away.
[12] O. R., 51, part 2, p. 698, ibid., 25, part 1, p. 809.
[13] O. R., 25, part 1, p. 796; ibid., part 2, pp. 757-58.
[14] O. R., 25, part 2, p. 758; 1 R. W. C. D., 302.
[15] Probably via Culpeper.

and XII Corps of the Army of the Potomac. More than that, Stuart stated that these columns of the enemy were headed for Germanna and for Ely's Ford on the Rapidan.[16] This was news of the greatest moment. It indicated, in the first place, that the Federals had a very large force of infantry twenty-one miles

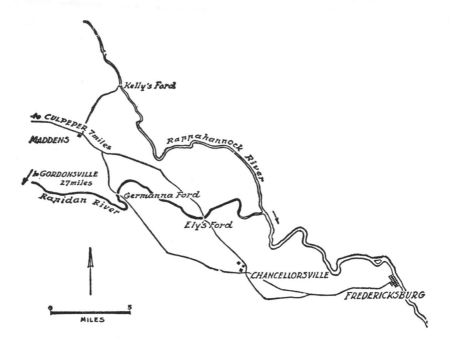

northwest of Fredericksburg; it meant, secondly, that some or all of these men were moving to turn the left flank of the Confederate army. For if the entire force encountered by Stuart had been making for Gordonsville, it would have been marching to the southwest and not to the southeast, into the angle between the Rappahannock and the Rapidan.

Aside from the threat thus presented of a turning-movement against Lee's position at Fredericksburg, there was immediate danger that if the Federals crossed at Ely's and Germanna Ford, they might throw themselves between Lee and Stuart and thereby deprive the army of its cavalry at a time when every road should

---

[16] *O. R.*, 25, part 1, pp. 796, 1046. Stuart stated that he advised Lee of the advance toward Germanna Ford; Lee mentioned both fords.

be watched. Lee wished to prevent this, if he could. He deliberately took the chance that the enemy's horse might prey upon
the railroads in his rear, and ordered Stuart to rejoin the main
army as soon as possible, delaying the Federals on their march.[17]

Shortly after 6:30 that afternoon, April 29, a courier arrived with
a report that the Federals had crossed at Germanna Ford. On
the heels of this messenger arrived another with the intelligence
that the enemy was also over the Rapidan at Ely's Ford.[18] This
removed all doubt as to the direction of the advance: the roads
from Ely's and from Germanna met at Chancellorsville, fourteen
miles west of Fredericksburg. The Federals evidently were seeking
to turn the flank from that direction and, presumably, to get in
the rear of the Army of Northern Virginia.[19] But in what strength?
That was a question the reports from the Rapidan did not answer.[20]
If it was a small column, it could be dealt with readily, but if it
was the main force of Hooker, all the troops at Fredericksburg
might have to retire in order to re-establish contact with the cavalry,
now presumably separated from Lee by the force marching on
Chancellorsville.[21] The larger question of where the major engagement was to be fought when the enemy had developed his
plan could wait on the immediate necessity of securing the flank
and getting in touch with the cavalry. The morning, Lee believed,
would almost certainly find the whole of the Army of the Potomac
on the south side of the Rappahannock.[22]

R. H. Anderson, commanding one of the two divisions left
behind by Longstreet, had three of his brigades above Fredericksburg, guarding two of the fords. Another brigade was near at
hand. The fourth had been ordered up.[23] Lee decided to pivot the
right of this division on the Rappahannock, above Fredericksburg,
and to swing it back roughly at right angles to the river. This
would cover his left, and would enable him to hold Chancellorsville, where the two routes of the enemy came together.

This movement began at 9 P.M. on the 29th, through a drenching
rain.[24] Anderson, to whom it was entrusted, was an able officer

---

[17] O. R., 25, part 1, pp. 796, 1046.
[18] O. R., 25, part 2, p. 759; cf. ibid., part 1, pp. 862, 870.
[19] O. R., 25, part 2, p. 756; ibid., part 1, p. 796.
[20] O. R., 25, part 2, p. 756.
[21] O. R., 25, part 2, p. 759.   [22] O. R., 25, part 2, p. 756.
[23] O. R., 25, part 2, p. 849.   [24] O. R., 25, part 1, pp. 809, 865.

of high courage but indolent and difficult to arouse.[25] Lee accordingly took the precaution specifically to order Anderson to go to the front and to direct the troop-movement in person.[26] Midnight found Anderson at Chancellorsville, where he met the two brigades that had been on the extreme left at United States Ford.[27] Meantime, Lee had ordered McLaws, commanding the other division of Longstreet, to put his troops in condition to move the next day with cooked rations, if he should be needed to support Anderson.[28] Lee did not place these two under McLaws, the senior. Instead, he took their movement in his own hands, leaving to Jackson the management of the Second Corps.

The scattered condition of the army, in Lee's opinion, favored the operations of the enemy,[29] but his disposition at the end of the day protected him against a surprise as fully as his limited strength permitted. Although he did not have all his cavalry at hand, he had not been caught wholly off his guard. The advance had come from the quarter where he had expected it. While he had as yet no adequate knowledge of the number of troops moving from the left, he held the roads of direct approach and had most of his disposable cavalry on his threatened flank. Should his expectations be at fault, and the main assault be delivered against his right, Jackson was there on good ground to oppose it with the whole of his corps.

Morning of the 30th saw little change on the front below Fredericksburg. Bridgeheads had been constructed during the night, and the Federals were busy digging a line of trenches to connect them, but the enemy showed no disposition to attack.[30] So quiet was he that a deer, trapped between the opposing forces, was chased by the men of both armies and was finally captured by the Federals without the firing of a single shot.[31] Lee himself had a touch of the malady from which he had recently suffered and he prudently counselled with Jackson in his tent.[32] Later in the morning he rode out with "Stonewall" and examined the Federal lines from

[25] Sorrel, 135.   [26] O. R., 25, part 2, p. 759.
[27] O. R., 25, part 1, pp. 796, 849.   [28] O. R., 25, part 2, p. 759.
[29] O. R., 25, part 2, p. 757.   [30] Early, 195–96.
[31] Major H. E. Young: "Lee the Soldier," in Robert E. Lee; Centennial Celebration of His Birth Held Under the Auspices of the University of South Carolina, on the 19th Day of January, 1907, pp. 14-15. Major Young dated this and other incidents on May 1, but all the evidence shows he was in error by one day.
[32] Ibid.

the ridge. Jackson was all for attacking. Lee's judgment was against it. He told Jackson he feared it was as impracticable to move against the enemy on the plain as it had been in December. The Union positions could be assaulted only at heavy loss. If the attack were not successful, it would be difficult to break off the battle under the fire of the Federal guns. However, Lee continued, with the deference he always showed in tactical matters when he had entrusted an operation to a subordinate, if Jackson thought it could be done, he would give the order. Jackson pondered and asked for time in which to study the situation. Lee consented.[33]

As Jackson went about his examination of the ground, with only a little long-range artillery practice to interrupt him, Lee turned to measures for aiding Anderson. Engineers were hurried to him to draw entrenchments[34] and Alexander's battalion of artillery, which had come up from the rear, was sent him.[35] President Davis was advised of the situation and was told that the enemy's object evidently was to turn the Confederate left.[36] Nothing was heard from Anderson during the morning, but between noon and 1 P.M. a courier arrived from the 3d Virginia Cavalry, announcing that the Federal infantry, who had crossed at Germanna Ford, were advancing. A wagon and artillery train with heavy infantry escort was said to be across at Ely's Ford. These columns were moving on Chancellorsville.[37] A little later, Anderson reported that he had been as far as Chancellorsville, and had been joined by the brigades from the United States Ford.[38] He had withdrawn to a good position east of Chancellorsville, Anderson said, and up to the time of writing had encountered only cavalry, moving from the direction of Chancellorsville, but he needed reinforcements.[39]

Lee promptly sent Anderson careful and detailed orders: He was to dig in at once and, if he could do so in time, prepare a line adequate for the additional troops that Lee hoped to be able to send him. Anderson was to advise whether he desired additional

[33] Fitz Lee, *Chancellorsville*, 22, quoting Lee directly. Long, *op. cit.*, 251, described the two generals on an eminence, examining the ground, but he mistakenly dated the interview on May 1, when Jackson had already left for Chancellorsville.
[34] *O. R.*, 25, part 1, p. 850.   [35] *O. R.*, 25, part 1, p. 809.
[36] *O. R.*, 25, part 2, p. 761; *Lee's Dispatches*, 85–86.
[37] 8 *S. H. S. P.*, 253.   [38] Mahone's and Posey's.
[39] Anderson's dispatch has been lost, but its contents can be reconstructed from his report, *O. R.*, 25, part 1, p. 850, and from Lee's reply to his letter, *ibid.*, part 2, p. 761.

artillery. In particular, he was to have his men keep two days' cooked rations on their persons and was to be prepared to remove his trains at any time should the occasion demand. Cavalry was coming up, Lee explained, and must be employed in apprizing Anderson of the enemy's movements, while retarding as much as possible the advance of the Federals.[40] To insure the ready dispatch of more guns to Anderson, should they be needed, Lee halted the artillery moving up from the rear.[41]

These orders to Anderson, which were dispatched at 2:30 P.M.,[42] were of historical importance. It was the first time, in open operations, that Lee had ordered the construction of field fortifications. He had thrown up works at Fredericksburg when he thought that he might wish to hold the heights with a small force, while keeping the rest of his troops for manœuvre, and now he reasoned that he could increase his defensive power on the left by putting his men under cover. There was suspicion on the Fredericksburg sector that the Federals were diminishing force.[43] Jackson, moreover, reported that he concurred in Lee's belief that an offensive on the troops below the town was impracticable.[44]

With only this scant information in hand, Lee had now to decide on his general plan. Opinion among his officers was much divided,[45] but he studied his intelligence reports with great care and made a long-range but careful examination of the strength and movements of the Federals on the Stafford Heights. At length he shut up his glasses. "The main attack will come from above," he said. And from that moment there was no doubt in his mind. He believed the Federals on the left were in large force, and that they had advanced almost as far as he could permit them to come without getting between him and Richmond. If, as he had concluded, it was not possible to drive back the Federals below

---

[40] O. R., 25, part 2, p. 761.   [41] O. R., 25, part 1, p. 810.

[42] General Alfred Pleasanton, commanding the cavalry attached to the advancing columns, subsequently stated that he captured a courier about 1 P.M., bearing a message from Lee to Anderson, complaining that he had heard nothing from him (4 Report of the Committee on the Conduct of the War, 27). In 3 B. and L., 174, General Pleasanton gave a different version of this alleged capture and said the dispatch was to McLaws. John Bigelow, Jr., in his Campaign of Chancellorsville (cited hereafter as Bigelow), 128 n., called attention to these discrepancies, noted the absence of the dispatch from the records of the War Department, and left the reader to infer that, in his opinion, General Pleasanton's memory was at fault.

[43] Early, 196.   [44] Fitz Lee, Chancellorsville, 22.

[45] Fitz Lee, Chancellorsville, 27.

Fredericksburg and then turn with his full strength on the enemy moving against his flank, only two courses were open to him: Either he must retreat southward, or else he must hold his position at Fredericksburg and strike at once with the greater part of his army at the columns marching on Chancellorsville. A retreat was the easier and safer course, so far as the immediate situation was concerned. General Pope, somewhat similarly placed by Jackson's march on Manassas, had not hesitated to retire precipitately. The alternative policy—to divide the army now and to give battle on the left—was to take great risks of destruction. Defeat on the left would necessitate the evacuation of Fredericksburg; disaster at Fredericksburg would bring the Federals on that sector to his right flank and rear. Late in March Lee had argued against the evacuation of the line of the Rappahannock because, as he said, "It throws open a broad margin of our frontier, and renders our railroad communications more hazardous and more difficult to secure." [46] This consideration weighed heavily with him now, and inclined him to hazard a battle to hold the front on which he then stood. Besides, only 20,000 men had been employed to repulse the assaults of Burnside's whole army at Fredericksburg in December. A lesser force might suffice to beat off the attacks of the divisions huddled under the river-bank. He probably reasoned, also, that a retreat was what Hooker might reasonably anticipate. An immediate offensive against the columns advancing down the south bank of the Rappahannock might disconcert his adversary and give the Confederates the advantage of a surprise in a broken, wooded country.

Lee's decision, therefore, was to prepare the army for a retreat, if that became necessary, but to retain a limited force at Fredericksburg and to strike swiftly on his left. Early's division, with one brigade from McLaws, supported by a strong force of artillery, would be held on the heights overlooking the plain where waited the Federal units now identified as under command of Major General John Sedgwick. McLaws was to move at midnight to reinforce Anderson, and Jackson was to follow at daybreak, with his entire corps, less Early.[47] McLaws had already been instructed to make ready for a move,[48] and both he and Jackson were now

[46] O. R., 18, 944.
[47] O. R., 25, part 1, p. 797: ibid., part 2, p. 762.   [48] O. R., 25, part 2, p. 759.

directed to send all the wagon-trains to the rear and to provide the men with two days' rations.[49] Jackson's mission, as set forth in orders, was to "make arrangements to repulse the enemy," but Lee's purpose was, if possible, to "drive the enemy back to the Rapidan."[50]

McLaws marched at midnight on April 30–May 1. The forehanded Jackson had his men aroused soon after that hour and was on the road, by the light of a brilliant moon, before dawn covered the earth with a thick fog.[51] About daybreak, also, Stuart arrived at headquarters, accompanied by Major von Borcke, and reported that the cavalry, after some romantic moonlight fighting, was on the flank of Anderson's column. The force of cavalry was small—only five thin regiments,[52] for he had detached two regiments under Rooney Lee to watch Stoneman. Two regiments were a petty force with which to oppose the thundering Federal columns, riding hard toward the railroad; yet the main army had its "eyes," and Lee no longer had to consider any difficult rearward manoeuvres simply to re-establish contact with the cavalry.[53]

Instead of riding forthwith to the left, Lee prudently went back on the morning of May 1 to the old lines on the heights behind Fredericksburg. The fog was very heavy[54]—fortunately, this time, for it limited the vision of the crew of the Federal observation balloon that rode high above it.[55] Finding that the Federals were not preparing an immediate advance, Lee directed that more artillery be brought up and that no additional batteries be sent to Jackson, who would be fighting in a country where there would be little opportunity for the employment of guns.[56] From Lee's Hill, he approved the disposition already made of the artillery and sent a battery down the Rappahannock to deal with two gunboats that were reported to be shelling Port Royal.[57] To General Early, who was left in charge, he gave precise instructions: Early was to conceal the weakness of his numbers and was to endeavor to hold his position against attack. In case he was compelled to retreat

---

[49] *O. R.*, 25, part 2, p. 762.
[50] *Lee's Dispatches*, 86. The telegram to Davis, quoted here, was dated "April 30?" by the editor, but he is now satisfied that it was sent May 1.
[51] 3 *B. and L.*, 203. [52] *Fitz Lee*, 255.
[53] 2 *von Borcke*, 208; 2 *Henderson*, 418; *O. R.*, 25, part 1, pp. 796–97, 1046–47.
[54] *Malone*, 32. [55] *W. W. Chamberlaine*, 57.
[56] *O. R.*, 25, part 1, pp. 810, 820. [57] *O. R.*, 25, part 1, p. 810.

before an overwhelming force, Early was to retire southward and was to protect the trains already moving in that direction. Should he discover that the enemy had sent away any large part of his troops, Early was to dispatch to the left as many troops as he could possibly spare; and if the enemy disappeared, Early was to move at once to rejoin the main army.[58]

With these directions and a final look at the lines, Lee started during the early afternoon of May 1 to the threatened sector. He was playing a desperate game, and he knew it.[59] He was leaving Early with only about 10,000 men, including the personnel of forty-five guns,[60] and he was about to lead 51,000, of all arms, against a foe who, if he were making his major offensive, might have nearly twice that number in and around the gloomy Wilderness of Spotsylvania.[61] There was no news of any Confederate reinforcements.[62] In a word, the weakened Army of Northern Virginia would have to rely upon itself, and itself only, to escape the jaws of the gigantic pincers that seemed to be closing upon it.

Riding down the Plank road, which led west from Fredericksburg to Chancellorsville, Lee joined Jackson just as the Confederate skirmishers were engaging the Federals.[63] Together with Jackson, who was dressed in full uniform,[64] Lee rode along the road to Zoar[65] church amid the cheering of the troops, who saw in the presence of their favorite commanders the augury of victory.[66]

In a short time, the Federals began to give way before McLaws and Anderson, who were advancing along the Orange Turnpike and the Plank roads. As Jackson had the situation well in hand, Lee soon rode off to the right to reconnoitre. He found that the enemy's left, which had not been attacked, was being drawn in along with the rest of the line. It was retiring to a front that rested

---

[58] O. R., 25, part 1, p. 800; Early, 197.

[59] Cf. Lee to Davis, May 2, 1863, O. R., 25, part 1, p. 765.

[60] Early, op. cit., 197, put his force at 9000, but after deducting his losses of 150 on April 29, the closest estimate the writer can make of his strength is 10,400.

[61] Deducting Early's casualties and the 1150 detached with W. H. F. Lee, the estimate of 51,000 plus Early's 10,000 at Fredericksburg checks closely with the previous figure of Lee's total strength, viz., 62,500. Most Southern writers put the total from 3000 to 5000 lower.

[62] Lee's Dispatches, 86.

[63] R. E. Lee to Doctor A. T. Bledsoe, Oct. 28, 1867; Jones, 159.

[64] Grimes, 29.   [65] Sometimes called Zion church.

[66] 3 B. and L., 204; Long, 252; 3 C. M. H., 379; W. H. Stewart: A Pair of Blankets, 81. Colonel Stewart, it should be added, was mistaken as to the time of this incident, which he placed in the early morning.

on the Rappahannock close to Scott's Ford and ran thence south and southwestward. The approaches were well picketed and the troops were spread out in a tangled country of close, second-growth timber, in very truth a wilderness, broken with small streams, cut by only a few roads and almost devoid of open ground. Every road seemed swept by batteries. The terrain resembled the Chickahominy Valley, where the Seven Days' Battles had been fought, except that the timber was not so large, while the swamps were small and widely scattered. Still more did it resemble, save in the absence of hills, a country that Lee never saw, but one that was to have a still more sinister name as the graveyard of tens of thousands —the Meuse-Argonne. An attack through the sombre thickets, where vision was limited to a few score yards, was out of the question. To enter the woods, in the face of an enemy who had selected and fortified his position, was to invite destruction. That was plain to Lee as he rode back to the Plank road.

There was something suspicious about the situation. The advance of Anderson and McLaws, which was still under way, was much too easy. The Federals seemed merely to be fighting a slow, rear-guard action. Prisoners affirmed that they belonged to Meade's V Corps and that they had followed Howard's strong XI Corps across the Rapidan. The XII Corps was likewise known to have passed the river: what had happened to it, and where was Howard? Had the XI and the XII Corps taken some other road? Was it possible that Hooker, from the abundance of his man-power, was employing the V Corps to screen a great movement farther around the flank toward the R. F. and P., or westward toward Gordonsville, whither early reports had led Lee to believe that Howard was moving? Stuart should know; Lee, at 4 p.m., sent him a message to ask what had become of the other Federal columns.[67]

After sunset Jackson sent word that the enemy had stopped his withdrawal and had checked the Confederate advance. As far as could be ascertained, the Federals were on a line extending southwestward from the front Lee had reconnoitred to a clearing in the Wilderness that bore the pretentious name of Chancellorsville, though it consisted of only one residence and its outhouses.[68]

[67] O. R., 25, part 2. p. 764.   [68] Long. 254.

Were these dispositions the answer to Lee's questionings? Had the Federals simply drawn back to a prepared position to await attack with their whole force?[69]

To ascertain more of the ground, Lee went forward a mile and more to the southeast angle of the crossing of the Plank road and the road that led southwestward to the Catherine Iron Furnace.[70] It was still daylight when he joined Jackson there, and they had to retire a short distance to escape the fire of a Federal sharpshooter, who, from the top of a distant tree, was trying to pick off the gunners of a Confederate battery that had halted nearby on the Plank road.[71]

The two walked back under the cover of the pine woods and sat down on a log.[72] Lee's first question was whether Jackson had discovered the strength and position of the enemy on the Confederate left. Jackson replied that Stuart's horse artillery had just been engaged in an artillery duel in that direction and had encountered a very heavy fire.[73] General Wright, co-operating with the horse artillery, had also found the enemy in strength in the woods.[74]

Jackson went on to explain how promptly the enemy had abandoned his advance and how easily he had been driven back to Chancellorsville. The movement was a feint or a failure, he said. The enemy would soon recross the Rappahannock. "By tomorrow morning," he insisted, "there will not be any of them this side of the river."

Lee could not believe that this would happen. He hoped that Jackson's prediction might be realized, he said, but he thought that the main army of Hooker was in their front, and he could not persuade himself that the Federal commander would abandon his attempt so readily.[75] Calling for Major T. M. R. Talcott and Captain J. K. Boswell, Jackson's chief engineer, he instructed them

---

[69] For a summary of the fighting on the Turnpike and Plank roads from Zoar or Zion church to the vicinity of Chancellorsville, see Lee's report, *O. R.*, 25, part 1, p. 797, Anderson's, *ibid.*, p. 850, McLaws's, *ibid.*, p. 825; Wright's, *ibid.*, p. 866. The full details, with admirable illustrative maps, are given in *Bigelow*, 243 ff.

[70] *Long*, 254.

[71] T. M. R. Talcott in 34 *S. H. S. P.* (cited hereafter as *Talcott*), 17.

[72] Marshall in *Talcott*, 12.

[73] *Talcott*, 16. For the report of this action, which Talcott did not give in detail, see the report of Major R. F. Beckham, *O. R.*, 25, part 1, p. 1048.

[74] See his report, *O. R.*, 25, part 1, p. 866.

[75] Marshall, in *Talcott*, 13.

to make a careful reconnaissance of the ground.[76] If their report was against an attack, as Lee expected it would be, then there was no alternative except to move by the left flank and to try to get in Hooker's rear, for Lee was satisfied from his reconnaissance that there were no openings on the Confederate right.

While the two were speculating on this, General Stuart rode up with a report from General Fitz Lee, who was operating beyond the Confederate left. Fitz Lee had discovered that the enemy's right flank, extended west beyond Chancellorsville, was "in the air," resting on no natural barrier, and therefore could be turned if it could be reached.[77] Very little Federal horse had been encountered. The main force of cavalry had evidently gone off under Stoneman. This news, of course, improved the prospect of a turning movement beyond the Confederate left wing. Secrecy and celerity were necessary for such a bold operation: both would be promoted if no considerable force of Federal cavalry was on the flank to delay the advance or to warn the Federal infantry.

But who could give information as to whether there were roads to the westward that led beyond the Union outposts, roads that were, if possible, entirely out of the enemy's sight? Stuart undertook to examine the ground and to find a guide. He soon rode off for that purpose.

Before midnight, Talcott and Boswell returned to the bivouac, where Lee and Jackson were still discussing what should be done. The two engineers had reconnoitred with care and reported unequivocally against an attack in front.[78] The enemy's position, they said, was strong, well protected by the woods and covered with an abundance of artillery.[79]

That settled the question in Lee's mind. He decided immediately against a frontal attack and resumed his conference with Jackson. "How," he asked, half to himself, "can we get at these people?" Jackson answered, in substance, that it was for Lee to say. He would endeavor to do whatever Lee directed.

Lee took his map, which showed most of the roads and, after a few minutes' study, pointed out the general direction of a move-

[76] *Talcott,* 16.
[77] Fitz Lee, *Chancellorsville,* 26; R. E. Lee to Mrs. Jackson, Jan. 25, 1866, 2 *Henderson,* 472.
[78] *Talcott.* 16.   [79] *Talcott,* 16.

ment around the Federals' right flank and to their rear. An attack must be made from the west, to turn the strong Union positions around Chancellorsville, so that the two wings of the army could make a united assault.[80] Jackson at once acquiesced.

"General Stuart," Lee went on, "will cover your movement with his cavalry." Jackson rose, smiling, and touched his cap: "My troops will move at 4 o'clock," he said.[81]

Remembering Jackson's repeated declaration that the enemy would recross the river that night, Lee added, in effect, that if Jackson had any doubt whether the enemy was still in position the next morning, he could send a couple of guns to the point where Stuart's horse artillery had been engaged that evening and could open fire on the enemy's position. That would soon settle the question.[82]

Jackson was thus entrusted with the execution of the plan that Lee had determined upon. Caution and speed were urged upon him. The council then ended. Jackson retired promptly to get a few hours' rest, as he would have to be up early to procure detailed information about the roads, before he set his column in motion.

Before Lee followed Jackson to the cold comfort of a bed on the ground, Reverend B. T. Lacy, a well-known chaplain in Jackson's corps, reported by order of Stuart, who had learned that Lacy had formerly had charge of a church in the neighborhood and had often travelled its byways.[83] The minister's description of the roads satisfied Lee that the movement he had ordered Jackson to make in the morning was not beyond the endurance of the troops and the horses. Relieved in mind, Lee spread out his saddle-blanket at the foot of a tree, put his saddle at one end of it for a pillow, covered himself with his overcoat and lay down.[84]

He was asleep when Captain J. P. Smith, of Jackson's staff, a young man whom Lee was fond of teasing, waked him with a report of the situation on the right, whither Lee had sent him earlier in the evening. Lee slowly sat up. "Ah, Captain," he said, "you have returned, have you? Come here and tell me what you have learned on the right." And putting his arm around the shoulder of the bending young officer, he drew him by his side.

[80] O. R., 25, part 2, p. 769. [81] Talcott, 16–17.
[82] Marshall, in Talcott, 13. [83] Long, 252.
[84] Long, 255; Smith, in 3 B. and L., 205.

Smith told him what he had found. Lee thanked him and then added that he regretted the young men around General Jackson had not saved him from annoyance by locating a Federal battery that had been causing trouble. You young men, he said in substance, are not equal to the young men of my youth. Smith saw that the General was rallying him and he broke away from the hold Lee tried to retain on his shoulder. The General laughed heartily—a strange sound in those grim woods and among those sleeping men marked for death—and then stretched out again.[85]

Silence fell once more over the pine thicket, silence and darkness, except for the faint light of a feeble fire that a waiting courier had lighted. An hour or so passed, and then the gaunt form of Jackson stirred. He rose, spread his borrowed cape over a brother officer who lay uncovered on the ground, and went to the fire. There, in a short time, he was joined by Mr. Lacy. Jackson made place for the chaplain on a cracker-box where he had found a seat, and quizzed him regarding the roads. Jackson concluded that those with which Lacy was most familiar lay too close to the enemy's lines. Telling the minister to seek a more covered route, Jackson sent him off with Major Hotchkiss, his topographical engineer.[86]

After Lacy and Hotchkiss had gone off, Colonel Long of Lee's staff woke up and found Jackson alone by the fire, shivering from the chill of the morning, against which he had no overcoat to protect him. Long slipped away and contrived to get Jackson a cup of coffee from an adjacent cook-camp. As the two stood talking, Jackson's sword, which was leaning against a nearby tree, fell with a clatter to the ground. Long picked it up and gave it to Jackson, who buckled it on. There was ill omen in this, as Long remembered the incident afterwards.[87]

Now the camp began to stir in the darkness. Lee woke up and joined Jackson.[88] They discussed the roads to the left and speculated, doubtless, on what the reconnaissance of Lacy and Hotchkiss would show. Whatever was done must be done at once, because even a careless enemy could not be expected to keep his right flank uncovered long when he had no cavalry to guard it. At Fredericksburg, Sedgwick surely would attack, also, if the Federals

[85] 3 B. and L., 205.
[86] Dabney, 675–76.
[87] Long, 258.
[88] 3 B. and L., 205.

discovered that the right flank of the Confederate army was weakened. The two generals did not have long to wait, for Lacy and Hotchkiss soon rode up. Hotchkiss picked up another cracker-box, set it between Lee and Jackson and placed his map before them. He explained that a crude trail, which he had drawn on the sheet, had been cut through the woods, well to the southwest and out of sight of the enemy. This ran into a better road that led northward and beyond the enemy's right flank. The proprietor of the iron furnace, who had opened the byway through the woods, would act as guide over it, in case his services were needed.

Lee had left the execution of the movement to Jackson, and had not prescribed a definite route or designated how many troops were to follow it. He now turned to "Stonewall," who was still studying the map. "General Jackson," said he, "what do you propose to do?"

"Go around here," Jackson said, and traced the route that Hotchkiss had marked.

"What do you propose to make this movement with?"

"With my whole corps," Jackson answered.

That was Jackson's own conception, his major contribution to the plan. He would not attempt a simple turning movement that would merely confuse the enemy and give an opening for a general assault. In moving to the enemy's rear, as Lee had planned, he would march with all his 28,000 men and would attack in such force as to crumple up the enemy and throw the whole right wing back against the fords. It was a proposal Lee had not expected, and it floored him. "What will you leave me?" he said, in some surprise.

"The divisions of Anderson and McLaws," Jackson answered, unabashed.

Two divisions to face an enemy who might easily have 50,000 men in a strong position! In case the enemy should learn that Jackson had been detached and should then resume the offensive at Chancellorsville and at Fredericksburg . . . However, the movement around the left flank to the rear of the Federals was the only means of retaining the initiative. If it were to be attempted at all, it should be undertaken in sufficient strength to roll up the enemy's rear. The boldness of the proposal stirred Lee's fighting blood; the benefit to be gained from the operation appealed to his military judgment. The thing could be done; it should be done. If Jackson could turn the flank, he would hold the line. "Well," said he, calmly, "go on." And as Jackson sketched his march, Lee jotted down notes for his own dispositions.[89]

It was now nearly daylight, and the dimming stars gave promise of a clear day.[90] In the bivouacs around headquarters, the troops were eating. The hungry horses were devouring such scant forage as the quartermasters had been able to find. The skirmishers were beginning their fire. Orders for Jackson's movement were fashioned quickly. Lee soon rode off to cover with his scant force that part of the line on the left that Jackson was about to abandon.[91] Lee directed Posey to extend his brigade to the left, and established headquarters temporarily on the side of the road to the Catherine Furnace.

He was there, about 7 A.M., when the head of Jackson's column began swinging to the southwest. A short distance behind the leading regiments rode "Stonewall" and his staff. Jackson drew rein for a minute or two and said a few words to Lee that nobody overheard. "Stonewall" pointed significantly ahead. Lee nodded. Jackson rode on.[92] Doubtless Lee's eyes followed the erect figure of Jackson. "Stonewall's" face was a bit flushed under the visor of the cap that was pulled far down over his blue eyes. He disappeared like a Norse god in the forest. As Lee looked, it must have been with confidence, with personal affection, and with admiration. "Such an executive officer," he said not many days thereafter, "the sun never shone on. I have but to show him my design, and I know that if it can be done, it will be done. No need for me to send or watch him. Straight as the needle to the pole he advanced to the execution of my purpose."[93]

---

[89] Hotchkiss in 2 *Henderson*, 432.   [90] *Malone*, 32.

[91] Captain W. F. Randolph, commanding Jackson's bodyguard, in *Southern Churchman*, April 11, 1931, is authority for the statement that Lee left the bivouac before Jackson did.

[92] 2 *Henderson*, 433; *Alexander*, 333.

[93] Lee to Francis Lawley, quoted in 2 *Henderson*, 477. The incidents of the night of May 1–2, which have here been put together without interrupting the story, have been the subject of a controversy that is analyzed briefly in Appendix II–5.

CHAPTER XXXIV

FATE INTERVENES AT LEE'S HIGH NOON

THE mission of Jackson was daring by every canon of war. Equally daring was the task to which Lee turned when Jackson's figure faded into the forest to the rhythm of the clanking canteens of his swiftly swinging soldiers. For Lee, defying the lesson of Sharpsburg, had divided his army into three parts—into four, if Rooney Lee's two regiments of cavalry, facing Stoneman, were counted as a separate unit. Jackson was carrying 28,000 men with him toward the right flank and rear of Hooker. Early's 10,000 were watching Sedgwick on the Fredericksburg sector, and Lee, with a scant 14,000, was left to hold off the main army of the Federals on a front of three and a quarter miles.[1]

Lee planned his dispositions quickly. Tactically and strategically, the day's work was to be his, for he had no officer with him above the rank of division commander and he was unwilling to trust either of the major generals with direction of the field. He sent back Colonel Chilton, in person, to Fredericksburg to repeat the orders of the previous day, which were for Early to hold his position, to detach troops to the Chancellorsville line if the enemy reduced force in his front, and to join Lee with his entire command if the enemy disappeared from the Fredericksburg sector.[2] Wilcox, who was watching Banks's Ford with his brigade, was similarly instructed to leave a small force there and to march in support on the Plank road in case the Federals showed no intention of crossing.[3] Then Lee moved Wright's brigade of Anderson's division from the Plank road up to the Furnace road, where it formed on the right of Posey.[4] The map[5] on page 527 shows the situation at

[1] The front here computed is that of the V and XII Corps from the Rappahannock to the left of Posey's brigade at 8 A.M. The XII Corps extended farther to the westward, but Lee made no effort to parallel the flank to its junction with the left of the XI Corps.
[2] O. R., 25, part 1, p. 800; Early, 201.   [3] O. R., 25, part 1, p. 855.
[4] O. R., 25, part 1, pp. 867, 871.
[5] Redrawn with the permission of the publishers, The Yale University Press, from Map 16, opposite page 274, in Major John Bigelow's exhaustive Chancellorsville.

8 A.M. on May 2. It represents not only the Confederate line but also the Federal positions, most of which were unknown at that time in detail to Lee.

Orders were to hold the line, with skirmishers well out, but not to provoke attack.[6] The guns were placed as advantageously as possible to cover the approaches,[7] but the prospect remained one of dire danger. Even when Kershaw came up to fill the gap between McLaws's left and the right of Anderson, the men were iix feet apart on some sections of the line.[8] They could not possibly hold their ground against a determined attack by the powerful enemy that faced them. If the divisions of Anderson and McLaws were forced to retreat, there would be a gap between Fredericksburg and Jackson's column; if Early were driven back, Lee's rear would be exposed and Jackson might be compelled to break off his turning movement; if Jackson were repulsed, the Federals might have opportunity of destroying him and then of turning on Lee and Early. Lee was fully conscious of the risks he was taking. "It is plain," he wrote in a dispatch to the President, "that if the enemy is too strong for me here, I shall have to fall back, and Fredericksburg must be abandoned. If successful here, Fredericksburg will be saved and our communications retained. I may be forced back to the Orange and Alexandria or the Virginia Central road, but in either case I will be in position to contest the enemy's advance upon Richmond. I have no expectations that any re-enforcements from Longstreet or North Carolina will join me in time to aid in the contest at this point, but they may be in time for a subsequent occasion. . . . If I had with me all my command, I should feel easy, but, as far as I can judge, the advantage of numbers and position is greatly in favor of the enemy." [9]

The morning opened quietly. Save when the skirmishers engaged angrily, or when the Southern batteries on the right growled in warning as the Federals showed themselves, the early hours were such as the army might have spent during the weeks of waiting in front of Richmond, eleven months before.

But what of Jackson? How was he faring on those narrow Wilderness roads that lent themselves so readily to ambuscade

---

[6] Cf. O. R., 25, part 1, p. 825.
[8] Fitz Lee, 246.
[7] For their location, see Bigelow, 270.
[9] O. R., 25, part 2, p. 765.

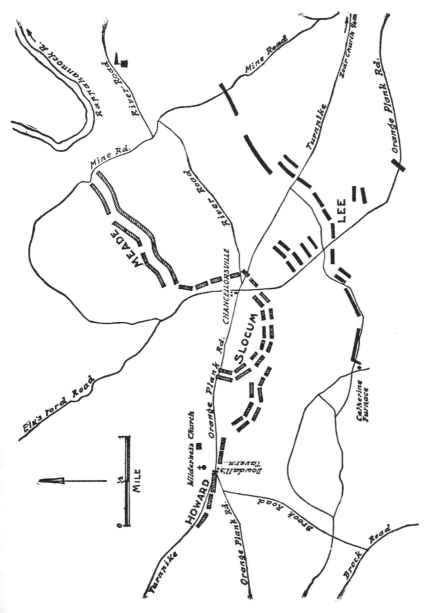

Situation around Chancellorsville, about 8 A.M., May 2, 1863, the exact position of the various Federal units being unknown to General Lee.

and surprise? About 10 o'clock there was a sound of artillery fire by a few guns to the westward, and at 11 this grew heavier.[10] As noon shortened the shadows, a sudden outburst of infantry fire was audible from the vicinity of the iron furnace past which Jackson's column was moving. Soon a courier brought ominous tidings—the enemy was attacking the wagon-train that was following the rear of the turning column! The possibility of frantic driving, wild confusion, and blocked roads were all conjured up by that dread phrase, "The enemy in the wagon-train."

Jackson, of course, could be counted upon to have made some provision against disaster from such a move, because he knew that Lee could not cover his line of march. However, Posey's brigade was sent toward the threatened point, and Wright was shifted to the left to support Posey. Ere long came the reassuring news that the enemy had been beaten off, that the trains were free,[11] and that Jackson had thrown back two brigades to cover his rear.[12] But as Posey's skirmishers were hotly engaged, he was left where he was to assist these brigades,[13] and an effort was made to place a gun where it would help him.[14]

As the afternoon wore on, it became apparent that Jackson had not been held up a second time on the early stages of his march. Nor had the enemy shifted troops from the line to meet him. Where visible in front of Chancellorsville, the Federals were not decreasing in force, though they seemed more numerous around Catherine Furnace. On McLaws's front there was some lively firing by Wofford's brigade around 3:15, but nothing to indicate a general attack by the Federals.[15]

Just as the fusillade on Wofford's lines began to die away, a message in Jackson's autograph was delivered to Lee. It was a single sheet, scrawled in pencil and reading as follows:

Near 3 p.m.
May 2d, 1863

General,

The enemy has made a stand at Chancellor's which is about 2 miles from Chancellorsville. I hope as soon as practicable to attack.

---

[10] *Bigelow*, 275.   [11] *O. R.*, 25, part 1, pp. 798, 851, 867, 871.
[12] Thomas's and Archer's, *O. R.*, 25, part 1, pp. 912, 924.
[13] *O. R.*, 25, part 1, p. 871.   [14] *O. R.*, 25, part 1, pp. 877-78.
[15] *Bigelow*, 284; *O. R.*, 25, part 1, p. 826.

I trust that an ever kind Providence will bless us with great success.

Respectfully,

T. J. JACKSON,
Lt. Genl.

Genl. R. E. Lee

The leadg division is up & the next two appear to be well closed.

T. J. J.[16]

This was good news and bad—good because it indicated that Jackson was far around on the enemy's flank, bad because its reference to a "stand" by the enemy seemed to destroy all hope that the attack Jackson was about to make on the enemy could be a surprise. Until further reports came, Lee could only listen for the sound of firing. Apparently nothing had happened between the time the courier left Jackson and the time he reached headquarters, for the only echo of battle that came from the west was that of Posey's skirmishers opposite the iron furnace.

Suspense was rising. The day was far gone. Unless Jackson's guns were soon heard, his action would have to be deferred until morning, and, being postponed, would almost certainly be discovered. Orders were issued to press the enemy as soon as Jackson opened, so as to prevent the dispatch of reinforcements to oppose him.[17]

The next news did not come from the west but from the east, and was enough to make excitable men turn pale. Early had left Fredericksburg! Without firing a shot, he was marching to join Lee; the strong positions on the heights had virtually been abandoned to the enemy, to be occupied at his pleasure; the rear was open to Sedgwick! It was all due to a mistake in the transmission of ever-dangerous verbal orders. Colonel Chilton, who had not been in good spirits for some time,[18] had reached Early's headquarters about 11 A.M. that day, and in some unaccountable fashion had confused the instructions he had been directed to

---

[16] The original, from the Virginia State Library, is reproduced in facsimile in 3 B. and L., 206.

[17] It is impossible, from evidence now available, to say when these orders were issued. Lee wrote, in his report (O. R., 25, part 1, p. 799), as if they were not sent until after the sound of Jackson's cannon reached headquarters. McLaws intimated (O. R., 25, part 1. p. 826) that the instructions reached him earlier.

[18] Cf. O. R., 25, part 2, pp. 745-46.

deliver. He had told Early that he was to leave one brigade at Fredericksburg, with artillery support, and was to march at once to Lee with the rest of his command. Early had protested in vain and then obediently had drawn out his guns and had put them on the road. Lee, of course, at once wrote him to correct the misunderstanding and to leave him full discretion, but he did not know what might have happened after Early had left the heights. The only reason for hoping that the enemy had not seized the positions was that no report to that effect had been forwarded by the brigade that had been left behind.[19]

In any case, the situation was one of acutest danger. Fredericksburg was exposed to the enemy; no further news had been received from Jackson about his advance or about the "stand" of the enemy; night was distant but two hours—it was a desperate moment in a desperate campaign. Yet, despite his recent illness, Lee did not show misgiving in a single doubtful word or impatient gesture. If Fredericksburg were occupied in force, or if Jackson had been balked in front of a line that had been strengthened at the news of his coming, then . . . but what was that rumble from the west, swelling like distant thunder above the rattle of Posey's skirmishers? Every ear was strained; every heart stopped for a moment. Then, as the fury of a cannonade swept over the wilderness, every eye brightened. It was Jackson at last, hurling his veterans desperately against the Federals to the wild music of his guns!

Quickly the word was passed to the right: Advance and hold the attention of the enemy; threaten him with attack, alarm him for the safety of his position. Not one man must Hooker be permitted to withdraw from his left to reinforce the right that Jackson was now crumpling up. As diligently as if engaged in a real offensive, the thin line sprang up and straightened and

---

[19] *O. R.*, 25, part 1, pp. 800, 811, 814, 1001; *Early*, 200–203. Here, again, there is an element of doubt as to time. Early left Lee's Hill at 2 P.M. (*O. R.*, 25, part 1, p. 812). He stated (*Early*, 203) that he received Lee's later letter, explaining Chilton's mistake, "a little before dark," which would be around 7 o'clock. As Lee's courier had to find him, it is reasonable to assume that the letter was not delivered until two hours after it was written. This would make the hour of its dispatch about 5 P.M. The only fault in this chronology is that it assumes that Chilton did not reach Lee's headquarters, or did not tell Lee of the orders he had given Early, until nearly six hours after he is known to have been at Fredericksburg, as it may be taken for granted that Lee wrote Early as soon as he was informed of the misunderstanding of orders.

stiffened and began steadily to move forward. Past the picket-posts it pressed, up to the Federal skirmishers, on toward the grim main position behind the felled trees in the thicket. The roads were to be covered, Lee said, and if any opening was found, the men were to make the most of it, but otherwise they were to content themselves with a demonstration and were gradually to incline to the left so as to join flanks with Jackson, if he succeeded in rolling up the enemy back on the centre. As the men approached the Federal entrenchments, they could see them lined with troops, against which the Confederate batteries played.[20] No sign was there anywhere of any evidence that the enemy sensed a bluff and was drawing men off to oppose Jackson, the sound of whose battle was rising louder and louder, in a glorious chorus. As Lee shifted to the left in a tactically flawless move, a gap was made in McLaws's division, but the 10th Georgia was deployed in its full strength as a skirmish line and so admirably performed its duty that the front seemed unbroken.

Lee was nearest at the time to Mahone's brigade and personally directed its advance. Watching the situation closely, he now ordered forward three companies of the 6th Virginia to make a feint as if the whole line were about to charge. The Virginians sprang forward, rushed over a difficult abatis and entered the enemy's works a little after dark. They could remain only a short time, as the Federals quickly rallied, but when the three companies returned they brought with them the beautiful colors of the 107th Ohio Regiment, which they delivered into Lee's own hands.[21]

The demonstration had served its purpose, for in the darkness that had now settled thickly over the Wilderness, the Federals could not move troops to their right in time to strengthen it. Lee ordered McLaws and Mahone back to their original lines and, with the rest of the army, listened in fascination to the swelling roar of Jackson's attack. It was evident that Jackson was advancing rapidly, but the volume of sound indicated a growing resistance. Soon the moon rose above the trees in a sky of floating clouds and vaguely illuminated the landscape,[22] but the western horizon was covered with a fiery curtain, draped into fantastic, ever-changing folds by the lighted fuses of the flying shells—a dazzling,

[20] O. R., 25, part 1, p. 826.   [21] O. R., 25, part 1, p. 864.   [22] Long, 256.

awesome sight.[23] Now the din diminished, now it rose again: salvoes and volleys, the nervous, uneven fire of scattered, frantic batteries, the rattle of long lines of muskets. Hour after hour the night battle continued, slowly drawing nearer and shifting southward. At 11 o'clock it was still in its fury; not until midnight did it die away into silence, like the sullen growl of an exhausted dog. Then, as Lee prepared to lie down in a little pine thicket, with an oilcloth over him to keep off the dew, the whippoorwills began their dirge. And never were they "known to sing so long and loud as they did that Saturday night at Chancellorsville."[24]

Weariness overcame the questionings of an anxious mind, and Lee went to sleep on the ground. About 2:30 he was awakened by the sound of two voices, one of them Taylor's.

"Who is there?" Lee called.

"It is Captain Wilbourn," Taylor answered.

Lee raised himself on his elbow, and pointed to his outspread blankets. "Sit down here by me, Captain, and tell me about the fight last night."

Captain R. E. Wilbourn, who was Jackson's signal officer, was tired from hard riding and harder action, but he had to tell a tale the like of which had never been recounted in all the grim annals of America's wars. Jackson had marched straight on when the wagon-train of his rear division had been attacked. After writing Lee from the vicinity of Chancellor's house, he had discovered the right flank of the XI Corps "in the air" just north of the turnpike, a mile beyond the Wilderness Church. The Federals, with their arms stacked, had been unsuspectingly cooking their supper. Not a sign had they given that they were anticipating an attack or had been warned to look for one. Jackson had then quietly extended his men in three lines on a wide front and had given the word. The bugles had sounded through the woods, and the corps had gone forward with a demoniac yell. The startled enemy had offered brief resistance and then had fled, Jackson in full pursuit. Wilderness Church had been reached and passed, the lines had pressed more than a mile farther eastward, and then, having rolled up the whole Federal flank, had been halted by

---

[23] *O. R.*, 25, part 1, p. 826.
[24] *Slocum and His Men*, 164, quoted in *Bigelow*, 328.

darkness and by stiffened resistance. Such a victory the army had never won, but . . . in the confusion, Jackson had ridden forward with a few of his officers, had been fired on . . . and had been wounded three times in the arms. He had been carried to the rear and was under a surgeon's care.[25]

Lee had heard Wilbourn without a comment or even an exclamation. At the announcement of Jackson's injuries, though Wilbourn said they were only flesh wounds, he could not contain himself. He moaned audibly and, for a moment, seemed about to burst into tears.[26] With deep feeling he said, "Ah, captain, any victory is dearly bought which deprives us of the services of General Jackson, even for a short time!"

Wilbourn had been with Jackson when he had been shot and he began to describe how it happened and how Jackson had been borne back to the lines under heavy fire and in extreme pain. The story was more than Lee could endure. "Ah," he said, with rising emotion, "don't talk about it; thank God it is no worse!"

Then he fell silent, pondering, perhaps, the calamity the army would sustain if Jackson's wounds proved more serious than they seemed. He battled with that gloomy thought until he noticed that Wilbourn was rising in the belief that Lee had ended the interview. Stopping him, he asked him to stay. "I want to talk with you some more," he said, and started to ask what position the

---

[25] Wilbourn's MS. account of this interview is summarized in *Cooke*, 238–39. The classic account of Jackson's assault, one of the finest passages in military historiography, is that of Henderson, *op. cit.*, 2, 439 *ff*. The fullest description of the action from the Federal point of view, with an elaborate defense of the conduct of the XI corps, is that of Augustus Choate Hamlin: *The Battle of Chancellorsville: The Attack of Stonewall Jackson*. Bigelow covered the whole operation exhaustively in his *Chancellorsville*, 271 *ff*. There are many narratives of the wounding of Jackson. One of the fullest was that of Captain R. E. Wilbourn in *Early*, 213 *ff*. n. Another was that of J. P. Smith in 3 *B. and L.*, 211 *ff*., republished in modified form in 43 *S. H. S. P.*, 50 *ff*. Dabney (*op. cit.*, 686 *ff*.), gave much valuable data; so did Mrs. Jackson (*op. cit.*, 427 *ff*.). In 1 *N. C. Regiments*, 667–68, is set forth the contention of the 13th North Carolina that it was not responsible for the wounding of Jackson. In *Blackwood's Magazine* for October, 1930, 487 *ff*., appeared a graphic account by an unnamed officer who took upon himself the responsibility for firing the volley that brought Jackson down. For this reference the writer is indebted to his correspondent, Newton Wanliss, Esq., of Ballarat, Victoria, Australia. Major Benjamin Watkins Leigh's account appeared in 6 *S. H. S. P.*, 230 *ff*. Major M. N. Moorman gave his in 30 *ibid.*, 110; the narrative of one of the litter-bearers was published in 10 *ibid.*, 143; General Lane's will be found in 8 *ibid.*, 493. A feeling narrative is that of the commander of Jackson's body-guard, Captain W. F. Randolph: *With Stonewall Jackson at Chancellorsville*. Doctor Hunter McGuire, Jackson's surgeon, was not with him when he was wounded, but is an invaluable witness on all that followed. See *infra*, p. 560.

[26] 8 *S. H. S. P.*, 230 *ff*.

troops held and who was in command. Wilbourn told him that A. P. Hill, as senior division commander, had taken Jackson's place, but that he, too, had been wounded slightly. Brigadier General Rodes had then assumed command, Wilbourn said, but Stuart had been summoned, as senior major general on that sector, to take charge of the corps. The leaders, Wilbourn went on, were anxious that Lee come in person to that flank.[27]

"Rodes," Lee broke in emphatically, "is a gallant, courageous, and energetic officer." And he asked where Stuart and Jackson were, that he might write to them.

Wilbourn volunteered that from what he had heard Jackson say, he thought the General had planned to seize the road to the United States Ford and to cut the enemy off from it that night or the next morning.

This reference to the resumption of the battle galvanized Lee. He rose on the instant. "These people must be pressed today," he said.[28] He wrote immediately to Stuart:

May 3, 1863—3 a. m.

General:

It is necessary that the glorious victory thus far achieved be prosecuted with the utmost vigor, and the enemy given no time to rally. As soon, therefore, as it is possible, they must be pressed, so that we may unite the two wings of the army.

Endeavor, therefore, to dispossess them of Chancellorsville, which will permit the union of the whole army.

I shall myself proceed to join you as soon as I can make arrangements on this side, but let nothing delay the completion of the plan of driving the enemy from his rear and from his positions.

I shall give orders that every effort be made on this side at daybreak to aid in the junction.[29]

In a few minutes the General had on his boots and spurs and ordered his staff to make ready. With his own hands he spread out for Wilbourn a breakfast from a basket some lady had sent him, and he told Wilbourn to lie down and get some sleep as

---

[27] For the assumption of command by Rodes, and the subsequent transfer to Stuart see *O. R.*, 25, part 1, pp. 887, 942; *Taylor's General Lee*, 168; *Fitz Lee*, 252.

[28] *Cooke*, 239.   [29] *O. R.*, 25, part 2, p. 769.

soon as he had finished eating. Lee had mounted when a second messenger arrived from the left in the person of Captain Jed Hotchkiss, Jackson's topographical engineer. He had other details of the battle and of the position of the troops. Lee listened to his report but would not let him tell of Jackson's wounding. "I know all about it," he said, "and do not wish to hear any more—it is too painful a subject." [30] When Hotchkiss prepared to ride off, Lee gave him further instructions for Stuart. "It is all important," he said in his dispatch to Stuart, "that you continue pressing to the right, turning, if possible, all the fortified points, in order that we can unite both wings of the army. Keep the troops well together, and press on, on the general plan, which is to work by the right wing, turning the positions of the enemy, so as to drive him from Chancellorsville, which will again unite us. Everything will be done on this side to accomplish the same object. Try and keep the troops provisioned and together and proceed vigorously." [31] Early was notified of what had happened and was told that the army hoped to make its victory complete that day. [32]

When Lee rode off to do battle for a junction with Jackson's corps, the situation was much confused. Stuart, Lee knew, was a mile and three-quarters northwest of him and would soon be advancing toward him. Wright and Posey, of Anderson's division, were facing west, a mile beyond the nearest point of the Confederate line held by the troops under Lee's immediate command. Stretching from the vicinity of the Plank road, running east and northeast, was the remainder of Anderson's division and the whole of McLaws's. Their faces were toward Chancellorsville. Presumably the lines of the enemy formed a great dipper, with the handle from northeast to southwest. The sides of the dipper were east and west and the bottom to the south. But what forces the Federals had outside this dipper, between his left and Stuart's right, Lee could not tell. His position was roughly as shown on page 536.

[30] 8 *S. H. S. P.*, 230 ff.
[31] *O. R.*, 25, part 2, p. 769. Hotchkiss, in 3 *C. M. H.*, 387. Captain (later Major) Hotchkiss quoted his own interview with Lee and said that "Captain Wilbourn . . . reached General Lee at about the same time . . ."; but it is evident from Captain Wilbourn's account and from the timing of Lee's dispatches to Stuart that Wilbourn arrived before 3 A.M. and that Hotchkiss came about 3:30 A.M.
[32] *O. R.*, 25, part 1, p. 815.

Lee now prepared to attack the eastern and the southern sides of the dipper with his own forces. He believed that if he did this and Stuart continued to press eastward, he could speedily uncover

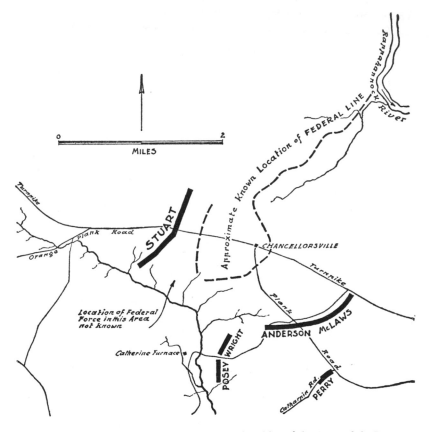

Position of Army of Northern Virginia and assumed position of the Army of the Potomac, about 5 A.M., May 3, 1863.

Chancellorsville and, in that way, more quickly than in any other, could unite the two wings of the army for a joint advance that would throw Hooker back against the Rappahannock. The situation, however, had changed during the night,[33] and rough work lay ahead. Perry's small brigade, which had been moved back from the line at daylight, was sent down the Catharpin road with

[33] *Bigelow,* 342.

instructions to move around to the furnace, to feel out the Federals and to form on the extreme left of Anderson's division.[34] Posey and Wright were to pivot on the eastern flank of Wright's brigade, were to face north, were to extend their line, and were to advance[35] simultaneously with the rest of Anderson's division and the whole of McLaws's.

The brigade commanders entrusted with this important movement knew nothing of the difficult ground through which they had to lead their troops. Their force was much too small to cover their assigned front adequately. They went to their task, however, with fine initiative, their left supported by three guns that Lee personally ordered into position.[36] Perry cleared the ground on his part of the front. Posey engaged hotly. Wright found himself called upon with 1600 to sweep the far-stretching tangle of woodland on a front of one mile. He wisely contracted his own line, throwing out a heavy skirmish line to connect with the brigades to right and to left, and pressed vigorously northward.[37] Lee himself started to the left to direct the junction of Stuart's column and his own.

As he approached Catherine Furnace, the fury of a battle to the northwest was borne upon him. Stuart had attacked before sunrise and was pushing forward. Thanks alike to the good judgment of Stuart's acting chief of artillery, Colonel E. P. Alexander, and to a bad blunder on the part of the Federals, Stuart had been able to seize an excellent artillery position known as Hazel Grove, about 2000 yards southwest of Chancellorsville, and had massed thirty guns there.[38] This strong battery gave him an immediate advantage. But on the left of Stuart's command the enemy was attacking violently. Stout brigades were shaken. Regiments whose flags were covered with the bloody names of many proud victories were broken. Reinforcements had to be hurried to that part of the line until the right was almost without reserves. The centre of the Second Corps was hard beset also. Its dispositions had not been tactically good. Some of the brigade commanders were fighting without knowledge of Stuart's plan or of the manœuvres of the troops to right or to left. From a knoll 750

[34] O. R., 25, part 1, p. 875. [35] O. R., 25, part 1, pp. 867, 871.
[36] O. R., 25, part 1, p. 878. [37] O. R., 25, part 1, p. 868.
[38] O. R., 25, part 1, pp. 821, 887; Bigelow, 347 ff.; Alexander, 342–43.

yards west of Chancellorsville, known as Fairview, the best position on the entire front, the Federal artillery was pouring a mur-
derous fire. Still Stuart's men pressed on; still their leader rode
recklessly up and down the line, cheering, singing, and exhorting
as if he were a cavalry colonel in the first exuberant days of the
war.

Was it possible that the butternut lines could sweep on and
pinch off the salient at Chancellorsville? Could it be that Lee's
bold plan to divide his army between Fredericksburg and the
Wilderness and then to divide it again in the Wilderness would
be crowned with an incredible victory? Or would those massed
thousands of infantry, backed by that superb artillery, dash out of
the thickets in some new *coup* and overwhelm the scant divisions
that were slowly closing in on them?

As the battle raged beyond the furnace, men were carried
beyond themselves and fought as if the fumes of gunpowder
were a mysterious hashish that gave them the strength of madness. Rarely in the whole war did frenzy mount to wilder
heights; never before had the exaltation of a common cause so
completely possessed the Army of Northern Virginia that mistakes were disregarded, enfilading fire was ignored, and attacks
from flanks and rear were met without a tremor and repulsed without a stampede. Above the din that the thickets seemed to amplify
into a paralyzing thunder, could be heard the fiendish rebel yell
rolling from the end of the line, clear and defiant. And in the
midst of it all, at the very climax of the battle, when failure to
effect a junction of the two wings of the army might mean ruin,
Lee sat calmly on his horse, conversing with a German military
observer, Captain Justus Scheibert.[39] As he saw the steady advance of the lines, he wondered what those young men would do
to improve themselves when the war was over, and he fell to
talking with Scheibert of the future education of the Southern
people.[40] It may have been at this bloody moment that he
sowed the seeds that were later to ripen into the resolution to
devote his own life after the war to the education of youth. The
Orange plank road pointed the way to Lexington.

[39] For Scheibert's presence at headquarters, see 2 *von Borcke,* 201.
[40] Scheibert, *Der Bürgerkrieg in den Nordamerikanischen Staaten,* 39.

As Lee discussed these things with Scheibert, the Confederate flags were planted on the works at Fairview and then went down under a wave of blue; another furious cannonade swept the ground and again the flags went forward; again there was a Federal rally and the lines gave way in confusion. From the southeast, Union troops that were withdrawing before Anderson's assault threatened the rear of the attacking force in front of Fairview. But the Confederates were following them fast. Perry's men were coming up. With one more thrust the enemy might be pushed back, the two wings of the army united, and the victory driven home. Lee rode over in person to Hazel Grove, found Archer's brigade of Stuart's command, and ordered the men forward. For 400 or 500 yards they advanced and then halted. Again they went on, dividing on either side of the open ground in front of Fairview and disappearing in the woods. In this manoeuvre, the right flank of Archer established contact with the left of Perry. A continuous line was now moving forward.[41] Quickly Lee sent word to Stuart that junction had been formed.[42] Soon a staff officer came back from Stuart, reporting his situation and asking for orders from Lee. "I found him," wrote this officer, "with our twenty-gun battery, looking as calm and dignified as ever, and perfectly regardless of the shells bursting round him, and the solid shot ploughing up the ground in all directions." [43] Lee was ready for the final blow: Stuart was ordered to advance with his whole command up the Orange plank road; McLaws and Anderson would co-operate.

The line now swept on without a break. On the Confederate right, McLaws met with little opposition, for the Federals saw their fate and were withdrawing toward an inner line that was little more than a vast bridge-head covering the avenues of retreat across the Rappahannock.[44] Mahone's task was easy.[45] Wright, Posey, and Perry met with resistance but soon were close to the plank road.[46] The vigilant commander of the newly formed artillery battalions hurried their batteries to Fairview. With Lee's consent, Colonel Tom Carter added his guns to those that were

[41] O. R., 25, part 1, pp. 800, 875, 925.
[42] 2 von Borcke, 239.
[43] 2 von Borcke, 239.
[44] O. R., 25, part 1, p. 826.
[45] O. R., 25, part 1, p. 862.
[46] O. R., 25, part 1, pp. 800, 851, 867, 871-72. 875, 878.

racing for the eminence.[47] Soon twenty-five pieces, manned by some of the best artillerists in the army, were at Fairview, with Chancellorsville in plain sight.[48]

By 10 o'clock these guns were beating a fast accompaniment for the approaching climax. The resistance to the advance of Stuart's left wing was immediately reduced. Troops facing Anderson fell back beyond the plank road. Like a wedge, the artillery at Fairview was riving the whole line. From that point the retreat of the Federals through the Chancellorsville clearing could be seen plainly, though their ordnance still stubbornly challenged the Confederate advance. The Chancellor house was breaking into flames from chance shots. The dry leaves in the woods and the abatis of the Federal defenses were afire, their smoke blending with that of the firearms. At intervals through the smoke, where the forest was thin, glimpses could be had of bright Confederate battle flags and shining bayonets as Anderson's men worked their way almost unopposed to the plank road.

The Federal artillery fire fell off. The batteries limbered up and disappeared. Where the horses were killed the guns were valiantly removed by hand. The blue infantry that had fought so vigorously at dawn were making for the thickets that lay between Chancellorsville and the river. Everything indicated a precipitate retreat to the fords and pontoon bridges on the Rappahannock. If all went well, the enveloping lines would tighten, the retreat would become a rout—and there would be no gunboats to stay Lee's hand, as they had ten months before on the James. Strategy and the valor of his small army had apparently achieved the impossible. The burning thickets would be the pyre of the puissant Army of the Potomac.

And now word came back that Chancellorsville had been taken. From Hazel Grove, Lee rode over to the plank road and thence eastward to the clearing, along the route the Federals had followed in their confident march from Germanna Ford. Everywhere was the debris of the lost battle, wrecked caissons,

---

47 *O. R.*, 25, part 1, p. 999.
48 Major Bigelow (*op. cit.*, 368 n.) insisted that the Confederates had forty-four pieces at Fairview and he cited Major W. J. Pegram's list of participating batteries to prove it; but he wrongly assumed that all the guns of McIntosh and of Carter reached the hill. Both Carter (*O. R.*, 25, part 1, p, 1000) and Pegram (*O. R.*, 25, part 2, p. 938), stated that the number of participating pieces was about twenty-five.

dying horses, abandoned rifles, knapsacks thrown away in the flight, blankets, oil cloths, cartridge boxes. Scattered playing cards, face up, told of interrupted games. Plundered haversacks showed where hungry Confederate skirmishers had stopped in their pursuit to gulp down the ample Federal rations. And the dead—some lay where the Confederate shell had blasted them into hideous masses of flesh; some had their weapons in their hands and had fallen with their faces to the rear; others had dragged themselves back with mortal wounds and had expired by the road. Where life still lingered, there was terror in the eyes, for now the thickets were burning fiercely, and from the copses came the screams of wounded boys, crying to be saved from a death worse than that of battle.

Past woods on the left of the road, Lee rode beyond Fairview, where, with elevated guns, the jubilant artillerists were firing at a distant target, retreating fragments of broken regiments. Beyond Fairview, the woods on the left gave place to the Chancellorsville clearing, in itself a paltry stake on which to gamble the lives of 125,000 men. But what a sight it was under the warm sun of that May noon! There in the centre of the picture was the Chancellor house, burning as if it had been a bonfire set to celebrate the victory. Beyond it, gray and raw against the thickets, were the abandoned Federal works, scarcely visible in the smoke and in the throng of men in butternut. Wright's brigade, coming up from the south, had been the first to reach the clearing; the rest of Anderson's division had quickly crowded up to the road. All of them, now, in the wild jubilation of victory, were eager to drive the enemy into the river. As Lee rode toward the Chancellor house they recognized him. Sensing that he had fashioned their victory, they broke into the wildest demonstration they had ever made in his presence.[49] "The fierce soldiers with their faces blackened with the smoke of battle, the wounded crawling with feeble limbs from the fury of the devouring flames, all seemed possessed with a common impulse. One long, unbroken cheer, in which the feeble cry of those who lay helpless on the earth, blended with the strong voices of those who still fought, rose

[49] M. D. Martin to J. J. Martin, May 8, 1863, 37 *Va. Magazine of History and Biography*, 226.

high above the roar of battle, and hailed the presence of the victorious chief. He sat in the full realization of all that soldiers dream of—triumph; and as I looked upon him," wrote one of his staff officers, "in the complete fruition of the success which his genius, courage, and confidence in his army had won, I thought that it must have been from such a scene that men in ancient times rose to the dignity of gods." [50]

It was the supreme moment of his life as a soldier. The sun of his destiny was at its zenith. All that he earned by a life of self-control, all that he had received in inheritance from pioneer forbears, all that he had merited by study, by diligence, and by daring was crowded into that moment. The life of stern duty that had carried him from a West Point classroom through the mud flats of Cockspur Island, across the pedregal to Padierna, over the passes in West Virginia, and to the brink of the Potomac at Sharpsburg, had brought him to that plain of military glory.

But it was not given to this man ever to know as a Confederate soldier a single hour when the fates that had favored him in body and in mind did not threaten him with ruin. As he turned modestly from the acclaim of his troops to direct the relief of the wounded Federals in the Chancellor house, a courier placed a dispatch in his hand. He fumbled at it with gauntleted fingers and handed it to Major Marshall to read to him. It was from Jackson. Nothing in it indicated that Jackson had dictated the paper in the first consciousness after an operation for the amputation of the wounded left arm. In brief, soldierly phrases, Jackson expressed his congratulations on the victory, and announced that he had been compelled by wounds to turn over the command of his corps to Major General A. P. Hill. Not for a moment had Lee forgotten his great lieutenant, but this note and the news that it had been necessary to remove the injured member shook Lee more violently than if one of the shells that were still roaring overhead had exploded under the flank of Traveller. His calm face was overcast with anguish on the instant. What was another victory if it meant that Jackson's flesh wounds were serious and that he might . . . ? Perhaps Lee would not let himself think

[50] *Marshall.* 173.

how the wounds might terminate. With shaking voice, choked by emotion, he bade Major Marshall reply to Jackson that the victory was his, that the congratulations were due him, and that he wished he had been wounded in his stead. Quickly Marshall wrote out the message and gave it to Lee to sign. It read:

"General:—I have just received your note, informing me that you were wounded. I cannot express my regret at the occurrence. Could I have directed events, I would have chosen for the good of the country to be disabled in your stead.

"I congratulate you upon the victory, which is due to your skill and energy." [51]

At the moment, the success of the operations that Lee generously credited to Jackson seemed to promise the immediate retreat of the enemy across the Rappahannock. Lee so advised the President. "We have again to thank Almighty God for a great victory," he said.[52] Speed was necessary if the victory was to be capitalized, but the troops were scattered and many of them had already been fighting since dawn. Lee felt compelled to call a temporary halt to rest the men and to organize the next stage of the offensive, which had to be conducted in one of the densest parts of the Wilderness against a position of unknown strength.[53] In the confidence of victory, the officers quickly reorganized their men, who, anxious to press on, were disposed on a long front, with Anderson thrown out on the right along the turnpike east of Chancellorsville.[54]

Then, again, as if they had not already done mischief enough in marring Lee's most spectacular victory by the wounding of

---

[51] *O. R.*, 25, part 2, p. 769; *Marshall*, 173–74. Hotchkiss (3 *C. M. H.*, 387) and Dabney (*op. cit.*, 702) made it appear that this note was dispatched soon after Hotchkiss came to headquarters before daylight on May 3, but Smith, who was with Jackson at the time, stated that it was received in reply to a note written at Jackson's dictation and presumably after 9 A.M. (3 *B. and L.*, 213–14). The internal evidence bears this out. It has also been stated that Jackson's note, which has been lost, made no reference to his wounds, but this seems contradicted by the opening sentence of Lee's answer.

[52] *O. R.*, 25, part 2, p. 768.

[53] *O. R.*, 25, part 1, 800. Von Borcke (*op. cit.*, 2, 241) said that this was done at 11 A.M. It is not certain whether Lee knew at this hour that Hooker had fortified a strong line north of Chancellorsville. In his report (*O. R.*, 25, part 1, p. 800), he mentioned a "strong position" that Hooker had "previously fortified," but this fact may readily have been discovered later in the operations.

[54] *O. R.*, 25, part 1, p. 851.

Jackson, those twin conspirators against the South, fate and circumstance, the Castor and Pollux of Northern success, again rode into the Wilderness. Just as Lee was about to give the orders for the resumption of the attack on the bewildered Federals, Lieutenant Andrew L. Pitzer, of General Early's staff, reached him with news of a disaster. Before dawn that morning the enemy had thrown a pontoon bridge across at Fredericksburg. A little later, General Sedgwick had made a demonstration below the town on Early's right. It had been easily repulsed. Then an attack had been made on the extreme left, near Doctor Taylor's, above Beck's Island. This, too, had been beaten off with the help of Wilcox's brigade, which had marched most opportunely from Banks's Ford.[55] Thereupon the enemy had assailed Marye's Heights, which were very thinly held.[56] Twice the Federals had recoiled and then, in a heavy assault, they had overwhelmed the position. Pitzer had seen them in force on top the dominating ground, and then, without waiting to communicate with Early, he had spurred on to inform Lee.[57] The enemy, by this time, was almost certainly in Lee's rear, marching down the plank road.

Fredericksburg lost, the left of Early's line turned, the main army now between Sedgwick and Hooker—this in the hour when one more blow, untroubled from the rear, had seemed to promise an overwhelming triumph!

---

55 For Wilcox's movements, see *O. R.*, part 1, pp. 825, 855.
56 *McCabe*, 359, quoting Barksdale in *Richmond Dispatch*, May 31, 1863.
57 *O. R.*, 25, part 1, pp. 800–801; *Early*, 211.

CHAPTER XXXV

Lee Loses His "Right Arm"

Lee did not blanch at the news of the disaster at Fredericks-burg. Nor did he hesitate. When a Mississippi soldier rode up a little later with another excited report, Lee simply said: "We will attend to Mr. Sedgwick later." [1] His position dictated his action. He could not strike Hooker with part only of his army. He would not retreat. Instead, he would demonstrate against Hooker's crippled host, would hold it in the Wilderness, and would detach troops immediately to join Early and to deal with Sedgwick's column. Whom should he send? Not Anderson, for he had been fighting since dawn; not any part of Jackson's corps, for it had been in desperate action two days. Obviously, McLaws must go, for his front was not in danger and his troops had not been heavily engaged; yes, and, as one of McLaws's brigades had been left at Fredericksburg, he would give him, in its place, Mahone's brigade of Anderson, which, on the 2d and on the 3d, had had little to do.

This time, too, he would take no chances that orders might be delayed or misunderstood. He would deliver them in person. Riding quickly to McLaws's front, he found the General and directed him to move Kershaw's and Mahone's brigades down the plank road at once to resist the enemy's advance. As soon as they were well on their way, he ordered McLaws to follow in person with his remaining brigades, those of Wofford and Semmes.[2] Early was notified that reinforcements were being sent to him and was directed to co-operate with McLaws in driving Sedgwick,[3] who was believed to have with him one corps and part of another.[4]

The detachment of McLaws left Lee with only 36,000 to 37,000

---

1 Statement of R. W. Royall, an eye-witness, Jan. 17, 1923.
2 *O. R.,* 25, part 1, pp. 801, 826, 830, 851.
3 *Early,* 220. 4 *O. R.,* 25, part 1, p. 801.

men to face Hooker.[5] Two brigades were reported on the move
from Richmond to support him, but as Stoneman's cavalry were
known still to be raiding along the lines of communication,[6] Lee
determined to hold these troops, Ransom's and Pettigrew's brigades, at Hanover Junction to guard the railroads.[7]

Establishing temporary headquarters in a little tent by the side
of the Orange plank road,[8] Lee now undertook to make a demonstration that would discourage Hooker from taking the offensive
on the strength of the news from Fredericksburg. Lee assumed,
of course, that the knowledge of the success on that sector would
lead Hooker to halt the move back to the north side of the
Rappahannock, but he believed he could hold him within his
lines. Summoning to his tent Brigadier General R. E. Colston,
who was in temporary command of Trimble's division, he gave
him instructions: "General," said he, "I wish you to advance your
division to the United States Ford road. I expect you to meet
with resistance before you come to the bend of the road. I do
not want you to attack the enemy's positions but only to feel
them. Send your engineer officer with skirmishers to the front
to reconnoitre and report. Don't engage seriously, but keep the
enemy in check and prevent him from advancing. Move at
once." [9] It was then 3 o'clock,[10] and the troops under McLaws
were on their way back toward Salem Church, four miles west of
Fredericksburg, a good position on which to meet an attack.
Heth's and Rodes's divisions were left where they were.[11]

From headquarters, Lee now rode to the right of the line and
instructed R. H. Anderson concerning his part in the game of
keeping General Hooker amused. Anderson was told to move his
division northward from the turnpike along the River road
towards the Rappahannock. This was a very important precaution, because the River road led into the Old Mine or Mountain road, which ran southeast from Hooker's lines and joined
the turnpike at Zoar Church. If Anderson blocked the River

[5] McLaws carried with him some 7000 men. The original strength of that part of
the Army of Northern Virginia on the Chancellorsville front, 51,000 had been reduced
by casualties of between 7000 and 8000.

[6] Cf. O. R., 51, part 2, p. 700.   [7] O. R., 25, part 2, p. 768.

[8] 3 B. and L., 233.   [9] 3 B. and L., 233.

[10] O. R., 25, part 1, p. 1006.

[11] O. R., 25, part 1, pp. 892, 945. Harry Heth was commanding A. P. Hill's division
and R. E. Rodes had D. H. Hill's.

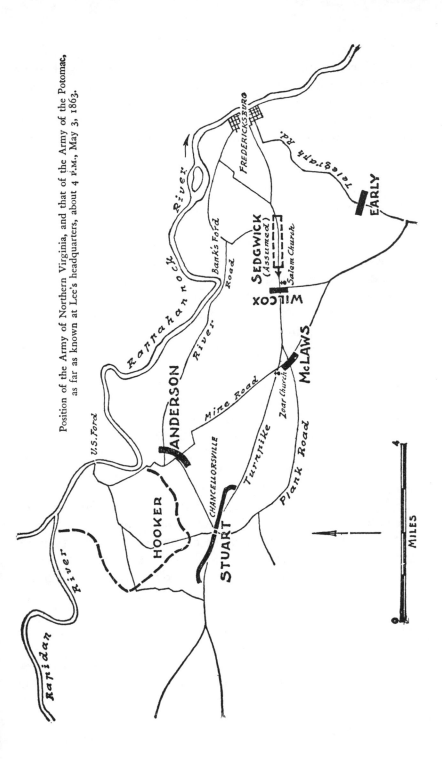

Position of the Army of Northern Virginia, and that of the Army of the Potomac, as far as known at Lee's headquarters, about 4 P.M., May 3, 1863.

road, he could threaten the enemy's communications and break up any movement undertaken down the Rappahannock from Hooker's line to form a junction with Sedgwick.[12]

By this time, in all probability, Lee had heard that Early had evacuated his positions on the ridges below Fredericksburg and had marched down the Telegraph road. He doubtless knew, also, that Wilcox, with splendid initiative, had withdrawn from Taylor's Hill to the plank road and was very stubbornly resisting the advance of Sedgwick's columns. The situation, then, as he appraised it about 4 P.M. was as shown on the preceding page.

It was, of course, a grave state of affairs, fraught with disaster if Lee's plans miscarried, but there is not a line in the reports to suggest that Lee viewed it otherwise than with the calmness he always displayed. The confidence neither of the commander nor of the army was shaken, when, about 5 P.M., there came the sound of a cannonade from the direction of Salem Church, followed by reports of an infantry engagement. Now, if ever, Hooker would assume the offensive; yet even on Anderson's front, where an irruption seemed most likely, the Federals did not attempt an advance. Instead, Anderson made a reconnaissance and projected an attack, though he found the day too far spent to launch it.[13]

For two hours and more the firing from the east continued. Taking it to mean that McLaws was attacking, Lee determined to develop whatever advantage McLaws might gain. He reasoned that as Early was on the Telegraph road, he was potentially on the flank of Sedgwick's columns on the plank road. The combined strength of Early and of McLaws should suffice to demolish Sedgwick. So, to the music of the cannonade, he wrote to Early and to McLaws outlining a plan whereby Early should come up on the enemy's left while McLaws attacked in front. "It is necessary that you beat the enemy," he wrote McLaws, "and I hope you will do it." [14] Just as he had seized the initiative in dealing with Hooker by advancing toward Chancellorsville, so now Lee purposed to put Sedgwick on the defensive.

The first news from McLaws's column indicated that the way had been prepared for the execution of this plan. Wilcox, who

---

[12] O. R., 25, part 1, p. 851.
[13] O. R., 25, part 1, pp. 851–52.   [14] O. R., 25, part 1, p. 771.

never appeared to better advantage than on that day, had made a stand at Salem Church, on the plank road, where he had been joined by McLaws. The Federals had come forward about 5:20, after artillery preparation. They had gained an initial advantage and had broken the front of one regiment but had been savagely repulsed. A second attack had been beaten off easily. Then Wilcox and Semmes, who was on the left, had rushed forward and had driven the enemy for nearly half a mile, retiring only when approaching darkness rendered their advanced position dangerous.[15]

In the security this news afforded, Lee prepared to bivouac for the night. Sitting down at a little fire, he was soon joined by Stuart, with whom he talked of the day's developments and of the probable resumption of the battle. Major von Borcke rode up presently and had to be told of the adventure that had befallen Captain Scheibert, the Prussian observer then attached to Lee's headquarters. Scheibert had gone off during the day to seek forage for the horse he was riding and at a nearby farmhouse had suddenly found himself confronted by six Federal infantrymen. Pretending that he was followed by a body of cavalry, Scheibert had bluffed the Union soldiers into surrender and then had marched them off and had presented them in person to Lee.

The recountal of this episode was much interrupted by the arrival of dispatches, which Lee had great difficulty in reading by the dim and flickering light of the tiny fire. Von Borcke slipped away and after some time returned with a box of candles. He had noticed them near the lines during the day and very daringly had gone back and had picked them up, almost under the noses of the Federal skirmishers. Lee was grateful, but, surmising that von Borcke had acquired them at no small risk to him, he gently rebuked him. "Major," he said, "I am much obliged to you; but I know where you got these candles, and you acted wrongly in exposing your life for a simple act of courtesy." [16] Perhaps Lee remembered how another warrior in an ancient contest with the Philistines, had poured out water

---

[15] O. R., 25, part 1, pp. 801, 858–59. General Lee stated in his report that Wilcox and Semmes advanced "nearly a mile," but this was from their positions and not from the point where the enemy's advance had been halted. The old toll-gate, where Wilcox halted, was about three-eighths of a mile from Salem Church.

[16] 2 von Borcke, 244–45.

that three mighty men had brought him "from the well of Bethlehem, which is by the gate."[17]

By the light of one of Von Borcke's candles, Lee read near midnight a message from McLaws, enclosing one from Early, in which that officer proposed that instead of attacking on the left of McLaws, as planned, he return to Marye's Heights, cut Sedgwick's communications with Fredericksburg and then move against the enemy in co-operation with McLaws. Lee forthwith had one of his staff officers write to McLaws approving the scheme, if practicable, but cautioning him to press the enemy and not to permit Sedgwick to concentrate on Early while that officer was between the Federal commander and the Rappahannock.[18]

Then, in an atmosphere of alarms and distress, with the wounded crying out from nearby copses for water,[19] Lee sought a little rest. What a day it had been! A lifetime had been crowded into it—the proud news of the victory on the left, the shocking report of the wounding of Jackson, the desperate advance on Chancellorsville, the triumphant hour amid the shouting troops and the burning forest, the ominous intelligence that Jackson's arm had been amputated, the announcement of the breaking of the line at Marye's Heights, the dispatch of McLaws, the battle at Salem Church—all had been crowded into the hours that had elapsed since he had been aroused by the arrival of Captain Wilbourn in the pine thicket, where the whippoorwills had been calling.[20]

When Lee took up his duties on the early morning of Monday, May 4, one of his first thoughts was of his wounded lieutenant. Reports were that Jackson was doing well. He had rallied from the operation, had slept, and was resting comfortably in a tent. Lee felt, however, that there still was danger of a raid by the

[17] II *Samuel* xxiii, 15–17.   [18] *O. R.*, 25, part i, p. 770.

[19] 2 *von Borcke*, 243.

[20] It is interesting to note that the lectionary of the Protestant Episcopal church prescribes for May 3, the date when Lee heard of the wounding of Jackson, the lament of David for an earlier Jonathan. It reads:

"O Jonathan, thou wast slain in thine high places.

"I am distressed for thee, my brother Jonathan: very pleasant hast thou been unto me! Thy love to me was wonderful, passing the love of women.

"How are the mighty fallen, and the weapons of war perished."

The lectionary of Lee's prayer-book contained a different passage.

enemy's cavalry from the direction of Ely's Ford, so he sent a guard to the vicinity of Jackson's temporary quarters and instructed the corps surgeon, Doctor Hunter McGuire, to remove him to a place of safety at Guiney's, as soon as this could be done without discomfort to the patient.[21]

Reconnaissance undertaken at daylight showed that Hooker had strengthened his position. On well-chosen ground, protected in part by streams, he had a heavy line, with abatis and ample batteries. Anderson was already preparing to feel out the enemy on the Confederate right,[22] but Lee quickly decided that it would be a waste of life to attack with less than his entire force. To concentrate all his units, he must first dispose of Sedgwick and remove the threat against his rear. He must take no chances with this. McLaws and Early might suffice to hold Sedgwick or even to defeat him, but it was wise to adhere to the sound old fundamental of presenting a superior force at the point of attack. Hooker must be held, if possible, with the artillery and the three divisions of Jackson's corps. Anderson should go to reinforce Early and McLaws.[23]

Scarcely had Anderson started and Heth moved up to Anderson's line, when Lee received a dispatch from McLaws, in which that officer explained the details of Early's plan of a joint attack. McLaws expressed doubt as to his ability to co-operate adequately with the troops he had and asked for reinforcements.[24] Lee replied that Anderson was marching to McLaws's support, and as the operation had now assumed magnitude, he decided to ride to the right in person to supervise it. Perhaps he was the more readily prompted to do this by his knowledge of McLaws, who as senior of the three division commanders would assume command. Lafayette McLaws was a professional soldier, careful of details and not lacking in soldierly qualities, but there was nothing daring, brilliant, or aggressive in his character. An excellent division commander when under the control of a good corps leader, he was not the type to extemporize a strategic plan in an emergency.[25]

[21] *Mrs. Jackson*, 438, quoting Doctor McGuire.   [22] *O. R.*, 25, part 1, p. 852.
[23] *O. R.*, 25, part 1, p. 802.   [24] *O. R.*, 25, part 1, p. 827.
[25] For McLaws's career. see 6 *C. M. H.*, 431 *ff*. A very just appraisal is given in *Sorrel*, 133.

When Lee reached the vicinity of Salem Church he found the situation less favorable than the dispatches had indicated. McLaws had postponed all operations pending the arrival of Anderson and knew very little about the dispositions of the enemy. The head of Anderson's column was close at hand,[26] but the remainder of it came up very slowly. As Lee awaited its appearance, trying to ascertain something definite about the enemy's whereabouts, his patience speedily exhausted itself. Worn by lack of sleep and exasperated by the snail-like pace of Anderson's men, he lost his temper and was in distinctly bad humor.[27] When at last Anderson's three brigades were on the ground, Lee ordered them farther eastward to fill the gap between McLaws's right and Early's left; but the country was rolling, there were no decent roads in the direction of Anderson's advance, and his progress was slow. McLaws must have been bewildered, for he did nothing whatever.

At length, with Anderson on his way, Lee rode around to Early's sector. He found him on an elevated position, in rear of Lee's Hill, across Hazel Run from Alum Springs Mill.[28] Early had a very good account to give of himself. Soon after sunrise he had marched up the Telegraph road and had recovered Marye's Heights and Lee's Hill. Barksdale's brigade had been sent to the stone wall below Marye's Heights, but had not occupied the town because it had discovered a strong force there, protected by rifle pits.[29] As far as the enemy's position could be ascertained in the broken country, Sedgwick had a line in some old Confederate gun positions stretching parallel to the Rappahannock in rear of the heights. At right angle to the troops in this position, who were subsequently found to belong to Howe's division, the main Federal line ran slightly south of west, close to the plank road, and extended to McLaws's front. From that point it ran north toward Banks's Ford, but how strong it was in that quarter and where it extended, nobody seemed to know.

Early's plan was to advance up the high ground in rear of the heights, and to turn the Federal position on the plank road, while Anderson attacked on his left and McLaws closed in from the

26 O. R., 25, part 1, p. 827.   27 Alexander, 356.
28 Early, 227, 230.   29 Early, 224-25.

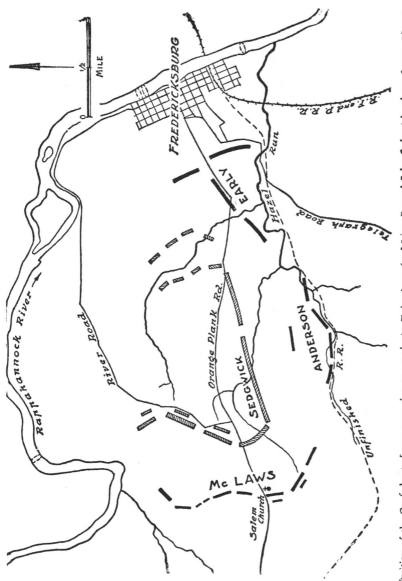

Position of the Confederate forces preparing to attack the Federals under Major General John Sedgwick, about 6 P.M., May 3, 1863, between Salem Church and Fredericksburg.

west. It was a plan that involved no little manœuvring over difficult terrain, but as it seemed feasible, Lee approved it and rode
back toward the centre.[30] The troops there were still having
much trouble in getting into position. All along the front there
was uncertainty both concerning the position of the enemy and
concerning the best crossings over the small streams that cut the
countryside into ravines. It must have been after 2 P.M. when Lee
returned to Anderson's front, and even then much time was lost
in reconnaissance. Lee urged speed and did his utmost to hurry
up the guns, but he could not complete the dispositions
promptly.[31] Six o'clock came before the troops were all in
position, as shown on the preceding page.[32]

At last the signal guns were fired, and Early and Anderson
advanced. They met with a hot resistance on some parts of the
line. Hoke's brigade came up on the left of Hays, and the two
fired into each other. Wright's advance masked that of Posey
and Perry and received in the open the concentrated fire of the
Federal artillery and skirmishers.[33] Kershaw and part of Wofford's brigade beat their way through thickets but did not reach
the enemy. McLaws's left was scarcely engaged at all. As darkness began to fall, a heavy fog crept over the ground and slowed
down the advance still more.[34] Despite all these difficulties, the
enemy was pushed back on the centre and on the right.

As soon as the advance had cleared the ground, Lee rode up to
the Downman house, on a ridge overlooking Hazel Run. Sending for Early, he got a report concerning the advance on the
right. All was well there, but if the Federals were hard pressed,
the force in Fredericksburg might attempt a diversion in Sedgwick's behalf. Early, in consequence, was directed to send two
brigades to strengthen Barksdale, and with the rest of his command was to draw a line perpendicular to the plank road.[35]
Accumulating reports from the other brigade commanders during the course of the next hour led Lee to believe that if the
enemy were vigorously and immediately assailed, he would be
forced across the Rappahannock that night. If he were allowed to

---

[30] *Early*, 227–28.　　　　　　　[31] *Alexander*, 357.
[32] This map was redrawn from No. 37 in Major John Bigelow's *Chancellorsville.*
[33] *Bigelow*, 414; *O. R.*, 25, part 1, pp. 802, 852, 869.
[34] *O. R.*, 25, part 1, p. 802.　　　　[35] *Early*, 232.

remain undisturbed where he was, he would entrench again during the night, would be ready to give battle the next day, and would hold up the return of the three divisions to Chancellorsville, where Hooker at any time might take the offensive. For this reason, Lee determined to push the advance in the darkness —the first time he had ever undertaken a night attack. Early was advised; McLaws was instructed about the movement of his brigades; Alexander and Hardaway were told to move guns within range of Banks's Ford and to shell it.[36]

Stuart, all ears, reported during the evening that he could hear the enemy moving vehicles on the Confederate left, beyond Chancellorsville, but whether this presaged a retreat or the beginning of an attempt to turn that flank, he could not say.[37] If it were the start of a new offensive by Hooker, then, obviously, the need of clearing the rear was greater than ever. When he learned of these activities on the extreme left, Lee thought of Jackson as well as of the army. He felt that the removal of "Stonewall" to Guiney's was imperative. A messenger was hurried off to instruct Surgeon McGuire to that effect. Remembering, too, that he had recently forbidden surgeons to accompany wounded officers to the rear and thereby perhaps to neglect the soldiers on the field, he specifically ordered Doctor McGuire to go with Jackson. The prompt recovery of the commander of the Second Corps meant more to the army at that time than anything else.[38]

Through the night the artillery boomed away at the unseen target of Banks's Ford,[39] but in the fog the weary infantry made no progress. At daylight, when the skirmishers advanced, the bird had flown. Sedgwick was across the river. Word came soon after from Fredericksburg that the brigade of Colonel Norman J. Hall at that point had also started back over the Rappahannock, had repulsed an attack to halt its retreat, and was regaining the north bank. Its pontoon bridge had been cut loose and was slowly drifting toward the Stafford side of the stream.[40]

---

[36] O. R., 25, part 1, pp. 802, 817, 821, 828, 880, 882, 1002; ibid., part 2, pp. 860–61. In The Richmond Times-Dispatch, Sept. 15, 1930, the statement was made that Lee gave his sash to Color-bearer E. S. Trainum for gallant conduct in this action.

[37] O. R., 51, part 2, p. 702.   [38] Mrs. Jackson, 438.

[39] O. R., 25, part 1, pp. 821, 880–81.

[40] O. R., 25, part 1, pp. 359, 802, 841; Bigelow, 422.

All was well on the Chancellorsville front. Stuart reported that a forced reconnaissance had shown the enemy in strength in his earthworks. As Stuart said nothing about any attempted advance on the part of Hooker, it was manifest that the Federal commander had obligingly waited for Lee to clear his rear without interfering with his plan of operations.[41] Lee could accordingly prepare to march again to Chancellorsville and confront Hooker. But as Sedgwick could readily return to the right bank of the river, Lee took precautions that his final blow at Hooker should not again be halted at the very moment it was poised. Early was sent back to Fredericksburg with his own division and Barksdale's brigade. The other troops were directed to start their westward march to the Chancellorsville front.[42] The units were badly scattered, however, and were showing exhaustion. It was slow work to reconcentrate them. McLaws got away in fair time with orders to relieve Heth on Anderson's line nearest the Rappahannock.[43] It was 4 P.M. before the roads were clear for Anderson,[44] and as he advanced, one of the worst storms of the spring broke over his tired troops.[45] Night found the head of his column still one mile from Chancellorsville.[46]

The day did not seem to have been altogether wasted. In fact, though there was natural regret that Sedgwick had gotten off so easily, the situation had been restored. It was practically what it had been on the afternoon of May 3, except that there were now no Federals on the south side of the Rappahannock at Fredericksburg. Lee was free to strike again, and that was what he had hoped to make possible when he had started after Sedgwick. But he had to count his hours. If he was to attack at all, it must be quickly, for Stoneman's raiding cavalry, divided now into a number of separate columns, had cut the line of the Richmond, Fredericksburg and Potomac Railroad and had been within sight of Richmond. Even telegraphic communication with the capital had been severed. Stoneman would of course retire across the Rappahannock if Hooker did, but any long delay in sending Hooker back to his starting point would prolong Stoneman's raid

41 O. R., 51, part 2, p. 702.   42 O. R., 25, part 1, p. 802.
43 O. R., 25, part 1, p. 829.   44 O. R., 25, part 1, p. 852.
45 O. R., 25, part 1, p. 869.   46 O. R., 25, part 1, p. 852.

and probably leave the army without food and without ammunition.[47]

The best news of the day was from Guiney's. Jackson had stood the trip to that point admirably. He was in the best of spirits, his wounds were beginning to heal, and he had eaten well. All the indications were for a speedy recovery.[48] As Lee retired on the night of the 5th, under a fly-tent at Fairview,[49] with every intention of delivering a general attack on the morning of Wednesday, May 6, his first prayer must have been one of gratitude to God for the improvement of him who was the spearhead of the army. When Hooker was given the *coup de grâce,* and Jackson was well again, that long-projected new offensive into Maryland might be started, and then. . . .

Orders were to advance the skirmishers all along the front at daybreak and to follow this with a general assault. That this would be bloody business, every one in the army recognized, but there was no hesitation and no misgiving. If the army had been able to turn the Federal right on the evening of the 2d and to break the line on the morning of the 3d, what was there to keep it from driving the enemy into the Rappahannock on the morning of the 6th?

At dawn the camps were astir, the scant rations were hastily eaten, the skirmishers were sent forward, the line of battle was being formed. At headquarters, Lee wrote a dispatch to the War Department,[50] reviewed the dispositions, found all in readiness, and was on the point of giving the order for the general advance when General Pender galloped up and rushed in. His skirmishers had already moved forward, he said—but Hooker was gone! The frowning lines in the woods were empty.

"Why, General Pender!" Lee exclaimed in amazement that nothing of this had been reported during the night. "That is the way you young men always do. You allow those people to get away. I tell you what to do, but you don't do it!"

Pender could say nothing. "Go after them," Lee cried, with an impatient gesture, "and damage them all you can!"[51]

---

[47] *Cf. O. R.,* 25, part 2, p. 775.
[49] Hotchkiss, in 3 *C. M. H.,* 392.
[51] 3 *C. M. H.,* 392.

[48] *Mrs. Jackson,* pp. 439–40.
[50] *O. R.,* 25, part 2, p. 779.

There was no damage the advancing divisions could inflict. Hooker had thrown up the sponge. Federal troops, guns, horses, and wagons were safely over the Rappahannock. The Confederates who had gone forward in the expectation of a bitter fight spent the forenoon in succoring the enemy's wounded, in exploring the lines, in commenting on the great strength of the works, in picking up booty and stragglers, and in gazing blankly into the woods that fringed the river. Lee gave them half a day for this curious recreation, then he had them recalled and formed. Leaving a few regiments to care for the wounded, to bury the dead and to collect the prizes of war, he started back to Fredericksburg with the main army.[52] Over horrible roads and through a drenching rain that began before night, the troops retraced their steps to their familiar camps.[53]

The weary army had now to be refreshed, the gaps had to be filled, and officers had to be designated to replace those who had been killed or disabled. A. P. Hill had already been ordered back on the 6th to the temporary direction of the Second Corps, for his injuries were slight, and Stuart was again with his beloved troopers.[54] To head D. H. Hill's old division, Lee asked the immediate promotion of Brigadier General R. E. Rodes, whose gallant leading of that command on May 2 had been

[52] O. R., 25, part 1, pp. 802, 852, 945.

[53] O. R., 25, part 1, p. 974. Hooker, first and last, had more than 80,000 men on the Chancellorsville front, but he used them very unwisely. Many of his best units were not put into action. After gaining a great advantage in crossing the rivers unopposed, he suddenly abandoned all idea of an offensive and, on the afternoon of May 1, yielded the initiative to Lee and recalled from good positions east of Chancellorsville the troops that had been marching directly on Lee's flank. The Confederate advance that seemed suspiciously easy to Jackson was, in reality, pursuit of a line that was deliberately retiring. On the 2d, Jackson's movement to the right flank of the Army of the Potomac was observed but was assumed to be a retreat. The attack on Jackson's wagon-train was intended as the first move in following this supposed retreat, but it was not pushed. Hazel Grove was abandoned on the 3d as the result of a tactical blunder. The defeat of the Federals on the 3d was facilitated by the exhaustion of the artillery ammunition and by an injury to General Hooker. He was standing by a pillar on the porch of the Chancellor house when it was struck by a round shot and the pillar was overturned, hurling him heavily to the floor. For several hours thereafter he was partially stunned and incapable of directing operations intelligently, but except for a brief time he did not formally turn over the army to his senior corps commander, Major General D. N. Couch. He seemed to lose all his fighting-qualities once he confronted Lee. Throughout the campaign he was greatly handicapped by his mistake in ordering away all the cavalry except one brigade. His decision to recross the river on the night of May 5 was made in the face of the opposition of some of his corps commanders. Communication between Hooker at Chancellorsville and Sedgwick at Fredericksburg was slow, and misunderstandings were numerous.

[54] O. R., 25, part 2, p. 782.

especially commended by Jackson in a message to Lee.[55] For the command of Trimble's division, which Brigadier General R. E. Colston had handled during Trimble's convalescence, Lee asked Major General Arnold Elzey or Major General Edward Johnson,[56] if the latter were able to do field duty. Davis sent him Johnson.[57]

Fortunately for the hungry men, the repair of the railroad from Richmond was completed on the 6th or 7th,[58] and when congratulatory orders were issued on the 7th,[59] the men had rations as well as honors to boast. They were allowed to rest till tired muscles were content. As Lee did not anticipate an early resumption of the offensive by the badly punished enemy, he directed Longstreet not to overtax his men by haste in rejoining.[60] One great concern that Lee felt, as he examined the depleted ranks, was for the strengthening of the cavalry and for the reinforcement of the army with new units. Stoneman's raid had been a failure, but it might be repeated. "[The Federal] cavalry force," he wrote the President, "is very large and no doubt organized for the very purpose to which it has recently been applied. Every expedition will augment their boldness and increase their means of doing us harm, as they will become better acquainted with the country and more familiar with its roads. . . . You can see, then, how difficult it will be for us to keep up

---

[55] *Lee's Dispatches*, 87; *O. R.*, 25, part 2, p. 774; *Mrs. Jackson*, 439. General Rodes had cherished small hope of being given command of the division and, with characteristic generosity, had urged General Ewell to seek assignment to it. "The whole Division I doubt not," he wrote Ewell, "would be delighted to have you as their Commander— Do not hesitate to avail yourself of every means of procuring this result—and be assured that I will be personally gratified to be under your command again" (R. E. Rodes to R. S. Ewell, *MS.*, March 22, 1863, for a copy of which interesting document the writer is indebted to Doctor P. G. Hamlin of Philadelphia, the biographer of General Ewell).

[56] *O. R.*, 25, part 2, p. 774. [57] *O. R.*, 51, part 2, p. 703.

[58] *O. R.*, 25, part 2, p. 781; *Mrs. Jackson*, 449.

[59] *O. R.*, 25, part 1, p. 805. The publication of these orders in the Northern press was made the occasion of a new personal attack on Lee. *The Boston Transcript* said that Lee's reference to a "signal deliverance" would have come more properly from the lips of his slaves than from his own. It printed a lengthy communication from a Northern soldier who had visited Arlington and, as he stated, had received from an old slave a blood-curdling report of Lee's cruelty. This story, evidently a variant of one that circulated before the war, was that Lee had ordered some Negroes punished for fishing in a brook when they had nothing to eat. The overseer having refused to whip a woman among the offenders, Lee was alleged to have lashed her with the utmost ferocity. "After Lee had lacerated the girl's body," the correspondent concluded, "he bathed the yet bleeding wounds in brine." The paper accepted all this as fact (*Boston Transcript*, May 14, 1863, editorial, p. 2, and article, p. 4, col. 2).

[60] *O. R.*, 18, 1049.

our railroad communications and prevent the inroads of the enemy's cavalry. If I could get two good divisions of cavalry, I should feel as if we ought to resist the three of the enemy." [61]

As for infantry, Lee urged that troops be brought from the departments of South Carolina, Georgia, and Florida, where he did not believe more soldiers would be needed during the summer months than would be required to man the water batteries. This, of course, raised the question of the proper employment of their commander, General Beauregard. With no flourish of words, and writing as if he himself could be replaced after his greatest victory as readily as any subaltern, Lee proposed that Beauregard be brought to the Army of Northern Virginia and put in command of it. [62]

But there was a more immediate concern than for the increase of the cavalry or the reinforcement of the infantry. One of Jackson's chaplains, Reverend B. T. Lacy, came to headquarters during the morning of the 7th on his way to find Doctor S. B. Morrison, Early's chief surgeon, whom Doctor McGuire desired in consultation. Jackson was worse, Mr. Lacy said. He had done very well on the 6th except for slight nausea, but at dawn Doctor McGuire had found unmistakable symptoms of pneumonia. There was fear, for the first time, that his illness might be fatal. [63] Lee would not admit the possibility of such an outcome. His own faith in God was so complete that he did not believe Heaven would deprive the South of a man whose services were essential to victory. He said to Lacy: "Give [Jackson] my affectionate regards, and tell him to make haste and get well, and come back to me as soon as he can. He has lost his left arm, but I have lost my right." [64]

What would become of the army if Jackson died? Where,

---

[61] *O. R.,* 25, part 2, p. 782.

[62] *O. R.,* 25, part 2, pp. 782–83. It is possible to construe this passage as simply meaning that Beauregard be given command in Virginia of the troops he brought from the South. Lee's words were: "But it will be better to order General Beauregard in with all the forces which can be spared, and to put him in command here, than to keep them there inactive and this army inefficient from paucity of numbers." Had Lee meant that Beauregard should have charge of only part of the army, it seems most likely that he would have said "put him in command *of them* here."

[63] The fullest report of the condition of Jackson, day by day, is Hunter McGuire: "Account of the Wounding and Death of Stonewall Jackson," *Richmond Medical Journal,* May, 1866.

[64] *Dabney,* 716.

among all his lieutenants, could Lee look for another man to execute with swift certainty the flank marches he so much employed in his strategy? Longstreet was a fine fighter, once the issue was drawn, but Longstreet was slow and contentious, always arguing for his own plan, even to the last minute, whereas Jackson, after advancing his own proposals, would execute Lee's orders as readily as if they were his own.[65] In the Army of Northern Virginia, he had no peer. For him to die would be in very truth for Lee to lose his "right arm."

That evening Jackson was reported better. The pneumonia did not seem to be filling the lung. But the next morning, Friday, May 8, as Lee went about the routine duties of the day,[66] gloom settled again. Jackson was weaker, the pneumonia was advancing, he was in mild delirium at intervals,[67] babbling orders and, with his old concern for the welfare of his men, repeatedly calling, "Tell Major Hawks to send forward provisions for the troops."[68] Despite these ominous symptoms, Lee would not give him up. Jackson *could* not die, he kept telling himself! He was unable to go to Jackson, both because he could not trust his emotions and because there was no one in whose hands he would feel safe in leaving the army. He had even been compelled to ask the President to come to headquarters for the discussion of important military questions, inasmuch as he felt that his own presence there was essential.[69] There was one thing, only one, that he could do for Jackson. That was to pray for him. On Saturday night, as the doctors shook their heads and expressed the fear that the outlook was hopeless, Lee went down spiritually to the brook Jabbok and, like Jacob, wrestled with the angel. Never in his life had he prayed with so much agony of spirit. While the army slept and Jackson in his stupor fought his battles over, Lee on his knees implored Heaven to grant to his country the mercy of the deliverance of Jackson from death.

When the troops began to gather for worship during the forenoon of the next day—a beautiful Sabbath that the commanding

---

[65] *Marshall,* 170.
[67] *Mrs. Jackson,* 441.
[66] *O. R.,* 25, part 2, pp. 786-87.
[68] *Dabney,* 719.
[69] *O. R.,* 25, part 2, p. 783. Longstreet was due to reach headquarters on the 9th (*O. R.,* 51, part 2, p. 705), but was entirely unfamiliar with the state of the army or the disposition of the troops.

general had recommended as a day of thanksgiving for the victory[70]—Lee was still unconvinced that Jackson would be taken. Eagerly he met the chaplain who came from Guiney's at Jackson's request to preach at headquarters. The face of the clergyman told his story: The doctors had given Jackson up and did not believe he could survive, except by a miracle. He was in virtual coma, breathing very badly, and muttering still of his warring. "A. P. Hill," he was saying, "prepare for action." And again: "I must find out whether there is high ground between Chancellorsville and the river . . . push up the columns, hasten the columns. . . ."[71]

Even in the face of this, Lee refused to believe it could happen. "Surely, General Jackson must recover," he said, in a shaken voice. "God will not take him from us, now that we need him so much. Surely he will be spared to us, in answer to the many prayers which are offered for him!"

The minister preached to a large company of officers and to a multitude of men who had escaped the fangs of death in the Wilderness, but it is doubtful if Lee heard much that the earnest and eloquent Mr. Lacy had to say. His mind was at Guiney's, with Jackson, and so were his prayers. When the service was over, Lee spoke again to the chaplain: "When you return, I trust you will find him better. When a suitable occasion offers, give him my love, and tell him that I wrestled in prayer for him last night, as I never prayed, I believe, for myself." And he had to turn abruptly away to conceal his emotion.[72]

Going to his headquarters tent, Lee found that his staff officers had just completed decoding an important dispatch from the War Department, which had been garbled in transmission. It was an argument for sending Pickett's division to Vicksburg as a reinforcement to General Pemberton. In Lee's eyes the proposal represented a choice between holding Virginia and holding the line of the Mississippi, and he so advised Seddon by telegraph. Then he wrote a fuller answer, to be transmitted by mail.[73] In this letter he mentioned the possibility that if the Army of Northern Virginia were weakened he might be compelled to

[70] 26 S. H. S. P., 8.
[72] Dabney, 725.
[71] Dabney, 719; Pendleton, 271.
[73] O. R., 25, part 2, p. 790.

withdraw into the defenses around Richmond. Perhaps that familiar phrase, the "Richmond defenses," set up a chain of memories in his mind—Jackson gaunt and exhausted in the swamps around Richmond, bewildered and taciturn; then the fiery zeal with which a transformed Jackson had urged an immediate advance on Pope after Lee had joined him at Gordonsville from Richmond; the start of the "foot-cavalry" that August afternoon on the dusty road from Jeffersonton to Thoroughfare Gap; the light that shone in Jackson's eyes when he came over to welcome the following army that Homeric day at Groveton; the heart-stirring sight of his hurrying bayonets over the ridge at Sharpsburg when the army would have been lost without him; the confidence with which he had met Longstreet's awkward jests while the fog was disappearing from the plains of the Rappahannock in December; that last glimpse of him as he sat in silhouette against the background of his marching men on that narrow road in the Wilderness. How gloriously "Stonewall" had redeemed the Seven Days and how much remained for him to do! If Jackson's dauntless will triumphed over the doctors' dark predictions as it had over the might of the enemy, then the army might take up anew the offensive that had been abandoned at South Mountain. Jackson would not be delayed the next time at Harpers Ferry. The fear of his name would cause the enemy to evacuate it; then he, the fast-moving, the sure-visioned, would reach Harrisburg and destroy the railroad bridge that linked East and West; the march might next be made to Philadelphia and . . .

There was a stir outside the tent, a moment of hesitation, and then some one brought in a bit of folded paper. It contained the brief and dreadful news. In the little cottage at Guiney's, Jackson had roused from his restless sleep and had struggled to speak. His mind had been wandering far—who knows how far? —but with an effort, in his even, low voice, he had said: "Let us pass over the river, and rest under the shade of the trees." And then, as so often on marches into the unknown, he had led the way.

General Orders,
No. 75

Hdqrs. Army of Northern Virginia,
June 24, 1862.

I. General Jackson's command will proceed tomorrow from Ashland toward the Slash Church and encamp at some convenient point west of the Central Railroad. Branch's brigade, of A. P. Hill's division, will also tomorrow evening take position on the Chickahominy near Half-Sink. At 3 o'clock Thursday morning, 26th instant, General Jackson will advance on the road leading to Pole Green Church, communicating his march to General Branch, who will immediately cross the Chickahominy and take the road leading to Mechanicsville. As soon as the movements of these columns are discovered, General A. P. Hill, with the rest of his division, will cross the Chickahominy near Meadow Bridge and move direct upon Mechanicsville. To aid his advance, the heavy batteries on the Chickahominy will at the proper time open upon the batteries at Mechanicsville. The enemy being driven from Mechanicsville and the passage across the bridge opened, General Longstreet, with his division and that of General D. H. Hill, will cross the Chickahominy at or near that point, General D. H. Hill moving to the support of General Jackson and General Longstreet supporting General A. P. Hill. The four divisions, keeping in communication with each other and moving *en échelon* on separate roads, if practicable, the left division in advance, with skirmishers and sharpshooters extending their front, will sweep down the Chickahominy and endeavor to drive the enemy from his position above New Bridge, General Jackson bearing well to his left, turning Beaver Dam Creek and taking the direction toward Cold Harbor. They will then press forward toward the York River Railroad, closing upon the enemy's rear and forcing him down the Chickahominy. Any advance of the enemy toward Richmond will be prevented by vigorously following his rear and crippling and arresting his progress.

II. The divisions under Generals Huger and Magruder will hold their positions in front of the enemy against attack, and make such demonstrations Thursday as to discover his operations. Should opportunity offer, the feint will be converted into a real attack, and should an abandonment of his intrenchments by the enemy be discovered, he will be closely pursued.

III. The Third Virginia Cavalry will observe the Charles City road. The Fifth Virginia, the First North Carolina, and the Hampton Legion (cavalry) will observe the Darbytown, Varina, and Osborne roads. Should a movement of the enemy down the Chickahominy be discovered, they will close upon his flank and endeavor to arrest his march.

IV. General Stuart, with the First, Fourth, and Ninth Virginia Cavalry, the cavalry of Cobb's Legion and the Jeff. Davis Legion, will cross the Chickahominy tomorrow and take position to the left of General Jackson's line of march. The main body will be held in reserve, with scouts well extended to the front and left. General Stuart will keep General Jackson informed of the movements of the enemy on his left and will co-operate with him in his advance. The Tenth Virginia Cavalry, Colonel Davis, will remain on the Nine-mile road.

V. General Ransom's brigade, of General Holmes' command, will be placed in reserve on the Williamsburg road by General Huger, to whom he will report for orders.

VI. Commanders of divisions will cause their commands to be provided with three days' cooked rations. The necessary ambulances and ordnance trains will be ready to accompany the divisions and receive orders from their respective commanders. Officers in charge of all trains will invariably remain with them. Batteries and wagons will keep on the right of the road. The chief engineer, Major Stevens, will assign engineer officers to each division, whose duty it will be to make provision for overcoming all difficulties to the progress of the troops. The staff departments will give the necessary instructions to facilitate the movements herein directed.

By command of General Lee:

R. H. CHILTON,
Assistant Adjutant-General.

APPENDIX II—2

JACKSON'S MARCH OF JUNE 24-26, 1862

The evidence is conclusive that Lee intended Jackson's march of June 26 to make it unnecessary for the columns of attack to storm the

Federal position on Beaver Dam Creek, the strength of which was well known to the army. In his report Lee said: "Jackson . . . was to advance at 3 A.M. on the 26th and turn Beaver Dam." Again "Jackson being expected to pass Beaver Dam above and turn the enemy's right, a direct attack was not made by General Hill."[1] Beyond all question, Lee expected this to be done as a part of the operations of June 26.[2] Jackson, however, in his report used this language: "On the morning of the 26th, *in pursuance of instructions from the commanding general, I took up the line of march for Cold Harbor.* . . ." After describing the difficulties encountered during the day, he went on: "That night the three divisions bivouacked near Hundley's Corner. While there some skirmishing took place. . . . We were now approaching the ground occupied by that portion of the Grand Army of McClellan which was posted north of the Chickahominy. . . . *As our route that day inclined toward the south* and brought us in the direction, but to the left of Mechanicsville, we distinctly heard the rapid and continuous discharges of cannon, announcing the engagement of General A. P. Hill with the extreme right of the enemy." He then recounted the happenings of the early morning of June 27 and said: *"Continuing to carry out the plan of the commanding general, I inclined to the left and advanced on Cold Harbor. . . ."*[3] Now, the words which have been italicized (they do not so appear in the text of the report) can create only one impression: Jackson considered it to be his mission to march for Cold Harbor. He did not regard it as an essential part of his mission to cross or to turn Beaver Dam *on the 26th.*

Thus there is a definite conflict between Lee's intention and Jackson's understanding of it. If Lee's intention was made known to his subordinate, in person or through published orders, then the blame for what happened on the 26th rests first and chiefly on A. P. Hill for advancing contrary to orders, and secondly on Jackson for not advancing farther. If, on the other hand, the plan of the commanding general was not clear, Jackson must be relieved of at least some of the responsibility for what happened on Beaver Dam Creek.

To settle this, recourse must be had to the language of the order, which it is to be assumed Lee sent Jackson. There is no positive proof that Jackson had the text, but as Lee personally drafted it, his known regard for detail would indicate that he did not omit so important a matter. Jackson's reference to "the plan of the commanding general," and his specific mention of "inclining to the left," which was enjoined in the order would indicate that Jackson had seen the document.

1 *O. R.,* 11, part 2, pp. 490–91.   2 See *supra,* pp. 111, 132.
3 *O. R.,* 11, part 2, p. 553.

How did the order read? It has been quoted in part on page 114, to prepare the reader for a possible misinterpretation of its terms by one of the commanders, and it appears as Appendix II–1, but a few of its sentences must again be quoted: "At 3 o'clock Thursday morning, 26th instant, General Jackson will advance on the road leading to Pole Green Church, communicating his advance to General Branch. . . ." Then followed the directions for the advance of A. P. Hill The order continued: "The enemy being driven from Mechanicsville, and the passage across the [Chickahominy] bridge opened, General Longstreet, with his division and that of General D. H. Hill, will cross the Chickahominy at or near that point, General D. H. Hill moving to the support of General Jackson and General Longstreet supporting General A. P. Hill. The four divisions, keeping in communication with each other and moving en echelon on separate roads, if practicable, the left division in advance, . . . will sweep down the Chickahominy and endeavor to drive the enemy from his position above New Bridge, General Jackson bearing well to his left, turning Beaver Dam Creek and taking the direction toward Cold Harbor. . . ." [4]

Jackson's successive movements, then, as set forth in the order were to be: (1) An advance to Pole Green Church; (2) liaison with A. P. Hill through Branch; (3) contact with D. H. Hill; (4) leading an *échelon* movement down the Chickahominy; (5) bearing well to the left; (6) turning Beaver Dam Creek and (7) taking the direction toward Cold Harbor. The orders said nothing about Jackson's "passing" Beaver Dam Creek in the sense of passing over it. Neither did the orders say specifically that Jackson was to turn the Creek *on the 26th,* though that undoubtedly was Lee's intention. The turning-movement was to be dependent upon the appearance of D. H. Hill in support, and upon the beginning then of an advance of four divisions in left *échelon.*

If Jackson had been in contact with Lee between the date the order was issued and the time set for its execution, he would, of course, have cleared up all points that seemed to be ambiguous. But it must be remembered that Jackson was out of touch with the commanding general after the evening of June 23, except as they communicated by courier, or by telegraph. On the evening of the 25th, telegraphic communication was interrupted. Jackson had, therefore, to rely on his previous instructions.

This much of the conclusion, then, is plain: If Jackson had been at

[4] *O. R.,* 11, part 2, pp. 498–99.

Pole Green Church earlier on the 26th, D. H. Hill would have been sooner in support and the advance *en échelon* could have been begun that day, as Lee intended. There is every reason to believe that this advance would have turned Beaver Dam Creek and would have obviated the delay and losses there, for McClellan had only one brigade of infantry and one regiment of cavalry facing Jackson's line of advance.[5] As it was, A. P. Hill attacked prematurely. Then, when Jackson's delayed march brought him to his intermediate objective, and he failed to find his support there, he did the natural and the proper thing: he held to the letter of his instructions, as he interpreted them. He did not hurry on alone to turn Beaver Dam Creek, because he did not understand either that it was necessary to do so that day, or that he was expected to execute the turning-movement without support. Quite reasonably, when he heard firing that indicated a probable change in plan, he may have expected that he would be notified if this change called for any new movement on his part. He put his forces at Hundley's Corner, however, where he would be in position to advance as soon as D. H. Hill was *en échelon*. The evidence does not warrant a charge of disobedience of orders in failing to cross Beaver Dam on the afternoon of June 26.[6] On the contrary, by every approach, the argument goes back to the initial mistake of A. P. Hill in advancing contrary to orders.

Two questions remain to be answered. First, did Lee propose unreasonable marches for Jackson on June 25 and 26? In other words, was his plan of action, as drawn on June 24, apt to be upset by such delays as occurred on the march? The order speaks for itself. On Jackson's own assurance that he would reach Ashland by the evening of June 24, Lee gave him a march of only six miles for June 25—from Ashland to the western side of the Central railroad—and for the 26th, with orders to start at 3 A.M., asked him to do only eight and one-quarter miles to get into position at Pole Green Church in time to turn Beaver Dam Creek.[7] Jackson certainly did not regard these marches as impracticable or even severe. In fact, it will be recalled[8] that he told Longstreet on June 23 that he could be in position on June 25. It was at Longstreet's instance that another day was allowed him. The plan was a reason-

---

[5] *O. R.,* 11, part 2, pp. 232–33, 389–90.

[6] Colonel H. L. Landers, formerly of the Historical Section of the Army War College, was the first, as far as this writer knows, to call attention to the plain indications in the report of General Jackson to that officer's belief that his mission was to reach Cold Harbor. To Colonel Landers's admirable MS. *History of the Seven Days' Battles,* to his splendid maps of the troop-positions in the engagements, and to his generous counsel in many particulars, this writer is so deeply indebted that he wishes to make this special acknowledgment.

[7] *O. R.,* 11, part 2, p. 498.   [8] *Supra,* p. 112.

able one in this particular. The fault was with Jackson's slow march on June 24–25, as he approached Ashland. Nor did he promptly notify the commanding general that he was behind his schedule. It was the morning of June 26 when Lee learned from Jackson that the march of the Army of the Valley had not brought it to the neighborhood of Ashland until the evening of the 25th.[9] At that time, according to Lee's order, Jackson should then have been below Ashland, close to the Virginia Central Railroad. Had Jackson notified Lee earlier that he was behind schedule, it might have been possible to put up a strong resistance to the threatening operations of McClellan on the 25th and to allow Jackson one more day in which to turn Beaver Dam Creek. It is possible that Jackson started his courier as soon as he found the telegraph-line down, but the conclusion seems unescapable that Jackson overestimated the marching-power of his men and underestimated the difficulties of moving in an unfamiliar country a force that was much larger than any he had ever commanded. Yet his self-confidence and his pride in his soldiers were such that apparently he hoped, until the last minute, to speed up their march and to maintain his schedule. The difficulties he encountered on the road, during his march on the 26th, were enough to slow him down, but, had he started earlier, they would not have upset the general plan.

If, then, Lee's plan was not at fault in expecting Jackson to reach the upper waters of Beaver Dam Creek in time to turn it on June 26, did Lee select the proper route for the turning-movement? Was Pole Green Church the right intermediate objective? According to the map Lee then used, the answer undoubtedly is in the affirmative. His map showed Pole Green Church only one and one-half miles by road from the crossing of Beaver Dam Creek at Colonel Richardson's, with roads leading around the head of the creek to Cold Harbor. Any trained soldier is apt to say that if he were defending the lower stretches of Beaver Dam Creek, and learned that a heavy hostile column was where Pole Green Church appears on Lee's map, in relation to the course of the creek, he would hasten to evacuate the bank of that stream. In fact, if Jackson had regarded the turning of Beaver Dam Creek as his mission, he might reasonably have concluded that he had done this, strategically, when he reached Hundley's Corner.

Unfortunately for Lee, the map was defective in two respects. First, the distance from Pole Green Church to the crossing at Colonel Richardson's was not one and one-half miles, as the map indicated,

---

[9] *Lee's Dispatches*, 15–16; see *supra*, p. 122.

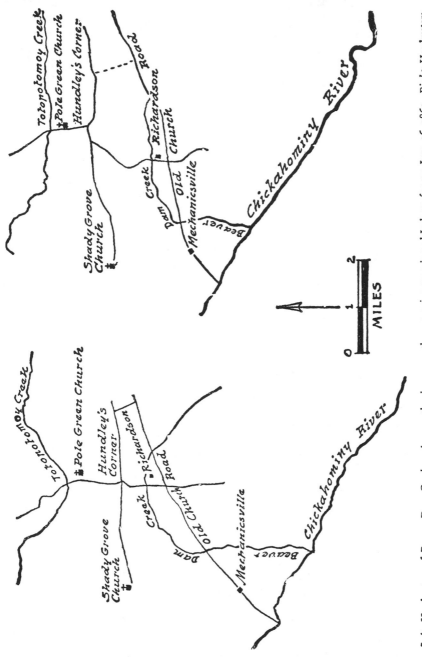

Left: Headwaters of Beaver Dam Creek as incorrectly shown on the campaign map issued Jackson for use June 26, 1862. *Right:* Headwaters of the same stream on the corrected Confederate map of 1864.

but two and three-quarters miles. From Hundley's to Richardson's was not seven-eighths of a mile, as the map showed, but one and seven-eighths—a very substantial difference in a turning-movement. In the second place, the map showed the upper waters of the creek bending sharply to the southeastward from Richardson's, when in reality the course of the creek above that point, as one went upstream, was almost due east. The Federals knew the terrain and must have realized that they could easily defend the creek until nightfall, with their right and rear safe until Jackson was well beyond Hundley's Corner. Had Lee possessed a correct map at the time he probably would not have directed Jackson to march to Hundley's Corner but to Bethesda Church, where he would have passed the headwaters of the creek and could have headed for Cold Harbor. The following sketches will show the difference between the map Lee had at this time and the correct map he used in 1864.

To sum up the case, then: Lee's demands on the marching-power of Jackson were not unreasonable; his logistics were sound; if the campaign map had been correct, the intermediate objective he assigned Jackson at Pole Green Church would have been proper. But Lee's written orders did not make it plain to a subordinate twenty miles away that the turning of Beaver Dam Creek on the 26th was his first mission. Jackson marched poorly on June 24, 25, and 26, and, if it was possible to communicate sooner, he erred seriously in not sooner notifying the commanding general that he had been delayed. Arriving when he did at his intermediate objective and failing to find his supports at hand, Jackson was justified under his interpretation of the letter of his orders in halting there for the night. Taken as a whole, it is a singular fact that comment on this operation has laid so much stress on Jackson's delay and has dwelt so little on A. P. Hill's violation of orders, in advancing before Jackson was in position. This advance was the immediate reason for the slaughter on Beaver Dam Creek.

APPENDIX II—3

THE REASON FOR JACKSON'S FAILURE AT WHITE OAK SWAMP, JUNE 30, 1862

D. H. Hill, son of the general of the same name, in his *North Carolina in the War Between the States*,[1] reviewed the various theories of Jackson's

---

[1] 2, 147.

failure to cross White Oak Swamp. These and the explanations given by other witnesses who are not cited by Hill fall under these six heads:

1. *Jackson failed because a crossing was impracticable.* This was the explanation Jackson gave in his report. He said: ". . . the marshy character of the soil, the destruction of the bridge over the marsh and creek, and the strong position of the enemy for defending the passage prevented my advancing until the following morning."[2] This was the view, also, of Doctor Hunter McGuire, Jackson's surgeon. "The ford," said he, "was miry and deep and impracticable for either artillery or infantry."[3] General McCall wrote in his report, without any knowledge of the brewing controversy and therefore with no thought of being cited as a witness: "I did not apprehend [Jackson's] ability to effect a passage."[4]

Such a view leaves out of account the possibility of crossing the swamp elsewhere than at White Oak Bridge, a possibility that will be considered presently. Colonel William Allan, Jackson's chief ordnance officer, and a soldier of experience and standing, is a credible witness in refutation of the view that the Federal position was impregnable. He asserted: "Jackson, ignorant of the country, had in the swamp and Franklin's veterans substantial causes of delay, but they were not such obstacles as usually held Jackson in check. Vigorous demonstrations at the fords above and below, as well as at White Oak Swamp Bridge, would probably have secured a crossing at one point or another, and the tremendous prize at stake was such as to justify any efforts."[5]

2. *Jackson might have crossed at some other point than White Oak Bridge and doubtless would have done so but his orders allowed him no discretion.* This was Henderson's conclusion. He wrote: [Jackson] "had been ordered by General Lee to move along the road to White Oak Swamp, to endeavor to force his way to the Long Bridge road, to guard Lee's left flank from any attack across the fords or bridges of the lower Chickahominy, and to keep on that road until he received further orders. Those further orders he never received; and it was certainly not his place to march to the Charles City road until Lee, who was with Longstreet, sent him instructions to do so. . . . [Jackson] said 'If General Lee had wanted me he could have sent for me.'" Henderson quoted Doctor Hunter McGuire to this effect: "It looked the day after the battle, and it looks to me now, that if General Lee had sent a staff officer, who could have ridden the distance in forty minutes, to order Jackson with three divisions to the cross roads, while D. H. Hill and the artillery

---

[2] *O. R.,* 11, part 2, p. 557.   [3] 2 *Henderson,* 51 n.; *McGuire Papers.*
[4] *O. R.,* 11, part 2, p. 389.
[5] *The Army of Northern Virginia in 1862,* p. 121.

watched Franklin, we should certainly have crushed McClellan's army. If Lee had wanted Jackson to give direct support to Longstreet, he could have had him there in three hours. The staff officer was not sent, and the evidence is that General Lee believed Longstreet strong enough to defeat the Federals without direct aid from Jackson." Henderson added: "Such reasoning appears incontrovertible." [6] But is it? Is it not invalidated by the evidence of Wade Hampton quoted in the text, evidence that had not been published when Doctor McGuire and Colonel Henderson wrote? Jackson's orders were simpler than Henderson makes them out to be. The dispatch of Ewell to guard the crossings of the Chickahominy, etc., was incidental to the main plan. Ewell's mission had been fulfilled and the last units were back with Jackson by 4 o'clock on the afternoon of the 30th.[7] Jackson must have known the part assigned him in the general plan, for he probably was in conference with Lee on the 29th and certainly on the morning of the 30th. Contrary to Henderson's and McGuire's statements, Jackson was notified that he was needed to reinforce Longstreet: Hampton saw Longstreet's aide on the north side of the swamp and was told why he had come.[8] In short, Henderson's whole argument rests on the assumption that Jackson received no orders while at White Oak Bridge; when that assumption is proved unfounded, Henderson's case collapses.

It is only fair to add Henderson neglected to say much that would have strengthened his case if he had been acquainted with it. There were three fords over the swamp above White Oak Bridge: First was Brackett's, one and one-half miles west of Jackson's road. Next was Fisher's, two and a half miles from Jackson. The third was Jordan's, distant three and three-quarter miles from the Confederate position.[9] Fisher's and Jordan's Fords had been uncovered by Huger's advance. If Jackson had moved his army to either of them, or had gone two miles farther upstream to the head of the swamp, he would have been able to cross unopposed. But here is the point that has escaped most commentators: At some undetermined hour of the afternoon D. H. Hill sent his engineer officer across the swamp urging Huger to attack Franklin and thereby force him to release his grip on the ground above White Oak Bridge. Huger sent back word that the Charles City road was obstructed.[10] If, therefore, Jackson had crossed at Fisher's or at Jordan's, or had gone around the head of the swamp, he would have found his divisions jammed in the Charles City road, in rear of Huger, and more

[6] 2 *Henderson*, 58.   [7] *O. R.*, 11, part 2, pp. 618.   [8] *Marshall*, 111.
[9] The location of Jordan's Ford, which seems to have been in some doubt with mapmakers and students of this campaign, is plainly established by *O. R.*, 11, part 2, p. 102.
[10] 2 *B. and L.*, 388.

useless, for the time being, if such a thing were possible, than if they remained where they were. Brackett's Ford was opposite the Federal
position. A crossing there would have to be forced. The only Confederate officer of high rank who visited Brackett's Ford that day and left
any account of it was General A. R. Wright. He said: "I ascertained
that the road debouched from the swamp into an open field (meadow),
commanded by a line of high hills, all in cultivation and free of timber.
Upon this range of hills the enemy had posted heavy batteries of field
artillery, strongly supported by infantry, which swept across the meadow
by a direct and cross fire, and which could be used with terrible effect
upon my column while struggling through the fallen timber in the
wood through the swamp."[11] The bridge at Brackett's had been destroyed that morning by order of General S. P. Heintzelman[12] and was
protected by Slocum's division. The troops defending the crossing at
Brackett's had only one 12-pounder howitzer at hand,[13] but there was
abundant Federal artillery nearby and unemployed. It is very doubtful
whether Jackson could have forced this position if he had tried; but it
is certain that he did not try and it is almost certain that he did not send
any one to Brackett's to see whether, if he tried, he could succeed.
Wright examined the ford after he left Jackson and made no mention of
having forwarded any report to him. The movements of Wright indicate that he felt that Jackson had released him to return as best he could
to Huger.

There remained for Jackson the ford that Hampton discovered below
White Oak Bridge. This was so close to Jackson's assigned route that
no man in full possession of his faculties could have regarded a crossing
at that point as contrary to his orders. If Jackson had been reasoning on
the 30th with his usual military acumen, he could only have hesitated to
make the crossing on the ground that he could not employ his artillery
in the attack, and therefore would lose heavily. He could not have been
precise in this, however, because he did not personally examine Hampton's ford, nor is it known that he sent any one to verify or to disprove
Hampton's statement that the enemy could easily be taken in flank from
that quarter.

Summing up this contention, it must be said that the evidence does
not justify the claim that Jackson failed to cross at some other point than
White Oak Bridge because it would have been a violation of orders. He
should not have crossed at Fisher's, at Jordan's, or above the head of
White Oak Swamp. He might not have been able to cross at Brackett's,
but he did not reconnoitre to see whether that route was practicable, and

[11] *O. R.*, 11, part 2, pp. 810–11.   [12] *O. R.*, 11, part 2, p. 99.
[13] *O. R.*, 11, part 2, p. 435.

he did not attempt to cross nor did he even examine the ground at Hampton's ford, which was so close to his assigned route that, to repeat, the most meticulous regard for literal compliance with orders would not have been violated by a crossing there. This general contention, then, must be put aside.

3. *Jackson did not exert himself to fulfil more than the letter of his orders because he did not wish to serve in a subordinate capacity—was unwilling, in short, to co-operate.* This was camp gossip at the time, and is not formally advanced by any serious student of the campaign. In the Valley, there had been nothing to suggest that Jackson was disposed to play a spectacular lone hand and not to co-operate. On the contrary, he had exhibited quick perception of what Lee had intended to do, and had displayed eagerness to execute his part of the larger plan, even to the point of appealing to general headquarters from Johnston's ill-advised order to abandon the pursuit of Banks. Jackson was ambitious. He may have preferred independent command—what self-confident soldier would not?—but he had fitted himself perfectly into the general design.

4. *Jackson felt that his troops were being called upon to do more than their part of the fighting and should be spared as much as possible.* This contention was advanced by D. H. Hill who said: "I think that an important factor in this inaction was Jackson's pity for his own corps, worn out by long and exhausting marches, and reduced in number by its numerous sanguinary battles. He thought that the garrison of Richmond ought now to bear the brunt of the fighting. None of us knew that the veterans of Longstreet and A. P. Hill were unsupported; nor did we even know that the firing we heard was theirs." [14] Alexander[15] commented thus on Hill's statement: "This . . . is but another form of a rumor which, to my knowledge, had private circulation at the time among the staff-officers of some of the leading generals. It was reported that Jackson had said that 'he did not intend that *his* men should do all the fighting.' "

D. H. Hill's statement is a theory, unsupported by evidence; Alexander simply repeated a rumor. Both are discreditable to Jackson, if he were physically and mentally himself during the campaign, and both are entirely at variance with everything else in his splendid career. It is true that Jackson's and Ewell's veterans from the Valley sustained fewer casualties than any other divisions of the army during the Seven Days,[16] but this may have been the result of other causes than of a desire to keep them from bearing their part of the burden of battle. If Jackson had

---

[14] 2 *B. and L.*, 389.   [15] *Op. cit.*, 152.   [16] See *supra*, p. 247, n. 128.

wished to spare his men, it is reasonable to suppose that he would have opposed the dispatch of his army to Richmond earlier in the month. Instead, he was willing, if not eager, to come, as the quotations from his letters[17] plainly show. Nor could any reasonable man argue that the Richmond garrison had been spared, at Jackson's expense, during the campaign. Jackson's and Ewell's divisions had marched farther but had fought less than A. P. Hill's men and no more than Longstreet's. Huger and Magruder had not been fully engaged but that was the result of circumstance, not of favoritism. Jackson was brought to Richmond because the safety of the Confederacy demanded it, and he was placed at the point where he could be most useful under Lee's plan. He was not called on to do "all the fighting" or an undue part of the fighting. Besides, less than half the troops then under Jackson had been engaged in the Valley. Whiting's troops and those of D. H. Hill were on all fours with the other divisions that had been in front of Richmond before Jackson's arrival. Jackson had neither the right, the reason, nor—there is every reason to believe—the disposition to spare them. Ignorant as he was of the terrain and poor as was the map, he was aware of the proximity of the James River and knew that if McClellan escaped, a great opportunity would be lost. There was an echo of this feeling in his remark to his staff, after he roused himself when he had fallen asleep at mess with his supper between his teeth—"let us . . . rise with the dawn and see if we cannot do something." [18] In his report he stated that the sound of Longstreet's cannonade "made me eager to press forward." [19] On the morning of July 1, as is explained in Chapter XIII, when Jackson met Magruder, and the latter proposed that his troops take the lead, Jackson insisted that his men form the van, as they were fresher: was that the act of one who wished to spare his own command? To say that a man of Jackson's military perception deliberately shielded his men, on the day of all days when the Army of the Potomac might have been destroyed, is to accuse him of a measure of skulking only one degree removed from treason.

5. *Jackson failed at White Oak Swamp and during the rest of the campaign because he underestimated the difficulties of handling a large force in a strange country.* This is the view of General Sir Frederick Maurice and is entitled to respect, coming from so distinguished a soldier. Undoubtedly this increased Jackson's difficulties, but it hardly accounts for all his shortcomings during the Seven Days, and it does not explain his behavior at White Oak Swamp.

[17] *Supra,* p. 103 *ff.* [18] See *supra,* p. 198.
[19] *O. R.,* 11, part 2, p. 557.

6. Jackson was physically and mentally exhausted and therefore temporarily incapable of reasoning with his usual accuracy or of acting with his accustomed energy. This is the explanation given by Major R. L. Dabney, Jackson's chief of staff. He said: "Two columns, pushed with determination across the two fords at which the cavalry of Munford passed over and returned—the one in the centre [adjoining White Oak Bridge] and the other [probably Hampton's] at the left—and protected in their onset by the oblique fire of a powerful artillery so well posted on the right, would not have failed to dislodge Franklin from a position already half lost. The list of casualties would indeed have been larger than that presented on the 30th, of one cannoneer mortally wounded. But how much shorter would have been the bloody list filled up the next day at Malvern Hill? This temporary eclipse of Jackson's genius was probably to be explained by physical causes. The labor of the previous days, the sleeplessness, the wear of gigantic cares, with the drenching of the comfortless night, had sunk the elasticity of his will and the quickness of his invention, for once, below their wonted tension." [20]

This is first-hand evidence from the man of all others in the army who was closest to Jackson at the time and knew him best. It is early testimony, too, for Dabney wrote in 1863–65. [21]

Dabney, also, is authority for the highly significant statement that Jackson fell asleep that night at mess, "with his supper between his teeth." Jackson's remark about an early start the next day, Dabney observed likewise, "showed that he was conscious of depression." [22] In 1896, when Henderson was preparing his *Stonewall Jackson,* a lively correspondence was exchanged among Doctor Dabney, Major Jed Hotchkiss, and Doctor Hunter McGuire, as to the reason Jackson did not cross the swamp. At the close of this correspondence Doctor Dabney offered to withdraw, in a proposed new edition of his biography, his claim that Jackson was exhausted. He said he would not assert his judgment on such a question in opposition to that of Doctor McGuire, [23] but before agreeing to this, he wrote a memorandum, presently to be quoted, that made his recantation pointless. Dabney, however, is not the only witness to Jackson's exhaustion. The General's courier, John Gill, observed it. Writing of the climax of the campaign of the Seven Days, he noted: "General Jackson had been in a bad humor for several days; the truth of the matter is that he and his men had been completely worn out by what they had gone through." [24]

[20] *Dabney,* 466–67.
[21] T. C. Johnson: *The Life and Letters of Robert Lewis Dabney,* 280.
[22] *Dabney,* 467.
[23] R. H. Dabney to Jed Hotchkiss, May 7, 1896, MS.—*McGuire Papers.*
[24] John Gill: *Reminiscences of Four Years as a Private Soldier,* 67.

Finally, Jackson himself may be called to the bar of history. On July 8, 1862, he wrote his wife: "During the past week, I have not been well, have suffered from fever and debility." [25] In confirmation of this evidence, it is pertinent to add that Jackson was a man singularly dependent upon sleep. In May, 1861, he had twice complained of physical distress on account of the loss of sleep. "I feel better this morning than I have for some time," he wrote on May 3, "having got more sleep than usual last night." And again, on May 8, "I am in good health, considering the great amount of labor which devolves upon me, and the loss of sleep to which I am subjected. . . ." [26] In July, 1861, before the battle of First Manassas, he had complained again: "One of the most trying things here is the loss of sleep." [27]

Now, if Jackson was particularly dependent upon sleep, had his experiences during the days preceding June 30 been of a sort to deprive him of it and thereby to produce mental exhaustion? The following record of his daily movement speaks for itself.

Night of June 22–23: No sleep subsequent to midnight, if any; riding after 1 A.M. to Richmond.

Day of June 23: En route to Lee's headquarters, at conference there and riding back.

Night of June 23–24: In the saddle. Total distance covered after 1 A.M., June 23, approximately 100 miles.

Day of June 24: A slow, difficult march.

Night of June 24–25: No record; probably sleeping; up very early for continuance of his march.

Day of June 25: Marching to Ashland.

Night of June 25–26: No sleep; in prayer and giving orders.[28]

Day of June 26: Marching from Ashland to Hundley's corner; skirmishing.

Night of June 26–27: Bivouacking on the battlefield; up at earliest dawn.

June 27: Marching from Hundley's Corner to Old Cold Harbor; battle of Gaines's Mill.

Night of June 27–28: On a battlefield covered with wounded; in conference with Stuart after midnight.

June 28: On the battlefield: dispatching Ewell to Dispatch Station; a day of tension.

Night of June 28–29: No record; probably a good night's sleep.

June 29: Rebuilding Grapevine bridge; preparing to pursue retreating enemy.

[25] *Mrs. Jackson*, 302.   [26] *Mrs. Jackson*, 151, 152.
[27] *Mrs. Jackson*, 168.   [28] *Dabney*, 440.

APPENDIX

Night of June 29–30: Aroused by rain at about 1 A.M.; moving thereafter; saw Magruder at 3:30 A.M.

In summary, during the eight days from noon, June 22, to noon, June
30, Jackson rode approximately 100 miles with no rest intervening except while in conference at Lee's headquarters; he lost all of four nights'
sleep or else had no sleep after midnight; he was probably up at dawn
on the four mornings following a night of sleep; two of these four nights
were spent on or close to fields where battles had been fought the preceding day; finally, on six of the eight days, he was either making his
hurried ride to Richmond or else was on the march with his troops,
under the most exacting conditions. If it be asked why Jackson showed
more of the physical effects of the campaign than did any other of the
division commanders, it may be answered that his strain began on the
night of June 22–23, whereas the others lost no sleep until the night of
June 25–26. Put in a form perhaps more dramatic than historically correct, it may be concluded that Jackson paved the way for failure at
White Oak Swamp by riding all night of June 22–23 and of June 23–24
and by praying all night of June 25–26. Magruder almost broke down
with less loss of sleep,[29] and though Lee required little repose and took
pains to get rest every night, he was close to exhaustion on the morning
of July 1.[30]

Jackson was full of vigor on June 27, and Doctor McGuire said he
never saw Jackson "more active and energetic than during the engagement" at White Oak Swamp; but it is a well-known fact that a man who
gets even a little sleep at night can perform his duties the next morning
and will not begin to feel exhaustion until the afternoon. That precisely accords with what is known of Jackson's behavior on the 30th.
Sending Wright away without dispatching a staff officer to see how he
fared, returning no answer to Longstreet by Captain Fairfax, sitting on
a log listening to Hampton's report and then walking off without a
word—this may be the picture of a man benumbed into irresolution and
paralyzed for action by utter exhaustion.

Major Dabney's comments in 1896 may now be quoted as final evidence in behalf of the view that Jackson was exhausted on June 30, 1864.
He said:

". . . But, consider the scene at [Jackson's] supper the night of the
30th when he actually went to sleep with a biscuit between his teeth and
nodded; and then waking with a start, said the words, which I print.
Don't they imply a consciousness of an ineffectual day? Nobody could
blame Jackson for being done out that day. Remember he had had a

[29] O. R., 11, part 2, p. 662.   [30] See *supra*, p. 200.

580

hard time since leaving Beaver Dam; not a wink of sleep the night at Ashland; not a regular meal after leaving Hundley's Corner Friday morning. Our headquarters wagon and servants all in the rear; no mess chest, no cook; no regular rations drawn; no mess tables set, Friday, Saturday, Sunday, Monday, nor Tuesday. Very little sleep Sunday night, which from 1 o'clock on was spent on horseback. I suppose he had neither breakfast nor dinner Monday. I know I had none, and I suppose he was no better off, and next to no meals for three days before, such were the terrible exigencies of his previous services. He must have been a man of iron indeed, had not body, brain, and animal spirits, felt the depressing effects. All the day Monday he was faithfully busy, as on other days, with his duties. With all his usual unselfish disregard for his own comfort, and his usual exposure of himself to danger. But he appeared to me to have less of his usual push and quick decision. To be more specific, I have related how Colonel Munford's regiment of cavalry crossed the miry stream, mounted the upland, made his reconnoisance, found Franklin's left wing in position and threatening him with artillery and wheeling away from it found a sheltered vale leading down to the water course and at the foot of it a practicable ford, across which he brought his regiment back to our side in safety. My thought was that where this cavalry came back to us, a column of infantry might have crossed to the front, and thus established itself upon Franklin's right flank. I did not suggest it; I did not take such liberties.

"Jackson seemed to have made up his mind that he would not risk the serious onset with the infantry unaccompanied by his artillery. Probably the gun carriages could not have been taken across this lower ford in safety; but this fact remains true; the next day, at Malvern Hill, we had to fight McClellan's triple lines with our infantry alone. Now I am well aware Jackson may have known facts which would have shown this idea of mine to be erroneous. I did not advance it in my printed narrative, I only stated what appeared to me the true explanation of our unquestionable check upon that useless day." [31]

To conclude, then, it was not ugly selfishness or sulky unwillingness to fight under Lee that led Jackson to leave the battle to others and to let the great opportunity pass. It was not altogether ignorance of the ground that held him back, nor, primarily, inexperience in handling large bodies of men. It was not the miscalculation of erring genius; it may have been the lack of calculation of an exhausted mind. It was not the absence of zeal when the great day came and passed; it may have

[31] R. L. Dabney to Jed Hotchkiss, April 22, 1896, *MS.—McGuire Papers.*

been excess of zeal in overstraining himself to make that day possible. His state of mind may have led him to exaggerate the difficulties of the terrain. This seems the most probable explanation. A positive, incontrovertible one cannot be given.

APPENDIX II—4

The Terrain of the Battle of Malvern Hill

Those who intend to study the battle of Malvern Hill tactically will find rather full general descriptions of the ground by Lee,[1] Wright,[2] and D. H. Hill,[3] but as the field has changed greatly during the last seventy years and is still changing as the advancing pines take the abandoned farm lands, a detailed description may be useful.

About a mile and a half east of the Willis Church-Quaker road an old byway ran south from the Long Bridge road. This byway was employed by Keyes in moving his troops and trains. Until June 30, he reported, "it had not had a wheel run over it for five years." Trees were rotting in it.[4] The Confederates did not use this route. They took up their positions on the left by moving along a narrow, wooded lane that led to the left (east) from the Willis Church road to the Poindexter farm.[5]

The Poindexter farm was at an elevation not much lower than that of the Federal right, but the wooded ravine of Western Run[6] was sixty feet below the hill on which the house stood. A field of wheat, covering more than a quarter of a mile, was standing on the eastern side of the farm.[7] Nearer the Willis Church road on the Poindexter farm, the land was broken and afforded some shelter for artillery.[8] From this open ground on the farm, woods extended for a quarter of a mile westward to the Willis Church road and southward to the ravine of Western Run. Opposite the Confederate left, the rising ground of the Federal right, south of the run, was open and part of it was in oats.[9]

From Willis Church southward to the run, the Willis Church road was wooded heavily on the right (west), except for one open space near the Methodist parsonage. On the left (east) of the road, there was a narrow fringe of wood stretching southward until one reached the quarter-mile belt of woods on the Poindexter farm.

[1] O. R., 11, part 2, p. 496.   [2] Ibid., 812.   [3] Ibid., 627.
[4] 1 Report of the Committee on the Conduct of the War, 611.
[5] O. R., 11, part 2, p. 527.   [6] O. R., 11, part 2, p. 267.
[7] O. R., 11, part 2, pp. 558, 567, 573–74.
[8] O. R., 11, part 2, pp. 573–74.   [9] O. R., 11, part 2, pp. 208, 267.

South of the run, as one began to climb toward Malvern Hill, the Willis Church road was wooded on the right for about 400 yards. Above that point, mounting to the top of the hill, there was, probably on the western side of the road, a fence and a hedgerow that offered some shelter.[10] From the end of this fence southward, along the right-hand side of the road, there were no obstructions to the crest of the ridge. Where it turned eastward, three-eighths of a mile from the lane leading to the Crew house, there was another fringe of wood on the south side.[11]

East of the Willis Church road, all the way from the run to the West house, the ground was clear, though broken by a few small ravines.

The ground occupied by the Confederate centre, west of the Willis Church road, was much more difficult. The Confederate approach from beyond artillery range had to be across a troublesome stretch of open ground near the Methodist parsonage and the Garthright house. This cleared land fell more than sixty feet to the swampy ravine of Western Run, and, south of that, consisted of a steep, heavily wooded hillside. The woods at this point were in the form of a broad V with the angle projecting several hundred yards farther southward toward the Federal position than anywhere else on the front. Opposite these woods the field was open for 300 or 400 yards to the Federal positions. The ground nearest the Federal batteries had been ploughed.[12] The whole of the centre, southward from the parsonage, was within artillery range.

Beyond D. H. Hill's front, on the Confederate right, the western side of the projecting V of woodland ran northwest for half a mile and then spread westward and northward. Most of this was heavy timber, chiefly oak, which were scarred during the course of the battle to a height of thirty feet.[13] There were, however, a pine thicket and occasional thick briar patches in front of Armistead's first position.[14] Cross-ravines cut this woodland,[15] with a troublesome mill dam about half a mile up Western Run behind Armistead's line.[16] In rear of the Confederate right, between the woods that ran westward and those that ran northward, was "Carter's field," with an orchard. Across this field ran the farm road down which Armistead and Wright had marched from the Long Bridge road. It was from near the southeastern

---

[10] O. R., 11, part 2, p. 737. It is not quite certain that this fence and hedge were on the western side of the road.
[11] O. R., 11, part 2, p. 275.   [12] O. R., 11, part 2, pp. 267, 557, 627, 643, 692.
[13] 18 S. H. S. P., 60; McDaniel, 8.
[14] O. R., 11, part 2, p. 833; 696; McDaniel, 8.
[15] O. R., 11, part 2, p. 696.   [16] Early, 79.

end of Carter's field that Pegram, Grimes, and Moorman opened on the Federals.[17]

Looking southward from Armistead's position, there seemed to be directly in front only a fence [18] and a gradual incline through a clover field [19] and onward for about 400 yards.[20] The ground occupied by the Federals appeared to be a strong but not an impregnable position once the assaulting troops were out of the ravine that led down to Western Run.[21] But in front of the right, beyond the extreme left of the enemy, was the long wheat field, with the grain, as noted in the text, cut and shocked.[22] This wheat field ran southward to the west of the Crew house hill in front of the Confederate right. On the eastern side of the wheat field, the hill gradually became more abrupt and was cut with ravines, until it rose almost to a bluff. The Crew house hill, in other words, as seen from the Confederate right, was a plateau on its eastern side, a hill on the northern face nearest the Confederates, and well-nigh a precipice on the western side, overlooking the wheat field.[23] The Crew house on top of this hill, and close to the bluff, was a large white frame residence on a brick foundation. In some of the reports this place is called Doctor J. H. Mellert's house.[24] It was burned in November, 1877, but the present building is said to rest on the old foundations. As mentioned in the text, the main Federal artillery position ran eastward from the yard of the Crew house, along the farm lane and across Willis Church road to and beyond the West house.[25] The Federal infantry were in support just to the south of the guns. The other artillery positions are given, about as accurately as they can be located, on Colonel H. L. Landers' excellent map. The original Malvern house, dating from the seventeenth century, was situated one mile south by east from the Crew house.

APPENDIX II—5

Who Devised the Left Flank Movement at Chancellorsville?

In his *Life and Campaigns of Lieut.-Gen. Thomas J. Jackson*, published in 1866, Reverend R. L. Dabney, D.D., formerly Jackson's chief of staff, stated that Jackson "proposed to throw his command entirely

[17] *O. R.*, 11, part 2, pp. 719, 728, 749.   [18] *O. R.*, 11, part 2, pp. 700, 826.
[19] *O. R.*, 11, part 2, p. 813.   [20] *O. R.*, 11, part 2, p. 712.
[21] *Cf. O. R.*, 11, part 2, pp. 812, 833.   [22] *W. W. Chamberlaine*, 25.
[23] *O. R.*, 11, part 2, p. 812.   [24] *Cf. O. R.*, 11, part 2, pp. 274, 811.
[25] The location of this lane has been changed a few feet, at one time or another since the battle, and has been heavily eroded at one point.

into Hooker's rear."[1] This language was accepted in the South as a claim, on Dabney's part, that Jackson was responsible for suggesting as well as for executing this movement. In the same year, Colonel William Allan and Major Jed Hotchkiss published their *Chancellorsville,* in which Hotchkiss, who evidently wrote that particular passage, quoted a conversation between Jackson and Lee which seemed to justify the claim Dabney had made.[2] This conversation, slightly elaborated, was repeated in a letter from Major Hotchkiss to Colonel G. F. R. Henderson and was accepted by him in his *Stonewall Jackson and the American Civil War.*[3] The substance of this contention is that the movement around the right flank of the Federal army was not suggested until the morning of May 2, when Major Hotchkiss and Mr. Lacy returned from their reconnaissance beyond Catherine Furnace. The whole of this incident is given in the text, p. 521 *ff.*

Some of General Lee's staff officers knew the facts and were quick to assert that the initiative as well as the responsibility were Lee's. A mild controversy developed. It culminated in 1906 in a review of all the circumstances by Colonel T. M. R. Talcott, of Lee's staff. Colonel Talcott concluded that Major Hotchkiss's claim to have brought word of a new road to the left was not well founded, and that the proposal for the flank movement undoubtedly originated with Lee.[4]

The controversy need never have arisen if the parties to it had realized that the council of war on the night of May 1–2 lasted for hours. Various individuals heard different snatches of it, as they came and went, and they mistakenly assumed that what they heard was all that was said. When Major Hotchkiss went off to reconnoitre with Mr. Lacy he knew nothing of what had happened earlier in the evening. He did not understand that Lee had already ordered the movement and had entrusted its execution to Jackson. The conversation he reported between the two would certainly have indicated that Jackson proposed the move, had there been no previous discussion. As it was, the leadership that Jackson seemed to assert and the questions Lee asked him take on a very different meaning when read as Jackson's explanation of how he intended to carry out a plan Lee had proposed in outline and had left for him to elaborate in detail. If this be kept in mind, and if the various versions of the last council be fitted together in their proper sequence, they present no material contradictions. Instead, they accord precisely with what is known of the manner in which Generals Lee and Jackson worked. Jackson looked to Lee, as

[1] P. 673.   [2] Pp. 41–42.   [3] 2, 431–32.
[4] 34 *S. H. S. P.,* 1 *ff.,* cited in the text as *Talcott.*

commander, for decisions on strategy; Lee almost always gave Jackson the largest discretion both as to the routes he should follow and the men he should employ in executing his orders.

The problem of the biographer, then, is not one of deciding where the weight of probability lies on the scale of contradiction. His task is simply that of taking scraps of a conversation that occurred at different hours and of piecing them together, like the bits of a jig-saw puzzle, into a consistent whole. This is not altogether easy, but it is possible to fix the approximate sequence of events, especially if one takes into account what the different witnesses omit as well as what they say.

Stuart's visit evidently occurred while Talcott and Boswell were reconnoitring; most of the conversation that Marshall quoted in his narrative must have taken place about the same time. After Talcott and Boswell reported, however, a definite decision had to be made and the route had to be chosen. The conversation therefore took on a more precise tone. The only difficult part in the picture is that relating to Reverend B. T. Lacy. Fitz Lee affirmed, doubtless on Stuart's authority, that General Lee saw the chaplain; yet Jackson's conversation with him before daylight, as reported by Dabney, who got the story from Lacy, indicated that Jackson had not previously talked with Lacy about the roads. The most reasonable assumption is that Lacy arrived after Jackson retired. He talked with Lee, but did not see Jackson until the latter woke up. This accords with the known fact Jackson retired ahead of Lee but was up earlier on the morning of May 2

If the case were not one where the evidence could be reconciled easily, the biographer could hardly hesitate in deciding from the preponderance of evidence that the proposal to turn the enemy's flank originated with Lee. The testimony of three members of General Lee's staff, Long, Talcott, and Marshall, is available and is in agreement that the main decision had been reached before the interview with Major Hotchkiss could possibly have occurred.[5] Hotchkiss was the only eye-witness to leave the inference that Jackson originated the plan, for Major Dabney was not present at the council. In his final account of the incident,[6] Hotchkiss repeated what he had said in his *Chancellorsville,* but he significantly expanded his original narrative so as to make it plain that Lee first proposed the move. Hotchkiss's contention, therefore, is narrowed down to the claim that Jackson chose the particular

---

[5] Long's account is in *op. cit.,* p. 252 *ff.;* Talcott's has already been cited, and Marshall's was given to Fitz Lee, *vide* his *Chancellorsville,* 27–28. Long wrote before 1886; Talcott before the same year, and Marshall in 1879. Talcott, as quoted, dates from 1906, but the review he published that year agrees in nearly every particular with what he wrote Long (see *Long,* 254–55), thirty years before.

[6] 3 *C. M. H.,* 38:.

roads that were to be followed and that Jackson first suggested that he take his whole corps with him. As this was never disputed by Lee's staff officers, the case was even stronger in 1906 than Colonel Talcott made it out.

Lee's own evidence remains to be taken into account. Late in 1865 Mrs. Jackson sent for his perusal the manuscript of Dabney's *Life.* He read it "for the pleasure of the narrative," as he subsequently told Mrs. Jackson, "with no view of remark or correction," and he took no notes. He was forced to return the manuscript before he could give it the critical reading Mrs. Jackson seems to have expected of him. In writing her, however, he mentioned a few errors into which Doctor Dabney had fallen through his desire to present Jackson's service fully. Lee said: "I am misrepresented at the battle of Chancellorsville in proposing an attack in front, the first evening of our arrival. On the contrary, I decided against it, and stated to General Jackson, we must attack on our left as soon as practicable; and the necessary movement of the troops began immediately. In consequence of a report received about that time, from General Fitz Lee, describing the position of the Federal army, and the roads which he held with his cavalry leading to its rear, General Jackson, after some inquiry concerning the roads leading to the Furnace, undertook to throw his command entirely in Hooker's rear, which he accomplished with equal skill and boldness . . ." [7] Dabney paraphrased this in his *Life,* but he substituted "proposed" for "undertook"—an unjustified change of language.[8]

Doctor A. T. Bledsoe, at one time chief of the Bureau of War in the Confederate War Department, wrote Lee in 1867 for his opinion of an article in *The Southern Review* on Chancellorsville.[9] Lee replied that he had not read the article in question, nor any of the books "published on either side since the termination of hostilities." He went on: "I have as yet felt no desire to revive my recollections of those events, and have been satisfied with the knowledge I possessed of what transpired. I have, however, learned from others that the various authors of the 'Life of Jackson' award to him the credit of the success gained by the Army of Northern Virginia where he was present, and describe the movements of his corps or command as independent of the general plan of operations, and undertaken at his own suggestion, and upon his own responsibility. I have the greatest reluctance to do anything that might be construed as detracting from his well-deserved fame,

[7] R. E. Lee to Mrs. T. J. Jackson, Jan. 25, 1866, conveniently accessible in 2 *Henderson,* 472–73.

[8] *Talcott,* 19.

[9] *Southern Review,* vol. 2, 461, Oct., 1867. The article was unsigned and may have been by Bledsoe himself.

for I believe that no one was more convinced of his worth, or appreciated him more highly, than myself; yet your knowledge of military affairs, if you have none of the events themselves, will teach you that this could not have been so. Every movement of an army must be well considered, and properly ordered, and every one who knows General Jackson must know that he was too good a soldier to violate this fundamental military principle. In the operations round Chancellorsville I overtook General Jackson, who had been placed in command of the advance as the skirmishers of the approaching armies met, advanced with the troops to the Federal line of defences, and was on the field until their whole army recrossed the Rappahannock. There is no question as to who was responsible for the operations of the Confederates, or to whom any failure would have been charged. What I have said is for your information . . ." [10]

Gamaliel Bradford[11] remarked: "The more I read this letter, the less I understand it." General Maurice[12] said of Bradford's comment "I agree with Lee that to any one with a knowledge of military affairs it is clear as daylight." It may be added that any one with a knowledge of General Lee's letter-writing after the war knows, further, that he was exceedingly careful and reserved, because his letters might find their way into print. While he laid down a general principle that Doctor Bledsoe's clear mind was certain to apply to his particular inquiry, Lee took pains to avoid a specific statement that might lead to controversy among a people whom he wished to see united, with their minds on their economic problems and not on the battles of the war. The letter gave no specific information and was not intended to do so, but the inference from it is reasonably plain.

Lee's official statements are the final evidence and, to those who are familiar with his method of writing, they are convincing proof that he initiated the proposal that Jackson so brilliantly executed. In his letter of May 2 to President Davis he described operations of May 1 and said: "I am now swinging around to my left to come up in his rear." [13] If the proposal had come from any one else or was in any sense an independent movement, Lee's meticulous regard for the performance of others would almost certainly have prompted him to say so. For example, in telegraphing Davis on August 27, 1862, regarding Jackson's move on Manassas, Lee specifically said: "The advance *under Genl. Jackson* last night broke up the Orange and Alexandria R.R. . . ." [14]

---

[10] R. E. Lee to Doctor A. T. Bledsoe, Oct. 28, 1867, *Jones*, 158–59.
[11] *Lee the American*, 151. [12] *Op. cit.*, p. 185.
[13] *O. R.*, 25, part 2, p. 765.
[14] *Lee's Dispatches*, 54. The italics are not in the original.

The language of Lee's report on Chancellorsville is equally significant. He said of the situation on the night of May 1–2: "It was, therefore, resolved to endeavor to turn [the enemy's] right flank and gain his rear, leaving a force in front to hold him in check and conceal the movement. The execution of this plan was intrusted to Lieutenant General Jackson with his three divisions." [15] In his telegrams, Lee usually spoke in the first person; in formal reports, especially where his own acts were concerned, he was in the habit of speaking impersonally, because those documents were printed. When he said "It was, therefore, resolved . . .," etc., he meant "I resolved . . ." He used the identical form when he wrote in the same report of his decision to divide the army and to hold Sedgwick with part of the forces while the rest were thrown against Hooker—a movement that undoubtedly originated with him and with him alone. His language was: *"It was, therefore, determined,* to leave sufficient troops to hold our lines, and with the main body of the army to give battle to the approaching column." [16]

Taking the evidence as a whole, it is difficult to see how the controversy could have lasted so long or could have confused so many students of the campaign. The facts are unmistakable: Lee originated the plan to turn Hooker's flank and to get in his rear; Jackson elaborated it by proposing to use his entire corps, and then executed the plan with assured genius.

[15] *O. R.,* 25, part 1, p. 798.
[16] *O. R.,* 25, part 1, p. 797. No italics in the original.

SHORT–TITLE INDEX TO VOLUMES I AND II

The Selected Bibliography for this work follows the Appendices to Volume IV. This Short-Title Index gives the names by which certain important sources mentioned once in the footnotes with the full title and the name of the author or editor are cited thereafter. Only to those manuscripts and publications that are the subject of frequent reference have short titles been assigned. The adopted short title appears on the left in italics, then the name of the author or editor, and, on the right, a longer, identifying title. In some instances these titles have been somewhat abbreviated, inasmuch as the Selected Bibliography contains full information.

Alexander. E. P. ALEXANDER. "Military Memoirs of a Confederate."
Anderson, C. C. ANDERSON. "Texas Before and on the Eve of the Rebellion."
B. and L. "Battles and Leaders of the Civil War."
Baylies. FRANCIS BAYLIES. "A Narrative of General Wool's Campaign in Mexico."
Beale, R. L. T. R. L. T. BEALE. "History of the Ninth Virginia Cavalry."
Bigelow. JOHN BIGELOW, JR. "Campaign of Chancellorsville."
Boyd. THOMAS BOYD. "Light Horse Harry Lee."
Boynton. EDWARD C. BOYNTON. "History of West Point."
Bradford. GAMALIEL BRADFORD. "Lee the American."
Brock. R. A. BROCK. "General Robert Edward Lee."
Brock, Miss. SALLY BROCK. "Richmond During the War."
Cent. U. S. C. "Robert E. Lee: Centennial Celebration of His Birth—University of South Carolina."
Cent. U. S. M. A. "Centennial of the United States Military Academy."
Chamberlaine, W. W. W. W. CHAMBERLAINE. "Memoirs of the Civil War."
Childe. EDWARD LEE CHILDE. "The Life and Campaigns of Gen. Lee . . . translated from the French . . . by George Litting."
Chilton Papers. "MS. Papers of Gen. R. H. Chilton."
C. M. H. C. A. EVANS, editor. "Confederate Military History."
Cond. M. A. "Condition of the Military Academy, 1824, American State Papers, Military Affairs."
Conner. P. S. P. CONNER. "The Home Squadron Under Commodore Conner."
Cook, Joel. JOEL COOK. "The Siege of Richmond."

Smith, J. H. Justin H. Smith. "The War with Mexico."

Sorrel. G. Moxley Sorrel. "Recollections of a Confederate Staff Officer."

Southern Generals. Anon. "Southern Generals, Who They Are and What They Have Done."

Stephens. A. H. Stephens. "A Constitutional View of the War Between the States."

Talcott. T. R. M. Talcott. "General Lee's Strategy at the Battle of Chancellorsville in 34 S. H. S. P."

Talcott MSS. (F). "Talcott MSS. (Freeman)."

Talcott MSS. (VHS). "Talcott MSS. (Virginia Historical Society)."

Taylor, C. E. Charles E. Taylor. "Letters in Wake Forest Student, March, 1916."

Taylor, R. Richard Taylor. "Destruction and Reconstruction."

Taylor's Four Years. W. H. Taylor. "Four Years with General Lee."

Taylor's General Lee. W. H. Taylor. "General Lee."

Thomas. H. W. Thomas. "History of the Doles-Cooke Brigade."

Thomason. John W. Thomason, Jr. "Jeb Stuart."

Villard. O. W. Villard. "John Brown, a Biography After Fifty Years."

von Borcke. Heros von Borcke. "Memoirs of the Confederate War for Independence."

Webb. A. S. Webb. "The Peninsula."

Welch. S. G. Welch. "A Confederate Surgeon's Letters to His Wife."

White. H. A. White. "Robert E. Lee and the Southern Confederacy."

Winston. R. W. Winston. "Robert E. Lee."

Wise. Jennings C. Wise. "The Long Arm of Lee."

Wise, G. G. Wise. "History of the Seventeenth Virginia Infantry."

Withers. R. E. Withers. "Autobiography of an Octogenarian."

Wolseley. G. Wolseley. "A Month's Visit to the Confederate Headquarters."

Wooten. D. G. Wooten. "Comprehensive History of Texas."

Worsham. John H. Worsham. "One of Jackson's Foot Cavalry."

WPLB. "MS. Letter Book of the Superintendent of West Point."

INDEX FOR VOLUMES I AND II

597

INDEX FOR VOLUMES I AND II